MW00630232

Pearls from Peoria

Pearls from Peoria

Philip José Farmer

Edited by Paul Spiteri

SUBTERRANEAN PRESS • 2006

First Edition

Trade Hardcover ISBN
1-59606-059-X

Subterranean Press
PO Box 190106
Burton, MI 48519

www.subterraneanpress.com

The Editor and Publisher gratefully acknowledge the permissions given to include the stories, articles and speeches within this anthology.

In an ideal world we would be able to list each and every occurrence of each of the published articles contained in this volume. That hasn't proven possible so we have contented ourselves with listing the American publishing history. Further information can be found on two excellent and comprehensive Philip José Farmer websites;

The Official Philip José Farmer Website   www.pjfarmer.com
Philip José Farmer International Bibliography   www.philipjosefarmer.tk

Contents

This collection is dedicated by Philip José Farmer to the brave men of SF, who have worked so tirelessly to see that this book could see print:

Rick Beaulieu
Jason Robert Bell
Charles Berlin
Christopher Carey
Mike Croteau
Keith Howell
Craig Kimber
Tracy Knight
Paul Spiteri
Mario Zecca

All true fans and friends of Philip José Farmer.

List of Illustrations

"Nobody's Perfect" *by Charles Berlin*

"Wolf, Iron, and Moth" *by Charles Berlin*

"Evil, Be My Good" *by Charles Berlin*

"A Scarletin Study" *by Keith Howell*

"Hunter's Moon" *by Charles Berlin*

"Writing Doc's Biography" *by Keith Howell*

"Savage Shadow" *by Charles Berlin*

"The Monster On Hold" *by Jason Robert Bell*

"The Princess of Terra" *by Keith Howell*

"The Source of the River" *by Jason Robert Bell*

"Oft Have I Travelled" *by Mario Zecca*

"Maps and Spasms" *by Jason Robert Bell*

Myths and Paramyths

"*Myths are to be taken seriously. Paramyths are also to be taken seriously, but they have an element of the absurd. But that element is just as serious as the nonabsurd. One becomes the other.*"

—*Philip José Farmer.*

Nobody's Perfect

Nobody's Perfect

First published in *The Ultimate Dracula,* Byron Preiss, 1991.

Commissioned by Byron Preiss for his anthology, Phil submitted a story of sexual and religious symmetry, a theme Phil previously explored in his 1962 novel *Fire and the Night.*
Vampires with high sexual energy also figure prominently in Phil's *Image of the Beast* and *Blown.*

Phil: "I'd always considered vampire stories, werewolf tales, and in fact, the whole Gothic field, as more-or-less disguised sex stories. Pornography of the weird. Why not bring the hidden stuff into the open."

Rudolph Redeemer had just finished sucking my blood. My brain glared like a klieg light, and my clit was pulsing.
I wanted to beg him to keep on sucking, but the girl in line behind me was shouting, "Move on, bitch!" The drums were rolling; the bugles were blaring. The audience jamming the concert hall was shrieking its lungs out.

Rudolph's bodyguards, just below the stage and in the wings, must've become even more alert then. A year ago, an assassin had shot Rudolph during this ritual. Three months later, the same thing had happened.

Dazed, knees weak, I started to walk toward the steps leading down from the stage. But he shouted, "You're the one I've been looking for for years! I think I love you!"

I was both thrilled and astonished. You expect such tender language to be whispered in the bedroom, the only noise your heavy breathing and the twanging of bedsprings and maybe "Wooed Screwed and Sued" shaking the walls. But I wasn't going to argue with him.

Blood was trickling down the corner of his mouth. He smiled, showing the dripping red steel canines fixed to his real canines. His eyes blazed. Really burned. That, as I found out later, was because he loved the new designer fix, God Trek. It makes your eyes look like the open doors to Hell, though some claim it swings wide the gates of Heaven. Whatever it does, it sure beats hero-in, crack, ballrush, and mindjam. Though, as I soon discovered, Rudolph took all of them.

But he wasn't on all that shit for the reason most people are. That is, to feel normal. He took it so he could feel human. Which I suppose is the same thing. I never was much for philosophy. What do I care about gurus and mahareeshis, they're all fakers, about karma and mantras, and whether or not Immanuel Kant had a cunt?

"Come to my apartment at midnight!" he yelled.

"I'm not a one-night stand!" I yelled back.

I was lying, and he knew it. But he grabbed the next girl, bent her backwards, cupped her breast with his left hand, and bit into her neck. Again, the drums roared, and the crowd shrieked like lost souls suddenly seeing hope. The girl had an orgasm or she was faking one, so much of that nowadays, but the men don't care. You is what you pretends you is, as a friend once said.

However, I sure hadn't faked anything. So maybe she was feeling the same exquisite cold fire that'd started in my toes and soared up through my body and numbed my brain with an ecstasy even mindjam and God Trek couldn't quite match.

Rudolph let loose of the girl and seized the pimply boy behind her. The youth may have been straight or gay, but he was shining with ecstasy. Part of it religious, part of it sexual, or is there any difference, much as I hate to say it? For sure, there's no difference when the Redeemer takes you into The Blessed Body, also no difference whether you're male or female when you accept initiation and communion at the same time. Only it's a reverse communion because Rudolph, the priest in this case and claiming to be God's vicar, drinks the wine of your blood. But you get a little of his holy saliva in your bloodstream.

At the steps, a girl sprayed germicide on the wound on my neck and slapped a Band-Aid over it. When I'd picked up my ticket, I'd signed a form releasing Rudolph Redeemer from all responsibility for any infections or emotional stress supposedly caused by the neck bite. Rudolph didn't worry about catching AIDS or anything. He claimed that vampires were untouched by human diseases.

Was I excited? Yes! But even while I was steaming under the silk, as they say, I was wondering if Rudolph really meant what he'd said. If he thought I'd be ready to put out and take in any time anywhere until the old thrill was gone, it seldom lasted, it almost always went, he was right. But if he thought he was going to keep on tapping me for blood, like a farmer milking a cow, he was wrong. I can't afford to lose much of my precious hemoglobin. I got enough trouble with anemia and pseudo-hepatitis. That

God Trek not only fucks up your blood, it's hell on the liver. At the time, though, it seems worth it.

Why had he picked me out? I'm not backward admitting I got gorgeous legs and big standing-out siliconeless tits and these, with my Liz Taylor face, I once thought, would make me a movie star. Nobody ever told me you had to have at least a moderately good acting ability to make it to the top. I was a genuine innocent, or maybe I was just stoned dumb. Too dumb to know the producers and directors would promise you anything if they could prong you.

Anyway, I wasn't the only goddess in that crowd, and he must've banged lots of divine bimbos. So, why me? Had he seen something making me stand out like a sex-crazed cockroach making it with a pecan in a can of mixed nuts?

I'd find out when I got to his apartment. Which was where? So, I was surprised and delighted when a man slipped me a note and said, "From The Redeemer." I opened it. It bore a hand-printed message (he probably wasn't sure I could read handwriting). The printing meant he must've seen me before the rituals started, probably by looking at a TV set scanning the crowd. He was still sucking blood from the initiates and so was too busy to have taken time off to get a message to me.

The note said that the driver of a yellow limousine would pick me up when the ceremonies were ended.

Now, that really did make me feel special! Or did he do that every show, pick out some beauty whose brains were in her snatch, who looked as if she'd already fallen from grace and was going to fall into his bed? For all I knew, a whole grope of groupies had been given notes like mine during this evening. Each was told to come at a different time. So, when my time was up, I'd get the bum's rush.

Glory, glory, glory! Even if a girl got bounced without a thank-you after an hour with Rudolph, she wasn't supposed to feel pissed-off. No way. You were lucky, one of the Chosen. You not only had something to brag about, you left with something else beside his sperm in you. It was the Redeemer's Kingdom Come in you, a house in Heaven, an eternal blessing, a never-failing assurance you were one of the Elect, an eternal queenship in the New Earth.

His followers knew that when Old Earth was redeemed by Rudolph, they'd become immortal. They would truly live forever, body and soul. Moreover, the women he'd laid had a special place in the heavenly mansion. It was like Rudolph paid you off for balling him, not with money but with a saint's halo. Beatified via a bloody communion. Canonized via penis.

After what seemed like an unendurable time because I wanted to be with The Redeemer right now, the closing ritual came on. Rudolph was hoisted up by the Bloody Communion musicians and his hands and feet were nailed to a crucifix formed by a combination of cross, star of David, crescent moon, and swastika. That last symbol got a lot of flak from nonbelievers, but Rudolph said it was the ancient Buddhist symbol, right-handed in form unlike the left-handed swastika the Nazis dishonored.

The blood ran out from his hands and feet, and the band, except for the drummer banging away, licked the blood running down along the shaft of the Holy Mantra. Then they clawhammered the nails out from the Mantra and carried Rudolph on their shoulders to the coffin and laid him in it and closed the lid.

This was done with a lot of wailing and breast-beating by the crowd. The musicians went back to their instruments and beat out the bars of "The Blood Is The Life." It sounded like a fusion of the blacksmithy of the ancient pagan deities and of angels working in the celestial armory, like the band was forging weapons for the Twilight of the Gods and Armageddon combined. The beat made you feel as if the end of the world was just around the corner.

At least, that's what a music critic had written. For once, he was not full of shit.

Then, after a long pause, during which the crowd fell silent, the band crashed into "Arise, Arise, And Shine, Light Of The World!" The coffin lid slowly rose. Then Rudolph sat up, and then he bounced. I mean, bounced out of his coffin from a sitting position and landed on his feet, smiling, his arms lifted and widespread.

The crowd roared, all 200,000 humans sounding as if they'd been squeezed into the form of a colossal lion and its gigantic throat was issuing a challenge to shake the walls of the temple, shake the walls of the cosmos itself.

I really felt exhalted, in a fine frenzy of joy. I didn't want to feel it. But I couldn't escape that flashflood of emotion charging out from all those people and shooting out from deep inside me. Nobody's perfect.

Rudolph stood there, arms still up, the wounds in his hands and feet beginning to close up like nightclubs after 4 a.m. Then the crowd filed out while singing "Arise!" Mightily shaken, though silent, I walked out slowly with the singers.

It was 11 p.m. in Los Angeles, but the lights outside the hall made it almost as bright as a smog-free high noon. A big crowd of anti-Redeemers was waiting for us. It wanted to eat us, like the lions waiting for the Christians. In this case, it was just the opposite. Actually, the people there were Christians of different sects and Jews, Moslems, Hindus, Buddhists, and even some neo-Voodooists. But the Fundies, a.k.a. literalists or holy rollers, were the most numerous and the most dangerous. If it hadn't been for the army of cops, the Fundies would've tried to beat our heads in with the signs they were waving at us.

"Vengeance is mine, saith the Lord." But these people were God's agents, and they were ready to carry out His plan. If any cheek was going to be smitten or turned, it wouldn't be theirs. But then, as I said, nobody's perfect.

An objective person—is there any such thing?—might've said they had plenty of reason to be spitting mad. Here's Rudolph Redeemer claiming to be a genuine vampire but at the same time a savior anointed by the Creator to make Earth green again and to solve most of its problems. And he has a couple million disciples who'd kiss more than his ass if he asked them to. Then this bloodsucking horny blaspheming sleazebag druggie who exposes his yellow-painted balls and purple-painted dick during his rituals claims to be the only true world-saver. Isn't that a little too much even in this country of free speech?

In the list of people who should be killed, Rudolph is on the top. More people hate him than hate the President of the U.S.A. or the current villains in the soap operas. He's been shot and also wounded by a bomb. Yet, a few minutes after the assassination attempts, his wounds are healed. So, he must be a genuine vampire.

In fact, if what his enemies claim is true, he must be a demon flown first-class from Hell, advance agent for the Anti-Christ, if he's not him in person. In each case, according to Fundie belief and logic, it's no sin to murder him. It's not even murder. So, the next time, the assassin should use a large-gauge shotgun or a bigger bomb. How about an anti-tank missile?

It was dangerous to be within a hundred yards of Rudolph, but hundreds of thousands took the risk gladly. And here was I doing the same. Gives you an idea of his charisma.

Everybody in the gigantic mob coming out of the hall was cursed at and railed at by demonstrators. A paper sack full of human shit sailed by my shoulder and splattered on a girl behind me. Cries of "Anti-Christ!" and "Hell-doomed bloodsucking demon!" and many more, some obscene, all hot with hate, rose like burning paper in a strong wind. Signs waved everywhere. THOU SHALT NOT SUFFER A WITCH TO LIVE. SATAN IS LOOSE, HIS NAME IS RUDOLPH, HIS NUMBER IS 666. One sign, JUDJMENT DAY SHALL SEPERATE THE SHEEPS FROM THE GOTES, revealed more than its maker's fervor.

Just before the yellow limousine drove up to the curb, I saw George Reckingham's big pumpkin face and his carrot-shaped nose. He was in the demonstrators' front row, which writhed like a wounded snake as the Fundies strove to break through the double line of sweating cops. He waved at me and shouted something. I shook my head to show him I couldn't hear him. Then he held up his hand, its thumb and first finger forming an O but I could read his lips; I'd been trained to do this.

"You took the first step and the second. God bless you and show you the righteous way on the third."

He meant that the first step was my getting clean of drugs, which I could never have done without his loving help. I don't think Hell has anything worse, though George wouldn't agree with that, but he never went through the fires himself. The second step was getting right with myself. The third step was something he argued against. He said it was far too dangerous for my soul to keep associating with drug addicts (none of this mealy-mouthed "chemical dependents" for him). And my soul was in the gravest peril if I got "friendly" (another euphemism) with the Anti-Christ.

He suspected that I'd be fucking a lot, too, just as I did before I met him. (No "having sexual relations" for him. He told it like it was.) Well, I knew that. No way am I going to give that up. A vagina clogged with dust and cobwebs was not in the Creator's mind when He made it.

He was a Fundie, but they're not clones. Don't let anyone tell you that. They got right wings and left wings and middle-of-the-roaders and farout fringe-dwellers. Even if all insist the Good Book must be taken literally, they disagree a lot about the interpretation of the letter and also of the spirit. But they have one thing in common. Faith in God moves all of them like castor oil moves the bowels. They can't fight against it.

The same thing was true of Rudolph's followers.

I smiled and waved at George and then stepped into the limo, and it drove away slowly into the traffic, which was a mess. How had the driver picked me out of the mob? Better not ask, I told myself. If black magic was involved, I didn't want to know it.

I was taken to a new apartment building on Wilshire in Westwood. I had to go through a security system with a hundred electronic eyes, through a battalion of guards who frisked me maybe more closely than they should have, and through who knew how many sensors before I stepped off the elevator into the penthouse. I was probably X-rayed on the way up in the elevator.

I was alone in rooms displaying squalid luxury or luxurious squalor. But the thing catching my eye was the big coat-of-arms over the fireplace mantel. I'd seen photos of it on TV and in newspapers. It was the arms of a Scottish noble family, the Ruthvens, from whom Rudolph was descended. Some unnamed person had had it made as a gift for Rudolph. But where the original arms showed a ram and a goat supporting the sides of the shield, the gift-giver had covered each with a huge hypodermic hardwood syringe. It was his jesting tribute to Rudolph's well-known drug habit.

Another item, one you wouldn't expect to find in a vampire's apartment, was a huge crucifix on the wall. That didn't surprise me because Rudolph had laughed about it during a talk show. "Crosses don't bother us," he'd said. "That's just folklore without a crumb of truth. Vampires, you know, were around in the Old Stone Age, long long before Christianity came into being. The movies have hyped the folklore so everybody thinks crucifixes scare hell out of us. Same for holy water. Hell, I keep bottled holy water in my apartment! I drink the stuff just to prove what nonsense it all is!"

The rooms hadn't been cleaned recently, and the air was thick with several currents of shit, mindjam stinking the worse. There were ashtrays piled high with cigarette and marijuana stubs, and on the tables, chairs, and floors were needles and syringes, a lot of them used, and plastic packages holding white or crimson powder and prescription containers with contents I guessed were nonprescription. Here and there were some Turkish waterpipes and laser-guided ass jabbers.

It was a narc's wet dream, but Rudolph didn't seem to be worried about being busted. With his money, he could buy several government agencies and the state and local cops, and probably had.

What surprised me, though, was a table set for two. It bore a number of covered dishes, all silver. Fifteen minutes later, some of his bodyguards came into the apartment and quickly checked out all the rooms with electronic detectors. When Rudolph came in, the guards left. His red hair flowed down past his shoulders, making him look like a Swedish guru. But his face was clean-shaven, and he wore a business suit. Brown, for God's sake!

"Well, Polly, how do you like the décor?" he said with that deep rich baritone that's enough to make any of Eve's daughters, no matter how puritanical, look around for the tree with the aphrodisiacal apples and a soft place to lie down on while eating the fruit.

"The décor?" I said. "I'll pass on comment. I'm not an arbiter of bad taste."

He laughed, and his deep blue eyes sparkled. He looked like Dracula about as much a wolf resembles a pit bull.

"You're honest, no suck-ass. Let's eat."

"Eat what?" I said.

Again, he laughed, and he gestured at the table. When I sat down, he moved the chair under me like I was a rock star and he was a head waiter, a real gentleman. I said, "All this food? I thought...?"

"Hey!" he said as he sat down. "That's superstitious bullshit. This is a cause-and-effect, energy-in, energy-out, a certain-amount-of-excrement-residue universe. No way can a vampire live just on blood. Unless you're a bat, and its mass doesn't require relatively much food. I need a balanced diet and bulk, just as you do.

"But I have to have a certain amount of blood to satisfy a vital psychic need. I've tried to quit twice, cold turkey, once in 1757 and once in 1888. I almost died. I mean, really died."

"You sure don't look your age," I said, and I felt stupid saying it. I wanted to be witty, to impress him. That's because, all of a sudden and very much against my will, I was in love with him. Just like that. It happens, though this was the first time I'd ever hurtled into love after a few minutes with the beloved. But I wasn't as happy about it as you might think. Every time I've gotten deeply involved with a man, I've ended up an emotional train-wreck, an airplane in the fog smashing against a mountain wall. I knew, I knew, oh, God, I knew, that this love wasn't going to turn out any better than the others! In fact, it was going to be the worst! I really knew!

But, what the hell! "Sieve the day!" is my motto. Drain off the bad stuff each day and keep the good stuff close to your heart. What a pukey sentimentalist! But it's what I am, no getting away from it.

We ate like vultures, and then it was off with the clothes and into the bedroom. There wasn't any coffin in it. That's another superstition. Vampires don't have to sleep in one, though they're sometimes good hiding places. And vampires can go out in the daylight but don't like to. It makes them very tired and very nervous and irritable. Like a heavy smoker trying to kick the habit.

By now, you can see that I really believed that Rudolph was what he said he was. I had believed it before then but not really, not deep deep down in me. It didn't make any difference to me. I loved him then, and I was absolutely crazy about him before the night, a long one, was over.

I didn't get into bed with him right away. He was lying there, ready for me, waiting for me to mount myself, a self-destructing butterfly, on his pin. But my eye was caught by a small framed painting on a table. I picked it up and looked at it. I wasn't trying to tease Rudolph, delay the big moment just to get him more excited. I'd just had a little shock. The woman in the painting was dressed in eighteenth-century clothes. She looked almost exactly like me!

"My mother," he said. "Dead since 1798."

It took a moment to get my thoughts together. Then I said, "You picked me out because I look like her? You got an Oedipus complex?"

He nodded. He said, "During three hundred and eighty-three years, I've been deeply in love about seven times. Each one looked like my mother. But I don't apologise. Nobody's perfect."

"You son of a bitch!" I said. "I thought you chose me because one look at me hooked you, because you knew I was a soul mate!"

"And so you are," he said.

"Hey, I might have your mother's face! But what about my personality? You might not like it when you get to know me well. How about all those others? Did they have your mother's personality?"

"Every one of them," he said, grinning. "Yet, each had a different personality. It didn't matter. My mother, poor beautiful wretch, was a multiple-personality case. About thirty-three in all, I believe. She died in a locked room in my castle when I was forty-six. But I loved every one of her personalities after I got over being confused, though three of them were murderers. So, you see, there won't be any trouble matching one of her personae to yours. Come here."

Though very angry about being just a fucking mother-substitute, I crawled into bed anyway. Before daylight came, I was over most of my fury. It was worn out, along with me. His body temperature wasn't unhumanly low like all the vampire stories say they are. But his sperm-shoot was shockingly cold whether it was in me, my mouth, or anus. (I'm not called Polymorphous-Perverse Polly for nothing.) They were like electrified icicles in me, sensations like I never had before and would die for to get again. Again and again and again.

We talked sometimes. I found out a lot about him. He had been bitten many times by a female vampire whom he deeply loved when he was thirty-one. Contrary to folklore, a single bite from a vampire could not change a normal person into a compulsive bloodsucker. The change took place only after an unbroken series of nightly feedings. That was why the thousands of youths whom Randolph had bitten only once during the rituals had not become vampires.

He called himself the Redeemer so he could organize youths into groups that would be dedicated to making this planet into a true Green Earth. He had not intended at first to be a religious leader, but his enemies had pushed him into it. He was not, he told me, Anti-Christ or a demon from hell. (He didn't convince me of that, though I didn't argue.) He'd been using drugs for two hundred years, but they hadn't hurt him a bit. (Another reason for me to believe he wasn't entirely human.) His motive for originating the bloody communion was partly selfish, partly humanitarian. By sucking all the blood from the kids during the ceremony, he satisfied his hunger for it, and he didn't have to kill anybody.

During the day, he didn't die. He just went into a sort of hibernation. His heart slowed way down but never stopped beating. That had been proven scientifically. But, when he was hibernating, he did have an almost flat brainwave.

"If my heart did stop entirely," he said, "how could it get started again?"

When dawn came, while I watched, he went into the sleep that was not quite the sleep of the dead. Though I was trembling with fatigue and fear and was sore all over, I got out of bed and went quickly into the kitchen. I found a screwdriver and went into the big front room. With it, I pried loose one of the huge syringes glued to the coat-of-arms. Then I mixed holy water (it couldn't hurt) from one of Rudolph's bottles with a lot of horse, the big H, heroin. I filled the syringe with it.

The liquid was so thick I wasn't sure it wouldn't clog the hardwood needle. I pressed the plunger enough to shoot a thin spray. Then I took the syringe into the bedroom. I would've preferred a hammer and a pointed wooden stake, but I had to work with the materials at hand. I don't suppose that the syringe and needle had to be made of wood, but my superiors had not taken any chances. They'd also made sure that the syringes would work before they'd mailed the coat-of-arms, along with a letter from a supposedly zealous disciple, to Rudolph.

He was lying flat on his back on the bed, uncovered and naked. His hands were folded on his chest as if he'd been laid out for a funeral. I put my hand on his chest, which now was cooling off. I was crying; my tears fell onto his chest. I'd thought I'd feel nothing except a fierce joy when I did this. But I hadn't foreseen, of course, that I would love him.

I told myself that the devil was the most seductive being in the world. And my superiors had warned me that his powers to charm were vast. I must think only of my duty to God and His souls. Anything I had to do to get to him and carry out my orders was justifiable and would be forgiven. I would, however, have to renounce fornication forever after I had completed this mission. I had verbally agreed to this, but my reservation about this was large. I wasn't going to give that up. It was heaven on Earth, and I certainly had that coming. On the other hand, it wasn't very likely that I would live long enough to ball anybody any more. In which case, I'd be spared having to sin again.

I inserted the sharp point of the hardwood needle between the two ribs just as I'd been taught to. I hesitated a moment, then drove the plunger down. He opened his eyes but never said a word. I think it was just a reflex. I hope to God it was. Anyway, he now had enough horse in his heart for him to ride on all the way to Hell.

I'd been told that maybe the substitute for the wooden stake, the wooden needle, plus the injection of heroin, might not be enough to kill him. After all, his body could repair itself devilishly fast. My orders were to cut off his head to make sure. But I couldn't make myself do that.

Weeping, I picked up the phone. I didn't call George Reckingham. He got me through the cold turkey and then led me to salvation. But he believed that murder was always a sin. That's why he'd left the Warriors of Jehovah and why he'd urged me to quit them. I wish I'd listened to him.

I phoned the Warriors' general. He picked up the phone so quickly he must've waited by it all night.

"It went as planned," I said, "It's done."

"God bless you, Polly! You'll sit at God's right hand!"

"Very soon, too," I said. "I can't get out of here without being caught. And I just can't kill myself so they won't be able to question me. I swore I would, but I'm a coward. I'm sorry. I can't do it. I just wish you, somebody, could've thought of how to get me out safely."

"Nobody's perfect," he said. And he hung up.

Wolf, Iron, and Moth

Wolf, Iron, and Moth

First published in *The Ultimate Werewolf*, Byron Preiss, 1991.

In this story Phil brings some common sense to the mythology of the werewolf. What kind of people would they be? How would they function in the modern world? Would they exhibit the very basic need to be with (or at least have knowledge of) their own kind?

In contrast to the controlling skin that Jean (in "Rastignac the Devil") is expected to wear, here we have the protagonist finding a cruel and sought after liberation in the disembodied epidermis he possesses.

***

L ess than Man, more than Wolf, he ran.
More than Man, less than Wolf, he ran howling with ecstasy through the forest.

He had no memory of being Man any more than he would remember being Wolf when he again became Man.

Whenever the storm clouds were torn apart briefly by the howling wind, the full July moon was revealed. It seemed to him, though vaguely, that his howling worked the magic that rent the clouds. But he had no conception of magic. He lacked words and The Word.

Lightning as white as cow fat crashed. Thunder like the death cry of a bull bellowed. Being Wolf, he did not think of these comparisons. The tips of the trees danced under the whiplash of the winds and seemed to him to be alive. He sensed that the thunder and lightning were the orgasms of Earth Herself locked in frenzy with the moon, though this feeling had no link to human thought and image. Being Wolf, he had no words to voice such feelings. Words could never image forth Wolf feelings.

He ran, and he ran.

Where a man would have seen trees, bushes, and boulders, he saw beings that had no names and were not connected or grouped by word or thought. They had in his mind no species or genus but were individuals.

The vegetation and the boulders he passed moved, changing shape slightly with each of his leaps, seeming to have their own life and mobility. Perhaps, they did. Wolf might know what Man could not know. Man knew what Wolf could not know. Though they occupied the same physical world, they lived in separate mental-emotional continuums.

A is A. Not-A is not-A. Therefore, never the twain shall meet. Not in the world of the mind. But werewolves…what are they? A plus not-A makes B?

He ran, and he ran.

Rain came from nowhere; he did not know that it was from above. Its nature changed when it dashed against the ground and splashed on his fur and into his eyes and on his nose. Raindrops had become something else, just wetness. He had no name for wetness. Wetness was a live being. It veiled his sight and his sense of smell. But the wind had carried the scent of lightning-frightened cattle to him before the rain absorbed the thousands of billions of scent molecules whistling by.

He floated over a wire fence and was among the cattle. He did bloody work there. The half-deaf farmer and his half-deaf wife and their stoned sons in the house a hundred feet away did not hear the loud cries of cattle-terror. The thunder, lightning, and booming TV censored the noise from the pasture. The wolf ate undisturbed.

"I've never seen a man gain weight so fast or lose it so fast," Sheriff Yeager said. "Seems to me it goes in a cycle too, regular as prune juice. You gain twenty or more pounds in a month. Then, come full moon, you seem to lose it overnight. How do you do it? Why?"

"If questions were food, you'd be fat," Doctor Varglik said.

Throughout the physical examination, the sheriff's pale-blue but lively eyes had fixed on the huge wolf skin stretched across the opposite wall of the room. It lacked the legs and the head, but its bushy tail had not been cut off.

"It doesn't seem natural," Yeager said.

"What? The wolf's skin? It's not artificial."

"No, I mean the incredibly rapid fluctuations in your weight. That's unnatural."

"Anything in Nature is natural."

The doctor removed the inflatable rubber cuff from Yeager's arm. "One twenty over eighty. Thirty-six years old, and you got a teenager's blood pressure. You can get off the table now. Drop your pants."

From a wall-dispenser, Varglik drew out a latex glove. The sheriff, unlike most men during this examination, did not groan, grimace, or complain. He was a stoic.

While he was bent over, he said, "Doctor, you still didn't answer my question."

The son of a bitch is getting suspicious, Varglik thought. Maybe he knows. But he must also think he's going bananas if he sincerely believes that what he's not so subtly hinting at is true.

He withdrew the finger. He said, "Everything checks out fine. Congratulations. The county'll be satisfied for another year."

"I don't want to be a nuisance or too nosey," Sheriff Yeager said. "Put it down to scientific curiosity. I asked you…"

"I don't know why I have such a phenomenally rapid weight loss and gain," Varglik said. "Never heard of a case like mine in a completely healthy man."

The wall mirror caught him and Yeager in its mercury light. Both were thirty-six, six feet two inches tall, lean, rangy, and weighed one hundred and eighty pounds. Both lived in Wagner (pop. 5000 except in tourist season), set along the south shore of Pristine Lake, Reynolds County, Arkansas. Yeager had an M.A. in Forest Rangery, but, after a few years, had become a policeman and then a sheriff. Varglik had an M.D. from Yale and a Ph.D. in biochemistry from Stanford. After a few years of practice in Manhattan, he had given up a brilliant and affluent career to come to this rural area.

Like most people who knew this, Yeager was wondering just why Varglik had left Park Avenue. The difference between Yeager and the others was that he would be checking out or had already checked out the doctor's past.

Despite their many similarities, they were worlds apart in one thing. Varglik was the hunted; Yeager, the hunter. Unless, Varglik thought, I can reverse the situation. But when did A and not-A ever exchange roles?

The doctor had removed the gloves and was washing his hands. The sheriff was standing in front of the wolf skin and looking intently at it.

"That's really something," he said. His expression was strange and undecipherable. "Where'd you shoot him?"

"I didn't," Varglik said. "It's a family heirloom, sort of. My Swedish grandfather passed it down. My mother, she's Finnish, wanted to get rid of it, I don't know why, but my father, he was born in Sweden but raised in upper New York, wouldn't let her."

"I'd've thought you'd've put it up on the wall above the fireplace mantel in your house."

"Not many people'd see it there. Here, my patients can see it while I'm examining them. Makes a good conversation piece."

The sheriff whistled softly. "He must've weighed at least a hundred and eighty. Hell of a big wolf!"

The doctor smiled. "About as big as the wolf that's terrorizing the county. But what would a wolf be doing in the Ozarks? Hasn't been one here for fifty years or more."

Yeager turned slowly. He was smiling rather smugly and without any reason to do so. Unless...Varglik's heart suddenly beat harder. He should not have been so bold. Why had he mentioned the wolf? Why steer the conversation to it? But, then, why not?

"It's a wolf, all right! I don't know how in hell it got here, but it's not a dog!"

"O.K." Varglik said. "But it had better be caught soon! The cattle, sheep, and dogs are bad enough! But those two kids!" He shuddered. "Eaten up!"

"We'll get him, though he's damn elusive so far!" the sheriff said. "Tomorrow morning, most of the county police, thirty state troopers, and two hundred civilian volunteers will be beating the bush. We're not stopping until we flush him out!"

Yeager paused, glanced sideways at the skin, then turned his head to face Varglik, "The hunt won't stop, day or night, until we get him!"

"Even the tourists are getting afraid," Varglik said. "Bad for business."

The sheriff turned to the pelt again. "Are you sure it's not artificial and you're not putting me on?"

"Why?"

"I don't know for sure. A minute ago, while I was looking at it, it suddenly seemed to glow. I thought my eyes were playing tricks on me. It had, still has, a light, very dim but a definite glow. I…"

"Aha!"

Yeager jumped a little. He said, "Aha?"

Varglik was smiling as if he were trying to conceal something behind it. His mirror image showed that too plainly. He uncreased his face.

"Sorry. I was thinking of the results of an experiment I made recently in my lab. I suddenly saw the answer to something that's been puzzling me. I apologize for not giving you my complete attention. It's rude."

Yeager raised his eyebrows. He was as aware as the doctor that the explanation was dragging one leg behind it. But he said nothing. He put on his Western hat and started toward the door. Hebe, Varglik's receptionist and nurse, appeared in the doorway.

"Phone call for you, Sheriff."

Yeager went into the front office. Varglik followed him to the office door and listened. Evidently, the wolf had gotten to Fred Benger's cattle last night and had killed four and crippled five. The Bengers had not heard anything, and the parents had not discovered the slaughter until they had returned from shopping in town. From Yeager's questions and his responses, Varglik deduced that the two sons were supposed to have put the cattle in the barn in the evening before milking them. But they had fallen asleep—passed out was closer to the truth—before the storm started. Old Man Benger's threats to kill his sons screamed from the phone. But he, like everybody in the county, knew that they were on drugs and were not to be trusted.

"I'll be right out," the sheriff said. "But don't tramp around the pasture and mess up the tracks."

He hung up and charged out of the office.

"The bastard knows!" Varglik muttered. "Or he thinks he knows. But he must also be suffering great doubt. He's very rational, not the least bit superstitious. He's struggling as much as I once did to believe this."

For years, both in his Manhattan office suite and in his Ozark office, the wolf skin had hung where his patients could see it and he could observe their reactions. Yeager was the first to see its glow! The first to comment on it, anyway. Only one kind of person could see the light. His father would call the person *Kväällulf.* The Evening Wolf. His mother would name him *Ihmissusi.* Man-wolf.

He went into the reception room to tell Hebe that he was lunching in his office. Hebe was gone. At the stroke of twelve noon, she had fled, a daylight Cinderella running away from the ball, the answering machine turned on, waiting for her to come back at one. If he ate in, he was supposed to monitor incoming calls. Today, he would let the machine do the work.

In his private office, he sat down and opened a box containing three beef sandwiches, two orders of French fries, a monumental salad, three bottles of beer, and a jar of honey. A huge bite of sandwich in his mouth, he opened a brown-covered envelope that had come in today's mail. Hebe, following his orders, had set it aside unopened for him. She must be wondering, of course, what the envelope that came every four months contained. Probably thought it was a kinky sex magazine, *Hustler* or *Spicy Onanist Stories* or *The Necrophile Weekly* with an updated list of easily accessible mortuaries and a centrefold of this month's lovely female corpse.

The glossy-paper magazine he pulled out was *WAW*, a very limited-distribution publication. How had the editors of the Werewolf Association of the World known about him? His letter of enquiry to WAW had been answered with a cryptic note. *We have ways.* The magazine, though in English, was published and mailed from Helsinki, Finland. A small section was devoted to articles about the problems of Asiatic weretigers, African werecrocodiles, South American werejaguars, and Alaskan and Canadian werebears and mountain lions. One article on the extinction of the Japanese werefox concluded that overpopulation and pollution and the consequent loss of forest space had caused its demise. The last line of the article was grim. The situation in Japan may soon be ours.

Another writer, under the obviously false by-line of Lon Chaney III, gave the results of his survey-by-mail of werewolf sex habits. The sampling showed that 38.3 percent of male and female lycanthropes were unconsciously influenced by their lupine phases. When in their phase, they preferred that the female be on all fours and that the male use the rear approach. They also tended to howl and yell a lot. This had led to trauma in 26.8 percent of the non-lycanthrope partners.

One of the most interesting articles speculated that the genes for lycanthropy were recessive. Thus, a werewolf could be born only to parents each of whom had the recessive genes. But the son or daughter had to be bitten by a werewolf before the heritage was manifested. Or the offspring had to obtain a skin taken from a dead werewolf. Hence, the extreme scarcity of lycanthropes.

Having gobbled down all the solid food, his belly packed and yet still feeling hungry, Varglik spooned out the honey from the jar into his mouth while he read the Personals column.

WM, single, 39, handsome, vivacious, affluent coll. Grad, loves Mozart, old movies, long walks in the evening, seeks young, lovely, coll. grad, polymorphous-perverse WF. Children no problem, won't eat them. Photo exch. Req. Write c/o WAW.

Jane, come home. I love you. All's forgiven. You may use the cat's litterbox. Ernst.

The magazine articles were serious scientific papers. But, surely, the WAW staff were making up most of the Personals column. Maybe to relieve the grimness of their lives. After all, being a lycanthrope was no fun. He should know.

Having read the magazine, he put it through the shredder. It hurt his bibliophile soul to do that, but the publisher's urgings to her subscribers to destroy their copies after reading them made good sense. On the other hand, the publisher might be keeping a small inventory of every issue hidden away, knowing that they could become quite valuable collector's items. His doubts about her intentions were probably unfounded. But being a lycanthrope, like being a dweller in the Big Apple, made one downright paranoiac. He had double reason to know that it was better to be suspicious than to be sorry.

It was also best to always play it safe. But the lycanthrope ejaculated all caution when the full moon was up. That had been yesterday. It did not matter. Two nights on either side of the full moon exerted almost as strong an influence. He was as helpless against the tug possessing him—soon to be a flashflood—as the moon was against the grip of its orbit.

Unable to fight the forces of change, not even knowing how to do it, he had once tried to cage himself during the metamorphosis. When its time was near, he had locked himself in a windowless room of his Westchester house with a side of beef as fuel for the re-transformation back into a man. Then he had pushed the key through the lock so that it fell on a paper in the hall just outside the door. As soon as he had felt the change beginning, a shudder running through him even more sweet and powerful than sexual arousal, he had smashed the furniture and bitten off the doorknob and howled so mightily that he would have awakened the entire neighbourhood if his house had not been so isolated.

He had no memory of his agonies during his frenzied attempts to escape to freedom. But the wrecked room and the wounds in his arms, legs, and buttocks where he had bitten himself were just as good evidence as if he had taped the drama. When he regained consciousness as a man, he was so crippled and weak from loss of blood that he had almost not been able to pull back under the door the paper holding the key.

Somehow, he had gotten up, unlocked the door, put on his clothes, cut and torn, over the wounds, and phoned a physician friend to come to his house to attend his wounds. The doctor had obviously not believed his story about being attacked by a large dog while walking in the woods, but he had not said so.

Since the police could not find the dog, Varglik had had to take a series of painful rabies shots.

That was his first and last attempt to cage himself.

A diligent and experienced detective, the sheriff would have found out about the supposed attack. A few phone calls or letters to New York would be enough. He would also have learned about the dogs and horses slain in the area, though the scenes of the killings were twenty miles from Varglik's house. Yeager would have learned about the mutilation-murders of two hikers and two lovers in the woods. The police suspected that the killer was a man who had butchered the four so that they would appear to have been killed and partly eaten by wild dogs. Yeager would tend to believe that the killer was neither man nor dog.

"It must drive him nuts to have to believe that," Varglik muttered. "Welcome to the funny farm, Sheriff."

Whatever Yeager did or did not believe or intend to do, Varglik could do nothing about what was going to happen to his persona. He could only control where he would be when the inevitable happened.

At six p.m., he left his office. The wolf skin, rolled up, was in the attaché case he carried. He waited in his house, eating a huge supper and afterwards munching on potato chips, until 10:30 p.m. Then he drove his car through town, watching behind him, going in an indirect route, stopping now and then to check for possible shadowers. Within thirty minutes he was on a gravel country road deep within the county just north of Reynolds County. After ten minutes, he pulled into a sideroad and stopped the car in the darkness of an oak grove. The only sounds except for his accelerating breathing were the shrillness of locusts and the booming of frogs in a nearby marsh. Then, the whine of mosquitoes zeroing in on him.

Hastily, he opened the car trunk, removed the skin, doffed his clothes, and put them through the open window into the front seat. His breath sawed through his nose. He panted. His body seemed to be getting warm, and it was. The fever of metamorphosis was nearing its peak.

The wolf skin was draped over his shoulders when he stepped out from under the shade to stand in the full shower of moonlight. Though he was not holding the skin, it clung like a living thing to his back.

The moonlight beams, pale catalytic arrows, pierced him. His blood thumpthumped. The great artery of his neck jumped like a fox caught in a bag. He reeled, and he fell through a cloud of shining silvery smokepuffs. His head and neck hairs rose; the curly pubic hair straightened out. An exquisitely pleasureful sensation rippled through him. He swelled like the throat sac of a marsh bullfrog. His nose ran; the fluid oozed over his lips, which were puffing outward.

Without his will, his arms lifted and straightened. His legs expanded as if blood had poured through the skin. His bowels contracted and expelled his feces with the sound of an angry cat spitting. He emptied his bladder in a mighty arc. Then his penis became enormous and lifted toward the moon until it had almost touched his belly and seemed to his darkening senses to howl shrilly.

Howling deeply with his mouth, he fell hard backwards on the ground. The wolf skin was still fastened to him as if it were a giant bloodsucking bat. He felt forces shooting through the ground and then through him like saw-topped oscillograph waves, chaotic at first then organizing themselves into parallel but curving lines. They shook his body until he had to claw deep into the dirt with his outstretched hands to keep from falling off the planet.

He shot out his spermatic fluid, again and again, as if he were mating with Mother Earth Herself. His human spermatozoa were gone, and his glands were already pouring Wolf fluid into his ducts.

After that, he knew nothing as Man.

Only the moon saw his hair and skin melt until he looked like a mass of jelly that had been formed into the figure of a man. After a minute or so, the jelly quivered, and it kept on quivering for some time. It shone as pale and semisolid as lemon jello. Or as some primeval slug that had crawled out of the earth and was dying.

But it lived. The furious metabolic fires in that jelly had already devoured some of the fat that Varglik had accumulated so swiftly. The fires would eat up all of it and then attack some of the normal fat before the process was completed. In the dawn of Varglik's awareness of what he was heir to, he had tried to diet. He reasoned that if he lacked the fat, he would lack the energy needed to carry out the metamorphosis. But the sleeping Wolf in him defeated him. Varglik could no more stop eating great quantities of food than he could stop sweating.

The jelly darkened as it changed shape. The arms and legs shrank. The head became long and narrow, and newly formed teeth shone like steel spears. The buttocks dwindled, and from the incipient spine, now a dark line in the mass, a tentacle extruded. This would become the tail. Smooth at first, then hairy. Other darknesses appeared in his head, trunk, legs and arms. These were at first swirling, the cells shifting as they were reformed by the magnetic lines generated by the Wolf in him.

The Wolf did not become conscious until the change was completed. The wolf skin had become a living part of the living jelly and then of the metamorphosis. That completed, what had fallen as two-legs rose as four-legs. He shook himself as if he had just emerged from swimming. He sat down on his furry haunches and howled. Then he prowled around, sniffing at the feces and the fluids. He investigated the car despite its repulsive and overpowering stench of gasoline and oil.

A moment later, he was running through the woods. He ran and ran. He loped through a world that had no time. He saw the bushes and trees and rocks he passed as living beings which moved. He saw the moon as an orb that had not existed until then. He had no concept of a changeless moon rising from above the Earth in its orbit. It was a new thing. It had been born with him.

But the wolf knew what it wanted. Flesh and blood. And, being a were-wolf, it desired human flesh above all flesh. Yet, like all creatures two-legged or four-legged, it ate what it could. Thus, he bounded over a fence and gripped the throat of a barking watchdog and carried it over the fence into the woods where he slew and ate it. That was not enough. He needed more prey to kill to thrill his nerves with ecstasy and to fill his belly for fuel for the change back into Man. He ran on until he came to a pasture on which horses grazed or slept. He killed a mare and disemboweled her and began tearing at the flesh until the aroused farmers came at him with flashlights and guns.

Then, in his wide circuit through the woods, he crossed a moonlight-filled meadow because sheep scent drifted across it to him. As he got close to the edge of the woods, he smelled, along with sheep, that flesh he most lusted for. A man stepped out from the darkness of the trees, the moon shining on the rifle barrel. He lifted it as Wolf leaped snarling at him.

———⇒≫●≪⇐———

Sheriff Yeager had not joined the hunting party just north of Benger's farm. Instead, outtricking his prey's every trick to detect a shadower, he had followed Varglik to the oak grove. He had sat in his car down the road until the wolf-howl had told him that what he had expected to happen had happened. After ten minutes, he had gotten out of the car and cautiously approached the grove. He was just in time to see the bushy tail disappearing into the dark woods.

Using his flashlight, he followed the pawprints in the wet earth. After a while, he heard distant shots. Guessing from which direction they came, he cut at an angle through the woods. Just before he got to the meadow, he saw the enormous wolf loping across it. He waited until the beast was almost ready to plunge into the forest, and he stepped out. His rifle cartridges contained no silver bullets. That was bullshit. A high velocity .30-caliber lead bullet would kill any animal, man included, weighing only one hundred and eighty pounds. The werewolf might seem to be of supernatural origin. But it was subject to the same laws of physics and chemistry as any other animal.

The bullet entered the gaping mouth, bounced off the roof of the mouth, tore down the throat, and angled into the liver. The wolf was dead and so was Varglik. Nor was there a change into the human body such as shown in many movies. The cells were dead, and the transformation principle could not act on the cells. The wolf remained Wolf.

Yeager did not want questions or publicity. He skinned the carcass and dug a grave and buried the wolf. In the process of re-metamorphosis, the skin would have fallen off, he supposed, separating from the body and other parts of the skin. But it remained whole now, the process of change having been erased with the end of life.

———⇒≫●≪⇐———

Now, the pelt was stretched out against the stone of the fireplace in the sheriff's house. Every night, its light seemed to Yeager to be getting brighter. He considered destroying it. He knew or thought he knew what he would do soon if the skin stayed within his sight or within the reach of his hand. He had to burn it.

The hungry wolf will try to get at the meat even if it sees the trap. An iron filing does not will not to fly to the magnet. The moth does not extinguish the flame so that it will not be incinerated.

Evil, Be My Good

Evil, Be My Good

First published in *World Fantasy Convention Program,* 1990.
Also published in *The Ultimate Frankenstein,* Byron Preiss, 1991.

While Philip José Farmer has taken his pen and reshaped many literary characters, from classic to pulp to modern and even to horror, this is his first and only treatment of the Frankenstein monster. In common with "Nobody's Perfect" and "Wolf, Iron and Moth," in "Evil, Be My Good" Phil reinterprets the fundamentals of myth from an original yet highly pragmatic viewpoint and, as in the preceding stories, Phil's sympathies lie with the "monster," the perfect symbol of the social outsider.

Phil: "I've always wondered what went on in Frankenstein's Monster's mind."

To Herr Professor Doktor Waldman,
University of Ingolstadt,
Grand Duchy of Bavaria

7 October, A.D. 1784

My Esteemed and Worthy Colleague:

This is indeed a letter from one whom you must long have believed dead and entombed. I, Herr Professor Doktor Krempe, your colleague for many years, am not as dead as you have thought. Bear with me. Do not reject this letter as the product of a crazed mind. Read it to its end, and consider well what is herein.

Though I am dictating this letter, the hands which are writing this letter are huge and clumsy, not my own small and artistic hands. Moreover, they are freezing, and so is the ink in the pot. The supply of writing materials is non-existent in this Godforsaken and icy desolation. The very limited amount available to me was brought from an icebound ship. Thus, I cannot give a detailed account of what happened to me since the time I was placed in my tomb.

Yes, this is, in a figurative sense, the voice of one everybody has assumed to be dead. It will be a shock, and it will seem to be an affront to both commonsense and logic. Only a professor of natural philosophy could possibly believe this narrative. I say "possibly" because even you, the most open-minded and liberal man I know, perhaps too much so, will find it difficult to put credence in it.

I repeat, please do not shred this letter because you believe that it is both fraudulent and written by a maniac. One item which will make you believe that this is an insane prank is the handwriting. You will compare it to the samples of my penmanship which are in your files, and you will readily see that the letter is not in my hand.

It is not. Yet, it is. Please keep reading. I will explain, though perhaps not to your satisfaction.

I am sending this by a native on skis from this utterly wretched outpost east of Archangel. I have great doubts that it will ever reach you. However, you are the only person who might think that my story could have some semblance of reality. I cannot send it to my wife. She would not understand anything in it; she would think it a cruel joke if it was explained to her.

Moreover, she has probably remarried. I must confess—a scandal no longer matters and you will keep it to yourself—that we did not, to put it mildly, care for each other.

To the breach, to my tale! Withhold your sense of disbelief until you have read the entire missive. Perhaps, then...but no, I doubt you will ever receive this.

The first stroke of lightning paralyzed me. That occurrence, as you know, was in September, 1780, on the grounds of our great university.

The second stroke of lightning, in November, of which you know nothing, freed me.

Yet, in many senses, the succeeding bolt put me in a prison far worse than the first. I could walk and talk after that stroke of hell's energy from the heavens. At the same time, I could not walk and talk. Another creature was walking and talking for me, though I did not want him to act as he acted.

(You are no doubt asking yourself, What second lightning stroke? Be patient. This and other matters will be explained soon.)

For many weeks after the first lightning bolt mummified me, as it were, I was faithfully attended by my wife, the nurses, and the best doctors in Ingolstadt. "Best" is only a relative ranking. All the physicians were quacks. They could have made some simple tests to ascertain if I was conscious and aware despite the fact that I could not move a muscle. But they assumed, in their ignorance and arrogance, that I was in a coma. And, to try to cure me, they bled me and, thus, assured that I did become unconscious from the loss of blood until my body restored the lost fluid!

May they all go to hell! And may that consist of being unable forever to move even their eyelids while they hear their wives, relatives, nurses, and attending quacks talk about them as if they were in their coffins! That condition, you stupid, lackwitted, and pompous practitioners of the unhealing arts, bringers of death to those whom Nature might have healed, would make you painfully aware of what your supposedly caring nurses and loving wives and servants really think of you!

I suffered more agonies than even the cruellest and most savage are doomed to endure forever. Murderers, mutilators, cannibals, blasphemers, freemasons, physicians, lawyers, bankers, and sodomists! You who have gone to hell and are destined to go! You will know little of real pain in that place! The tortures of the damned dead pale beside the tortures of the innocents who must live in the hell of the totally paralyzed!

I, Herr Professor Doktor Krempe, twice dead though not really dead, am back from two tombs, to write this! Yet, it is not my hand that moves the pen!

I owe all of my second hell to my student in natural philosophy, the ever-egregious, hubris-swollen, and morally unprincipled Victor Frankenstein. I knew what his private opinion of me was because another student reported it to me. Frankenstein, that smug, self-centred, self-righteous, utterly irresponsible, and totally spoiled infant in a man's body, that overbearing and utterly snotty student, said that I was short and squat and the repulsiveness of my hoarse voice was only exceeded by that of my face. Also, he told my informer that only the mercy of God kept my stupidity from being fatal to me. So enraged was I on hearing this from my informant on that dismal October evening that I ignored the cold and driving rain and the perils of the ravening night skies to venture forth on foot to confront the slanderous scoundrel in his own quarters. And I was struck down by a lightning bolt en route to Frankenstein's quarters to confront him. Is there Justice? Is there a God who believes in Justice?

Later, I was able to revenge myself upon him, though it was done through a very strange vicar, satisfyingly savage. What was not satisfying, I admit was my revenge. OUR revenge, I should say, and you will soon know what I mean by OUR! Nothing that could be done to Frankenstein on Earth or in hell would transform the fire in my bosom to sweetness and light, for which seemingly un-Christian statement I am fully justified.

Yet, according to the word of God as printed in the Holy Bible, I must forgive even my worst enemy. Otherwise, I go to hell, too. Is it worth it? I ponder this question often. My chief thoughts revolve around one possible solution to my dilemma. Did Frankenstein commit an unforgivable sin? The particular sin he committed is certainly not listed in the Holy Book. That unique offense against God, I suppose, would also make his sin an original sin. Thus, there are two more grave questions to concern the theologians, and God knows they have enough now that they cannot answer. Are there two unforgivable sins? Are there two original sins?

Unfortunately, or fortunately, they will not have to concern themselves with these matters. No one will ever know about the pair of double sins unless this account gets to a civilized nation. Or unless somebody else writes a book about the monstrous Frankenstein and his monstrous creation. That seems very unlikely. And it would, if it were written, probably be printed as a romantic novel, a fiction. Who among the unenlightened public, the ignorant masses, would believe it if it were presented as fact? For that matter, what learned man would put credence in it?

The day came that I died. That is, the purulent frauds attending me declared me dead. You can imagine, though the mental picture must be only a shadow of the real horror, how I felt! I strove to protest, to cry out aloud that I was still alive! I struggled so violently within myself, though in vain, that it was a wonder I did not have a genuine stroke! I was taken to the undertakers for the washing of my body, dressing me in my best suit, and obscene joking about the size of my genitals. I did manage, finally, to flutter my eyelids. Those drunken incompetents never noticed! Afterwards, while lying in state and listening to the comments about me from those hypocrites, my wife and relatives, I fought once more to blink. But, this time, I failed.

Fortunately for me, the practice among the English wealthy of embalming the body had not become as yet popular in Ingolstadt. Even if it had, my wife would not have permitted it because of the expense. As a result, I lived, though I can truly say that I wished it had been otherwise. I dehydrated, of course, while lying in state, two states, in fact. The other was the state of hell on Earth.

My dear colleague, put it in your will that a knife be driven into your heart before you are buried! Make sure that you are indeed dead before being buried!

The funeral was held—no doubt, you were there—and then the coffin was closed. Immediately thereafter, I was placed in the tomb. I expected to die quickly though horribly when the air in my coffin was used up. But my very shallow breathing made the oxygen last longer. Then, just as I was about to perish, the coffin lid was raised.

You must have already guessed, from my previous remarks, whose face I saw by the light of the torch in his hand. Young Victor Frankenstein, of course!

With him were two scroungy and scurvy fellows he had hired to assist him. They lifted me from the coffin and wrapped me in an oiled cloth enclosing ice chunks and put me in a wagon. In bright daylight! But my tomb was in a remote section of the cemetery, and he was in a desperate haste.

When the cloth was unrolled, I found myself in a filthy and cluttered room. His quarters off campus, I assumed. It looked like the typical degenerate student's room except for the great quantity of expensive scientific equipment. The usual stench of unwashed body and unemptied chamber pot was overridden by the odor of decaying flesh. I cannot go into detail about what followed because of the limited supply of paper and the increasingly wretched penmanship of the creature who is writing this. His hands are getting colder and colder, so I must not indulge myself any more. I must compress this incredible narrative as much as possible.

To be brief, Frankenstein dared to believe that he could make an artificial man out of dead bone and tissue and give the assemblage life! He would do a second time what God had done first! Man, the created, would become a creator! His creature was not visible since it was in a wooden box packed with ice and some preservative that he had discovered through his chemical researches.

I had believed and still believe that this scion of an aristocratic family was the acme of arrogance, stupidity, and selfishness. But God, for some unknown reason, had endowed this detestable being with the genius of Satan. The youth knew what he was doing or he blundered into success, probably the latter.

Yes, success!

He placed me in a box filled with ice, sprayed me with some substance I cannot identify, and then proceeded, though the cutting was not as painful as I had anticipated.

What happened when I began bleeding, I do not know. I can only surmise that he knew then that I was living. But, instead of making efforts to revive me, he continued his blasphemous and murderous work. I had known that he despised me, but I had not fathomed the depths of both his hatred of me and his relentless and conscienceless pursuit of a goal only a madman would desire or attempt to achieve.

I awoke late at night. The lightning stroke which he had drawn down from the storm clouds by means of a rod had revivified the body in which I found myself. Its body lived, and so did its brain.

However, the brain was mine!

How that fool of an inexperienced student had managed to connect the encephalic nerves to the others is beyond me. I would not have attempted it despite my deep knowledge of anatomy.

Though I am well known for my mastery of language, I do not have the words to describe the sensations of being only a brain installed in vitro in an alien body. And what a body! As I was to discover later, it was eight feet in stature and was a disparate assemblage of human and animal parts. As the workmen say, built from scratch.

Of course, I did not know at the moment of awakening that I was not in my own fleshly shell. But it did not take me long to realize the true state of location when the monster lifted my hands. MY hands! They were a giant's, yet they had to be mine! Slowly and clumsily, I rose from the huge table on which I—no, not I, he—had been placed before Frankenstein pulled down the blazing vital fluid from the sky. I was aware not only of my own sensations but of the creature's. This was very confusing and continued to be so for some time before I was able to adapt myself to the unnatural situation.

I said that his sensations were also mine. His thoughts, feeble and chaotic though they were in the beginning, were perceived by me. Integrated by me would be a better description. And, perhaps, I should not describe the thoughts as such. The monster had no language, thus, no words with which to think. He did have the power of using mental icons—I suppose even a dog has that—and his emotions were quite humanlike. But he had no store of images in his brain, which was a veritable *tabula rasa*. Everything that he first saw, smelled, touched, and heard was new to him and impossible for him to interpret. Even the first time he experienced bowel rumblings, he was astonished and frightened, and, if you will pardon the indelicacy, his morning erections disturbed him almost as much as they disturbed me.

How am I to express comprehensibly the relationship of his brain to mine? In the first place, why should his brain be a blank tablet when he was brought to life? (It was, in reality, my brain, but I shall henceforth refer to that portion of my brain used by him as being his own brain.) His own brain should, on revivification, have contained all that it possessed before I died. It did not. Something, shock or some unknown biological or even spiritual mechanism wiped it clean. Or pushed the contents so deep that the creature had no access to them.

If part of the brain was scoured clean, why did a part remain untouched? Why was my consciousness pushed into a corner or, as it were, under the cerebrumic rug? I have no explanation for this phenomenon. The process of creation should not have been like God creating Adam but like God bringing Adam back to life after his longevity of nine hundred and thirty years. Adam would have remembered the events of his stay on Earth.

Our mental connection was, however, a one-way route. I was aware of all he felt and thought. He was totally unaware that a part of him was not he. I could not communicate with him, strive though I did to send some sort of mental semaphore signal to him. I was a passenger in a carriage the driver of which knew nothing of horses or the road he was on or why he was holding the reins. Unlike the passenger in this example, who could at least jump out of the vehicle, I could do nothing about my plight. I was even more helpless and frustrated than when I had been paralyzed by the first stroke of lightning. I was also more frightened and despairing than when in that "coma." That was a natural and not unheard-of situation. This was unnatural and unique.

I saw through the monster's eyes. (These, by the way, were long-sighted. Frankenstein had botched the selection of the visual orbs just as he botched everything else, though he desired to make a perfect human being. Why, in the name of God and all His angels, did Frankenstein build an eight-foot high man? Was that his idea of a being who would not stand out in a crowd?)

As I said, I saw through the eyes of this blasphemy in flesh. Though they needed glasses for reading, their deficiencies were not responsible for the peculiarity of my visual acuity. I saw as if I were peering through the big end of a telescope. What the creature saw as normal-sized, I assume, I saw as if reduced in size. At the same time, the images I received were as if the large end of the telescope were dipped just below the surface of a pond of clear water. The intersection of instrument and fluid made for a peculiar and somewhat blurry picture.

This distortion extended to my hearing also. Thus, the construction of the eyes was not the cause of this irritating phenomenon. It must have been the construction of the brain or, perhaps, a faulty connection between him and me that interfered with proper reception by me. Or perhaps that was the manner in which the creature saw and heard.

Great God! How I do run on! I know that both my time and the quantity of paper are limited. One may give out before the other does. Yet I, always noted for the clarity, conciseness, and absolute relevancy to the subject of my lectures to the benighted, apathetic, and thick-headed students of our university, am as silly and talkative as any one of the hundred passengers on Sebastian Brant's Ship of Fools. Forgive me. I have so many statements to make so that you will understand the story of Frankenstein, his monster, and myself.

Just now, the monster, despite my mental urgings, faltered in his copying of my mental dictation. It is not the cold in this shack which contributes to his weakness. It is the frigid finger of death touching him and, hence, me. I must hurry, must compress. However, as you must realize, you would not be reading this if I had not been successful in reactivating him into continuing the task I have set him without his knowing what he is doing or the reason for it.

He is falling apart, literally. It is my belief that he would have done so much sooner if Frankenstein, that unhappy combination of fool and genius, had not injected some chemical in him to prevent his organs, collected from different individuals and different species, from reacting poisonously upon each other. The chemicals used to effect this have, however, dissipated their strength.

Yesterday, his right ear fell off. The day before, his left leg swelled up and turned black. A week ago, he vomited all the polar bear meat and seal blubber that have been his—our—main ingredients of diet. He has been unable to keep much down since then. Most of his teeth are rotting.

Let us hope that I can keep pushing him until he hands over this letter to the messenger.

That hopelessly irresponsible Frankenstein was so horrified when his creation became alive that he ran away, leaving the monster, innocent as a baby and as full of potential good—and evil—as an infant, to his own devices.

I could do nothing but go along with the monster in his pathetic efforts to understand the world into which he had been involuntarily thrust. All of us, of course, had no say about our entering this harsh and indifferent universe. But most babies have someone to take care of their needs, to love them, and to educate them. This creature was, of all mankind, and it was human despite the doubts of itself and its maker, the most forlorn infant of all. Though I at first loathed him, I came to sympathize with him, indeed, to identify with him. Why not? Is not he myself, and is not myself he?

Onward more swiftly. As the end of his—our—lifespan approaches, so must the end of this letter be hastened.

No time for details, no matter how much they demand to be illuminated and explained.

The creature fled from Ingolstadt to the mountain forests nearby. He learned much about himself and the world and the people in this area. He longed for acceptance and love. He did not get either. He learned how to make and use fire. He approached a village in peace and was injured by the stones cast at him. He took refuge in an unused part of a cottage and spied upon the occupants, once-wealthy French aristocrats exiled and now living in poverty.

His eavesdropping enabled him to learn how to speak French. Part of that was my doing. I had by then managed to send him some messages of which he was not conscious. These were not commands which he obeyed or anything making him conscious of my presence, but the information stored in my brain, which included an excellent knowledge of French, oozed through to him.

(Incidentally, I discovered the most intimate details of the electrical, chemical, and neural constructions and functions of the human brain. Alas! No time

to impart this stupendously vital information which would propel our knowledge of the brain to the high stage which I imagine the citizens of the twentieth
century will enjoy. But I cannot resist informing you that the treelike organization of the nerves is a delight to the explorer. My travels up and down its trunks,
branches, and twigs were the only joy I have had during my incarceration in the
monster's body. I was, in a sense, a great ape swinging from branch to branch in
the orderly jungle of the neural system, learning as I traveled. I discovered that
the splanchnic nerve is actually three nerves and all control the visceral functions
in various manners. I call them the Great, the Lesser, and the Least. I especially
loved the Least Splanchnic Nerve, a modest, unassuming, and yet somewhat
cheeky transmitter with unexpected after-effects, a rosy glow, in fact.)

The creature—it has never had a name, a lack which has greatly depressed
its self-esteem but heightened its fury and its lust for revenge: you have no idea
what being nameless does to a human being—finally revealed himself to the
occupants of the cottage. He expected compassion; he got repulsion and horror. The occupants fled. He burned down the cottage and then wandered aim-
lessly around. He rescued a girl from drowning and was wounded by a gun for
his heroic deed. This ingratitude intensified his hurt and rage, of course. Then
he came to Geneva, Frankenstein's native city.

Here he murdered Victor's brother, the child William. While he was doing
this, I screamed at him, if a voiceless being can be said to scream. No use. The
monster's hands—my hands—choked the life out of the infant.

The man-made thing encountered his maker and got him to promise to
make a female for him. Victor went to the Orkney Islands and did as promised. But, disgusted, suffering from Weltschmerz—with which the monster
was also afflicted—Victor destroyed the female, which was as huge and ugly as
her male counterpart.

Oh, the catalog of horrors! The ravening creature murdered Henry
Clerval, Victor's best friend. He raped and murdered Victor's bride on their
wedding night. After that hideous deed, he declared that evil would henceforth
become his good. He was sincere when he said that. But the words were not
his in origin even if they were his in spirit. They were a paraphrase of Satan's
defiant statement in Milton's Paradise Lost. "Evil, be thou my good."

Yes, the monster had read that noble work. It contains, as you know, some
of the greatest lines in poetry. However, there are boring passages which stretch
their dryness to an intolerable length. The reader feels as if he were a parched
traveller lost in a Sahara of iambic pentameter.

I was the unwilling actor in a tragedy which was real, not Miltonic. You
cannot imagine the agony and the shame I experienced while the monster was

performing his ritual of lust and murder upon Elizabeth, Frankenstein's bride. Yet, I must confess that I also shared the ecstasy of his orgasm; though, soon after I was transported, I loathed myself.

Frankenstein, after he was put in prison because he went temporarily mad—temporarily?—after his father's death, began to track down his creation in order to slay him. After much time and wanderings, both Frankenstein and his creature were in the Arctic, travelling on dogsleds. Victor became very sick but took refuge on an icebound ship. After telling his story to an Englishman aboard the vessel, he died.

Meanwhile, the ice pack broke up. The passage to warmer climes was open. But the monster came aboard just after his creator died. He had by then been stricken with the pangs of conscience, perhaps because he felt dimly my own reactions to his satanic deeds, though I was eager as he to slay Victor, and these, in a twisted way, caused the monster to repent.

I do not think that he had sufficient reason because of this to decide to kill himself. He was far more the injured of the two. What did Frankenstein expect? That the creature, like a true Christian, would turn the other cheek? He had not been instructed in Christianity and, anyway, how many of those so instructed would have forgiven such great evils done to them?

In fact, that the monster did have a conscience so tender and highly ethical trumpets forth his innate goodness.

But it may be that my mental urgings were by then influencing him, however small their voices. I had been trying to get him to kill himself, for his sake and, I have to admit, for my own. What a miserable life I had been leading! Starving and freezing with him, hurt with him, sick with fury and desire for revenge with him. I wanted our lives—actually, a single life—to end.

One of the unforgivable sins is suicide. But I was not killing myself through my direct action. The nameless and pitiful unnatural creature would be doing it. My hands were clean; his would be dirty. But he would not have to burn in hell for that deed. He had no soul. Nor would I burn. I had died once and should have gone to Heaven. Instead, Frankenstein, the foul incarnation of the archdemon, had brought me back to life. For that blasphemous crime, Frankenstein would exist forever after death as a shade on the plain of burning sands in the seventh circle of Hell. There, an eternal rain of fire would fall on him. There, according to the great Italian poet, Dante, are the blasphemers and the sodomites, the violent against God, which Frankenstein certainly was. There also are the usurers, that is, the violent against Art. Frankenstein belongs in their ranks. He violated God's Art by making the monster. Thrice accursed, thrice tortured!

His monster finally forgave him, but I cannot do that. Thus, the monster is more Christian than I. Theological and philosophical question for you, colleague. Does that indicate that God should or must endow the monster with a soul? If he does, to whom belongs the brain of that soul? What is my brain is his brain and always the twain shall be one. The implications are staggering. A whole college of St. Aquinases could consider that one question for aeons.

To resume. The creature—and myself—declared to the Englishman on the ship where Frankenstein died that he would build a funeral pyre and lie down upon it until his loathsome body was burned to ashes. Of course, you will find this ridiculous. Where, in this Arctic wasteland, could he find a single branch for fuel?

Then he boarded a large piece of ice and floated away. During the interval before the ice island came to land, I managed finally to communicate with the other part of my brain. It was a one-way form, that is, I could impart some of my mental suggestions or commands to him, though he was not aware of my presence or of the command. I do not know how I finally did it. I believe that it was his weakening state of health, his decaying flesh, that enabled me to overcome whatever obstacle had previously existed.

He—we—wandered over the snow-and-ice covered land until we came to this remote outpost inhabited by a few miserable natives. We were given food, disgusting fare but nutritious, and a shelter scarcely worthy of the name. Now, I could transmit my commands, though they became distorted in the passage as if they were flags manipulated by a drunken semaphorist. No doubt, this was because of the rapidly decaying state of the monster's neural system. Of course, that affected me, and my transmissions may also have been at fault.

The main problem is that, the weaker and more disorganized the creature's brain becomes, the easier it is for me to influence him but that very removal of mental obstacles decreases the monster's efficiency in carrying out my messages.

To put it in the colloquial, you pay for what you get. Also, the more progress you make in solving a problem, the more problems you encounter.

I really cannot see now how legible the handwriting is. The objects I observe through his eyes are getting smaller and smaller. And the watery veil now seems to have swirling particles in it. These are becoming more numerous. It may not belong bfore them coleisce to from a seemerly slodid well.

Ferwale...is end...Dog forgove...menster. Me too...evn fregiv his creatr... Farknesten...Dog...nodDog...min, God...God...furgiv...nodpar...pardin... pardon...fregiv...all...rweched...humn...beins...evn monste...humn too... iverbudy...for!gev...al...Gd...God...fregiv me

Mother Earth Wants You

First published in *And Walk Now Gently Through The Fire…*, Chilton Book Company, 1972.

A story that takes us far into our future where gender supremacy is a matter of life and death. Phil had previously explored the White Goddess myth in his 1960 novel, *Flesh*. In both stories sex and violence are posited as inevitably linked.

Phil: "Both sex and violence are linked to my name because violence usually accompanies sex in my stories. That is because they usually deal with the sicknesses of our attitude towards sex."

Covey and The Man stopped to rest when they got to the top of the high steep hill. Covey looked across the plains below at the little white city several miles away, at the groves of tall trees and the square cornfields and the bright canals and little river. The land was indeed fair.

The Man stood behind Covey, his hand on Covey's shoulder while he spoke softly into his ear. The hand kept squeezing, as if telegraphing a digital code. Whatever the letter of the message, its spirit was nervousness. And no wonder. They were only twenty feet from the sacred grove, where Her power was strongest.

Covey was as nervous as The Man. Wasn't his wife sitting under the central lingam? Wasn't she covered with a blue robe and hood? Wasn't a man approaching her and wouldn't she rise in a moment and drop the robe, revealing a masked face and what the man had to take whether or not he liked what he saw? Once a man crossed the outer ring of trees, he was within sight and sound of Her, and he must go through with the ritual. Otherwise, the earth would tremble and then open up and swallow him. Also gulped down would be the sacred grove and the lingams and her equipment for seeing and hearing. And Her sacred vessel, Covey's wife. But this did not bother Mother in the least, as far as anybody knew.

The Man, still squeezing Covey's shoulder, said "Renounce Her! And then you will have the world! The world which She claims to be! But She lies, of course! She does not exist!"

Covey turned around, and the hand fell away. The Man's eyes, irises, pupils, balls, were bright red, as if they had sucked in underground fires and refused to let them go. His hair was shoulder-length, red-bronze, and shimmery in the light of the halo spinning just above the tips of his goat horns. His beard was pale orange; his nose, eaglish. His hands were perforated, and when he lifted one to point upwards, the sky shone through its wide opening.

"There, in the sky, there is where the true deity is."

"Then you know for sure that the priestesses are lying about Her?" Covey said. "She doesn't really exist?"

The Man did not answer. He was fading away into the sunlight. He was Covey's doubts metamorphosed into human shape, though he sometimes seemed more real than Covey himself.

Did The Man really exist? Was he hiding in the woods, begging or stealing bread and wine, sleeping with the foxes in their holes or the sheep in the meadows? Was The Man whom Covey saw the mental projection, the astral forerunner sent by The Man because he was still afraid to expose his flesh and blood where Mother could seize him?

Covey walked towards the grove. The outer ring was composed of twelve times twelve elm trees. The inner ring was seven times nine ash trees. Inside it was a triangle of nine giant oaks. Inside the delta was a round thick shaft of oak painted a reddish pink with blue veinlike lines and topped by a dark red dome creased across the top. Set into each quadrant of the shaft, just below the overhang of the dome, was one of Mother's eyes-ears. The priestesses' technical term for them was "teevee transceivers." Their hidden copper wires went deep, ending in a vein of copper or iron or some similar metal, if Covey had not been misinformed.

From the vein, which was a nerve of Mother Earth, modulated currents flowed. These were shaped by the great brain which could never be seen because it was so deeply buried. It was a brain of stone and metal and was invulnerable, if the priestesses did not lie.

The Man said that they did lie. They were the handmaidens of the Mother of Lies.

But the Priestesses said that The Man was the Father of Lies.

The Man said that they had confused him, on purpose, of course, with his own ancient enemy. How clever of Her.

Covey stopped before he quite reached the outer ring. The masked man was rising from Penelope, who lay on the grass with the white legs, the black triangle, the pinkish rings shimmering in the peculiar sunlight that was found only in the sacred groves. The blue mask was still on her face. Anonymity had to be preserved. Mother did not care for personalities. She wanted only the communication of bodies, the most archaic of speech. The only permitted modulations were the curve and angle of protoplasm and the grunts, cries, moans, and the short savage arcs and ellipses and the final vibrations every way free.

The man walked past Covey, removing his mask as he stepped out from under the branches of the outer ring. His expression was both satisfied and religious, as it should have been. He wore a wide-brimmed straw hat, a blue cloak, a bright green kilt, and calf length red boots. He was sweaty and dirty; hay and seeds were stuck in his hair; he stank of horse manure and onions. He looked as if he was a farmer, and he probably was. He had come up from the fields during his lunch hour and, now spiritually refreshed, he was returning to his work. Blessed indeed was he by the Mother.

And the peasant would undoubtedly have good seed. Perhaps he was the one who would provide Penelope with a lusty child.

Penelope had had three children by Covey. Each, living but obviously unhealthy, had been carried by a priestess into the house where, after a short prayer to Mother, she had lifted the infant high so that the eye-ear might see. And, after a few seconds, a single ideogram had appeared on the screen.

The priestess had looked at the white stylized sickle crossed by the five lines representing a sow's head, and she had said loudly what she had read.

"Death!"

And so the baby had been carried to a trough and plunged under water and held there until it was dead. Then it went back into the earth in some field where the roots of wheat or corn would feed upon it.

That was right, and, in the long run, much more merciful. The baby would not grow up to suffer nor would it transmit its imperfections.

It was also right that Covey's wife should sit in the scared grove and wait for strangers. She had a right to prove that she was not responsible for the sick babies. Or, if she did have a baby by a stranger and it was like the others, then she would have shown that Covey was not at fault. And Covey could then divorce her and get another wife.

He did not want to divorce her, no matter what happened. He loved Penelope with an intensity of which Mother might not have approved if She had known about it. He did not mind too much that his wife sat in the grove. (Or do you? The Man had whispered into his ear more than once.) If she had a healthy child, or if she didn't, she must come back to him.

But Penelope said that she was not coming back. The second day after entering the sacred grove, she had told him that. She would not tell him why. Perhaps, she was ashamed to tell him that she preferred variety. Perhaps, she had become very religious and loved to serve Mother in this way. Perhaps…Who knew? All he did know was that she did not want anything more to do with him. Was there something about him that now repulsed her? Did she smell The Man when he appeared? But no, that could not be. The Man had not appeared until after she had told Covey that she wanted no more to do with him.

"Penelope!" he cried.

She sat up and looked around her while the sacred woodpeckers flew up out of the wood in alarm at his shout. She drew her cloak about her, and the sight of the white body withdrawing into the blue cloth made him sick with a frustration of love.

"Penelope! I've come to take you home!"

"What, again?" she said faintly.

He looked up past the blur of her face inside the deep hood at the glassy eye set under the wooden glans of the pillar. His image and his worlds were being transmitted—who knew how many hundreds or thousands of miles?—to that great brain inside the world. To the brain. No messages could reach Her heart, because She had no heart.

His own heart was a boulder rolling down a steep hill, thudding into other rocks, bouncing, smashing into obstacles, flying off and hitting other rocks, his ribs. His knees were loosened, their pinions removed by his great fear of Mother.

But he shouted at Penelope again. There was no law that a husband could not try to talk his wife out of the sacred grove. As long as he stayed on this side of the outer ring of trees, he was not transgressing.

"Go away!" Penelope said.

"I'll love the child!" he shouted. "You know that! I'll love it just as I love you! And if it turns out that you can't have a healthy child, I still want you! We can adopt a child! Mother only permits each couple one child, if it is their flesh and blood! But She permits a couple to adopt as many as they can!"

"I stay here until Mother grants me a healthy child!" Penelope shouted back. "In any event, you and I are through!"

"But why?" he yelled.

She was silent. Perhaps she did not know herself, not that not knowing why she did a thing had ever kept her from giving him a dozen reasons for doing it.

Covey fell silent, and, suddenly, he felt someone behind him. Then a hand was on his shoulder and squeezing dots and dashes. And there was an extra brightness to the sunshine which could only come from the halo.

"Your wife is using the baby as an excuse," The Man whispered. "She likes being a whore. And since a sacred whore is beyond criticism or censure, she will remain one. Mother Earth protects and feeds her. And so she will stay in the grove until…"

"You will become old and ugly!" Covey shouted. "Men will come to you no more! Mother will see what is happening and will kick you out! Where will you go then? I won't be waiting for you! You can work as a house or field hand until you get too old to work and the priestesses of the House of the Sow come for you because you have no one to support you!"

Two men, looking curiously at him from behind their ritual masks, walked by him and under the branches of the outer ring. One was dressed in leather and carried a leather sack full of copper pots and pans on his back. The other wore a cap made of horses' tails and carried a bundle of buggy whips. Such was to be Penelope's lot. Field hands and traveling salesmen, and, on weekends, the unmarried youths and old bachelors from the white city of the plains.

He watched them as they stopped before Penelope, spoke a few words to her, received her blessing, and then sank on their knees for a short prayer to Mother. He continued to watch until they were done. Penelope certainly was pleased with them, and the two seemed to be pleased. One left a large copper pot as a gift and the other gave two buggy whips.

"Why do you watch?" The Man said behind him.

"I can't help it" Covey said. "Penelope is very religious, isn't she? She truly worships Mother with her body."

"Swine!" The Man said, and Covey wondered about this. To call someone a swine was a high compliment. Pigs were sacred to Her, but on special feast days, four times a month, She permitted men to eat them. They were delicious.

The two men left the grove grinning.

"They are laughing at you," The Man said. "They heard you. They know you are her husband."

"Their attitude doesn't seem reverent enough," Covey said.

"No man sneers at another unless he is willing to back up his sneer with his sword," The Man said.

"Mother would see us fight, and She would be displeased, since She did not give us permission."

"Go after them. I bring a sword, not peace, you know," The Man said. "Catch them down the hill, out of Her sight, if you are afraid of Her."

Afterwards, Covey wondered why he had obeyed The Man. He did hate the two, even though he had no right to do so. Yet he could not take out his hatred on them, even if they had not seemed reverent and should have been chastised.

Later, he would see the contradiction. Why get angry at men who lacked reverence when he was so doubtful about Mother himself?

But he wasn't being logical, and he did need a vent for his anger. He followed the two down the path, calling after them when all three were out of Mother's sight. They turned, and, seeing his angry face, started to draw their swords. Doubtless, they had intended only to warn him off. At that moment, however, he needed the slightest excuse to attack, and he thought he had it.

"Draw on me, will you?" he shouted. "Wasn't having my wife enough?"

The latter must have startled them, since it sounded so irrational to them. They were slow in their responses, perhaps because the fear of madness made them cautious. They may have thought it would be better to try to talk him out of his madness.

Covey slashed at them, cutting one's neck in half and chopping off the sword hand of the other.

Afterwards, he grew sick. He did not vomit because of their blue faces or the blood. Mother's children saw much of the butchery of animals and of voluntary human sacrifices. The cat clawing inside his belly was the thought that these two had just left a religious service and he had allowed his secular feelings to interfere with Her worship.

Or had he, he asked himself as he began to recover from his sickness? The service had been completed; the men had left the holy ground.

But all ground was holy, since all earth formed Mother's breast.

Some ground was more holy than others, however.

The Man, looking down on the bodies, said, "This is the first step in the war against Her."

"I wish you wouldn't say things like that," Covey whispered. "They scare me."

He was more than scared. He wanted to run and run until he was out of sight of the hill and the dead men. But he would never be out of sight of Mother. No matter how carefully he moved around, sooner or later he would come within view of one of Her eyes.

How had he gotten into this horror?

"Horror is the daughter of doubt," The Man said.

"I notice you said *daughter*, not *son*," Covey replied.

"It's important to make such distinctions," The Man said. "Distinctions are the guideposts along the road to truth."

The Man seemed to be getting more solid. The sunlight was running into obstacles inside his image. It was bouncing back and back as if it glanced off crystals forming in his body. Perhaps The Man was a ghost and fed off the blood of living things.

Perhaps, though, The Man was what he claimed to be. Perhaps he wasn't just the exteriorized persona of the man-god which sleeps in the lower brain of every human being. Mother had striven to put this Man to sleep forever. But he would not lie down and sleep; he must be up and out.

Covey wished again that he had not been chosen as the vehicle for the return of The Man. How easy to believe wholeheartedly in Mother, to sink down on your knees before Her sacred trees and Her eyes-ears and cry out to Her and then see Her answers to your prayers on the screens, the flickering ideograms which said Yes or No and, almost always, Go with my blessing, my son.

Mother had so much more to give than The Man. She was the whole earth, and she fed and clothed Covey and gave him stone and wood for house and fire and the beasts of the field to ride and to eat and to work for him and gave him Her daughter to be his wife. (However, as The Man pointed out, She also took all this away if She felt like it.) Whereas, The Man was the son of the beaten and discredited god of the sky. True, without air, life was not. But even this precious element came from Mother. Without Her grass and trees, air would become poison. So, even The Man and his father had lived only at Mother's sufferance. They had ruled at Her sufferance, too, though you would never have known it if you believed their arrogant boasts.

Long long long ago, so the priestesses said, Mother had ruled over all Her body. And then evil arose, and the men of the North and the desert tribes turned to their own image and formed from worship of themselves the father god and, eventually, his son. They slew the worshippers of Mother in their own lands and then they swarmed out of their lands into other lands. And, eventually, they killed or forcible converted the worshippers of Mother. But a few of Her people survived, living in the midst of the father-god worshippers and disguised as such.

Mother was patient. She waited. And man invented science and he flourished and multiplied. Beyond reason. And then Mother Herself: Her waters, Her soil, Her air, became poisoned.

About this time, so the priestesses said, women began to throw off the patriarchal yoke. And a woman discovered that Earth was not just a ball of matter circling the sun. She was a sentient being, a self-conscious entity. She had blood and bone, organs, a skin, and a brain. Or the mineral analogs of such.

Mother Earth, it was discovered, talked. The puzzling configurations of electromagnetic fields which supersensitive instruments had detected were words of Her language. She was transceiving to-from the moon and the other planets. Mother Earth and hot little Mercury and hot mist-hidden Venus and little red Mars and the vast icy remote giants Jupiter, Saturn, and Uranus, and the even icier and more remote Neptune and Pluto, talked.

And so the scientists decoded the speech of the spheres (no easy task because of the scarcity of recognizable referents), and they assigned ideograms to the units of the language.

The next step was to talk to Mother Earth Herself.

Meanwhile (as the priestesses said), mankind was dying. Man was killing himself off in his own poisons, dying in his self-fouled nest.

Mother Earth twitched Her skin.

In other words, She generated earthquakes, sank lands, and lifted oceans. The survivors swore they would never again offend Mother.

The only science permitted now, or, to be more exact, technology, was that needed to make and maintain the electronic equipment to communicate with Mother. Hence, the sacred groves and temples, the phallic pillars and the glassy eyes-ears of Mother. Hence, the abhorrence of all but the simplest machinery needed to plow Mother's skin. Hence, the rule of state and church by women. Hence, the passing of tolerance, for it was only when faith weakened that tolerance for other faiths was born. But if a faith have the truth, then it should not put up with anything that denies the truth.

All this had seemed to Covey, at one time, to be the way things should be. And Covey was still not sure that it wasn't the way things should be.

But, one day he had walked by the great grave-shaped hill where the body of the father god was said to lie. Never mind that other areas had similar graves with similar claims. Covey had looked once at the hill and then turned his gaze away. The gigantic body interred in there had long ago rotted. But the bones must still nourish evil, and it was best not to loiter in their neighborhood. And then, as he strode along the base of the hill, anxious to get away, his eyes averted, he saw The Man rise from the earth and stand before him.

Terror had locked the joints of his skeleton. Here was the ancient enemy who would not stay down. Or, at least, the son of the enemy. Covey was confused about which was father and which was son, since the priestesses who taught school did not seem to know the distinction themselves. At least, if they did, they had never made it clear.

Since that day, Covey had not been able to get rid of The Man.

Perhaps it was The Man who was responsible for the troubles between Penelope and Covey. The Man denied this. He said that it was Mother who had caused them. She was the one who insisted that a woman should have the last word in everything. Whereas, the man should be the head of the family, the state, the church. Women should be subservient to their natural lords. As for the thing called equality, forget that. Equality existed only in mathematics. Wherever two or more were, there was also a pecking order.

Naturally, so The Man said, Mother favored women. She felt closer to beings of Her own sex. Yes, Mother Earth, even if She were a planet, a massy ball of rocks and iron and soil and water and air, was a female. But who, then, was the father? Who seeded Her, who planted in Her womb?

Covey did not argue about that. Mother was a woman. No doubt of that. As a child, and even more as a juvenile, he had had his dreams of Mother coming to him through the blackness of the night. She was a tall woman, mountainously breasted, massively buttocked, hugely thighed. She was blonde, and She was white everywhere except for the dark cavernous delta. Even Her eyes were pale.

The schoolchildren were encouraged to describe their nocturnal encounters, and the juveniles told in class of their couplings with Mother, their ecstatic emissions.

Sometimes, the boys saw Her as the queen of the land. The queen was a woman they had seen in the flesh when they went to the great white city to the east, and so she was easily visualized. But it was understood that she was not the queen when she appeared in dreams. She was the symbol of Mother, of course.

The girls dreamed of lying with the king, who sat on a throne lower than the queen's and who was sacrificed when his manly vigor ran out. But the girls understood that he was a symbol of Mother, though a third-hand one, in a sense. Sometimes, the girls told of meeting Mother in their dreams and of being embraced, held against those brobdingnagian breasts, and of sucking. The wonderful milk refreshed them, and they went back to dreaming of the king.

And what of Covey's dreams of The Man.

They had all been nightmares.

The Man had explained that this came about because of the conflict in Covey's mind. Once he had rid himself of his evil love for Mother, then the nightmares would go away.

"When my father ruled, Mother used to come to man in his dreams as a terrible hag or a lovely vampire." The Man said. "Now that She is ascendant, She sees to it that my father, and myself, play the role that my father once gave to Her."

Definitions meant nothing now. Only deeds mattered. And the deed was done. He had murdered two men.

"You have three choices," The Man said. "You can run and hide and try to form an underground. You can run and take refuge in the fairy reservation. Or you can throw yourself on Mother's mercy.

"Let's take the last two first. The reservation is for homosexuals and criminals who want a sanctuary. But it's not much of a refuge, since, every now and then, Her soldiers come in and thin down the population, just as the forest rangers crop the deer population when it's too large.

"You can throw yourself on Her mercy. The lightest sentence you could get would be to serve as a eunuch priest in one of Her temples. There you can swing censers and sweep floors and develop all of the vices and none of the virtues of a woman.

"You can become an outlaw, and you can find others who dream of The Man, and, in time, you can start a revolt against Mother. Believe me, there are many men like you. With enough of them, you could destroy the sacred groves, rip out Her eyes-ears, make Her deaf, dumb, and blind, and render Her helpless. And then you will see how easy it is to overcome women when you have the muscle and they lack Mother's direct help."

While Covey stood in thought, he had control of events taken from his hands—if he had ever had any control. A woman screamed. Below him was a woman clad in a blue robe and hood. She must have come up to sit also in the sacred grove, but she had almost stepped on the two bodies. Now, after screaming three times, she turned and ran back down the path.

Covey overtook her, and, knowing that words were useless, cut her head off.

The Man, standing behind him, said, "The blood of my father's enemies feeds him. I hear him stirring in his grave."

"And what will my blood, when it is spilled, do for him?" Covey said.

"The blood of his martyrs is like a sea that's broken a dike. It spreads his worships."

Covey felt as if he were a chess piece. First, Mother moved him. Then, The Man. Then, Mother. And so on.

"And my father can do more for you than Mother," The Man said. "She promises only that you will be born, will live a while, may have a happy life if you follow Her laws, and then will assuredly die forever. I can promise you a life after death."

"Can you keep that promise?" Covey said.

The Man was silent, and, when Covey turned, he saw that he was fading away again.

Covey sliced off the men's genitalia, climbed back up the hill, entered the grove, and cast down his offerings at the feet of Penelope, though they were to Mother, not to her.

"Mercy, Mother!" he said. "I have killed two of your sons and one of your daughters! I was mad! Because of love of a woman!"

She would surely understand that.

"And I have come to my Mother because She promises only what She can fulfill! Out of Her womb we come, and back into Her womb we go! And that is all She offers, because that is all there is!"

Penelope had moved away until her back was against the lingam. She stared at the bloody organs and the bloody sword. Surely, Covey thought, she must know that if Mother says I am to die, then she will die, too.

Covey waited. And he felt a faint stirring behind him, something light and airy but still solid enough to displace some air. Had The Man dared to materialize within the sacred grove?

If Mother saw The Man standing behind him, She would have no mercy at all.

He turned. The sunlight was being troubled by an alien presence. Mists were forming. The beams were being refracted and reflected.

"Go away!" Covey said. "Are you mad?"

"Do not be afraid," a thin voice said. "I am with you."

"That is what makes me afraid," Covey said, but he faced the lingam again. At that moment, as if She had been waiting for him to see, She flashed the ideogram for death upon Her eye. It flickered in and out. "Death! Death! Death!"

A hand clamped down on his shoulder. The Man said, "Do not die like an ox or a lamb! Battle like a hero! And, who knows, you may get away and collect others like you around you! There are plenty who dream of The Man and of his father stirring in his grave."

Covey shouted and swung his blade, Penelope's scream was cut off, as was her head. Covey picked up a large rock and heaved it. It shattered Mother's eye-ear so that She would not be able to see him running off down the hill. Not that that mattered, since the other eyes would know that he could have gone in only one direction, inasmuch as they had not seen him.

Covey ran down the hill and along the dirt road and then across fields and meadows and through woods and across brooks and ravines. At each second he expected the earth to shake and to crack around him and perhaps under him. He had hoped that She would be in a rage and shatter the earth for miles around Her. To kill one, She would kill a thousand innocents. Too bad. So much the worse for them. But they could be replaced, and the survivors would fear Mother's anger even more.

Covey was hoping that She would lose Her temper. He would take his chances on being wiped out in the general catastrophe. And if he escaped, he would then have put a number of Her eyes-ears out of commission. While the techs were repairing the damage, he would be at the next sacred grove, upsetting Her and causing Her to strip Herself of Her own communications.

The Man, running along behind him, said, "Wait a minute! Use your brains! Think! You can't do much by yourself. But if you got a large enough gang, and they made Mother destroy Her own eyes-ears over a large enough area, then She would be rendered deaf, dumb, and blind. And you'd have a chance to do something against the army She'd send in. You might even eventually strip Her of all Her senses. Then She would be helpless. She would rage and cause widespread destruction, perhaps, but after a while She'd forget. And mankind could walk unafraid over Her breast. And men would regain their natural place in society."

"I'll think about it," Covey said. "But why hasn't She quaked this area? What is She thinking of?"

The Man told him to stay away from the sacred groves until he had gotten enough converts to test Her strength. Covey waved him away. His curiosity was too strong. He had to find out what She was up to. Who knew but why She had decided to ignore human beings all of a sudden? Perhaps She had tired of this tiny breed of monsters that was always pestering Her.

"You're crazy!" The Man said. "I know the old Bitch from a long way back. Mark my words…"

Towards evening, Covey found another hill on top of which was a sacred grove. He climbed it with his plan and determination hardened. He would kill the sacred whore, or whores, he found under the pillar. He would allow Mother to see him do it, and then he would run. Surely, this time, She would break open the earth for miles around. But he would escape; he was convinced of that.

"You're suffering from guilt and you want to die!" The Man said. Dusk had fallen on the land below and darkened somewhat the grove. At the foot of the lingam sat a shrouded figure.

Covey did not put on his cloak or mask. He would let Mother know he was coming, let Her have time to get angry.

The figure stood up as he neared it. It dropped the cloak.

Her body was white and beautiful.

She dropped her mask, and he saw a skull.

He yelled with horror and then cried, "Mother Death!"

His momentary inaction had given her the chance to use the weapon, or ritual tool, that she had hidden behind her. The sickle cut through his members with a single stroke.

Other figures emerged from the gloom of the trees beyond. They seized him and carried him off while the priestess removed the skull mask. She was beautiful; she had long honey-colored hair, lips as red as blood, and wild staring eyes.

She stooped and picked up his genitals, held them up so that Mother could see them, and tossed them upon his belly.

The man holding his legs got between him and the woman, and Covey saw her no more. But there was little more he would ever see. The shock and the loss of blood were carrying him off even faster than the eunuch priests.

"A corner of a field down there needs feeding," one of his carriers said.

The other grunted.

Covey felt a hand on his shoulder. He saw, as if it were smoke passing, The Man.

"She's a wily old Bitch," The Man said. "She's learned that She just hurts Herself if She rips up the earth to get at one person. So She sent a daughter after you. Or sent one to wait for you, rather."

The darkness was almost complete. He seemed to be riding as a passenger, a very small passenger, in his own head.

"You will die, too," he said to The Man. "You were born of me. I couldn't have children, so I conceived you. You will die when I die."

The panic in The Man's voice was only the ghost of panic. But Covey felt it strongly.

No! I exist! I am an idea! Ideas aren't born in a mind! They float around, and they enter a mind if there is an opening for them.

Covey was too small and weak to reply. Mother had been weeding out men like himself, slowly, generation after generation, but surely. And he was the last of his kind. With him would die The Man. The idea even of The Man.

Both of them, however, would be of some use. The corn would appreciate them; the earth would be richer for a long time to come because of them.

Mother knew best.

Opening the Door

First published in *Children of Infinity*, Franklin Watts, Incorporated, 1973.

On plate 14 of William Blake's *The Marriage of Heaven and Hell*, Blake talks of 'The cherub with his flaming sword' and 'the doors of perception,' both strong influences on this story.

This story was part of a collection aimed specifically at young adults with the intention of showcasing science fiction. Phil's story does much more and maturely treats such themes as impending adulthood, death, loss, rejection and familial responsibilities.

Phil has long had an enthusiasm for Blake, starting a decade preceding this story with the start of The World of Tiers series—based on Blake's Urizen books from where many of Phil's characters were taken.

⚜

The voyage from sixteen to seventeen was dark and silent.

Up above, he knew, were light and air, blue clouds, white skies. No, it was the other way around. Blue skies. White clouds. And the wind shushed, the waves slapped, the gulls screamed. And somewhere, far off, human beings spoke.

He cruised along in the dark of the deep. He felt the pressure—its cold, its indifference.

Sometimes, he could put up a periscope. He could drive it up through the congealing and freezing substance. He could drive it up, up, until it was near the surface. He knew that it was near, where water and air met—or parted—because he would see a glimmer. And the voices became stronger.

Then he would cry out through the periscope. But nobody answered. And though he tried to keep going up, he would sink. The glimmer would dissolve, and the cold and pressure would return.

And something huge would move near in the darkness. Menacing, it moved. Breathing in darkness and pressure and cold, and breathing out horror, it would move nearer.

Then he ceased being a submarine. It was so unexpected. It was like having the world pulled out from under you and another shoved in. Light was born. White was up above and on both sides, except where dark instruments and gray faces of cathode-ray tubes emerged. Faces moved around him as if he were the sun and they the planets.

No. He was in a hospital room. The faces were those of men and women who must be doctors. After a few seconds, he recognized two faces.

His mother was weeping. This was not unexpected. But she had gotten older. His father's face was rigid. Nothing new. But he seemed to have aged also.

His mother's tears fell on his face. Salt water. Was it for this that he had struggled up from the briny deep? For more brine? The briny shallow? And the face of his father. Was it for the thermosetting plastic of those features that he had propelled himself so desperately upward?

His parents' faces fell away. A man's face appeared. He was, the face said, Dr. Deet. He was in charge of N-PWR. Neural-Parallel World Research. He had personally supervised the care and instrumentation of Clark for over a year. From the day that Clark had been brought in.

He remembered his name then. He was Clark Norris. He was just sixteen and had been driving his father's new steamer. There was the Yield sign, and Clark hadn't yielded, and something vast and dark and screaming had overtaken them.

It was not all his fault, Dr. Deet explained. The big steam semi had not had its lights on.

That did not matter, Clark thought. His girl, Diana, and Bob, Mavis, Angela, and Larry were dead. Buried over a year ago.

And why did you bring me back from the dead?

He could not hear his own voice. However, he could see it. On the ceiling was a screen, and his words flashed across it.

His mother wailed.

Dr. Deet said, "You've not been dead, though there were times when we were not sure that you were still living."

His parents came and went many times. He groped around on the bottom of the ooze now and then. Other times he dreamed, and he knew that he was dreaming and that this was the first time in a long time that he had dreamed. And the doctors floated up before him and then were snatched away, as if they were balloons.

At first, he did not want to admit it. But after a long while, after many talks, he told Deet that, yes, he now knew that he had no legs or arms. He did not have a tongue. Yes, he could easily see and feel, he was hooked up to electronic devices. He watched his own words flashing across the screen. His speech was like lightning, but it struck only himself.

"Now I know who I am," he said.

"Who?" Dr. Deet asked.

"In the midst of all the chatter a year ago, we were talking about the game—rather, they were. I was asking myself, Who are you? Will you ever know? That's why I didn't see the Yield sign. Perhaps because I felt like yielding to no one at that time. It seemed to me that I'd been yielding all my life."

"And now you know who you are?" Deet said.

His face passed from Clark's tunnel of view.

"I know who Diana, Bob, Mavis, Angela, and Larry are," Clark said. "They're dead. No problem there. And I know who I am. Clark the almost dead. No problem there. From almost to completely is a short step. Of course, I can't take that step. I have no legs. That's a problem there."

"We all know that," the doctor said. "No self-pity, please. Now, for your information, you haven't been in a genuine coma. Shortly after you were hooked up, you began seeing—no, experiencing—this."

His mother must have entered while he and Deet were talking. Or perhaps she'd been there for a long time. No, she would never have kept quiet for a long time. Now, she wailed and she said, "Oh, no!"

Dr. Deet ignored her and signaled to someone. A gray screen on the ceiling turned to two shades of black. The lighter was an oblong in the center of the screen. After a while, something gleamed flickering and palely behind the oblong.

"This is a recording of what you saw while you were—ah—unconscious," Deet said.

"What is it?" Clark said. Then he said, "Of course. I'm in N-PWR. Never mind. I know what you're doing to me."

"You've made contact," Dr. Deet said. His voice was low but fierce. "This is the best contact we've ever recorded. I don't mean just by you. By anyone."

"It doesn't look like much to me," Clark said. "Black on black."

"It's consistent. That's the thing, it's consistent. And it keeps getting stronger. The flickering, I mean. It's increasing in frequency and brightness."

"I have a big imagination," Clark said. He drifted off, vaguely aware that his mother was crying. Where was his father? Probably glaring at her because she was weeping. When he got her home, he would lose his silence. Then he would start yelling at her to quit crying, to quit making a scene.

When he awoke, he saw the screen with the oblong and the flickering. If this was a replay, it was of a more recent vision. The oblong had gotten blacker, or the area around it had paled. And the flickering ran along something bladelike.

"It's acquiring shape," Deet said.

"Or shape is acquiring it," Clark said. He did not know what he meant by that.

"Who gave you permission to stick those electrodes into my brain?" Clark added.

Deet told him what he already knew. His parents had signed the papers. They had done so because all his hospital bills would be paid by the research center.

That was the logical thing for them to do, he told himself. Why should they beggar themselves, put themselves in debt for the next how many years?

If he had a son, wouldn't he do the same?

He groaned, and peaks of light traveled across the voice screen.

He would never have a son.

It was no use thinking of his lost limbs or his lost life as husband and father someday. It was better to think of the implications of his being in the N-PWR.

He might really be in contact with another world. To be exact—if there could be exactitude in this field of research—he was in touch with a parallel universe.

The principle that only one object could occupy a particular area of space at any one time did not seem to be true any longer. Many worlds could be "polarized," could exist "at right angles to each other," and so could occupy the same point in matter. Of course, the matter of one universe would not be the matter of another, which is why thousands, or even billions, of worlds filled the same "space" but did not rub against each other.

A scientist named Pearson, however, had maintained, and had "proved," that these worlds did, in fact, influence each other. Rather, the beings of one world could get into mental communication with those of the world next door. They did so through an unconscious method of transceiving, one that operated without the transceiver's knowledge or wish.

Pearson had detected in the brain the very weak wave that sent out complexly modulated forms. And he had located the area of the brain—a minute colony of nerves—that received at the same time it transmitted. Whatever barrier it was that kept the physical aspects of one universe from colliding with the other, this barrier was no obstacle to the waves.

Pearson also claimed that the power of fantasizing did not exist. Fancies, dreams, daydreams, wild thoughts did not originate in the fancier, the dreamer, the wild-thinker. They were glimpses of another world, brief drinkings-in of the foam of alien seas forlorn.

Most scientists did not accept Pearson's theory of the origin of fantasy in the human brain. But they did accept the fact that some people were more gifted than others in making contact with other worlds. And they could not deny that it was the most imaginative who were the most gifted at making this contact.

Now that even more powerful electronic amplifiers had been developed, N-PWR was on the verge of another breakthrough.

"If you want to know who you are," Deet said, "you're the Columbus of the parallel worlds."

"Did Columbus know who he was?" Clark said.

"We're not dealing with spiritualism or with time travel," Deet said.

By then, the oblong had become even darker. But it was like dark glass. Through it, the definitely sword-shaped light could be seen. And something tall and thin and peculiarly shaped was forming behind the blade. At times, it looked manlike.

"Almost like an angel with a flaming sword," Deet said. "It could be a guardian at the gate of the new Eden."

"Does it want to keep me out?" Clark said.

Deet hastened to explain that he had been using anthropocentric terms. Even scientists who knew better were always couching their terms in such images. But he did not literally mean that the oblong was a gate or that the strange phenomenon of the blade and the figure was an angel holding a sword. In fact, what they saw on the tube was not the "real" thing. It was a hybrid of the psychic and the physical. It was a silhouette formed by Clark's mind and by the limitations of the electronic amplifier itself. After all, the tube could only show what the circuits were designed to interpret. And man had built the circuits.

"And what lies behind the mask of what we see?" Clark said. "What is the reality?"

"Only an intelligent young man, a very young man, or an old fool asks such a question," Deet said.

"My legs and arms and tongue and most of my lower jaw and my ability to move anything but my eyes are gone," Clark said. "I'm only half-here. Half-matter. The ratio of psychic to physical has risen, and so I'm closer to reality. You follow me? I'm entitled to ask that question."

"Very well," Deet said. "But that doesn't mean that you're entitled to an answer."

Clark watched the screen. At first, it did not change much. After a while, the oblong seemed to swing out from one side a little.

Deet, seeing it, became excited.

"You're influencing it with your conscious mind! That's not a recording!"

"No," Clark said. "I haven't been trying to influence it with my thoughts at all."

"Then you're able to influence it while you're conscious, even if your unconscious is doing the work."

After a few minutes, Clark became tired. The oblong swung shut.

"Where are my parents?"

"Your father is working, of course," Deet said. "Your mother is attending class-es at the university. I thought she told you she was going back to get her degree."

"Weren't they here all the time while I was unconscious?"

"At first. But when it looked as if you might never come out of the coma, or that it might take years, they quit coming so regularly. They're only human, you know. And now that you can cooperate with us scientists, you can spend your time more profitably than by just talking to your parents. They have to have their lives, too, you know. As it is, they do spend a lot of time here. At least two or three hours every day."

"And so now when they can talk to me, and when I need them, they're gone."

"What would you talk about?" Deet said. "The last few times they've been here, you and they had nothing to say to each other."

"We would have improved with practice," Clark said.

"After sixteen years?" Deet said.

"Seventeen."

"You were, for all purposes, gone for a year."

Clark did not answer. Deet said, "N-PWR is your father and your mother." He touched Clark's forehead. "Anytime you want to talk, day or night, the mid-dle of the night, anytime, I'll be here."

Clark had never felt so helpless, so frustrated, so scared, and so angry.

After a while, he said, "The door's swinging open again."

Deet wasn't looking at the voice-screen then, but he did happen to see the Parallel World screen.

"I wonder?" he said.

"Wonder what?" Clark asked.

The oblong was slowly turning outward, as if it really were on hinges.

"If the desire to escape your, ah, condition, could enable you…but no, it's too fantastic."

"Could what?"

"Enable you physically to transport yourself through that gate? Or through what is, obviously, a gate to you? After all, there have been many unexplained disappearances. People disappearing in plain view of many witnesses, as if they had stepped into another world. And there have been many cases of airplanes or ships disappearing without a trace. An entire squadron of naval planes fly-ing over the Caribbean in fine weather, and then…nothing. But you've read Charles Fort. You know what I'm talking about."

"You mean that if I think hard enough, I can open that gate and go into the other world?"

"And have arms and legs again, talk with a tongue, run, play as you did before."

"How could that be?"

"How? How would I know?" Deet said. "But I'm just talking. Besides, there is your guardian angel with the flaming sword. How would you manage to get by him?"

"What do you mean?"

"If you want to escape through that doorway, you also want to stay here. Otherwise, why do you put a guardian there? One who's armed to keep out intruders."

"I'm not putting him there," Clark said. "According to the theory, the world next door is as independent of effect of thought on its physical substance as this one is. How could I put a guardian there unless I dreamed up that universe? In which case, you're seeing only the electronic manifestation of my fantasies."

"I don't think you've created that world," Deet said. "But I do think you somehow managed to locate a doorway that has a guardian. For your own purposes, whatever they are."

"Get my parents," Clark said. "Let them see what's happening. Then, maybe…"

"Ah, so that's it," Deet said. "Very well. I can have them here inside half an hour."

But they did not come. They did send word they would be at the center during the evening, sometime after supper.

"You told them it was an emergency?" Clark said.

"I told them you wanted them now."

"But you didn't convince them. Why? Is it because you're afraid that if my parents and I start having a good relationship the contacts with that other place might vanish? Is that it? Or maybe you never even called them? Maybe you never said a word to them? You wouldn't want your experiment ruined, would you? You're as bad as they are."

"You're getting hysterical," Deet said.

"Then step back over here so I can see your face!"

"I know best what's good for you," Deet said.

"And where have I heard those words before?" Clark said.

The voice-screen became an explosion of light.

One of the women doctors screamed.

A few seconds later, Deet screamed.

Something wet splashed over Clark's face. He had no tongue to lick his lips, but he knew it would be salty if he could taste it.

The blade now seemed more like a pair of scissors than a sword. It flashed and flashed soundlessly, though heavy thumps followed every flashing.

There was silence. The thing stood at the foot of the bed so that Clark could see only the head. Its eyes flamed, and then it was gone.

From the corridor came screams.

These were cut off. Then, faintly, from the corridor below—or was it from the one above?—more screams. It must have gone upstairs. It would be making a clean sweep of the hospital before it moved out into the street.

Clark wished he could die. If he died now, that thing would have to go back through the gate. Deet had been mistaken. It had not been at the gate to keep intruders out. It had been waiting for the gate to open wide enough for it to slip through.

And it had not killed Clark because he, in some mysterious way, was its gate. To kill him was to shut the gate.

The screen in the ceiling was flashing, "Help. Help. Help."

But there would be no help, and the lightning blades would snip and snip. They would close, but they would always be clean, no matter what they passed through, and then the thing would find his parents. And they would never know, never know.

Or would they, in a flash of light from the thing's eyes, see *his* eyes?

The Wounded

First published in Fantastic Universe, Volume 2, Number 3, October 1954.
Also published in Farmerage, Volume 1, Number 2, October 1978.

The nature of us all is to crave Cupid's injury when it is absent but to experience its sublime pain when inflicted. This story graphically puts this into context. That this mythical character is turned from inflictor to inflicted by a mortal female shows a propensity to be manipulated normally lacking in Farmer's protagonists.

Those Polaroid glasses they give you at the 3-D movies were the cause of my downfall.

When the show was over I went into the lobby and stood there a moment while I studied my schedule. I was supposed to go to a big party given by one of the prime numbers of the Four Hundred. I didn't have an invitation, but that never bothered me. Biggest gate-crasher in the world, that's me.

I heard a gasp and looked up to see this beautiful young woman staring at me. She had forgotten to take off her 3-D glasses and that, I instantly realized, was the trouble. Somehow, the polarization was just right to make me visible. Or let's say that I was always visible but nobody recognized me.

The view she got enabled her eyes to make that subtle but necessary shift and see me as I really am.

I thought, *I'd have to tell Mother about this.* Then I walked out fast. I ignored her calls—she even addressed me by the right name, though the accent was wrong—and I hopped into a taxi with my violin case under my arm. I told the cabbie to lose the taxi in which she was tailing me. He did, or seemed to.

As soon as I entered the penthouse, a house detective seized my arm. I pointed to the violin case under my arm. His piggish eyes roved over it as he munched upon a sandwich he held in his other hand. He was one of the wounded, always eating to stuff the ache and the hollowness of it.

"Listen, kid," he said, "aren't you sort of young to be playing in an orchestra?"

"I'm older than you think," I replied. "Besides, I'm not connected with this orchestra."

"Oh, a soloist, heh? A child prodigy, heh?"

He was being sarcastic as many of the wounded are. I could pass for twenty-five any day or night.

"You might call me that," I said truthfully.

"One of our hostess' cute little surprises, heh?" he growled, jerking a thumb at the tall middle-aged woman standing in the middle of a group of guests.

She happened at that moment to be looking at her husband. He had a beautiful young thing backed into a corner and was talking in a very intimate manner to her.

The light was just right so I could see the flash of green deep within my hostess' eyes. It was the green of a long-festering wound.

Her husband was one of my casualties, too, but his clothing covered the swelling of the injured spot. The girl he was talking to was pretty, but she was one of the half-dead. Before the party was over, however, she would come to life with the shock of pain. When I hit them, they know it.

I glanced around at the partygoers, many of whom exhibited the evidences of their wounds like the medieval beggars who hoped to win sympathy and alms by thrusting their monstrous deformities under your nose.

There was the financier whose face-twisting tic was supposed to spring from worry over business. I alone knew that it wasn't business that caused it, that he looked to his wife for healing, and she wouldn't give it to him.

And there was the thin-lipped woman whose wound was the worst of all, because she couldn't feel it and would not even admit it existed. But I could see her hurt in the disapproving looks she gave to those who drank, who laughed loudly, who spilled cigarette ashes on the rug, who said anything not absolutely out of Mrs. Grundy. I could read it in the tongue she used as a file across the nerves of her husband.

I wandered around a while, drinking champagne and listening to the conversation of the wounded and the unwounded. It was the same as it was in the beginning of my profession, a feverish interest in themselves on the part of the unwounded and a feverish interest in their healers on the part of the wounded.

After a while, just as I was about to open my violin case and go to work, I saw the young woman enter—the one who had recognized me. She still had the 3-D glasses. She carried them in her hand now, but she put them on to glance around the room. It was just my luck for her to be one of the invited. I tried to evade her search but she was persistent.

She swept triumphantly towards me finally. She carried a large cardboard box in her arms. She halted in front of me and set the box at her feet. Certain she could identify me from now on, she then removed her glasses.

She was very beautiful, healthy-looking, and with no outward signs of her wounds.

If it hadn't been that her eyes were so bright I'd have thought she was one of the half-dead. But there was no mistaking the phosphorescent glow of the warm wound deep within her eyes.

I glanced at my watch and said coolly, "What's on your mind, Miss?"

"I'm in love with you!" She said it breathlessly.

I had trouble suppressing a groan. "Why?" I said, though I knew well enough.

"You're the one who did it!" she replied. "Did you think that, recognizing you, I would ever let you go?

"Marry me."

"That'd be no good for you," I said. "I would never be at home. I keep all kinds of hours. Your life would be worse than that of the wife of any traveling salesman. Besides," I added, "I don't love you."

Usually that floors them. But not this one. She rocked with the punch and calmly pointed at my violin case.

"You can remedy that," she said.

"Why in Hades should I? Do you think that any sane person would deliberately hurt himself in that manner?"

"Am I not desirable?" she asked. "Would I not be good to come home to? Don't you often long for somebody you can talk to, somebody who will get your meals and listen to your troubles, somebody who *cares*?"

Well, of course I've heard those exact words a billion or more times before. Not that they were always directed at me. Nevertheless, there was something new in them.

"And," she repeated, "am I not desirable?"

"Yes," I said, looking at my wristwatch and getting uneasy because of the delay. "But that has nothing to do with it. When my marriage was annulled— oh, somewhere back in the eighteenth century, or was it the sixteenth—I swore by all the gods I'd never marry again. Moreover, Mother says I'm too busy…"

"Are you man or mouse?" she flashed.

"Neither!" I flashed back. "Besides, Mother is my employer. What would I do if she fired me? Become like one of those?"

I glanced contemptuously at the guests.

She knew what I was thinking, for she cried, "Look at me! I'm wounded! But am I like them? Am I one of the halt, the lame, the blind? Am I like that detective who swells himself into a gross human balloon because he stuffs the growing void of his hurt with food?

"Am I like our hostess, whose green wound caused her to drive away two husbands because it festered so deep she went into a delirium of unfounded imaginings about them? And then got a third who fulfilled the image she'd built up of the first two?

"And am I like that thin-lipped woman who deep-freezes her wound because she is mortally afraid of pain? And do I behave as some of these women here who throw themselves at every man who might give temporary healing, all the while knowing deep within them that the wound will become more poisonous?

"Is it my fault if most of these people don't cultivate their wounds, if they grow sickly and twisted and ill-smelling plants from them instead of the lovely and colorful and sweet flower that grows in me?"

She seized my shoulders, said, "Look me in the eye! Can you see what *you* and you *alone*, did? Is it disgusting, gangrenous? Or is it beautiful? And if it does turn poisonous, whose fault is it? Who refused to heal me?"

Her eloquence was overwhelming. I trembled. I wasn't affected when I overheard other wounded addressing their potential healers thus. But when *I* was talked to in such a manner, I shook, and I remembered the early days when my first wife and I had tended each other's injuries.

"Sorry," I mumbled, abashed before this raging yet tender mortal. "I must be going."

"No you don't!" she said firmly. She stopped and lifted the lid from the paper box. I saw it was crammed with those damned 3-D glasses.

"After I tailed you here," she said, "I returned to that theater and bought a hundred tickets and with them got these. Now, if you don't come with me where we can at least talk, I'll pass them out and everybody will see you for what you are. And don't think for a moment that those who've suffered because of you won't tear you limb from limb and string you up on the highest chandelier!"

"Nonsense," I mumbled.

I felt suddenly shaky. And so unnerved was I that I rushed away from her and out into the hall. All I wanted to do was to get into the elevator, alone and unobserved, and speed away with the speed of light, half way around the world.

Do you know, I think that that clever young wench had planned that very move? She knew I'd be so upset, I'd forget my violin case. For, as I stood fretting before the elevator door, she stepped into the hall and called, "Lover!"

I turned—then I screamed, "No! No!" I backed away, my hands spread despairingly before me.

No use. The bow she'd taken from my case strummed. The arrow struck me in the heart...

Later, when I tried to explain to mother, I found myself forced to defend myself against her contention that I had *wanted* the mortal to wound me, that I was putting my own selfish desires above my duties to her and our profession. My argument was weakened by my secret belief that she might be right.

Mother raged, but my clever wife—these modern women!—showed Mother that she and her son could not alone keep up with the expanding population. A good part of the world belonged to the half-dead, and they would continue to take it over unless we got some speed and efficiency into our work.

Mother became convinced. That is why I now have so many helpers—hired through a detective agency—and why we all now carry sub-machine guns in our violin cases instead of the picturesque but obsolete bow.

Modern times demand modern methods; there are so many to be wounded that we just simply *must* use the spraygun technique. There is no more individual attention, true, but then that never really mattered. What you do with your wound is up to you. Find your own healer.

I, Cupid, have found mine and it truly pleases me.

Heel

First published in If, Volume 1, Number 2, May 1960.
Also published in Farmerage, Volume 1, Number 2, October 1978.

Homer's Iliad describes the manipulation and cajoling of mortals by gods with awesome powers; in Phil's story these 'gods' are shown as advanced beings with godlike powers but who retain the desire to manipulate for their own (less altruistic) reasons.

Phil revisited the theme of the ultimate movie in "The Making of Revelation, Part 1" written exactly twenty years later in 1980. This story can be found in Phil's anthology *The Purple Book*.

<hr>

"Call me Zeus," said the Director.

"Zeus?" said his wife, a beautiful woman not over a thousand years old. "What an egomaniac! Comparing yourself to a god, even if he is the god of those—those savages!"

She gestured at the huge screen on the wall. It showed, far below, the blue sea, the black ships on the yellow beach, the purple tents of the Greek army, the broad brown plain, and the white towers of Troy.

The Director glared at her through hexagonal dark glasses and puffed on his cigar until angry green clouds rolled from it. His round bald head was covered by a cerise beret, his porpoise frame by a canary yellow tunic, and his chubby legs by iridescent green fourpluses.

"I may not look like a god, but as far as my power over the natives on this planet goes, I could well be their deity," he replied.

He spoke sharply to a tall handsome blond youth who wore a crooked smile and a bright blue and yellow tattoo spiraling around his legs and trunk. "Apollo, hand me the script!"

"Surely you're not going to change the script again?" said his wife. She rose from her chair, and the scarlet web she was wearing translated the shifting micro-voltages on the surface of her skin into musical tones.

"I never change the Script," said the Director. "I just make the slight revisions required for dramatic effects."

"I don't care what you do to it, just so you don't allow the Trojans to win. I hate those despicable brutes."

Apollo laughed loudly, and he said, "Ever since she and Athena and Aphrodite thought of that goofy stunt of asking Paris to choose the most beautiful of the three, and he gave the prize to Aphrodite, Hera's hated the Trojans. Really, Hera, why blame those simple, likeable people for the actions of only one of them? I think Paris showed excellent judgment. Aphrodite was so grateful she contrived to get that lovely Helen for Paris and—"

"Enough of this private feud," snapped the Director. "Apollo, I told you once to hand me the script."

Achilles at midnight paced back and forth before his tent. Finally, in the agony of his spirit, he called to Thetis. The radio which had been installed in his shield, unknown to him, transmitted his voice to a cabin in the great spaceship hanging over the Trojan plain.

Thetis, hearing it, said to Apollo, "Get out of my cabin, you heel, or I'll have you thrown out."

"Leave?" he said. "Why? So you can be with your barbarian lover?"

"He is not my lover," she said angrily. "But I'd take even a barbarian as a lover before I'd have anything to do with you. Now, get out. And don't speak to me again unless it's in the line of business."

"Any time I speak to you, I mean business," he said, grinning.

"Get out or I'll tell my father!"

"I hear and obey. But I'll have you, one way or another."

Thetis shoved him out. Then she quickly put on the suit that could bend light around her to make her invisible and transport her through the air and do many other things. Out of a port she shot, straight toward the tent of her protégé. She did not decelerate until she saw him standing tall in the moonlight, his hands still raised in entreaty. She landed and cut the power off so he could see her.

"Mother, Mother!" cried Achilles. "How long must I put up with Agamemnon's high-handedness?"

Thetis took him by the hand and led him into the tent. "Is Patroclos around?" she asked.

"No, he is having some fun with Iphis, that buxom beauty I gave him after I conquered the city of Scyros."

"There's a sensible fellow," said Thetis. "Why don't you forget this fuss with King Agamemnon and have fun with some rosy-cheeked darling?" But a painful expression crossed her face as she said it.

Achilles did not notice the look. "I am too sick with humiliation and disgust to take pleasure in anything. I am full up to here with being a lion in the fighting and yet having to give that jackal Agamemnon the lion's share of the loot, just because he has been chosen to be our leader. Am I not a king in Thessaly? I wish—I wish—"

"Yes?" said Thetis eagerly. "Do you want to go home?"

"I *should* go home. Then the Greeks would wish they'd not allowed Agamemnon to insult the best man among them."

"Oh, Achilles, say the word and I'll have you across the sea and in your palace in an hour!" she said excitedly. She was thinking, *The Director will be furious if Achilles disappears, but he won't be able to do anything about it. And the Script can be revised. Hector or Odysseus or Paris can play the lead role.*

———⟫●⟪———

"No," Achilles said. "I can't leave my men here. They'd say I had run out on them, that I was a coward. And the Greeks would call me a yellow dog. No, I'll allow no man to say that."

Thetis sighed and answered sadly, "Very well. What do you want me to do?"

"Go ask Zeus if he will give Agamemnon so much trouble he'll come crawling to me, begging for forgiveness and pleading for my help."

Thetis had to smile. The enormous egotism of the beautiful brute! Taking it for granted that the Lord of Creation would bend the course of events so Achilles could salvage his pride. Yet, she told herself, she need not be surprised. He had taken it calmly enough the night she'd appeared to him and told him that she was a goddess and his true mother. He had always been convinced divine blood ran in his veins. Was he not superior to all men? Was he not Achilles?

"I will go to Zeus," she said. "But what he will do, only he knows."

She reached up and pulled his head down to kiss him on the forehead. She did not trust herself to touch the lips of this man who was far more a man than those he supposed to be gods. The lips she longed for...the lips soon to grow cold. She could not bear to think of it.

She flicked the switch to make her invisible and, after leaving the tent, rose toward the ship. As always, it hung at four thousand feet above the plain, hidden in the inflated plastic folds that simulated a cloud. To the Greeks and

Trojans the cloud was the home of Zeus, anchored there so he could keep a close eye on the struggle below.

It was he who would decide whether the walls of Troy would stand or fall. It was to him that both sides prayed.

———>•<———

The Director was drinking a highball in his office and working out the details of tomorrow's shooting with his cameramen.

"We'll give that Greek Diomedes a real break, make him the big hero. Get a lot of close-ups. He has a superb profile and a sort of flair about him. It's all in the Script, what aristocrats he kills, how many narrow escapes, and so on. But about noon, just before lunch, we'll wound him. Not too badly, just enough to put him out of the action. Then we'll see if we can whip up a big tearjerker between that Trojan and his wife—what's her name?"

He looked around as if he expected them to feed him the answer. But they were silent; it was not wise to know more than he.

He snapped his fingers. "Andromache! That's it!"

"What a memory! How do you keep all those barbaric names at your tongue's tip? Photographic!" and so on from the suckophants.

"O.K. So after Diomedes leaves the scene, you, Apollo, will put on a simulacrum of Helenos, the Trojan prophet. As Helenos, you'll induce Hector to go back to Troy and get his mother, the Queen, to pray for victory. We can get some colorful shots of the temple and the local religious rites. Meantime, we'll set up a touching domestic scene between Hector and his wife. Ring in their baby boy. A baby's always good for ohs and ahs. Later, after coffee break, we'll..."

Apollo drifted through the crowd toward the Director's wife. She was sitting on a chair and moodily drinking. However, seeing Apollo, she smiled with green-painted lips and said, "Do sit down, darling. You needn't worry about my husband being angry because you're paying attention to me. He's too busy shining down on his little satellites to notice you."

Apollo seated himself in a chair facing her and moved forward so their knees touched.

"What do you want now?" she said. "You only get lovey-dovey when you're trying to get something out of me."

"You know I love only you, Hera," he said, grinning. "But I can't meet you as often as I'd like. Old Thunder-and-Lightning is too suspicious. And I value my job too much to risk it, despite my overwhelming passion for you."

"Get to the point."

"We're way over our budget and past our deadline. The shooting should have been finished six months ago. Yet Old Fussybritches keeps on revising the Script and adding scene after scene. And that's not all. We're not going home when Troy does fall. The Director is planning to make a sequel. I know because he asked me to outline the Script for it. He's got the male lead picked out. Foxy Grandpa Odysseus."

———>•<———

Hera sat upright so violently she sloshed her drink over the edge of her glass. "Why, my brother means to kill Odysseus at the first opportunity! My brother is mad, absolutely mad about Athena, but he can't get to first base with her. She's got eyes only for Odysseus, though how she could take up with one of those stupid primitives, I'll never understand."

"Athena claims he has an intelligence equal to any of us," said Apollo. "However, it's not her but Thetis I meant to discuss."

"Is my stepdaughter interfering again?"

"I think so. Just before this conference I saw her coming out of the Director's room, tears streaming from her big cow eyes. I imagine she was begging him again to spare Achilles. Or at least to allow the Trojans to win for a while so Agamemnon will give back to Achilles the girl he took from him, that tasty little dish, Briseis."

"You ought to know how tasty she is," said Hera bitterly. "I happen to know you drugged Achilles several nights in a row and then put on his simulacrum."

"A handy little invention, that simulacrum," said Apollo. "Put one on and you can look like anybody you want to look like. Your jealousy is showing, Hera. However, that's not the point. If Thetis keeps playing on her father's sympathies like an old flute, this production will last forever. Frankly, I'd like to shake the dust of this crummy planet from my feet, get back to civilization before it forgets what a great script writer I am."

"What do you propose?"

"I propose to hurry things up. Eventually, Achilles is supposed to quit sulking and take up arms again. So far, the Director has been indefinite on how we'll get him to do that. Well, we'll help him without his knowing it. We'll fix it so the Trojans will beat the Greeks even worse than the Director intends. Hector will almost run them back into the sea. Agamemnon will beg Achilles to get back into the ring. He'll give him back the loot he took from him, including Briseis. And he'll offer his own daughter in marriage to Achilles.

"Achilles will refuse. But we'll have him all set up for the next move. Tonight a technician will implant a post-hypnotic suggestion in Achilles that he send his buddy Patroclos, dressed in Achilles' armor, out to scare the kilts off the Trojans. We'll generate a panic among the Trojans with a subsonic projector. Then we'll arrange it so Hector kills Patroclos. That is the one thing to make Achilles so fighting mad he'll quit sulking…"

"Patroclos? But the Director wants to save him for the big scene when Achilles is knocked off. Patroclos is supposed to put Achilles' armor on, storm the Scaian gate, and lead the Greeks right into the city."

"Accidents will happen," said Apollo. "Despite what the barbarians think, we are not gods. Or are we? What do you say to my plan?"

"If the Director finds out we've tampered with the Script, he'll divorce me. And you'll be blackballed in every studio from one end of the Galaxy to the other."

Apollo winked and said, "I'll leave it to you to make Old Stupe think Patroclos' death was his own idea. You have done something like that before, and more than once."

She laughed and said, "Oh, Apollo, you're such a heel."

He rose. "Not a heel. Just a great scriptwriter. Our plan will give me a chance to kill Achilles much sooner than the Director expects. And it'll all be for the good of the Script."

That night two technicians went into the Greek camp, one to Achilles' tent and one to Agamemnon's. The technician assigned to the King of Mycenae gave him a whiff of sleep gas and then taped two electrodes to the royal forehead. It took him a minute to play a recording and two to untape the electrodes and leave.

Five minutes later, the King awoke, shouting that Zeus had sent him a dream in the shape of wise old Nestor. Nestor had told him to rouse the camp and march forth even if it were only dawn, for today Troy would fall and his brother Menelaos would get back his wife Helen.

Agamemnon, though, who had always been too clever for his own good, told the council of elders that he wanted to test his army before telling them the truth. He would announce that he was tired of this war they could not win and that he wanted to go home. This news would separate the slackers from the soldiers, his true friends from the false.

Unfortunately, when he told this to the assemblage, he found far less men of valor than he had expected. The entire army, with a few exceptions, gave a big hurrah and stampeded toward the ships. They had had a bellyful of this silly war, fighting to win back the beautiful tart Helen for the King's brother, spilling their guts all over foreign plains while their wives were undoubtedly playing them false with the 4-Fs[1], the fields were growing weeds, and their children were starving.

In vain, Agamemnon tried to stop the rush. He even shouted at them what they had only guessed before, that more was at stake than his brother's runaway wife. If Troy was crushed, the Greeks would own the trading and colonizing routes to the rich Black Sea area. But no one paid any attention to him. They were too concerned with knocking each other over in their haste to get the ships ready to sail.

At this time, the only people from the spaceship on the scene were some cameramen and technicians. They were paralyzed by the unexpectedness of the situation, and they were afraid to use their emotion-stimulating projectors. By the flick of a few switches the panic could be turned into aggression. But it would have been aggression without a leader. The Greeks, instead of automatically turning to fight the Trojans, would have killed each other, sure that their fellows were trying to stop them from embarking for home.

The technicians did not dare to waken the Director and acknowledge they could not handle a simple mob scene. But one of them did put a call through to one of the Director's daughters, Athena.

Athena zipped down to Odysseus and found him standing to one side, looking glum. He had not panicked, but he also was not interfering. Poor fellow, he longed to go home to Penelope. In the beginning of this useless war, he had pretended madness to get out of being drafted. But, once he had sworn loyalty to the King, he would not abandon him.

Athena flicked off her light-bender so he could see her. She shouted, "Odysseus, don't just stand there like a lump on a bog! Do something or all will be lost—the war, the honor of the Greeks, the riches you will get from the loot of Troy! Get going!"

Odysseus, never at a loss, tore the wand of authority from the King's numbed hand and began to run through the crowd. Everybody he met he reproached with cowardice, and backed the sting of his words with the hard end of the wand on their backs. Athena signaled to the technicians to project an aggression-stimulating frequency. Now that the Greeks had a leader to channel their courage, they could be diverted back to fighting.

There was only one obstacle, Thersites. He was a lame hunchback with the face of a baboon and a disposition to match.

Thersites cried out in a hoarse, jeering voice, "Agamemnon, don't you have enough loot? Do you still want us to die so you may gather more gold and beautiful Trojan women in your greedy arms? You Greeks, you're not men.

---

[1] Someone unfit for military duty

You're women who will do anything this disgrace to a crown tells you to do. Look what he did to Achilles. Robbed him of Briseis and in so doing robbed us of the best warrior we have. If I were Achilles, I'd knock Agamemnon's head off."

"We've put up with your outrageous abuse long enough!" shouted Odysseus. He began thwacking Thersites on the head and the back until blood ran. "Shut up or I'll kill you!"

At this the whole army, which hated Thersites, roared with laughter. Odysseus had relieved the tension; now they were ready to march under Agamemnon's orders.

Athena sighed with relief and radioed back to the ship that the Director could be awakened. Things were well in hand.

———————

And so they were—until a few days later when Apollo and Hera, waiting until the Director had gone to bed early with a hangover from the night before, induced Hector to make a night attack. The fighting went on all night, and at dawn Patroclos ran into Achilles' tent.

"Terrible news!" he cried. "The Trojans have breached the walls around our ships and are burning them! Diomedes, Agamemnon, and Odysseus are wounded. If you do not lead your men against Hector, all is lost!"

"Too bad," said Achilles. But the blood drained from his face.

"Don't be so hardhearted!" shouted Patroclos. "If you won't fight, at least allow me to lead the Myrmidons against the enemy. Perhaps we can save the ships and drive Hector off!"

Achilles shouted back, "Very well! You know I give you, my best friend, anything you want. But I will not for all the gold in the world serve under a king who robs me of prizes I took with my own sword. However, I will give you my armor, and my men will march behind you!"

Then, sobbing with rage and frustration, he helped Patroclos dress in his armor.

"Do you see this little lever in the back of the shield?" he said. "When an enemy strikes at you, flick it this way. The air in front of you will become hard, and your foe's weapon will bounce off the air. Then, before he recovers from his confusion, flick the lever the other way. The air will soften and allow your spear to pass. And the spearpoint will shear through his armor as if it were cheese left in the hot sun. It is made of some substance harder than the hardest bronze by the hand of man."

"So this is the magic armor your divine mother, Thetis, gave you," said Patroclos. "No wonder—"

"Even without this magic—or force field, as Thetis calls it—I am the best man among Greek or Trojan," said Achilles matter-of-factly. "There! Now you are almost as magnificent as I am. Go forth in my armor, Patroclos, and run the Trojans ragged. I will pray to Zeus that you come back safely. There is one thing you must not do, though, no matter how strong the temptation—do not chase the Trojans too close to the city, even if you are on the heels of Hector himself. Thetis has told me that Zeus does not want Troy to fall yet. If you were to threaten it now, the gods would strike you down."

"I will remember," said Patroclos. He got into Achilles' chariot and drove off proudly to take his place in front of the Myrmidons.

The Director was so red in the face, he looked as if his head were one huge blood vessel.

"How in space did the Trojans get so far?" he screamed. "And what is Patroclos doing in Achilles' armor? There's rank inefficiency here or else skull-duggery! Either one, heads will roll! And I think I know whose! Apollo! Hera! What have you two been up to?"

"Why, Husband," said Hera, "how can you say I had anything to do with this? You know how I hate the Trojans. As for Apollo, he thinks too much of his job to go against the Script."

"All right, we'll see. We'll get to the bottom of this later. Meanwhile, let's direct the situation so it'll end up conforming to the Script."

But before the cameramen and technicians could be organized, Patroclos, leading the newly inspired Greeks, slaughtered the Trojans as a lion kills sheep. He could not be stopped, and when he saw Hector running away from him, he forgot his friend's warning and pursued him to the walls of Troy.

"Follow me!" yelled Patroclos to the Greeks. "We will break down the gates and take the city within an hour!"

It was then Apollo projected fury into Hector so that he turned to battle the man he thought was Achilles. And Apollo, timing to coincide with the instant that Patroclos flicked off his force field, struck him a stunning blow from behind. At the same time a spear thrown by a Trojan wounded Patroclos in the back. Dazed, hurt, the Greek started back toward his men. But Hector ran up and stabbed him through the belly, finding no resistance to his spear because Patroclos had not turned the force field back on. Patroclos hit the ground with a crash of armor.

"No, no, you fool, Apollo!" shouted the Director into the radio. "He must not die! We need him later for the Script. You utter fool, you've bumbled!"

Thetis, who had been standing behind the Director, burst into tears and ran into her cabin.

"What's the matter with her?" asked the Director.

"You may as well know, darling," said Hera, "that your daughter is in love with a barbarian."

"Thetis? In love with Patroclos? Impossible!"

Hera laughed and said, "Ask her how she feels about the planned death of Achilles. That is whom she is weeping for, not Patroclos. She foresees Achilles' death in his friend's. And I imagine she will go to comfort her lover, knowing his grief when he hears that Patroclos is dead."

"That's ridiculous! If she's in love with Achilles, why would she tell Achilles she is his mother?"

"For the very reason she loves him but doesn't want him to know. She at least has sense enough to realize no good could come from a match with one of those Earth primitives. So she stopped any passes from him with that maternal bit. If there is one things the Greeks respect, it is the incest taboo."

"I'll have him knocked off as soon as possible. Thetis might lose her head and tell him the truth. Poor little girl, she's been away from civilization too long. We'll have to wind up this picture and get back to God's planet."

Hera watched him go after Thetis and then switched to a private channel. "Apollo, the Director is very angry with you. But I've thought of a way to smooth his feathers. We'll tell him that killing Patroclos was the only way to get Achilles back into the fight. He'll like that. Achilles can then be slain, and the picture will still be saved. Also, I'll make him think it was his idea."

"That's great," replied Apollo, his voice shaky with dread of the Director. "But what can we do to speed up the shooting? Patroclos was supposed to take the city after Achilles was killed."

"Don't worry," said Athena, who had been standing behind Hera. "Odysseus is your man. He's been working on a device to get into the city. Barbarian or not, that fellow is the smartest I've ever met. Too bad he's an Earthman."

During the next twenty-four hours, Thetis wept much. But she was also very busy, working while she cried. She went to Hephaistos, the chief technician, an old man of five thousand years. He loved Thetis because she had intervened for Hephaistos more than once when her father had been angry with him. Yet he shook his head when she asked him if he could make Achilles another suit of armor, even more invulnerable than the first.

"Not enough time. Achilles is to be killed tomorrow."

"No. My father has cooled off a little. He remembered that the Script calls for Achilles to kill Hector before he himself dies. Besides, the government anthropologist wants to take films of the funeral games for Patroclos. And he overrules even Father, you know."

"That'll give me a week," said Hephaistos, figuring on his fingers. "I can do it. But tell me, child, why all the tears? Is it true what they say, that you love a barbarian, that magnificent red-haired Achilles?"

"I love him," she said, weeping again.

"Ah, child, you are a mere hundred years or so. When you reach my age, you'll know that there are a few things worth tears, and love between a man and a woman is not one of them. However, I'll make the armor. And its field of force will cover everything around him except an opening to the outside air. Otherwise, he'd suffocate. But what good will all this do? The director will find some means of killing him. And even if Achilles should escape, you'd be no better off."

"I will," she said. "We'll go to Italy—and I'll give him perpetuol."

Thetis went to her cabin. Shortly afterward, the doorbell rang. She opened the door and saw Apollo.

Smiling, he said, "I have something here you might be interested in hearing." He held in his hand a small cartridge.

Seeing it, her eyes widened in surprise.

"Yes, it's a recording," he said, and he pushed past her into the room. "Let me put it in your playback."

"You don't have to," she replied. "I presume you had a microphone planted in Hephaistos' cabin?"

"Correct. Won't your father be angry if somebody sends him a note telling him you're planning to ruin the Script by running off to Italy with a barbarian? And not only that but inject perpetuol into the barbarian to increase his life span? Personally, if I were your father, I'd let you do it. You'd soon grow sick of your handsome but uncouth booby."

Thetis did not answer.

"I really don't care," he said. "In fact, I'll help you. I can arrange it so the arrow that hits Achilles' heel will be a trick one. Its head will just seem to sink into his flesh. Inside it will inject a cataleptic agent. Achilles will seem to be dead but will actually be in a state of suspended animation. We'll sneak his body at night from the funeral pyre and substitute a corpse. A bio-tech who owes me a favor will fix up the face of a dead Trojan or Greek to look like Achilles'. When this epic is done and we're ready to leave Earth, you can run away. We'll not miss you until we're light-years away."

"And what do you want in return for arranging all this? My thanks?"

"I want you."

Thetis flinched. For a moment she stood with her eyes closed and her hands clenched. Then, opening her eyes, she said, "All right. I know that is the only way open to me. It's also the only way you could have devised to have me. But I want to tell you that I loathe and despise you. And I'll be hating every atom of your flesh while you're in possession of mine."

He chuckled and said, "I know it. But your hate will only make me relish you the more. It'll be the sauce on the salad."

"Oh, you heel!" she said in a trembling voice. "You dirty, sneaking, miserable, slimy heel!"

"Agreed." He picked up a bottle and poured two drinks. "Shall we toast to that?"

Hector's death happened, as planned, and the tear-jerking scene in which his father, King Priam, came to beg his son's body from Achilles. Four days later, Achilles led the attack on the Scaian gate. It was arranged that Paris should be standing on the wall above the gate. Apollo, invisible behind him, would shoot the arrow that would strike Achilles' foot if Paris' arrow bounced off the force field.

Apollo spoke to Thetis, who was standing beside him. "You seem very nervous. Don't worry. You'll see your lovely warrior in Italy in a few weeks. And you can explain to him that you aren't his mother, that you had to tell him that to protect him from the god Apollo's jealousy. But now that Zeus has raised him from the dead, you have been given to him as a special favor. That is, until living with him will become so unbearable you'd give a thousand years off your life to leave this planet. Then, of course, it'll be too late. There won't be another ship along for several millennia."

"Shut up," she said. "I know what I'm doing."

"So do I," he said. "Ah, here comes the great hero Achilles, chasing a poor Trojan whom he plans to slaughter. We'll see about that."

He lifted the airgun in whose barrel lay the long dart with the trick head. He took careful aim, saying, "I'll wait until he goes to throw his spear. His force field will be off...Now!"

Thetis gave a strangled cry. Achilles, the arrow sticking from the tendon just above the heel, had toppled backward from the chariot onto the plain, where dust settled on his shining armor. He lay motionless.

"Oh, that was an awful fall," she moaned. "Perhaps he broke his neck. I'd better go down there and see if he's all right."

"Don't bother," said Apollo. "He's dead."

Thetis looked at him with wide brown eyes set in a gray face.

"I put poison on the needle." Said Apollo, smiling crookedly at her. "That was my idea, but your father approved of it. He said I'd redeemed my blunder in killing Patroclos by telling him what you planned. Of course, I didn't inform him of the means you took to insure that I would carry out my bargain with you. I was afraid your father would have been very shocked to hear of your immoral behavior."

Thetis choked out, "You unspeakable...vicious...vicious...you...you..."

"Dry your pretty tears," said Apollo. "It's all for your own good. And for Achilles', too. The story of his brief but glorious life will be a legend among his people. And out in the Galaxy the movie based on his career will become the most stupendous epic ever seen."

————>⊙<————

Apollo was right. Four thousand years later, it was still a tremendous box-office attraction. There was talk that now that Earth was civilized enough to have space travel, it might even be shown there.

Ralph von WauWau

"I've always loved my Ralph stories because he has few human failings."
—*Philip José Farmer.*

A Scarletin Study

A Scarletin Study

First published in *The Magazine of Fantasy & Science Fiction,*
March 1975.
Also published in *Sci-Fi Private Eye,* ROC, 1997.

The title apes the first ever Sherlock Holmes story; "A Study
in Scarlet" and written under the pen name Jonathan Swift
Somers III, whose biography appears later in this collection.
Sherlock Holmes has appeared regularly in Phil's fiction;
whether under an alter ego (as illustrated here); a main character (as
in The *Adventures of the Peerless Peer)* or as a cameo (in *Doc Savage
and the Cult of the Blue God*—which debuts in this collection).

Phil: "When I reread these stories and articles, I am amazed
at what I then planned to do—and didn't. But I still hope someday to write 'The Wonder of the Wandering Wound.'"

Foreword

Ralph von Wau Wau's first case as a private investigator is not his most com
plicated or curious. It does, however, illustrate remarkably well my colleague's peculiar talents. And it is, after all, his first case, and one should proceed
chronologically in these chronicles. It is also the only case I know of in which not
the painting but the painter was stolen. And it is, to me, most memorable
because through it I met the woman who will always be for me the woman.

Consider this scene. Von Wau Wau, his enemy, Detective-Lieutenant
Strasse, myself, and the lovely Lisa Scarletin, all standing before a large painting in a room in a Hamburg police station. Von Wau Wau studies the painting while we wonder if he's right in his contention that it is not only a work of
art but a map. Its canvas bears, among other things, the images of Sherlock
Holmes in lederhosen, Sir Francis Bacon, a green horse, a mirror, Christ coming from the tomb, Tarzan, a waistcoat, the Wizard of Oz in a balloon, an
ancient king of Babylon with a dietary problem, and a banana tree.

But let me begin at the beginning.

Chapter I

HERR RALPH VON WAU WAU

In the year 1978 I took my degree of Doctor of Medicine at the University of Cologne and proceeded to Hamburg to go through the course prescribed for surgeons in the Autobahn Patrol. Having completed my studies there, I was duly attached to the Fifth North-Rhine Westphalia Anti-Oiljackers as assistant surgeon. The campaign against the notorious Rottenfranzer Gang brought honors and promotions to many, but for me it was nothing but misfortune and disaster. At the fatal battle of the Emmerich Off-Ramp, I was struck, on the shoulder, by a missile which shattered the bone. I should have fallen into the hands of the murderous Rottenfranzer himself but for the devotion and courage shown by Morgen, my paramedic aide, who threw me across a Volkswagen and succeeded in driving safely across the Patrol lines.

At the base hospital at Hamburg (and it really is base), I seemed on the road to recovery when I was struck down with an extremely rare malady. At least, I have read of only one case similar to mine. This was, peculiarly, the affliction of another doctor, though he was an Englishman and he suffered his wounds a hundred years before on another continent. My case was written up in medical journals and then in general periodicals all over the world. The affliction itself became known popularly as 'the peregrinating pain,' though the scientific name, which I prefer for understandable reasons, was 'Weisstein's Syndrome.' The popular name arose from the fact that the occasional suffering it caused me did not remain at the site of the original wound. At times, the pain traveled downward and lodged in my leg. This was a cause célèbre, scientifically speaking, nor was the mystery solved until some years later. (In "The Wonder of the Wandering Wound," not yet published.)

However, I rallied and had improved enough to be able to walk or limp about the wards, and even to bask a little on the veranda when smog or fog permitted, when I was struck down by Weltschmerz, that curse of Central Europe. For months my mind was despaired of, and when at last I came to myself, six months had passed. With my health perhaps not irretrievably ruined, but all ability to wield the knife as a surgeon vanished, I was discharged by a paternal government with permission to spend the rest of my life improving it. (The health, not the life, I mean.) I had neither kith nor kin nor kinder and was therefore as free as the air, which, given my small social security and disability pension, seemed to be what I was expected to eat. Within a few months the state of my finances had become so alarming that I was forced to completely alter my life style. I decided to look around for some considerably less pretentious and expensive domicile than the Hamburg Hilton.

On the very day I'd come to this conclusion, I was standing at the Kennzeichen Bar when someone tapped me on the shoulder. Wincing (it was the wounded shoulder), I turned around. I recognized young blonde Stampfert, who had been an anesthetist under me at the Neustadt Hospital. (I've had a broad experience of women in many nations and on three continents, so much so in fact that I'd considered entering gynecology.) Stampfert had a beautiful body but a drab personality. I was lonely, however, and I hailed her enthusiastically. She, in turn, seemed glad to see me, I suppose because she wanted to flaunt her newly acquired engagement ring. The first thing I knew, I had invited her to lunch. We took the bus to the Neu Bornholt, and on the way I outlined my adventures of the past year.

"Poor devil!" she said. "So what's happening now?"

"Looking for a cheap apartment," I said. "But I doubt that it's possible to get a decent place at a reasonable rate. The housing shortage and its partner, inflation, will be with us for a long time."

"That's a funny thing," Stampfert said. "You're the second...person...today who has said almost those exact words."

"And who was the first?"

"Someone who's just started a new professional career," Stampfert said. "He's having a hard go of it just now. He's looking for a roommate to share not only expenses but a partnership. Someone who's experienced in police work. You seem to fit the bill. The only thing is..."

She hesitated, and I said, "If he's easy to get along with, I'd be delighted to share the expenses with him. And work is something I need badly."

"Well, there's more to it than that, though he is easy to get along with. Lovable, in fact."

She hesitated, then said, "Are you allergic to animals?"

I stared at her and said, "Not at all. Why, does this man have pets?"

"Not exactly," Stampfert said, looking rather strange.

"Well, then, what is it?"

"There is a dog," she said. "A highly intelligent...police dog."

"Don't tell me this fellow is blind?" I said. "Not that it will matter, of course."

"Just color-blind," she said. "His name is Ralph."

"Yes, go on," I said. "What about Herr Ralph?"

"That's his first name," Stampfert said. "His full name is Ralph von Wau Wau."

"What?" I said, and then I guffawed. "A man whose last name is a dog's bark?" (In Germany 'wau wau'—pronounced vau vau—corresponds to the English 'bow wow.')

Suddenly, I said, "Ach!" I had just remembered where I had heard, or rather read, of von Wau Wau.

"What you're saying," I said slowly, "is that the dog is also the fellow who wants to share the apartment and is looking for a partner?"

Stampfert nodded.

Chapter II
THE SCIENCE OF ODOROLOGY

And so, fifteen minutes later, we entered the apartment building at 12 Bellener Street and took the elevator to the second story. Stampfert rang the bell at 2K, and a moment later the door swung in. This operation had been effected by an electrical motor controlled by an on-off button on a control panel set on the floor in a corner. This, it was obvious, had been pressed by the paw of the dog now trotting toward us. He was the largest police dog I've ever seen, weighing approximately one hundred and sixty pounds. He had keen eyes which were the deep lucid brown of a bottle of maple syrup at times and at other times the opaque rich brown of a frankfurter. His face was black, and his back bore a black saddlemark.

"Herr Doktor Weisstein, Herr Ralph von Wau Wau," said Stampfert.

He grinned, or at least opened his jaws, to reveal some very long and sharp teeth.

"Come in, please, and make yourself at home," he said.

Though I'd been warned, I was startled. His mouth did not move while the words came from his throat. The words were excellent standard High German. But the voice was that of a long-dead American movie actor. Humphrey Bogart's, to be exact.

I would have picked Basil Rathbone's, but *de gustibus non disputandum.* Especially someone with teeth like Ralph's. There was no mystery or magic about the voice, though the effect, even to the prepared, was weird. The voice, like his high intelligence, was a triumph of German science. A dog (or any animal) lacks the mouth structure and vocal chords to reproduce human sounds intelligibly. This deficiency had been overcome by implanting a small nuclear-powered voder in Ralph's throat. This was connected by an artificial-protein neural complex to the speech center of the dog's brain. Before he could activate the voder, Ralph had to think of three code words. This was necessary, since otherwise he would be speaking whenever he thought in verbal terms. Inflection of the spoken words was automatic, responding to the emotional tone of Ralph's thoughts.

"What about pouring us a drink, sweetheart?" he said to Stampfert. "Park it there, buddy," he said to me, indicating with a paw a large and comfortable easy chair. I did so, unsure whether or not I should resent his familiarity. I decided not to do so. After all, what could, or should, one expect from a dog who has by his own admission seen *The Maltese Falcon* forty-nine times? Of course, I found this out later, just as I discovered later that his manner of address varied bewilderingly, often in the middle of a sentence.

Stampfert prepared the drinks at a well-stocked bar in the corner of the rather large living room. She made herself a tequila with lemon and salt, gave me the requested double Duggan's Dew o' Kirkintilloch on the rocks, and poured out three shots of King's Ransom Scotch in a rock-crystal saucer on the floor. The dog began lapping it; then seeing me raise my eyebrows, he said, "I'm a private eye, Doc. It's in the best tradition that P. I.'s drink. I always try to follow human traditions—when it pleases me. And if my drinking from a saucer offends you, I can hold a glass between my paws. But why the hell should I?"

"No reason at all," I said hastily.

He ceased drinking and jumped up onto a sofa, where he sat down facing us. "You two have been drinking at the Kennzeichen," he said. "You are old customers there. And then, later, you had lunch at the Neu Bornholt. Doctor Stampfert said you were coming in the taxi, but you changed your mind and took the bus."

There was a silence which lasted until I understood that I was supposed to comment on this. I could only say, "Well?"

"The babe didn't tell me any of this," Ralph said somewhat testily. "I was just demonstrating something that a mere human being could not have known."

"Mere?" I said just as testily.

Ralph shrugged, which was quite an accomplishment when one considers that dogs don't really have shoulders.

"Sorry, Doc. Don't get your bowels in an uproar. No offense."

"Very well," I said. "How did you know all this?"

And now that I came to think about it, I did wonder how he knew.

"The Kennzeichen is the only restaurant in town which gives a stein of Lowenbrau to each habitué as he enters the bar," von Wau Wau said. "You two obviously prefer other drinks, but you could not turn down the free drink. If you had not been at the Kennzeichen, I would not have smelled Lowenbrau on your breath. You then went to the Neu Bornholt for lunch. It serves a salad with its house dressing, the peculiar ingredients of which I detected with my sense of smell. This, as you know, is a million times keener than a human's. If you had come in a taxi, as the dame said you meant to do, you would be stinking much more strongly of kerosene. Your clothes and hair have absorbed a certain amount of that from being on the streets, of course, along with the high-sulfur coal now burned in many automobiles. But I deduce—olfactorily—that you took instead one of the electrically operated, fuel-celled, relatively odorless buses. Am I correct?"

"I would have said that it was amazing, but of course your nose makes it easy for you," I said.

"An extremely distinguished colleague of mine," Ralph said, "undoubtedly the most distinguished, once said that it is the first quality of a criminal investigator to see through a disguise. I would modify that to the *second* quality. The first is that he should smell through a disguise."

Though he seemed somewhat nettled, he became more genial after a few more laps from the saucer. So did I after a few more sips from my glass. He even gave me permission to smoke, provided that I did it under a special vent placed over my easy chair.

"Cuban make," he said, sniffing after I had lit up. "*La Roja Paloma de la Revolucion.*"

"Now that is astounding!" I said. I was also astounded to find Stampfert on my lap.

"It's nothing," he said. "I started to write a trifling little monograph on the subtle distinctions among cigar odors, but I realized that it would make a massive textbook before I was finished. And who could use it?"

"What are you doing here?" I said to Stampfert. "This is business. I don't want to give Herr von Wau Wau the wrong impression."

"You didn't used to mind," she said, giggling. "But I'm here because I want to smoke, too, and this is the only vent he has, and he told me not to smoke unless I sat under it."

Under the circumstances, it was not easy to carry on a coherent conversation with the dog, but we managed. I told him that I had read something of his life. I knew that his parents had been the property of the Hamburg Police Department. He was one of a litter of eight, all mutated to some degree since they and their parents had been subjected to scientific experiments. These had been conducted by the biologists of *das Institut und die Tankstelle fur Gehirntaschenspielerei.* But his high intelligence was the result of biosurgery.

Although his brain was no larger than it should have been for a dog his size, its complexity was comparable to that of a human's. The scientists had used artificial protein to make billions of new nerve circuits in his cerebrum. This had been done, however, at the expense of his cerebellum or hindbrain. As a result, he had very little subconscious and hence could not dream.

As everybody now knows, failure to dream results in a progressive psychosis and eventual mental breakdown. To rectify this, Ralph created dreams during the day, recorded them audiovisually, and fed them into his brain at night. I don't have space to go into this in detail in this narrative, but a full description will be found in "The Case of the Stolen Dreams." (Not yet published.)

When Ralph was still a young pup, an explosion had wrecked the Institute and killed his siblings and the scientists responsible for his sapiency. Ralph was taken over again by the Police Department and sent to school. He attended obedience school and the other courses requisite for a trained *Schutzhund* canine. But he was the only pup who also attended classes in reading, writing, and arithmetic.

Ralph was now twenty-eight years old but looked five. Some attributed this anomaly to the mutation experiments. Others claimed that the scientists had perfected an age-delaying elixir which had been administered to Ralph and his siblings. If the explosion had not destroyed the records, the world might now have the elixir at its disposal. (More of this in "A Short Case of Longevity," not yet published.)

Ralph's existence had been hidden for many years from all except a few policemen and officials sworn to silence. It was believed that publicity would reduce his effectiveness in his detective work. But recently the case had come to the attention of the public because of Ralph's own doing. Fed up with being a mere police dog, proud and ambitious, he had resigned to become a private investigator. His application for a license had, of course, resulted in an uproar. Mass media persons had descended on Hamburg in droves, herds, coveys, and gaggles. There was in fact litigation against him in the courts, but pending the result of this, Ralph von Wau Wau was proceeding as if he were a free agent. (For the conclusion of this famous case, see "The Caper of Kupper, the Copper's Keeper," not yet published.)

But whether or not he was the property of the police department, he was still very dependent upon human beings. Hence, his search for a roommate and a partner. I told him something about myself. He listened quietly and then said, "I like your odor, buddy. It's an honest one and uncondescending. I'd like you to come in with me."

"I'd be delighted," I said. "But there is only one bedroom..."

"All yours," he said. "My tastes are Spartan. Or perhaps I should say canine. The other bedroom has been converted to a laboratory, as you have observed. But I sleep in it on a pile of blankets under a table. You may have all the privacy you need, bring all the women you want, as long as you're not noisy about it. I think we should get one thing straight though. I'm the senior partner here. If that offends your human chauvinism, then we'll call it quits before we start, amigo."

"I foresee no cause for friction," I replied, and I stood up to walk over to Ralph to shake hands. Unfortunately, I had forgotten that Stampfert was still on my lap. She thumped into the floor on her buttocks and yelled with pain and indignation. It was, I admit, stupid—well, at least an unwise, action. Stampfert, cursing, headed toward the door. Ralph looked at my outstretched hand and said, "Get this straight, mac. I never shake hands or sit up and beg."

I dropped my hand and said, "Of course."

The door opened. I turned to see Stampfert, still rubbing her fanny, going out the door.

"*Auf Wiedersehen*," I said.

"Not if I can help it, you jerk," she said.

"She always did take offense too easily," I said to Ralph.

I left a few minutes later to pick up my belongings from the hotel. When I re-entered his door with my suitcases in hand, I suddenly stopped. Ralph was sitting on the sofa, his eyes bright, his huge red tongue hanging out, and his breath coming in deep happy pants. Across from him sat one of the loveliest women I have ever seen. Evidently she had done something to change his mood because his manner of address was now quite different.

"Come in, my dear Weisstein," he said. "Your first case as my colleague is about to begin."

Chapter III

THE STATEMENT OF THE CASE

An optimist is one who ignores, or forgets, experience. I am an optimist. Which is another way of saying that I fell in love with Lisa Scarletin at once. As I stared at this striking yet petite woman with the curly chestnut hair and great lustrous brown eyes, I completely forgot that I was still holding the two heavy suitcases. Not until after we had been introduced, and she looked down amusedly, did I realize what a foolish figure I made. Red-faced, I eased them down and took her dainty hand in mine. As I kissed it, I smelled the subtle fragrance of a particularly delightful—and, I must confess, aphrodisiacal—perfume.

"No doubt you have read, or seen on TV, reports of Mrs. Scarletin's missing husband?" my partner said. "Even if you do not know of his disappearance, you surely have heard of such a famous artist?"

"My knowledge of art is not nil," I said coldly. The tone of my voice reflected my inward coldness, the dying glow of delight on first seeing her. So, she was married! I should have known on seeing her ring. But I had been too overcome for it to make an immediate impression.

Alfred Scarletin, as my reader must surely know, was a wealthy painter who had become very famous in the past decade. Personally, I consider the works of the so-called Fauve Mauve school to be outrageous nonsense, a thumbing of the nose at commonsense. I would sooner have the originals of the *Katzenjammer Kids* comic strip hung up in the museum than any of the maniac creations of Scarletin and his kind. But, whatever his failure of artistic taste, he certainly possessed a true eye for women. He had married the beautiful Lisa Maria Mohrstein only three years ago. And now there was speculation that she might be a widow.

At which thought, the warm glow returned.

A. Scarletin, as I remembered, had gone for a walk on a May evening two months ago and had failed to return home. At first, it was feared that he had been kidnapped. But, when no ransom was demanded, that theory was discarded.

When I had told Ralph what I knew of the case, he nodded.

"As of last night there has been a new development in the case," he said. "And Mrs. Scarletin has come to me because she is extremely dissatisfied with the progress—lack of it, rather—that the police have made. Mrs. Scarletin, please tell Doctor Weisstein what you have told me."

She fixed her bright but deep brown eyes upon me and in a voice as lovely as her eyes—not to mention her figure—sketched in the events of yesterday. Ralph, I noticed, sat with his head cocked and his ears pricked up. I did not know it then, but he had asked her to repeat the story because he wanted to listen to her inflections again. He could detect subtle tones that would escape the less sensitive ears of humans. As he was often to say, "I cannot only *smell* hidden emotions, my dear Weisstein, I can also *hear* them."

"At about seven last evening, as I was getting ready to go out..." she said.

With whom? I thought; feeling jealousy burn through my chest but knowing that I had no right to feel such.

"...Lieutenant Strasse of the Hamburg Metropolitan Police phoned me. He said that he had something important to show me and asked if I would come down to headquarters. I agreed, of course, and took a taxi down. There the sergeant took me into a room and showed me a painting. I was astounded. I had never seen it before, but I knew at once that it was my husband's work. I did not need his signature—in its usual place in the upper right-hand corner—to know that. I told the sergeant that and then I said, "This must mean that Alfred is still alive! But where in the world did you get it?"

"He replied that it had come to the attention of the police only that morning. A wealthy merchant, Herr Lausitz, had died a week before. The lawyer supervising the inventory of his estate found this painting in a locked room in Lausitz's mansion. It was only one of many valuable objects d'art which had been stolen. Lausitz was not suspected of being a thief except in the sense that he had undoubtedly purchased stolen goods or commissioned the thefts. The collection was valued at many millions of marks. The lawyer had notified the police, who identified the painting as my husband's because of the signature."

"You may be sure that Strasse would never have been able to identify a Scarletin by its style alone," Ralph said sarcastically.

Her delicate eyebrows arched.

"Ach! So that's the way it is! The lieutenant did not take it kindly when I told him that I was thinking of consulting you. But that was later.

"Anyway, I told Strasse that this was evidence that Alfred was still alive. Or at least had been until very recently. I know that it would take my husband at least a month and a half to have painted it—if he were under pressure. Strasse said that it could be: one, a forgery; or, two, Alfred might have painted it before he disappeared. I told him that it was no forgery; I could tell at a glance. And what did he mean, it was painted some time ago? I knew exactly—from day to day—what my husband worked on."

She stopped, looked at me, and reddened slightly.

"That isn't true. My husband visited his mistress at least three times a week. I did not know about her until after he disappeared, when the police reported to me that he had been seeing her...Hilda Speck...for about two years. However, according to the police, Alfred had not been doing any painting in her apartment. Of course, she could have removed all evidence, though Strasse tells me that she would have been unable to get rid of all traces of pigments and hairs from brushes."

What a beast that Scarletin was! I thought, how could anybody married to this glorious woman pay any attention to another woman?

"I have made some inquiries about Hilda Speck," Ralph said. "First, she has an excellent alibi, what the English call ironclad. She was visiting friends in Bremen two days before Scarletin disappeared. She did not return to Hamburg until two days afterward. As for her background, she worked as a typist-clerk for an export firm until two years ago when Scarletin began supporting her. She has no criminal record, but her brother has been arrested several times for extortion and assault. He escaped conviction each time. He is a huge obese man, as ugly as his sister is beautiful. He is nicknamed, appropriately enough, *Flusspferd.* (Hippopotamus. Literally, riverhorse.) His whereabouts have been unknown for about four months."

He sat silent for a moment, then he went to the telephone. This lay on the floor; beside it was a curious instrument. I saw its function the moment Ralph put one paw on its long thin but blunt end and slipped the other paw snugly into a funnel-shaped cup at the opposite end. With the thin end he punched the buttons on the telephone.

A police officer answered over the loudspeaker. Ralph asked for Lt. Strasse. The officer said that he was not in the station. Ralph left a message, but when he turned off the phone, he said, "Strasse won't answer for a while, but eventually his curiosity will get the better of him."

It is difficult to tell when a dog is smiling, but I will swear that Ralph was doing more than just exposing his teeth. And his eyes seemed to twinkle.

Suddenly, he raised a paw and said, quietly, "No sound, please." We stared at him. None of us heard anything, but it was evident he did. He jumped to the control panel on the floor and pushed the on button. Then he dashed toward the door, which swung inward. A man wearing a stethoscope, stood looking stupidly at us. Seeing Ralph bounding at him, he yelled and turned to run. Ralph struck him on the back and sent him crashing against the opposite wall of the hallway. I ran to aid him, but to my surprise Ralph trotted back into the room. It was then that I saw the little device attached to the door. The man rose glaring and unsteadily to his feet. He was just above minimum height for a policeman and looked as if he were thirty-five years old. He had a narrow face with a long nose and small close-set black eyes.

"Doctor Weisstein," Ralph said. "Lieutenant Strasse."

Strasse did not acknowledge me. Instead, he tore off the device and put it with the stethoscope in his jacket pocket. Some of his paleness disappeared.

"That eavesdropper device is illegal in America and should be here," Ralph said.

"So should talking dogs," Strasse said. He bowed to Mrs. Scarletin and clicked his heels.

Ralph gave several short barks, which I found out later was his equivalent of laughter. He said, "No need to ask you why you were spying on us. You're stuck in this case, and you hoped to overhear me say something that would give you a clue. Really, my dear Lieutenant!"

Strasse turned red, but he spoke up bravely enough.

"Mrs. Scarletin, you can hire this...this...hairy four-footed Holmes..."

"I take that as a compliment," Ralph murmured.

"...If you wish, but you cannot discharge the police. Moreover, there is grave doubt about the legality of his private investigator's license, and you might get into trouble if you persist in hiring him."

"Mrs. Scarletin is well aware of the legal ramifications, my dear Strasse," Ralph said coolly. "She is also confident that I will win my case. Meantime, the authorities have permitted me to practice. If you dispute this, you may phone the mayor himself."

"You...you!" Strasse sputtered. "Just because you once saved His Honor's child!"

"Let's drop all this time-wasting nonsense," Ralph said. "I would like to examine the painting myself. I believe that it may contain the key to Scarletin's whereabouts."

"That is police property," Strasse said. "As long as I have anything to say about it, you won't put your long nose into a police building. Not unless you do so as a prisoner."

I was astonished at the hatred that leaped and crackled between these two like discharges in a Van de Graaff generator. I did not learn until later that Strasse was the man to whom Ralph had been assigned when he started police work. At first they got along well, but as it became evident that Ralph was much the more intelligent, Strasse became jealous. He did not, however, ask for another dog. He was taking most of the credit for the cases cracked by Ralph, and he was rising rapidly in rank because of Ralph. By the time the dog resigned from the force, Strasse had become a lieutenant. Since then he had bungled two cases, and the person responsible for Strasse's rapid rise was now obvious to all.

"Pardon me," Ralph said. "The police may be holding the painting as evidence, but it is clearly Mrs. Scarletin's property. However, I think I'll cut through the red tape. I'll just make a complaint to His Honor."

"Very well," Strasse said, turning pale again. "But I'll go with you to make sure that you don't tamper with the evidence."

"And to learn all you can," Ralph said, barking laughter. "Weisstein, would you bring along that little kit there? It contains the tools of my trade."

Chapter IV

LIGHT IN THE DARKNESS, COURTESY OF VON WAU WAU

On the way to the station in the taxi (Strasse having refused us use of a police vehicle), Ralph told me a little more of Alfred Scarletin.

"He is the son of an American teacher who became a German citizen and of a Hamburg woman. Naturally, he speaks English like a native of California. He became interested in painting at a very early age and since his early adolescence has tramped through Germany painting both urban and rural scenes. He is extremely handsome, hence, attracts women, has a photographic memory, and is an excellent draftsman. His paintings were quite conventional until the past ten years when he founded the Fauve Mauve school. He is learned in both German and English literature and has a fondness for the works of Frank Baum and Lewis Carroll. He often uses characters from them in his paintings. Both writers, by the way, were fond of puns."

"I am well aware of that," I said stiffly. After all, one does not like to be considered ignorant by a dog. "And all this means?"

"It may mean all or nothing."

About ten minutes later, we were in a large room in which many articles, the jetsam and flotsam of crime, were displayed. Mrs. Scarletin led us to the painting (though we needed no leading), and we stood before it. Strasse, off to one side, regarded us suspiciously. I could make no sense out of the painting and said so even though I did not want to offend Mrs. Scarletin. She, however, laughed and said my reaction was that of many people.

Ralph studied it for a long time and then said, "It may be that my suspicions are correct. We shall see."

"About what?" Strasse said coming closer and leaning forward to peer at the many figures on the canvas.

"We can presume that Mrs. Scarletin knows all her husband's works—until the time he disappeared. This appeared afterward and so we can presume that he painted it within the last two months. It's evident that he was kidnapped not for ransom but for the money to be made from the sale of new paintings by Scarletin. They must have threatened him with death if he did not paint new works for them. He has done at least one for them and probably has done, or is doing, more for them.

"They can't sell Scarletins on the open market. But there are enough fanatical and unscrupulous collectors to pay very large sums for their private collections. Lausitz was one such. Scarletin is held prisoner and, we suppose, would like to escape. He can't do so, but he is an intelligent man, and he thinks of a way to get a message out. He knows his paintings are being sold, even if he isn't told so. Ergo, why not put a message in his painting?"

"How wonderful!" Mrs. Scarletin said and she patted Ralph's head. Ralph wagged his tail, and I felt a thrust of jealousy.

"Nonsense!" Strasse growled. "He must have known that the painting would go to a private collector who could not reveal that Scarletin was a prisoner. One, he'd be put in jail himself for having taken part in an illegal transaction. Two, why would he suspect that the painting contained a message? Three, I don't believe there is any message there!"

"Scarletin would be desperate and so willing to take a long chance," Ralph said. "At least, it'd be better than doing nothing. He could hope that the collector might get an attack of conscience and tell the police. This is not very likely, I'll admit. He could hope that the collector would be unable to keep from showing the work off to a few close friends. Perhaps one of these might tell the police, and so the painting would come into the hands of the police. Among them might be an intelligent and well-educated person who would perceive the meaning of the painting. I'll admit, however, that neither of these theories is likely."

Strasse snorted.

"And then there was the very slight chance—which nevertheless occurred—that the collector would die. And so the legal inventory of his estate would turn up a Scarletin. And some person just might be able to read the meaning in this—if there is any."

"Just what I was going to say," Strasse said.

"Even if what you say happened did happen," he continued, "his kidnapers wouldn't pass on the painting without examining it. The first thing they'd suspect would be a hidden message. It's so obvious."

"You didn't think so a moment ago," Ralph said. "But you are right...in agreeing with me. Now, let us hypothesize. Scarletin, a work of art, but he wishes to embody in it a message. Probably a map of sorts which will lead the police—or someone else looking for him—directly to the place where he is kept prisoner.

"How is he to do this without detection by the kidnapers? He has to be subtle enough to escape their inspection. How subtle depends, I would imagine, on their education and perceptivity. But too subtle a message will go over everybody's head. And he is limited in his choice of symbols by the situation, by the names or professions of his kidnapers—if he knows them—and by the particular location of his prison—if he knows that."

"If, if, if?" Strasse said, throwing his hands up in the air.

"If me no ifs," Ralph said. "But first let us consider that Scarletin is equally at home in German or English. He loves the pun-loving Carroll and Baum. So, perhaps, due to the contingencies of the situation, he is forced to pun in both languages."

"It would be like him," Mrs. Scarletin said. "But is it likely that he would use this method when he would know that very few people would be capable of understanding him?"

"As I said, it was a long shot, Madame. But better than nothing."

"Now, Weisstein, whatever else I am, I am a dog. Hence, I am colorblind. (But not throughout his career. See "The Adventure of the Tired Color Man," to be published.) Please describe the colors of each object on this canvas."

Strasse sniggered, but we ignored him. When I had finished, Ralph said, "Thank you, my dear Weisstein. Now, let us separate the significant from the insignificant. Though, as a matter of fact, in this case even the insignificant is significant. Notice the two painted walls which divide the painting into three parts—like Gaul. One starts from the middle of the left-hand side and curves up to the middle of the upper edge. The other starts in the middle of the right-hand side and curves down to the middle of the lower side. All three parts are filled with strange and seemingly unrelated—and often seemingly unintelligible—objects. The Fauve Mauve apologists, however, maintain that their creations come from the collective unconscious, not the individual or personal and so are intelligible to everybody."

"Damned nonsense!" I said, forgetting Lisa in my indignation.

"Not in this case, I suspect," Ralph said. "Now, notice that the two walls, which look much like the Great Wall of China, bear many zeros on their tops. And that within the area these walls enclose, other zeros are scattered. Does this mean nothing to you?"

"Zero equals nothing," I said.

"A rudimentary observation, Doctor, but valid," Ralph said. "I would say that Scarletin is telling us that the objects within the walls mean nothing. It is the central portion that bears the message. There are no zeros there."

"Prove it," Strasse said.

"The first step first—if one can find it. Observe in the upper right-hand corner the strange figure of a man. The upper half is, obviously, Sherlock Holmes, with his deerstalker hat, cloak, pipe—though whether his meditative brier root or disputatious clay can't be determined—and his magnifying glass in hand. The lower half, with the lederhosen and so on, obviously indicates a Bavarian in particular and a German in general. The demi-figure of Holmes means two things to the earnest seeker after the truth. One, that we are to use detective methods on this painting. Two, that half of the puzzle is in English. The lower half means that half of the puzzle is in German. Which I anticipated."

"Preposterous!" Strasse said. "And just what does that next figure, the one in sixteenth-century costume, mean?"

"Ah, yes, the torso of a bald and bearded gentleman with an Elizabethan ruff around his neck. He is writing with a pen on a sheet of paper. There is a title on the upper part of the paper. Doctor, please look at it through the magnifying glass which you'll find in my kit."

Chapter V

MORE DAWNING LIGHT

I did so, and I said, "I can barely make it out. Scarletin must have used a glass to do it. It says *New Atlantis*."

"Does that suggest anything to anybody?" Ralph said.

Obviously it did to him, but he was enjoying the sensation of being more intelligent than the humans around him. I resented his attitude somewhat, and yet I could understand it. He had been patronized by too many humans for too long a time.

"The great scholar and statesman Francis Bacon wrote the *New Atlantis*," I said suddenly. Ralph winked at me, and I cried, "Bacon! Scarletin's mistress is Hilda Speck!"

(*Speck* in German, means *bacon*.)

"You have put one foot forward, my dear Weisstein," Ralph said. "Now let us see you bring up the other."

"The Bacon, with the next two figures, comprise a group separate from the others," I said. "Obviously, they are to be considered as closely related. But I confess that I cannot make much sense out of Bacon, a green horse, and a house with an attic window from which a woman with an owl on her shoulder leans. Nor do I know the significance of the tendril which connects all of them."

"Stuck in the mud, eh, kid?" Ralph said, startling me. But I was to get used to his swift transitions from the persona of Holmes to Spade and others and back again.

"Tell me, Doc, is the green of the oats-burner of any particular shade?"

"Hmm," I said.

"It's Nile green," Lisa said.

"You're certainly a model client, sweetheart," Ralph said. "Very well, my dear sawbones, does this mean nothing to you? Yes? What about you, Strasse?"

Strasse muttered something.

Lisa said, "*Nilpferd!*"

"Yes," Ralph said. "Nilpferd. (Nile-horse.) Another word for hippopotamus. And Hilda Speck's brother is nicknamed *Hippopotamus.* Now for the next figure, the house with the woman looking out the attic and bearing an owl on her shoulder. Tell me, Strasse, does the Hippo have any special pals? One who is perhaps, Greek? From the city of Athens?"

Strasse sputtered and said, "Somebody in the department has been feeding you information. I'll…"

"Not at all," Ralph said. "Obviously, the attic and the woman with the owl are the significant parts of the image. *Dachstube* (attic) conveys no meaning in German, but if we use the English translation, we are on the way to light. The word has two meanings in English. If capitalized, Attic, it refers to the ancient Athenian language or culture and, in a broader sense, to Greece as a whole. Note that the German adjective *attisch* is similar to the English *Attic.* To clinch this, Scarletin painted a woman with an owl on her shoulder. Who else could this be but the goddess of wisdom, patron deity of Athens? Scarletin was taking a chance on using her, since his kidnapers, even if they did not get beyond high school might have encountered Athena. But they might not remember her, and, anyway, Scarletin had to use some redundancy to make sure his message got across. I would not be surprised if we do not run across considerable redundancy here."

"And the tendrils?" I said.

"A pun in German, my dear Doctor. *Ranke* (tendril) is similar to *Ranke* (intrigues). The three figures are bound together by the tendril of intrigue."

Strasse coughed and said, "And the mirror beneath the house with the attic?"

"Observe that the yellow brick road starts from the mirror and, curves to the left or westward. I suggest that Scarletin means here that the road actually goes to the right or eastward. Mirror images are in reverse, of course."

"What road?" Strasse said.

Ralph rolled his eyes and shook his head.

"Surely the kidnapers made my husband explain the symbolism?" Lisa said. "They would be very suspicious that he might do exactly what he did do."

"There would be nothing to keep him from a false explanation," Ralph said. "So far, it is obvious that Scarletin has named the criminals. How he was able to identify them or to locate his place of imprisonment, I don't know. Time and deduction—with a little luck—will reveal all. Could we have a road map of Germany, please?"

"I'm no dog to fetch and carry," Strasse grumbled, but he obtained a map nevertheless. This was the large Mair's, scale of 1:750,000, used primarily to indicate the autobahn system. Strasse unfolded it and pinned it to the wall with the upper part of Germany showing.

"If Scarletin had put, say, an American hamburger at the beginning of the brick road, its meaning would have been obvious even to the *dummkopf* kidnapers," Ralph said. "He credited his searchers—if any—with intelligence. They would realize the road has to start where the crime started—in Hamburg."

He was silent while comparing the map and the painting. After a while the fidgeting Strasse said, "Come, man! I mean, dog! You…"

"You mean Herr von Wau Wau, yes?" Ralph said.

Strasse became red-faced again, but after a struggle he said, "Of course. Herr von Wau Wau. How do you interpret this, this mess of a mystery?"

"You'll note that there are many figures along the yellow brick road until one gets to the large moon rising behind the castle. All these figures have halos over their heads. This puzzled me until I understood that the halos are also zeros. We are to pay no attention to the figures beneath them.

"But the moon behind the castle? Look at the map. Two of the roads running southeast out of Hamburg meet just above the city of Luneburg. A *burg* is a castle, but the *Lune* doesn't mean anything in German in this context. It is, however, similar to the English *lunar*, hence the moon. And the yellow brick road goes south from there.

"I must confess that I am now at a loss. So, we get in a car and travel to Luneburg and south of it while I study the map and the painting."

"We can't take the painting with us; it's too big!" Strasse said.

"I have it all in here," Ralph said, tapping his head with his paw. "But I suggest we take a color Polaroid shot of the painting for you who have weak memories," and he grinned at Strasse.

Chapter VI

FOLLOW THE YELLOW BRICK ROAD

Strasse did not like it, but he could not proceed without Ralph, and Ralph insisted that Mrs. Scarletin and I be brought along. First, he sent two men to watch Hilda Speck and to make sure she did not try to leave town—as the Americans say. He had no evidence to arrest her as yet, nor did he really think I believe—that he was going to have any.

The dog, Lisa, and I got into the rear of a large police limousine, steam-driven, of course. Strasse sat in the front with the driver. Another car, which kept in radio contact with us, was to follow us at a distance of a kilometer.

An hour later, we were just north of Luneburg. A half-hour later, still going south, we were just north of the town of Uelzen. It was still daylight, and so I could easily see the photo of the painting which I held. The yellow road on it ran south of the moon rising behind the castle (Luneburg) and extended a little south of a group of three strange figures. These were a hornless sheep (probably a female), a section of an overhead railway, and an archer with a medieval Japanese coiffure and medieval clothes.

Below this group the road split. One road wound toward the walls in the upper and lower parts of the picture and eventually went through them. The other curved almost due south to the left and then went through or by some more puzzling figures.

The first was a representation of a man (he looked like the risen Jesus) coming from a tomb set in the middle of some trees. To its right and a little lower was a waistcoat. Next was what looked like William Penn, the Quaker. Following it was a man in a leopard loincloth with two large apes at his heels.

Next was a man dressed in clothes such as the ancient Mesopotamian people wore. He was down on all fours, his head bent close to the grass. Beside him was a banana tree.

Across the road was a large hot-air balloon with a bald-headed man in the wicker basket. On the side of the bag in large letters were: O. Z.

Across the road from it were what looked like two large Vikings wading through a sea. Behind them was the outline of a fleet of dragon-prowed long-ships and the silhouette of a horde of horn-helmeted bearded men. The two leaders were approaching a body of naked warriors, colored blue, standing in horse-drawn chariots.

South of these was a woman dressed in mid-Victorian clothes, hoopskirts and all, and behind her a mansion typical of the pre-Civil War American south. By it was a tavern, if the drunks lying outside it and the board hanging over the doorway meant anything. The sign was too small to contain even letters written under a magnifying glass.

A little to the left, the road terminated in a pair of hands tearing a package from another pair of hands.

Just before we got to Uelzen, Strasse said, "How do you know that we're on the right road?"

"Consider the sheep, the raised section of railway, and the Japanese archer," Ralph said. "In English, *U* is pronounced exactly like the word for the female sheep—*ewe*. An elevated railway is colloquially an *el*. The Japanese archer could be a Samurai, but I do not think so. He is a *Zen* archer. Thus, *U, el*, and *zen* or the German city of Uelzen."

"All of this seems so easy, so apparent, now that you've pointed it out," I said.

"Hindsight has 20/20 vision," he said somewhat bitterly.

"And the rest?" I said.

"The town of Esterholz is not so difficult. Would you care to try?"

"Another English-German hybrid pun," I said, with more confidence than I felt. "*Ester* sounds much like *Easter*, hence the risen Christ. And the wood is the *holz*, of course. *Holt*, archaic English for a small wood or copse, by the way, comes from the same Germanic root as *holz*."

"And the Weste (waistcoat)?" Ralph said.

"I would guess that that means to take the road west of Esterholz," I said somewhat more confidently.

"Excellent, Doctor," he said. "And the Quaker?"

"I really don't know," I said, chagrined because Lisa had been looking admiringly at me.

He gave his short barking laughter and said, "And neither do I, my dear fellow! I am sure that some of these symbols, perhaps most, have a meaning which will not be apparent until we have studied the neighborhood."

Seven kilometers southeast of Uelzen, we turned into the village of Esterholz and then west onto the road to Wrestede. Looking at the hands tearing loose the package from the other pair, I suddenly cried out, "Of course! Wrestede! Suggesting the English, *wrested!* The hands are *wresting* the package away! Then that means that Scarletin is a prisoner somewhere between Esterholz and Wrestede!"

"Give that man the big stuffed teddy bear," Ralph said. "OK, toots, so where is Scarletin?"

I fell silent. The others said nothing, but the increasing tension was making us sweat. We all looked waxy and pale in the light of the sinking sun. In half an hour, night would be on us.

"Slow down so I can read the names on the gateways of the farms," Ralph said. The driver obeyed, and presently Ralph said, "Ach!"

I could see nothing which reminded me of a Quaker.

"The owner of that farm is named Fuchs (fox)," I said.

"Yes, and the founder of the Society of Friends, or The Quakers, was George Fox," he said.

He added a moment later, "As I remember it, it was in this area that some particularly bestial—or should I say human?—murders occurred in 1845. A man named Wilhelm Graustock was finally caught and convicted."

I had never heard of this case, but, as I was to find out, Ralph had an immense knowledge of sensational literature. He seemed to know the details of every horror committed in the last two centuries.

"What is the connection between Herr Graustock and this figure which is obviously Tarzan?" I said.

"Graustock is remarkably similar in sound to Greystoke," he said. "As you may or may not know, the lord of the jungle was also Lord Greystoke of the British peerage. As a fact, Graustock and Greystoke both mean exactly the same thing, a gray stick or pole. They have common Germanic roots. Ach, there it is! The descendants of the infamous butcher still hold his property, but are, I believe, singularly peaceful farmers."

"And the man on all fours by a banana tree?" Strasse growled. It hurt him to ask, but he could not push back his curiosity.

Ralph burst out laughing again. "Another example of redundancy, I believe. And the most difficult to figure out. A tough one, sweetheart. Want to put in your two pfennigs worth?"

"Aw, go find a fireplug," Strasse said, at which Ralph laughed even more loudly.

"Unless I'm mistaken," Ralph said, "the next two images stand for a word, not a thing. They symbolize *nebanan* (next door). The question is, next door to what? The Graustock farm or the places indicated by the balloon and the battle tableau and the antebellum scene? I see nothing as yet which indicates that we are on or about to hit the bulls-eye. Continue at the same speed driver."

There was silence for a minute. I refused to speak because of my pride. Finally, Lisa said, "For heaven's sake Herr von Wau Wau, I'm dying of curiosity! How did you ever get *nebanan?*"

"The man on all fours with his head close to the ground looks to me like ancient Nebuchadnezzar, the Babylonian king who went mad and ate grass. By him is the banana (Banane) tree. Collapse those two words into one, a la Lewis Carroll and his portmanteau words, and you have *nebanan* (next to)."

"This Scarletin is crazy," Strasse said.

"If he is, he has a utilitarian madness," Ralph said.

"You're out of your mind, too!" Strasse said triumphantly.

"Look!" And he pointed at a name painted on the wall. Neb Bannons.

Ralph was silent for a few seconds while Strasse laughed, and then he said, quietly, "Well, I was wrong in the particular but right in the principle. Ach! Here we are! Maintain the same speed driver! The rest of you, look straight ahead, don't gawk! Someone may be watching from the house, but they won't think it suspicious if they see a dog looking out of the window!"

I did as he said, but I strained out of the corners of my eyes to see both sides of the road. On my right were some fields of barley. On my left I caught a glimpse of a gateway with a name over it in large white-painted letters: Schindeler. We went past that and by a field on my left in which two stallions stood by the fence looking at us. On my right was a sign against a stone wall which said: Bergmann.

Ralph said delightedly, "That's it!"

I felt even more stupid.

"Don't stop until we get around the curve ahead and out of sight of the Schindeler house," Ralph said.

A moment later, we were parked beyond the curve and pointed west. The car which had been trailing us by several kilometers reported by radio that it had stopped near the Graustock farm.

"All right!" Strasse said fiercely. "Things seem to have worked out! But before I move in, I want to make sure I'm not arresting the wrong people. Just how did you figure this one out?"

"Button your lip and flap your ears, sweetheart," Ralph said. "Take the balloon with O. Z. on it. That continues the yellow brick road motif. You noticed the name Bergmann (miner)? A Bergmann is a man who digs, right? Well, for those of you who may have forgotten, the natal or Nebraskan name of the Wizard of Oz was Diggs."

Strasse looked as if he were going to have an apoplectic fit. "And what about those ancient Teutonic warriors and those naked blue men in chariots across the road from the balloon?" he shouted.

"Those Teutonic warriors were Anglo-Saxons, and they were invading ancient Britain. The Britons were tattooed blue and often went into battle naked. As all educated persons know," he added, grinning. "As for the two leaders of the Anglo-Saxons, traditionally they were named Hengist and Horsa. Both names meant *horse*. In fact, as you know, *Hengst* is a German word for stallion, and *Ross* also means horse. *Ross* is cognate with the Old English *hrossa*, meaning horse."

"God preserve me from any case like this one in the future!" Strasse said. "Very well, we won't pause in this madness! What does this pre-Civil War house with the Southern belle before it and the tavern by it mean? How do you know that it means that Scarletin is prisoner there?"

"The tableau suggests, among other things, the book and the movie *Gone With The Wind*," Ralph said. "You probably haven't read the book, Strasse, but you surely must have seen the movie. The heroine's name is Scarlett O'Hara, right, pal? And a *tavern* in English, is also an *inn*. Scarlett-inn, get it?"

A few minutes later Ralph said, "If you don't control yourself, my dear Strasse, your men will have to put you in a strait jacket."

The policeman ceased his bellowing but not his trembling, took a few deep breaths, followed by a deep draught from a bottle in the glove compartment, breathed schnapps all over us, and said, "So! Life is not easy! And duty calls! Let us proceed to make the raid upon the farmhouse as agreed upon!"

Chapter VII

NO EMERALD CITY FOR ME

An hour after dusk, policemen burst into the front and rear doors of the Schindeler house. By then it had been ascertained that the house had been rented by a man giving the name of Albert Habicht. This was Hilda Speck's brother, Albert Speck, the Hippopotamus. His companion was a Wilhelm Erlesohn, a tall skinny man nicknamed *die Giraffe*. A fine zoological pair, both now behind bars.

Hilda Speck was also convicted but managed to escape a year later. But we were to cross her path again. ("The Case of the Seeing Eye Man.")

Alfred Scarletin was painting another canvas with the same message but different symbols when we collared his kidnapers. He threw down his brush and took his lovely wife into his arms, and my heart went into a decaying orbit around my hopes. Apparently, despite his infidelity, she still loved him.

Most of this case was explained, but there was still an important question to be answered. How had Scarletin known where he was?

"The kidnapping took place in daylight in the midst of a large crowd," Scarletin said. "Erlesohn jammed a gun which he had in his coat pocket against my back. I did as he said and got into the back of a delivery van double-parked nearby. Erlesohn then rendered me unconscious with a drug injected by a hypodermic syringe. When I woke up, I was in this house. I have been confined to this room ever since, which, as you see, is large and has a southern exposure and a heavily barred skylight and large heavily barred windows. I was told that I would be held until I had painted twelve paintings. These would be sufficient for the two men to become quite wealthy through sales to rich but unscrupulous collectors. Then I would be released.

"I did not believe them of course. After the twelve paintings were done, they would kill me and bury me somewhere in the woods. I listened often at the door late at night and overheard the two men, who drank much, talking loudly. That is how I found out their names. I also discovered that Hilda was in on the plot, though I'd suspected that all along. You see, I had quit her only a few days before I was kidnapped, and she was desperate because she no longer had an income.

"As for how I knew where I was, that is not so remarkable. I have a photographic memory, and I have tramped up and down Germany painting in my youth and early middle age. I have been along this road a number of times on foot when I was a teenager. In fact, I once painted the Graustock farmhouse. It is true that I had forgotten this, but after a while the memory came back. After all, I looked out the window every day and saw the Graustock farm.

"And now, tell me, who is the man responsible for reading my message? He must be an extraordinary man."

"No man," I said, feeling like Ulysses in Polyphemus' cave.

"Ach, then, it was you, Lisa?" he cried.

"It's yours truly, sweetheart," the voice of Humphrey Bogart said.

Scarletin is a very composed man, but he has fainted at least once in his life.

Chapter VIII
THE CONCLUSION

It was deep in winter with the fuel shortage most critical. We were sitting in our apartment trying to keep warm by the radiations from the TV set. The Scotch helped, and I was trying to forget our discomfort by glancing over my notes and listening to the records of our cases since the Scarletin case. Had Ralph and I, in that relatively short span of time, really experienced "The affair of the Aluminum Crèche," "The Adventures of the Human Camel" and "The Old-School Thai" and the distressing business with the terrible Venetian, Granelli? The latter, by the way, is being written up under the title: "The Doge Whose Barque Was Worse Than His Bight."

At last, I put the notes and records to one side and picked up a book. Too many memories were making me uncomfortable. A long silence followed, broken when Ralph said, "You may not have lost her after all, my dear Weisstein."

I started, and I said, "How did you know I was thinking of *her?*"

Ralph grinned (at least, I think he was grinning). He said, "Even the leadbrained Strasse would know that you cannot forget her big brown eyes, her smiles, her deep rich tones, her figure, and her et cetera. What else these many months would evoke those sighs, those moping stares, those frequent attacks of insomnia and absentmindedness? It is evident at this moment that you are not at all as deep in one of C. S. Forester's fine sea stories as you pretend.

"But cheer up! The fair Lisa may yet have good cause to divorce her artistic but philandering spouse. Or she may become a widow."

"What makes you say that?" I cried.

"I've been thinking that it might not be just a coincidence that old Lausitz died after he purchased Scarletin's painting. I've been sniffing around the painting—literally and figuratively—and I think there's one Hamburger that's gone rotten."

"You suspect Scarletin of murder!" I said. "But how could he have killed Lausitz?"

"I don't know yet, pal," he said. "But I will. You can bet your booties I will. Old murders are like old bones—I dig them up."

And he was right, but that adventure was not to happen for another six months.

The Doge
Whose Barque Was
Worse Than His Bight

First published in *The Magazine of Fantasy & Science Fiction,*
November 1976.

The character Cordwainer Bird is a pseudonym first used by
Harlan Ellison and a year after this story Phil used the pseudonym himself when he penned "The Impotency of Bad Karma."
Ellison eventually wrote a story for *Weird Heroes 2*, at Phil's insti-
gation, featuring the eponymous Bird. Yet more elliptically, Phil
wrote Bird into Doc Savage's genealogy in the paperback edition
of *Doc Savage, His Apocalyptic Life.*
In his preface here, Phil gives Somers birth date as 26 January
1910. In his biography of Somers (which follows this piece) his
birth date is given as 6 January 1910. We can give credence to
this second date as it links with the birthday of Sherlock
Holmes. So, is the 26th a typo? Let's not forget that 26 January
is Phil's own birthday.
Although Phil only penned two completed Ralph stories,
Spider Robinson added an episode to the cadre with "Dog Day
Afternoon" which featured in his *Time Travelers Cash Only.*

Editorial Preface

"A Scarletin Study", the first of the Ralph von Wau Wau series, appeared
in the March, 1975, issue (of *The Magazine of Fantasy & Science Fiction*—
Editor). Those interested in biographical details about the author may refer to
Kilgore Trout's "Venus on the Half-Shell" (Dec., 1974, and Jan., 1975 issues
of *The Magazine of Fantasy & Science Fiction*; Dell Publications, February,
1975). Since then, your inquisitive editor has unearthed some information
unprovided by Trout. Somers was born in Petersburg, Illinois, on January 26,
1910. His grandfather was a judge; his father, an aspiring but unpublished

poet. Their epitaphs and a fragment of Somers III's blank verse epic can be found in Edgar Lee Masters' *The Spoon River Anthology*. Somers III was partially paralyzed by polio at the age of ten. Though he has never been out of his native town, he often soars from his wheelchair to freewheel via the exploits of his fictional heroes. The two most popular are John Clayter, spaceman *extraordinaire*, and Ralph von Wau Wau, unique private eye. Ralph, it's true, hasn't exactly stepped into Sherlock Holmes' or Sam Spade's shoes. He isn't built for it. But he is unmatchable at sniffing out evil. And how many male detectives, totally unclothed, can enter a ladies' restroom without causing an uproar?

—1—

It was on a bitterly cold night and frosty morning toward the end of the winter of '79 that I was awakened by a long wet tongue licking my face. It was Ralph von Wau Wau. The streetlight under which our Volkswagen was parked shone upon his eager face and told me that something was amiss. Rather, I'd missed a miss.

"Come, Weisstein, come!" he cried. "The dame is afoot!"

He spoke in English, for some reason preferring its use when we were alone.

"Good Heavens!" I said. "Surely, you can't mean Fraulein Saugpumpe?"

He chuckled and then switched from Basil Rathbone's voice to the one he preferred when he was especially sarcastic. You would swear that you were hearing Humphrey Bogart in *The Maltese Falcon*.

"Who else have we been watching for five straight days and nights, sweetheart?" he said. "Pippi Long Stockings? She just went around the corner. Get on the stick, Doc, and step on the gas. Or would you prefer to keep on dreaming of Frau Scarletin?"

He pressed the specially installed button on the dashboard. The door swung shut. He can open and close the door by bending his paw at right angles to his leg and pulling the handle out. But he usually uses the mechanism actuated by the dashboard and a toggle switch under the fender. Those familiar with our adventures will remember that we fitted the Volkswagen with this device during the rather horrendous events of "The Hind of the Baskerbergs."

I started the motor and put the gear into first. As we drove away from the curb, headlights suddenly struck us and a loud deep horn blared. I slammed on the brakes, and Ralph bounced into the dashboard and fell on the floor. The huge Diesel truck roared by, missing our left fender by an inch.

"Are you hurt?" I said as Ralph climbed back to the seat.

"No, but you're going to be, pal. Unless you take your mind off that skirt and get with it."

"I really prefer that you not refer to Frau Scarletin in that manner," I said stiffly.

"My apologies, my dear fellow," he said, reverting to his favorite alternate voice. "I had no intention of insulting one who, for you, will always be The Woman. But please do concentrate on the business at hand. Our quarry is a slippery one, a real fox, no pun intended."

I had by then driven the car around the corner. No sooner done than I pulled over to the curb and stopped.

"She's getting into a taxi," I said.

"I'm not blind," Ralph said. "Undoubtedly, she's heading for the airport."

"However could you know that?" I cried.

"To anyone else, she would merely be going to the opera. She's dressed for it, she had no luggage, only a small purse, and in forty minutes *Fidelio* begins. But it is not the magnificent Beethoven she is interested in.

"I was in the alley a half a block away when she came out of the door of her apartment building. Fortunately, the wind was in my favor. I was able to obtain an excellent olfactory profile of her. She'd been drinking heavily. Now, we know from the *Polizei* psychological profile of her that when she is relaxed she drinks California brandy. Though she'd also been smoking heavily, I was able to detect through the odor of American cigarettes—Camels, I believe—the telltale molecules of four-year old California brandy stored in re-used white oak barrels.

"Without fear of contradiction I can state that the emitted fumes were of a brandy of 84 proof: pH, 4.48; total acid, 14.3; aldehydes, 5.9; esters, 1.6; fusel oil, 45.5; furfural, 0.18..."

I pulled the car from the curb to follow the taxi, crying at the same time, "Spare me the details, Ralph! I know your nose is an ambulatory chemical-analysis laboratory!"

He chuckled. "If you had memorized the profile as I have, my dear Weisstein, you would recall that she is terrified of flying. Only in extreme emergencies will she travel otherwise than by car or train. She can only overcome her neurosis by imbibing considerable amounts of alcohol. When she entered the building six hours ago, she looked contented and she had been drinking moderate quantities of Armagnac. It's apparent that she's received a phone call necessitating an airplane flight. You do follow my line of reasoning, my good fellow?

He paused, grinning, his tongue hanging out, a triumphant light in his big brown eyes."And I suppose you know where that is?" I said somewhat testily. I was, I admit, in a bad mood.

I had been interrupted almost at the climax, if I may use the word, of a most pleasant dream. It would be indiscreet to go into its details.

"*Its citizens are a race apart, comparable only to themselves,*" he said.

"Venice!" I cried, recognizing Goethe's phrase. "But how…?"

I shot the VW into a parking space near Dammtorstrasse 28. Saugpumpe's taxi had stopped before the *Staatsoper* and she was getting out.

"Ha!" I said. "For once, you have erred, Ralph! She *is* attending the opera!"

"Really?" he said. "Have you also forgotten that the police report stated that she is tone deaf?"

"Whenever did that keep people from going to the opera?" I replied. "Perhaps she is meeting a gentleman inside, enduring what is to her a meaningless gibberish for the sake of male companionship."

He switched to Bogart. (From now on, I will refrain from identifying his differing voices except when necessary. I trust the reader can distinguish from the style of speech whether he is speaking in the persona of the Great Detective or the hard-boiled dick of San Francisco.)

"Bushwa, pal. She's shaking her tail, I mean, ducking her shadow. She still thinks she's the meat in a Hamburger police bun. She doesn't know the shami—that's the plural of shamus, sweetheart—were pulled off five days ago."

I groaned. Perhaps Ralph preferred English because only in that language can one make appropriate—or inappropriate—puns preserving the peculiar flavor of those two immortal mythics. Personally, I prefer Dr. Thorndyke.

A few minutes later, we were standing by the entrance to the opera house. We were in Guise No. 3, I with dark glasses and a cane, holding a leash attached to Ralph's harness. We stood there twelve minutes, the only interruption being a doorman who asked if he could do anything for us. I told him that we were waiting for my wife.

Presently a man in evening clothes came out, passing us with only a glance. The doorman whistled a taxi for him, and he was carried off.

"He looked mad," I said. "Perhaps his date stood him up."

"That was Saugpumpe, you simp! Get the lead out! Hump it! We'll lose her!" And he dragged me along willy-nilly behind him. Ralph weighs one hundred and sixty pounds, about seventy pounds more than the average German shepherd dog. Besides his father was half Canadian timber wolf.

As we got into the VW, he said, "I smelled her. OK, I apologize. I keep forgetting you don't have my keen nose. That disguise would've fooled me, too, if I'd just eyeballed her. Maybe. Didn't you dig that hipswaying? She was trying to walk like a man and almost succeeded."

"I thought he might just be a little, you know, on the ambiguous side," I said.

"Always the gent, ain't you, Doc?"

As we drove away, I said, "How do you know she's going to Venice?"

"That's where the long green, the loot, the mazuma is just now. And where the carrion is, the hyenas gather. In this case, Giftlippen and his sidekick, Smigma. Things must be about ready to pop open. Otherwise, Giftlippen wouldn't have called in his old lady."

"But," I said, "Giftlippen and Smigma are dead! They were blown to bits last year at Marienbad when the Czech police ambushed them. You know that. You set up the trap for them."

"How many wooden pfennigs have you got in the bank, Doc?"

—2—

As Ralph had predicted, her taxi went straight to the Northern Aircross, the airport at Fuhlsbuttel. I hope my foreign readers will forgive me if I mention, with some pride, that it is the oldest airport in Europe. It also has some of the longest lines at the ticket counter in the world. Ralph stayed in the car while I waited by the counter and ascertained that Saugpumpe was indeed going to Venice. Fortunately, she was so intoxicated that her normal perceptiveness was missing. She didn't notice me. Also, I suppose she must have been sure she had eluded her shadows, if any.

She was still in her male clothes, passing as a Herr Kleinermann Wasnun. I returned to the parking lot, where I got out of the trunk our forged ID's and other papers. Among these was a health certificate from a licensed veterinarian, required for a seeing-eye dog traveling to a foreign country. I wrote in the date since it is invalid if issued over fifteen days before leaving. I then muzzled Ralph, another requirement; and with a suitcase which is always packed for such emergencies, we proceeded to buy a ticket. (A blind man's dog travels free.) Of course, we couldn't board Saugpumpe's airliner. Even she would have thought it suspicious that we would have been at the opera and on her plane, too. She took a Lufthansa directly to the Lido Airport, and we left on an Albanian airliner to Rome. Not, however, before I had phoned Lisa Scarletin. When I hung up, I found that Ralph had been eavesdropping.

"You look like one of Dracula's victims," he said. "She really chewed you out, didn't she?"

"Yes. She said this was the last time. She gave me seven days more. If the case isn't wrapped up by then, I can either abandon it and return to Hamburg. Or…"

"Or forget the wedding bells, heh? Well, Doc, you can't blame her. She hardly ever gets to see you, and you lead a very dangerous life. Besides, women regard their competitors as bitches, but a male dog...unforgivable! I won't crowd you. You're a big boy now. You can make your own decision."

"Either way, I lose!" I cried.

"That's life for you." But his involuntary whine betrayed him. He was as upset as I.

The flight was pleasant enough, though marred by three minor incidents. One was when a scowling Albanian commented, in his native Gheg, about us. I leaned down to Ralph, who was lying in the aisle by my seat, as regulations required. "What did he say?"

"How the hell can I talk with this muzzle on?" he said.

Reassured that I could hear him—after all, the voder in his throat doesn't depend upon his lip movements—he said, "Something about a capitalist dog."

"What?" I said. "I shall certainly complain to the stewardess. After all, the Albanian Airline is trying to drum up business, and they certainly won't get any good will if they allow their passengers to be insulted."

"For cripes' sake, pipe down!" he said. "He was referring to *me*. And quit talking. They're staring at us."

Sometime later he rose while I was eating. Through a lifted lip, he said, "How's the rabbit stew?"

"Delicious. But I can't give you some. You know I can't unmuzzle you to eat."

"It ain't rabbit, Doc. It's *cat!*"

I suddenly lost my appetite. And I was furious, but I could not complain. I didn't want to draw any more attention to myself. Besides, how could I explain that I knew the difference between cat and rabbit without admitting that I was well acquainted with the taste of both?

About an hour before we landed at Rome, Ralph again put his head on my lap. "I can't stand it any more," he said. "I gotta go!"

"No. 1 or No. 2?" I said.

"Do you want a demonstration in the aisle? Let me into the toilet before I bust."

It was most embarrassing, but Ralph insisted on the intensity of the urgency in terms which would affront the more delicate of my readers. In fact, they affronted me. Even more furious, I rose and tap-tapped my way down the aisle with the leash in my other hand. The passengers started, but they assumed of course that I was the one in need. Once at the door of the toilet, which fortunately was in the rear, I observed that no one was looking. I quickly opened the door and Ralph bounded in and sat down on the seat. I shut the door, but a few seconds later it occurred to me that if anyone did look back he might be surprised. I went into the toilet quickly and locked the door.

"I was wondering what you were doing out there," Ralph said. "I don't know what the Albanians consider a low sanitation level, but they might object to a mere canine using their facilities."

"Hurry up," I said. "The other toilet's occupied, and somebody might want to use this one at any moment. If he should see us emerge together from this place, well..."

"Can it, Doc! No pun intended. I've been able to adapt to living as a human in most respects. But I am a dog, and in some things I'll always be a dog. For Homo sap, Number 1 relief is a continuous process, quickly done. For me, it's intermittent, and it's long, though highly pleasurable. So keep your shirt on."

I sweated, and then at last Ralph was finished, and I opened the door. And what I'd dreaded, happened. A fat, frowzy, and elderly woman was waiting outside. Her expression of impatience, and perhaps of some slight pain, became astonishment. Then revulsion. She poured out a flood of furious protest mixed with some invectives, I'm sure, though I didn't understand a word of it. Ralph growled, and even though muzzled he scared her. She backed up, screaming for the stewardess. There was quite a commotion for a while. I got back to my seat and sat down, and then the stewardess, speaking German, asked me for an explanation.

"It's simple," I said. "The dog was suffering, and so I took him where he would no longer have to suffer."

"But that is for the passengers," she said, though she was having difficulty repressing a smile.

"The dog is a passenger," I said. "And I didn't see any sign forbidding use by animals. Besides, he's much cleaner than her," and I pointed to the fat woman glaring at us from across the aisle.

"Oh, you mustn't say that!" she said. "She's a commissar!"

But she returned to the woman; they talked for a while, and that was the last I heard of that. However, after disembarking, Ralph pulled me up alongside the woman, who was trudging across the field carrying a large attaché case. He lifted his lip, said something, and then dropped back. She looked back, this time with a frightened look, and then broke into a waddling run.

"All right," I said. "What did you say?"

"Do you know Albanian for *up yours?*"

"Ralph," I said, "that was stupid. We've had a lot of publicity. She might put two and two together and..."

"And come up with *vier,*" he said. (I should explain that the German word for *four* sounds much like the British English *fear.*)

"Anyway," he continued, "she'll convince herself she was mistaken. It's been my experience that nobody really believes in a talking dog until he's been around me for a while."

"Nevertheless, that was stupid. It could jeopardize our mission."

"I'm human, all too human. Likely to give way to self-destructive impulses. I apologize again. You're entitled to that remark. God knows how many times I've called you stupid. I've regretted it later, of course. After all, it's not your fault you don't have my high IQ"

—3—

For the reader who knows nothing about Ralph—though it seems incredible in this day of global TV—I'll recapitulate his career. Ralph was the result of experiments by psychobiologists at an institute in Hamburg. They were able to raise the intelligence of various animals through the implantation of an artificial protein. These developed into billions of cerebral nerve synapses, making the brain not much larger but immensely more complex.

German shepherd dogs were not the only experimental animals at the institute. The scientists had succeeded in raising the intelligence of all their subjects and also increased the size of many. The sentient beasts had included donkeys, bears, otters, rodents of various kinds, and a gorilla.

The person believed to be chiefly responsible for the IQ-raising techniques was Professor Pierre Sansgout. He was a biologist who had been fired from the University of Paris because he preferred German beer to French wine.

Blackballed everywhere in his native country, he had gone to work for the Hamburg institute. Apparently, the explosion that killed everyone but Ralph at the institute was Sansgout's fault. From the few notes escaping destruction, it was learned that his pet project was the mutation of bees which would directly produce mead. According to a note, he had done this, and the alcoholic content of this mead was eighty percent. However, he, and the institute as a whole, had become victims of oversuccess. The source of the explosion was traced to a giant hive on his laboratory table.

Ralph was now twenty-nine but was as vigorous as a man of the same age. No one knew how his lifespan had been extended. The explosion had also destroyed the records. There was speculation that the scientists had discovered an age-delaying "elixir," which had been injected into the beasts. But no one really knew.

Ralph was a pup when the explosion occurred. Legally, he was a *Schutzhund,* the property of the Hamburg Police Department. He came close to being destroyed—"murdered," Ralph said—by the HPD because of his slow growth, which matched the pace of a human infant. But when he uttered a few words while on the way to the gas chamber, he was saved. The HPD realized what they had and gave him an education.

Investigation revealed that a voder had been implanted in his throat. This was connected to cerebral circuits which enabled him to switch it off and on and converted his linguistic thoughts into spoken words. As he grew older, larger voders were implanted. At the present, the voder contained circuits enabling him to speak with a perfect accent all twelve of the world's great languages and a number of the minor.

However, Ralph wasn't fluent in all of these. He had not as yet mastered all. Nor could he speak all of these with perfect grammar or a large vocabulary. But he was learning. The voder also contained different voice circuits. Hence, he had two male, one female, and one child's voice. He could also whistle, meow like a cat, utter ten different bird calls, and the decibel level ranged from that of a bullhorn to a whisper.

Every four years, the voder had to be removed and its tiny atomic battery replaced.

On becoming a juvenile, Ralph went to work for the HPD. He soon became famous because of his success in solving crimes. Eventually, he tired of this and applied for freedom and a license as a private detective. Those familiar with my chronicles will know that he had to endure a trial to establish his legal right to become a German citizen. Ralph won, but he also had to pay back the HPD for the expenses of his education. Thus, though he often earned fabulous fees, he was still sending large monthly amounts to the HPD.

A bitter aggravation of his financial distress had been brought about by the very villain we were tracking, Giftlippen, Baron Rottenfranzer. Before taking up a criminal career, Giftlippen had been an eminent literary critic and an affluent literary agent. Though a native and resident of the tiny principality of Liechtenstein, his influence was enormous all over the world. When Ralph's novel, *Some Humans Don't Stink*, came out, Giftlippen had turned thumbs down on it. His venomously unfair and viciously scornful articles had resulted in small sales for the book. (He even had the audacity to claim that it was authored by a ghost writer.)

Recently, we'd heard that the English translation was selling well. But the American royalties had not yet arrived. I once asked Ralph how it was possible for a distinguished and highly educated man like Giftlippen to become a crook.

"From literary critic to criminal is only a short, almost inevitable, step," Ralph had replied bitterly.

Smigma had been a noted Polish author of didactic fairy tales. He was also Giftlippen's good friend and client. His fiction, however, was only a sideline. He was a high official in the communist propaganda bureau. Then a strange thing happened after he'd suffered brain damage in a car crash. He found himself unable to utter a falsehood. This, of course, rendered him unfit for writing propaganda or fiction. (This characteristic would trip him up in "The Case of the Jesting Pilot.") It also made him dangerous to the state. He fled Poland and joined Giftlippen.

In the case titled "A Scarletin Study," I recount my own career as a physician for the Autobahn Patrol Medical Department. During an encounter with the murderous Rottenfranzer Gang—oil-hijacking specialists—I suffered a wound which hospitalized me. I retired and took up private practice without much success. During this time I met Ralph, who was looking for a human to share the expenses of his apartment. I abandoned my practice and became Ralph's full-time partner.

It was an exciting life, but now I had to make a choice between Lisa and Ralph. She would accept no more excuses that I was sorely needed by Ralph.

While we were waiting for our plane, Ralph explained why we were going to Venice.

"Here's the setup, Doc. Venice has slowly been sinking at the rate of 2.08 centimeters annually since 1920. It doesn't sound like much, but Venice is flush with the surface of the sea. In addition, the tides and seiches that sweep through the lagoon from the Adriatic cause a lot of trouble. And the atmospheric pollution from the factories of Mestre, the nearest mainland city, is destroying the art treasures, the building exteriors, the paintings, the statues, et cetera.

"The islands of Venice are sinking because of withdrawal of water through wells. The water-bearing strata are subsiding. And it won't do any good to pump water back in, according to the scientists. Venice seemed doomed.

"Meanwhile, a short time ago, a savior, or a man who claims to be a savior, appears. He's a strange man with a strange story. His name *was* Giuseppe Granelli. He was born and raised in the back woods of the Italian Alps. His village was destroyed in a landslide. He was the sole survivor, though crippled for life. But during his convalescence he had a selcouth experience."

"Selcouth? What does that mean?" I said.

"It's an archaic English word meaning *unusual* or *strange*, my unlearned colleague. Granelli had a series of visions which revealed to him that he is the reincarnation of the most famous Doge of Venice, Enrico Dandolo, died 1205. He adopted the name and came to Venice in his wheelchair. There he proclaimed his real identity and his mission and organized the Venice Uplift Foundation. Despite the sound of its title, it is not an organization to raise money to buy a bra for the goddess of the sea."

"Spare me," I murmured.

"Dandolo's ideas for salvation sound feasible, though they'll cost a hell of a lot of money. He aroused vast enthusiasm. Mazuma pours in from art lovers, rich and poor, from all over the world. We kicked in twenty marks ourselves, remember, Doc? Had to skip a few meals but we considered it worth it."

"*You* did," I said. "Lisa was upset when I took her out to a Colonel Sanders' instead of the Epicurean's Club."

"Economics always wins over esthetics. Anyway, the Fund's funds are kept in a Venetian bank. So far, eighty million dollars American, and more coming in. And in two days the various festivals will start, including the traditional Marriage of the Sea of the Doge."

"And you think this vast sum will tempt Giftlippen? And he'll attempt a robbery during the confusion of the festivals?"

"Bingo! Give the man a kewpie doll! Look, I could be wrong. But it'll be the first time. Why should Giftlippen's mistress suddenly take off for Venice? It's because Giftlippen isn't dead, and he needs her for more than just sexual satisfaction."

"And Saugpumpe will lead us to Giftlippen?"

"We'll nail him. And we'll be financially independent. The reward offered for him, dead or alive, by the West German government has not been withdrawn. He's supposed to have perished, but the bureaucrats haven't gotten around to canceling the offer. It's still in effect, legally, and if we get him, we can legally collect. Five million marks. Think of that. You'll take your half and marry Mrs. Scarletin with your head held high. You won't be a down-at-the-heels quack marrying a rich widow."

"I don't care for your choice of words," I said. But it was an automatic response. I had gotten used to Ralph's taking his resentments out on me. Even though he had proved a hundred times that he was smarter and more educated and competent than most humans, he was still patronized by many. To them, he was just a freak. There were many who didn't believe that he was just a freak. There were many who didn't believe that he was truly sentient. I've even read articles where it was hinted that he couldn't speak at all, that I was a ventriloquist. The worst, in his eyes, were those who talked down to him, who insisted on petting him. He couldn't stand this. Not even I was allowed to pat his head. Lisa was the only exception so far.

He had once explained to me why she was granted this privilege.

"Dogs are inherently pack animals. I don't mean beasts of burden. I mean members of a pack. In a pack there's always one leader to whom the others defer and make submissive gestures. This is in the wild state, you comprehend, my dear fellow. But domesticated dogs have the same instincts, which is why they adapted to human society so well and why dogs have become the favorite pets of most people. But they're all psychologically mixed up by domestication. Some are one-man dogs, will allow only their master or mistress to pet them. Other dogs will allow any familiar human or stranger to pet them. Every human is, to them, a pack leader.

"I have the same instincts, but I am also, in a sense, human. I regard myself as the leader, whether the pack is Canis or Homo. But there's something about Mrs. Scarletin, call it charisma or whatever, that makes me want her to pet me. It's humiliating, in a way, because I'm more intelligent, more perceptive, and stronger. But that's the way it is."

"That's the way it is with me, too," I said.

—4—

Coming in at 12,000 feet, I could see the whole of the Laguna Veneta and much of the mainland in the late April sun. Two islands form part of the barriers which almost seal off the lagoon from the Adriatic: the Lido and Pellestrina. The former looks like an extended human shinbone; the latter is little more than a semideserted thin flat reef, now frequently awash. Between the two is a strait through which the high tide poured to send water swirling around the islanders' ankles.

Within the lagoon were the 116 closely spaced islands. A motor and train causeway connected Venice to the mainland. Smoke poured from the stacks of hundreds of factories in Mestre.

We sank down, then came in low over the Lido. Looking down, I could see the famous golf course at the western end. A minute later, we had landed on the airport at the other end. The Lido is, I believe, the only island on which vehicles are permitted. We took a Fiat taxi to our hotel. Since we did not have much money, and wanted to be inconspicuous, we had reserved a room at the Rivamare, a third-rate hotel facing the Adriatic. The Lido was crowded and festive, as were all the major islands. We were lucky to get rooms at this time, when Labor Day, Accension, Corpus Christi, and the Marriage of the Sea coincided on May 1. Moreover, the Doge Dandolo had been attracting large crowds even out of season.

The taxi driver cheated me, which infuriated me. But since I was supposed to be blind, I couldn't protest. I ordered a bottle of Falerno, two bowls of *burrida*, and a dish of *capotano* for me and of *fegatino* for Ralph. We finished them off with *cassata siciliana*, a rich cake with ice cream.

I then spent some time on the phone, calling hotels on the main island. Finally, the clerk at the Danieli informed me that a Herr Wasnun was registered there. We at once took a vaporetto, a steamboat, to the Riva degli Schiavone, a promenade facing the lagoon by the Canale di San Marco. A cluster of hotels was along here. The most famous, and expensive, was the Danieli.

"George Sand and Alfred de Musset stayed there in Room 13," Ralph said. "The Doge Dandolo resides there. More to the point, Fraulein Saugpumpe is there. She didn't have any trouble getting a room there; it had been reserved for her for a long time. So I suspect that our quarry, Giftlippen, is also residing there. The *arschloch* always did travel in style.

"Also, you'll notice that the Banco di Manin is nearby. That's where the Fund's money is deposited. But I suspect that Giftlippen has more in store for Venice than just cleaning out a bank. I have to give him credit; he does think big."

We were on the point of strolling to the Danieli when our attention was attracted by a commotion on the waterfront. At first we thought it was a brawl, a fight between the supporters of Dandolo and his opposition. A number of Italians decried him because of the stand of the Church. As I said, Dandolo claimed to be a reincarnation of the greatest of the Doges. Reincarnation is contrary to Catholic theology, of course, and the Pope had denounced Dandolo as a heretic and a fraud. Despite this, the majority of Catholics supported the Doge. They wanted Venice saved. Moreover, they regarded this affair as one more event in the love-hate relationship between the Pope and the Italian people.

"If they can give the man in the Vatican the finger, without endangering their immortal souls, they'll gladly do it," Ralph had commented.

The news media had crackled with reports of brawls between the pro- and anti-Dandolists. But the melee, the screaming and shouting and cursing and fistfighting, were not caused by theological disagreement. After we got close, we saw that it was a mob scene being filmed for a movie. Suddenly, two men and a woman were pushed into the water, a man yelled, "Cut!" and silence clamped like a giant hand over the mouths of the actors.

But only for a moment. The director began yelling—screaming, rather— and I suddenly realized that the screaming had been done mostly by him. He had an extremely shrill voice, one which carried like a factory whistle for a long distance. He was an extraordinary person, one who'd attract attention anywhere.

He was only four feet high but looked as if he were thirty-five years old. As I found out later, he was actually forty-five. He had long straight hair as black as the bottom of an oil well. His eyes were a beautiful robin's-egg blue. His face was hawklike but handsome. The stocky body was perfectly proportioned. So, though he was often referred to as a "giant dwarf," he was actually a midget, though too tall even to deserve that appellation.

It would be indiscreet to record the scorn, the invective, the denunciations of incompetency he hurled at the actors. Suffice it to say that he gave them the worst tongue-lashing I've ever heard. Also, the most entertaining. The man was an artist, a poet, extemporaneously pouring out demosthenics which must have cut the actors to the heart yet made me want to fall on the marble walk with laughter. Of course, I wasn't the recipient of the words and so could enjoy them.

The assistant director argued with him that the scene had been extremely vigorous and loud. There was nothing phony-looking about it.

"Yeah!" the little man screamed. "Everybody knows you Italians are very dramatic! You can ask somebody to please pass the antipasto, and you look and sound as if you're threatening murder and mayhem! But everybody knows you're mostly bluff and bluster and you just like to hear the sound of your own voices! You're all soap opera characters in real life and about as convincing!

"What I want is sincerity, understand, sincerity! I want you to be really mad at each other! Hate each other's guts. Don't just shake your fists! Slam each other in the breadbasket! Twist a few balls; that'll get some sincerity out of you.

"OK! Take your places and this time do it for real. Think of your opponent as someone who's spit on the pope *and* balled your mother. He has knocked up your sister and won't marry her. He's also the editor of a newspaper, and he's just put in big headlines that your aunt is running a whorehouse. As if that isn't enough, he's revealed that your daughter has run off with a married man, a *German* tourist!"

At this point the actors began yelling at him. His voice rose again, blanketing out the others like a lid put on a pot of steaming soup. By this time, the three who'd fallen into the water had climbed out. They stood near him, dripping with the stinking sewage-clotted liquid. One of them was a tall woman with a beautiful face and a superb figure. Her scanty wet clothes clung tightly to her body. All of a sudden, I was no longer in a hurry.

One of the actors was talking to the director. It seemed that he was the agent for the actors' union and he was protesting that they were not being paid to hurt each other.

"I'll pay you! I'll pay you!" the little man screamed. "Godalmighty! Every time I want you to do something extra, put a little sincerity into your shams, you want more *Lire!* Are you sure you're not members of the Mafia? It's extortion, pure essence of extortion, blackmail, financial rape, a currency copulation, *lira* lewdness, a Giovanni jazzing! You're bankrupting me!

"OK! Let's shoot it again and do it right this time, You think film grows like spaghetti! Do you think at all? Look, I'll tell you what'll make you mad enough to shuck off your insincerity like a stripteaser drops her panties! Think of your opponent as me! And I've just told you you're the illegitimate son of a Sicilian!"

That did it. No Italian will admit that Sicilians are real Italians, or so I've often been told by them. The North Italians look down upon the South Italians, and both look down on the Sicilian. I don't know who the Siciliano looks down on. The Maltese, perhaps.

The mob held a brief but spirited discussion. The agent said a few words to the director, something like "*Ah fahng goo*," and all, including the cameraman, walked off. For a moment, the big midget was speechless, than he shouted, "You're fired! Discharged for incompetency! Come back, do you hear? Come back or I'll put barnacles on your gondolas! Oh, my God, why did I ever come to this garlic swamp?"

Yelling, he hurled the camera into the canal and stamped around as if he would leave his footprints in the marble.

"Childish tantrums," I said to Ralph.

Ralph said, "I know who he is! He's the famous, or infamous, Cordwainer Bird!"

Immediately I recognized him. Bird was an American, an inhabitant of Los Angeles who had, in recent years, been much in the world's eyes. Originally, he had been a science-fiction writer, author of works well known in his peculiar genre. These included such strange titles as "I Have No Can and I Must Go," "Pane Deity or Up Your Window," "The Breast That Spouted Cholesterol into the Arteries of the World," "The Whining of Whopped Whippets," and "Dearthbird Stories."

At the same time, he had managed to rise to the top as a TV and movie writer. But his inability to tolerate tampering with his scripts by the producers, their mothers-in-law and mistresses, directors, actors, and studio floorsweepers had gotten him into trouble. After several incidents in which he almost strangled some powerful producers, he was blackballed in Hollywood.

Simultaneously, he was frustrated in his efforts to impress the literary critics of New York. He wrote several mainstream novels which the "East Coast Literary Mafia"—as he called it—reviled. He became destitute, which was the normal state of most science fiction writers. But he was a fighter, and he vowed to smash the Manhattan cartel, which existed to encourage native Gothamites whose shoddy works counterfeited emotions and destroyed the imagination of readers. He sold his stately mansion in Sherman Oaks at a loss and hitchhiked to New York. There he engaged in a guerrilla war with the critics and their allies, the publishers, distributors, and truck drivers' union.

And here he was, Cordwainer Bird, apparently making his own movie.

At that moment he saw us. He stopped, stared, then bounded grinning toward us.

"Wow! What a magnificent dog!" he said to me. "Is it all right to pet him?"

I wasn't surprised at this request. Many people desire to do this. And Bird's reputation as an ardent canophile was well known.

"There's only one person he's permitted to do so," I said. "But you can try. He won't bite, though."

Bird reached out a hand. I was surprised and, I must admit, somewhat jealous, when Ralph submitted to his stroking.

"Holy, Moly!" Bird said. "I think I'm in love! Listen, I don't want to offend you, but I'd like to buy him! Name your price."

This was too much for Ralph. He growled and lifted his lip, baring teeth that would have given a hungry leopard second thoughts. The idea of being sold, as if he were just an animal, offended him.

"Hey!" Bird said. "He acts like he knows what I'm saying!" Coaxingly, he said, "Come on, pal. I wouldn't hurt your feelings for anything. Say, what's his name?"

He thrust out his hand again and stroked Ralph's ear.

"He's not for sale," I said. I tugged at the leash and Ralph trotted on ahead of me. But he kept looking back as if he regretted having to leave.

Suddenly, Bird was in front of me. Before I could resist, he had, removed my large dark glasses and ripped off my false mustache.

"Ah, ha!" he said. "I thought so! *Herr Weisstein und der wunderhund,* Ralph von Wau Wau! I might've thought another German shepherd could be as big as Ralph. But it was evident he understood every word I spoke. Wow! Weisstein and von Wau Wau!"

"You sure blew it, sweetheart," Ralph said to me.

I sputtered with indignation. "Really," I said. "What could I have done? What did I do to give us away? It was your reaction that aroused his suspicions."

"Never mind that." He spoke to Bird. "For Pete's sakes, be a pal and give him his glasses and mustache. We're on a case!"

Bird smote his forehead with his hand. "Holy Jumping Moses! You're right! I am a dummy."

Unfortunately, the hand with which he struck his forehead was holding the mustache. It stuck to it when his hand came away. He handed me the glasses and then started to look around. "Where'd it go?"

I ripped it off his skin and replaced it with trembling hands. "By now all of Venice must be on to us," I said.

He looked quickly around. "No, nobody's looking this way. You're okay. So far. Listen, I don't want to horn in if I'm not welcome. But I've been looking for some real excitement. Life has been an emotional downhill slide since I cleaned out the New York establishment. I'd like to be dealt in this. I have certain talents which you could use. And it'd be a great honor to work with the great von Wau Wau. I'd do it for nothing, too. But don't tell my agent I said so."

"The best thing you could do for us would be to swear to keep silent about us," I said frostily.

I spoke to Ralph. "Isn't that so?"

"My dear fellow," Ralph said. "It *isn't* so. We're up against a great criminal, the deadliest biped in Europe. I've studied Mr. Bird's exploits in New York, and I believe we could use him with great advantage to our mission."

I was struck dumb with astonishment. Ralph had always said he wouldn't dream of taking in another partner. He had enough to do to put up with me. Of course, he was jesting when he spoke so disparagingly of me. But though he liked me, perhaps—dare I say—even loved me, he resented having to depend upon a human. As he once said, "Weisstein, you are my hands." Of course, he had to spoil it by adding, "And all thumbs, alas!"

But there was some sense in what he said. We could use a man of Cordwainer Bird's caliber. By which I mean that, though he looked like he was a BB gun, he shot a .44 Magnum. Besides, if he got mad at us, he could expose us. And that might be fatal.

At an outdoor restaurant we outlined to him our mission over a bottle of *soave* and a plate of *baccala*. Bird, however, refused the wine. He neither smoked nor drank, he said. He didn't seem to like it that Ralph lapped up the wine from the platter by my feet, but he said nothing.

"Bend an ear, buddy," Ralph said. "You're in the midst of shooting a flicker. You'll have to forget about that now. Can you stand the expense, all that money tied up?"

"No sweat," Bird said. "I'm backing and producing this myself. I'll show those Hollywood phonies a thing or two. I wrote the script myself, too. It was originally titled *Deaf in Venice*. But I decided on a more eye-catching title. I'm great on that, you know. How about *Ever Since I Met Her in Venice, I've Had Trouble With My He-ness?*"

"You'll need a wide screen," I said.

At that moment, we heard a blare of trumpets and a banging of drums. Everybody got up from their tables and ran to the crowd pouring out of the hotels and streets. I called to a man hurrying by, and he said, "*I'l Doge Dandolo!*"

We stood up and looked out across the Canale di San Marco. A boat had appeared from around the island of San Giorgio Maggiore. I recognized it at once, having seen it many times on TV. It was magnificent, coated with gold, propelled by sixty oarsman, an exact replica of a late medieval barque. On a platform in the stern stood some people dressed, like the oarsmen, in twelfth-century Venetian costumes. After a while, we could see the Doge himself. He sat in a wheelchair, an extraordinarily large one, also coated with gold. It was said to be self-propelled with a steam engine fueled by a small atomic reactor. As the barque stopped by the *riva*, a gang of flunkies from the Danieli Hotel ran out and placed an ornately carved gangplank onto the boat.

Ralph said, "Watch for Saugpumpe, amigo. I'll nose around and try to pick up the scents of Giftlippen and Smigma."

I released the leash and he trotted over to the crowd cheering on the quay. Bird left on his task, a rather distasteful one. He had to dive down into the stinking waters and recover his camera. Ralph had said that he could pose as a TV-news cameraman. He could take pictures which we could study later, hoping to identify our quarry in the crowds. Also, posing as a newsman, he could be seen everywhere without arousing suspicion.

I remained on my chair to observe both the crowd and the hotel entrance. I had difficulty not keeping my attention strictly on Dandolo. He was a huge man with a disproportionately large head. His features were exactly those of the late Doge whose reincarnation he claimed to be. They were immobile, waxy, their deadness the result of the landslide which had buried him for three days. He could, however, move his lips and jaws. He always wore fur gloves, reportedly to conceal hideous scars. A tigerskin robe covered his legs.

The wheelchair and its occupant rolled off the platform and down the gangplank. He was surrounded by his retainers and the hurrahing crowd, but I got up on my chair to get a good view before I remembered that I was supposed to be blind and hastily got down, I saw him clearly. By his side was his chief assistant and valet, Bruto Brutini, a small bespectacled man, prim-faced, bald and bearded.

He carried an ornately chased golden bowl full of shelled walnuts and pecans. Dandolo dropped his hands into this and threw a dozen at a time into his mouth. His addiction to nuts was well known.

Presently, the *riva* was almost deserted, the crowd having collected around the hotel entrance. Ralph came back and allowed me to leash him again. "Order another bottle of *soave*," he said, his tongue hanging out. "That was dry work."

"Any luck?"

"No, damn it. For one thing, both Dandolo and Smigma were too heavily perfumed. It overrode every other odor in the crowd. I wonder why they used perfume instead of taking a bath. Perhaps it's because that's what the old doges did. Dandolo is said to be a stickler for authenticity."

Cordwainer Bird rose out of the water, shoved the camera onto the stone, and walked dripping to us. He looked excited; his robin's-egg blue eyes shone.

"You aren't going to believe this. But I was under the barque when it came in."

"You bumped your head?" I said.

He stared. "Yeah. How'd you know?"

"A wish fulfillment," Ralph said, staring at me. I blushed. There was no fooling him. He knew that I was jealous, though I had tried not to show any sign of such an unworthy feeling. He claimed that he could smell emotions in humans, that they caused a subtle change of body odor. He would have made a great psychiatrist, not only because of his olfactory and emotional sensitivity and high intellect. People have no hesitancy in revealing all to a dog.

"Oh?" Bird said. "Listen, you guys, I did bump my head, but not on the bottom of the barque. I rammed it into metal six feet below the barque! Curved metal!"

"What was it?" I said.

"Hell, man, it was a submarine!"

I gasped, and Ralph whined.

"Yeah, there's a tiny submarine attached to the bottom of the barque!"

—5—

"*Donnerwetter!*" Ralph said, reverting in his surprise to his native tongue. Then, "Of course, what a blockhead I am! All the clues were in front of my nose, and I failed to smell them! How humiliating!"

"What are you talking about?" I said.

"The Doge Dandolo is Giftlippen!"

"However did you deduce that?"

"You mean *infer*, not deduce, don't you?" he said. "How often must I point out the difference? Actually, to be exact, I *gathered*. Check your Webster's."

"For crying out loud!" Bird said. "This is no time for lexical lessons! What's going on?"

"I had thought that Giftlippen would be here because of the Venice Uplift Fund millions," Ralph said. "But I erred again in underestimating that archvillain. He created the fund in order to steal it. But I'm sure that's part of a much bigger rip-off. Exactly what, I don't as yet know."

"But...the clues?" I said.

"It's too early to tell you. Besides, I think I also know the true identity of Giftlippen. It's only a theory, you understand. I prefer not to say anything about it until theory has become fact. But we may proceed on my premise that Dandolo is indeed Giftlippen, who is...never mind that now."

"If this is true," I said. "we must inform the Venetian police."

Simultaneously, Ralph said, "Don't be a sap, pal," and Bird said, "You're out of your gourd."

"One, the police would claim the reward," Ralph said. "And we need the money badly. Two, Giftlippen has a habit of bribing a strategically situated policeman or official to tip him off. Sometimes, he even plants one of his own men in a high place long before he pulls a job. The Venetian fuzz may be safe, but we can't take a chance."

"We'll give the big cheese our own *shazam!*" Bird cried.

Bird, I found out later, often reverted in moments of intense excitement to the speech he'd picked up from the comic books he'd read when a youth. Hence, his sometimes old-fashioned and often obscure phrases.

(For the benefit of my German readers, I'll explain that *shazam* was a word endemic in, I believe, the Captain Marvel comicbooks. Uttered by the captain and his juvenile partner, Billy Batson, it gave them superman powers. The American audience will have no trouble recognizing it. Neither will the French, who take comics seriously and even grant Ph.D. degrees for theses on this subject.)

"This turn of events pulls the rug from under us, sweethearts," Ralph said. "If Giftlippen or Smigma eyeball us, we'll be candidates for the morgue. This blind-man-and-his-seeing-eye-dog act isn't going to fool them. Not after our Kuwait adventure, heh, Weisstein?"

He was referring to that series of extraordinary events which I have chronicled as "The Shakedown of the Shook Sheik."

Ralph suddenly growled. Bird said, "Oh, oh!"

I turned. We were surrounded by seven Arabs. All wore dark glasses and were dressed in flowing robes. The faces of two were shrouded by their hoods or whatever Arabs call them. But they were not concealed enough to prevent me from distinguishing the massive waxen features of the Doge under a fake beard and the prunish lineaments of his assistant. They were all barefoot, and the wind was blowing from us to them. That accounted for their being able to take Ralph by surprise. Their wide loose sleeves had been pulled over their hands, but we could see the silencers attached to automatics.

"You three gentlemen will walk onto the barque with us," Smigma said in a thin high voice with a Polish accent. "Believe me, at the first sign of making a break, we will shoot you down."

I looked around. A number of oarsmen were coming toward us. They would block off the view of the passersby. If we were shot, they'd doubtless just pick us up and carry us off as if we were drunks—a not uncommon sight during the festivals.

That Smigma had addressed us as "three gentlemen" told me that they knew Ralph's identity.

We said nothing as we were conducted up the gangplank to the center of the boat. A hatch was raised and we were prodded down a ladder into a narrow cabin. Ralph could manage a ladder by himself. Another hatch gave entrance to the submarine attached to the bottom of the barque. We went past the small control room to a cell near the bow and were locked inside. This was so confined that we had no room to sit down. After a few minutes, we felt the craft begin moving and could detect faint vibrations as the propellers pushed us toward an unknown destination.

Ralph quit cursing himself for a dunderhead in six languages, including the Scandinavian. "I suspect, my esteemed but also dumb colleagues," he said, "that Saugpumpe led us into this trap. Giftlippen would want to get me, his most dangerous antagonist, out of the way before he proceeded with his dastardly plot. So, he allowed his mistress to remain under our observation until the last moment."

The only sound then was Bird banging his forehead on the steel bulkhead and muttering, "You cretin, you! Taken like a babe in diapers! Oh, the ignominy of it all!"

After a while, Ralph said, "You'll suffer even more brain damage if you keep that up." That was his way of subtly calling Bird a blockhead. There was one thing about Ralph. Though he had little hesitation in self-reproach, he hesitated even less in reproaching others.

We could do nothing. We couldn't even see the control room, since our door was windowless. After an hour, we felt the sub slow down. Then it stopped, the door was opened, and we were ushered up the ladder. We emerged into a vast cavern illuminated by floodlights. The cave had no visible entrance, which meant that it was beneath the surface of the sea. Our craft lay next to a stone platform; almost level with the water. Near it was docked a much larger submarine. Like our vessel, it had no conning tower. Beyond it was a blue sausage-shaped bag of rubber or plastic about sixty feet long and ten feet wide.

Ralph said, "Aha! That sub is a World War I U-boat! I recognize it. It was stolen from the Kiel Marine Museum a year ago! Giftlippen plans far ahead of time, the cunning fellow. He's removed the conning towers because of the extreme shallowness of the lagoon. Otherwise, the towers would project above the surface."

"And the bag?" I said.

"To be towed behind the U-boat. It must contain a metal skeleton to keep it from collapsing. Also, compartments to be flooded for submersion. Plus others for transporting the loot and much of his gang back from Venice. Doubtless, he has a large crew planted there, ready to carry out his foul plot."

Prodded by a rifle, we crossed the platform into a tunnel hewn out of rock. This led us for thirty paces to stairs also cut out of the rock. We ascended these into another tunnel made of stone blocks. A man pulled a lever; a section of the wall ground open. We entered a dungeon filled with rusty instruments of torture, a disheartening sight, passed through it and up a narrow winding stone staircase, and came out through another wall-door into a kitchen. It looked exactly like the kitchen of a medieval castle, which, indeed, it was.

After traversing a wide stone corridor, we came into a vast unfurnished room. We climbed up dusty staircases and presently were locked inside a twelfth-story stone cell. I looked through the steel bars of a small square opening in the southeast wall. The castle was set on a hill about fifty feet high. Since the rest of the country hereabouts was so flat, I deduced that the hill was artificial. The builder of the castle had piled earth here centuries ago.

The seaward side had been cut to make a perpendicular front and then a stoneblock wall had been erected against it to prevent erosion. (I couldn't see this from my window, of course, but I found out these details later.)

The castle was about half a mile from the shore. An arm of the lagoon a hundred yards wide extended from the shore to the base of the hill. It was the avenue for the sub which had brought us here. Once it, too, had been lined with great stone blocks, but many of these had fallen. A number jutted above the water just below the walls.

Ralph stood up on his hind legs by me. "You can see the islands from here," he said.

Normally, he wouldn't have been able to see that far. Dogs are short-sighted. But he was wearing contact lenses.

"Well, I know where we are," he said. "In the ruined and long-abandoned castle of Il Seno. He was a thirteenth-century Venetian, confined by the Council of Ten to his castle. The Council didn't mind his piracy as long as it was restricted to non-Venetian vessels. But Il Seno wasn't very discriminating.

"His name, by the way, means 'The Bight' in Italian. And this little recess in the land was also called Il Seno. It's still referred to by the locals as Il Seno del Seno. The Bight of the Bight. And here we are, the bitten among the bighters. A bitter pun, if you will excuse me."

"The desperate among the desperadoes," Bird said. "Okay, now what'll we do?"

At that moment the Judas window in the steel door opened. Giftlippen's enormous head appeared beyond it. "Have you any complaints about the accommodations?" he said in a deep baritone voice. He spoke in German with a Liechtensteiner accent.

"Cut the comedy, crook," Ralph said. "What I want to know is what do you intend for us? I would have thought you'd have kaputted us at once."

"What? And deprive me of the esthetic pleasure of forcing you to watch the rape of Venice?" Giftlippen said. "You, who screwed up my greatest coup? No, my shaggy friend, ever since you thwarted me in Kuwait, I've been planning this very scenario. I want you to view, as helpless spectators, my second-greatest coup. Actually, my greatest, since the Kuwait caper was a failure.

"You'll see the whole thing. Here"—he handed a long telescope to me— "and you won't be able to do a damned thing about it."

He broke into a weird blood-chilling cackling. Bird said, "Sounds just like my uncle, Kent Allard, alias Lamont Cranston. I've heard Giftlippen has a fabulous collection of old radio-show records."

"It *is* a recording," Ralph said enigmatically.

"Tomorrow is the ceremony of the Marriage with the Sea," Giftlippen said. "Ah, wait until you see the priceless wedding gifts the Venetians will be giving me. Of course, they don't know about their generosity yet, and I regret to say that it will be one hundred percent involuntary. But it's the gift that counts, not the intention."

"And after the wedding?" Ralph said.

"Do you know the history of this chamber?" Giftlippen said. "It's rather grim. This is the place where the daughter of a noble starved to death. Il Seno abducted her, locked her in it, and told her she could eat when she agreed to share his bed. She refused. I think it only esthetically appropriate that my greatest enemy suffer a like fate."

He paused to chomp on some nuts.

"Legend has it that she ate her own flesh before she expired. A classic case of diminishing returns. Now! There are three of you, and I have a wager with my esteemed colleague, Smigma, that one of you will put off the inevitable for a while by dining upon the other two. My money is on you, von Wau Wau. You're a dog, and dogs are always hungry. Your canine heritage will triumph over the human. You'll eat your friends, though you may weep walrus tears while doing so."

"By the heavens!" I cried. "You're a fiend! You're not human, you foul beast!"

"I'll go along with that, pal," Ralph said.

Bird snatched the telescope from me and drove its end through the window into the huge face. Giftlippen cried out and fell away. Smigma's face, a safe distance away, succeeded his. He cursed us in Polish, and then the window was slammed shut.

"At least, he'll never forget Cordwainer Bird," the little man said. "His nose crumpled up like a paper cup!"

"I doubt he was hurt," Ralph said. But he refused to elaborate on that statement.

"Hell, they haven't built the cell that can keep me in!" Bird said. He began inspecting the room, testing the steel bars, tapping the walls. Presently he went back to the bars, of which there were three. They were about a half-inch in diameter, a foot long, and set into holes drilled in the stone. Bird grabbed one with both hands and braced his feet against the wall. He pulled mightily, the muscles coiling like pythons beneath his skintight shirt. The shirt split along the biceps and across the back under the pressure. The bar bent as he pulled. Sweat ran out, soaked his clothes, and fell onto the floor to form a little pool. And the bar popped out.

Bird fell backward but twisted and somehow landed on his feet. "Like a cat!" he cried and then, "Begging your pardon, Ralph!"

"My dear fellow, I don't share the common canine prejudice against felines," Ralph said. "Oh, occasionally my instincts catch me off guard when a cat runs by, and I go after him. But reason quickly reasserts itself."

"That's quite a feat of strength," I said. "But even if you get the other bars out, so what? It's a fall of a hundred feet to the base of the castle. And fifty more if you should miss the slight projection of the cliff. Not to mention the boulders sticking out of the sea at the bottom."

"There are birds that can fly but can't dive. And birds that can dive but can't fly. This Bird can do both."

"I admire your confidence but deplore your lack of good sense," I said.

"Don't be such a Gloomy Gus, sweetheart," Ralph said. "Anyway, it's better to go out like a smashed bulb than flicker away while your battery dies by agonizing degrees."

"It's no wonder Giftlippen denigrated your novel," I said.

"The most unkindest cut of all," Ralph said, wincing.

Bird laughed and bent, literally, to the herculean task of ripping out the other bars. After much groaning and panting and screech of steel riven from stone, plus a miniature Mediterranean of perspiration on the floor, the way was open.

"Disbarred like a shyster!" Bird cried triumphantly. The window was too small for any person of normal size to wriggle through. Bird, however, wasn't handicapped in this respect. In fact, what some would regard as a handicap was in this case an advantage. If he'd been larger, he could not have gotten through the window.

"But how in the world can you launch yourself from the ledge?" I said. "The window is flush with the outer wall. By no means can you attain an upright position on it. Surely, you don't plan on dropping headfirst from it?"

Bird eyed the opening, said, "Get out of the way," and backed to the door, which was directly opposite the window.

"I'll get you guys out of this mess," he said. "Never fear."

As I shouted a protest, he ran at blinding speed across the room and dived through the window. I'll swear he had no more than half an inch clearance on all sides. I expected to see him bash his head against the stone, much like those cartoon characters who attempt a similar feat. But he sailed through and disappeared. For a moment we stood stupefied, like drunken stand-ins; then we rushed to the window. I got there first and stuck my head through the window. Behind me, Ralph cried, "For heaven's sake, Weisstein! Tell me, tell me, is he all right?"

"So far, so good," I said. "He's still falling."

Even as I cried out to Ralph, Bird cleared the edge of the cliff by a hair's-breadth. Then he was hurtling down alongside the cliff. I expected to see him strike one of the two boulders at the sea's edge. But he shot between the two, disappeared, and the water spouted up after him.

I said, "He went in cleanly. But who knows what the impact of the water after that fall will be? And if the bottom is shallow...?"

I waited for a sign of him while Ralph, reverting in his excitement, barked. I looked at my watch. Twenty seconds since he had plunged through the blue-green surface. Sixty seconds. At one hundred and thirty seconds, I withdrew my head and looked sadly at Ralph. "He didn't come up."

"Look again."

I turned just in time to see a black head break loose. And, a moment later, a brown arm wave at me. "He made it!" I shouted. "He made it!" I grabbed Ralph's two front paws, pulled him upright, and we danced around and around together.

Finally, Ralph said, "You're not following properly. Let me down."

I did so. Ralph recovered his breath, then said, "*Viola un homme!*"

For the benefit of my readers who don't understand French, this means, "What a man!" I recognized it as the phrase uttered by Napoleon after meeting the great Goethe. And, unworthy emotion, jealousy struck again.

Ralph, of course, smelled it. "My dear fellow," he said, "there's no blame attached to you. I'm sure that if you weren't too big to get through the window, you would have tried it. If you'd also been crazy. Bird was small enough, and insane enough, to attempt it. Let us hope that…"

At that moment a strangled cry came from the door. We turned to see Smigma staring stricken through the Judas window.

—6—

Everything happened very quickly after that. Giftlippen, still in his Arabian robes and cloud of perfume, stormed in. He was followed by armed men. I was astounded to see that Ralph was right. His nose was untouched. The archvillain looked through the window, whirled, and shouted, "We can still get him!" He gave orders for some men to go after him in the mini-submarine and others to go in a helicopter. We were then conducted downstairs to another tower room. My hands were tied behind my back. The door was slammed shut and bolted.

A half-hour passed. Suddenly, the door was unbolted and opened. Giftlippen and Smigma came in with six men. The former's face as impassive and pale as ever, but the latter's was twisted and red. Giftlippen roared, "The Yankee runt got away! But the chopper's still looking for him! He won't dare to come out from the coastal bush until nightfall! By then it'll be too late! I'm moving the schedule up! Too bad! It would have been esthetically appropriate to pull off this job during the Marriage! But you and your friends have no sense of the beautiful, von Wau Wau! So, instead of marrying the bride, we abduct her! Ha! Ha!"

We were hustled back to the cave. The large submarine and the giant plastic bag were gone. Presently we were outbound on the mini-sub. When the boat stopped, an hour had passed according to my luminous watch. Ralph said little during the transit, and I uttered nothing except a few groans. My thoughts, I must admit, were not, like his, directed to means of getting us out of this mess. I could only curse myself for my stubborn and stupid resistance to Lisa. Why had I not said yes, I will marry you at once, abandon this dangerous life? I could now be sharing connubial bliss, not to mention the delights, with Lisa, surely the daintiest thing in slacks that ever walked this planet.

On the other hand, Ralph would have been alone, would have died without a single friend to give him moral support at the fatal moment. How sad to die companionless. And how I would have grieved, have been stricken with remorse, have cursed myself for a coward, if I had not been at his side. On the other hand, there was Lisa....such were my thoughts during that gloomy trip in our dark narrow cell.

The craft stopped with a bump. The cell door was opened to let us into the control room. A man snapped the leash on Ralph's harness while another held a gun to his head. A man wearing a gas mask climbed the short ladder, opened the hatch, and looked out. He removed the mask and shouted down, "All clear!" I followed Ralph to emerge on the deck of the barque by the Riva degli Schiavone.

Ralph sniffed and said, "There's a strange odor in the air."

I could smell nothing except the sewage-laden canal waters. What struck me was the silence. Except for the distant drone of a helicopter and the faraway chug of a *vaporetto*, there was not a sound. The loud babble of the festive crowds was gone. No wonder. Everywhere I looked, bodies sprawled unmoving upon the *riva* and the plaza of St. Mark.

"Great Scott!" I cried. "Are they all dead?"

"Fortunately, no," Ralph said. "That strange odor is the residue of an anesthetic gas. That helicopter must have laid down a cloud of it, rendering all the citizens unconscious. Undoubtedly, all the islands nearby, including the Lido, were also subjected to the gas."

Ralph and I were taken to the poopdeck. The end of his leash was looped through an oarhole and tied. I was made to stand by him; a guard with a Browning automatic rifle was stationed about six feet from us.

Giftlippen strode up to us, his robes flapping in the stiff breeze which had sprung up. He gestured toward the city with his gloved hands.

"You are indeed privileged," he said. "You'll be the only nonparticipant witnesses to the crime of, not the century, but of the ages. Unfortunately, you won't be able to report it. But I am allowing you enough time to savor its full flavor. And to contemplate what idiots you were to think you could outwit me. Within one hour, we will have the greatest treasures, those that can be moved, anyway, stowed away."

He waved a hand at the big submarine, which was just to the north of us. Men were lowering paintings, statuettes, chests, and boxes into the giant sausage behind it.

Motorboats roared up, docked, and discharged other treasures: bags of jewels, figurines, statuettes, reliquaries, and paintings. All beautiful, priceless, unique. Among the paintings I recognized N. B. Schiavone's *The Adoration*, Titian's *The Annunciation*, Bellini's *Madonna of the Trees*, Vecchio's *Saint Barbara*.

Due to their limited time, the bandits could not take the care needed in moving these fragile works. Fortunately, all had been sprayed with Giftlippen's plastic as part of his professed pollution-prevention program. This saved them from being scratched or chipped. But it broke my heart to see them so rough-ly handed down into the hatches of the giant bag.

Giftlippen said, "The VUF funds have been removed from the bank. In fact, all the banks nearby have been looted. I'll hold the works of art for several years, then ransom them. But the world is going to pay me for those I've had to leave behind. You see, they've all been sprayed. What the authorities don't know, as yet, is that the plastic is actually acidic. It will in time eat up the paintings and the surfaces of the statues, whether stone or bronze. I shall inform them of this and then demand a large—exorbitant, in fact—sum for the formula of the solvent to neutralize the acid effect. Only I know this."

"What is to prevent the Venetians from removing the acidic plastic?" Ralph said.

"They can't dissolve the plastic by any known means," Giftlippen said tri-umphantly. "Scraping it off will cause a friction which will accelerate the acidic effect."

He paused. "Magnificent, isn't it? I expect to reap a profit, tax free, of about three billion American dollars."

Again, he broke into that hideous freezing cachinnation.

"And all the time, while a world-wide search is being made for me, I'll be watching them, almost within arm's reach of them."

A moment later, men brought aboard two large tables and set them down on the middeck. Others put piles of plates and tableware on the tables. Still others staggered up laden with baskets full of bottles of wine. Four men deposited two huge kettles on a table. Another set by them an enormous bowl of antipasto. Saugpumpe removed the kettle lids, and I smelled spaghetti and spaghetti sauce.

Good Heavens, I thought. Surely they are not so confident that they are going to have a leisurely meal on the return trip?

Ralph said, "You have about a hundred and fifty men in your band? Do they share in the profits? Or do you intend to rid yourself of most of them? I would think a bomb planted on the barque, set to go off after you've escaped in the mini-sub, would eliminate forty or so. And you must be thinking of flooding the compartments in the bag which will carry most of the others."

I expected Giftlippen to react violently to this. Even if Ralph's speculations were unfounded, the crew might become very suspicious. Enough to decide to make sure there was no double-cross by killing him.

But he only laughed again. He said, "You'd make a great criminal, von Wau Wau. But then crooks and cops are only two sides of a coin, aren't they? And you can't always be sure which is obverse; which, reverse."

He spoke to the guard. "Shoot them if they try to communicate to anybody but me or Smigma."

He walked away, leaving us, me, at least, with gloomy thoughts. Ah, Lisa, I will never see you again!

The gangsters were using small motorcycles towing long low wagons. Both were collapsible and apparently had been transported here in the plastic bag. They were busy, roaring off into the city and returning with wagons laden with treasures.

Presently, the *vaporetto* I'd heard chug-chugged up and docked. Its deck was filled with men and piles of objects.

"How long can they go undetected?" I said. "Surely, the causeway into Venice will be full of cars and the train loaded with tourists? If the traffic is stalled because of the gas, won't the authorities at Mestre investigate?"

"Giftlippen has undoubtedly cut all lines of communication," he said. "And bribed some officials in Mestre to create confusion and delay."

"And Bird, if he survived, won't be able to venture out from the bush until dark, I said. "By then it'll all be over. Still, Giftlippen knows that Bird can reveal his secret. He surely isn't going to return to the castle."

"Not unless Bird is caught. You must realize, my dear fellow, that the chopper has undoubtedly laid down a cloud of the anesthetic gas over the area in which Bird is hiding. When the gas is blown away, a search will be made on the ground for the unconscious Bird. If he isn't found, Giftlippen will take an alternate route to safety. He must be impatiently waiting for a radio message that Bird has been snared."

At that moment Smigma gave a shout and hurried up to Giftlippen. He was holding a walkie-talkie. They conferred for a moment. Smigma was smiling broadly. After a minute, Giftlippen walked to us. He said, "Your athletic, but stupid, colleague has been captured! He'll be taken back to a tower cell. From there he can witness your end. It'll make a fine display, and his agony will be increased by knowing that you will be in the explosion!"

"Ah," Ralph said quietly. "You *are* going to blow up the barque! And we'll be in the casualty list?"

"If there's enough of you left to identify," Giftlippen said. "You see, by the time the barque is halfway across the lagoon, airplanes and helicopters from Mestre will be over the area. My agents there can stall an investigation only so long. A time bomb in the barque will go off. Investigators will find only pieces of bodies and the art treasures left from the 'accidental' explosion. The barque will contain only works of lesser value."

Cackling, he walked away. He began shouting at the men who were coming aboard laden with paintings and boxes. I almost felt sorry for them. They would also be victims of the man's diabolical cunning.

"Ralph," I said, "this is it…"

Ralph whined, his nose pointed toward the open hatch, his nostrils expanding.

"What is it?" I said.

"What I'd hoped for. *I am Sir Oracle, and when I ope my lips let no dog bark!*"

I recognized the quotation as from Shakespeare's *The Merchant of Venice*, Act 1, scene i. But what he meant by it, I didn't know. He was always doing this to me, making obscure references through quotations. Very aggravating.

"*If I can catch him once upon the hip, I will feed the ancient grudge I bear him.*" This was also from *The Merchant of Venice*.

"What in heaven's name are you getting at?" I said.

"Look at Giftlippen and Smigma. They're jumping with joy. *Some there be that shadows kiss; Such have but a shadow's bliss.*"

"Will you stop that?" I said. "And enlighten me?"

"*I would not have given him for a wilderness of monkeys.*"

"It's *it*, not *him*," I said. "Same play, Act III scene i, line 130, I believe."

"*But, since I am a dog, beware of my fangs.*"

"Act III, scene iii, line 6," I said. "Ralph, this is no time to show off."

The guard was looking at us curiously. Ralph winked and said, "A bird in the hatch is worth two in the bush."

"Oh!" I said. "You mean…?"

I jumped, and Ralph started. Simultaneously, at least a dozen explosions in the city gouted flame and fragments. As their reverberations died, Smigma shouted at the men to get aboard. They hurried up, bearing their loads, onto the barque, the U-boat, and the floating bag.

"He's started fires to make a diversion," I said, staring at the thick black plumes of smoke. "Listen, Ralph! Now's your chance to make a break for it! Snap your leash and run like mad! I'll knock down our guard, keep him from shooting!"

"What, and leave you, my dear friend?" Ralph said. "No! I am touched at your offer of sacrifice. But we'll play this game out together, lose or win, side by side."

I am not ashamed to record that these words of loyalty and love almost made me cry.

A helicopter swept over, and the men cheered. Then, laughing joyously, they disappeared into the U-boat and the bag. Those who came aboard the barque did not, as I had expected, grab the oars and start rowing. The barque started moving as if by magic. But it was the tiny submarine attached to it that was the motive power. It wasn't progressing very fast. It would at this rate only get a few miles from the island before the police showed up. The crew must have known that, but they didn't seem worried. I surmised that Giftlippen must have given them some sort of explanation to put them at ease.

Saugpumpe beat on a gong and yelled at them to come eat and drink, to celebrate their ill-gotten wealth. Poor fools, they crowded around the tables and dished themselves up heaps of spaghetti and antipasto. They grabbed the numerous bottles of wine and toasted each other and their leader. Giftlippen had retreated to the poopdeck to sit on the wheelchair and eat nuts while Smigma and Saugpumpe helped fill the plates and uncapped the bottles.

Within fifteen minutes, the men had become very drunk. Far too drunk for the alcohol alone to account for it, even at the rate they drank. They were whooping and yelling, staggering around, speaking slurredly, and singing off-key.

"Giftlippen is helping us, though he doesn't know it," Ralph muttered. "He's cutting down the odds against us. When the time comes for action, move swiftly, Weisstein. We'll still be unarmed. And I don't know when the bomb will go off. Or where it is, either."

We had gone about two miles when one of the men yelled louder than the others. Everybody followed the direction of his finger. There were small objects above Venice, moving so slowly they had to be helicopters.

Giftlippen arose. Smigma and the woman looked at him. He nodded. Some of the men abruptly collapsed and lay snoring heavily on the deck. Others were glaze-eyed and looking around stupidly.

Our guard had not drunk or eaten anything. Obviously he was in the plot. At the moment, he was watching the aircraft.

"Back up to me and spread your bonds as far as they'll go!" Ralph whispered.

I did so, and his teeth snapped down on them, the lips brushing wetly against my wrists. He had the powerful jaws of a German shepherd and even more strength than the average because of his size and the genes of his wolf grandfather. Two snaps, and the thin ropes were severed.

"Stand still! Wait!" Ralph said. "The timing must be of the exquisite!"

I couldn't see him, but I could imagine him moving back to get some slack in his leash. It had a concealed breakaway in it, designed for just such emergencies as this.

Giftlippen was nearing the hatch. Smigma and the woman were by the table. I supposed they were anticipating objections from the crew. Both now held submachine guns they had picked up from under the table. A dozen more men had crashed upon the deck. Those still on their feet were swaying or reeling crazily around.

Of the U-boat and the bag it was towing, there was no sign. It must have dived as soon as possible.

Giftlippen stopped and looked at his wristwatch. "We have ten minutes before the bomb goes off!" he shouted. "Everybody below!"

The guard turned for one last check to us. I did not move. Still carrying his rifle, he hurried toward the hatch. Smigma and Saugpumpe threw down their weapons and trotted toward it also. Giftlippen turned and yelled at us, "*Bon voyage!*" and he broke into that maniacal laughter.

"Ready, set, GO!" Ralph said. He lunged; the leash snapped; he sped past me, a black and brownish-gray blur, silent death.

Smigma and Saugpumpe yelled and stopped. Giftlippen whirled so fast he fell down, his feet caught in the floor-length robe. The guard spun, firing the rifle before he had completed his circle. Ralph gave a bound, and his jaws closed on the man's throat.

I was already charging across the deck, intending to pick up the automatic rifle. But as I did, I saw Cordwainer Bird pop up from the hatch.

The guard was on his back, his throat torn open. Ralph wasted no time on him. He sped growling toward Giftlippen, who was back on his feet by now. Smigma and the woman turned and ran back toward their weapons. Giftlippen yanked a huge automatic pistol from beneath his robe and pointed it at Ralph. I yelled a warning to him, but Ralph didn't have a chance unless Giftlippen missed him. At that short range, it was not likely.

Bird had seen this, however, and he made a split-second choice. Instead of going after the others, he hurled himself at Giftlippen. In what is called in American football a blocker's tackle. I believe, or perhaps it was an illegal clip, his shoulder took Giftlippen's feet from under him. Giftlippen flew backward screaming, and crashed upon the deck. His automatic skittered spinning out of his reach.

Bird was up on his feet as if he were made of rubber. Ralph ran by him, his target Smigma and Saugpumpe. Bird, passing by the fallen man to assist Ralph, kicked out sideways. The side of his foot struck Giftlippen in the face, and he collapsed again.

I picked up the rifle and fired several rounds into the air to get the attention of the villains. Everybody ignored me. Ralph leaped high and knocked Smigma sprawling. Saugpumpe bent down to get her submachine gun, but Bird was flying through the air. As if he were broad jumping, his feet preceded him. She rose and turned to fire at us, just in time to receive Bird's feet in her face. She performed a splendid, if involuntary, backward somersault. Thereafter, she took no interest in the proceedings.

"I always wanted to do that to a woman!" Bird yelled exultantly from the deck where he had fallen. "Anyway, she looked like my sixth wife, the bitch!"

Smigma had gotten to his feet. Ralph crouched for another leap. Smigma grabbed the nearest thing he could find for a weapon, the enormous bowl of antipasto. He lifted it above his head, and the contents spilled down blinding him. Smigma, shrieking, cast the bowl hard but missed Ralph. Ralph leaped, but this time not for the throat. He grabbed the man's arm and bit down. Then the two were thrashing around on the deck.

Giftlippen rose, crouching. I stared in horror at his face. It had been broken by Bird's kick, literally crumbled. As I stood frozen, he reached up and tore away the rest of the covering. I could not believe my eyes. Then he quickly doffed his robe and kicked off his slippers. I was even more incredulous. This state of shock, I am ashamed to admit, was my undoing. Before I could lift my rifle and start firing, his hand moved and the sinking sun glittered on something streaking toward me.

The fellow, if I may call him that, had depended upon the shock of recognition to paralyze me. It succeeded just long enough for him to pluck a knife from the scabbard at his belt and hurl it. I felt a shock in my right arm; the rifle clattered on the deck; I was suddenly weak. I looked down. The knife had penetrated the muscle of my right shoulder. It wasn't a fatal wound, but it certainly was unnerving.

Giftlippen, chattering, was on me then, had knocked me down, had gone on. I sat up while Bird and Ralph ran toward the poopdeck. I groped for the weapon, could not find it, and thus was unable to prevent Giftlippen's escape.

He was quick, oh, so quick! Even the speedy Bird and the swift Ralph could not catch him in time. He had leaped into the wheelchair, punched some buttons on the control panel, and then was gone. Hidden, rather, I should say. Panels had slid up from the sides of the enormous wheelchair and closed over him. Behind a glass port, his mouth worked devilishly. The two giant front teeth, incisors like daggers, or perhaps I should say, a rodent's, gleamed.

His hands moved again, and the muzzles of two automatic rifles sprang out of the sides. I rolled off the slight elevation of the poopdeck, falling to the deck.

Bullets chopped off pieces of the teakwood and then were spraying the deck. Bird dived down the hatch, headfirst, the deck exploding around him. Ralph raced forward and then rolled in toward me, safe from the fire.

He looked at the protruding dagger. "Are you hurt, buddy?"

"Not severely," I said. "But what next?"

"He could hold us here, but he'll abandon ship at once. The bomb's too close to going off. Ah, there he goes!"

The rifles had suddenly ceased their terrifying racket. A few seconds later, there was a splash. Ralph stood on his hind legs. He said, "All clear now."

I stood up. There was no sign of the wheelchair or the thing that had been in it. But it was obvious where they had gone. The railing had been destroyed by the rifle fire to make a passage to the sea.

"There's no use trying to get him now," he said. "That wheelchair is obviously submersible, and it's also jet-propelled. He'll go underwater to the shore. But, unless he has another disguise cached away somewhere, he will be easily spotted."

"Yes," I said. "There's nothing that will attract more attention than a six-foot six-inch high squirrel."

—7—

There was no opportunity for explanations. Somewhere in the barque, a time bomb was ticking away. We could have escaped in the mini-sub, but that would have meant leaving sixty or so people to perish. They did deserve to die, but we would not abandon them. It was impossible to carry them into the submarine in the little time left. Besides, there wasn't room for that many.

Bird stuck his head out of the hatch. Ralph shouted at him to look for the bomb. There was only five minutes left. We would help him after we secured Smigma and Saugpumpe.

Bird said, "Right on!" and he disappeared.

Both the culprits were still unconscious. I tied up the woman while Ralph stood guard in case the man aroused. Then I used his belt to bind him. He was a sorry-looking mess, covered with lettuce, mushrooms, anchovies, sliced peppers, and a garlicky oil.

Ralph chuckled and said, "I smote the saladed Polack."

"A slightly altered line from a speech by Horatio, *Hamlet*, Act I, scene i," I said. "Good heavens, Ralph, this is no time for your atrocious puns."

We hastened below deck where we found Bird frantically opening boxes. Though handicapped by my wound, I pitched in. Ralph, cursing his lack of hands, paced back and forth.

"Jumping jellybeans!" Bird said. "Only two minutes to go!"

"It's too late to get into the sub," I said. I was sweating profusely, but I like to think that that was caused by my wound, not panic.

"Sixty more seconds, and we'll have to jump into the sea," Ralph said. "Wait! I have it! Quiet, you two! Absolutely quiet!"

We stood still. The only sound was the lapping of the waves against the hull. Ralph stood, ears cocked, turning this way and that. He had a much keener sense of hearing than we two humans. Even so, if the timing mechanism was not clockwork or if it was covered with some insulating material... Suddenly, he barked. Then he said, "Damn! My instincts again! That box on the pile by you, Doc! Third one under!"

I toppled off the top two with one hand while Bird and Ralph danced around. "Forty-five seconds!" Bird shrilled.

The third box was of cardboard, its top glued down. Bird jumped in and tore it open savagely. Ralph stood up on his hind legs to look within. All three of us stared at a curious contrivance. It was of plastic, cube-shaped, and had two small cubes on its top. On the inner side of the left-hand one was a metal disk. Moving slowly from the inner wall of the other one was a thin cylinder of steel. Its tip was only about two-sixteenths of an inch from the disk.

As we stared, the slender cylinder moved a sixteenth, of an inch.

"Quick, Weisstein, the needle!"

I snatched my handkerchief from my pocket, but I wasn't quick enough to satisfy Bird. He grabbed it from me and interposed a corner between the disk and cylinder. One more second, and the electrical contact would have been made. I shudder even now as I write of this and a certain sphincter muscle tightens up.

Bird threw the bomb overboard. "Whew! Okay, I'll get the sub going, and we'll mosey back to Venice. But first, *what* the hell was Giftlippen? I know what I saw, but I still don't believe it."

"I had suspected for some time that it was Nucifer," Ralph said. "There were clues, though only I had the background to interpret them. You see, one of the institute animals supposedly wiped out by the explosion was a giant squirrel. Nucifer, Professor Sansgout called him. Nut-bearing. From the Latin.

"Obviously, he wasn't killed. He took to a life of crime, murdered the real Giftlippen, and took over his gang. Smigma joined the gang after Giftlippen was well launched on his career, you know. He may have been surprised to find that his friend and agent was now a giant rodent. On the other hand, Giftlippen was always a little squirrelly. I should feel bad about the Liechtensteiner's murder...but, after the way he murdered my book... well, no matter.

"Anyway, when Giftlippen—Nucifer, I mean—decided on the Venetian caper, he set up a whole new identity. He triggered off that landslide...cold-blooded massacre of the villagers...and emerged as Granelli, the reincarnation of Doge Dandolo.

"But now he was in the public eye. So, he put on a wax-and-putty head to conceal his bestial features and gloves to disguise his paws. He stayed in a wheelchair when on display, covering his unhuman legs with the tigerskin. He stuck his bushy tail down a hole in the chair's seat. When he was in that Arabian costume, he strapped his tail to a leg, as you saw.

"He also made sure that his distinctive squirrel's odor was covered by a heavy perfume. He knew that I was on his trail and that I could expose him after one whiff."

"But why did Smigma also use perfume?"

"Same reason. After Smigma's accident, he suffered a metabolic imbalance, you know. He emitted a cheesy odor which even humans could detect.

"The immobile features, the covering of the legs, the gloves, the perfume all suggested to me his true identity. His addiction to nuts cinched the matter."

"Elementary," I said.

"No, alimentary."

Bird started away. I said, "Wait a minute. However did you manage to appear so conveniently—for us—inside the barque?"

"Easy," Bird said, grinning. Then: "Well, I won't lie to you; it wasn't a breeze. I swam toward the sea to give the impression I was escaping that way. But I returned, working my way through the fallen blocks of stone. Then I swam through the tunnel to the cave. I almost didn't make it. I got to the mini-sub before the bandits came down. I hid in its engine room, behind the batteries. When everybody left the sub, I came out. I used the sub's radio to send a fake message that I'd been captured. I was taking a chance. If the chopper overheard me, they'd warn Smigma. But Smigma turned the walkie-talkie off right after he got my message.

"First, though, I listened in on him and the chopper. That way, I learned the codewords they were using for identification. Giftlippen's—Nucifer's—was California. Isn't that strange? No other names of states were used."

"The squirrel's a double-dyed villain," Ralph said. "But he has a sense of humor. California has the world's biggest collection of nuts."

—8—

Nucifer eluded detection. Smigma later escaped from prison and rejoined Nucifer. How Ralph and I caught up with them is described in "The Four Musicians of Bremen."

Bird used the walkie-talkie to summon the police. They arrested the few crooks in the cave. I say few because, as Ralph had suspected, the gang in the plastic bag had been drowned by their compatriots in the U-boat.

All the art treasures were recovered. And it turned out that Nucifer had lied about the acidic effect of the plastic spray. The authorities would have had no way of knowing this, of course, and undoubtedly would have paid millions for a useless formula.

We stayed two weeks for the festivities in our honor. We were made honorary citizens of Venice, and a local artist was commissioned to cast in bronze a commemorative monument of us. It can be seen today in St. Mark's Square. It's well done, though it always causes children, unacquainted with our story, to ask why the dog is grabbing the big squirrel by its tail. Artists, like TV/movie directors, feel no obligation to be historically accurate.

While we were waiting at the Lido Airport, I made another long-distance call to Lisa. Ralph paced back and forth nervously, whining now and then despite his vow to repress this canine characteristic. Cordwainer Bird sat on a bench nearby, writing in longhand his latest novel, *Adrift Just Off the Eyelets of My Buster Browns*. Both, seeing my approach, stopped what they were doing. Bird rose from the bench, though not very far.

"She gave the final ultimatum, Ralph," I said. "It's either she or you. I had to make the final decision right there."

"No need to tell me what it is," he said. "If your long face wasn't enough, the odor of resignation mixed somewhat with that of repressed joy, would inform me."

"Then it's good-by," I said, choking.

"*Das Ewig-Weibliche/Zieht uns hinan*," he said.

"*The Eternal-Feminine/Draws us on*," I said. "The last line of Goethe's *The Gothic Chamber*. He was a wise man."

"A very horny one, too. I'll miss you, Doc. It'll be a new and exciting life in Los Angeles—provided I can get my citizenship papers in the States. But..."

The loudspeaker blared, informing us in Italian, French, German, and English that passengers for Hamburg must enter customs. At least, I thought that was what was said. Like airport announcers everywhere, he managed to make almost everything unintelligible, no matter what the language.

Bird said, "I'll go change our reservations for the plane to L.A." He held out his hand. "Sorry about this, Doctor. I don't like to rip off Ralph from you. But it's your decision."

"Don't blame yourself," I said. "Sooner or later, it would have come. But be sure to get in touch with me."

"I'm not much for letter writing. Ralph'll have to do that. *Auf Wiedersehen*, Doc."

He walked away. I looked at Ralph. Then my German reserve shattered, and I knelt down and put my arms around that furry neck and wept. Ralph whined, and he said, "Come on, buck up, sweetheart. You know it's all for the best. You'll lead a dog's life, it's true. But that ain't necessarily bad. Take it from one who knows."

I stroked his ears, shed a few more tears, then rose. "*Auf Wiedersehen.* Though I have this feeling that I'll never see you again."

"Hit the road, Doc, before my guts lose their anchors. *Gott!* If only I had tear ducts! You humans don't know how lucky you are. But we'll see each other now and then. Maybe sooner than you think."

I picked up my bags and walked away, never once looking back. I thought he was just talking to make me feel better. I didn't know how prophetic his words were. Or how distressed I would be to see him. But that is all chronicled in the bewildering adventure of adulation and adulteration, private sin and public confession, branding irons and preachers: "The Scarletin Letter."

Jonathan Swift Somers III: Cosmic Traveller in a Wheelchair

First published in *Scintillation,* 13, June 1977.

Having read the two Ralph stories here is an introduction to their fictional author. As part of Phil's interlinking, Leo Queequeg Tincrowder is a distant cousin and Jonathan Swift Somers III himself is the fictional grandson of the Jonathan Swift Somers immortalized in Wallace's *Spoon River Anthology.*

Leo Queequeg Tincrowder makes a passing appearance in "Fundamental Issue," also in this collection.

Jonathan Swift Somers III is probably most famous to Phil Farmer fans as the favourite author of Simon Wagstaff, the protagonist in *Venus on the Half-Shell.*

Note from Philip José Farmer: In the November 1976 issue of *Fantasy & Science Fiction,* it was announced that a group in Portland, Oregon, called The Bellener Street Irregulars were going to be publishing something called *The Bellener Street Journal.* The journal was to be dedicated to the study of the canine detective, Ralph von Wau Wau. *The Bellener Street Journal* never even saw a first issue, however, due to inexplicable complications within the group.

The following biographical sketch of Jonathan Swift Somers III was written for the journal, and was to be published along with a lost story by Dr. Johann H. Weisstein and a story by Jonathan Swift Somers III entitled, "Jinx."

Petersburg is a small town in the mid-Illinois county of Menard. It lies in hilly country near the Sangamon River on state route 97. Not far away is New Salem, the reconstructed pioneer village where Abraham Lincoln worked for a while as a postmaster, surveyor and storekeeper. The state capital of Springfield is southeast, a half-hour's drive or less if traffic is light.

A hilltop cemetery holds two famous people, Anne Rutledge and Edgar Lee Masters. The former (1816-1835) is known only because of the legend, now disapproved, that she was Lincoln's first love, tragically dying before she could marry him. "Bloom forever, O Republic, From the dust of my bosom!"

These are from the epitaph which Masters wrote for her and are inscribed on her gravestone. Unfortunately, the man who chiseled the epitaph made a typo, driving Masters into a rage[1]. We authors, who have suffered from so many typos, can sympathize with him. However, we have the advantage that we can make sure that reissues contain corrections. There will be no later editions in stone of Anne Rutledge's epitaph.

Masters (1869-1950) was a poet, novelist and literary critic, known chiefly for his *Spoon River Anthology*. There is a Spoon River area but no town of that name. Masters chose that name to represent an amalgamation of the actual towns of Lewistown and Petersburg, where he spent most of his childhood and early adulthood. Lewistown, also on route 97, is about forty miles from Petersburg but separated by the Illinois River.

The free verse epitaphs of Masters' best-known work were modeled after *The Greek Anthology* but based on people he'd known. These told the truth behind the flattering or laconic statements on the tombs and gravestones. The departed spoke of their lives as they had really been. Some were happy, productive, even creative and heroic. But most recite chronicles of hypocrisy, misery, misunderstanding, failed dreams, greed, narrow-mindedness, egotism, persecution, madness, connivance, cowardice, stupidity, injustice, sorrow, folly and murder.

In other words, the Spoon River citizens were just like big-city residents.

Among the graves in the cemetery of Petersburg are those of Judge Somers and his son, Jonathan Swift Somers II. Neither has any marker, though the grandson has made arrangements to erect stones above both. Masters has the judge complain that he was a famous Illinois jurist, yet he lies unhonored in his grave while the town drunkard, who is buried by his side, has a large monument. Masters does not explain how this came about.

According to Somers III, his grandson, the judge and his wife were not on the best of terms during the ten years preceding the old man's death. Somers' grandmother would give no details, but others provided the information that it was because of an indiscretion committed by the judge in a cathouse in Peoria. (This city is mentioned now and then in the *Spoon River Anthology*.)

The judge's son, Somers II, sided with his father. This caused the mother to forbid her son to enter her house. In 1910 the judge died, and the following year the son and his wife were drowned in the Sangamon during a picnic

[1] The tombstone reads 'Ann Rutledge,' rather than 'Anne Rutledge'

outing. The widow refused to pay for monuments for either, insisting that she did not have the funds. Her son's wife was buried in a family plot near New Goshen, Indiana. That Samantha Tincrowder Somers preferred not to lie with her husband indicates that she also had strong differences with him.

Jonathan Swift Somers III was born in this unhappy atmosphere on January 6, 1910. This is also Sherlock Holmes' birthdate, which Somers celebrates annually by sending a telegram of congratulations to a certain residence on Baker Street, London.

The forty-three year old grandmother took the year old infant into her house. Though the gravestone incident seems to characterize her as vindictive, she was a very kind and probably too indulgent grandmother to the young Jonathan. Until the age of ten, he had a happy childhood. Even though the Somers' house was a large gloomy mid-Victorian structure, it was brightened for him by his grandmother and the books he found in the library. A precocious reader, he went through all the lighter volumes before he was eleven. The judge's philosophical books, Fichte, Schopenhauer, Nietzsche, et al, would be mastered by the time he was eighteen.

Despite his intense interest in books, Jonathan played as hard as any youngster. With his schoolmates he roamed the woody hills and swam and fished in the Sangamon. He gave promises of being a notable athlete, beating all his peers in the dashes and the broad jump. Among his many pets were a raven, a raccoon, a fox and a bullsnake.

Then infantile paralysis felled him. Treatment was primitive in those days, but a young physician, son of the Doctor Hill whose epitaph is in the *Anthology*, got him through. Jonathan came back out of the valley of the shadow, only to find that he would be paralyzed from the waist down for the rest of his life. This knowledge resulted in another paralysis, a mental freezing. His grandmother despaired of his mind for a while, fearing that he had retreated so far into himself he would never come back out. Jonathan himself now recalls little of this period. Apparently, it was so traumatic that even today his conscious mind refuses to touch it.

"It was as if I were embedded in a crystal ball. I could see others around me, but I could not hear or touch them. And the crystal magnified and distorted their faces and figures. I was a human fly in amber, stuck in time, preserved from decay but isolated forever from the main flow of life."

Amanda Knapp Somers, his grandmother, would not admit that he would never walk again. She told him that he only needed faith in God to overcome his "disability." That was the one word she used when referring to his paralysis. Disability. She avoided mentioning his legs; they, too, were disabilities.

Amanda Somers had been raised in the Episcopalian sect. She came from an old Virginia family whose fortune had been ruined by the Civil War. Her father had brought his family out to this area shortly after Appomattox. He had intended to stay only a short while with his younger brother, who had settled near Petersburg before the war. Then he meant to push on west, to homestead in northern California. However, he had sickened and died in his brother's house, leaving a wife, two daughters and a son. The wife died a year later of cholera. The surviving children were adopted by their uncle.

Amanda came into frequent contact with the fundamentalist Baptists and Methodists of this rural community. Though she never formally renounced her membership in the Episcopalian church, she began attending revival meetings. After marrying Jonathan Swift Somers I, she stopped this, since the "respectable" people in Petersburg did not go to such functions. Now, however, with her husband dead and her grandson crippled, she went to every revival and faith healer that came along. She insisted on taking young Jonathan with her, undoubtedly hoping that he would suddenly be "saved," that a miracle would occur, that he would stand up and walk.

This went on for two years. The child objected strongly to these procedures. The tense emotional atmosphere and the sense of guilt at not being "saved" wore him out. Moreover, he hated being the center of attention at these meetings, and he always felt that he let everybody down when he failed to be "cured." Somehow, it was his fault, not the faith healer's, that he could not rid himself of his paralysis.

During this troubling time, several things saved young Jonathan's reason. One was his ability to get away from the world into his books. The library was large, since it included both his grandfather's and father's books. Much of this was too advanced even for his precocity, but there were plenty of adventure and mystery volumes, and even fantasy was not lacking. Moreover, though his grandmother had some narrow-minded ideas about religion, she made no effort to supervise his reading. She gave him freedom in ordering books, and as a result Jonathan had a larger and more varied collection than the Petersburg library.

At this time he came across John Carter of Mars, Tarzan of the Apes, Professor Challenger and Sherlock Holmes. In a short time he had ordered and read all of the works of Burroughs and Doyle. A copy of *Before Adam* led him to Jack London. This writer, in turn, introduced him to something besides fascinating tales of adventure in the frozen north or the hot south seas. He gave young Jonathan his first look into the depths of social and political injustice, into the miseries of "the people of the abyss."

It was not enough for him to read about far-off exciting places. Unable immediately to get the sequel to *The Gods of Mars*, he wrote his own. This was titled *Dejah Thoris of Barsoom* and was one hundred pages, or about 20,000 words, quite an accomplishment for an eleven year old. On reading Burroughs' sequel, *The Warlord of Mars,* Jonathan decided that he had been out-classed. Years later, however, he used an idea in his story as the basis for *The Ivory Gates of Barsoom,* his first published novel. This was his first John Clayter story. Clayter is, of course, a name composed of the first syllable of Tarzan's English surname (Clayton) and the last syllable of John Carter's surname. At the time of this novel, the spaceman John Clayter has not lost his limbs.

More than books saved young Jonathan, however. His grandmother brought him a German Shepherd (police) pup. The child loved it, talked to it, fed it, brushed it, and threw the ball for it in the big backyard. Jonathan insisted on naming the male pup Fenris, after the monstrous wolf in Norse mythology. Fenris was the first of a long line of German Shepherds, Somers' favorite breed. Today, Fenris IX, a two-year old, is Somers' devoted companion.

There is no doubt that Somers modeled his fictional dog, Ralph von Wau Wau, upon his own pet. Or is there no doubt? The Bellener Street Irregulars insist that there is a real von Wau Wau. In fact, Somers is not the real author of the series of tales about this Hamburg police dog who became a private eye. The Irregulars maintain that Somers is only the literary agent for Johann H. Weisstein, Dr. Med., and for Cordwainer Bird, the two main narrators in the Wau Wau series. Weisstein and Bird are the real authors.

When asked about this, Somers only replied, "I am not at liberty to discuss the matter."

"Are the Irregulars wrong then?"

"I would hesitate to say that they are in error."

So, perhaps, Somers is really only the agent for Ralph's colleagues.

There is one objection to this belief. How could Weisstein and Bird have written true stories about their life with Ralph since these stories took place in the future? The dog's first adventure took place in 1978, yet this appeared in the March 1931 issue of the magazine, *Outré Tales.* ("A Scarletin Study" was reprinted in the March 1975 issue of *The Magazine of Fantasy & Science Fiction.*)

Somers' answer: "There are such people as seers and science fiction writers. Both are able to look into the future. Besides, to paraphrase Pontius Pilate, 'What is time?'"

Another of the bright lights that kept him from becoming overwhelmed by gloom was Edward Hill. This man was the brother of the same Doctor Hill who had pulled Jonathan through his sickness. Edward, however, had chosen the career of artist. Though he managed to sell some of his landscape paintings now and then, he needed extra money. At Doctor Hill's suggestion, Mrs.

Somers hired him to tutor Jonathan in mathematics and chemistry. Later, Edward gave lessons in painting. During the warm months, he would put Jonathan and Fenris in his buggy, and the three would travel to a hillside or the riverbank and spend the day there. Jonathan would paint with Edward's eye on his progress or lack thereof. But they did much more than work at their pallets. Edward would bring insects and snakes to Jonathan and expound on their place in the ecosystem of Petersburg and environs.

These were some of the happiest days of young Somers' life. It was a terrible blow when Edward died the following year of typhoid fever.

Jonathan might have slid into the sorrow from which Edward Hill had rescued him if he had not met Henry Hone. Henry was the son of Neville Hone, a chiropractor who had just moved to Petersburg. A year older than Jonathan, he was a big happy-go-lucky boy, though he too suffered from a handicap. He stammered. Perhaps it was this that drew him to Jonathan, since misery is supposed to love company. But Henry, ignoring his verbal disadvantage, was very gregarious. He played long and hard after school with his schoolmates, and he did well in his classes. It was not shyness that made him spend so much time with Jonathan. It must have been a sort of elective affinity, a natural magnetism of the two.

The fact that he was Jonathan's next-door neighbor helped. He would often drop in after school or come over to spend part of Saturday. And it was he who got young Somers started with physical therapy. He talked Mrs. Somers into building a set of bars and trapezes in the backyard and constructing a little house on the branch of the giant sycamore in the corner of the yard. Every day Jonathan would haul himself out of his wheelchair by going hand over hand up a rope. At its top he would transfer to a horizontal bar and thence up and down and across a maze of iron pipes. In addition, he would pull himself up a rope which was let through a hole in the floor of the treehouse. A seat was built for him inside the treehouse, and in it he would look through a telescope at the neighborhood.

Moreover, the bars and the treehouse attracted other children. Jonathan no longer was forced to be alone; he had more companions than he could handle.

If Henry Hone aided Jonathan Somers much, Jonathan reciprocated. One of the many things that interested Jonathan was the artificial language, Esperanto. By the age of twelve he had taught himself to read fluently in it. But, wishing to be verbally facile, he enlisted Henry. At first, Henry refused because of his stammer. But Jonathan insisted, and, much to Henry's joy, he found that he could speak Esperanto without stammering. Both boys became adept in the language and for a while a number of their playmates tried to learn Esperanto, too. These dropped out after the initial enthusiasm wore out. But Henry and Jonathan continued.

On entering high school, Henry took German and found that in this language, too, his stammer disappeared. It was this that determined Henry to go into linguistics. Eventually, he got a Ph.D. in Arabic at the University of Chicago. He continued to correspond with his friend, in Esperanto, though he never returned to Petersburg after 1930. His last letter (in English) was from North Africa, sent shortly before he was killed with Patton's forces.

It was Henry who talked Jonathan into attending high school instead of staying home to be tutored. Arrangements were made to accommodate Jonathan, and in 1928 he graduated. This decision to go to high school kept Jonathan from becoming a deep introvert. He made many friends; he even dated a few times in his senior year.

A photograph of him taken just before his illness hangs on the wall of his study. It shows a smiling ten-year old with curly blond hair, thick dark and straight eyebrows, large dark blue eyes, and a snub nose. Another picture, shot about six months after his attack of infantile paralysis, shows a thin hollow-cheeked face with dark shadows under the eyes and brooding shadows in the eyes. But his high school graduation photograph reveals a young man who has made an agreement with life. He will not sorrow about his lot; he'll make the best of it, doing better than most men with two good legs.

After getting his diploma, Jonathan thought about attending college. The University of Chicago attracted him, especially since his good friend Henry Hone was there. But that summer his grandmother broke her hip by falling out of a tree while picking cherries. Not wishing to leave her until she was well, Jonathan embarked on a series of studies designed to give him the equivalent of a university degree in the liberal arts and one in science. A room was fitted with laboratory equipment so he could perform the requisite experiments in chemistry and physics. He also took correspondence courses in electrical and mechanical engineering and in radio. He became a radio ham, and when he had a powerful set installed, he talked to people all over the world.

Jonathan had decided at the age of ten that he would be a writer of fiction. This determination firmed while he was reading *Twenty Thousand Leagues Under the Sea*. He too would pen tales about strong men who voyaged to distant and exotic places. If he could not go himself in electrical submarines or swing through jungle trees or fly dirigibles or journey in space ships, he would travel by proxy, via his fictional characters.

When he was seventeen he wrote a novel in which the aging Captain Nemo and Robur the Conqueror fought a great battle. This was rejected by twenty publishers. Jonathan put the manuscript in the proverbial trunk. But he has recently rewritten it and found a purchaser with the first submission. *The Nautilus*

Versus the Albatross will appear under the nom de plume of Gideon Spilett. For those who may have forgotten, Spilett was the intrepid reporter for *The New York Herald* whose adventures are recounted in Verne's *The Mysterious Island.*

Jonathan wrote twelve works (two novels and ten short stories) when he launched into the career of freelance writer. All of these were rejected. His thirteenth, however, was accepted by the short-lived *Cosmic Adventures* magazine in December 1930. Payment was to be on publication, which was February 1931. The magazine actually appeared on a few stands here and there, but it collapsed during the distribution. Jonathan never received his money nor were his letters to the publisher ever answered. However, he did sell the story, "Jinx," to the slightly longer-lived *Outré Tales* magazine. This had had five issues, all chiefly distinguished by stories by Robert Blake, the mad young genius whose career was so lamentably and so mysteriously cut short in an old abandoned church in Providence, Rhode Island, on August 8, 1936. Somers' "Jinx" was to be featured with Blake's sixth story, "The Last Hajj of Abdul al-Hazred." But this publication also folded, and neither Blake nor Somers were paid. Jonathan corresponded with Blake about this matter, and Blake sent a copy of his story to Jonathan. As of today, it has not been published, but Jonathan hopes to include it in an anthology he is editing. "Jinx" did not go out again until 1949, when Somers dug it up out of the trunk. It was returned by the editor of *Doc Savage* magazine with a note that the magazine was folding. Though Somers claims not to be superstitious, he decided that "Jinx" might indeed be just that. He retired the story to his files. However, it too will be included in the anthology.

Somers' second published story, and the first to be paid for, was a Ralph von Wau Wau piece, "A Scarletin Study." As noted, this was published in the March 1931 issue of *Outré Tales*. (The editor of *Fantasy & Science Fiction* failed to note the copyright in his introduction.) It is evident to the Sherlockian scholar that the title is a rearrangement of the title of the first story about Holmes, "A Study in Scarlet." The initial paragraphs are also paraphrases of the beginning paragraphs of Watson's first story, modified to fit the time and the locale of Somers' tale. All Wau Wau stories begin with takeoffs from the first pages of stories about the Great Detective and then the story travels towards its own ends. "The Doge Whose Barque Was Worse Than His Bight," for instance, starts with a paraphrase of Watson's "The Abbey Grange." "Who Stole Stonehenge?," the third Wau Wau in order of writing, begins with a modification of the initial paragraphs of Watson's "Silver Blaze."

This is Somers' way of paying tribute to the Master.

Of all his characters, the most popular are the canine private eye, Ralph von Wau Wau, and the quadriplegic spaceman, John Clayter. Those who have been unfortunate enough not to have read their adventures first-hand can find an outline of many of these in Kilgore Trout's *Venus on the Half-Shell.* This might serve as an introduction, a sort of appetite whetter. It was Trout who first pointed out that all of Somers' heroes and heroines are physically handicapped in some respect. Ralph, it is true, is a perfect specimen. But he is disadvantaged in that he has no hands. And, being a dog, he needs a human colleague to get him into certain places or do certain things. Sam Minostentor, the great science fiction historian, has also remarked on this in his monumental *Searchers for the Future.* Minostentor attributes this propensity for disabled protagonists to Somers' own crippled condition. Somers is consequently very empathetic with the physically limited.

However, Somers seldom shows his characters as being bitter. They overcome their failings with heroic efforts. They treat their condition with much laughter. In fact, they often make as much fun of themselves as their creator does of them. Some of this humor is black, it is true, but it is nevertheless humor.

"I had a choice between raving and ranting with bitter frustration or laughing at myself," Somers said. "It was bile or bubble. I drank the latter medicine. I can't claim any credit for this. I acted according to the dictates of my nature. Or did I? After all, there is such a thing as free will.

"My stuff has often been compared to my cousin's stories. That is, to Kilgore Trout's. There is some similarity in that we both often take a satirical view of humanity. But Trout believes in a mechanistic, a deterministic, universe, much like that of Vonnegut's, for instance. Me, I believe in free will. A person can pick himself up by his bootstraps—in a manner of speaking."

Jonathan was plunged into gloom when his grandmother died in 1950 at the age of ninety. There was not much time for despondency, however. She was no sooner cremated than he was informed that he would have to sell the huge old house in which he had lived all his life to pay for the inheritance taxes. To prevent this, he wrote eight short stories and three novels within six months. He saved the house but exhausted himself, and while resting his black mood returned. Then a new light brightened his life.

One of his numerous correspondents was a fan, another Samantha Tincrowder. She was his mother's cousin once removed and sister to the well-known SF author, Leo Queequeg Tincrowder. Samantha had been born in New Goshen, Indiana, but, at the time she became a Somers aficionado, she was living in Indianapolis. Somers' letters convinced her that he needed cheering up. She quit her job as a registered nurse and came to Petersburg for an extended visit. Within two months, they were married. They have been very happy ever since, the only missing element being a child. Their interests are similar, both loving books and dogs and the quietness of village life.

Though his home is a backwater, a sort of tidal pond off the main streams of the highways, Jonathan Somers quite often gets visitors. At least once a month, fans or writers drop in for a few hours or a day or so. Bob Tucker, who lives in nearby Jacksonville, often comes by to help Somers empty a bottle of whiskey. On one occasion, he even brought his own. I live in Peoria, which is within about a two and a half-hour drive of Petersburg. I go down there at least twice a year for weekend visits. Another guest is Jonathan's relative, Leo Tincrowder. Neither Leo nor I, however, would be caught dead drinking Tucker's brand, Jim Beam, which we claim is fit only for peasants. The subtleties and the superbities of Wild Turkey and Weller's Special Reserve are beyond the grasp of Tucker's taste.

Jonathan Herowit stayed with Somers for six months after his release from Bellevue. (Somers has empathy for the mentally disadvantaged, too.) Eric Lindsay, an Aussie fan, stopped off during his motorcycle tour of the States after the Torcon. And there have been many others.

Somers' fans will be interested in his current project.

"I plan to write a novel outside the Clayter and Wau Wau canons. It'll take place almost a trillion years from now. It'll be titled either *Hour of Supreme Vision* or *Earth's Dread Hour*. Both titles are quotes from the Spoon River Anthology. The latter is from that fictitious epitaph Edgar Lee Masters wrote for my father, poor guy!"

"You don't have many years of writing left," I said.

He looked puzzled, then he smiled. "Ah, you mean Trout's prediction that I'll die in 1980." He laughed. "That rascal put me in his novel just long enough to kill me off. Had a boy riding a bicycle ram into me. Well, that could happen. This town is hilly, and the kids do come down the steep streets with their brakes off. I did it myself before I got sick. But the way I feel right now, I'll live to be eighty, anyway."

I drove away that night feeling he was right. His yellow hair has turned white, and his beard is grizzled. But he looks muscular and hairy-chested, like Hemingway when he was healthy. His gusto and delight of life and literature seem to ensure his durability. His readers can look forward to many more adventures of John Clayter and Ralph von Wau Wau and perhaps a host of other characters.

Somers' old mansion is only a few blocks from the corner of 8th and Jackson Street, where Masters' boyhood house still stands. A sign in front says: "Masters Home, Open 1-5 P.M. Daily Except Monday." I wonder if someday a similar sign will stand before Jonathan Swift Somers' home. I wouldn't be surprised if this does happen. But I hope it'll be a long time from now.

Lost Futures

Seventy Years of Decpop

Seventy Years of Decpop

First published in *Galaxy*, Volume 33, Number 1, July 1972.
Also published in *Best Science Fiction* for 1973, June 1973.

This story is curious in that it was both touted on the cover
of Galaxy as a lead novel when it was first printed, and thought
of highly enough to appear in *Best Science Fiction* for 1973 edited by Forrest J Ackerman. Then it just disappeared. It has not
been reprinted in any of the many retrospective anthologies, and
it has not appeared in any of the many collections of Philip José
Farmer stories. In his Hugo Award winning short story "Riders
of the Purple Wage," the citizens in the story live in a future
where the government has switched from an economy of scarcity to an economy of abundance. In this story we see a possible
future situation where making the switch just might be the only
way forward for mankind.

As with most of Farmer's best work, the narrative may focus
on one individual, but the real story is how society as a whole
reacts to circumstances beyond its control.

Written in 1972 it is interesting to note Phil writing about 24
hour news channels, telephones with caller recognition and Viagra!

April, Year One

Jackson Canute, on that terrible morning, faced three things he did not
want to face.

One, his baby-food business would have practically no customers in less
than two years.

Two, the probabilities were that he was not one of the naturally resistant.
According to the latest information only one in 20,000 persons had not been
rendered permanently sterile.

Three, like almost every adult he was experiencing the end-of-the-world
syndrome, as it was to be called.

Number three he thought he could handle. He had always prided himself
on his self-control, his flexibility, his adaptability.

Number two? He would not know whether or not he was sterile until he took the test Clabb had described in his letters.

Number one? Conversion.

But his wife, Ellen, was phoning him and he knew by her whiteness, her drawn face, her wide eyes, that she was going to be hysterical about all three and nasty about number two.

His secretary, Jessica, had asked him if she should put the call through and he had said she should.

Get It Over With was his philosophy.

He pressed the button and Ellen asked, "Why did you take so long about answering?"

"You're not the only one shaken up," he said. "I heard the news on the radio just before I drove into the parking lot."

"It's awful, isn't it?" she said. "Just terrible! Horrible!"

"If it's true," Jackson said.

"It certainly is true!" Her voice rose, fluttering like a frightened bird. "They verified all the important things before they released the news. How do you explain the sudden drop in pregnancies in the last four months? It was all Clabb's[1] doing! He explained the whole thing in his letter—the one they read. How he built toy factories all over the world, except in the Iron Curtain countries, and how only he knew that the aerosol he'd had his scientists make was being blown out into the winds and carried all over the world and how it affected only man and the higher apes and how only one person in twenty thousand—"

"Clabb's letter was read over the radio and I heard it again on the TV in my office."

"They say Clabb has disappeared. No one has the slightest idea of where he went."

"Naturally," Jackson said.

"Please come home," Ellen said. "I'm just about to go to pieces."

"I was planning on coming home—was just going to call you," he said. It was evident that she meant to wait until he got home before she reproached him. "But first I have to make some calls. It takes time and money to convert a business and—"

"What do you mean?"

He explained and she said, "What if you can't get a loan to change over? Nobody's going to want to invest in the future because the future isn't going to exist. It—"

---

[1] Every head of state on Earth received a letter from Jacob Clabb. By the time scientists had determined that Clabb's formula was not a crackpot's work the planet's birth rate had dropped noticeably. There was no longer any reason to suppress the news. Clabb had disappeared without a trace. One theory was that Clabb may have become mentally unbalanced following the Great July Choke in New York City in 1976.

"You're getting hysterical."

He regretted saying that as soon as he had said it. In Ellen's mind to be accused was to be guilty. She broke up and was still screaming when he cut her off. He checked Dr. Seward's office number but received no answer. He tried the doctor's home. Mrs. Seward answered. Her makeup was wrecked by tears and her slurred speech indicated she had been drinking.

"Ronald's at General Hospital," she said. "He's got six would-be suicides on his hands and more coming in. And I'm not so sure that I'm not going to be one of his patients if he doesn't come home."

"Call a good doctor," Jackson said, hoping the dry approach would calm her down. And then, seeing her anger, he said, "I'm just kidding, Jane. Look, why don't you go over to my house? You and Ellen can buck up each other until I get home. Or maybe that's not such a good idea. Ellen's no post to lean on just now. Go to Willa's. She's pretty steady."

"She's one of Ronald's pill-takers!" Jane Seward said shrilly. "Good God, man, don't you know this is the end of the road for humanity?"

"I don't know any such thing," Jackson said. "Look, go over and talk to Ellen until I get home. Meanwhile, consider the figures. Even with only one—"

He stopped. She had cut him off. He pressed Jessica's button. "Call my wife. Tell her I'm on my way home now. I will actually be making some phone calls, but they shouldn't take too long. By the way, you look as if you were being sensible about this."

"I'm too numb really to know what's going on inside me," she said. She smiled. She was beautiful enough when her face was composed—when she smiled she was striking.

Her face faded from the screen. He spoke Arnold Rawley's number, but according to his secretary Mr. Rawley was not in. She did not know where he was. He was not at home, because she had called there and his wife had said that he should have been at work.

Canute phoned Mike's, a tavern on Highview Road near Highview Woods, where Canute and Rawley lived. Mike's was a small but elegant place. It had become a sort of "neighborhood" tavern. The neighbors were some of the wealthiest and most influential men in Busiris.

Mike answered. In a few seconds Rawley's flushed face was on the screen.

"Jackson!" Arnold said. "Come on down! We're celebrating the end of the world! No more babies! Jesus!" The tears ran down his cheeks.

"You have six children," Canute said. "You've got it made."

"Yeah, but I won't have any grandchildren. They ought to hang Clabb when they find him! No, hanging's too good for him—they ought to crucify him, except that would be blasphemous. They ought to nail—"

"Cut it out," Canute said. "Why the hell are you crying in your beer—scotch—anyway at this time of the morning? You don't even know that everything Clabb says is true. With six kids you've got a chance of one's being fertile even if all the claims in those letters are verified. I have work to do and I need you. I want to get started at once to convert—that much I'm sure of. I'm calling an emergency meeting of the board of directors and you should be working out the legal foundations. But you won't be in any shape today, I can see. What about your partner? Is he off on a bender, too?"

"Young Luckenvor? Not that cold fish."

"I'll call him then," Canute said. "I expect to see you sober tomorrow. At eight."

Rawley glared.

"Young Luckenvor's not the only cold fish."

"I can get hysterical with the best of you," Canute said, "when there's occasion for it. It's not as if the sky was falling down, Chicken Licken."

He phoned Rawley's office again. Mrs. Tengrow, the secretary, said that Luckenvor was in the Hospital, according to a call she had just received from Mrs. Luckenvor. He had driven into a lamppost, wrecked the car, broken a collarbone and then suffered a broken arm when another car broadsided into his. The other driver had been arrested for drunkenness. Luckenvor had not yet been arrested, though he, too had been intoxicated—and where was Mr. Rawley?

"Why would Luckenvor be drunk so early in the morning?" Canute asked. "Mrs. Tengrow, when was the news about Clabb's letter first released?"

Mrs. Tengrow was sixty, childless, and did not care much for the direction in which the world had been going for the last forty years.

"Oh, the first announcement was during the late late show."

"Many people must have heard about it before dawn," he said. "But I never thought Luckenvor—" He cut himself short, told Tengrow where she could locate Rawley. "But I advise you not to ask him to come to the office. He should go home. In a taxi."

Mrs. Tengrow pursed her mouth but said nothing.

Canute made several calls to board members, asking them to call others for a meeting at the Golden Boar's Head at the earliest possible moment. His secretary would arrange for the private banquet room and take care of other details.

He listened to Jessica on his callbox. She was still talking to Ellen. He turned and went out the back way, though Jessica had probably rotated the phone so that Ellen could not see him if he passed Jessica's desk.

———>•<———

He was glad to see the tall white pillars and reddish-brown roof of his house ahead. Something was uncoiling from the ice-shot mud in his entrails. It was sending vibrations up through his flesh.

Humanquake, he thought. *I wonder what degree this is on the personal Richter scale…*

If he could cast his reactions into such channels he was safe from breakup.

He stopped the car on the curving drive, turned off the steam and sat for what seemed a long while behind the wheel. Finally the big carved-oak door opened and Ellen came out. He left the car and walked toward her. She flew to him as if she were a self-thrown basketball, his arms the hoop. He held her for a long while, but, seeing passersby in cars turning their heads to look, he finally released her and urged her into the house. There he did what seemed to him the best way to comfort her—and himself—even though she weakly protested. But she lost her reluctance after a few minutes. She soon understood that they were making the most significant gesture they could—they were, in a sense, shaking their fists or thumbing their noses at the catastrophe that hung over mankind. And there was the hope that this would result in conception and prove that they were not going to share in the larger fate of the world.

———>•<———

Canute did not get much accomplished the next day. Rawley could not make it to work. Even if he had not been so hung over he would have stayed home to settle down his wife. The board of directors membership was still suffering from shock and refused to attend a meeting until the numbness wore off.

The third day Jackson took his time leaving the breakfast table. Ellen was fairly calm, though at times her chin would start trembling and tears would appear. They watched the early morning news together. International, national and local news came in that order. Three elephants of bad portent, two holding the tails of their predecessors in their trunks. Most programs had been canceled for news or special programs. These consisted largely of "authorities" lecturing or being interviewed or talking with other authorities. There were also views of reactions, public and private, from all over the world.

Shortly before he left for the office Jackson said, "Busiris has a population of about two hundred thousand. That means that only about ten adults in Busiris are naturally resistant. Ten! And if half are women, how many can bear children? A person can be naturally resistant, but that doesn't necessarily mean he or she is fertile."

The President of the United States was to speak at 8:00 P.M. One commentator thought that Lister was sure to make the same announcement as the premier of China and the president of France. They had stated that the FCP, the Fertility Check Project, was mandatory for every citizen between sixteen and fifty. The test itself was a contribution by Clabb described in one of his letters. A needle dipped in clabbonite—Clabb's own name for it—was drawn across the skin of the arm or hand deep enough to bring blood. Ten minutes later, if the person were naturally resistant to Clabb's aerosol, a red inflammation approximately a centimeter wide would appear on each side of the scratch. Enormous batches of the clabbonite were being prepared by every nation. Public servants were being trained in administering the test.

Some commentators thought that the legality of the FCP in the United States would be challenged. Most suits would be of the civil rights variety— Jehovah's Witnesses, for example, could object to the drawing of their blood.

Canute kissed Ellen and drove to his office. She still had not reproached him for his having insisted on putting off having children until he was thirty and she was twenty-six. She was more restrained than he had thought she could be. Perhaps she was waiting until the results of the FCP tests were known.

Jessica was waiting at the office with a list of what she had accomplished the day before. Rawley would be in at 10:30, ready to discuss the legal actions needed for conversion. The board of directors and a few major stockholders would be at the Golden Boar's Head for lunch at 12:00. The meeting would start at 1:00. Mr. Joshua Tabbs of the First United Federal Savings and Trust was ready to meet him at 10:00 the next morning if Canute had the go-ahead on the conversion from the board.

"How did he sound?" Jackson asked.

"Upset."

"I was hoping he'd sound friendly—as he does when he's favorable to a loan. But that's too much to expect. Everybody's upset. They're either too jittery or too controlled."

Jessica looked up from her note pad. Her eyes were naturally large and makeup made them enormous. They were a lovely violet under the contact lenses she always wore in his presence. He suspected that their real color was blue. No doubt a lovely blue.

"Mr. Canute, what do you think about this FCP? Do you think everybody will have to take the test?"

"I see no other way out," he said. "The world—humanity, rather—can't afford to let a single fertile person go unused."

"But what about unmarried persons?"

"Jessica, the normal social sanctions don't apply. When survival is threatened conventions go out the window."

She glanced down at her full breasts, then looked up at him.

"But what if, say, someone like me were—uh—fertile and the man I loved wasn't?"

"No trouble," Jackson said, looking at his wristwatch. "Artificial insemination is available."

"But what if my husband didn't want to bring up another man's child?"

"You've got no idea how much social pressure is going to be brought to bear on people like that," Canute said. "Listen, Jessica, today's a very important one for Canute Baby Foods, Incorporated. Screen my calls even more thoroughly than usual. Use your judgment."

"How soon do you think the FCP will get going?"

"What? Oh, I don't know. Several months maybe. If Congress makes it a law. I'll be in my office. Send Rawley in as soon as he shows."

———⋙●⋘———

The morning went smoothly. Rawley, red-faced, red-eyed, moved sluggishly, but his brain was functioning. Once he understood that Jackson did not want to talk about Clabb or the FCP, he stuck to business. But when he was leaving he said, "What the hell will my wife and I do if none of our six kids are fertile?"

"The oldest are seventeen and sixteen, right?" Jackson said. "They're old enough to take the test now, so you will soon know the score. The others are twelve, eleven, nine, and seven, right? So you have to wait until they pass puberty and then find out. Meanwhile I suggest you think about their reactions, not yours."

"I am, I am," Rawley said. "Their reactions, as you call them, are mine. When they cry I cry."

"And when you—"

Jackson stopped.

To suggest that Rawley quit dissolving his backbone in booze and give his children a good example would only anger him.

"What?" Rawley said.

"Nothing. Good luck to your kids. Good luck to all kids."

The probabilities were against it, but one of Rawley's children might be fertile, one of Busiris' lucky ten. If they were lucky. Being fertile was going to bring on them an enormous amount of public scrutiny and concern. And disappointed psychotics would be a danger to them. The lucky might have to become semiprisoners, guarded by the state for their own good.

The luncheon and board meeting were attended by several wealthy older women who owned large blocks of stock. They were not concerned about their own sterility or fertility—they were past the age even to be tested under the FCP. But they had children who were worried. Jackson answered all questions calmly and with an optimism he did not believe was founded in reality. But his object was to get them in a frame of mind for a rational consideration of the financial difficulties that Canute Baby Foods, Inc., faced. A few could not grasp the idea that baby foods would be out of customers in two years or less.

"But that means that my son's infant disposables will be gone, too," Mrs. Wilmort said.

"Many businesses will become obsolete," Canute said. "It's easy to think of the obvious ones. But many more will be affected as time goes on. One trend will be constant and we would all do well to keep it in mind. From now on all businesses will have an ever-decreasing number of customers. The expanding economy, along with the expansion of population, is a thing of the past."

"The stock market is still declining," Mrs. Dammfrum said.

"It'll stabilize and start up again," Jackson said, not really believing it would. The mental depression of the world always generated a financial depression.

"That goddamned Clabb!" Mrs. Mondries said. Jackson smiled. She was a self-righteous, stickily prudish person. He would have thought nothing could bring such an outburst from her. Which showed how much he knew.

The meeting following the luncheon was perfunctory and lasted only minutes. Jackson got his clearance to convert and buzzed Jessica to move his meeting with Tabb ahead to that afternoon. No one had much heart for business.

Reverend Cottons, a prominent stockholder and a nondenominational preacher, gave the parting blessing. He prayed that God would have pity on His children and cancel Clabb's evil deeds, stick His finger in, as it were, and resurrect the dead wrigglers and eggs. The reverend was a tall handsome man of fifty-six who could project considerable charisma or a reasonable facsimile thereof. Along with this went a virility that both males and females of his church seemed to relish. Horniness and divinity, Canute thought, had always been allied deep in the layman's mind—somewhere in the nether layers of human awareness the desire to worship the goddess of fertility lurked eternally.

Even Canute, who belonged to no faith, felt more optimistic after Cottons had finished his prayer. It was all but impossible to believe in sterility in the reverend's juicy presence.

———————

At three in the afternoon Canute was in Tabbs' office. The banker was a lean, bald-headed man with small eyes, the greenish color of which suggested new dollar bills. He was all smiles and little jokes, but he was also unwilling to make a decision.

"I can't take an objective look at what your conversion involves until this panic is over," Tabbs said. "You understand, don't you?"

"Of course," Canute said. "But I don't have much time to start moving."

"I realize that. But you haven't stated exactly what you intend to convert to. And the canned food business is highly competitive, isn't that so?"

"It is. I can give you the figures for the whole canning industry next time we meet. At this time, as I said over the phone, I just want to get an idea of your interest in making me a loan."

"Before you go to somebody else? Believe me, Jackson, our relationship has been such that I have great—the greatest—confidence, in you. You're only twenty-eight but your success in running your father's business has been remarkable. Under almost any other circumstances I wouldn't hesitate to say that we would advance whatever you required. But under other circumstances you wouldn't be wanting to convert, would you?

The bank, too, has to face changed conditions."

Bankers dealt in hard facts and figures, but they were the most plastic of people. Or the most ectoplasmic.

"I can understand why you want to wait," Canute said. "Only I can't afford to wait."

"I appreciate that," Tabbs said. "Look, it'll take you some time to decide exactly what you want to do, how much the operation will cost, what losses you'll suffer during the shutdown and changeover and so forth. By the time you've got your facts in hand we may be in a better position to understand what's going on. In other words, the dust will have settled and we can see how near the mountains are."

Canute rose at the same time as Tabbs. Tabbs looked a little annoyed that Canute had anticipated him.

They shook hands and Tabbs said, "I am very sorry. But—"

"The bank comes first, of course," Canute said and wondered why Tabbs felt it necessary to apologize.

"My daughter became pregnant about four months ago," Tabbs said. "So she escaped this tragic thing. You might say our family made a deposit just in time. What interest she'll bear—"

Canute smiled but did not laugh because he was not sure that Tabbs wasn't being serious.

"Congratulations," he said. "You'll be a grandparent at least once. And perhaps your daughter may be one of the lucky ones."

"Better than having gold in the bank," Tabbs said. He ushered Canute out as if he were concentrating on the treasure in the dark vault of his daughter's womb.

———◦———

Out on the street Canute felt deflated. He had known the market was bad, but he had not, somehow, expected to be turned down. But he wasn't angry at Tabbs. Tabbs had to face a different future along with everyone else.

The First United Federal was at the end of the short leg of a large suburban shopping center in the form of an *L.* Canute decided to take a stroll around it. He could observe the state of business and also do some thinking about the conversion. The sidewalks and stores seemed as crowded as ever and nothing in the faces or movements of the shoppers indicated that a catastrophe had occurred. Many still did not understand—emotionally anyway—the depths of the event. And the disaster was not one that had occurred quickly—like a tidal wave or a volcanic eruption—and would be soon over. This was an invisible calamity. Its effects would assume reality slowly—so slowly that most people would not begin to see the overall results plainly for five years. Even then the visible effects would not be overwhelming or too frightening. With 60,000,000 people dying each year, five years would see 300,000,000 dead all over the world. The deceased would leave a sizable gap behind them. Put together, they would fill a monstrously large and terrifying cemetery. But they would not be collected— they would be scattered everywhere. The Earth would absorb them quietly and, at the local level, the survivors would not notice much difference. Cities and towns would not be quite as crowded. Empty apartments and houses would be more numerous but not depressingly so. Births had recently averaged more than 125,000,000 yearly. Subtract the annual deaths of 60,000,000, and the world had yearly gained 65,000,000 persons. In effect, Earth had annually taken on the additional burden of a new nation—another France or Germany, say. That gain had been suddenly cut off. Some years would have to pass before the full scope of the loss became visible to citizens other than statisticians.

Canute walked down the short leg and the long leader of the *L* to the liquor store. It was crowded—the clerks were moving jerkily, trying to serve all customers at once. All the liquor stores, according to a comment by a TV newsman, were breaking sales records. Some of the customers looked as if they had drunk up everything at home and had been forced to go out for more, whether or not they could now see or walk straight.

⟶✺⟵

He walked back to the parking lot. The date was April 15. The sky was blue and cloudless. It had rained three days before—the grass was green and the trees were budding. It was a fine day to be alive. Yet, as T.S. Eliot had written, "April is the cruelest month." Mankind was facing its end. Or was it? Clabb's letter had made it plain that he thought he was giving humanity its only chance to survive. Perhaps he was right. Even so, this was still the cruelest month of Canute's life.

He drove back to his office. Kalender, the business agent of the canning workers' union, was waiting for him.

Canute shook his hand and said, "I was wondering how long it would take you to realize the implications."

Kalender did not ask, *Implications of what?* He said, "You're giving me credit for more intelligence than I have. I should have seen it, but I didn't. Shock, I suppose. I hope it was shock, not stupidity. But I saw Millman's show last night and he said that in five years kindergartens the world over would be empty. And in six, all first grades. I sat up and yelled at Richie—she's my wife, you met her at—"

"I know," Canute said. "A lovely woman. Well, come on in. I would have called you by tomorrow anyway."

Kalender's suit came from the same tailor as Canute's—his tie, however, was a trifle more flamboyant. He had long ago gotten over his original, somewhat belligerent manner toward Canute. He listened without interruption while Canute told him what he had done so far and what he hoped to do.

"We still have to walk out on July first if the industry doesn't give in." Kalender said.

"You really think they'll vote for a strike with the economy in such questionable shape and with the future so debatable?"

"You forget they passed up a pay increase last year because of Lister's anti-inflation speech. I was surprised when they voted against a strike. But this year they're hurting even more. Prices—well, you know. The thing is, even if they don't want to strike on account of they'd like to help you make the conversion, they have to. This is national, and the canning workers not in baby foods won't be affected by your special situation. We'll have to go along with national headquarters."

"Maybe you could get a dispensation from them," Canute said.

Kalender smiled slightly. "I don't think I'll get anywhere, though I'll try. The central office always takes the view that the minority must suffer if the majority will profit. And—"

Canute said, "In ten years Busiris' two hundred thousand population will be down to about a hundred and eighty-two thousand. Sales of canned foods—of everything, in fact—will be dropping. Now, Busiris' decrease in population doesn't sound like much. And Canute Foods, after conversion, will do the bulk of its business outside Busiris. But the overall decline in the number of consumers will inevitably force the closing of much of the canning industry in fifteen years. The effects will be felt long before then. Here and there factories will close down—never to reopen."

Kalender leaned forward and said, "You trying to scare me?"

"Think about it and you'll scare yourself."

<hr/>

Canute drummed his fingers on his desktop and then said, "According to our present contract, the company has to pay a full weekly wage to each worker laid off during any shutdown for maintenance, repair, conversion, etc. But not during a strike. So—"

"I thought you'd bring that up." Kalender paused to light a cigar. "If you wait until the strike to start converting, you won't have to pay your workers during the shutdown. The national office is aware of this—I talked to the headquarters for an hour last night about it. Phoned them a half-hour after I realized what was going to happen. They said—all this is confidential, off the record, you know—that the new contract will take care of that. The company will have to reimburse its workers a hundred percent of the pay lost during a shutdown, strike or no strike. The reimbursement can be stretched out over six months, doesn't have to be paid at once. We know that the industry has its problems and we'll go along—to a certain extent."

Jackson Canute leaned back, put his hands behind his head and looked up at the pale blue ceiling with its glowing traceries: mandalas, crux ansatas, cosmic eyes, dollar signs, pyramids, infinity signs, ying and yang.

"I object in principle. But in practice I can't see that it makes much difference. If you don't strike we have to pay you during shutdown. However, I don't know what view the banks will take of the strike and the shutdown pay. They might decide that they can't make the loan. Banks take the long-range view, you know, and they won't have any trouble extrapolating the effects of decpop, as the newsmen are calling it. The canned food industry is highly competitive. You know that as well as I. And our establishing a foothold is going to take time, will cost us much and possibly—I might even say most likely—will result in failure.

"And even if we—notice the we, since you workers are as much a part of Canute Canned Foods as the managers and stockholders—even if we do get a good share of the business, enough to keep us going, we won't be able to keep up the gross indefinitely. Sales, as I said, will inevitably decline for the entire industry. And then the dog-eat-dog struggle ends in one dog, top dog. And within forty years—with two billion four hundred million of those now living dead and with very little replacement—the world population will be about one billion six hundred million. Still sounds like a lot, doesn't it? Well, it's eight million less than it was in nineteen hundred.

"Seventy years from now there will still be several million centenarians, nonagenarians and so on. And several hundred thousand young fertile people. Maybe. If society doesn't crumble long before then, which it may well do. As you know, modern society, capitalist, communist, or socialist, depends on an expanding economy. Which—"

"I know," Kalender said. "And the banks know. But even so, if the banks quit making loans because of this they will go out of business. Won't they hang on to a business-as-usual policy as long as possible?"

"I hope so."

Canute talked some more about what could be done. But in the end the two returned from the abstract and the unlikely to the coming next six months. Finally Kalender decided to leave.

"Usually these preliminary talks straighten both of us out on the realities and the potentials," he said. "No matter what our public statements, we both knew pretty well what we will end up doing. But this time—who knows? It's up to the banks—"

"They're just part of the total picture," Canute said. "They're depending on many things to help them make up their minds. One of which, a very important which, is the President of the United States. Maybe he'll say something significant in tonight's speech."

Kalender left. Canute felt depressed. Even reminding himself that depression was anger turned inward did not help. What was he angry at? The union? Because of its shortsightedness? Its members were acting according to the old rules—and if they didn't see that new rules had to be adopted they were no more blind than the managers and the bankers. Perhaps the President, who was a flexible and unconventional man—too much so for many voters— would come up with new rules. But even if he did—could he get his nation to accept them?

—————

Canute had invited to dinner the Rawleys; his vice president, Markham and wife; Mrs. Luckenvor (who came after visiting her husband in the hospital); Jack Ward, a construction company owner and a powerful politician; the city manager and his wife and Manfred Schiller, a black economics professor at Traybell University.

The dinner went only so-so—talk was punctuated by frequent total silences despite the tested ability of everyone present to keep a conversation going. Afterward the party moved into the big TV room to view Lister's speech.

The President was a lean-faced man of fifty-three. His voice had a compelling resonance—it made most voters want to believe him. Normally he managed to look both grave and cheerful at the same time, but tonight a bleakness seemed to override his spirit. Or perhaps, Canute thought, his viewers had turned off their cheerfulness receptors.

Canute was disappointed that the President did not propose some bold new economic measures. However, he had no right to expect them. As he had told himself earlier, it was too early for these. The major part of the speech concerned the setting up of fertility tests for the entire nation, exclusive of the too old and the too young, of course. The first tests would be given on June 28 and the FCP Department, newly created, would handle the project. Professional medical personnel was not needed to make the tests or even interpret their results. Within four months the nation should know what its "fertility resources" were. Scientists' projections placed these at approximately 13,250 persons. The aged were excluded. Youngsters whose natural resistance to the aerosol could be determined but whose actual fertility would not be known until they matured sexually were included in the statistical projection.

Lister emphasized several times that the fertiles would be given special treatment from now on. He did not say what the special treatment was to be.

The President said that the world had no reason to panic. The overpopulation problem had been solved overnight, as it were, whether or not the world liked the nature of the solution. What had happened was a catastrophe, but it was not the end of man. Far from it. People were not dying any faster or in any greater numbers. The only difference that had immediate impact was that the world was not having to handle daily the arrival of enough babies to populate New Orleans, Louisiana, or Newark, New Jersey.

Lister took a hopeful view of the situation.

However—and here Lister's voice trumpeted as if for a cavalry charge—the old methods of dealing with society, economics and so forth could no longer be used. This was a new and unprecedented situation. Fresh approaches would have to be developed. There would be much resistance to some of these, since most people were naturally conservative, naturally resistant to swift change. But everyone would soon see that the old methods were now useless.

The new departures would be described in a future speech. Meanwhile no cause for panic or even pessimism existed on either individual or national levels...

The party at Canute's listened quietly to the various commentators on the President's speech. Next came extracts of other speeches made by heads of other states from all over the world. In essence these made the same points Lister had made.

Canute finally turned off the set. Everybody began to talk excitedly at once. Even those who were suspicious of Lister's "methods" were not gloomy. They seemed to take a joy in arguing that there was no sense in abandoning the present system for even more socialism or for communist-type institutions. It was evident that the President's speech had uplifted everybody, even those who would fight against his measures to deal with the crisis.

"What do you think about it, Jackson?" Rawley said.

"Whatever the new system is, some men will come out on top and some will go down," Canute said.

"And you hope to be on top, right?" Rawley asked.

"I believe that I'm flexible enough," Canute said.

"Well, I hope you're flexible enough to get a loan for the conversion. Say, maybe that's one of the things Lister was hinting at? A Federal loan could keep Canute Baby Foods, Incorporated, in business."

The trouble with Rawley, Canute thought, was that he insisted on thinking in the same old grooves.

June, Year One

Jackson and Ellen Canute had received a letter from the newly created Fertility Checkup Project Department two weeks earlier. They were to report at the Reywoods High School for their tests on the morning of June 28th. Instructions included a procedure to follow if the Canutes objected to taking the test on religious or civil-rights grounds. Arrest was automatic, but under the Emergency Vital Resources Law the arrestee would be released immediately on bail. The law required that the case be tried within a week before a special judge and a jury of twelve peers. This was unheard-of speed for the courts, but the fertility resisters, as the news media dubbed them, had total priority. The Government, which was the people, could not afford to miss one potential parent. The President, during a press interview, had stated that mankind's existence depended upon one in every 20,000 persons—and that one must be found. He pointed out that similar laws with much harsher methods of enforcement and penalties were being passed in less democratic nations.

A new law had been passed by the time June 28th came around. It required resisters to be subjected to physical and psychiatric testing. The theory was that anyone who would not cooperate in saving mankind had to be psychotic. Part of the test was drawing a needle across the skin so that blood welled. Most of those scratched failed to react with inflammation and these were quickly released without a trial. A number of suits were filed against the U.S. government before testing even began and eventually the U.S. Supreme Court declared the law unconstitutional. But by then everybody, objector or not, had been tested.

Jackson and Ellen drove to the high school on the hot June morning. A traffic jam delayed them for ten minutes. Then they had to cruise around the big parking lot until someone pulled out. A little steam-driven Volkswagen tried to beat them into the parking place. It was going in the wrong direction, ignoring the signs and arrows all over the place.

Ellen had been sullen and withdrawn that morning and Jackson was angry about this. That was why, when he saw the Volkswagen cut around the car that had just left the parking place and swing sharply inward, he kicked down on the accelerator. He and Ellen were jerked back. Canute swung the wheel. Ellen gasped and put one hand on the dashboard and the other on his right arm. He blew the horn, but the driver of the little car, grinning at him from under a thick mustache, made no effort to slow down. Jackson swore as the Volkswagen crashed into his left fender.

He and Ellen sat still for a moment, shaking and pale. The impact bag before them was shrinking with a long drawn-out gasp.

"You all right?" Jackson asked.

Ellen said, "I think so. I'm just scared, that's all."

"I was doing eight and he was going about thirteen," Jackson told her. "That's a twenty-one-kilometer impact."

"I'm glad you're so cool and quick-thinking," Ellen said. "You're so cool that now I'll never have a baby!"

"We haven't had the test yet, remember?" He unfastened his safety belts and opened the door. He knew that if he stayed in the car he would really take off on Ellen. He climbed out and examined the damage to his car. The fender had crumpled, but the little car's bumper, hood and radiator were pushed in. About a thousand dollars' worth of damage for the other man—a hundred for himself.

A guard appeared, a recorder hung around his neck and a microphone in his hand. The driver of the Volkswagen got out, but his woman passenger stayed inside. She was a pretty girl of about twenty and held a baby. It was screaming loudly. But the mother was safety-belted and both she and the baby had been protected by the impact bag. The driver, also young, wore one of the new Marie Antoinette wigs, green wraparound glasses, dangly crystal earrings and fluorescent pink-and-green striped Louis XVI suit. He was pale and angry.

"I got a baby in the car," he said.

<hr />

Canute was taken aback. But he quickly recovered. He asked, "So why were you driving the wrong way, speeding and endangering the infant by trying to beat me into the parking place, to which you had no right?"

The officer stopped in front of them, flicked on the recorder and said, "I called the regulars. Meanwhile, your ID card, please."

Jackson handed it to him and the officer stuck the card into the recorder. A tiny light gleamed and he removed the card, handed it back to Jackson. He then asked the young man for his card.

The young man gave it to him, but said, "I've got a baby in the car and this guy paid no attention to him—"

A crowd had gathered. A number of them must have seen the accident, but only one, a middle-aged lady named Greenbaum, volunteered to be a witness.

The young man, a Mr. Dutton, continued to harp on the fact that his infant son had been a passenger. And that Canute had ignored the baby and crashed right on through.

Jackson did not understand Dutton's insistence on this completely irrelevant point. What did the baby have to do with this, except that its presence should have made Dutton more careful with his driving? Then he heard comments, some subdued, some loud, from the bystanders and understood what Dutton was getting at. The young man was entirely in the wrong, but he knew that things had changed—that babies were now the most precious of all mankind's possessions. And he was appealing to the crowd on the basis of this. He was succeeding. More and more hostile looks and remarks were directed at Canute.

Canute felt like hitting Dutton. But he also felt helpless. Emotion was winning over logic in this situation. It would not win in a court battle, of course. Or would it? Jurors were human.

The city police arrived and took down their evidence. A service truck towed away Dutton's car. Canute drove his into the parking space and helped Ellen out.

Ten minutes after the needles had been drawn across their wrists neither of their scratches had yielded inflammation.

Ellen waited five minutes past the reaction time—since people did vary—then began weeping quietly.

Jackson guided her out by the elbow. As he passed the Duttons, he heard the wife say, "I can't help it that I'm all right and you're not, can I? Is it my fault? And what good is it anyway? We're married, aren't we? And we have a baby already, don't we?"

Despite Ellen's grief Jackson could not help smiling. Later he would feel a little ashamed because of his momentary exultation and still later he would be sorry for Mrs. Dutton. He found, some years afterward, that her baby had died and that she had divorced Dutton and married a fertile man.

Such news made the papers.

At the moment he had little time to think about the Duttons. Ellen sobbed violently in the car. He tried to put his arm around her and draw her to him, but was shoved away. He gave up and drove home and when she locked herself in her room he went out, got into the car and drove to Mike's.

July, Year One

Jackson Canute had studied the reports of his business analysts. They confirmed in specifics what he had been sure of in general. The canning industry was overcrowded and would face a steadily declining market from now on. Even if Canute's company could get a loan, bank or Federal, conversion would simply postpone bankruptcy to the near future.

Another complication was that the distributors for the canners had raised their demands. They wanted an official increase of a cent a can for their services and an under-the-table increase of a cent a can. The organization that controlled the distributors—Canute did not doubt they were owned by a crime syndicate—was trying to grab all the profit it could before the market went to hell.

Six banks, starting with First United Federal, had turned down Canute. Canute had then called in Kalender and told him that it would make no difference if the union struck or not. Kalender, even though he had expected this, turned pale.

"What about a Federal loan?" Kalender asked.

"If we could get it—and I doubt we could—by the time we cleared the red tape we would be too late," Jackson said. "It looks as if we'll all be on welfare. And when I say all I include myself."

"That isn't something to joke about." Kalender looked grim. "You've got money in the bank, powerful friends—and you're a graduate biochemist with a degree on the side in business administration."

"It's none of your business, but I have enough in the bank to pay for three months' living and maintenance on my Highview Drive mansion. And my powerful friends can't get me a job if none is available."

Kalender's surprise was thinly filmed over with pleasure. Something in him rejoiced in an employer's ill fortune and could not be entirely hidden. Canute did not resent this. Kalender's reaction was a human one.

"It takes time to dispose of the company," Canute said. "I can't just lock up and walk away. It'll be six months or more before all the paperwork and legal procedure are gone through. I hate to think of the board of directors' meetings, the stockholders' meetings, the meetings with lawyers and Uncle Sam's representatives and so on—to nausea."

Kalender stood up. "You think it's going to be easy to tell my men they're out on the streets?" He shook hands with Canute. "Good luck."

"Good luck to you, too," Canute said. "But we'll be seeing each other quite often for several months, anyway. It's funny isn't it? We'll see each other more while we're getting rid of the business than when we were prosperous."

August, Year One

Busiris, Illinois, had at this time exactly 200,302 inhabitants. Of these twelve were naturally resistant to the aerosol and presumably fertile. Four were married to sterile partners. Four were under sixteen years of age. One was a Roman Catholic nun who had objected to being tested but had finally given in. One was a lesbian living with another lesbian. One was a hopelessly insane twenty seven-year-old woman. The twelfth was a forty-five-year-old man, divorced, childless, diabetic, a misogynist and a firm believer in the theory that God intended that mankind should perish. Hence, under no circumstances, would he provide his seed for the survival of humanity.

Other cities all over the world revealed similar patterns.

The rural village of Boseman, a few miles west of Busiris, had a population of 500 with not one naturally resistant person.

The metropolitan area of New York City had approximately 13,000,000 population of whom 650 were resistant.

Of Earth's approximately four billion population, 200,000 were resistant. The figures were not quite accurate, since there were some pygmy, Negrito, and Amazon Indian tribes that had escaped the test. Of the 200,000 about half were women.

Of these 100,000, about 25,000 did not seem available for reproduction for one reason or another, including sterility. That a person was resistant to Clabb's aerosol did not mean that he or she was fertile. And, if the fertile women married to unfertile men were included among the unavailable women their total rose to 85,000.

"What we must do," the Chinese premier said in his famous Peking Statement, "is make the unavailable available."

"We will persuade but never coerce," the prime minister of England said.

"Mother Russia demands the utmost in sacrifice from her children," the Soviet premier said.

The Pope, at the time the first complete statistics were compiled, had still not made any public statement regarding the attitude of the Church toward the new situation. But he was reported to be working on it.

"Now is the time for every citizen to act for the general good first and for himself next," the President of the United States said. "Laws must be enacted to permit the citizen to do this."

Lister, interviewed the next day, said that he would make specific proposals at a later, more appropriate time. By this, according to some news analysts, Lister meant when the public temper had been readied to receive radical proposals favorably. The analysts were vague about what they meant by radical.

The drunks standing at the bar in Mike's were vague, too, in their remarks about the speech and the professional comments on it. But they were precise enough in their adjectives directed at the President and the analysts.

"Listen, Jackson," Rawley said, pushing a dense front of bourbon against Jackson's face. "I think Lister, the weirdo's friend, is working up to something really radical. Like real radical, you get me? He hinted, just hinted, mind you, in his speech last month—you remember, you were at my place for dinner—that our present system isn't up to handling this crisis. He didn't say what he meant by 'system.' But he isn't putting anything over on me. I know his record. I know whom he used to hobnob with and whom he'd really like to have in his cabinet. I know all about his speeches on the economy of abundance when he was a young Congressman. So—"

Jackson listened for a while. When Rawley ordered another drink Jackson said, "If the house is so termite-ridden it's too late for the exterminator, ready to fall down, then you tear it down and build a new one. You don't just shore it up."

"What?" Rawley asked.

"The economy's going to hell, has been for a long time. It's been unable to handle its problems at even a sixty percent efficiency for years. You know that—you just won't admit it. And now that this has come along we can't just fight it with the old tired-and-untrue methods, you follow me, Rawley?"

The lawyer was slipping away, his head drooping and his nose almost in his drink. Jackson stopped talking and began the task of getting him to his car so he could drive him home. Rawley's wife could take a taxi and pick up Rawley's car later.

September, Year One

The President made his famous Blessing in Disguise speech the day before Labor Day. The entire speech lasted sixty minutes and was undoubtedly the most "compressed" that any president had ever made.

Jackson, working late that night, viewed it in his office. He sat at his desk with a glass of bourbon and ice and sipped while Lister made history.

Lister began by saying that the deed—Clabb's—was done and could not be canceled. Now was the time for the people of America—and of the world—to shed their grief and depression. If they were to survive as a viable society and bequeath their few children a viable society—and ensure that civilization endured—they must perform not miracles but prodigies. What they had to do would be difficult, but not impossible. They must shed old habits of thought and action. They must become new men.

And Clabb had opened the way for them, whether or not he had intended doing so. The pollution problem was taking care of itself and would continue to fade away as the population became smaller and smaller. And although unemployment had increased enormously, this was only a temporary situation. Lister anticipated a labor shortage in the near future if his plans were put into effect. The nation would prosper as never before from the grassroots upward. Poverty would disappear. Anybody who wanted an education would be able to get it free. Earth would be beautified and the generation born after the Clabb Effect had run its course—the fertile generation—would be taken care of. It would not inherit a world that had fallen into howling savagery, as so many continued to predict. It would inherit a world that was as close to paradise as fallible human nature could create.

What the President and his advisors envisioned was a society progressively cybernated. Every industry or service that could be equipped with electronic brains and mechanical organs and limbs would be so equipped. Success would ensure that the means of production—from mines to factories to transportation to the final dispensing of goods to the consumers—would be as efficient as possible.

This automation would not deprive people of their jobs. On the contrary, more jobs than there were people to fill them would be available. The total efforts of the entire population were needed to build the cybernated society and, as people passed away—Canute lifted his glass in a silent toast to the soon-to-be-dead, among whom would be himself, maybe—the computers and the machines would take over. Cybernated farms, for example, would continue to produce unfalteringly, regardless of population changes or shifts. Citizens would actually be liberated—worthwhile work would replace toiling for survival.

And how the hell are you going to cybernate the farms without turning the privately owned ones into state-owned combines—and what will happen to the farmers who are dispossessed?" Canute asked his TV set out loud. "To-morrow you'll be accused of being a Communist—and the day after you'll be shot by some madman."

Lister, it became obvious, had asked himself the same questions. He took some pains to make sure his audience understood him. Private farmers, he promised, would be given cybernated equipment and trained in its use. Those who wanted to learn how to repair and maintain the equipment would go to free schools. Those who would not or could not master the necessary skills could call on a pool of technicians.

What Lister did not say at that time or later—events simply worked out that way—was that if a farmer died and left no heirs the Government would buy his place and turn it into a state farm. And if the deceased had heirs the treasury department would permit adjustments in the inheritance tax if the heirs would sell the property to the Government.

Lister also did not mention that the repeal of the Twenty-second Amendment to the Constitution was already quietly on the way and that it would become effective in time for him to be elected to a third term. And a fourth, fifth and sixth.

Despite the many strong objections to Lister's programs later on most of the nation was thrilled and cheered by his speech that night. Out of bad would come good—at least prosperity for everybody. He was truly the leader of his people—courageous, adaptable. At last, after a series of—from the historical viewpoint—inept Presidents, a great man had risen.

———

Jackson Canute received a telephone call two weeks to the day after Lister's speech.

"The White House, Mr. Canute," Jessica said in a quivering voice.

The President? Canute's heart banged like a loose valve.

His caller was not Lister but one of the President's large staff of undersec-retaries. He asked how Canute was, said that he was glad in response to

Canute's: "Fine—" and promised that Canute would receive a letter from the President himself, or at least one originally composed and signed by him. It would confirm this call and spell out in more personal detail the President's plans. This was merely an overall briefing on what Canute might expect.

Canute knew, in outline, the purpose and the setup of CONES, The Committee of National Economic Standards. The news media had talked and printed enough about it. Now he was being asked if he would serve on the local board—if, in fact, he would help organize it under the supervision of the local chairman. The chairman had recommended Canute because he knew that Canute would not be occupied with his business and because Canute had the necessary qualifications. One of these was that he was a prominent member of the President's political party and a good friend of the chairman. But there was more to it than that, of course.

Canute said that he would give a verbal acceptance now and a written one later. He thanked the secretary and watched the fading image with great satisfaction.

Jessica was too disciplined to ask him what the call had been about. Canute, not being consciously sadistic, summoned her and gave her the news. Jessica looked even more beautiful when she was thrilled—and she was certainly at her most beautiful now. The contrast between her and Ellen, who had been looking and acting more and more haggish lately, was strong and troubling. Jessica never bothered Jackson and obviously adored him. Her reaction to the sterility problem continued markedly different from Ellen's. If she suffered grief she had not allowed it to show or sour her outlook. She had been married once, briefly, and though she had never said much about it, she had mentioned a year ago— she and Jackson had been working late—that any man she loved would have to compete with her dead father. Jackson had decided then and there that their relationship would always be that of employer and employee. He would never compete with a ghost, he had told himself. More than once.

Jessica was so thrilled now that she kissed him quickly on the lips and then, laughing, ran back to the outer office. Jackson had not kissed a woman for ten days—Ellen had begun to turn her cheek to him and for the past four days he had quit trying for even that.

Well, marriage meant more than kisses and every mentally stable woman got over her depressions. If Ellen were to become happy again Canute would be happy. He did not know what more he could do to bring her out of her pit. He had tried everything he could within the little time phasing out Canute Baby Foods, Inc., allowed him these days. He had tried to get her to go to a psychiatrist or go with him to a marriage counselor. But she had refused. These men could not make her fertile, she had said. She had emphasized men, making it plain that he was a member of that guilty set. Probably, more accurately, he was in an inner circle consisting only of himself—the man who had put off having children.

He had asked her if she would like to adopt a child. She had said no—she wanted one of her own. He had thought she might change her mind and had investigated possibilities. They were non existent—he was far too late. The day after the release of Clabb's letter the orphanages had been avalanched with requests for adoption.

Ellen was also suffering from the shock of being no longer married to an affluent man. She had objected vigorously—had even thrown ash trays at him—when he had told her that the house must be put up for sale, though there was little chance it could be sold without a great loss. The real-estate market had caved in.

Now, however, the CONES position would pay him $100,000 a year. Inflation made that equal to about $45,000 of ten years ago. He wouldn't suffer and he could keep the house, but he certainly was not going to be affluent again. He and Ellen would have to watch the budget very closely. And it might be best to sell at a loss that could be partially deducted from his income tax if he purchased a smaller home in the same year.

He poured bourbon into two glasses of ice and called Jessica back for a toast. She would not be out of a job after all, he told her. As a CONES board member he would need a battery of secretaries—whom she could boss. He would have enough budget to pay for them. Not to mention—as he did not—that he was going to have considerable influence and power as a CONES official.

So here's to our future, Jessica!

April, Year Three

With an annual death rate of nine per 1,000 inhabitants Busiris should have lost 5,400 citizens in three years. But the suicide, homicide and fatal accident rates had risen sharply. The population, instead of 194,600, was now approximately 183,800. However, the suicides and homicides seemed to be leveling to pre-Clabb times.

The lack of births and the attrition by death were so far almost unnoticeable. When Canute drove to work or downtown—or sometimes just around the town—he saw few empty houses. The only sights that really hit him were the day nurseries.

The nurseries were completely shut down. He saw children playing on the school grounds during recess, but he knew that the kindergartens and low grades would soon be empty. For years the schools had been steadily getting more overcrowded. But before long classes would be cut down in size and more teachers per pupil would be available.

Canute, as a CONES board member—chairman now, in fact—was also educational supervisor. He toured the schools from time to time, though most of the overseeing was done by a secretary. In three years his budget had tripled and he now had twice as many people working for him as at the beginning. He had much power, but his responsibilities and work had also increased. He had been feted a number of times, approached by many who wanted favors, and had been beaten badly by four men who had called him a "tool of the Government," among other things. He was lucky. One CONES member had been shot in the brain late at night as he got into his car in the parking lot. The killers had pinned a button to his bloody coat—above the letters FFF was a hand holding a lighted torch. Fighters For Freedom. The underground revolutionaries. Unlike the underground of the past, this group was composed of "reactionaries," men who wanted the old system kept intact, who still insisted that the old structures were suited for solving the new problems.

As it had turned out, a jealous husband had hired three men to murder the CONES official and had succeeded for a time in putting the blame on the underground. The jealous husband had happened to be the man responsible for Canute's appointment to the board, its first chairman. The resultant scandal had been used by opponents of the Government in an effort to discredit its policies. Canute had been appointed the new chairman and had accepted the position in the midst of heavy criticism. One of his bitterest critics—and the most influential—was the editor-publisher of the *Busiris Journal-Sun*. Caleb Tooney was sixty years old, a lifelong conservative and a big stockholder in the huge Earthmover Diesel Works of Busiris. He was also a vigorous enemy of Lister and his policies. Many of his editorials prophesied that Lister would have to suspend certain portions of the Constitution, such as civil rights, if he were to carry out his plans efficiently. That Tooney could print his editorials seemed to be the best refutation of his prophesies.

July, Year Five

When the *Buriris Journal-Sun* building burned down the police chief blamed arsonists. He produced evidence that the fire had been set, but found nothing to help him make an arrest. Some psychotic might have set it simply because he liked to watch the flames. Tooney claimed privately that the Government intelligence people had set the fire, though he did not directly accuse Lister.

Canute wondered.

He told himself that the fate of humanity was at stake. Strong Government measures had to be taken, measures that he himself would have condemned as criminal in ordinary circumstances, but might consider justified in the light of current emergencies.

He next told himself that he was indulging in cowardly rationalizations. What good if man survived if he had to build a repressive society to survive in? Actually Tooney's paper had acted as a safety valve for those who needed to blow off steam. It had been ineffective in hindering CONES. And it had called attention to the blunderings, the arrogances and the fracturing of people's rights, all of which the Government now and then was guilty of.

Whatever good or evil the paper had done, it was now through. Tooney was a stubborn old man. He tried to raise funds and get bank loans to rebuild his plant. He had been unable to collect his insurance because he had apparently failed to hire a sufficient number of security guards and set up the expensive alarm system the insurance people had specified. Tooney took the matter to court. The case was not tried until a year later and then it dragged on for six years in the lower and then the higher courts before Tooney lost. Meanwhile a more liberal syndicate announced plans to start a new paper, the *Busirian*. It never got off to a good start. The citizens of Busiris had to subscribe to out-of-town papers, usually a Chicago or St. Louis sheet, or catch the news on the local TV channel. In time one nationwide network dropped all programming except for news and eventually replaced the printed medium.

Canute checked around and saw a pattern suddenly taking shape around the country. Fires, bankruptcies, labor trouble, loss of advertising, sudden raises in taxes and outright vandalism were killing the remaining newspapers. In many cases nothing spectacular happened to a paper—except that a local TV station had become a full-time news agency and people quit subscribing. The Government was lending money to the TV news stations but not to the newspapers. It always had reasonable grounds for its refusals. The best was that it did not want to invest the taxpayers' dollars in a losing proposition.

October, Year Seven

Decpop had reduced the citizens of Busiris to 176,625. The loss of 23,677 was somewhat noticeable but still not spooky. In fact, there were no empty houses in the better residential areas. When an owner died heirless—or his heirs were bought out—the Government gave loans to certain selected citizens of the poverty sections. These folks moved into the hitherto exclusive areas.

Jackson Canute lived in the most exclusive district. Six black families owned homes within two blocks of his. The blocks were, however, exceptionally long, the equivalent of three ordinary blocks. The heads of the black families were lawyers, doctors and college professors.

As Jackson passed through the neighboring district, which had homes in the $75,000-$500,000 class, he saw a score of black faces in hitherto honky homes. Their occupants, he knew, had once lived in the middle-class black area on the west side. Now they had moved up.

The people in poverty areas won their Government loans—and the chance to move—in restricted lotteries. But the winners Canute discovered without being able to prove his point, were carefully chosen. They were ambitious types who wanted to advance, who could be counted on to continue to conform to the Government's definition of "responsible citizens." The Government was trying to siphon off the ghetto people with discretion. Others besides Jackson discovered the trend and there were riots and court actions. The riots were contained by law enforcement officials and the court actions dragged endlessly. The protesters included both blacks and whites and each had reason to cry injustice.

As chairman of the CONES board, Canute had more actual power than the city manager of Busiris. He used it to organize a survey of the South Side poor whites. He discovered far fewer qualified candidates than the black ghetto produced—virtually no professional people and almost as few qualified on the basis of real ambition. Jackson recognized the social factors behind the phenomenon, but he could not help or alter those. He concluded that the Government was trying to make the necessary social transition as easy as possible and was, for once, conducting itself in a sensible manner. He did, however, discover enough whites to balance the blacks who had been moved into the neighborhood adjacent to his own. He began to move them whenever there was an opening. This resulted in accusations of discrimination by blacks—as well as by some whites—and his days and nights grew even more troubled.

Power was its own high pay, but its by-products were nerve-twisting ulcer-generating and also fatigue-causing. Even behind the buffer of his secretarial battery Jackson was beset with letters, phone calls, people catching him outside his office, waiting on the porch of his home. Once a note wrapped around a rock was thrown through his living-room window. The note held money to pay for the window, but Jackson had the man arrested anyway.

Ellen left him the next day. The rock throwing was only one of a long series of incidents she had complained about. But she and Jackson had been quarreling more and more—their reconciliations were fewer and lasted a shorter time.

Yet, if he had been able to spend more time with her, if she had not also been bothered by the petitioners, they might have been able to make peace.

Year Eight

Jackson missed Ellen, but not very much. He married Jessica six months after his divorce. They were fairly happy, though she complained about his frequent absences. She continued to work for him, but he was gone much of the day from the office and much of the evening from home. She did have her bad times about being sterile and sometimes had nightmares about the end of the world. But these were infrequent and, in any event, she did not blame him for them.

Then Jessica thought she was pregnant. Pseudopregnancies had become a common phenomenon during the first ten years after Clabb. Often the pseudopregnancy was actually a large tumor, swiftly growing and all too frequently malignant and metastatic. It was as if a deep, unconscious desire in certain women to reproduce and so save humanity caused the growth of cells—certainly some such feeling kept many from early treatment. The growth was usually wild and resulted in the deaths of many women—so many that the annual death rate jumped from nine per thousand (in the first three years after Clabb) to eleven per thousand by the eighth year.

Jessica died at the end of the eighth year.

Perhaps this type of malignancy was, some psychologists speculated, one of the results of the end-of-the-world syndrome. Generally, the syndrome itself was a vague phenomenon, hence difficult to grapple with and conquer. It was like a question that could not be precisely phrased and so was unanswerable. Not many people went insane because of it. But it took the joy out of much of the work and the play. It bleached the skies, painted the Earth pale and it malformed men's unconscious minds.

Jackson Canute liked to think that he was exempt from this feeling. Up to Year Zero B.C. (Before Clabb, the news media facetiously had dubbed it), he had had work that had at least satisfied him. He had been a useful member of the community, administering an industry that supplied infants with nutrition. Now he was administering what was essentially a phasing-out operation. But it was the most gigantic and longest phasing out in history and he was playing an important part, even if only on a local scale. He loved more than anything to run an organization, to plan ahead on a large scale and to deal directly with people on the small scale.

Other people were not so happy, but that was the way things went and part of his job was to try to improve their dispositions.

But his basic goal, of course, was the greatest good for the most people—which meant that a minority was sure to be unhappy.

⟶⟶❦⟵⟵

He had been responsible for handling the case of Miss Scroop, the lesbian whom the FCP tests had revealed as fertile. She had announced that she was willing to have children. Her stipulations were that the conception must be brought about by artificial insemination and that she could legally be married to her lover, Miss Windsor.

The great furor over this climaxed in the eighth year after Clabb. *Time* (still a magazine and not a TV station at this time) ran three articles on the two women, giving Canute much favorable publicity. Miss Scroop's employer fired her when she made her announcement and, when Canute could not get the employer to take her back, he hired her as a secretary. The two women received many threatening letters—Canute himself received a hundred. (No telephone calls were made, since every phone automatically showed on its screen the number of the other instrument.) Some public-spirited citizens beat up Miss Scroop's ex-employer.

Miss Scroop insisted that she would not bear children unless she could be legally married. That the Illinois legislature immediately made this possible showed how public opinion had changed. No lawmaker in the state would have dared to propose such an enabling act a year earlier.

Ten months later Mrs. Windsor, as she now called herself, bore the first of five children. Jackson watched the interview as she left the hospital with the baby.

TV interviewer: "Mrs. Windsor, are you happy?"

Windsor: "Oh, very. My mate, Glenda, is also very happy."

Interviewer: "Is it true that you're planning to bring up your baby as a lesbian?"

Windsor: "You (censored), if I weren't holding my child I'd kick you right in the (censored). Get out of my way, you (censored) man, you!"

The interviewer had dared to say in public what many had said in private or in letters to the news media editors.

In her final interview with *Time* Mrs. Windsor stated that the child would be raised "properly."

"Of course, I was raised by two heterosexuals and look how I turned out. So who knows about Sappho?"

Eventually the two Windsors and the child left Busiris to live in Nova City, the Federal establishment outside Asheville, North Carolina. There they resided in a house some called palatial and there they were free of harassment.

The fertile nun, Sister Gratian, had been released from her vows on the condition she marry and have children. The only fertile man of her faith in Busiris became available when his wife died during childbirth. Mr. Bunding married Sister Gratian, who left him the day after their wedding night. She gave no reason and Mr. Bunding was speechless. Mrs. Bunding lived for a year in an apartment at the other end of town from her husband and then went to Nova City. However, she bore Mr. Bunding six children, all by artificial insemination. The church did not object to the procedure as long as the donor was her own husband.

———————

Nova City had been established by the Federal Government as a center for the "maintenance of the nation's greatest resources." Precedents had been set by several other countries, notably China, Japan, Indonesia, Israel, the United Arab Republic, Brazil and the U.S.S.R. These nations had made it mandatory for fertile women to bear at least seven times and substantial bonuses were awarded for each child. The U.S. Congress liberally funded Nova City and did its best to attract fertile couples to residence there. There were protests that the free and luxurious living for the fertiles was discriminatory. The reply, disseminated over the news media, was that not all discrimination was bad. Not if it helped humanity—and especially the United States of America—to survive.

Some radicals proposed that all nations agree to support a single international community where all the fertiles of the world could be gathered. This would form, in effect, a new state. The common language for its citizens would be the newly revised Esperanto or Loglan III—and in time all mankind would have rid itself of the problems and evils of national boundaries, nationalism and differing languages.

The idea sounded good to many, but it was, of course, impossible to get any nation to accept the concept as a workable reality. Each hung on to its own fertiles.

———————

San Marino, the tiny Italian-speaking nation, had one fertile. She and her husband and six children took the highest offer and migrated secretly to the United States to live in Nova City. Furious protests rose from other nations especially Italy, which had hoped to get her. The husband of the woman was sterile, but he showed a remarkable liberality in view of his faith and permitted his wife to have six more children by artificial insemination. Outcries were heard in the United States that the Federal Government was promoting immorality, but the majority of citizens seemed to approve. It was felt that the need to survive overrode conventional morality.

———————

The Republic of South Africa (in Year One) had 150 fertile white, 23 Asian and 271 black women. The Republic set up separate equivalents of Nova City for each of the three categories of persons. The Asian women all perished with husbands and children when their transport plane crashed en route to their establishment. A year later the 271 black women died when an ammunition dump next to the establishment exploded. The Republic officials made several explanations about why the dump had been set up next to the black "national resources." Neither the plane crash nor the explosion were ever proved to be anything but accidents. But the black population was enraged, and civil war—or a rebellion, depending upon whose side you were on—flamed. Before the whites finally stamped out the uprising, a raid on the white fertiles resulted in their massacre—only five survived. The black underground vowed to get these, but the five were smuggled out of the country and came to the U.S., which promised them the highest standard of living.

West Samoa began with four fertile women. This scarcity was common throughout the Polynesian area. Many South Pacific nations and territorial possessions did not have the critical minimum of fertiles needed to ensure the perpetuation of their human populations. A Greater Polynesian Confederation was advocated with all the fertiles relocated on Tahiti, the original homeland (according to some authorities). This was rejected by the nations owning the islands or having mandates over them. Nevertheless, all the fertile men and women of the South Pacific area were sneaked out of their homelands and established in West Samoa. (By now this practice was being called, among other things, wombnaping.) A war between England and the U.S. on one side—defending the Greater Polynesian Confederation—and the French and Chileans on the other side—they wanted their Polynesian fertiles back—seemed to be a possibility if the news media of the countries involved were to be believed.

The Polynesian experiment worked surprisingly well. The East African Bantu Union, formed for the purpose of putting together the fertiles of Zambia, Malawi, Kenya, Rwanda, Urubu, and Mozambique, failed. Tribal differences were too great to surmount—the fertiles eventually went back to their home territories and the Union broke up.

Canada was the world's second largest nation in area but had a population of only 21,100,000 in Year One. It had 1038 white, 13 Indian and four black fertiles. Every one of the Indians belonged to a different tribe. Of the blacks, one lived in Toronto, one in Quebec, one in Saskatoon and one in Vancouver. The 13 Canadian Indians invited the 33 fertile Amerinds in the United States to come live with them on the shore of the Great Slave Lake, where a new Indian nation would be started. The idea was that the small group would form the nucleus of a tribe that would eventually spread out into the North American wilderness. They would live much as had their pre-Columbian ancestors, except that they would have certain indispensable gadgets, of course.

The U.S. objected to its Indians leaving its territory (this was while it was defending the Polynesians' rights to leave theirs). The 33 Indians sneaked into Canada anyway and, while extradition proceedings were dragging, Canada and the U.S. merged into the United States of North America, the U.S.N.A. The newly created tribe—calling itself The First Men—adopted English as its common language. Many years later, when the tribe had expanded through the great land which had reverted to wilderness, it presented the curious phenomenon of Amerinds speaking English and named, because of their origin, Slavs. (Slav was the pronunciation of Slave, from The Great Slave Lake.)

July, Year Twenty

Busiris had lost 40,000 of its citizens, mostly to the graveyard. It had also gained fifty, but had lost them to Nova City. These were the children of the children who had been under sixteen in Year Zero, B.C. They had moved out with their parents. It was strange, Canute thought, to drive through the city and not see a single person under twenty. In fact, not many under thirty were visible.

The number of empty houses and vacant lots was beginning to be noticeable. The Government now tore down houses as soon as they became ownerless. The lots were turfed, planted with trees and flowers. They not only gave a parklike appearance to residential areas, but ensured that when the reexpanding population eventually arrived it would find a more welcoming vista than over grown ruins.

The long-range plan was to level all of the city gradually, step by step, death by death—one future day a visitor might never know that Busiris had stood here until he came to the stele in the middle of a forest. The stele, already in the project stage, would carry a brief record of the city's history. Even the cemeteries were planned for obsolescence—the wild would take them over when all the living had left.

Canute's grave would be lost with the others—his name, however, would be on the stele. "For all eternity," a government official had told him.

Canute had smiled. How many vanished monuments had been set up for all time? And how long did it take Time to prove that for all human artifacts there was no such thing as forever? Marble was only a little more enduring than bone—then it, too, went the way of all matter shaped by man.

The official had correctly interpreted Canute's smile. "But this stele will be of inertum—indestructible. It will last forever!"

Canute had shrugged. "But I will be dead and no children of mine will see my name."

One morning he drove through the South Side, ostensibly on an official checkup, actually just to take a drive. Twenty years ago the area had consisted of slums, tenements and Federal housing projects, breeding grounds of crime, disease and misery. Its habitable buildings, tenanted mostly by blacks but with a minority of poor whites, had needed maintenance. Its yards had been grass-less and littered with paper, cans, cigarette butts. Its driveways had been cluttered with rusty or torn-down cars. The uninhabitable buildings had stared through broken windows past obscene letterings and drawings.

Today no sign of the ghetto remained. The inhabitants had been moved into the better residential districts. All buildings had been razed, removed and replaced by grass and trees. The area was now bounded by a man-made lake, stocked with fish.

Protests had accompanied the changes and much conflict had arisen between those moved into choicer areas and people already living there. But the friction had not been as bad as had been expected and twenty years—and relative freedom from want—had reshaped the deghettoized into reasonable facsimiles of middle class citizenry. The misery and even bloodletting of two decades ago had been generally forgotten.

Jackson was thinking, as he drove his electric car slowly through the South Side, that Busiris had been lucky in its transitional procedures because it had had a small minority of poor people. The New York City metropolitan area, with its immense minorities, had not yet solved its problems. Nor would it until they were cut down to size even more than had been done. Its pre-decpop population had been 15,000,000. A normal death rate would not have made too radical a change in it, but the suicide and murder rates had increased greatly and the terrible August riots of twelve years ago had cost the area approximately 1,000,000 deaths. The burning of Harlem during the riots, the spreading of the fire to other areas, had resulted in 200,000 deaths in six days. The army, navy and national guard had taken over and a dispersion of the populace had been arranged, partly under Federal auspices.

In the general dispersion—the Second Diaspora some called it—Busiris had received 350 of the dispossessed. Most of these were of Puerto Rican descent. Canute had housed them where he could—in the emptied orphanages and grade schools, dwellings vacated but not yet torn down—and then he had fed them out, little by little, to various residential districts. He had easily found jobs for them— at that time a labor shortage had been a major problem. Their adaptation to a middle-sized Midwestern city had not been easy, however, and Canute, as a sort of ombudsman, had put in many weary hours trying to make them happy.

One of them had been Maria Gutierrez, a computer programmer, beautiful, dark-eyed, red-haired, in her early twenties. Canute's affair with her had begun during Jessica's final illness and after her death he had married Maria.

He was sure that the disparity in their ages would cause trouble, but meanwhile he was enjoying her, especially since she did not complain much about his seldom being at home. Maria had a low-keyed sexual desire. She responded quite satisfactorily but never complained about wanting more. All in all, she was a fine wife for a man in his middle years who was often tired from his labors.

Canute glanced into his rearview mirror and saw a steamwagon tailgating him. It bothered him to be followed so closely while he was taking a pleasure drive and he slowed to let the other driver pass. The car did pull around, but it suddenly cut in, forcing Canute to kick the brake pedal in all the way. The tires screeched as the steam engine quit and locked the four wheels. The hood of Canute's car rammed into the wrap-around bumper of the wagon.

The man who got out of the car looked familiar to Canute. But not until he saw the revolver did full recognition dawn. He was shocked. Twenty years had passed since the young fellow in the Volkswagen had tried to beat him into the parking slot at the Reywoods High School—the man looked older now, but the stubborn wrongness about him was the same. That wrongness, now emphasized by the pistol, had first jogged Canute's memory.

"What do you want?" Canute asked, feeling his insides coiling coldly. The muzzle of the pistol—a Colt .45 six-shooter, probably a hundred years old and a real collector's item—looked enormous.

"To pay you back," the man said and then he must have fired the pistol.

Canute awoke to pain, dimness and confusion more than once. Eventually he was fully awake in a hospital bed. One bullet, undoubtedly the first, had struck the side of his head a glancing blow. The second had gone into his chest at an angle and come out along the front of his breastbone. The third had pierced his right thigh.

"A police car came along, otherwise the maniac would have emptied his gun into you," the doctor said. "He fired at the police instead and they were forced to kill him."

"But why would he want to kill me?" Canute said. "The incident in the parking lot was minor—and happened twenty years ago."

"He's been in a Los Angeles mental hospital for ten years," the doctor said. "I've read the whole transcript. According to his psychiatrist, he has blamed you for his baby's death and his wife divorcing him. He claimed a bump the baby got when your cars collided caused the tumor that killed him. There is, of course, no evidence whatever that that's what happened—and in any case, the police records here show that he was responsible for that old accident. Anyway, he escaped six months ago. He stole the revolver and ammunition from a Dodge City museum on his way here. The police learned that a stranger was in town—"

"A stranger in town? Since when has it been illegal to be new in a town?"

"You're still not thinking clearly," the doctor said.

"Oh, yes," Canute said. He thought for a moment. "Yes, I see."

The police force had swelled enormously since Year Zero. Lister had insisted on enough manpower at local levels to keep down riots and help maintain full employment. The standards for the police had been raised at every level, local, state and Federal, and all levels were in constant communication with each other. The numbers of the police had been maintained despite the decline in population. Any policeman was likely to know everyone in his precincts and strangers were immediately spotted. It had become routine for motorized patrolmen to compare any stranger's features with mug shots and films transmitted over the car's phone. Los Angeles must have had Dutton's photos on the air.

The doctor left. When Canute awoke again a nurse was standing beside his bed. She was attractive and younger than Jackson Canute.

She smiled and said, "Good afternoon, Mr. Canute. I'm Amanda Tilkeson. How do you feel?"

"Better, after seeing you," he told her.

"Thank you, Mr. Canute. The sensors indicate you're in very good shape. You should be hungry."

"I am," he said.

"The roboserver will bring you your meal," she said. "But the aids will bring your supper.

"Good."

Canute watched her walk away. The hospital was so completely cybernated that one nurse could manage a whole floor. But Lister had said—no doubt a medical psychologist had written that particular speech—that cybernation was only an aid in hospital care and that the sick needed humans around.

———>•●•<———

Canute had written his autobiography in his off-moments during the past ten years. Publishing individual works was now the Government's business and Jackson had had no trouble getting his life story and thoughts into print. What would or would not sell no longer decided acceptance of a book. Lister had long ago announced publicly that he wanted "every voice in the land to be heard."

The Government could not, of course, print and distribute a million copies of every book submitted to it and it would have been undemocratic to set up committees of learned and distinguished critics to screen out the "bad" stuff. The problem had been tackled at first by printing cheap editions of every manuscript submitted, regardless of merit, and limiting the number of copies. Distribution had been through the "feedies" or Federal stores. The books had been given to those who asked for them. When the supply was gone no more books had been printed unless they had received a good rating by readers. About half of the readers had used the rating machines in the stores and about one-eighth of the books had been reprinted in larger editions and for wider distribution.

The system had soon proved unworkable—it was too happenstance. Many worthwhile works had been lost forever while trash survived. Critics had discussed books on television shows and often they had decided a book's fate. Sometimes the critics had had personal axes to grind. The situation had served, however, to define the problems and point up a need and soon Lister had had his top cyberneticists working on solutions.

They had come up with one.

Every citizen today was issued a number of linders. These, named after their inventor, George Linder, consisted of "books" thirty centimeters square by six centimeters thick and weighing thirty-two grams. Each contained, on delivery, ten thousand blank pages. The owner could then get from the feedie a cassette (the size of a match folder) containing, in coded electronic form, an entire book. He would plug the cassette into the back of the linder and connect the works to the household electric power source. With the book on a flat surface, he would rub the indicated spot on the cassette with his thumb or the end of a pencil and the linder would start operation. Minutes later, the cassette would trill and the owner could disconnect the power source. Opening the linder he would find the book he wished to read printed out, with illustrations in color.

When the owner was through with the book he could erase it. If he intended to read the particular work again he kept the cassette. Otherwise he returned the cassette. The linders were reusable almost indefinitely.

The cassettes could also be plugged into a TV adapter to display the contents of the book on the screen. A manual remote-control device regulated the speed of the display.

For the first time in history anybody who wanted to publish could do so within certain limits. The original printing of the work of any previously unpublished author was confined to fifty thousand cassettes. If there was a demand for more, the Government would fill it. Publishing credits entitling an author to larger printing accrued automatically and were based on reader demand.

———————

Canute's autobiography had been received well in Busiris but outside the city he was little known. Amanda Tilkeson, the nurse-technician, dropped into his hospital room now and then to discuss the book with him. She admired it very much. Canute did not really think much of its intrinsic interest or literary merits, but it was pleasant to have someone admire it. Maria had read it but had said that she had had difficulty getting through it. Canute discovered another bond between himself and Amanda. She was a fishing and boating nut, as was he—Maria hated to get out on the water—and they talked about water sports.

All in all, after the pain lessened he could get out of his cybernated bed into a cybernated wheelchair, Canute enjoyed the hospital stay. Maria, very much concerned at first, began to reveal a side of herself he had not seen before. She seemed to resent the rapport between Canute and Amanda—possibly she was remembering her own first meetings with him while he had still been married to Jessica.

She now said that the reason she had not liked his autobiography had been that it reminded her of how much he had neglected her. When he told her that it was news to him that she felt neglected at all she went into a tirade.

Don't give me that *jazz* about sacrificing yourself for others! You like what you're doing! You prefer working to being with me. I bore you. But your work doesn't. So you're being selfish—you're not doing what you do to help people. You couldn't care less for them."

"What's the difference?" he asked. "It's the results that count. "And whether I help all these people because I want to help or because I feel a compulsion to do this sort of work doesn't matter. I admit I'm selfish and shallow. So what? The local affairs run smoothly—people are taken care of and helped and I'm happy, regardless of my motives."

"Then why don't you care about making me happy?"

He was honestly puzzled and surprised, but he did not particularly care.

"If I sat around at home watching TV and discussing your problems in raising our dogs—then *I* would be unhappy. It's up to you to find something to keep yourself from being bored. I've asked you a thousand times to come down to work in the office."

"That makes me so tired I could vomit!"

She left him with a cold kiss on his cheek and a frown. Amanda came in shortly and, though she said nothing she acted as if she had been listening in on the intercom. Her expression was one of sympathy.

"If you got married again," he asked, "would you want to work or be a housewife?"

"Work," she said. "If I could have children—well, that would be different. I had one child just before Clabb. She's twenty-five now and sterile. But she's working in Nova City."

She stopped. A red light was pulsing on the instrument panel. Outside, the footsteps of a woman hurrying toward the room could he heard. A nurse entered.

"Mr. Guglielmo's dead!" she told Amanda. "And just a minute ago he seemed in fine health—"

She did not cry but she looked as if she would like to.

"He was such a good man!" she said. "Even if he was a rotten writer—"

Canute had never heard of the man.

"You just gave him a nice epitaph," he told the nurse. "Better that than the other way around."

April, Year Thirty-five

Busiris, Illinois, had a population of 100,000. Its youngest citizen was thirty-five years old, its oldest, 101. The death rate was accelerating as the median age rose. Materially man had "never had it so good," Lister's successor kept telling the U.S.N.A. This was true—yet the suicide rate, once stabilized, had again started to inch upward. Use of liquor and marihuana was on the rise—more and more citizens seemed to be committed to slow self-destruction. The

HSGs—hypersexogenics—were making superstuds and supermares of the older citizens. They sometimes suffered unfortunate side effects—heart failures or strokes. The Government had tried, not too vigorously, to take the HSGs off the market, but the resulting storm of protest forced the authorities to make them available again. Some citizens claimed that the Government did not really care—that it would just as soon kill off its older citizens as quickly as possible—but few paid any attention to this cynical reasoning.

Canute was sixty-three and feeling, at times, the old wounds from the South Side Park shooting. He still held the CONES chairmanship but had turned over most of his duties to younger members. Maria had died three years ago, possibly because of a dose of HSG she had taken, though the coroner said that this could not be proven. Canute had married Amanda Tilkeson after a decent interval.

Today he and Amanda were on a fishing trip. They had left home before dawn. He still lived in the mansion on Highview Drive though the place was becoming more of a problem than a pleasure. He was forced to do most of the painting, repairing, plumbing, wiring and so forth himself. The professional plumbers, electricians and painters were too few and to prone to go off on extended vacations. Their services could seldom be obtained. Canute had attended a homeowner's training school and had learned just about everything he needed to know to maintain a house—even so he had sealed off most of the mansion. He and Amanda contented themselves with about six rooms.

They drove before sunrise along the top of the bluff overlooking miles of the moonlit Illinois River, then descended. At the foot of the bluffs they cut across an area that had once been crowded with the modest homes of workers of the Earthmover Diesel Company. These were now gone—a young forest rose in their place. Canute took the river road to the Ivory Club, the members of which still kept their exclusiveness. He and Amanda set out on the river in his comfortable, steam-driven four-sleeper—they anchored on the other side of the river, away from all signs of civilization, and watched the sun come up over the hills.

The river was different from what it had been during mornings Canute remembered from his boyhood. The water was pure. He could look down into it for many feet and see the fish as the sun rose higher.

The stock was as it had been when the white man had first come here— he saw large river trout, pike and catfish.

He set out his lures and sat looking across the river, west and south, where the downtown section of Busiris had been—rather, still was. The city hall and jail, the Federal, state and city official buildings were there, but they were only two stories high and hidden by the tall trees. The high buildings—the old courthouse, the Busiris Life Insurance building, the Champlain Hotel, the Earthmover Diesel Building—had all been torn down. To go downtown was to go into another park.

"You know, Amanda," he said softly, "there are still people who curse Clabb. But he saved the world—he really did. If things had gone on as they were, with the expanding population and increasing pollution and breakdown of the economic and educational systems, mankind would have reverted to savagery. Some day, maybe, a statue will be erected to Clabb and he'll take his proper place in the history books."

"I wonder whatever happened to him," she said.

"He'd be eighty-six years old now, so he may be dead. But if he isn't he ought to know that he stands a chance of being ranked among the greatest— if not the greatest—at least by some people. With Lister next."

"I still don't like his having deprived me of having more children."

"Look at it this way," Canute argued. "He saved you the possibility of heartbreaks, of bitterness, of disappointment."

"My children would have loved me, taken care of me in my old age," she said.

"Don't get mad," he said. "But your children and you would probably have perished years ago. Or, if you had survived you'd be living in some stacked slum or wandering the Earth, looking for a chance to breathe. And you wouldn't have gotten any geriatric care, either. You'd be an arthritic, mostly toothless old woman instead of the beautiful and healthy, almost girlish woman you are."

Jackson knew by now how to make a wife happy.

On the way home he and Amanda passed a demolition rig taking down the old Williams mansion, which had been built a hundred and ten years ago. Dr. Williams and his wife had died within a few days of each other. The rig consisted of several big machines and one man who controlled everything through the console in his vehicle. He sat there, watching the machines work together.

April, Year Seventy

Of the four billion Earth population alive seventy years ago, 500 million remained. Several million might still be alive in another thirty years. In another thirty-five years, perhaps a dozen or so.

There were thirteen million who had not been alive when Clabb published his letter. The children of the fertiles had been having artificially induced twins, triplets and even quintuplets during the past twenty years, but this custom was tapering off. Why fill the world again faster than Nature desired?

Busiris had a population of 35,000, none of whom was under seventy years old. The town was being phased out and it was probable that it would have a zero number of citizenry in five years or less. More and more were needing hospital care and the "younger" ones just were not up to taking care of the older, even with the cybernated facilities available. Even computers—some said especially computers—broke down. Their electromechanical eyes and hands and feet failed and technicians and engineers were needed to repair them. There were few of these left in Busiris and outsiders were being brought in with increasing frequency to attend to emergencies.

The helpless aged were being moved to Chicago, where the Government—the youngest in the nation's history—had built a hospital-metropolis, already planned for obsolescence. In about fifteen years the hospital city itself would be a ghost town and exactly what was to be done with the superannuated phantoms roaming its corridors had not yet been decided. Probably the nonagenarians would be moved again, this time to Indianapolis. Illinois would then be even emptier of man than it had been when the pre-Columbians lived there. The roads were still being maintained by cybers tended by a small staff of septuagenarians under middle-aged supervisors—children of the fertiles and themselves fertile.

Canute, ninety-eight years old, sat in a cybernetic chair and watched TV through organ-bank eyes he had been given twenty years before. His hearing organs, his heart, many miles of veins and arteries, were plastic. His brain and circulatory system had been subjected for three years to a chemical that broke up and helped flush out the fatty deposits. Despite all these biological auxiliaries Canute felt that he was going to die any minute now. Something, somewhere in his body, had broken.

The President of the U.S.N.A. was speaking. He was only thirty years old. His face and head were clean-shaven, the style of the last twenty years for young men. He wore a black velvetone sleeveless shirt piped with gold and a knee-length canary-yellow kilt with embroidered red, white and blue chevrons and that was all. And he was—yes, he was proposing that the U.S.N.A. join the World Federation.

The concept of the World Federation had first been voiced by the premier of the SIND (Swedish, Icelandic, Norwegian, Danish) Union. The proposal, now endorsed by President Windom, was that within the next twenty years, since most of the pre-Clabbians would soon be dead, the post-Clabbians of the entire world migrate to a megalopolis to be built near Nice, France. Its citizens would have one nationality—Terran—and the language would be Loglan IV, the ancestor of the synthetic world language created in the middle twentieth century. From this megalopolis, to be named Terra City, the World Federation would expand outward and there would never again be more than one nation. New provinces would be created, but they would be part of the Commonwealth.

The surviving old people of all nations would be transported to a geriatric complex in Terra City as soon as facilities permitted.

President Windom did not stress this last—he did not wish to arouse the prejudices of the old citizens while they were still relatively numerous. One thing was obvious—the citizens of Terra City would be getting rid of the racial problem forever. It had, of course, already vanished to large extent—the fertiles had been encouraged to interbreed freely and their children had upped the tempo.

Windom himself would once have been called a black who was married to a white woman. Now few people used such terms. The World Federation planners envisioned a single race of Man, whose ancestors were of all the races.

Except the Amerinds of Canada, Canute thought, who would probably refuse to enter Terra City. And generations hence, when Europe, Africa, Asia, South America and Australia had been reoccupied by the expanding human race—what about North America? Once again it would be the property of the red man. What then? Would a highly civilized, highly cybernated society of the Terrans face a barbaric sylvan society of the Amerinds? War? Conquest again? Or would man by then have learned his lesson?

Was it a good sign that the youth of all the nations seemed so alien to its still surviving ancestors? The phenomenon was not unprecedented, though the generation gap, the communication gap, had never been so wide. Pre-Clabb and post-Clabb simply did not understand each other.

The national Government had long since been taken over by the post-Clabb people and President Windom's generation had stretched the gap further. All extra-Nova City citizens had been disenfranchised. They could elect state and local officials, but the Federal Government was forever out of their control.

Windom had declared four years ago that the old people no longer understood the young ones who had been raised and educated in Nova City. Disenfranchisement had followed. Many angry oldsters had raged about revolution, but the structure of their highly cybernated economy of abundance put them at the mercy of the central authority. Pressure on a button would cut off electric power anywhere in the nation. And nothing electromechanical would move. Besides, the oldsters had no weapons and were, to put it plainly, too old to act anyway.

The Nova Citizens and their counterparts the world over were said to be almost entirely free of mental illnesses and neuroses. They acted on a rational basis, were free of superstition and prejudice and had even rid themselves of the sexual jealousies that man had always prized as an integral part of his morality. Their society stressed total personal freedom among its members to cooperate in the enrichment of human experience and progress—whatever these meant.

Canute sat and half-dozed, dimly aware that the President had long ago quit speaking and that a comedy show and a documentary had followed and another of the many nostalgia programs was beginning. This one, it happened, was set in the year 1990.

Canute took a stimulator tablet and sat up to watch it. The nostalgia shows were more funny than the comedy shows. The year 1990, as Canute remembered it, was not something to get mushy or even slightly regretful about.

Two minutes passed and he was just beginning to chuckle at the commentary when suddenly the show was cut off.

Canute sat up still straighter. His heart began to hammer as he heard the news announcement. President Windom had just been shot and killed. The assassin had then killed himself. He had been a member of the President's inner circle of friends, though lately they had been known to have disagreed on certain policies and particularly on Presidential appointments. The assassin's wife had recently accepted—against her husband's wishes—a confidential White House post...

Canute settled down in his chair and laughed a little shrilly. His faith in the instability and corruptibility of human nature had been restored. There would be no supermen, no utopia. There would continue to be need for men like himself, unflappable, adaptable—men who could make a non-utopian society work simply by selfishly doing their jobs.

Not a thing wrong with a little selfishness, as he had once pointed out to Maria. Clabb had unselfishly destroyed a generation—and probably himself. Lister had selfishly teamed up with men like Jackson Canute to save what was left. Windom's assassination had been an equally unselfish act—it had destroyed the assassin. Somewhere a man was waiting to save himself—and quite incidentally his fellows—from this latest disaster.

Jackson closed his eyes. It gave him, the always rational man, satisfaction to know that mankind remained as capable of madness as ever.

Other men's madness gave sanity a chance...

Jackson Canute suddenly felt both human and invincible. *Play it cool,* he told himself, *and perhaps even when death comes...*

Fundamental Issue

First published in *Amazing Science Fiction,* Volume 50, Number 3, December 1976.

Phil's story uses satire to tear through the curtain and put on display the utter absurdity of over two hundred years of judicial nonsense that created the American legal system of today. Amazingly it could just as easily have been written yesterday and be just as effective. His use of acronyms such as LIFE and FRIG drives home the inanity of the modern governmental/judicial need for language manipulation through acronyms and high-minded obfuscation.

Phil does not have a particularly high regard for lawyers and in *Venus on the Half-Shell,* when left to run their own society, ended up locking everyone in prison; including themselves!

The science fiction story writer, Leo Queequeg Tincrowder (a distant cousin of Jonathan Swift Somers III), is Phil's own creation and was first introduced in "The Two Edged Gift," a section of Phil's *Stations of the Nightmare.*

"Stuck…"

"What did you say?"

Eldred A. Goll held up his hand for silence.

Christine closed her mouth.

"…will be delayed for an hour. Departure time is now 3:35. Passengers on Flight 395 will please report at Gate 23…"

"Oh, no! Not another hour!"

His wife looked at her wristwatch, though the big lobby clock was on the pillar directly before them.

"It's St. Louis time," he said. "Why don't you set your watch back two hours."

"I'm running on my time, not theirs."

"Would that were true."

He paced back and forth. The men, women, and children on the benches looked at him incuriously. He stroked his short, white, and bushy beard, grown during the month and a half in Hawaii and the Fiji islands. Christine had complained, though teasingly, that it scratched her face. She rather liked it now.

"You look like a United States Supreme Justice should look like," she had said. "Distinguished, full of years and wisdom. Not to mention something else," she added.

She was referring to what she delicately called his "affliction."

Nobody recognized him, though there had been much news media publicity about his marriage. Christine was a young woman. Only, *only* forty! She had been a babe in arms when he was thirty-one. She had just entered kindergarten when his first wife had died.

"Cradle-robber," she had called him during their honeymoon. She liked to tease, and he liked her for doing it. It had made him feel younger. But now he felt his age. He was seized, in more than one sense by the decision he must make. *The Decision*, as he pictured it in his mind. It was bright white, like the title of a movie. *The Decision*. Starring E. A. Goll and eight wise old men in black. With a cast of four hundred million.

No, a cast of five billion. This case was not the concern of one nation. Truly, the world was a global village. Spit to windward, and every person on Earth felt moisture.

But, and however—and there were always throngs of buts, ifs, howevers mixed with the whereases—he should not be considering the global reverberations. It was his duty—and he saw it clearly, didn't he?—to focus on one matter. The Constitution as it applied to the case.

Why, then, was he going to Watahee, New York, to see the situation for himself. What business did he have there? He had studied the documents, the statistics, the briefs everything that was expected, more than was expected.

He had all he had to know in his mind.

But it—the all—was stuck in his mind. It wouldn't budge. Probably this was because the all was not really the all. There was more. There was always more.

There were the human beings in Watahee who could be grievously affected by his decision. And there were the other people throughout the United States who would be affected just as profoundly. What moved in one place moved everything in other places. Throughout the world. No one smiled with the lips alone or cried with the eyes alone. The entire face, like a flag in the wind, rippled. The throat closed or opened. The heart slowed or raced. The glands were blocked or poured out stimuli or inhibitors. The whole body responded negatively or positively. Or some parts responded negatively; other parts, positively.

Sometimes, the reaction, though moving millions of substances invisibly within the body, froze the outer body. Stasis.

Christine said, "You look haggard, and your face is flushed. Come here. I want to feel your forehead."

He bent over. Her palm felt cool. He straightened up as she said, "You do feel *warm*. But you're not *burning* up. I think you have a low-grade fever."

"Proof I'm still alive," he said. "Not that I need it. Listen." He looked around. Nobody seemed to be listening. "I think I'm going to get some action."

"I hope so," she said. "But you've taken so much medicine you should be ready to explode. I think it's all those pills that are making you sick. If you'd just taken my advice..."

"Where would you get prune juice on Tonga-Tonga?" he said, trying to smile.

She seemed to be receding, to be dwindling.

She was no Alice who had taken a pill, however. On the contrary. *He* had swallowed the pill(s).

"Really, why won't you see a doctor?"

"Because I'm only temporarily indisposed. Because I'm due in Washington in five days. You know that. Because I want to go to Watahee first, and I won't be able to if I spend several days in bed."

He added, "I'll be gone a minute darling. I want to pick up a newspaper."

He returned with the bulky Sunday edition of the *Post-Dispatch* under his arm. He settled down by Christine saying, "Do you want any particular section?"

"Which one is the crossword puzzle in?"

This was the question-and-answer response, ritualized, repeated every morning at home. He didn't know why. Perhaps it was to keep the lines of communication open. When they were in Alexandria, she knew where the puzzle was. Its location never varied. Yet, he went through the business of looking at the index on the front page, noting that it was in section C on page 3.

Sometimes, he thought her passion for crossword puzzles was similar to that of a knight seeking the Holy Grail. No, that was a not quite correct metaphor. She was looking for The Word. Somewhere, in one of thousands of puzzles, she would find The Word. And all would become brightly illuminated. Then, she would know the meaning of life, its goal.

Or she would know its absurdity and its meaninglessness.

The danger in such quests was that it might be successful. The Grail could turn out to be only a rusty old chamberpot.

As for himself, he had quit looking for The Word since he was eighteen. No, not true. He must amend that. He had *found* The Word in The Law. The

Law was The Word. In the beginning was chaos and peril. But The Law—The Word—had imposed order and safety.

He sighed as he unfolded the comics section. Here were more Words. *Peanuts* and *The Wizard of Id* showed forth more wisdom than a hundred books of philosophy. Here, compressed in a small space, ready to uncoil to light-years' length, was real Wisdom. Laughter, sad or uproarious, at our human plight, at the state of the cosmos.

It was also therapy for him. Having chuckled at the illogical logic or logical illogicality of Charlie Brown and Gang and the egoistic inhabitants of the Kingdom of Id, he felt better. He was renewed. It was a hundred times better to read the comics for preparation for a stiff day in court than to scan the briefs.

Despite his fever and his painfully swollen abdomen, he smiled at this Sunday's theater of the absurd.

But page 2 of the A section hit him as if it were a club. It was three half-columns headed: LANDMARK DECISION STOPS FUSION-POWER DISPOSAL PLANT CONSTRUCTION.

Though he knew all the details of the story, he read the article.

"An upper New York utility is appealing to the U.S. Supreme Court a landmark ruling which has stopped construction of a combined fusion-power-sewage-trash disposal plant near Wahatee, N.Y.

"Officials of Gotham Interior Power stated yesterday, 'The 2-1 decision of the Court of Appeals for the 2nd Circuit seems to have substituted its judgement for that of the Nuclear Regulatory Commission in a highly technical area.'

"Meanwhile, citizens' groups and environmentalists saluted the court's decision in Schenectady to halt construction of the Wahatee complex.

"The court ruled Wednesday that the NRC violated its own guidelines by allowing the utility to build the $900,000,000, two thousand-megawatt plant near the Wahatee National Park and a city of more than 25,000 persons. The court called for an immediate halt to the complex's construction.

" 'The decision was a great victory for the public,' said James Mansard, attorney for the People's Interest Legal Limb, one of the groups seeking to close down the complex."

There was much more, though not a hundredth of what was actually involved.

Theoretically, the Wahatee project promised great things. It would end the electrical power shortage that had browned-out and blacked-out so much of the nation in the past decade. Also it would help to solve the ever-increasing problem of sewage and trash disposal.

The Laser-Ignited Fusion Energy (LIFE) system was new but had been thoroughly tested for three years in a pilot project. The experts had declared it safe.

Basically, and simply, it operated thus. A high-power laser beam ignited frozen pellets of deuterium-tritium (heavy hydrogen isotopes). At temperatures between 85 and 100 million Kelvin (hotter than the sun), the isotopes became a plasma or ionized gas.

The energy of the resultant fusion explosions was confined in a tritium-bleeding lithium "blanket" and channeled to generate electric power by means of conventional steam cycles.

One of the reactors would be used for destruction. It would receive a steady flow of sewage, plastic trash, acids and even nerve gases that would otherwise have to be dumped into the ocean or stored underground. They would be as destroyed as if they had been orbited into the sun.

These materials would be piped or transported through a gigantic pipe-truck-railroad system built by a private-enterprise combined with government aid. This system would give jobs to hundreds of thousands, boom the economy, and revitalize the dying railroads.

It all sounded extremely practical and absolutely necessary.

Yet, many people objected to it, and they have voiced their objections where they had the most effect—in the courts.

He grimaced, and stood up slowly. "If you'll pardon me, dear. I must venture to that bourne into which no woman is permitted."

She smiled slightly, seeming to move closer, to become larger. He wondered if he was swaying. He certainly felt light-headed.

"As long as you keep up that bridegroom's banter, you can't be deathly ill," she said. "But if you take too long, I'll send in someone after you."

"Don't tell him who I am."

He headed for the door marked MEN.

———⟫●⟪———

The racket was not deafening, but in his condition he found it upsetting.

He pushed in on the door and entered. He faced a blank wall, set there to keep passersby from seeing the occupants while the door was open, though they wouldn't have seen anything except men at a line of washbowls. The second entrance was on the left. He went through that, stepping slightly to one side to avoid bumping into a man who seemed to be in a hurry to get out.

The racket was coming from around the corner to the right. He stepped in and paused, catching, for a moment, a view of himself in the long mirror over the washbowls. He certainly looked tall and distinguished, resembling the great Justice Hughes.

A fine white powder flew through the air, swirling around him, settling down on his suit. He made a noise of disgust and brushed the white stuff from his lapels. What was going on?

Four men, wearing white overalls and yellow hardhats, were watching one man hacking away at the wall. On the back of the laborer in big orange letters was *Acme Destruct-Construct Co.*

A bomb!

A terrorist had hidden a bomb inside the men's room and then phoned the airport authorities!

Good sense reasserted itself immediately. If there was a bomb scare, the airport would be in an uproar of evacuation. And any wall-destruction would be done by airport and police personnel.

Nevertheless, his heart was beating hard. He felt even dizzier. He grabbed the edge of a bowl, feeling its wetness, and steadied himself. The worker stopped swinging his pickaxe, and for a minute there was a comparative silence. The worker turned to join his fellows in staring at him.

One of them, a short squat unshaven fellow with a huge jaw, said, "You okay, Pops?"

What would the man say if told that "Pops" was a U.S. Supreme Court Judge? Probably he would say nothing. He'd just laugh.

Why not? He was a "skilled" worker making an annual wage that equaled, if it did not exceed, the salary of the world-famous jurist. If he and the hardhat compared fringe benefits, he would be scratched at the starting post.

So much for the ever-growing egalitarian philosophy: I'm just as good as you. Or, to put it more realistically, I'm just as mediocre as you. Americans had extended the original premise that all were equal in the eyes of the law. They now insisted that all were equal in *every* respect. Which meant ignoring the obvious, which was that people were not born equal in intelligence, drive, temperament, or physical constitution.

But Uncle Sam would cancel Mother Nature's inequities through legislation. That was the American Dream.

He became aware that all five were staring at him. Not one had stepped forward, however. They were only mildly concerned, perhaps not even that. Nor were they going to get involved.

Yes. He was right. They had shuffled back up against the wall. They were removing themselves as far as possible from a contamination that they could not define but felt deeply. The feeling sprang from the Old Stone Age man, the savage that lived in every human being, that 6000 years of civilization could not kill.

If he had been one of their own, he'd be treated differently. If his hair wasn't so neatly cut, so short, his beard so well-trimmed, his clothes so expensive, he'd be immersed in their concern.

So much for the denial of the existence of class differences.

This was the Great American Schizophrenia.

Then the one who had spoken walked toward him, close enough so that Goll could see the broken veins in the eyes and smell the tobacco and cheap booze on his breath.

The face was harshly angled and tough, that of a professional wrestler who had made fame and fortune as the "villain," the "ugly," in the ring.

But the eyes were soft and so was the voice.

"You feeling sick, Pops?"

No, just slightly ashamed, Goll thought. I'm wrong again. The savage was there, alright. But savages could be sympathetic, empathetic, sometimes more so than their urban relatives. And this man was a human being, which meant that he was both savage and civilized. Sometimes, one "being" got the upper hand over the other; sometimes both expressed themselves at the same time. Or in bewildering irrational alternation.

"I'll be all right," he said. "Thanks. It's just a slight indisposition."

The softness died in the man's eyes. That "slight indisposition" marked him as one of the Others. There were visual and verbal clues to "class," and now the old man had flashed both.

The hardhat stepped back. Goll said, "I'll be okay." But it was too late. Nothing he could say or do now would reinstate that sudden concern. The two feet of physical separation might as well be a light-year.

The hardhat turned away, his broad back as expressive of indifference as his face. One of the men picked up a crowbar and began banging away at the wallboard with no great show of strength or enthusiasm. The others watched, ready to check him if he worked too swiftly. The tempo had been determined by many factors, one of which was making the job last as long as possible.

It was irrational for them to do so. Slow work meant fewer profits for their employer. The citizen who wanted to buy a new home couldn't afford it because of the towering cost of materials and labor. The decrease in homes bought and office buildings erected resulted in unemployment for the construction workers.

Surely, they could see that.

No, they couldn't.

"I'll get mine, Jack."

It was stupid and selfish.

But then—they'd had good teachers. The owners of industries, their employers, had shown them the way.

And why was he considering such things? They had nothing to do with the Decision, the law as limned in the light of the Constitution. He was sick.

———⟫●⟪———

At that moment, the door swung open. A group of men—what else?— burst in, talking loudly, laughing. They were young, exuberant, and very tall. A couple were human sky-scrapers.

Obviously, they were basketball players on their way to or coming from a game. If it was the latter, they'd won. He'd seen too many teams in airports on their way home, anything but conquering heroes. They were always glum, silent, brooding self-reproachful. *If only I hadn't missed that free throw...*

The youngsters lined up. The two tallest—the black must be at least six-foot-nine—were side by side. They looked down, cracking jokes that surely must have originated in the Old Stone Age. The white laughed loudly and said, "Hey, everybody! Get this! Another myth destroyed!"

The black laughed, showing huge white teeth, and slapped the white on the back with his free hand.

"Don't jive me, man! You know I was out in the cold longer than you. Wait'll it warms up. Then you'll see Saskatoon, Saskatchewan!"

"Where'd you get them googly blue eyes!" a black at the end of the line shouted.

Though he felt even a little warmer and dizzier, though the cramps were hurting some, Goll smiled. An Arab who had just emerged from a stall and was now washing his hands—with particular care to the left—was eavesdropping. He looked puzzled. He might be very fluent in American English, but the punchline references would be obscure. He wasn't native-born and so was unacquainted with the "dirty" jokes endemic among the male population—not to mention the female.

As he walked slowly past them, he considered the change in times, in attitudes. It had only been a little over two decades, yet it seemed far in the past. WHITE ONLY. COLORED. They did not mean what they said. If you were a Nigerian potentate or diplomat, blacker than most America blacks, dressed in flowing robes, you could enter the WHITE ONLY. The sign should have said: WHITE AND NON-AMERICAN COLORED ONLY.

The tabu markers had gone down, not without terror and bloodshed. First, at the airports and railroads and bus depots. Uncle Sam had jurisdiction over interstate commerce. "Federal interference" many called it. But even Eishenhower, not by any means known as a nigger-lover, "seed his duty and done it." As President of the United States, he had to execute, to enforce, the National Law. And so, Little Rock. And so, thousands of little and big Little Rocks.

The Law was above prejudice and persecution. Or it was supposed to be. No rich murderer, however, had gone to the death cell. Money talks. The logical thing to do was to make sure that money did not talk, that wealthy murderers were executed. But that seemed impossible. So, the illogical triumphed. Nobody, rich or poor, was to be hung or gassed.

Well, "nobody" wasn't quite right. A person who killed a president or a federal policeman while he was on duty could be executed. But that would change. Wasn't John Doe, as valuable in the eyes of God, and of democracy, as the head of the nation?

The Constitution. That greatest organ of state fashioned by men. An organ organic. Fixed in form but adaptive in function. A capacity for growth inherent in its structure. In 1896 the nine old men in black had ruled (*Plessy v. Ferguson*) that "separate but equal" facilities satisfied the requirements of the 14th amendment (1868).

That was that. Or so it seemed.

But one generation dies, and the next doesn't see things through the same prism. The light shifts in intensity and color when the refractive instrument is turned. The light is the same as before, but now it's seen differently.

And so, the nine old men in black—no longer the same old men though the color of the robes was unchanged—corrected the errors of their predecessors. They ruled (*Brown v. Board of Education*) that states that segregated white and Negro children in the public schools had violated the Constitution.

In a few months he and his eight colleagues would be sitting upon another case. *The Prophet v. State of California.* The First Amendment provided that Congress would make no law respecting an establishment of religion, or prohibiting the free exercise thereof. This had not been construed to protect immoral acts practiced within a religion. Thus, polygamy was licentious and so illegal. But the cult of *The Temple of the True God* claimed that polygamy was a vital part of their religion. When its founder, *The Prophet* (this was his legal name), was arrested, he had hired the best lawyers in California. Everybody had supposed that the case would be thrown out of the state supreme court, but it had been passed on up. Goll had hoped that the Apellate Court would stop it. No, the buck was passed again, though the U.S. Supreme Court could refuse to accept the appeal. Goll himself, however much he dreaded its consideration, felt that he should do so. And, surprisingly, so did his colleagues. Though they may have had different motives than he.

222 PHILIP JOSÉ FARMER

Twenty years ago the case would have been decided at the lower level, and The Prophet would be in jail by now. But the Zeitgeist, the spirit of the times, had changed swiftly. There were so many people living without benefit of clergy, so much group sex going on. At least, they'll be married was the most common opinion in a recent national survey.

The opinion of the majority of citizens must not be an influence. The only issue was the correct interpretation of the Constitution.

And so now what had once been a dead issue, buried for all time, had crawled out of the grave.

The banging on the wall became more noisy; the voices of the young men died. The cramps, gurglings, the rumblings within increased. He was in a near panic. After all this time, a sudden urgency. No doubt it had been brought about more by psychology than physiology. When the way was open, it was closed. Check and balance. Now that the way was closed, it was open. Check and balance.

The door to a free stall swung out. Reprieve. He hesitated. It was difficult to find a clean public restroom almost anywhere. Americans were supposed to be the most sanitation-conscious people on Earth. They were not, as anyone who had visited Japan knew. If one judged by the state of its public restrooms, he would conclude that the United States was inhabited by swine. This indictment would include the restrooms of many of the posh restaurants. How many times had he gone into a stall and recoiled with repulsion? The recent occupant of this cubicle had charged out as if ashamed of his behavior or as if an emergency demanded he break all laws of common decency to get to it. He didn't even have time to press on the flush valve. And the seat and the floor would look as if a chimpanzee had lived in the enclosure. The recent occupant would disdain to wash his hands. He would go swiftly to his emergency, spreading disease or its potentialities wherever he went. On dollar bills, coins, gum and cigarette machine pushbuttons, doorknobs, while shaking hands, and so on and so on.

There had been over two hundred years of public education in this country, with special stress of the findings of Pasteur. Yet at least half the citizens acted as if unaware of the linkage between germs and disease.

The culprits were not confined to the "poor." Not by any means. Goll knew a number of senators and big business executives who omitted washing their hands after excreting—unless someone they knew was observing them. Not always then. They acted as if they, personally could not be dirty. Others, yes. But not they. Bacteria died on contact with them. They sweat a sort of holy water which rendered them always pure. Immaculate deception.

As for the great "unwashed," the ghetto dwellers, the rednecks, the lower middle class, they just didn't care. They'd lived with dirt from birth; it was their natural environment. Try and get a landlord to repair the broken plumbing or to gas the cockroaches. Just try.

On the other hand, the landlord maintained that to fix the plumbing and exterminate the vermin was waste of money. In a short time, the tenants would have filled the pipes with rags—too poor to buy toilet paper or they'd rather spend their money on lottery tickets or beer—and the filth would quickly accumulate and bring the cockroaches and rats in.

This was true. But it was a vicious circle, and no one knew the point at which the circle had first been drawn. And no one knew how to break it. Or really cared.

Goll hesitated. He dreaded to enter the filthy chamber, but he felt moved to do so. While he stood there, he lost his chance. A hand reached past him, banged palm up against the door, and banged it hard against the inner wall. If anyone had been sitting there, leaning forward contemplatively, he would have suffered an injury on the head.

Goll was startled. The tall, thin, distinguished gray-haired man was U.S. Senator Thomas Roffe. Evidently he was in such a hurry that he hadn't looked at his long acquaintance, Chief Justice E. A. Goll. No, that wasn't it. The beard was a successful disguise.

He was out of luck for sure. And, knowing this, he felt a surge of distress.

The silvery tip of Roffe's head was visible above the top of the door. It was motionless for a moment. Was he also contemplating with repulsion the spoor of a citizen, perhaps one of his own constituents? Was he about to charge out with the same reckless inconsideration? Would he look around desperately, then perhaps recognize Goll?

No. The top of the head moved back, and a hand holding a tilted flat bottle rose into view. Its amber liquid content diminished rapidly.

The senator's need was not what Goll had first thought. It was no secret in Washington that Roffe was an alcoholic. Nor was it a matter of particular comment or concern. He was just one of the crowd, since there were more problem drinkers in Congress, proportionately, then in any other profession. Or, for that matter, any sector of society.

"The hand that tilts the bottle turns the wheel of state."

Roffe was thirsty, but Roffe was not going to be caught drinking in the cocktail bar upstairs. He had a public image to preserve. He also had a private image. Ten to one, Goll thought, Roffe's wife was standing in the corridor, waiting for her husband. A member of the W.C.T.U., she kept a close eye on her husband. But, like all drunkards, he knew a hundred places of concealment and refuge.

The door near him swung open, and a man walked out. At least the fellow had had the decency to flush. Goll put a quarter in the slot and entered. After some laying on of paper protection—throwaway armor, he thought—he settled down. His groan was half-pain, half-anticipatory relief, like a hen hopping to lay an outsize egg. Here he was within his nest, though the world clamored and howled outside. The banging and shouting of the workers at the wall, the chatter and laughter of a new influx of invaders just off a plane, all these beat around him.

But he had great powers of concentration. At least, in his normal state he did. Now, the slight fever, the dizziness, the sense that time and distance were somehow stretched out—like taffy made from a gummy poison—and the fist closing and opening within him, these distracted him.

He closed his eyes, and as if it were on a screen saw:

PREAMBLE
We the people of the United States, in order to form a more perfect Union…
"…more perfect Union…"

Either a thing was perfect or it was imperfect. It couldn't be "more perfect."

How could the founding fathers, masters of the English language, have started off with the wrong, the ungrammatical, foot?

Easily explained. The late eighteenth century had not as yet fallen prey to the pedants. Samuel Johnson and Dryden had not managed to convince the schoolteachers and the university academics that there was a "right" and a "wrong" English. It was perfectly acceptable in 1787 to write "more perfect." Just as it was acceptable for Shakespeare to declare that this was "the most unkindest cut of all." It was the spirit, not the grammar, that counted.

It was a wonder that the academics hadn't tried to rewrite the Preamble and Shakespeare. They must have thought of it but hadn't dared tamper with near-sacred works.

Somebody spoke just outside his door, and he brought himself back to his subject with a jerk. Had he almost fallen asleep? Or had the feverishness sneaked up on him?

He looked through the thin crack between door and wall. He wasn't mistaken. That *was* the voice of Omness. Omness, the founder and executive president of W. H. Omness Realty Enterprises. And that was a slice of his profile, thin, but enough to identify him for sure. Goll had seen him twice on the national news. First, when Omness was under investigation because of a suit brought against him by a homeowners' group. The charge: one of Omness' companies, Famous Realty & Investment Gains, had built a vast tract development on Wahatee with shoddy materials and without due consideration for the mud slides resulting from spring rains. Also, his company had failed to report correctly the dividends due the homeowners. They were supposed to reap a share of the profits, a gimmick that had seduced the buyers by the thousands. But the setup was so complicated that no one, not even the federal auditors, could make sense of it.

Second, Omness was suspected of violating the antitrust act. Investigation had disclosed, so far, that he controlled over half of the realty, savings and loan companies, and construction industries in New England, New York, and New Jersey. All through dummy corporations, of course.

It was a mess, Goll thought. But then, wasn't it always?

And what was Omness doing here? The answer wasn't as obvious as it seemed.

For one thing, a large attaché case was leaning against the wall by his legs.

Goll couldn't see the other people, but Omness wouldn't be talking to himself.

Goll leaned forward, turned the locking knob, and pushed the door slightly ajar.

Omness was walking away, giving Goll a full view of that cherubic profile. A chubby jolly man, that Omness, inspiring confidence and liking.

And there was Senator T. Roffe standing by the case, not looking at it, swaying slightly, blinking.

Omness disappeared around the corner into the crowd and the clamor and banging.

Goll closed the door and turned the knob. Roffe had turned his head toward him. If he thought someone was observing him, he would automatically suspect a government agent was shadowing him.

Befuddled as he was, he would know enough to walk out without touching that case. That is, he would if it contained what Goll thought it did. He could be wrong. Omness might have forgotten it; it might contain only underwear and toilet equipment.

It might not even be Omness' property.

He looked through the crack again. Roffe had moved closer to the case. The front part of his flushed, bug-eyed profile was visible. It revolved and he was facing in the opposite direction. He reached into his coat and, yes, of course, he was bringing the flask out again. And the rest of the bourbon was going down. He was nerving himself to the next step, uncaring if anybody saw him boozing.

Goll's view was cut off for a moment. A short squat dark man, clad in an Army jacket with faded corporal's stripes, a red-and-white checked shirt, dirty green levis, and dirty tennis shoes, had passed by. The relatively light skin and straight black hair and the hawkish profile were those of an East Coast Indian. Probably he was an Iroquois. What was he doing in St. Louis? High steel work, perhaps. If he was working, that is. The construction industry was in a slump.

Goll continued staring through the crack. Roffe was gone. Was he mistaken? The furtive transaction might be all in his mind, the case belonged to some forgetful harassed traveler. Or—? It contained a bomb...?

No. Surely not. A terrorist would leave his explosives where it would be difficult to locate. That is, he/she would if he/she were anywhere near rational.

Goll was seized with cramps. Terror and panic were moving him in no mysterious way, doing what mere anxiety could not do. At any other time, it would have been more than welcome. But it was keeping him from fleeing at once. He could not leave, though survival demanded it. The loss of dignity, the humiliation, the disgrace, were hands holding him down.

But if that did indeed hold a bomb...

He relaxed, and the gurgling and cramps died. He even managed to smile slightly. He had allowed his fevered imagination to run away with him. There was no evidence that the case held a bomb. Not the slightest. And yet he, who ordered his mind his life, around evidence, had abandoned in one moment of fear all his principles. Coolness, calmness, meticulously careful calculation, had fallen away from him.

He looked through the crack again. Roffe was back, standing by the case, looking around rather stupidly. Was that supposed to be an expression of innocence?

Suddenly, a brown hand swooped into his field of vision. It closed on the handle of the case. The case was lifted. The Indian flashed by, leaving Roffe startled, frozen, and helpless.

Roffe's eyes were bugging even more. He opened his mouth as if to call out. For a moment, his protruding eyes and gaping jaws made him look like one of Goll's pet goldfish. Where a fish sucked in water, Roffe was sucking in agony.

Would he dare raise a cry after the thief?

No, he wouldn't. He wasn't that drunk. He had to stand there, undoubtedly dying within from frustration and rage. There went—how much? How big a bribe would Omness pay Roffe? Fifty thousand dollars? No, that would have been a fairly large payoff for a project of the magnitude of the Wahatee plant a few years ago. But inflation has raised everything, including bribes. It might have held a hundred thousand, perhaps two to three hundred thousand dollars.

What would the thief think, how react, when he opened the case? He'd be expecting to find some shaving equipment, some clothes he could sell for a few dollars. Would he be frightened away by the largeness of the amount, think he'd intercepted a courier case in a Mafia drop-off? Would he grab a few hundred dollars and abandon the rest in a garbage can? Or would he drop dead from a heart attack?

That was his worry. Goll himself had enough to consider in his case. He had witnessed two crimes, and yet he could do nothing about it. He must keep silent. He, a Supreme Court Justice, could not tell anyone about it.

It wasn't just that it would be degrading and humiliating to reveal the circumstances. The news media would make a big joke of that; the public would have a fine time laughing at him. He could imagine the remarks, the dirty stories arising from the incident.

No. It wasn't that. Regardless of what kind of figure he would make, he would give his testimony. He would not draw back. That is, if he had any evidence to give. But he did not.

There was not the slightest proof that Omness had owned the case. The senator had made no move to pick it up. Undoubtedly, he had intended to do so. Otherwise, why would he have looked so stricken when the Indian snatched it?

A moment later, he heard a thump and looking out saw the senator lying, on the floor, face up. Men quickly, crowded around him. Goll stayed where he was. He couldn't help Roffe. If he came out, he might be recognized, and too many would wonder why a supreme court justice and a very influential senator happened to be in the same men's room, especially if the case did contain money and did come to the authorities' attention. There was nothing to be proved, but people would wonder if there was some sort of collusion between them. No one would believe that it was just a coincidence. Omness could deny having been in the men's room.

The attendants came and hauled the unconscious Roffe off on a stretcher. From the remarks of one, Roffe's heart was still beating. It was likely, Goll thought, that the senator had suffered a stroke. Whether it was caused by Roffe's age and excessive drinking or reaction to the theft—or both—no one would ever know.

Goll's mind and legs felt numb. He'd been too long in a mental and physical stasis.

He stood up and, leaning against the door with one hand, moved his legs. Pain shot through his legs as the blood stirred. The sounds of destruction, halted during the uproar over Roffe, broke out again. He did some shallow kneebends and then resumed his position, the archaic attitude.

Why didn't he give up, quit trying?

No, he wasn't one to quit. Beside there were indications that if he stuck to the task...

Two men, youths by their voices, were standing near the door. They were talking loudly, enabling him to hear snatches of what they said through the bang and rip of the destruction.

"...science-fiction book...by Leo Queequeg Tincrowder...short stories... new...for the bicentennial edition...yeah, I like him though I don't always understand...listen, you gotta read this one...what?...*Columbia Takes A Constitutional*...mean?...you know Constitutional!...taking a walk for your health...you haven't?...well, anyway, haw! haw!...mad scientist...yeah, I know...cliché...but Tincrowder...clichés in a new light...so, this scientist runs the Constitution through a computer...no, he didn't just drop it into the slot...punched the buttons...

"Then...haw! haw! the data's fed by the computer into a protein machine...what?...so the Constitution can be made flesh, it's turned into a real living human being...

"And the mad scientist calls her Columbia, see? What else? She's beautiful, statuesque...no, she doesn't carry a torch...living embodiment of the ideal America...goes for a walk...strolling in Central Park, see, that's where the constitutional comes in...look, Tincrowder always has double, sometimes triple meanings...

"So, Columbia walks through Central Park. And she's mugged and raped! Haw, haw!

"Oh, oh, someone's through. See you, Jack."

Goll had laughed at the ending of the story, but as he thought about it, he got angry. It was easy to criticize, to condemn America. Easy because there was so much that needed criticizing and condemning. God knew that; man knew that. America had been violated, raped, by its citizens. In the beginning was a vast land with seemingly inexhaustible riches. Use them up, there's always more. The Garden of Eden has no limits.

At the same time, citizen had violated, raped, citizen. The rich had exploited the poor, using violence, mainly through the police, to enforce the exploitation.

Slavery of the black wasn't the only open sore on the fair face of Columbia. The factories and the coal mines of the North were forms of slavery, as evil as and more insidious than its Southern counterpart.

But there was the Constitution, a device created by our Founding Fathers to establish and enforce justice and opportunity and the pursuit of happiness. (Though happiness was wisely not defined.) Many of the Fathers had been slave-owners, and those that weren't were not averse to exploiting the poor.

But there was the Constitution, the statement of the ideal, written by themselves. They had not dreamed that their creation was the instrument which would free the slaves (though it would put them in a worse form of slavery). Nor that it would then give ex-slaves and the exploited poor and exploited women a chance for freedom.

The Constitution was said to be the most nearly perfect document of state ever conceived. It was said to be self-regulating.

Goll thought that the first statement was true. The second was false. The Constitution was not self-regulating. It did not operate like a positive-feedback self-maintaining, self-powered, self-correcting servo-mechanism-computer.

It had to be operated by people. It was there, ready to be used. But it wouldn't work unless people used it. And there were too many who had ignored and were ignoring it. Or using it (for a time, at least) for their own selfish purposes. But when the persecuted, the exploited, felt that the machine wasn't working properly, then they could make sure that it was. Despite all attempts to block them, they could get to the control panel and could get the proper buttons punched. And then the machine started up, and the regulating, the correcting, began.

The control panel was, in a sense, the U.S. Supreme Court.

The discrepancy between the ideal (as stated by the Constitution) and the actual (America as it was) was often great. Sometimes, seemingly unbridgeable.

And it took time, oh, so much time, to force the ideal and the actual closer, closer, never quite bringing it together.

Meanwhile, hundred of thousands, millions, suffered and died.

But the old Adam and Eve had always been in humankind and always would be. Americans were not a separate species; there was as much of "original sin" or "Old Nick" in Americans as in any other nationality. But no more than in others.

The Constitution was designed to inhibit the old Adam/Eve and to protect the vulnerable. In one sense, it was a vaccine against evil. One which, however, required frequent booster shots.

Goll groaned then as body and mind strained.

Was the Wahatee case responsible for both blockages? Cause and effect were subtle, especially in a person's body.

The project would combine atomic power and sewage-trash disposal. It would provide electrical power to a large part of central and upper New York. Eventually, it would power half of New York City. And the complex would receive through a gigantic pipe system a vast amount of the metropolis' sewage and via trucks and railroads vast quantities of unbiodegradable trash.

But what if there was an accident? LIFE had been tried out in a pilot project for three years, and it had functioned one hundred percent. But that was no guarantee that it was malfunction—or accident—proof.

Goll remembered a 1974 case. The operators at a Lake Michigan-located nuclear power fission plant were transferring slightly radioactive water from one tank to another. The tank being filled overflowed, spilling the radioactive water onto the ground.

Investigation revealed that the electronic systems that were supposed to flood the reactor with cooling water in such an emergency had not operated properly.

Some electrical wires had been mistakenly connected in reverse.

Human error. Human error resulted in human tragedy, sometimes on a large scale.

That same year, more than 1400 "abnormal occurrences," as the NRC termed it, had occurred. Last year, there had been more than 1800 "abnormal occurrences." Only seven of these were, however, "directly significant" to safe reactor operation or radiation release. And no injuries or property damage had occurred.

There had been 929 cases which constituted a violation of federal technical standards.

To ensure a "minimum casualty list," the NRC had decreed that no nuclear plant could be built within two miles of cities with a population of 25,000 or more.

Gotham Interior Power had complied. When it started building its plant, the town of Wahatee, located a mile away, had only 9,000 inhabitants. Then, as should have been foreseen, workers and their families moved in. And Wahatee had a population of 35,000 now and was growing daily.

Most of the 35,000 were out of work at the present. And they would continue to be so unless the Appellate Court decision was reversed.

They'd have to move away to look for other jobs.

That meant that the houses they'd purchased from Omness' company would go back to it. And Omness could not resell them. He'd suffer a staggering loss.

Never mind that his company was presently under investigation for using shoddy materials. That had nothing to do with this case.

Besides, though the houses were poorly constructed, their purchasers were getting them cheap. And their houses were being steam-heated at a very low price. The water used for cooling the nuclear plant was piped directly to them in its resultant hot state and the electricity was provided at a low rate by the plant. These two features were selling points advertised by Omness.

Forget all that, Goll told himself. Forget that—possibly—Omness is bribing Roffe and no telling how many other people. At least, he isn't putting poor materials or unsafe construction into the plant. He wouldn't dare do that even if he weren't being watched by the federal inspectors.

All other things, hanky-panky or humanitarian, had to be put aside.

Under the Atomic Energy Act of 1954, the AEC (then the regulatory organ), could not issue a construction permit if it would be "inimical to...the health and safety of the public."

Both the administrative and technical staffs of the NRC stated that the Wahatee plant was safe.

Goll had studied its report and agreed that it was safe—if it operated as it was supposed to do.

If it did not, then a major accident might result, which would mean a major catastrophe. The city of Wahatee and the Wahatee National Park tourists, numbering 12,000 in any one day during the summer, might be killed.

But no nuclear plant had so far blown up.

It was true that the LIFE generator was not nuclear. Its principle of operation was different. Yet it had been tested, and the NRC had passed on its reliability. But what kind of pressure might have been put on the official to declare for its reliability?

That was why he had decided to go to the area itself to inspect it and to talk to the people involved. The people would not be just the officials; they would include the People, the citizens of the town itself.

Sometimes, he thought of the Supreme Court, yes, admit it, of himself, as a giant eagle hovering in the sky. Like the eagle-spirit of some of the western Indian tribes. A protecting spirit, a father eagle. Soaring high up there, keeping a fierce and paternal eye upon his wards below.

He was the embodiment of the impartiality and the majesty of The Law.

He had to smile at this thought now. Consider his circumstances. He was anything but an eagle swooping, a spirit soaring. He was human, and at this moment in one of those comical or disgusting—depending on the viewpoint—postures inescapable to humankind.

But the twofold, or bipartisan, struggle within himself was real and relevant to the issue. Never mind the particular physical situation.

He was caught in a bind, in a tension between two conflicting demands. Whichever side he pondered had both advantages and disadvantages, like everything else in life. Even the conservation group fighting the construction of the complex was in a contradictory position. It had opposed the plant because of the possible danger of radiation and implosion to the people in the area. At the same time, it had had to admit that the LIFE generator could eliminate half of the pollution choking this nation, not to mention the Atlantic and Pacific oceans.

We the People
Of the United States, in Order...to promote the general welfare...
And what, in this case, would promote the general welfare?

Voices reached him, gently parting the curtain he had put up between himself and the outside. The sound of whirling water partly drowned them, but he recognized them as those of the two youths. The one had just left the stall next door; the other had apparently been waiting for him.

"...reading this short story by Tincrowder while you were on duty...says Cousteau predicted the oceans'd be dead within fifty years...now...data's all in...he's right...nothing being done about it...oil from crankcases...thrown away...spills...sulphuric, nitric acids...all draining down sewers...rivers... seas...junk, crap, plastics like you wouldn't believe...yeah?...so...when oceans die, eighty percent of our oxygen factory's dead...not with a bang, a whimper... cough...go blue in the face and choke..."

The gulping noise increased at the same time there was a lull in the hammering and screeching around the corner.

"He's only a science-fiction writer," one youth said. "What does he know? Science-fiction writers don't have a good track record when it comes to predicting."

"It isn't their function to predict accurately," the other said, a defensive tone in his voice. "They speculate about the future; they invent every possible kind of future. Anyway, this death-of-the-oceans-bit isn't fiction anymore. It's straight scientific extrapolation. Unless we do something about it, there won't be any future. Not for us or our kids, you can bet on that."

"Then it's time we quit regarding the future as a plaything for science-fiction writers and readers," the first said gravely. "It's time the lawmakers take over and regulate the future."

"With their track record?" the second said. "Besides, even if the legislators knew anything about science, which most of them don't, they won't or can't do anything unless the public wants them to do it. And John Doe and Mary Roe ain't going to worry about it until it's too late."

There was silence for a moment, punctuated by a crash from the front part of the room. Somebody bellowed in anger; it sounded like one of the hardhats. There was some cursing, then the room became relatively quite again.

Goll heard a match scraping. One of the youths had lit up a cigarette.

"Yeah," one said. "You're always talking about pollution and how dumb the public is about it. But here you are, smoking, personally polluting yourself. That's dumb, Bill, dumb. You know what's going to happen to you personally, not too far in the future, if you don't quit smoking. Yet you won't. So how can you expect Mr. and Mrs. Enmasse to take a long-range view of something that they think doesn't affect them personally? They know what's going to happen, what's been predicted, anyway, if we don't quit messing up the world. But that's only relevant to the Other Guy, the one that lives someplace else. It can't happen here, not to me. I'm okay, Jack."

"Oh, let's go," the other said. "What're we hanging around here for? Talk about your pollution, haw, haw!"

Still talking, they left.

It was as if they had provided the touchstone, or the key, or call it what you will, Goll thought. Within a short, though painful, minute, he was free. Free and open, he thought, chuckling weakly to himself. He no longer felt feverish or blocked, physically or mentally.

It was "general Welfare" that counted. Not just that of the people of the United States but of all peoples, though The Law decreed that that of the United States must come first. And general Welfare was a broader, or more extensive, term than the Founding Fathers could have dreamed of. Yet, in their unconscious wisdom, they had anticipated future requirements. *The general Welfare* did not just imply the immediate future, the short-range welfare. It implied the long-range effects of promotions for the future.

Whatever dangers the LIFE generator-destroyer threatened, it was vitally necessary. The possible—local catastrophes—had to be balanced against the inevitable—worldwide catastrophe.

Never mind that Omness and others of his breed were cheating wherever possible, piling one fortune on top of another as if multimillions of dollars would make them immortal. The evil they did must be balanced against the good. Though their motives were bad, the beneficial effects outweighed by far the malignant.

Indeed, if it weren't for men like Omness, the energetic, aggressive, often vicious, schemers, conspirators, builders, amalgamators, call them what you will, not much would get done for the general Welfare.

Well, maybe that was an exaggeration, and, like most statements, required numerous qualifiers if the truth were to be expressed.

In essence, it was true.

And there was always The Law, as interpreted by the Constitution, to adjust, to regulate, to correct malfunctions.

Goll felt much better, much stronger, now that he knew what his decision would be.

Of course, he was only one of nine. But he was sure that the majority would agree with him. In one way or another, in the complicated yet basically simple ways that move people, his colleagues would arrive at the same decision.

He walked around the corner to the washbowls. And he stopped, staring.

The wall was down, and a rough passageway had been cleared through various obstructions, leaving a view of the room beyond. In it, several women stood by a line of washbowls, staring at him and the hardhats.

Goll quickly washed his hands, keeping his eyes on the mirror before him. His seventy-one year old face did not have the expression of peace and calm and quiet contentment it should have. Outrage and shock patinaed it. It wasn't a case of "future shock," as Toffler called it. It was "now shock." The future was here today, not ten years from now.

And, judging from the comments of some of the men, the Supreme Court would soon be considering the constitutionality of this new shock. What article of the Constitution, he thought, could apply to this case? Well, hopefully, it would be settled at a lower level.

As he left, he turned to look at the sign above the doorway. Yes, just as he'd thought. The MEN was gone. In its place: PERSONS' CONVENIENCE.

His wife looked around as he settled down beside her.

"What's going on?" she said, nodding at the sign. She was too short-sighted to make out its letters.

"Change," he said. "It's not determined yet whether it's progress or regress."

"You look much better. Did everything, uh, come out all right?"

"All systems are go. I feel fine."

She stabbed the point of her pencil at the crossword puzzle. "Do you believe in coincidence?"

"Only when it happens."

"Would you believe it? One of the words I have to figure out was *Wahatee!*"

"This has been a strange day," he said. "What was its definition?"

"It's from an Oneida Indian word meaning *He sat down.* Why in the world would the Indians name a place something like that? *Who* sat down? Why? What happened there to make that so memorable?"

"Perhaps he was a chief who sat down to make an important decision. Who knows? Great decisions and deeds spring from little ones. Perhaps the Oneida knew that, and so they memorialized the little one."

The voice of the announcer spoke again. Goll plucked the number of their flight from the mumble. He stood up.

"Come on. We have to keep on going."

Some Fabulous Yonder

First published in *Fantastic Stories of Imagination,* Volume 12, Number 4, April 1963.
Also published in *Strange Fantasy,* Number 8, 1969.

"Some Fabulous Yonder" first appeared in a much different form in the science fiction magazine *Fantastic Stories of the Imagination* in April 1963. Cele Goldsmith, the editor of the publication, cut out phrases, sentences, and paragraphs throughout the novelette, probably for the sake of space in the magazine. However, the most egregious editing of the manuscript occurred at the story's climax, where almost an entire page was excised. This considerably lessened the impact of the story's conclusion. The version included in this collection is taken from Farmer's original manuscript and restores the text deleted from previous publications.

The novelette is also of note because it occurs in the same universe as Farmer's Carmody series. The story begins with FECAB agent Raspold learning of the surrender of John Carmody. Raspold, the protagonist of "Some Fabulous Yonder," also appears in another Farmer story, "Strange Compulsion" (later published under the title "The Captain's Daughter").

Notice the meaning of the name Nge and what the characters later discover on Voittamaton. Also reflect on the story's title, the nature of this civilization's interstellar frontier, and the motives of the characters. Farmer is adept at showing us what it means to be human.

———◆———

Raspold was in a tavern in Breakneck, capital city of the Federation planet, Wildenwooly. He was drinking, but only in the line of duty. The bartender had some very interesting information for him, and Raspold was elated. He was finally getting someplace; the trail, once so cold, was now warmer.

Then a messenger (from Saxwell Space Links) walked into the tavern and handed him a sealed envelope. He tore it open and read. The message was in code and was to the point.

JOHN CARMODY TURNED HIMSELF IN AND IS NOW AT JOHNS HOPKINS REHABILITATION CENTER. REPORT AT ONCE TO ME.
　　R.A.

Four hours later, Raspold was talking to his chief, Richard Ali'i. He had had to wait at the spaceport of Breakneck for two hours for a scheduled ship. The trip between Wildenwooly and Earth—20,000 light-years—took, in wristwatch time, ten minutes. He spent an hour going through Customs and Sanitation. Another hour was consumed in taking various taxis and tubes to the headquarters of the Chief of Federation Extra-Terrestrial Criminal Apprehension Bureau (FECAB). This was deep within the bowels of Under Copenhagen.

Richard Ali'i was a big and handsome man of middle age, dark-skinned and black-haired but with blue eyes (Samoan and Norwegian immediate ancestry).

"Whatever made Carmody surrender?" said Raspold. "Are you sure he hasn't got some nasty scheme up his sleeves?"

"Thought of that. But his turning himself in seems to be genuine. Apparently, he was on Dante's Joy. Strange things happen there. I'll tell you about it sometime. Just now, we've got something that can't wait."

He paused, lit up a Siberian cigar, and said, "It's about No. 2. Rather, I should say, No. 1, now that Carmody's, uh, abdicated."

"Heinrich Nge?"

"Yes. I've had ten agents on his trail for the past four years. Five of them disappeared. Two were murdered. One is off somewhere. I can't get hold of him, maybe he's been done away with too. The tenth…well…he was bought."

Raspold was genuinely shocked. "A Fecab?"

"Thoroughly screened. But tests are given by human beings, and human beings are…fallible. The evidence is undeniable. McGrew took a bribe, sold out to Nge. We'd never have known if he hadn't been badly hurt in a drunken brawl in Diveboard. Under drugs, he babbled like a maniac. Not for long. Something in his body exploded, blew him to bits, killed a doctor and a Metro inspector. The explosive must have been surgically implanted. And set off by remote control, for McGrew was in no condition to do it himself, even if he'd wanted to."

———⟫●⟪———

"Diveboard?" said Raspold. "Then Nge, or one of his men, must be on the planet. That bomb must have been set off by radio."

"We think so. However, I'm not through yet. McGrew in his babbling told us something we would never have known otherwise. You remember the disappearance of the Federation destroyer *George A. Custer* two years ago?"

"Between Earth and Aldebaran?"

"Yes. Maiden voyage. Thirty men aboard. Translated from Earth, was supposed to appear above Einstein ten minutes later, ship's time. But she never did, and no one knew what happened. Now, we know. Nge highjacked her."

Raspold's hand, searching for a package of cigarettes in his purse, stopped. He said, "Highjacked? If I didn't know you so well, sir, I'd think you were kidding."

Ali'i permitted himself a rare smile. "I wish I was. No, Nge did the impossible. Or improbable. With one man. A member of his organization who had contrived, somehow, to become a crewmember. Released a deadly gas through the ventilation system of the destroyer, thus killing all the crew except himself. Then, piloted the bird to a rendezvous at some planet McGrew didn't name, and turned the *Custer* over to Nge. Must have been a damned good pilot. He did the translation all by himself."

"So, what's he going to do with the *Custer*?" said Raspold. The cigarette flared, but his hands shook as he drew it from the pack, and the hand that lifted the cigarette to his lips shook a little.

"I don't know. Or didn't. We fed this new data into ATHENA. And ATHENA, after checking this against what it knew about Nge, came up with a reasonable, if astonishing, probability. Maybe not so astonishing, considering Nge."

Raspold wanted to urge Ali'i to continue, kill the suspense, but he knew better. Ali'i spoke in his own time.

Finally, after blowing out three clouds of smoke, and staring at them like a contemplative dragon, Ali'i said, "Voittamaton."

"Voittamaton?" Raspold's brows wrinkled. He said, "Wait a minute! I got it! Fifty years ago…Miika Versinen…sure…I saw a dramatic recreation of his life. Ran as a three-part series. And, of course, I read about him when I was a kid."

He looked at Ali'i as if he still thought Ali'i was joking. "You mean Nge's going to use the *Custer* to storm Voittamaton? Even after Versinen failed so miserably and so bloodily?"

Ali'i nodded grimly.

Raspold raised his hands and shrugged his shoulders. "We won't have to worry about him any longer. Or any of the men with him. Why not let him go ahead?"

"Because, in the first place, we don't know for a certainty that that is what Nge plans to do it. It's only a high probability. Second, Voittamaton is taboo, off limits. Third, we have to stop Nge now before he hurts innocent people while preparing for the expedition against Voittamaton. Fourth, I want our department to get him—now. There are about ten Federation agencies of Earth alone trying to catch him, and the Great Light alone knows how many from other Fed or non-Fed planets. Fifth, why do you, a supposedly intelligent man, waste my time with such a stupid question?"

Raspold flushed, and he said, "Spur of the moment thought. I'd like to see the bastard get his comeuppance, which he will, if he tackles Voittamaton. Probably, a horrible comeuppance."

"Well," said Ali'i, "I—we—Earth want him *now*. And, despite what I said a moment ago, I think you're best qualified to do it."

He smiled slightly and said, "You haven't got a nose like a bloodhound's for nothing."

Raspold fingered his large slightly bulbous nose and said, "Thanks. I still wish, though…"

"Wish what?"

"That Carmody had not surrendered. Now, I'll never know which is the better man. I think I'd have caught up with him in the end."

"Great Light! We're running an organization—a very large and expensive one—to put an end to the activities of Federation criminals! Not to glorify you! Raspold, you're an egotist!"

"Who isn't? I'm just more honest than most."

———

Twenty minutes later, Raspold had sketched his plan, received his authorization and a draft for 5000 C, and was on his way. It took an hour for him to get back to the port. In the meantime, one of Ali'i's secretaries had arranged for a seat on a nonsked jumper. Because Raspold was going to Diveboard, a non-Federation "open" planet, he had to have a passport. Ali'i's secretary had given him a forged one bearing the name of Dick Ricoletti. Ricoletti was a sub-citizen of the Middle North American Department, Lifelong Limited Privileges Resident of Lesser Laramie. Raspold had spent some time in that city and could speak the dialect quite well. Not that he expected to run across anyone acquainted with it but he liked to present a perfect character.

His passport carried his portrait, his fingerprints, retinaprints, ear-lobeprints, blood type, EKG-patterns, and voiceprint. When Customs and Sanitation took these and matched them against the passport's, they would discover nothing wrong. And, when they wired the prints to ATHENA for double-checking, they would receive from ATHENA assurance that the prints belonged to Dick Ricoletti, Social Security No. Such-and-Such, Terrestrial Citizen No. Such-and-Such, and so on. What Customs and Sanitation did not know was that, when the inquiry about Ricoletti was plugged into ATHENA, it went to a data block that had been inserted by the FECAB.

Raspold leaned against a wall and smoked a cigarette while waiting for this procedure to be completed. He was a tall man, about 12 centimeters above average height (1.7 meters), but looked taller because of his thinness. His broad and tightly muscled arms and shoulders and chest contrasted strangely with the girlish thin waist, narrow hips, and slender legs. These were very long in proportion to his torso. He was wearing an auburn wig with a high-piled curly coiffure of the latest fashion. The hairs of the scalp beneath the wig were just beginning to grow back. When they emerged, they would be brownish-black. His eyes, normally a deep brown, were now a light purple. The wig and contact lenses had to come off during customs inspection but no one had commented. Almost every passenger wore them.

His features were as Nature had given them; no surgeon's knife or plasti-flesh for him. His forehead was high; his eyebrows, black and thick and meeting over the nose; his nose, big and thick, looking like a bloodhound's. The lips were medium sized and had only a smudge of lipstick and that red, not the fashionable green flecked with gold. On his left ear, he wore a huge golden ring with a large golden green pendant.

———⟫•⟪———

Presently, he walked out with the other passengers to the *Willowisp*, a twenty-seater craft belonging to a small line. The pilot, however, was a retired Federation Navy navigator. After the passengers were seated, the pilot gave his usual description of the trip they would make; the translation of 180,000 light-years in exactly nothing flat (objective and subjective time), the shorter translations, and the time it would take to fly to Diveboard's spaceport after the final "jump."

Raspold paid no attention; he had heard similar lectures over a hundred times. The passengers took his concentration, and, after examining each in the minutest detail, he decided that they were what they seemed to be. A couple of import agents going to Diveboard to set up business, and the rest, emigrants. These mostly came from the subclasses, men and women who could no longer endure the crowded apartments and jammed streets of the great enclosed cities, the low standards of living, the tribute paid from their meager wages to local politicians and their thugs, their ratings as lower class citizens (which their children might escape but not them). They had scraped enough money together to buy the expensive tickets to the far-off sparsely settled planet on the rim of the Galaxy (enticed by TV-shows of life on that planet), agricultural equipment, tools, guns, clothes, and whatever else they thought they might need. Now, they were facing a new life, ill-equipped, most of them, for the strange life on the frontier planet. But they all had dreams of some fabulous yonder, some place where there would be no formal classification of social and economic scale, more than enough fresh air to breathe, silence, trees, grass. And where they would be their own men and women.

Raspold felt sorry for them. They would find that what they had regarded as chains on Earth were, in many ways, walls to protect and guide them. Now, chainless, wall-less, they would be naked, helpless or inadequate, unsure of how to act. And their life would be hard, hard beyond their powers of conception.

He thought of Versinen. Miika Versinen. Translated into English from the Neo-Finnish of the colonial planet Toivo, Micah the Bloody. Versinen was the first and the greatest of the space pirates. A yellow-haired bearded giant who looked like an ancient Viking. He carried a broad axe at his belt, a weapon useless in warfare but quite adequate for splitting his prisoners' skulls in half. He was a madman but a successful one. Until he heard of that dark planet beyond the rim of the Galaxy. The sunless body traveling outwards toward Andromeda. An Earth-sized planet bereft of atmosphere, seemingly devoid of life from its beginnings. Yet, there were mysterious structures on its surface. Over a million of them, pillars with globes on their ends. They glowed; they looked like an army of phantoms.

The first Federation expedition to attempt to explore, a Naval force of a destroyer, a tender and a laboratory-carrier, had failed. Ten kilometers above the surface, the power in all three vessels had been cut off, and the ships crashed. The crews were killed except for a navigator. Finding that the power was now restored, he had escaped in a one-man hopper and succeeded in translating back to Diveboard, the nearest planet.

A second Federation force tried to land. The power of all six vessels was cut off while they were still in orbit. Then, restored. The fleet had left, and the planet was marked off-limits.

But Versinen listened to rumors, to wild tales. The inhabitants of the dark runaway possessed great powers and great riches. The men who conquered them would be the most powerful and the richest beings in the Galaxy. Versinen decided that he would be that man. Reckless, he brought his fleet of ten vessels out of translation only a kilometer above the surface and dived to the surface before his power could be extinguished. Three of his vessels miscalculated, for the translation drive was not as accurate at that time as it was now.

Two crashed. One translated below the surface, and there was an explosion that left a giant crater and thousands of the globed pillars flattened to the ground.

What happened after that is for speculation. Two of the pirate fleet still lie where they landed, several kilometers from the cavern's mouth. The third, the *Kirves*, was located in orbit around Diveboard; its only occupant, Versinen. He was mumbling and nonresistant. For a long while, all he could distinctly say was, "Voittamaton! Voittamaton!"

"Unconquerable! Unconquerable!"

Later, at Johns Hopkins, he quit talking and became catatonic. All efforts to arouse him failed. For ten years, he was a human blob. Then, one day, he opened his eyes, and gave a thick scream.

"I don't want to die!" he cried. "I can't! I must not!"

He muttered, "They're both horrible. But life is better."

A few minutes later, he was dead.

The pilot's voice brought him out of his reverie. They had made the final translation 50 myriameters from Diveboard's surface. From now on, they would proceed by gravitic drive.

An hour later, Raspold was through the lax Customs of Diveboard and walking its streets. It was high noon on Earth and almost dusk here.

He walked slowly to give the impression of a man out on a sightseeing tour. Occasionally, he stopped and looked about him, always making sure he scanned the faces behind him. After several blocks, he was certain that any tail he might have knew his business well enough to keep out of sight. Or that several men were involved, one following him for a distance, then radioing through his wrister to the man ahead.

Raspold wondered if he should contact the agent Ali'i had told him about. How did he know he could trust Jack Yee? He knew of the man but he did not know him personally. And, while Ali'i, his chief, was not likely to make a mistake about a man, he could. Yee might have been alright until Nge got to him and offered him such a large bribe that he had corrupted him. Or used some other means to make him his man. Unlikely, but Raspold did not feel like taking any chances whatever. Not, that is, until it was worthwhile. Meanwhile, he would see what he could do on his own.

Raspold found that, aside from the uneasiness of his situation—and he was not one to be thrown into a sweat easily—he was enjoying his stroll. The city of Diveboard was much like Breakneck, the capital of Wildenwooly. It was built of a medley of log structures, of quick-drying foam shells supported by sprayed beams, a few buildings of native stone; granite, limestone, or pressed concrete, roughly dressed planks, even of paper impregnated with hardo. The streets were the only evidence of planning. These were wide and ran straight and crossed each other at right angles. Some, those nearest the spaceport, were paved with the cheap and quickly laid hardo. The rest were dirt.

The men who thronged the streets were a varied lot. Many were recent immigrants from Earth but many were human beings from the colonial and independent planets: Toivo, Tserokia, Novaya, Big Sudan, Po Chi-i, Heinlein, Maya, Last Chance, Goibniu, and two dozen or more others. A minority among the human beings but not rare were oxygen-breathing non-humans. Sinister (to human eyes) Felicentaurs from Capella, the huge Ursucentaurs of Ross 128 III, feathery bipedal Gkuun from Taure IV, pygmy Flickertails from Van Houden, a big-turbaned Pachydermoid from Puppis, and a near-human type with slanted purple eyes and bulging cheekbones. Raspold had never heard of them before.

The men who jostled each other on the paved and the dusty streets came from many social classes and professions. Richly dressed and some obvious tourists, commercial spacemen in their blue, white, or gold uniforms, poorly dressed farmers or ranchers, buckskin-clad hunters or prospectors, and the nondescript. There were a few gravity-fed units coasting through the streets or high in the air, some electrical fuel cell-powered modes of transportation, and even a nuclear-powered truck. By far the most popular mode of transportation, that which gave an archaic air to the scene, were the buggies and wagons drawn by the furry equinoids of Diveboard. Whatever the immigrant could afford to import from Earth, he drove. And if he didn't have the money for a Terrestrial means of travel, he used the native resources.

⸻⸻

Raspold saw a chair sitting on a sidewalk. Beside it was a sign in big black letters in Lingo: LEG-PAINTING.¼ S. A LEG. Below was a name in English: JIM QUINN, PROPRIETOR. Standing behind the chair, his tools of trade on a small table beside the chair, was a medium-sized, chunkily built youth with bright orange hair—his own, judging from the shagginess—and a toothy smile. Raspold said to the youth, "I have long legs. Going to charge extra for them?"

Quinn grinned and said, "No, sir. Anything I lose on you, I'll make up when a fellow with short legs comes along."

Raspold sat down and placed his right foot on the short stool provided. Quinn took a bottle of clear liquid from his table and squeezed a shot of the liquid into a cloth in his other hand. Then, he began rubbing Raspold's right leg with the damp cloth. The red, white, and blue barberpole stripes painted on Raspold's leg ran together. After Quinn had wet a large area, he took a dry cloth and began to rub the area. The pale flesh beneath began to show.

"Earth?" said Raspold.

"Middle Dublin, 3rd Sector, sir," said Quinn. "My parents were second-class C, although my old man got first before he died. Played the bassoon in the Greater Dublin Symphony for twenty years. Me, I dint have no musical talent. Back to second-C for me until I was a majority. Then, to third. But my mother taught me to read and write. And you know there's lotsa second-C that can't do that. I worked at everything: sold pot, ran messages for a wardman, studied for a construction worker's license but dint have the money to pay for a license. Did a lot of other things. Finally, got tired of no money, being shoved around. And cubehappy. Couldn't stand being crowded all the time, couldn't breathe anymore. Then, luck, pure blind dumb luck! Stepped into a public bath and found a dead man. Some old guy that musta been slumming; he had some M's in his purse, so he couldn't have come from the Middle Sector. Musta had heart failure. No one else in the place. I took the M's and runned. Used some of the credits to find out where I could get hold of an outlaw jumper. Paid most of my M's to the agent and the pilot and took the jump to here with ten others. Landed with just enough money to buy me this chair, stool, table, and leg-painting tools. But I'm doing O.K. now. Someday, I'll be a big man on Diveboard. And I can breathe, I can breathe."

"You don't miss the big city and all its refinements?"

"Sometimes. You know, the gang, the girls. But I wouldn't ever have amounted to anything; I'da always been a drunken C. Here, things get tough, rough; you gotta fight like hell sometimes. But what the hell, you had to back on Earth. And here you're fighting for something besides a bonebare existence. It's exciting."

Raspold examined his legs and said, "You're doing a good job. Paint them black. Solid. No stars or crescents."

Quinn looked up, winked, and said, "You dint really need a paint job, sir. What's on your mind?"

"You must get around, hear a lot," said Raspold. "There's two S for this job if you can give me a little information."

"I come happy for two S," said Quinn, grinning bucktoothedly. "Yeah, I hear, see. But it might cost you."

"There are people in this city who have money. Where do their women—wives or what have you—go to buy their clothes, get their wigs cleaned and curled, get a sono?"

"Rene Gautier's," said Quinn. "Best place in town. Only place, in fact."

"You just earned 3 S," said Raspold. "Now, you've probably set up your business near Gautier's..."

"Yeah," said Quinn, grinning. "He's my only competitor. But not really a competitor, because only the fullpurses can afford him. But I place my chair near him a lot, because I like to see the dangoes that waltz in and out. Some pretty goodlookers."

"That's what I want to know," said Raspold. "Has one of Gautier's customers ever been a beautiful woman who uses Erector Set Perfume?"

"What's that?"

"A natural perfume from Umchawa. Used to be, anyway. It's been synthesized but is still by far the most expensive. The man who smells it has an immediate erotic reaction, if he's capable of one."

Quinn hawhawed. And he said, "Oh, you mean h...n perfume! Yeah, I smelled it twice, both times when I was working in front of Gautier's. The first time, I didn't think anything of it, the woman was such a dish. Second time, I was painting a customer's legs when she went by, and told me what it was. I couldn't figure out why a woman would be wanting to have it on her when she was walking on the streets. You'd think she'd cause a riot...get...Say! Maybe she was walking the streets! Naw, she dint have to, she was too beautiful, too well dressed."

"How tall was she?"

"Oh, about an inch or two higher than I am. That is, after I quit smelling that stuff, wow!"

"Lots of jewelry?"

"Loaded."

"She comes to Gautier's regularly?"

"Not that I know. I saw her last Thirdsday or Secondsday two weeks before that. Say, haven't I given you more'n 3 S' worth?"

"Five S now. Tell me a little more, and it's six. Was she alone?"

"Once. Other time, she had another woman with her. A blastoff, too, but she wasn't wearing that Erector Set stuff. Wow! Say, I don't like giving too much credit. You wanta bring your bill up to date?"

Raspold took six S out of his purse and handed it to Quinn. He said, "You're an intelligent man, and, therefore, curious. You must have asked around about that woman."

"What for? What chance would I stand with a woman like that? Maybe someday, after I make my pile...Yeah, I asked around. Nobody knows her name, and Gautier sure isn't going to give out any information. The tight-lipped little fairy. But I can tell you one thing that'll be at least worth a half-S. Haw, haw! She don't live in town."

"Half it is," said Raspold. "What does she ride in?"

"Believe it or not, a horse and buggy," said Quinn. "A Diveboard horse, not one of the Earth kind. She drives like a maniac. But it ain't hers. She rents it from Tak Alvarez; he's got a livery stable out at the edge of town. I painted his legs a coupla days ago. He says she walks in from the forest, from nowhere, and rents the outfit. Then, coming back from Gautier's, she leaves the horse and buggy with Ted, and walks off into the forest. So..."

Somebody could be waiting for her in a grav, thought Raspold. He said, "Many people live in the country around here?"

"More every day. Diveboard's population has doubled in the last ten months. Mostly poor would-be farmers or hunters or prospectors."

"Any rich ones?"

"A few. There're two nobody knows much about. Word is that they're big-shot criminals who've piled it and want to take it easy. Which they can do. Earth can't touch them; this's a Free Planet."

"I know. Now, what're the names of these so-called criminals?"

"Nobody knows the name of one of them. The other calls himself Gottfried von Fulka."

Quinn knew no more than that about von Fulka. Except that his house—mansion, rather—was on an island in a lake about fifty miles north of the cap-ital. The house was built about two years ago; von Fulka had not moved in until a year later.

"Alvarez' livery? It's on the north side of town?"

"South."

Raspold rose and examined the paint on his legs. "Very good," he said. "You'll go far in your profession—whatever it may be in the future."

"Another S-worth of advice," said Quinn, squinting shrewdly at him. "If you're thinking of hanging around Gautier's until this chick shows up, forget it. Gautier goes to her now."

Raspold's brows, thick and black, rose and he said, "You earned it. How do you know this?"

"Oh, I get around."

"Details, please," said Raspold, holding out, not an S but an Un with a large M on it.

Quinn's eyes widened, and he said, "Gautier drives a long red Wang. He's easy to spot, even late at night, especially here where lotsa people stay up all night for one reason or another. He's driven out on the North Road twice about two in the morning and didn't show up until the next night. Where'd he go? That road ain't passable for a sport car once you get ten miles outta town. And he ain't shacking up with no farmer's daughter. If he was, everybody in town'd know it. No, he parks his car someplace, and somebody picks him up. The Erector Set chick hasn't shown after she made those two trips, so…"

"The mountain goes to Mohammed. Or vice versa."

"More advice. Gautier may be one of the boys, but he's a hard nut to crack; he came here because he got into some trouble on Earth."

Raspold handed him the M and said, "Part of that is for silence. And loyalty in the future. I want you to work for me. More where that came from."

"How do you know you can trust me?" said Quinn. "I want to get ahead, and I know I need money for that. Suppose…"

Raspold shrugged. "I'm taking a chance. But those who betray me…"

"I'll hitch my wagon to your star, mister…?"

"Call me Dick Ricoletti for the present," said Raspold. "It wouldn't be good for either of us if you knew my real name. And I warn you, even talking to me as you have been doing may be very dangerous."

"If I scared easily, I wouldn't be here," said Quinn.

Raspold asked where the best restaurant in town was and then walked off. He strolled through the bustling colorful noisy streets, following Quinn's directions, until he came to The Soulful Cow. This establishment, a two-story building of rough-hewn logs of reddish wood, was a combination tavern and eating-place. A blast of chatter and laughter blew from out the open doorway, with a mixed odor of tobacco, beer, and frying steaks. Raspold stepped into a huge room filled with people and smoke. The great dark-red beams overhead were festooned with heads of native animals and signs in various alphabets, ideograms, and syllabaries. A bar, cement-topped, ran the length of the northern side of the building. Men stood two or three deep along it, and over a dozen bartenders sweated to keep their customers from dying of thirst. At the rear was the kitchen, open to view, and here were the cooks, their helpers, and waiters, preparing the only course The Soulful Cow served. Steaks, potatoes, butter, beans, and a dark bread.

Raspold's mouth watered. He had had steak on Wildenwooly, but it had been his first in an Earth month. On Earth, he could rarely afford true meat, but here, where cattle was one of the chief industries, and transportation from the plains to the city was not so expensive, he could have all the steak he wanted. At home, up to ten years ago, only the wealthy could afford such meat. Then, as the colonial planets built up herds, the fleets began importing meat in much larger quantities. Now, a well-to-do man could afford steak or pork once or twice a week. In another five years, even the poor might be able to do so.

He found an empty seat at one of the long plank tables. A mixed group sat there: sailors off merchant vessels, two Federation Space Navy P.O.'s, a few buckskin-clad backwoodsmen, some cowboys who might have stepped off the pages of a Western novel, even to the levis, hats, and moustaches; a couple who had the bleak hard look of asteroid-miners, and some other tough looking men who could have been anything.

His waitress might have been pretty under the many layers of paint and powder she wore; her brief uniform showed a well-built body; she made it evident in the first minute that she added to her income by taking willing customers upstairs—after her four hours of duty as a waitress were over.

Raspold declined this and ordered a stein of native dark beer with his meal.

He listened to the conversation up and down the table as they talked in the loud free voices of frontiersmen.

"...Joe musta forgot to recharge is 'suader," said a cowboy. "E turn it toward the bull, and the bull dont move the way e want it to. It charge, the damn orse rear up, and throw poor ole Joe. Time we get to im, e dead wi a broke neck. Is own fault, though, cause I tell im alla tim, 'Joe, you sloppy bastard, you gotta member tha you cant rely alla time on a sono to move em dogies long. One day, you battery run dry, then you gotta do like they done in the ole days, wen men was men...'"

"...I run into this stewardess offa the *Phoenix*, you know, a Saxwell freighter, 50,000-tonner, F-class, when boths our birds was docked at New Amsterdam—you ever been there?—and I'm telling you, she..."

"...staked her out, and everything looked OK, nothing on the scanner cept a coupla blips we knew was other asteroids, no good cause we'd assayed em before, and the Andy started acting funny, you know, you been through it before, and one a your partners thinks he aint getting a fair share, and so I say to Sibelius..."

"...sure, I could go to Earth and get this scar taken off and be my andsome old self, aw aw!, but I don't want spend the money. I need it for a grubstake, I gotta stand of timber about five undred mile north a ere that belong to nobody bu me, by a river and a lake that's bound to be a site for a big town some day, and I gotta contract, but..."

"...so I say to her, 'Lissen Sphinxie, I ain't see a human female for two year, and the longer I'm here, the more human you look...'"

"...yes, I have a Ph.D. in metallurgy and I was starving to death teaching on Earth. So, I decided to borrow all I could, pack up the family, and..."

The only ones at the table who seemed to be companionless were Raspold and a man who sat directly across from him. This fellow was easily the biggest human being in the place. Also, the broadest. His forearm looked as thick as Raspold's thighs. His chest looked like two drums of muscle. His hair was black and straight, and the handsome face was brown. His eyes were a light green.

He sat brooding, his huge right hand almost completely enfolding the tall stein of beer.

From time to time, he took a swallow from the stein. As he did so, his green eyes looked at—and through—Raspold. Yet Raspold was sure that the big man had taken in every detail of Raspold's face and dress.

Presently, a youth came in and bent down by the big man and whispered into his ear.

Raspold was startled, for the youth was the red-haired leg-painter, Quinn. Quinn, straightening up, gave Raspold a wink and a grin, and he walked away. Raspold wondered if Quinn meant these for a friendly greeting or a signal that this man had something to do with his quest.

—————⊷•⊶—————

Raspold rose and strode after Quinn. He caught him just outside the tavern, out of sight of anyone sitting within it.

"You working for that dark giant?" he said.

"Sorry," said Quinn. "I don't tell one of my clients another's business. It ain't ethical. It also ain't healthy."

"How much?" said Raspold.

Quinn's face, lit by a lamp above and to one side of him, darkened.

"You haven't got enough," he said.

Raspold laughed and said, "That tells me a lot about you. Maybe I can trust you, after all. O.K. I'll find out for myself. But you can do something for me. There's a Q in it for you. You know a man of Terran Chinese descent named Jack Yee? I don't know where he lives just now; he moves around a lot."

Quinn nodded and Raspold took a notebook and a pen from his purse, tore out a leaf, and began writing. Finished, he handed the leaf to Quinn.

"I could get into contact with him right now, but I don't want to use the waves, and I've got some business to take care of just now. When you see him, don't say a word. Just hand him this paper. Got it?"

"His place might be bugged?"

"Right. And don't bother trying to read this. It's in code."

"You must be on Heinrich Nge's trail," said Quinn.

Raspold had trained himself to keep a poker face, but he could not help betraying some surprise. "How do you figure that?"

"I hear a lot, see some. Word's around that he's here somewhere on Diveboard. A coupla his men been seen in town last few months. And the word also is that Raspold's in town, hot on Nge's trail."

Raspold smiled slightly and said, "Communications engineers ought to investigate the possibility of the grapevine. For swiftness, it beats the speed of light. Well, now you know you're in hot water up to your neck, and you're likely to get drowned. Want to back out?"

"It's exciting," said Quinn. "And I got a chance to make a big profit."

"I don't think you mean a profit from Nge," said Raspold. "As soon as you've delivered the message to Yee, come back here and tell me you've done it. Although I may not be here by then."

Quinn walked off, and Raspold returned to his seat at the table. By then, his dinner was before him, and he ate it with great pleasure. His enjoyment was not a bit tempered by the hard stares the big man across the table was now giving him. But, when Raspold had paid his bill and rose to leave, the big man also stood up. Raspold walked out of the tavern; he knew that he was being followed.

⟫◆⟪

Diveboard's moon, almost as large as Earth's, shone fitfully through a half-clouded sky.

"Mister," said a rumbling voice behind him. "A word."

Raspold turned around, noting that the man was keeping his distance. If he intended to attack, he meant to do it with a weapon. Raspold idly fingered the new pendant on his earring.

The fellow spoke in Lingo but used strange phonetic values that showed he had not learned it as an infant along with his native tongue but in later life.

"My name is Big Chuck Woodwolf," he said, not offering his hand. "I'm a Tserokian."

Raspold said, "I've been to Tserokia."

Woodwolf flashed a smile and said, "You speak my language?"

"Regretfully, no. My name is Ricoletti. What do you want?"

"O.K. We'll use that name. I think I know who you really are, but I won't say. Listen, you heard of the big raid that Heinrich Nge made on Sequoyah a year ago?"

Raspold nodded. Sequoyah was the capital city of Tserokia, a T-type planet colonized seventy years before (when interstellar travel had first started) by a thousand Cherokees. Since then, the population had expanded to thirty million, largely through the immigration of other racial groups and nationalities. The immigrants had become naturalized or, as the Tserokians phrased it, "adopted," and had learned to speak Cherokee. But that tongue was dying out, replaced by the standard Federation speech, Lingo, and the racial continuity of the original colonists (already half-white) had been broken. Big Chuck himself probably descended from at least three races and two dozen nationalities. But he thought of himself as Cherokee.

Two years ago, six months after the destroyer *Custer* had been highjacked, a fleet of ten vessels had appeared over Sequoyah. The *Custer* was one of them. Before anyone knew what was happening, the fleet had landed, looted the planetary treasury, the government museum, and had also kidnapped a number of good-looking Tserokian women. There was no doubt who was the leader of the pirates. Heinrich Nge. He had left a letter saying that he had enjoyed his visit there, thanked them for their gracious hospitality, and promised to return when their treasury was refilled. Also, complimented them on the beauty of their women. The letter bore the image of the scorpion (Nge was Swahili for *scorpion*).

"My sister, Tuli, was one of the girls taken by the pirates," said Woodwolf. "She's the most beautiful woman I've ever seen; she was to marry the richest man on Tserokia. He's dead now; killed by the pirates during the raid. I loved my sister."

"And you're trying to find her by tracking her down through Nge," said Raspold.

"You're way ahead of me, mister, but you're one hundred percent correct."

"Why tell me this?"

"Because I figure you're looking for him, too. And a man of your experience and resources stands a better chance than I do to find him. However, I know some things you don't. If we work together..."

Raspold considered. Woodwolf might be an agent of Nge. He could be approaching him with this story with the intent of capturing him. If so, he might give Raspold a chance to find Nge.

"Would you be willing to submit to questioning under *chalarocheil?*" said Raspold. "I'm not one to take unnecessary chances."

"Not the least bit backward about it, mister, uh, Ricoletti."

"In that case, it may not be necessary. Let's go someplace else and talk.'

Woodwolf started to lead, but Raspold said that he preferred to pick the place himself. Woodwolf smiled and said, O.K."

———————

Raspold merely walked across the street and stopped before the dark front of a farm equipment store. They were outside the illumination area cast by the nearest lamp, and he could watch the door to the Soulful Cow. Big Chuck Woodwolf began talking at once.

"I would have been handicapped in looking for Nge if I hadn't gotten the financial backing of my sister's fiancé's family," he said. "They gave me carte blanche; they want Nge as much as I do. Almost. They want him brought to court. I just want to kill him with my own hands."

He flexed his huge hands and said, "I went to Wildenwooly, Diveboard, Peregrino, Liang, Krona, all the 'free' planets. I figured that Nge might be found in a place where the Feds could not legally touch him. Then I went to Earth several times and also visited a dozen non-human planets. No luck at all.

"Then, instead of just running around, sniffing here and there like a dumb hound trying to find a lost trace, I sat down and did some thinking. If I were Nge, which God forbid, where would I go? And why? Nge wants to be the biggest man in the Galaxy. He wants power and wealth. How can he best do this? By looting the biggest treasury in the Galaxy, that's how. And what is that? Voittamaton.

"But Voittamaton is well-nigh invulnerable. So, if Nge needs men, ships, weapons to take Voittamaton, he will steal the ships and rob someplace to give him the money to buy men and weapons. So, he highjacks the *Custer*, and he loots Sequoyah. He now has money and firepower. But he also needs a base of operations. What inhabited 'free' planet is closest to Voittamaton? Diveboard, on the rim of the Galaxy, and only ten light-years from Voittamaton."

Raspold smiled. This man, using the little mass of gray matter within his skull, had come to the same conclusion as the skyscraper-tall computer, ATHENA.

"I come back here. I hung around taverns, the marketplace, found out who knew the most, tapped into the grapevine. I even became partner in some small robberies here to get the confidence of the underworld. However, I'll repay the men I robbed after this is over. I got a conscience.

"One night, while I was hanging around the Twelfth Street Tavern, a man I recognized entered. I didn't know his name, but I remembered seeing him during the raid on Sequoyah. I couldn't forget that face; we'd blazed away at the opposite ends of a hall with guns. He wounded me with his rifle, almost killed me. Now, I could reach out and get his neck between my hands and squeeze once. Pretended I was a planetpicker who'd tried to keep a planet to himself and been cashiered out of Federation Service. Down on my luck. He was cagey at first but he got drunk, and he said he might possibly have something for me to do—if I was made of strong stuff. Wouldn't say any more, and I figured that he wasn't likely to. I knew that the little device in his body might be transmitting our conversation to some monitor who only had to press a button and blow the both of us to kingdom come. He knew it, too.

"So, I told him that The Soulful Cow was a better place for steaks, drinks, and women, and we staggered out into the street. When we came opposite the entrance to an alley, I chopped him alongside the neck and dragged him back into the dark end. When he came to, he was bound tight and had a gag over his mouth. I used my little flash to show him what I'd written on a piece of paper. It told him what I wanted to know. What was his name? Where was my sister? Where was Nge?

"He had one hand free so he could write an answer. He wasn't about to try to speak. If his speech was being monitored, he wouldn't live more than a minute. Neither, probably, would I, but I had to take the chance. I had also written that, in return for the information, I'd let him loose. That I knew he wouldn't say anything to Nge, because Nge would kill him at once—or worse.

"He glared at me, but his hand shook when he wrote his answer.

"*Go to hell.*

"Brave talk. But I took his sandal off and ignited my cigarette lighter and held the hot wire between his big toe and the next. He didn't dare scream. I took the wire away and gestured to him to write. He must have made up his mind by then, for he began to scribble. He let the paper fall, I picked it up and read.

"His name was Howie Guy. My sister was still alive; Nge had taken her for one of his mistresses. She was all right except that she was now three months pregnant. She was at von Fulka's place. He didn't know if Nge was there now or not, for Nge often took off for visits elsewhere. He didn't know where.

"I asked him some more, by paper, of course; where von Fulka's place was? Who was von Fulka? Did Nge intend to attack Voittamaton?

"He wrote that Nge was von Fulka."

Woodwolf stopped talking. He was breathing heavily.

"So what happened?" said Raspold coolly.

"I'd promised to let him go free," said Woodwolf. "I keep my word. And I did. I untied him, after relieving him of a knife and a gun and knocking him out again. Then, I phoned the police but didn't give my name, of course. Told them that I'd seen Howard Guy and another man at the end of that alley. Guy was tied up; the other man was writing something on a piece of paper and showing it to Guy, and Guy was doing the same thing for him. I even told them about the hot wire between Guy's toes."

"You said you'd let him go free," said Raspold. "Was that...?"

"I'm not through talking yet. The police didn't get hold of Guy; I knew they wouldn't. I kept my word. It wasn't three minutes after the call that a big explosion took place right in the middle of Twelfth Street. Fortunately, nobody but Guy was involved.

"You see, I know, like everybody else, that Nge has his contacts in the local police force. Maybe the one I called up. The contact must have radioed Nge, and Nge wasn't taking any chances on Guy spilling anything.

"Kind of poetic justice, huh? Hoist by his own petard, you might say? By the way, what is a petard?"

"Well, - a bomb," said Raspold.

"What do you know!"

⟹⦁⟸

They started to walk down the street. But, hearing the frenzied barks of a dog and the equally frenzied cries of a man, they turned.

There, two blocks behind them, a youth ran as fast as he could, shouting for help. Several yards behind him bounded the dog, a large mongrel that looked as if he had a heavy dash of German shepherd in him.

"Looks like Quinn," said Raspold.

"Yeah," said Woodwolf. "And that dog...oh, oh!"

He broke the magnetic clasps of his shirt with his left hand and with his right reached under the shirt. Raspold, having previously noted the bulge under his left armpit, was not surprised to see the hand emerge clutching a pistol.

"Damn, damn!" groaned Woodwolf. "Nge must have stolen some piece of clothing from Quinn and set the dog to track down the owner."

Raspold saw the picture. He drew his gun, a .32 Weckel, and ran diagonally across the street. He shouted, "Quinn, out of the way!"

Quinn saw them and must have understood the waving of their guns, although he was too far away to hear them above the dog's barking. He sprinted for the sidewalk nearest him, which was Woodwolf's side of the street. The dog swerved to overtake Quinn. Raspold, aiming carefully, pressed the trigger.

The gun bucked twice, and the dog went whirling sidewise in the dust. Quinn kept on running. Meanwhile, Big Chuck Woodwolf had run into the middle of the street, and he fired immediately after Raspold. The dog, crumpled in a heap, moved a few inches under the impact of the .45. Quinn dived into an alley between two buildings. Woodwolf, only a few yards from the dog, threw himself flat on the dirt. Raspold, suddenly realizing his vulnerable position, did the same.

He was deafened, and the ground trembled under him. Dust swirled into the street; the plastic sheet of the store window near the dog blew inwards in a solid sheet, and the crash of objects falling off the store shelves was in the ears of the three as they rose and sped down the street.

After running for several blocks, they stopped to pant beside the side of a building. "Don't your citizens get nervous with all these explosions?" said Raspold.

"They love excitement," said Quinn. Then, "Oh, my God, that was close! But I'm O.K. Listen, Mister Ricoletti or whatever your name is, I couldn't deliver your note! Your friend, Jack Yee, was dead! I went to his room, he lives on the second story of Krishna's Hotel, and I knocked. There wasn't any answer. So, naturally, I tried the knob. The door was unlocked. I hollered again, cause I dint want my head blown off. Still no answer. I push the door, it swings in, and there's Yee on the floor. I go to him, look him over. He's dead but from what I don't know. Poison, maybe, or gas. So, I get to hell out of there with your note still in my hand."

"Nge must have discovered his identity," said Raspold, thinking that now, as far as he knew, he was the only FECAB agent on Diveboard.

"I was walking back," said Quinn, "when a car drove by. It stopped, and a door opened, and the dog jumped out. He stood there a moment, whining and sniffing. Then, like a hound out of hell, he ran for me, barking. I didn't know what was going on, but I didn't like the looks of it. I ran, and the dog came after me. Something told me I better not stop and try to talk to him. You showed up, and…"

He paused, then wailed, "Nge's after me, too!"

"He won't get you unless he gets us, too," said Raspold. He was considering every aspect swiftly. He could take a jumper back to Earth, talk to Ali'i, get a crew of FECAB, and return. But he couldn't take a legal ship, for Nge's men would be watching the spaceport. However, the police, if working with Nge, could arrest him and turn him over to Nge. If he hired an illegal jumper, he might fall into Nge's hands just as easily as if he tried the legal route. Nge must have the word around among the underworld that he wanted Raspold.

Even if he got to Earth, Nge would be gone by the time he returned. He might already have left Diveboard on the expedition against Voittamaton.

"Any place in town that rents cars or gravs?" he said to Quinn.

"Yeah. Jock Barry. But he's as crooked as a pretzel. He could be a stoolie for Nge."

"We won't rent one from him. We'll steal it," said Raspold.

They walked to Barry's place, a single-story foam structure on the edge of town. It was three in the morning; the building was dark. While Big Chuck stood guard, Raspold shot the big lock off the front door. He and Quinn entered and picked out a Bluebolt four-seater gravity-drive. Unfortunately, there were no keys available. So, he stuck the muzzle of the pistol against Barry's ribs as the owner came charging out of his rooms in the rear. Barry did not argue; he handed over the gun in his hand. And, a moment later, the keys. Raspold, wanting to make sure that Barry would not contact Nge—if he had intended to do so—took him along in the Bluebolt.

Big Chuck took over the controls and lifted the runabout just above the treetop level. He steered it northwards, toward von Fulka's house on the island 80 kilometers away. After five minutes, he landed the Bluebolt in an open space. Here, Raspold, after making sure that Barry had no wrister or other means of wireless communication on his person, told Barry to start walking toward home. If Barry followed a trail nearby, he would come out on a dirt road that would lead him back to town.

Barry looked as if he would like to curse them, but he did not open his mouth until just as they took off.

Big Chuck Woodwolf laughed and said, "Raspold, what would your chief say if he knew you were committing crime to fight criminals?"

Raspold smiled sourly and said, "FECAB has no jurisdiction here. So, if I'm caught, I'll get no help from it. No legal help, that is. The point is that Nge is too dangerous to permit at large. Any methods used—within reason, that is—to snare him are permissible. From my viewpoint anyway. Fight fire with fire."

Ten minutes later, the big Tserokian slowed the Bluebolt. The lake was in sight. It sparkled in the light of Diveboard's full moon, almost the size of Earth's. The house on the island in the middle of the lake gleamed whitely. No lights came from its windows.

Big Chuck, following Raspold's orders, slid the Bluebolt down the bank, into the lake, and under the surface. The little runabout was waterproof; the overhead doors were shut; they had air enough to last them until they reached the island. The car spurted forward in the darkness of the waters; the tiny pilot light by the compass lit only Big Chuck's features, which were grim and hard.

The Bluebolt presently struck the shallow mud of the island. The Tserokian lifted it slowly above the surface. They were on the beach, just outside the thick forest surrounding the house. There were no roads to the house. Raspold debated with himself whether they should proceed on foot, then decided against it. Big Chuck lifted the Bluebolt to a position level with the tops of the trees. The car, bending the treetops before it, proceeded toward the house. When they came to the clearing around the house, they stopped.

Quinn, sitting behind Raspold, had trouble keeping his teeth from chattering. Raspold said, "You want to stay here in the forest? We may all get killed. Or worse."

"It's my teeth that are cowardly, not me," said Quinn. "No, I owe Nge something for trying to kill me. Besides, if he lives after tonight, my life's not worth a non-Fed C."

"I don't see how they could be expecting us," said Raspold. "But with Nge, you never know. If it's a trap, we go into it."

"I got a nose for traps," said Big Chuck. "Smells like death. The question is, whose?"

A thick stone and cement wall about ten feet high surrounded the house, which was about forty meters from the wall. The house was a two-story structure also built of native rocks and cement. It looked as if it had from ten to twelve rooms. Against the northern wall stood a stone garage.

Raspold had Big Chuck guide the Bluebolt completely around the house. He was well aware that anyone looking out of the dark windows could see a glint of moonlight on the silvery Bluebolt. At any moment, he thought, guns will start firing. And we'll know where we stand.

"There are windows but no doors," he said. "They must get to the rooftop via grav and go down through a trapdoor. So will we."

"Nge isn't the man to sleep without guards of some kind." said Big Chuck. "That is, if he is in there. We don't even know that. Something's in there."

"Wait a minute," said Raspold. "You have to think about one thing. Nge's the greatest booby-trapper in the world. If he's left the house for keeps, he'll likely trigger it. If he knew I was coming to it, he wouldn't, for he's sworn to take me alive. But maybe he doesn't know I've tracked him this far."

He told Big Chuck to take the Bluebolt back across the forest-top to the beach. Here the car descended, and they slid a few feet above the beach around the island until Raspold saw what he was looking for. A log washed up by the waves, a log about one decimeter in diameter and two meters long. The three got out of the car, picked up the log, and laid it at right angles to the front and back seats. Quinn and Raspold held the log steady while Woodwolf piloted the car straight up into the air to a height of 20 meters.

The car moved until it was over the house, still silent and white in the moonlight. There was a very slight wind; Raspold estimated that they would not have to compensate for it.

Woodwolf locked the controls and rose from the pilot's seat to help them. With his strength added to theirs, one end of the log rose easily and was held vertically by the side of the car.

Raspold said, "Let her loose," and the log dropped. They sat down quickly, strapped themselves with the safety belt, and Big Chuck rolled the car fifty degrees along its longitudinal axis so that they could get a good view over the side.

The log, black in the silver moonlight, was almost on its target by the time they were ready to look. It was turning end over end very slowly; when it struck, it was horizontal, and the roof received the impact of the full length.

A bright flash appeared. Big Chuck slammed the Bluebolt into sudden flight, and the occupants were pressed back against the seat. For a moment, they were deafened.

Raspold looked back and saw planks and stones and other objects flying up higher than the car. If they had stayed, they probably would have been hit.

"I think," said Raspold, after he felt the others could hear him, "the mere opening of the rooftop door would have set off that mine. Anyway, we know one thing. Nge, if he was there, has left. Probably for Voittamaton. If he really dares."

⟫●⟪

They shot back to the city. Raspold went to the Terrestrial Consul and identified himself. After telling part of his story to the Consul, he had no trouble getting passports for himself and Woodwolf. Quinn decided to stay on Diveboard and continue in business. The passports gave the two immunity from police seizure (such a right had been granted in the contract with Earth ten years previously). He and the big Tserokian took a nonsked to Earth. An hour after getting through Customs, Raspold stood in the office of Ali'i.

"If your surmises are correct," said Ali'i, puffing away on a big cigar, "and if what I've read of Voittamaton is true, we can forget about Nge. He's as good as dead."

"We can't know for sure," said Raspold. "I want permission for myself, Woodwolf, and a pilot to go to Voittamaton. A small ship might be undetected by Nge. But if a big force showed up, we'd just scare him. He'd go into translation, and we'd have to start the whole chase over again."

"Woodwolf?"

"Swear him in as a temporary agent with limited powers and under my supervision," said Raspold. "If you don't, the damn fool will go to Voittamaton by himself. And he might get in the way, cause god-knows-what kind of mess. He's a good man, and he knows Nge's history, his behavior patterns, as few do."

"You'll have to take full responsibility for him and his actions," said Ali'i. He pressed a button and spoke into the box on his desk.

"Miss Petersen, show Mr. Woodwolf in."

Raspold and Big Chuck spent two hours with Ali'i, and then they went off to sleep for two hours while Ali'i made arrangements. Waking up completely refreshed, they removed the Morpheus electrodes from their temples and went to get breakfast. Afterwards, Ali'i introduced them to their pilot.

Raspold recognized him at once.

"Glad to see you're on the team," he said. "We couldn't have a better man."

He introduced Big Chuck to Aga-Oglu, a tall broad-shouldered man with a narrow face, a big curved nose, and deeply sunken eyes. Later, when Raspold was alone with the Tserokian, he said, "He's a native of Kagan. Was a member of the Baudelairean Gang. I was the only one who arrested him. About three years ago. He was rehabilitated and discharged from Johns Hopkins a year ago. Now, like a lot of rehabs, his experience with the criminal world is being used to good advantage by FECAB."

"You aren't a rehab?" said Big Chuck.

"If I'd been a criminal," said Raspold, "I'd never have been caught." He smiled to soften the egotism of the statement, but Big Chuck was not sure that Raspold was at all facetious.

Aga-Oglu called them, and they boarded the ship. Their take-off time was 13:47.22; to be delayed a second meant that new data would have to be fed into the ship's computer and a new translation period arranged for.

An hour later, subjective time, they were in a wide orbit about thirty thousand myriameters from Voittamaton. The nearest star was the sun of Diveboard, some ten light-years away. The rim of the Galaxy was so far away that it looked like a rough luminous disc seen edge on. And there was so little light that the planet, relatively close, was invisible.

"There it is," said Aga-Oglu, indicating the ghostly white circle on the screen before him. The image faded out and strengthened in 45-degree sectors, and on each side of the circle were little bursts of whiteness.

"Those little flashes are too big to be vessels," said Aga-Oglu. "Orbital debris; asteroidlets, maybe."

He flicked off the active scanner and turned on the passive.

"Now what?"

"We land," said Raspold.

Aga-Oglu shrugged and said, "I'll set the computer to land us in thirty minutes. We ought to be in our suits, have everything else ready by then? O.K.?"

Raspold nodded, and the three began to prepare for the landing. Twenty minutes later they were in their space suits and strapped to their seats. Aga-Oglu had turned the scanner on for another two minutes, long enough for the computer to receive all necessary data. Then, three minutes before the translator was to go into action, he turned the scanner on again. The computer rechecked their position and verified the setting of the translator "gauge."

"We make it in one big jump," said the pilot. "A series of small translations might allow Nge or whatever is on that planet to detect us between times. I've set the translator for minimum tolerance. We won't materialize any closer than one kilometer. We could try within that distance, but we'd run the risk of materializing under the surface. Two objects trying to occupy the same space. Boom! No more worries for us."

They all took a last drag of their cigarettes, then closed the visors to their helmets. A tiny alarm clanged; a big 12:00 glowed on the face of the clock. They sat like three stone statues, eyes fixed on the clock. 12:00.1, 12:00.2, 12:00.3, and on and on until the fiery numbers said 12:05.

Raspold's hands were tightly clenched around the arms of his seat, and they remained tight when, after the blink of his eyes, he saw 12:05.1.

Aga-Oglu went into savage action. He pressed the button that switched the controls to manual, and he rammed two control sticks forward. The vessel accelerated, and the occupants felt themselves pressed back against their seats. The window in front of them suddenly cleared; they were automatically visual now. They clamped their jaws to keep from crying out. The surface was rushing toward them; they were going to crash!

But Aga-Oglu knew what he was doing. He had shot the craft downward as swiftly as he dared after coming out of translation so that he could get on the surface before their power was cut off by whatever it was that had cut off the power of that Federation expedition so many years ago.

Twenty seconds later, they had landed as gently as a lover's touch.

Aga-Oglu's cheerful voice came through the helmet-phones.

"Well, that's one less worry. Now what?"

The entire upper half of their ship was transparent, and they could see the surface of the planet. Rather, could see what the darkness permitted.

It was more than they had expected. Something gleamed outside. Somethings. Tall and white, apparently casting a self-generated and feeble glow. Everywhere around them. So close they pressed against the vessel. Aga-Oglu had, with magnificent skill, landed them—wedged them—in an aisle of the phantom objects.

Raspold examined the one closest to him. It was a slender round pillar which rose to a height of five meters. At its top was a globe approximately two meters in diameter. This was only partially white; it bore irregular blackish blotches. The globe on the stele next to it also had the patches, but these were of a different pattern. And, on each stele, running from top to bottom, were characters. Alphabetical letters?

Raspold turned away from them. "How close are we to The Mouth?" he said, using the same word that Liedl, Versinen's lieutenant, had used when describing the opening in the mountain.

Aga-Oglu, looking at a card in his hand, said, "We were supposed to make a final translation within at least ten kilometers of The Mouth. The scanner took a fix while we were landing. We're just nine kilometers away. Straight North. How's that, huh?"

"Did it pick up any of Nge's ships?"

"No. How could it? If his fleet landed in the forest..."

Aga-Oglu read two other cards, and he said, "No more atmosphere than the Moon. Funny, too, when you're on a planet only a little smaller than Earth. Should at least be a frozen atmosphere, gas-snow."

Raspold considered. They could lift the ship above the globed steles and make a dash for The Mouth in it. Or two could get into each of the one-man "hoppers" stored in the rear of the bigger ship and advance between the aisles of the steles and beneath the cover of the globes. That meant that the Kagan would have to remain in the ship.

Aga-Oglu protested.

"If we have to come running," said Raspold, "I want everything triggered to go the moment we drive into the hopper-port. And if we don't return within two hours, you are to leave without us, at once, and report to Ali'i. That's an order."

He made sure his watch synchronized with Woodwolf's and Aga-Oglu's, shook hands with the Kagan, and walked to the hoppers. These were small rugged craft much used by spacers in asteroid mining. The two in the port had been especially beefed up for service on a large planet; they were capable of speeds up to six hundred kilometers an hour and could cruise at one hundred kilometers an hour for six hours before needing refueling. Each was armed with two .45 machine guns located in the forward end of the thick runners (like a sled's) placed at the underpart of the craft.

The two climbed into the seats, closed the ports on each side, and checked the controls and instruments. Raspold gave the order to Aga-Oglu to open the hopper-port. The pumps sucked the air content into the ship. The huge door swung swiftly open. The hoppers, Raspold's in the lead, rose a few inches and moved out of the port.

Raspold rotated the hopper so that it faced the north and lifted it over the *Pulex* and down into the aisle in front of it. Woodwolf's craft followed him.

Raspold began to increase his speed swiftly, but, after several seconds, while the tall white pillars and their globes shot by him, he lifted his hand in signal to Woodwolf. And he slowed the craft, looking in the rearview mirror to make sure that the big Tserokian wasn't going to hit him. When he had come to a halt, he lifted the hopper level with the globes. And he examined the nearest ones. He shook his head and proceeded slowly enough to allow himself a good look at those passing on his right. He crawled past them for a minute. Then, as if making up his mind, he lifted his hand again, and shot the hopper forward, reaching one hundred km p/h in five seconds. Again, the white and silent aisle sped by in a blur; the huge hole at the base of the mountain—outlined on the scanner—expanded before him. He stopped the hopper two kilometers from it, and Woodwolf landed directly behind him. Raspold flipped the switch that would put them in tight-beam communication—he wanted no one to tap in on the beam—and he said, "I slowed down because there was something familiar about the patterns of dark patches on the globes. Didn't they look to you as if they represented continents? As if the globes were supposed to be planets, and the white portions are seas?

"I didn't think so," said Big Chuck, "But, now that you point it out..."

"You don't suppose they do represent planets?" said Raspold. "Markers? Markers for what? Possessions?"

"This place gives me the spooks," said the Tserokian. "It looks like one big graveyard. The biggest in the world."

The hairs on the back of Raspold's neck rose. He said, "Maybe it is."

"What do you mean?"

Raspold shrugged and said, "I really don't know. But the whole thing is curious. A thousand square miles of nothing but globes on steles. For what purpose?"

"Maybe somebody in there has the answer?"

"If he—it—does," said Raspold, "I hope he feels like talking."

He reached for the controls, then stopped. Above and ahead of him, above the mountain, a luminous round object had appeared. It was, at first, a pale globe, dinner-plate sized. Which meant that, at this distance from him, it must be at least fifty meters in diameter. It could have been hanging, undetected, all this time; now, it had started to pour out light. And, in a few seconds, the light had strengthened, had become as bright as the Earthly sun.

"What the hell's going on?" said Woodwolf.

"Something just came out of the cave mouth," said Raspold. "Something small. It flew up the mountainside, went over the top."

———————

He sat for several seconds, rigid in his seat, before speaking. "Maybe it's a decoy. But let's go after it, anyway."

He shut off the beam and shot the hopper at an angle which would take it just above the sharp point of the mountain. Woodwolf followed him. Raspold, clearing the peak, saw that the mountain was part of a range of similar jagged cones. And he risked a quick look behind him and saw that the monuments were white as bleached bones under a desert sun. And that nowhere in the illuminated area was a sign of Nge's fleet. Perhaps, he thought, Nge had taken his ships into the cavern mouth. He had never reached the surface perhaps.

His mother ship, the *Pulax*, was still sitting wedged in the aisle. He could imagine Aga-Oglu's frantic reaction to the light, and he hoped the man would stay where he was, as ordered.

The hopper almost struck the top of the peak, then it was by. And Raspold saw the thing that had flown from the cave. It was not more than thirty meters from him and was hanging in space, facing him, as if waiting for him.

It was the strangest creature that Raspold had ever seen, and he had seen many. It had a long reddish-brown body roughly centaur-shaped. The lower torso gave a bilobed impression; there was a deep groove running its length where a spine would be in any other creature and where one might be in this. Six spindly and grotesquely long limbs hung downward from the lower torso and ended in something like a human foot. The upper torso had narrow shoulders and a neck and a head and two arms as spindly and overly long as the "legs." These ended in enormous hands with fingers that made Raspold think of spider legs.

The face was that of a demon. Humanoid, it had a chin, acromegalically developed. A nose that looked like a parrot's beak. Great forward-leaning ears. Two long independently moving fleshy strips sprouting from each cheek. The forehead was very low; the skull was hairless. The eyes were set in fleshy slants.

It was the tail that startled Raspold the most. A thick pillar, almost as long as the body, it ended in a thick oval four-lobed pad.

The creature was a nightmare, something out of an opium smoker's dreams. It had no right to exist, to be unprotected by a spacesuit, to have limbs where limbs were not needed to move, to have a nose where no air was, to have ears where sound had no medium through which to travel, to have a mouth where it could not talk.

It moved, seemingly by a biologically generated control of gravity. It lived without artificial devices where nothing could live naturally.

Raspold decided to break the silence between the hoppers; he activated the radio. With all the maneuvering they might have to do, they could not afford to jockey around until lined up for tight-beamed transmission.

"Watch the tail!" he said to Woodwolf. "If Versinen wasn't raving mad, these things use those pads as weapons."

"Here come four more," said Woodwolf's voice.

Raspold spun the hopper around so he could see past the Tserokian's craft. Four similar creatures were just coming over the peak.

A shadow appeared above him; he looked upward and at the same time placed the hopper into a reverse motion so savage that the upper part of his body strained against the belts holding him. The thing—which he mentally termed the "space station," darted after him, its long arms held out towards him.

He stopped the hopper and threw it forward, intending to ram the creature. But the scorpion shot off at an angle.

Woodwolf's hopper darted towards Raspold's. It tilted upward and flame appeared at the open end of one of the runners beneath the hopper.

The scorpion, struck by a series of .45 slugs, turned end over end, its legs and arms flailing. Then, as if it had suddenly lost its power over gravity, it began to fall straight.

Raspold steered his hopper over to Woodwolf's and at the four scorpions. These scattered, increasing the gap between them, some going up and some down. He had lost his chance to get all of them with one sweep of the machine-guns. But he did center one and gave it a burst. It was hurled backward, cartwheeling, and then began to fall swiftly.

There was a thud, and he looked upward to see a face upside down, pressed against the port on his left. The scorpion was clinging to the top of the hopper and was peering down at him.

For several seconds, he looked into the eyes above the falcon's beak. They were black, innocent of white of pupil or any other color. A ball of jet.

Then, he turned his hopper over and over in a violent maneuver to throw the creature away. But the thing clung tightly, and the four-lobed pad on the end of its tail came down against the right port and pressed against it.

Immediately, the irradiated plastic began to melt.

Raspold snatched the .45 automatic from its holster by the edge of his seat. He fired twice into the window, the muzzle centered on the pad. Normally, the bullets would have come flying back from the plastic. But, weakened by the melting, the plastic was no obstacle. The bullets plunged into the fleshy looking pad, and the pad jerked away.

Woodwolf's hopper suddenly appeared, the ends of its runners on a level with the top of Raspold's craft. Flame shot out from the open end; the scorpion's face disappeared. And reappeared on the other side of Raspold's hopper as it fell away.

That left two. No, one. For another had attacked Woodwolf, and to do so it had to pass by Raspold. He fired, knocked it spinning away, followed, dived after it, gave it four more bursts, and saw it fall toward the peak.

Now, the two men maneuvered their hoppers to herd the scorpion and catch it in a crossfire. But the creature, shaking its fist at them in a too-human gesture, turned and fled. Its speed must have been at least three hundred kilometers an hour; it went over the peak and disappeared, presumably toward the cavern mouth.

Raspold checked the hole in the plastic port. It was about the size of his hand, but he didn't worry about it. The cabin had no air in it; the access ports had been closed for protection against micrometeorites.

"If we go into the cavern," said Raspold, "we may encounter thousands of these. You know how little chance we'd have then."

"Yeah," said Big Chuck. "Maybe most of them were too busy with Nge to bother us. And what about Aga-Oglu? We'd better check on him before we do anything else."

Raspold looked out of the corner of his eyes at the bright-as-the-sun globe above him. He was sure that the scorpions were not responsible for that. Whoever had released them against the two Terrans had placed that globe there. And that indicated an intelligence at least as high as a human being's.

"We'll check on Aga-Oglu," he said. "Keep silence unless it's necessary to break it."

They dipped at an angle to the peak and stopped just above it. The rows on rows of globes and pillars were as before, ghostly, chill, white. The *Pulex* lay where it had been. The Kagan, Raspold knew, would see them when they came down along the face of the mountain. He'd know they were all right.

They dropped down the almost vertical face of the peak. But, before they reached the great opening below them, they were in darkness again. The globe had been extinguished.

Raspold felt cold. They were being watched. How? By whom? He did not know. But he assumed that he would soon find out. Probably not to his pleasure.

Just below the top of the cavern, he stopped. Why go on? Why not be sane, be discreet? Return to Earth, tell them what had happened. It was more than likely that Nge had met defeat at the hands of whatever lived in the bowels of Voittamaton. If the Federation wanted to, it could send a fleet back, a fleet which could land as they had and could shoot missiles with thermonuclear warheads into the cave. Get rid of the menace once and for all. Or, if Voittamaton were truly invincible, then Nge could be marked off the books and the planet could be left alone forever.

He sighed. The old proverb was true. Curiosity killed the cat, and Raspold had a cat's curiosity. He could not endure not knowing what had happened to Nge, what was the power within this dark planet.

He broke the silence and said to Woodwolf, "I'm going on in, but you don't have to be stupid too. Go back to the *Pulex*. Nobody is going to think one less whit of you."

"I hope you're not ordering me to return," said the Tserokian. "I don't want to be guilty of insubordination. But if I have to, I will. I swore I'd find my sister or find out what happened to her. And I swore I'd get Nge."

"It's your neck," said Raspold.

He directed the craft into the cave, just beneath the arch of rock. And he stopped almost at once. He had expected to be surprised but not so soon.

Below him, at least five hundred meters below, was the floor of the cave. He could see it easily because it glowed with a light. A strange light that illuminated only the area of the floor and cast no glow above a definite demarcation. The ships of Nge's fleet were clearly illuminated by the light. They rested on the floor in ranks of six, the stolen destroyer *George A. Custer* and the other largest ships in the front rank and the others, graded according to size, behind them. All had various ports open, the ports out of which the pirates must have proceeded on foot or in hoppers. The front ranks were by the wall at the far end of the cave, the wall that had stopped further progress on their part. And the personnel of the vessels must have gone through an opening of the wall, an opening large enough for ten men abreast but too small for the ships.

Raspold wondered where the light came from. Then, as he dropped down two hundred meters for a closer look, he saw that the surface of the lighted area had a shiny appearance. It was almost as if the entire floor of the cave had been covered with a thick plastic which trapped light issuing from some unseen source.

He gasped and dropped down again and then paled.

The floor *was* solid with some clear material. The ships were caught in it, embedded like insects in amber!

Raspold almost turned back at this point. If the power within Voittamaton could spring a trap like this, could release some gluey or flowing plastic substance and imprison big ships like this, then light it up for display purposes, what chance did only two men have? Who knew but what the light was for his benefit?

The ports were open; therefore, the men who had left the fleet must have gone through that archway in the far wall. But the men that must have been left behind in the ships were trapped. Doomed to die of starvation.

He thought, why didn't they just translate? The plastic could not hold them if they used the drive.

The answer was obvious. They did not have the power. It must have been cut off by an outside agency, just as the power in that Federation expedition had been cut off. So, the men would not die of starvation. They would die of choking as soon as they used up the air in the ships and then that in their spacesuits.

He had a thought, one which did not please him. If the plastic material also filled up the entrance to the next chamber or cave, he would have to turn back.

He guided the hopper over the embedded ships and to the archway. And found that the luminous material stopped several meters short of it. There was more than enough room for the hoppers to pass through.

—————⟶⦿⟵—————

The entranceway did not lead immediately to another cave, as he had expected. It was the opening for a tunnel, cut out of solid rock, that curved not quite imperceptibly to the left and led gently downward. Raspold had turned on the searchbeam so that he could see where he was going; the light splashed off an oily blackness of hard-seeming stone. Then, a bright glow was ahead, the tunnel ceased, and they were in another cavern.

This was so huge that it looked like the interior of a pocket world. It was well-lighted from an invisible source—nothing new in Raspold's technology—

and the floor, polished granitoid stone, held thousands of objects. These were arranged in rows; the aisles between were broad enough for five hoppers abreast. The objects were in groups and stood on black metal platforms about two meters high. It became evident, as they advanced down the aisle, that they were in a museum. The objects consisted of paintings, stone and wooden sculptures, wood and stone and metal weapons, furniture, models of dwellings: tents, houses, large buildings, and boats, wagons, chariots. And, standing stiffly and silently beside the artifacts, the makers of the artifacts.

These looked at first like wax dummies. But Raspold lifted his hopper and went closer. And he was sure that the statues were stuffed specimens, superb examples of taxidermy. They were members of some centauroid species with which he was unfamiliar.

After a while, they came to an aisle that crossed the one they were on at right angles, and Raspold decided to turn onto that. He drove for several kilometers until he met another aisle which continued in the same direction as the aisle he had originally been on. Turning down this, he at once saw that another type of sentient was represented on the platforms. These were bipedal, humanoid, their legs from the knees downward incased in tubes of clear plastic-like material. As they passed the platforms, they saw that the groups were arranged to show the stages of physical and cultural evolution of the various subspecies among the bipeds. Near the end of the aisle, they were passing platforms with highly developed artifacts, artistically and technologically.

They crossed an aisle at right angles to this one, and started down it. And found that this represented the same progress in evolution for a centauroid race of quite a different type than the first they had seen.

Raspold lifted the hopper until he could see far across the gigantic chamber. There, barely within the limits of his vision, was what he had expected. He gestured to Big Chuck and shot over the heads of the thousands of silent figures until he was at the desired aisle.

He did not need to break silence to tell Woodwolf what these represented. The subhuman figures were familiar enough to both of them, from their schoolbooks. After a minute, they were going by inescapably recognizable sentients. Homo sapiens.

———>≫●≪<———

Raspold sped down the aisle while the prehistory and history of man flashed by. Ten kilometers, and he was at the end. Beyond, a sea of empty platforms.

He did not turn then and go down the aisle that ran at ninety degrees to this. He knew that if he did he would see the present development of all the extra-Terrestrial sentients he knew and many many more he did not know. How far that aisle extended was a matter of conjecture. It went so far it passed the horizon, out of sight. But he was willing to bet with any taker that every sentient group that presently inhabited this Galaxy was represented.

Presently? Probably many that had existed but did no longer. When he had risen high to take a look, he had seen quite a few rows that had ended long before the others, that had empty platforms at the end of their lines.

Did the vast prairie of empties before him wait for further steps in evolution of the human race? Or did the curator of this museum consider that Homo sapiens was through, and the empties were to be filled with new sentients?

Raspold shivered, and lifted the hopper high. He rose to the top of the chamber, over two kilometers high, and looked for doorways. He found one, an entrance that looked small from where he was. But, when he came close to it, it was huge. An archway a hundred meters high and two hundred broad. And it was a thousand meters thick.

On emerging from the entrance, they found themselves in another cavern as Brobdingnagian as the last. And their eyes widened and their lips parted with gasps of wonder as they gazed upon mountain after mountain of piled-up jewels. Diamonds, emeralds, rubies, topazes, every precious stone that they knew of and many more they did not. The twinkling glittering masses, heaped higher than ten-story buildings, were composed of cut jewels of every size, from thumbnail dimensions to diamonds taller than a man.

Raspold wondered why Nge had not stopped here, taken all he could carry, and returned to his fleet. Perhaps, he had, and found his fleet trapped forever and had come back to find the possessor of these treasures and either kill him in revenge or force him to unspring the trap.

More likely, though, he had not retraced his steps. Nge might be tempted to grab and run but he would resist it. More than a share of this, he would want the knowledge and the power of the owners of this world. If he had those, he could easily be the most powerful man—being—in the Galaxy. And he could take whatever he wanted.

Or so Nge would reason, thought Raspold. I think like a criminal, and that is how I would think.

If even a portion of these were dumped on the market, they would be very cheap. Maybe not. There were a thousand worlds in the Galaxy that he knew of and a probable ninety-nine thousand more to be found. These could be spread out very thin.

He repressed the impulse to take several of the larger jewels with him and sped as swiftly as discretion allowed toward the opposite wall of the cavern. Here he found another archway just like the last one, but he paused before it. Big Chuck maneuvered directly behind him, and they established tight-beam transmission.

"It's still not too late," said Raspold. "We'd not be criticized at all if we return to Earth. We've invaluable information. The discovery of a form of life that can live in airless space and biologically control gravity is enough to justify us. Especially, if we pick up several of the bodies of the scorpions we shot down and give them to the scientists for dissection. And we can take some of the jewels. They're not stolen from Federation people, not as far as we know. We'd be entitled to keep them. You could buy the biggest ranch on Tserokia; I could resign from FECAB, set up my own agency.

"But there are stronger factors. I believe that we're as helpless before the inhabitants of Voittamaton as newborn kittens before a hungry wolf. From what I've seen, we don't have a chance."

"I'd always wonder about my sister," said Big Chuck. "And I want to make sure that Nge doesn't escape."

"He's as good as dead, if not now dead. If your sister is with him, she's lost too,"

"I'm going on ahead," said the Tserokian.

Raspold sighed and said, "O.K. Where angels fear..."

He drove the hopper down the archway. This was even longer than the previous one. And, as they neared its opposite end, they saw that it was obscured, flickering, like a flawed sheet of plastic on which light was playing.

But the flickering was an immaterial property; Raspold's hopper went through it as if it did not exist. He, however, breathed relief when nothing happened, for he expected it to be some sort of beam that would trigger off an explosion or a sheet of lightning or God-only-knew-what.

Then, they were inside another cavern.

The hopper lost the two decimeters of height above the floor. Raspold was startled, but he saw at once that every light on his instrument panel had gone out and all dials indicated zero. His power was cut off.

A shadow fell on his hopper, and then it resolved into dozens of scorpions. They grabbed his hopper and rose with it to a height of fifty meters before he could decide what action to take. By then, he knew that he could do nothing except go along for the ride. If he shot the scorpions, he'd be dropped and killed.

Besides, he knew that the inhabitants of Voittamaton had finally taken action against him, that they had been waiting for him, and had sprung the trap. In one way, he was glad. At least, the tension of waiting for attack was gone.

Behind him, Woodwolf's hopper was also being carried.

———————

Raspold looked through the spaces between the cloud of brown bodies around his craft. This chamber was even more fantastic. Its walls were plated with gold, and the gold was set with patterns of jewels. There were niches here and there in which were sets of statues and paintings of various sorts. The artwork, however, differed from that he had seen in the first chamber. This, it was evident, was all of a piece. The work of one group of sentients. The paintings were bizarre, many almost incomprehensible. And the statuary represented beings he had never seen before. Creatures that could only be termed dracocentaurs. Except that they had six lower limbs. The upper torso was scaled, and the arms were very long but humanoid. The face looked like an intelligent dragon's.

Abruptly, the hopper fell as those carrying it let themselves drop. For a few seconds, he wondered if he were to be killed as an eagle kills a tortoise, by dropping it and breaking its shell. But the scorpions applied deceleration, and he was gently lowered onto the floor. Immediately, the plastic ports shattered, fell outward, and huge hands with spidery fingers reached in and took his automatic from him. Then, the belts were unfastened, and he was dragged out of the craft and set on his feet.

The visor to his helmet was opened, and it was then he knew that the chamber had atmosphere. When he was whirled around, he saw that Nge and his men had also been caught. They were standing in orderly rows, and they were unarmed and as naked as the day they were born. Two hundred or so men and women, he calculated, for they were in twenty rows of ten each.

Behind him, Woodwolf cried out, "Tuli! Tuli!" and he spoke a long string of phrases in his native tongue.

So, Woodwolf's sister was one of the women. That part of his quest was ended, anyway. He had found her.

And he recognized Heinrich Nge. The man was standing in the first row but half a pace ahead of the others. The giant's massively muscled body was beautiful, shining copper in the golden light. The face, high-browed, aquiline-nosed, thick-lipped, was set in scowling lines; he looked like a statue of an ancient Pharaoh carved from a polished close-grained dark-red stone. His hands, like those of everybody in the ranks, were free. But his feet could not move, and, as Raspold was carried closer, he saw why. Every human being had his legs embedded inside a block of some transparent material.

Shocked, he thought of the stuffed beings in the museum. Their legs, also, were set inside similar cubes.

Carried horizontally, looking upward, Raspold saw that the ceiling of the gigantic chamber was covered with scorpions hanging upside down or else drifting slowly near the top. He turned his head to both sides and saw that, behind the human beings and on both sides, the floor was packed with creatures.

Perhaps the most terrible aspect of the scene was that they uttered not a sound.

He and Woodwolf were carried before the front row of the prisoners, also silent, and there the suits were swiftly removed from them. Their underclothes were stripped off, and scorpions carried in two metallic boxes. Inside the boxes was a clear liquid. The feet of each man were thrust into a box despite their struggles, and a scorpion dropped a tiny pellet into the liquid in each box. Within a few seconds, the liquid had become a jelly. In half a minute, the jelly had become a solid. The men and the boxes were lifted into the air, and the boxes were slid from the material. And the men were set back on their feet. Raspold found that he could stay upright without any difficulty; his feet were far enough apart.

Before he had been too occupied with what was happening to him to take a good look at the thing—things—about ten meters in front of the human beings. Now, he saw that a ball of some glassy stuff hung in the air at a level with his head. The ball had a diameter of about thirty meters and colors played inside the sphere as if a hundred living rainbows were chasing each other. On top of the ball, sitting or lying in a depression, was a dracocentaur.

It was about twenty meters long, exclusive of the long, scaled, and barbed tail which hung down on the other side of the ball but now and then rose into the air and waved about like a cat's tail. The upper torso reared into the air, propped up by the elbows of the long arms. The face was huge and frightening; the eyes were enormous. From each cheek hung a long tendril of pale flesh. The mouth, when opened, revealed quite human teeth, teeth that looked grotesque in that mouth, in that half-human, half-dragon face.

The eyes were black, completely, and Raspold, who had always scoffed at the cliché that eyes could show the character of a person, now repented. Those eyes looked ancient, ancient, ancient beyond the ken of his mind. Their blackness was that of interstellar space itself. No, that of extra-Galactic space, frightening in the emptiness and foreverness.

Raspold stood humble and quaking and silent, like some suppliant before the greatest of all kings. Behind him, the others were silent, too, except for the inevitable coughing, and the coughs bounced off the faraway wall and came back magnified and hollow.

———❦———

Finally, the dracocentaur opened its mouth, and the black and flexible lips spoke. They spoke in Lingo, but it was with phonetic values strange to Raspold's ears, so that he thought at first that it was an entirely foreign language. The structure of the creature's mouth was such that it could not quite master some of the phones.

"You came through the Place of Dead Worlds before you entered my home!" it said in a loud roaring voice. "Did not that make you think? Think that you could do nothing against one who has seen those globes form out of primeval gas and become balls of flaming gas and then cool off and give birth to brainless life and then to creatures that can talk and then give death as the parent sun cooled or became a nova? Nothing against one who was born before this Galaxy condensed out of interstellar gas? Against one who may see this Galaxy die? Die? And see another rise from the ashes?"

Raspold felt as if his bones had crystallized into ice. So that was what the globes on the aisles represented! He had passed through the greatest graveyard in the world, the graveyard of planets long dead. But what sort of creature was this that could mark the passing of a world by setting up a monument? And wait for eons for another to die and set up another marker? How long, how immeasurably long, since the first stele and globe?

The dracocentaur stopped talking and looked at them for several minutes. Then, it said, "No. You would not stop to think. You would not dare to stop. Your greed blinded you. As it has every creature that has tried to storm this world. Long before your ancestors were even one-celled sea creatures."

Raspold did not think he had the courage. Yet, he spoke. And, afterward, he thought it was the bravest act of his life.

"You are wrong! I did not come here to steal. Neither did my companion. And some among the others did not come of their own free will. They were brought along as prisoners. And my friend and I came only because we hoped to catch these criminals and take them to institutions of rehabilitation before they went too far."

The being on the sphere opened its mouth, whether to smile or snarl, Raspold could not tell. He could not interpret the expressions of this sentient.

Its eyes focused on Raspold. It said, "I know."

There was another silence while the brain that had outlived mountains of granite considered them.

Then, "I cannot worry about your petty problems—how petty you cannot guess—of good and evil. You are all one to me. Would you distinguish between the moral characters of a swarm of gnats, if these minute insects were capable of ethical behavior?"

"I would," said Raspold boldly. After all, what did he have to lose? Moreover, would a being as powerful, as ancient as this, be irritated by a being like himself?"

Perhaps. A lion will swat at a fly.

"One insect considers another," said the dracocentaur. His look seemed to say, "So?"

I talked to your predecessor, Versinen," said the being. "He went mad. Rather, more mad. Because I showed him what awaited him when he died."

<hr />

It paused and seemed to stare through them, the walls of stone, the mountain, and out to the stars. Or, beyond the stars.

"What waits for us all," it said. "What terrifies even me."

Now, for the first time since Raspold had entered, Nge spoke. He bellowed, "You are lying! After death, there is nothing! Nothing! You are trying to frighten us! You do not know! You do not know!"

The dracocentaur waited until the echoes of Nge's frenzied cries had ceased. Then, it said, "I know."

Again, it fell silent, and the brain within considered thoughts beyond the scope of man. Raspold shivered, though it was quite warm within the chamber.

It said, "The one who came before Versinen was a creature whose kind you do not know. They perished some hundreds of thousands of years ago—your Earth years, that is. He came seeking knowledge, not treasure to loot. I showed him what waited for him, for us all. He left crazy. Not as insane as Versinen, because he had greater stability. But he returned to his planet and told what he knew. I think that his revelation had something to do with their swift decline and death."

"What do you intend to do with us?" said Big Chuck Woodwolf. "I only came here to get my sister and make Nge pay for what he has done."

"During which, you injured some of my children," said the being. (Raspold thought of him now as Voittamaton; man must name everything.)

"Your children? These?" said Woodwolf, gesturing at the scorpions.

"Yes. For much longer than you can conceive, I was alone here. You see, my people have been practically immortal for a—to you—immeasurably long time. We were scattered over this Galaxy and others. Then, one by one, they died. Some by accident, for we are not truly immortal. Most by suicide. They had lived too long. Only I am left. I would have killed myself, too, but I lived long enough to find out what waits for us after death. And I dared not.

"But one of the things that made life intolerable was that we quit having children. We saw that life was, in the end, only futility. Moreover, after eons, we lost the desire to mate, to reproduce. You people are just beginning to encounter the numerous problems immortality brings. Wait until you are semi-immortal, like us. Then...

"However, recently—a thousand or so of your years ago—I thought, why not have children? They will be some companionship. Not much. Some. So, I removed several millions of egg cells from suspended animation, and changed their structure somewhat so that they can live and operate in space as well as in atmosphere of any type. They are also the only truly omnivorous sentients in the Galaxy. They can eat anything: rocks, trees, plants, animals. They can survive on radiant energy, too, though this is only enough to keep the spark of life from going out. Naturally, they derive most benefit from eating flesh.

"These you see now are pre-adolescents. They have been developing for several hundreds of your years. Soon, they will be adolescent and will be reproducing. Then, when this planet becomes too crowded, they will be venturing into the stellar systems in your Galaxy. Look out then!

"But these do not represent the greatest danger to you. There is a storm gathering on the Galaxy nearest to this, beings who are far more dangerous than my young. But you need not worry about them for a hundred years or more.

"However, you may be able to fight these youngsters. They are intelligent but ignorant. Savages. I will teach them nothing. It will be interesting, I hope, to see how they develop, but I doubt it. Interest dies as immortality grows."

"What about us?" shouted Nge. "We are not immortal! We want to live as long as we can! We cannot hurt you, and it will cost you nothing to let us loose!"

"You plead for your lives? Beg?"

"I beg for nothing!" said Nge. "I will not go down on my knees to you and whine for my life! I do not want to die, but if I have to kiss your scaly tail, I will die first! But I do say that we can be no danger to you. So, why not let us go? Especially, if what you say is true about an afterlife? Why condemn us to something you cannot face yourself?"

A horrible rictus opened Voittamaton's mouth. He said, "So! You do not believe what I told you about death? You are only using what I said to argue with me. Well, I will not argue."

He was silent again for a while. Then, "I admire courage and the will to live. Even if I know they mean nothing. Perhaps, that is why I brought my young to life."

He gave a quite human shrug of his shoulders, and...

Raspold did not at first grasp what had happened. Seemingly, between the blink of his eyes, he had been transported from the chamber of Voittamaton to the interior of a spaceship. He was in the lounge (he had seen enough of these to know), and stars hung outside the transparent viewport of the lounge. Whether the transition had been instantaneous or he had been made unconscious and transported here, he did not know and would never know.

The important thing was that Nge and his crew and Tuli and Chuck Woodwolf and himself were here. They were standing on a great heap of jewels, a layer of diamonds and other precious stones at least a foot thick.

Beyond the lounge was the open doorway to a corridor. And, far down the corridor, another open door. The entrance to the bridge. The pilot's chair was empty; nobody was at the controls.

———⊷⊶———

Nge and his crew still had their feet encased in the transparent blocks. But the blocks were gone from the legs of himself, Woodwolf, and a woman who must be Woodwolf's sister.

All three of them were standing side by side and in the midst of Nge and his men.

Raspold, the shock clearing, saw the situation as arranged by Voittamaton. The ship was accelerating or the gravitic field was on. Otherwise, they'd have been floating in free fall. The way to control of the ship lay open. Whoever got there first would get control. The pirates, though outnumbering the three, were handicapped by the blocks. The three were surrounded by enemies; they would have to fight their way to the bridge.

Voittamaton must be chuckling in his dragon throat, he thought.

Raspold shouted, "To the bridge, Woodwolf!"

He picked up a diamond as large as his head, and, holding it in both hands, smashed it into the face of the man nearest him. The man went down and knocked over several beside him. It was as if a bowling ball had struck a set of pins.

Raspold leaped over the bodies and struck again. Behind him, the giant Tserokian whooped and also began striking out. But with his fists.

Woodwolf was hit back and he reeled for a second. His sister pushed him forward again, and he seized a man and hurled him sidewise against the mob. The man's body knocked over a dozen of those standing by him.

Then, the big figure of Nge, almost as huge as Woodwolf, appeared before him. Nge threw an emerald the size of his fist at Raspold; Raspold ducked. The stone hit a man in the face, and the man howled with pain.

Nge seized hold of Raspold's arm and pulled him in toward him. Raspold, dirtiest among dirty when it came to fighting for survival, brought his knee up against Nge's crotch. Nge screamed and clutched himself and doubled over and fell writhing.

Then, Woodwolf had grabbed Nge's neck between his big hands and was squeezing. He paid no attention to the hard blows of fists from those nearest him.

"Woodwolf!" shouted Raspold. "Don't kill him! We have to get to the bridge!"

He was in a frenzy. If they lost now because of Woodwolf's obsession to kill Nge…

Something struck him in the jaw; his knees buckled under him, and blackness and flashes of light were all he saw. His head began to clear almost at once, but several other fists banged away at him. These struck his shoulders and ribs. They hurt but did not fuzz his thinking. And Tuli was helping him up. Tuli, whose swollen belly should have been her only concern but was taking blows to help him.

"If you don't forget about Nge!" howled Raspold into the giant Tserokian's ear, "your sister will die! Don't you care about her?"

Woodwolf looked up, and, for the first time, seemed to realize what he was doing. He bounded up, leaving the unconscious Nge lying on the jewels, and he picked up Raspold and lifted him above his head.

"So!" roared Woodwolf, and he gave him a toss that sent him flying over the heads of those nearest him. Down he came, irresistible, and knocked over those beneath him. He scrambled up, striking, clawing, while behind him the berserk Tserokian howled with battle fury. There were two men between him and the door; these went down and backward and could not get up fast enough to stop him.

Then, he was in the pilot's seat and there, dead ahead, looming so hugely it looked as if it would crush them, was the bulk of a planet. It filled the screen except for one corner cut by an arc.

Raspold was too old a spacehand to be alarmed by its seeming proximity. Instead, he located and found the transceiver controls. And, within a minute, he was in contact. The planet was Diveboard.

—————

Two days later, Raspold, Woodwolf, Tuli, and Aga-Oglu were sitting at a table in a bar in Upper Copenhagen. Raspold threw several bills on the table and said, "That'll buy us a couple of rounds. Then, I'm broke until payday."

Tuli smiled at him (the most beautiful smile in the world, thought Raspold, always given to hyperbole), and she said, "Just think. Two days ago we were the richest human beings in the Galaxy. Whoever would have thought that Nge would escape from jail the same night he was locked up and steal the ship back? While we slept in the hotel?"

"You don't know Nge," said Raspold. "If he weren't such a murdering monster, I could grow fond of him."

"We'll get him yet," said Woodwolf. "We can start looking for him again just as soon as I get Tuli settled back home."

"Not until my chief is through with me," said Raspold. "He's still angry because I didn't bring the ship right to Earth. It was no use my telling him that the Diveboard authorities wouldn't let me. And he acts as if he thinks our story isn't true."

"Tell him to go to Voittamaton himself and find out," said Aga-Oglu.

"I wouldn't tell my worst enemy that," said Raspold. He shivered. Those empty never-ending eyes and the dreadful voice telling with flat certainty of the horror beyond death…no. It was best not to think about that.

"Loan me enough to buy another martini," he said to Woodwolf. "Let's drink and be merry, for tomorrow…"

Planet Pickers

Previously unpublished.

Having read "Some Fabulous Yonder" you may be interested in seeing an early, but uncompleted, draft of the story. "Planet Pickers" was Phil's original title for the story that was first published as "Some Fabulous Yonder" in *Fantastic Stories of Imagination,* April 1963. Although this version was aborted after nearly 6000 words it is included here to show how Phil first approached the story. Also note that this version does not yet have the link to John Carmody and that any reminders Phil wrote to himself are included.

Diveboard had been discovered some years before by a lone planetstriker. It was a T-type or Tellurian planet circling a GO star that hung on the rim of the Galaxy, a hundred thousand light-years from Earth. He reported back to the corporation for which he worked and to the Bureau of Extra-Terrestrial Sociology. It was a 'wild virgin', planetstriker's slang for a world ripe and ready for the plucking. The Tellurian-Stellar Federation at once sent a battleship and two troopships loaded with Marines and workers. A garrison was built close to the optimum location for a city destined to become the capital of a new colony. A spaceport was constructed; a charter was given to Saxwell I.S.C., the company which had financed the planetstriker; and émigrés began pouring in. Earth, overcrowded Earth, could use a dozen planets like Diveboard as a siphon for their crowded people. Within five years its capital city, also named Diveboard, had a steadily growing population of eighty thousand, and the country roundabout it, two million.

One late Mayday, a tall broadshouldered earthman named Hadley Wolman stepped off a liner-freighter and rode into town. He was tall and had long wavy red hair of a hue hard to catch in any of the dyes then so popular for men. His features were rough and asymmetrical, yet handsome in a powerful way. His nose was too curved and his jaw too bold to meet classical standards, but the way he carried himself and the thrust of his dark blue eyes made women take a second look at him. Perhaps his clothes might have attracted them, too, for he was something of a dandy, a regular sartorial nova. The ring that hung from his left ear was large and golden and had a tiny topaz carved in the form of a parrot sitting within like a bird on a bar. His suspenders were quilted and spangled, his dickey glittered green and gold, depending on which way the light struck it, his puffkilts were deeply slashed, his shaven legs were painted canary yellow with thin scarlet stripes running around and around them—barberpole fashion. Even among men who gloried in garish attire, he stood out.

However, some of the dudish effect was countered by the long scar that ran along his left cheek—obviously a saber scar. Also, the mark of a college man, for dueling had come back into fashion among the students.

Hadley Wolman went straight to the bank and thereupon established his credit. Within a week, he had set up on Rhapsody Street a large and very chic dress shop for women, equipped with the latest fashions from New York and Paris. Inasmuch as it only took ten hours for a ship to get from Earth to Diveboard, Wolman's was not very far behind the actual shops on Earth itself. However, it did take much more money to transport articles across the Galaxy than from Paris to Peoria, so Wolman's was only for the very well to do.

The proprietor quickly became known as a character, which reputation however did not harm his shop in the slightest. During the daytime he spent practically every second the place was open attending to business on the front floor. He greeted every woman that came in but he made no attempt at all to be agreeable. Far from it, he was frequently insulting to his customers, especially if they asked for a dress that was too small or that was not suited to their figure. Despite this novel approach at business relations, he succeeded. Women came back for more. The fact that his advice was, aside from its acidity, solid and penetrating and that they did look better if they took it, may have helped some. Whatever the cause, every woman who had the money came to his place; many of them were tourists from the liners or from the nearby planets of Saki and St. Bessarion.

At nights Hadley Wolman would show up at Maybe Hassan's Café, a tavern built out of red ebony planks and close to the spaceport. Here he drank and talked and sang until one, then left to make a steady way homewards. He was a very generous spender and, therefore, very popular. Despite this, about once a week, he got into a fistfight with a spacer or tourist-slummer, or a marine from the nearby garrison. The latter at first delighted in baiting him because of his "novaish" appearance; the fact that their own off-duty dress was as bright and uninhibited did not seem to occur to them. They persisted in calling him Pretty Legs until the night he took on three of them at once. Though he knocked out one and broke the nose of another and the shins of a third, he took quite a beating and was carried out by Maybe Hassan himself, who brought him to with a bucket of cold water. Hadley Wolman went to the dentist the next day, had the roots of six broken teeth pulled and toothbuds put into the empty sockets. Within a week he looked as good as new, and the Marines no longer insulted him but insisted on standing him drinks.

"Mothaged," they swore, "you're a character. Whatever made you go into the ladies wear business?"

Three sheets to spaceward by this time from the whiskey they had bought him, he would leer at them and twist his mouth so his saber scar became a red question mark and would say, "If you want to catch a mouse, you don't poke about every nook and cranny and hole in the house. You set a trap baited with cheese and let the mouse come to the trap."

They dug their horny thumbs into his ribs and shouted, "Merrymotha, we catch you. You want to marry a rich woman, heh? So you set up this place where you can meet one, heh?"

"Nothing of the kind," he would say with dignity, though a grin was struggling to break loose. "Good night, gentlemen." And he would walk out of Maybe Hassan's, weaving slightly.

However, if anybody had followed him, they would have noticed that once out of sight of the café, he at once broke into a steady pace, one that was not at all like a man who had been drinking all night. They might have deduced that he had taken alcohol-oxidizer pills, and that he was as sober, actually, as the mythical judge.

One morning, after he had taken part in a brawl which involved the police he was busily advising a matron of one hundred and thirty whose curves were becoming bulges in spite of the slimming effects of a diet and of longevity shots.

"Madame," he said loftily, sneering down the side of his aquiline nose and his saber scar at the same time, "if you insist on emphasizing your broadness with a skirt with broad horizontal stripes, instead of trying to give an illusion of slimness with thin vertical stripes, if you persist in this myth that you have good taste and youth both, then I shall have to…"

He stopped and glanced keenly at the front door. Two women had just entered and stood by the doorway, waiting to be served. Both were strikingly beautiful despite the fact that they were dressed rather plainly. At first glance they looked as if they must be in some service or other, for both wore jackets and slacks instead of the civilian's skirt with the long sidesplit and the balloon hem. However, his practised eye at once told him they must be the women of farmers or hunters or else planetpickers. Since it was doubtful if the former would have money enough to enter his place, he concluded that the two had just gotten off their ship and were looking for something decent to wear for a vacation in Diveboard.

He turned over his centenarian customer to one of his girls and walked towards the two. Halfway across the room his step slowed down just a trifle—as if a thought had struck him—and his eyes narrowed. But he greeted them in a suave manner unusual for him and invited them to inspect his wares.

"I have models, Mesdames," he said. "The only couturier within five hundred light-years to so have. Would you care to select some dresses and then see how they look upon the models?"

The two women looked at each other as if they were not quite sure, then, as something seemed to pass between them, they both nodded their heads and said, "Yes, we would like to, very much."

Hadley Wolman then took charge of the two, ignoring his other customers to the extent that they stared at him and then at the newcomers as if wondering what on earth they had. He seated them upon the most comfortable sofa in the place, the only formfit chairs in Diveboard, and then proceeded to give orders which sent his employees bustling. Mrs. Cary and Miss Carmon relaxed for a moment then stepped into the booths where their measurements were taken. Afterwards they sat down again on the formfits to watch the models as they paraded before them.

Hadley, however, turned over the handling of the models to his manageress, saying to the two women that he would return in a moment as soon as he finished the ordering of some more dresses.

He locked the door of his office, sat down behind his desk, and dialed a certain number that was not on the city directory. At once, the screen on his desk flickered, and the face and shoulders of a man formed before him. The man was thin and longfaced and dark, with black eyes that looked as if they'd become so black because they'd absorbed so much of the sin they'd witnessed.

"Hello, Hadley," he said, "What's up?"

"Two women just came," Hadley said. "A Mrs. Cary and a Miss Carmon—so they say. But they look like Curtia Perry and Kris Munro, to me. Moreover," he added, glancing down at the piece of paper that he held in his hand, "their bodily measurements fit almost exactly to Perry's and Munro's."

A clicking rattled from a box at his elbow. He said, "Ah, here's the photo now," and pulled from a slot an envelope with a number of developed photographs. "These," he said, "were taken by the camera hidden in the dressing booths. He held them up for Raspold to see. "Dead ringers for Curtia Perry and Kris Munro, heh? They haven't even bothered to change the color of their hair or eyes. And I'll bet their fingerprints are the same too."

Raspold whistled. "That's them, all right. A couple of beauties, aren't they? Especially that Perry woman. I love very dark and luscious brunettes like that."

"I suppose so," said Hadley indifferently. "Are you going to check the port, to see if they landed there? I don't suppose they would take that chance, though. They must have landed on the other side of this planet and then come into the city on a gravyboat."

"I've already punched the signal for the port authorities to check," Raspold said, "If you want to hang on…hey! Here she is." He looked at a piece of paper on which was punched a code.

He shook his head. "No. Nothing doing there. Twenty ships landed today, but no passengers who looked like them. You might be right about their having landed on Diveboard's other side."

"Too bad the government can't afford to put radar stations around the whole planet," said Hadley. "But then, if they could have, we'd never have been able to set up our trap. The Perrys and Munros would have been scared off."

"Never mind that," said Raspold. "The point is, Hadley, that your trap has worked. I would have said we had only one chance in a hundred million of ever finding Perry again, yet here they are."

"They found us," said Hadley. "But we haven't caught them yet. What are your orders? Do I arrest the girls now?"

The chief of the Criminal Office of the Bureau of Extraterrestrial and Anti-Exploitation shrugged his bony shoulders, "You're handling this, Hadley. I've complete faith in you. All I'm doing is holding men in reserve and at your orders."

Hadley shook his auburn head and allowed a faint grin of self-satisfaction to touch the corner of his lips. The smile was more for Raspold's benefit, however, than for anything he really felt inside. It was true that he had solved all his cases so far very swiftly and successfully—including the famous Baboon red case which had received so much publicity—but he knew that he had come out alive from several of them only because he'd happened to get the breaks. However, he could not tell Raspold that because Raspold hated false modesty and being utterly without modesty himself, could not conceive of it in anybody else.

"Well, here's the way I look at it, Ras," he said. "We could arrest the women now, but if we do we can't use chalarocheil or any other truth drug until a court says we can. Damn this Free Will Law, anyway. I know it's for the protection of the citizen against any totalitarian tendencies on the part of our government, but it surely is a help to criminals."

Raspold nodded sympathetically and said, "Watch that redheaded temper of yours, Hadley. Let's get down to business."

"Heck, Ras. As I was saying, if I arrest them and they refuse to talk, it'll take at least a week, maybe two, before we can get a court to agree to force chalarocheil on them. And if they've landed on Diveboard just for a shopping trip—and I wouldn't put that past Curtia Perry, knowing what I do of her behavior pattern chart—then we may never catch Faber Perry or Lars Munro.

" If, however, they're in the city someplace else, or in a ship outside the city, we may be able to follow the women back to the boat. I'd rather do that. Besides, there's always the chance of false arrest—though it seems very negligible just now—and you know what a mess we get into when we do that."

Raspold nodded again sympathetically, his long sharp nose bobbing up and down like a meat cleaver in the hand of a nervous butcher.

"Yeah, if we pull another fiasco like we did on Wildenwooly in the Strickland Funny Face Case, the Free Will Law'll be invoked to throw me out on my ear. And maybe some of my men, too. Well, go ahead, Hadley. I'll keep in radio touch with you, and hold several men ready. What're you planning on doing next?"

"Selling a mess of clothes," said Hadley, grimacing. "If they want the clothes sent to an address, I'll follow up that lead. If they insist on taking them with them, I follow them."

Raspold laughed at the look of pain on the big man's face.

"What's the matter, baby? Is all this ladies' underwear and skirt selling getting you down?"

Wolman exploded. His face became as red as his hair.

"You're batherskitching right I'm getting fed up! In the first place, I have to wear this costume and hear these tough guys calling me Pretty Legs until I can't stand it any longer and then get in a brawl. And this hanging around all day in the odor of perfume until I could choke on it and having to listen to talk about this and that size and this and that pattern and don't you think this looks divine on me and handling all these laces and frills is about to get me down. I want to breathe some good clean air again and be able to relax among men."

Raspold smiled grimly and said, "Greater love hath no man for his duty than that which you are now displaying, Hadley. But hang on. The game may be ended soon. And you're lucky, if you come to think of it. So far, nobody's shot at it."

Hadley glanced at the watch on his wrist and punched a little button on one side of it. "Set for the 370 band, Ras. Next time I contact you, it'll be through this."

Raspold set his watch and said, "I'll leave its alarm on so it'll wake me up if you happen to call when I'm sleeping. So long, and good luck, Hadley."

Hadley flicked the switch, glanced at the mirror, powdered his nose, and combed his hair again. Then he strode back into the main part of the store, aware that many admiring glances followed him from his customers. He spoke to those who had just come in but brushed by them, making for the brunette and the blonde who were still sitting in their formfits, watching the models parade by.

Under the pretense of giving advice to a dowager who looked thirty-five but was actually eighty-five, he watched the two. Curtia Perry—for that was her real name—was much the more interested of the two. She was buying practically everything that was shown to her, from the most intimate of lingerie to fur coats of Albirean Rousch and Wildenwooly 'pelter. Hadley, noticing a two thousand credit fur coat she bought, decided that it must be winter on whatever planet she had been hiding on. He also wondered where she had gotten the money to pay for it and decided to phone Raspold at the earliest opportunity and tell him to check the pawnshops, the money fences, and the objets d'art dealers, all of whom could have given the women this money for certain highly desirable goods.

The blonde—Kris Munro, if he were right about her identity—seemed to take only a perfunctory interest in the clothes. Now and then she chose something that would look good on her, but more often her eyes roved around the shop, looking for something. Her fingers, he noted, drummed on the arm of her chair. Obviously nervous and dragged here by the vain Curtia.

At that moment their eyes met, and it was as if she had punched him on the chin. Something passed between them, something so unexpected and astonishing that he had to drop his eyes, a thing he never did before anybody's gaze.

Upset, he turned away from her and buried himself in doing something else until he could recover.

"I've had it." He muttered, and then cursed under his breath and said, "So what?"

But he couldn't fight off the feeling that had threatened to overwhelm him.

"This is ridiculous," he said. "You don't just fall in love with a single look from a woman, especially one that you suspect of being a criminal. All this stuff about love at first sight has been proven by the psychologists to be absolutely unfounded. It just happens in novels or poetry."

He lifted a dress off a rack and inspected it blindly, though an outsider would have thought he was looking keen-eyed at it.

"Of course, Dante fell in love with Beatrice in one swell foop—I mean fell swoop of his eyes. And there were others who did the same. But I'm no thirteenth

288 PHILIP JOSÉ FARMER

century poet. I'm a hardboiled twenty-second centurion who's been around, and when I say around I don't mean the corner, I mean the known galaxy and some parts that aren't so well known. So what's wrong with me that I allow this little thing between a blonde—albeit a beautiful one, still not the only one I've ever seen—and myself, Hadley Wolman, Operative No. 7 for the Criminal Office of the Anti-Exploitation Department of the Extra-Terrestrial Bureau of Sociology? What's wrong with you Wolman, aren't you feeling well?"

He turned around to flash a glance at the girl. She certainly was beautiful, with long blonde hair coiled into a bun at her back, a face almost classically perfect except for a tendency on the part of her nose to turn up, a superb figure, and long slim legs. Aside from that, however, there was nothing that would have especially attracted him, he thought. He'd seen other women just as beautiful and some even more so.

Well, he could argue, but there it was. She had him.

And when her eyes met his again and she gave a little start and quickly looked away then stole a glance at him out of the corner of her eye, he wondered if she could possibly have felt the same thing he did. It seemed almost too good a thing to expect. After all, Beatrice had not returned Dante's fervent devotion.

He saw a saleslady approach Curtia Perry, the dark beauty, and say something to her. The woman raised her eyebrows, said a few words to the blonde, rose, and walked, with her hips swaying, to a viewbooth. Hadley would have liked to take the opportunity of talking to Kris Munro alone, but his sense of duty prevented him. He swiftly walked back to his office, where he locked the door behind him and pressed a button on the underside of his desk. At once, the line to Booth No. 3, where the brunette was, was open to him. On the screen before him he could see the face of the man who had called Curtia.

He sucked in his breath with surprise and delight. The fat and purple face before him was that of Curtia's husband. Faber Perry!

Perry's skin was almost purple, and his jowls shook.

"What are you doing in that dress shop, Curtia?" he almost roared. "You know that you weren't supposed to go any place but to Maybe Hassan's. Have you been there yet or did you stop off at this place first?"

"You know I couldn't stop here until I'd seen Maybe," coolly replied Curtia, a sneer distorting her lovely face and complacently patting her long black hair. "Otherwise I'd have had no money with which to buy clothes."

Despite himself, Hadley chuckled. He had analyzed Curtia Perry's behavior pattern down to the last notch in the code-card. It would be like her to be unable to resist a spending spree on garments even if it endangered her plans.

It was this very factor that had caused him to set up this shop on this faraway planet—one choice out of thirty he could have made—and to sit back and wait for the fly to walk into the spider's parlor. (Go back, put this in the beginning about his calling it the Spider's Parlor Dress Shop.) Memnon, the colossal memory bank of Earth's Civilian Statistics Department had given Curtia Lang's B.H.P. and indicated to him her besetting weakness. With only that, and one other factor to go on, he had gambled that she would eventually show up on Diveboard. And now here she was with, apparently, everybody but Lars Munro, Kris' brother, in the trap. With a little skill he could snare him, too.

Perry's bellowing voice said, "Get those clothes and get the hell out here, Curtia. My God, if I'd known you were going to pull a stunt like this, I'd have gone in myself. But no, you said it'd be much safer if you did it because they might recognize me!"

Curtia's voice was low and controlled. "Quit bellowing like a fat stupid boar, Faber. Do you want everybody on Diveboard to know you're here? Kris and I are almost through, we'll bring the clothes with us and be with you in about twenty minutes."

A tremor ran over the jelly-tissue of Perry's face as he visibly struggled to master his temper.

"Dear," he said sarcastically, "If you aren't here within those twenty minutes, I'm leaving without you."

So, thought Hadley, Perry was probably speaking from the ship itself, using a radiotelephone hookup.

He pressed another button under his desk and spoke into a box set to one side. "Operator 5, Wolman speaking. Special service. Get me a line on the party speaking to the party in No.3 booth, number DS—3378, please."

While waiting for the operator's report, he listened to the rest of the conversation. Apparently, Perry had no idea at all that he could be watched; he thought himself absolutely safe.

"How did you find me?" Curtia asked, her face mask-like as if she really didn't care.

"You were supposed to be here an hour ago," Perry replied. "I knew that there are only two things that could make you late. One, the police had nabbed you, which seemed unlikely. Or, two, you wanted to spend some of that money to clothe your body. It wasn't hard to go down the list of couturiers, starting with the largest and most expensive."

"Very clever, Faber," she said. "Well, is there anything else you have to say before I cut you off?"

"Yes, you fool. Get out here on the double before your vanity ruins our plans!"

There was a click, and Perry's face faded from the screen. Hadley at once spoke to Operator 5. "Did you trace the call?"

"Yes sir. It's from Oursler's Tavern, a place about two miles east of the city."

"Thank you," said Hadley. He pressed the little button on the side of his watch and said, "Raspold?"

Instantly, as if he'd been waiting, came the husky voice of the Super. "Yes?"

"I think that Perry probably has his ship hidden in the woods about two miles east of here, close to a place known as Oursler's Tavern. It's probably under some of those red ebony trees that grow out that way. But I'm afraid that if you'd send some gravyboats out that way looking for him, you might scare Perry off and Munro too—if Munro is with him. It'll be best if I follow the women and coach the boats along by radio."

"Meanwhile," said Raspold, "I'll have Maybe Hassan's raided within the next ten minutes. We ought to be able to seize whatever it was that the women sold to him. And maybe we can identify the world from which their goods came. If we can, then we know definitely what they're up to. If we can't..."

"Then," finished Hadley Wolman for him, "we know that Perry has discovered a new planet and that he's trying to keep it to himself for his own selfish purposes. And we arrest him and the women?"

Raspold nodded. "Chances are that Lars Munro is on their beast, too. Even if he's not, we should be able to get the courts to give us permission to use a drug on them and get out of them the location of their find. Well, so long, Hadley. I'll be keeping in touch with you, and as soon as I find out what Maybe Hassan has in his house, I'll tell you that, too."

Hadley checked his watch, then left his office and returned to the display room of the store just in time to see the two women paying for their purchases. He at once hastened up to them and asked if everything was alright.

The blonde gave him a swift sidewise glance, then looked away. He could see that the muscles of the back of her neck were quivering and that her hand was also shaking. But whether it was because she felt what he did or whether it was the strain she must be under he did not know.

All he did know was that at the sight of her he felt again that sudden throb in his chest. He was not such a tyro that he did not recognize what it meant. On the other hand, he was mature enough to know that he had best fight against it and also to wonder if he were cracking up. It seemed to him that a man with his love-em-and-leave-em temperament, one who had always avoided any permanent entanglements and who loved some fabulous yonder of far off and undiscovered planets far more than he had any woman, should be proof against such a thing—such a calf-love that only a callow youth should experience.

Perhaps, he thought to himself, it is because I never felt this thing when I was young but repressed it in favor of adventure, that it has smoldered all these years, ready to break out when it found a weak point.

Perhaps…

Anyway, here it was, and he found himself in the agonizing position of spying upon this woman with the goal of arresting her, perhaps before the day was over.

Meanwhile, the black-haired Curtia, the woman whom ordinarily he would have been more interested in because of the experience and wisdom that shone from her every gesture and look, this Curtia whose vanity had yet betrayed her wisdom, smiled at him and looked at him intently with a look that he had seen on the faces of a hundred other women on a dozen other planets. She recognized in this big broadshouldered redhead with the ironic scarface and coolly-mocking ways the kind of man who knew her and whom she liked best to be with. Of course, she had no way of knowing what in impression the rather silent blonde by her side had made on him. Here her womanly intuition went astray, as it sometimes has a manner of doing. Perhaps it did so because Hadley carefully restrained himself from giving any signs of his feelings for Kris, and woman's so-called intuition is really a very sensitive yet sharp eye for seeing certain subtle actions and catching certain inflections of voice and movement. Whatever it was, it misfired this time. He was very careful to pay all of his attention to her. Of course, part of his policy was just good police work. She seemed to him to be running the show and therefore the logical person to focus upon. Moreover, it seemed to him that the blonde, Kris, was quiet and nervous because she did not have her heart in what she was doing. For a moment he thrilled with the idea that perhaps she had been forced into this and might turn out to be relatively innocent.

Then that thrill died away as he remembered her part in the affair, and he knew that she was as guilty as anybody else and that when the time came to pay the penalty, she must do so.

(Revise: Perry's at Maybe's, on the outskirts of town. C & K went into town just to pick up a few articles, but she insisted on buying clothes. When HW follows them into Maybe's, he's kidnapped during raid, finds that the planetpicker's beast is inside Maybe's hangar. Also, it was Monday night, when stores stayed open late, so CP thought she'd have better chance of getting by in the dark and busy city.)

So it was that he was not quite his light hearted and amusing self when he escorted the two out to their waiting car. One of the reasons he went of course was to check on the type of vehicle they were using. He saw at once that it was a three wheeler sedan rented for the day from the rental agency. He also glimpsed in the car's backseat a jumble of objects: several boxes containing small cans of expensive foods, a long box which he guessed held firearms, another that might hold ammunition, several other packages, a number of the latest mikes—some of which were brand new novels, detectives, adventures, love stories, and once, the title of an old classic—*Raintree County*. This latter, he liked to think, was Kris's choice of reading matter.

Curtia got into the driver's seat; Kris sat beside her. Hadley put his hand on the door and leaned over so his face was close to the brunette's. "Look," he said, "if you two aren't doing anything special tonight. I'd like to take you out. What about taking in the town? I know all the best places and the dives, places like Snatcher White's, Maybe Hassan's, and the Coal Sack. You could get a chance to wear some of your gowns."

Neither of them flinched at the mention of Hassan's. Curtia smiled at him and said, "Believe me, we'd like to, but we'll be leaving tonight. Besides, I don't think my husband would like the idea."

"Well," he said, "if you should change your mind, I'll be at Maybe Hassan's tonight until twelve. Then I go to Snatchy's."

Curtia hesitated a moment, glanced at him keenly, then, as if she'd decided she was on safe ground, said, "I'm surprised to hear you say that Hassan's is a dive. We're staying there, and our rooms are quite nice."

"Oh, I didn't mean it's sloppy or dirty or anything like that," he hastily said. "It's just that the barroom gets rather rough in the evenings. Why don't you and your husband and you, Miss Carey, go down there tonight before you leave? You could at least allow me to buy you one drink. After all, you two were my best customers today, you know."

He smiled and poured on the personality.

"I think it's only fair that two such beautiful women as you should allow me to see you in those clothes you bought before you go. After all, though I see many women, it's not often I see any as gorgeous as you two."

He laughed and looked directly at Curtia as if to say with his eyes, "It is you that I am speaking to, you that I think so beautiful. But of course I can't say so out loud without hurting your companion's feelings."

He thought, "Ah, Kris, if only I could be saying this to you alone. If only you weren't a criminal and I weren't an investigator who must, before long, arrest you. Why did this have to be? Why did you do it?"

Curtia gave him a dazzling smile that would have twisted him all up inside himself if he hadn't been so much taken with Kris. She said, "Well, we're leaving after midnight, so perhaps we might come down to the Red Star Room just for one drink. Since you've been so flattering and so kind…"

Hadley checked in his mind the schedules for birds leaving the port. There was a freighter that also took passengers clearing ground at one o'clock. But he was sure that the Perrys and Kris Munro wouldn't be leaving on it. They'd be going on their own bird, which must be hidden somewhere in the forest close to Hassan's. Unless, indeed, they had landed on the other radarless side of Diveboard and then had taken a gig—or gravyboat—to the city.

Whichever was true, they were covering up fairly well. They must have checked the port schedules too so they wouldn't be tripped up by saying they were going to take a bird that just wasn't listed.

The Terminalization of J.G. Ballard

Considered as a Fall Off a Barstool
Or
Why I Want To Dick Dick

Previously unpublished.

Phil's parody of JG Ballard evokes all of Ballard's trademark styles; outrageous sub-headings, cataclysmic imagery and obsession with sex and cars (as seen in Ballard's watershed novel *Crash*).
In anagrammatic disguise, JG Ballard has already appeared in a published Phil Farmer story, "The Last Rise of Nick Adams."

Phil: "I admire Ballard's writing style and offshoot thinking. But nothing is sacred. I had a lot of fun writing doing this, and a lot of fun rereading it after all these years."

In and Out of the Last Chance Saloon

VECTOR PRODUCT: A vector c the length of which is the product of the lengths of two vectors *a* and *b* and the sine of their included angle, the direction of which is perpendicular to their plane and the sense of which is that of a right-handed screw with axis *c* when *a* is rotated into *b*. Ballard's sense was that of a left-handed screw, which accounted in the best scientific manner for his backward toppling from the barstool. Prior claims must be awarded, however, to the weight of the crumpled Cadillac radiator grille projecting from his anus. This tended to exert a simultaneous downward and counter-clockwise force which he vainly compensated for by a tight grasp on a bottle of beer.

SQUEEZING PSEUDOREALITY: Another tenuous hold on the world of angles, icons, and imaginary sexual perversions was the rectal face of U.S.A. President Dick flickering on the misshapen TV set over the bar. Explaining why. Everybody had been watching him intently, which was why Ballard came in unnoticed, limping, trailing the radiator grille and part of a licentious plate. Nor did they observe him extracting a spark plug from his ear.

A BIPSYCHO BUILT FOR DUE: Bartender/proprietor Al Jarry was a Frenchman. He wore a huge crucifix on a chain around his neck. On the mirror behind him was pasted a blowup of Jarry on a bicycle, leading the race uphill. He slid a beer down the counter to Ballard, giving him at the same time a peculiar isosceles look. Ballard read the coded glance as easily as if it had been a linear declaration of the intrapatellar distance of Minnie Schwartz, meter maid well known in this neighborhood. "Put it on the bill," Ballard murmured, looking at the Frenchman through the glass and its liquid contents, yellow like the sands of a final beach suspended in offshore water. The President's face opened in a smile as meaningless as an erased tape, as mechanical and joyless as the squeezing of a hand-operated rubber anus. Jarry rang up *No Sale* on the cash register.

THE TROPIC OF DESCENT: Thrown off balance by the removal of the glass, he began toppling backward and slightly to the left. Haven't I done this before? he asked himself. As usual, no reply, linear or curved. He felt a definite sense of inverse sexuality or perhaps it was obverse. Converse? Whatever the configurations of desire, the heavy grille was making him play Humpty Dumpty. In a corner an old man quit sipping his absinthe to cry a bon voyage. He was Hank Miller, whom Ballard owed more than any though hardly anyone knew it.

THE FREE LUNCH IS NAKED: "Happy landing!" shouted Bill Burroughs, looking up from the soft eggs hard-boiled in booze, potato salad mixed with mayonnaise of pederasty, pastrami sandwiches imported from nostalgia of old St. Louis (wouldn't you?), and morphine-sprinkled pretzels. Ballard had let old Bill stand for many a drink, but old Bill didn't care. Not as long as he could look at his right toe.

SIGN LANGUAGE FOR THE BLIND: His eyes were splintered, like smashed-in headlamps. The President's smile was a half-unzipped fly on an old pair of trousers. The open skylight showed him a balloon floating beneath a pale-ale moon, towing on a banner the gigantic face of Rosie Schmidt, down with terminal flatulence in the hospital around the corner.

WHY I WANT TO HUMP HUMP, TOO: Even in his rapid too-linear descent, during which he could not avoid the unavoidable images of Humpty Dumpty, Hubert Humphrey, and Humphry C. Earwicker, he had presence of mind enough to remove his pocket calculator. As his body arced back, he click-clicked estimates, castanets in the ears of science. The President's facial contortions were causing sexual-death wish fantasies among 86.2% of the tavern's patrons. Eleven percent of this regressive post-drip tendency was generated by visual reaction to the President's tiny yellow crooked teeth, incorrectly added digits in a sum of no-confidence. They had no business being there. Not even in the face of a used-car dealer or operator of a third-rate junkyard.

COLLISION OF SHADE AND LIGHT: The flickering from the TV set formed bizarre runes on the wall, notes in an unknown tongue voiced by mad syphilitic seers of a lost race, the shavings from a psychosomatic totempole. Others were fractured profiles of Janie Jones and Mary Brown, two friendly neighborhood whores. The lamppost under which they stood cut a line at exactly ninety degrees to the horizontal of the street surface. This line, in turn, went asymptotically around the earth, which is definitely pear-shaped at times. It all meant something, but the Roman letters of the code looked Arabic at this speed of descent.

THE CELTIC BULL, R.C. & W.C. SPECIALIST: "Go it, Sassenach!" Jim "Weak Eeyes" Joyce yelled. Ballard waved at him. He owed the defrocked priest (or was it prefrocked?) much, too. But his grief at not being able to repay him did not overcome his cool scientific detachment, which enabled him to estimate that 12% of the Irishman's death wish was the square root of the length of his (Ballard's) sideburns.

THE ACME PLUMBING COMPANY: The Spanish plumber, Sal Dali, and his Greek senior partner, Euclid, looked up from the disemboweled grandfather clock cum commode. Dali had pulled the works out of shape; Euclid was trying to straighten their corners. They'd bought many a drink for the English kid, and now it looked as if they'd never get paid back.

LOST IN THE CASTLE: Frankie Kafka woke up under a table. His head hurt as if a Rolls Royce had run over it. The throbbing of blood in his temples reminded him that quasars, too, pulsed in distant space. Where was he? Who was he? Why was he? Who had bought the last drink? He frowned. Ontogeny recapitulates a fill of gin, he…Ballard flashed by, the end of the crumpled grille dug into the wooden floor, acting like a vaulter's pole, Ballard being vaulted, and then the violent parting of man and grille sounding like the popping of a plumber's helper when lifted from the drain of a stopped-up sink. A man opened the door in time to let Ballard fly past him into the street. Frankie heard the screech of brakes and tyres, smelled the burning fiberglass, napalmed by friction, conceptualized the skidmarks as parallel lines which formed an absurd geometry with the spheres of the victim's buttocks, felt the smash and rumble, like a bowel movement, as vibrations ran through the earth and up the floor from the collision of light pole and car. Frankie shuddered and wished that he was a cockroach.

LOCUS TOCUS: Ballard staggered back in. He presented the optimum injury profile. Part of that profile was the bonnet ornament from a classic model 1932 Pontiac sticking out from between his buttocks. The patrons were later interviewed by psychometrists from General Motors. Asked to name their most unforgettable traffic accident, 95% unhesitatingly chose Ballard. "You can't drive out of the parking lot without running over him," old Hank Miller said, "He's definitely autopolymorphous perverse. We'll never see his like again."

THE BANALITY OF ANALITY: The only dissenter was Al Jarry. "The motorcar, it is for queers. Now you take the bicycle. That's a real man's weapon." tests under extreme laboratory conditions proved that Jarry attained a proximal erection only at Golgotha. Case dismissed.

POST-IMPACT TRISTE: Ballard staggered in a stylized mode of *angst* towards the bar, causing 30.286% of the patrons to conceptualize blind cae(cums?)(ci?). The mouthparts of the President rearranged to form the breaking-apart of a jet-propelled Chevy composed of prepuces and vaginas. The third prepuce from the left remarkably resembled the face of Jerry Williams, janitor for the apartment building across the street and reformed Southern Baptist.

THE GEOMETRY OF ACCIDENCE: Not without pain which recalled the crash of tropical surf on brown beaches, the swift unrolling of toilet paper in the dead of night, the beauty of the sesquipedalian adjective *pseudoepiphenomeno-logical,* Ballard clambered back onto the stool. The mirror behind the bar reflected his face, a pileup of angles at the entrance to the on-ramp of parturition.

ONE FOR THE ROAD: "Drink up, and get out," the bartender said. Find some other place. And for God's sake find something else to amuse you besides traffic accidents." "Cancer?" Ballard said, but Jarry was giving good advice. If he didn't get out soon, he'd be trapped in the unyielding conjunctions of the terminal tavern with the dying and the dead. Going forever around and around in the Piccadilly Circus of stale repetition instead of speeding on the highway of the great open spaces where every road was a new one and there were no circles. "I'll go," he said, "but I want to make it clear that though I owe you all a great deal, I have acknowledged my debt. And I am my own model, not just a modification of last year. Right, fellows?" "Right," they said. "Good luck, kid." Satisfied, Ballard staggered out, the metallic head of chief Pontiac wagging a final farewell to the habitues. He headed wrong way on a one-way street, ecstatic from the traffic noises, notes from that inevitable opera, *The Marriage of Ford and Freud.*

Psychological Tales

The Blind Rowers

First published in *Knight*, Volume 5, Number 11, March 1967.

A tale of temptation, redemption and revenge; of sex and religion. The story is violent, sexually charged and deals with moral ambiguity.

This is probably one of the rarest pieces in this collection having only once before been in print and then in a publication not so easily accessible (unless you could reach the top shelf!). In what is essentially a Jacobean revenge story Phil subverts the genre of men's magazines by illustrating a non compliant female who metes out painful, embarrassing and fatal punishment when the male desires conflict with her morality.

Over the railing and into the Aegean Sea hurtled Joan McReady. She fell six feet, struck the water with her left shoulder, and went down. Two strokes upward brought her head above the surface. She looked up to see Platon Neusis standing in the moonlight.

He shook his fist at her and screamed in Romaic, reverting in his fury to his native tongue. He was a handsome man of thirty-five, but for the past six hours he had been getting uglier with each drink of Scotch and each refusal from her. Son of a multi-millionaire's widow, tall, blond, athletic, cosmopolitan, he was used to having his way with the women who accepted an invitation to go yacht-cruising with him. But he had not gotten his way.

Joan McReady, a secretary for a UN health unit, had met Platon at a party in Athens. From the first, she had had misgivings about his intentions. Even after dating him for two weeks, during which he had not gone beyond goodnight kisses, she did not trust him. Her friends had told her that he was a Don Juan. Also, she knew that the men of his country took "nice" girls to meet their mothers. So far, he had talked much of his mother, too much, but had not even hinted that he would like to introduce Joan to her.

When she had been invited to go on a cruise to Sikia, his native city on the northern coast of the Aegean, she had replied that she would love to go. That is, she would if others were going also. He assured her she would not be alone. There was another couple, a charming French couple. But they had gotten off at a small village south of Sikia, where they intended to stay for several weeks. Platon had suggested that he would like to continue to Sikia and see an uncle.

Once more, Joan had asked if she would be the only one aboard. He was smooth, as smooth as a hawk slipping through the air, and had never made a move or said a word that she might consider objectionable. He assured her again, and the ship left for Sikia on a moonlight cruise.

The captain and two crewmen were not on the yacht. Joan asked about them; Platon replied that they were on liberty. She reminded him of his promise. Smiling, he said that she was not alone. He was there.

The ship was then only half a mile from shore, and she could easily have swum the distance. She shrugged and told herself not to act like a fool. She could take care of herself. She was a little edgy for a while. Platon talked of the beauty of the landscape of his hometown and of the accomplishments of his uncle. Joan relaxed.

The ship moved on, and after an hour and a half, Platon, commenting that the sea was so smooth and beautiful, stopped the motors. He began drinking and soon, under the full moon and a full load of Scotch, made the proposals that were at first circuitous and then outright and even obscene. Joan did not try to be diplomatic. She was furious. Soon, they were yelling at each other. He tried to grab her; she clawed him; over the railing she went.

Joan refused to give him the satisfaction of hearing her scream or beg for help. She was so angry that she almost yielded to the impulse to try to swim to shore. Even when he continued to rage at her and showed no signs of throwing a ladder down to her, she did not get frightened. But when he disappeared and the motors coughed, and the yacht drew away, she became panicky. Still, she would not plead with him. Only when the white hull of the yacht was on the point of vanishing did she call out.

There was no answer, no moonlit whiteness getting larger. She was alone with the waves.

She still could not believe that he would not cool off and return after he had taught her a "lesson." But what if, when he came back, he could not find her? She was so small, and the sea was so large. And what if—unthinkable but nevertheless thought—he did not return?

The mainland shore was now at least fifteen miles away. The waters were not rough, and she was an excellent swimmer. She could stay afloat a long time, but she could not swim fifteen miles. Even if she could, she did not know which way to go. The moon was directly overhead. If only she had been more observant of the constellations and could guide herself by them...

She thought, *I'll panic if I don't do something. I can't just float here, waiting for that bastard Platon to come back. I'll swim in the direction his yacht went. No. He wasn't headed back to the shore. Or was he?*

First, she had to get rid of even the slight weight of her clothes. Her blouse and skirt slid off. After a slight hesitation, she removed her bra and panties. Modesty was non-survival. No man could see her, and the heaviness of water-soaked underclothing might mean a mile or two less of swimming.

Like a broad heavy hand, the sea closed around her. Its grip was not strong, but it promised a tighter squeeze later. It was not cold now, but it would become cold.

She swam slowly so that she could save her strength. Now and then she turned on her back and floated, though this resulted several times in a choking mouthful or stinging noseful.

But she kept on, and dawn swam out across the waves to meet her. The sun shone on nothing but water.

It seemed an easy thing to do, to quit moving her arms and legs and slide down into the waters and let the sea take her.

Twenty-five years old, and no one has taken me, she thought. *No man. I have resisted too strongly. I have said no too many times. I wanted it all to be right and proper, and no man was quite right. Now, I will be taken anyway. But by no man.*

Something long and hard slipped along her thigh and brushed against her crotch. She shrieked and turned and glimpsed the silver-and-black length of a fish.

Sharks? Were there sharks in the Aegean? She had never seen any. And that was no shark. A little fish not more than six or seven inches long

"I will swim until I have no strength left," she said.

An hour later, if the climb of the sun was a correct indication of time, she had reached the end of her strength. Treading, gasping, arms and legs heavy, as if logged with salt and water, she looked around the horizon. And she saw, to her right, a mass breaking the smooth line.

Clouds or land?

Whichever they were, she had to find out. Somehow, she would get there.

Fortunately, the current was carrying her towards the darkness. She floated and resisted the temptation to swim. Slowly, the infringement on the copyright of horizon became not clouds, but land. A squat hill, shaped like a crooked sausage, bent at an angle in the middle. There were large grey buildings halfway up. Later, a black sand beach at the foot of the hill.

A man was standing on the beach, a tall bearded man in a black robe and black cylindrical hat. He saw her, but he made no effort to help her. He turned and ran away, flapping his arms, the wide sleeves like the wings of a great clumsy bird attempting to take off. He ran up a flight of wooden steps zigzag-ging up the face of the cliff.

Why doesn't the damn fool come in after me and get me? she thought. *He can see I'm on the point of drowning. I can't stay up much longer. Can't he swim?*

Even though the shore was now only fifty yards away, she had to turn on her back and float. She did not have the energy to make two more strokes. Looking up at the sky, she thought, *Maybe that monk thinks I'm Venus riding out of the waves, having slipped off my scallop shell. And he's gone to spread abroad the news of another miracle, reinstate the old pagan religion. Or something.*

She giggled in near-hysteria. Then, hearing the growl of surf become a roar, she turned over and tried feebly to swim. She went up and down a valley, slid down its white-crested and green slope, and rolled over and over, going under at the bottom of the slope.

Coughing, she came up out of the waters. Now there were four men on the black sand, and others running down the crazy wooden steps. All were in robes and bearded. One of the men on the beach was white-haired and white-bearded. All had their heads turned away from her.

"Look at me!" she screamed. The wind tore her words apart. The waves swept her into the shallows, and she was on her hands and knees, sand grinding and cut-ting into her palms and knees, the receding sea trying to suck her back into the deep.

"Help me! *Look* at me!"

Two monks sidled towards her like huge black crabs. They held long poles, and their heads were turned away. One, however, was watching her out of the corner of his eyes. He thrust the end of the long wooden staff at her, and she grabbed for it and clung with all the strength—it was not much—that she had.

The monk shouted something and tore the pole from her grasp. Then it drove back at her. She put up her hands to stave it off but felt its hard end grinding into her breastbone. The monk lunged, and she was driven back out into a wave and knocked over by it.

"What are you doing? Are you crazy?" she screamed. Her lungs burned with the effort.

The white-haired man, his eyes shut, walked toward her. Two men, each hold-ing an elbow, directed him, although they could see her no better than he. When the three felt the water of the dying thrust of the surf on their bare feet, they stopped.

She had thought that they had not heard her, but the old monk, instead of speaking Romaic, used broken but fluent English. What was she doing *here*? His words came to her against the wind and the crash of surf, and she could make out only a word here, a phrase there. She heard enough to catch the sense. Sense? It was senseless.

What a question! An idiot could see she was a castaway. Did he really think that she had deliberately swum from the mainland to this insane place to entice these men with her naked body?

Summoning strength from a reservoir she had thought emptied, she shouted, "You fools! I fell off a ship! I mean, I was thrown off! Please let me ashore! I'll die if you don't! Die!"

The old man took two more steps into the water, and he cried, "No female, animal or human, has set foot on this island for a thousand years, my daughter! We cannot allow you even to touch the shore!"

"For the love of God, I'll die! Please!"

The old monk roared, "We cannot have the sanctity of this island violated! It would be unclean forever! Indeed, how do we know what lusts of the devil would be unleashed if you came among us! Naked in your shamelessness! The man who first saw you said you were as naked as our mother Eve. He will pay a heavy penance for seeing you. He might even blind himself to make sure this does not happen again!"

Death, which had seemed to recede into the sea, was as close as ever. These men were fanatics. Reason, compassion, humanity—these meant nothing.

"Give me a robe!" she yelled. "I'll cover my body! And my face, too, if that offends you! Please! I can't last much longer! I don't want to die!"

The old man opened his mouth wide in a grimace, and she saw that he had only a few teeth and these were black. At the same time, the young monk who had shoved her back with the pole turned his head fully towards her. He smiled. His teeth were even and healthy-looking. His eyes were large, moist, dark, and long-lashed. Even with his thick curly beard, he was handsome.

"I'm coming ashore!" she screamed. "You'll have to kill me to stop me! And my blood will be on your hands! You murdering eunuchs!"

For answer, the old man pointed to his left. Fifty yards away, six monks were bending their backs into shoving a rowboat into the surf.

"You must get into that! You will be given a robe to cover your nakedness! My brothers will row you to the mainland! But you will have to steer! They will be blindfolded to remove them from temptation! Go straight, west, keeping the hill as a landmark! When it is out of sight, keep steering westward! Follow the sun! Then you will see the mountains of the mainland!"

He covered his eyes with his hands and said, "Do not speak to my brothers or touch them! They will have to scourge themselves, and even then…"

Joan did not wait to hear the rest. She had to get to the boat before she collapsed. Everything, the island, the sky, the sun, the sea, was shifting, flowing into each other. Only the old monk was stable and definite, a black tower in chaos.

Too tired to wade, she floated and paddled weakly toward the boat. The waves kept driving her into shore. They knocked her over on her side and carried her, bumping and scraping against the sand, to the edge of the beach. Twice, she tried to crawl upon the sand and get out of reach of the waves. Each time, the young monk placed the blunt end of the pole against her ribs and shoved. She winced with the pain and glared with anger at him. He stared directly at her, seemingly not caring if the others saw that his eyes were open. But then, they had their eyes shut and could not see him. Or, if they did, they could not accuse him without accusing themselves.

Moreover, he could not be expected to push her away with the pole unless he could see her. Perhaps he had been authorized by the old monk to do so.

When she managed to reach the boat, which was now two waves out and lifting and rising in one spot, kept from drifting back by the rowers, she was reeling. She stretched out a hand to a monk who was standing up and holding out a robe to her. His head was turned away. The others were blindfolded.

She grabbed the edge of the robe and pulled. The monk, losing his balance, toppled over into the sea beside her. The robe, which had slipped out of both their grasps, floated billowing towards the shore. The monk rose out of the water, risked one look, turned his head away from her, and struck out from the beach. He looked frightened.

Joan was trying to get the strength to call to the others in the boat and tell them they had to help her aboard when she felt a strong hand on her elbow. Another hand seized her buttocks in a powerful bowler's grip.

She cried out with pain, surprise, and injured dignity. A man laughed behind her. Up she went, kicking, forgetting her weakness in the shock of feeling those fingers. She went over the side of the boat and onto the deck, scraping the skin off her shins. She turned over on her back to see the face of the young monk appear, followed by his soaking black robes.

He now had on a blindfold, but it was placed high enough for him to peer out from beneath it. He said, "The abbot...say...you go to mainland. He give you...directions? We keeping the...what you call them...blindfooleds?...over eyes. You steer. You know how steer?"

"I know," she said. She took the tiller while he sat down in the position vacated by the monk who had fallen into the water. The young monk chanted, and the six began to row. Presently, Joan turned her head to look behind her. The figures on the beach were tiny.

"Do you have food and water? Especially water? I'm dying!"

The young monk, eyes bright from the reflection of her body, jerked his head at a basket and said, "Bread, wine, water there. But you not die. You too good flesh to die. Strong, healthy flesh."

She left the tiller and crawled to the basket. As she grasped its handle, she felt the monk's bare foot sliding over her breast. She recoiled but did not let the basket go.

He grinned at her and said, "You eat. Get strong. Weak woman is no good..."

She returned to the tiller and opened the bottle of water and drank, forcing herself to swallow the water slowly. Then she ate half a piece of bread, holding it with one hand while she steered with the other. Her eyes became heavy; the sun warmed her body; there were a million tiny golden needles, hypodermics all, shooting sleep into her. She shook her head and told herself she had to stay awake.

Suddenly, she was being shaken by the young monk. One hand was on her shoulder, and it was some time before she became aware of what his other hand was doing.

Her voice was like a crow's. She squawked harshly, "Quit that! Or I'll scream!"

He stepped back from her, but he was smiling. He said, "You sleeping for two, maybe three hours. Plenty time yet. I steering. We not going straight, but not in a hurry. You eat more, get strength quick."

She ate rapidly, biting off huge chunks of the black bread and parts of the cold fish, and washing them down with long swallows of water. Food had never been so exquisite, and she did not care if the water was sanitary or not.

It was no wonder they were going in circles, she thought. The young monk had not been rowing and was not now. He stood near her while he finished off a bottle of wine.

"You strong now?" he said in a low voice.

"A little," she replied. She looked around the boat. "Don't you have anything I can cover myself with? What will I do when I get to the mainland?"

He grinned and slipped off his robe. He was wearing nothing under the robe. "Here. You want my robes?"

"You dirty peasant," she said. "Get back to your bench and start rowing. And tell me which way to steer. If you don't do it—right now!—I'll tell your friends what you're doing."

"They not understand English," he said. "And they not believe you. The abbot tell them not listen to you. Devil try seduce them through you. Maybe you what you say; maybe not. They to stop their...airs?...if you talk. And if they stop their airs, they not able to row. So you keep mouth shut."

He threw the bottle into the sea and said, "You true blonde, heh? You not dye your hair, right?"

"I'll scream so loudly they'll have to listen. And if you think they won't take their blindfolds off, you don't know men."

He inched towards her. His hands were half-closed, moving inwards towards each other and towards her. They were long slim hands with delicate fingers. They reminded her of the hands of Platon Neusis. He played a piano beautifully; he often spoke of playing for hours for his mother. And shortly before he had thrown her overboard, he had boasted of how his hands played women, played symphonies with them.

"You scream; I throw you to the fish. Please. Not make me add one more sin. If it is sin to kill a devil sent to make men sin."

"And how will you explain my disappearance?" she said. "You can't get away with it."

"I tell them you crazy. You come out of sea, a crazy naked woman, a devil. You go back into sea. They be happy."

He stopped his hands a few inches from her and leaned toward her. His skin was like dark, fine-grained marble. However, long dark hairs sprouted out of his nostrils. *Like horns,* she thought. *What made me think of horns?*

"You're the devil!" she said. "Stay away from me!"

"Don't be scared. You keep mouth shut. I won't hurt you. What you expect, anyway? You can't go naked like this."

He pointed at her breasts and hips. "You white there. You take sunbath with coverings for evil things of woman. You white like the flesh in my dreams. You white!"

"You have a lot of guts talking about the evil things of women! You're the evil one! You'd rape me! Murder me!"

"I can't help," he said. "It's you sin, you fault. Three years I fight off devil at night when I try sleep. Even so, he sends womans—white like ghosts but solid like flesh—to my dreams. Then I wake up and pray. Night go by. Dawn come. I not sleep. Three years of fighting the devil. Now, just as I defeat the devil, can sleep, forget womans, you come out of the sea. Like the devil send you. And I tired of fighting!"

He launched himself at her, his hands closing around her throat and the force of his body throwing her backwards. Her head struck the wood of the deck with a shock that made her see bright planets with rings around them. His mouth was on hers, and it was no young god's, unless the Olympians were fond of garlic.

Joan fought, convinced that it made little difference in the eventual outcome whether she submitted, cooperated, or resisted. He would have to kill her to keep her from talking, and he knew it. So she would fight.

Suddenly, his lips left hers, his hands loosened, and his face twisted. Shaking, moaning, he rolled away from her.

"Too much years. All this in me, all the womans in my dreams. I burst, like a goatskin with too much wine in it."

Joan gripped the tiller handle to keep from falling. She felt faint. But she managed to snarl feebly at him.

"Goatskin? You smell like a goat! I hope you're satisfied now."

She could see that he was not.

She rose, wobbling, and grabbed the blindfold of the nearest rower and pulled it upwards and off his head. He cried out and snatched for the cloth, though he still kept his eyes shut. Joan lunged past the young monk and began to pull the blindfold off another monk. Then, seeing the young monk coming towards her, she struck the two rowers in the faces with her fists. The nose of one began to bleed and the mouth of the other was cut with a finger-nail. They beat the air with their hands but refused to open their eyes.

"Are you all crazy?" she yelled. "Help! Help!"

The rowers sat stiffly, their oars motionless, faces rigid. They seemed to be listening to inward voices. They were silent; the young monk was silent; the only noise was the sea muttering and a gull mewing overhead.

"All right, all right, you deaf and dumb statues! Then I'll do it!"

She tore an oar from the hands of a grey-haired monk and raised it over her head. It felt heavy, too heavy, but she kept it up and then brought it down towards the young monk. He lifted his hands to protect himself and jumped backward. The blade of the oar hissed and thunked into the deck. The shaft flew from her hands and struck a monk on the shoulder. He cried out and half-rose, then sat back down.

The young monk charged, hurled into her, and bore her down. She fell heavily, her breath driven from her. There was an inch of water on the deck, and she was rowed backwards over it by the monk. By the time she had regained her wind, it was over. At least, for the time being.

"Now, you be a good girl," he said. "I not kill you, it not is necessary, see? Just keep mouth shut. Who knows? Nobody believe you anyway."

Joan had two older brothers who had told her what to do if she were attacked. It was too late for defense but not for revenge. She knew exactly where to squeeze with all the strength left.

He writhed, his teeth clamped to keep from crying out. She rose and picked up the empty bottle of water and struck him against the side of the head. She was too weak to swing with much force, and his thick hair gave him some protection. Nevertheless, his eyes unfocused for several seconds.

He struggled to his feet while clenching his groin with both hands. She ran at him. He lifted his hands to ward off her raised bottle. It struck his wrist and was torn from her fist, but she grappled with him. She hooked her heel behind his and pushed. They fell, this time with her on top, and toppled over the side of the boat and into the sea.

On striking the water, she loosed her hold on him and began swimming toward the boat. A scream and a cry in Romaic made her turn around. She saw his hands, reaching upwards for something to hold, slide beneath the surface.

There was nothing she could do for him—or wanted to do. She lacked the strength even to save herself. The monks were rowing again and the boat was drawing away at speed beyond her ability to match.

No use calling out. Only one thing to do. Hope. Hope that the boat because it had no steersman and lacked one rower, might come back in a circle.

It did not turn back to her. It dwindled, became a dot, then nothing.

Once again, she was alone, blue around, blue overhead, blue underneath. Somewhere down there, the young monk, his passion spent, was sinking to the bottom. And if help did not come soon, she would be joining him.

Coldly, wearily, she thought. *This is life for you. I fight for virtue. Why? I would rather lose it than my life. What good am I to anyone but the fish if I drown? Never again. Let them do what they want to. I want to live...*

The only lover I ever knew. No lover, really. And he died, just as I will die. For his sins? No, because the fool never learned how to swim.

Well, what if he couldn't? I can swim. And a fat lot of good it does me. This is life for you. Never again. If I'm saved—oh, God, I hope I'm saved!—I'll become the biggest...

Something flashed white on the horizon.

It became larger while she fought to keep from screaming wildly and wasting her energy. It was the yacht, and it was soon alongside her. Platon, his face anxious, threw her a lifebelt and then hauled her aboard.

He wrapped a blanket around her, helped her below-decks and into a bunk. He gave her hot coffee, bread and cold meat. And after she had eaten, she looked at him, wondering if it was all to begin over.

"I am sorry, sorry beyond words!" he said. "I cooled off fifteen minutes after I—ah—pitched you off the ship. I came back, but I couldn't find you. I've been looking for you ever since, praying, cursing myself for a drunken swine, a murderer."

His eyes were bloodshot and puffy; his face, lined; his voice, shaky.

"Have you really been swimming all this time? What a woman! I would not have thought it possible! It is a miracle! And you have suffered so much because I thought you were one of those easy American girls playing hard to get. What an idiot, what a criminal, I am! Please forgive me!"

You don't know how easy it would be for you now, she thought. I have neither strength nor will to fight. I don't think I want to fight, ever again. Not physically, anyway. But what am I saying? In the water, I swore...

Platon took her hand in his. He said, "I think you are the most beautiful and the most amazing woman I have ever met. Even more than my mother! Yes, I say it openly. More than my mother! To prefer drowning to seduction by me, me, at whom women throw themselves! And to swim so far, so long, until I find you again! I tell you, it's a miracle!"

He kissed her hand. "Joan. I love you! I will take you to meet my mother! And I will say to her..."

She smiled slightly. If it turned out that Platon had saved more than one life when he had picked her up from the sea, if she felt life stirring within her in a few months...well, he was as much responsible for what had happened as the young monk. No, much more. Much, much more.

She said, "Yes. I'd like to meet your mother. But don't jump to any conclusions. I'm not so sure I want to even consider a man who's capable of murder."

"Murder! I would not dream of lifting my hand against you! You are a saint! I worship you!"

"And after you've gotten over your spasm of conscience?" she said. "Help me back to the deck Platon. I feel stifled down here."

Near the railing, she turned to him. He was blond and blue-eyed and handsome, and his eyelashes were long and thick and dark. They reminded her of the lashes of the young monk. They were rotting now or being torn by fish or dissolving in the belly of a fish.

Platon took her hand again and kissed it. He said, "Your hand is so cold, my darling. But I swear that I will warm it and keep it warm forever."

She seized his hand and pulled him towards her, reached down, and squeezed. He shrieked and doubled over and then went over the railing as she shoved him with her foot.

She stood at the railing and looked down as he writhed and splashed and shouted. For a moment, she thought of taking the ship away and leaving him there. Then she thought. *No. He must live.* She threw down the ladder.

Platon crawled aboard. He lay gasping for a while and then said. "I do not blame you. You must have been very angry. You must have suffered terribly. But now you've paid me back. We can start off even again, can't we?"

She looked down at him. She felt cold, but she did not shiver. She thought. *Paid back? You have just started to pay.*

Hunter's Moon

Hunter's Moon

Previously unpublished.

Phil readily admits that he was easily discouraged when he first started writing. That this story languished in a trunk for over 50 years is a tragedy that this collection is glad to, finally, redress.

Psychologically driven and laden with Freudian imagery, a vivid picture of small town life and the hypocrisy that draws parallels with Phil's 1960 novel *Fire and the Night*. As Phil observed in 1977, *Fire and the Night* dramatised the idea that sex and religion were only two sides of the same coin.

Phil: "This is one of the 4 or 5 stories I wrote before I sold my first published story, 'O'Brien and Obrenov'. I sent these 4 or 5 to Whit Burnett, editor, with his wife, of the literarily prestigious periodical, *Story*. Whit liked my submissions, but his wife didn't. I put them all in the trunk."

The bartender's voice was low.

"Mac, the parents in this town'll tear you apart. You got to quit poking and prying into things they think're sacred. Use your head. If you don't, it'll be broken."

McTyon grinned and said, "Lynch law? I don't believe it. Not here and now. This is Redstag, Minnesota, and I'm free, white, twenty-six, and I'm not suspected of rape. I'm just a high-school teacher of sociology and general science. My only crime is stepping on the toes of a few narrow-minded parents of my students. I'm not scared."

"Sure, you didn't win that D.S.C. at Bloody Ridge for nothing. Trouble is, you got too many guts. You shouldn't have conducted that survey among those kids without asking the principal's permission. And don't tell me again that you didn't ask Hansen because he was out of town. You could have waited till he got back or else asked the Board Chairman. But you knew Lund would turn you down, too, even if you are sweet on his niece.

"Maybe Lund would have refused *because* you date his niece. He'd already run outta his house two men who asked for her hand in marriage. O.K., O.K., don't get mad! Anyway, Hansen is now saying that you're working for Kinsey."

"Ha! Hansen and the Board know better. They're well aware the survey papers were sent by the sociology department of Centerwest U., they know it wasn't connected in any way with Kinsey and didn't even have the same goals. All I did was supervise the survey and make sure the students remained anonymous, and I mailed the questionnaires back to the university. What's more, no student was forced to take it."

"Makes no difference," said Bob. He sighed and then waddled off to the end of the bar at a call from his other two customers.

Darkly, McTyon's image stared back at him from the mirror upon the wall behind the bar. It was that of an average-sized man with broad shoulders, a blocky face with brown wavy hair, thick chevron-shaped eyebrows, blue eyes dark in this subdued light, a long straight nose scarred across the bridge by a shell fragment, a full mouth, and a deeply cleft chin that thrust forward a little too much.

Above his image was the reflection of the mounted head of a large buck, hung over the entrance behind him. Its glass eyes stared emptily at him each time he looked into the mirror. As McTyon sipped more and more beer, reluctant to leave the warmth for the long cold walk to town, he had become increasingly aware of the head. The flickering of the colored lights from the jukebox, combined with his angle of vision, had given the stiff head an almost quivering aliveness. The eyes bulged out of their sockets, its thick brown hairs bristled with fear, and the mouth curved open, about to slaver foam. It looked as if wolves were about to leap at its throat.

That thought caused him to glance at the ends of the long mirror, above each of which hung the stuffed head of a wolf, shot not a mile outside Redstag. Their eyes flashed brightly but blindly from the jukebox's shifting lights.

Below the head to his right stood Ericssen and Sonderquist, their faces long and narrow and thin-lipped, like those of Puritan Pilgrims, the foambrimming schooners held just below the level of their sharp chins forming the seventeenth-century white collars.

Bob returned and rang up the sale. Bending over the tap to refill Mac's glass, he said, "Promise to keep your temper, and I'll tell you something. O.K.? Those two guys've been shooting off their mouths about your survey. Sonderquist says no kid of his can be insulted with unhealthy questions about his personal life. He says you're hinting that Redstag's kids and the people who raised them ain't pure."

McTyon put his glass down upon the bar so hard that the beer splashed over his wrist and the two at the end of the bar looked up from their murmuring talk.

"Easy, easy," said Bob softly but urgently. "Don't pop off to Sonderquist, or you'll get me in dutch. I'm telling you this because I like you, but I don't want no trouble. And he's only saying what all Redstag is saying."

"All right!" said McTyon fiercely, leaning over until his face was only six inches from the other's. "I'll keep your nose clean. But you listen. No matter how free I am in my outlook, I am not, as some citizens of Redstag maintain, an atheist. I consider myself a Christian, and I go to church because I like to, not because other people expect me to. I've done some thinking about my religion, and I've come to the not-so-original conclusion that one of Christianity's essential claims is that no one, *but no one*, is good or pure. And I can quote chapter and verse to back me up, if you care to hear them.

"Another claim you'll find is that you can't be true to yourself or God until you take a long, hard, and unafraid look into yourself and don't back away from what you see but do something constructive about it. In other words, so says the Good Book, let's admit we're all sinners and root out what's wrong."

"Can't prove it by me," said Bob, shrugging.

McTyon ignored the interruption.

"This survey was designed to test my students' honesty in the sexual field. I thought that perhaps it might not only help the learned doctors at the university find out a little bit of what's rotten in our society, it might lead some of the kids to a soul-searching. And whatever the faults of the survey, it's much better than refusing to admit there are dark and shameful things in each of us. You don't kill the cockroaches in the kitchen by refusing to clean it up or even to admit it's infested."

Suddenly, McTyon rose. "I'm tired of this. Think I'll go home. I bagged three rabbits. Want one?"

"Yeah. Sure. Thanks. The missus'll like that."

"Don't be so anxious to get rid of me."

A few minutes later, he slipped the strap of his hunting-bag over his shoulder and gripped the handle of the case which held his shotgun.

"So long," he said loudly to Bob and the two patrons.

The latter nodded but did not speak. Their eyes were dark and glazed, and they seemed as immobile as the wolfheads. Nevertheless, McTyon felt he'd gained a moral victory by forcing them to acknowledge his leave-taking.

Under a sky clear and slick as ice, he walked briskly over the snowpacked road. Far to his left, a locomotive whistled, its headlight feeling through the night like a blind man's cane. When he came to the cross of railroad tracks and highway, he stopped to stare at the full moon. The two halos around it made it look like a giantess's eye. The globe itself formed an opaque pupil. The iris, the inner ring, was a pearly grey edged by a light rose-red. The outer ring was a blue-grey also rimmed with rose-red.

"Beautiful, beautiful," he murmured. "But cold, cold. Artemis, nocturnal goddess of the hunt, remote, inviolable, strange, frozenly virginal. Artemis, O Artemis, I, McTyon, a mere man and mortal, salute you!"

Shivering, he turned from the skies to look beyond the broad field that lay to his right. Diagonally across the sweep of snow, set far back from the road, was the house of Mr. Lund. Even at that distance it was large, its old-fashioned gables and dormers and cupolas bulking many-angled and black. It was too bad the Lunds were not home or had gone to bed. He'd like to propitiate Mrs. Lund with a rabbit, and, with that to ease his way, discuss with Diane's uncle this problem of the survey. Moreover, he'd get a chance to talk to the lovely Diane. Not that he didn't see her five times a week, for she taught English at Redstag Consolidated, but that he couldn't see too much of the woman he was beginning to fall in love with. Lovely Diane. Silent but lovely.

At that moment, the blind face of the house winked. A square of light appeared in the middle of the first story, revealed by the lid of a shade being raised. Impulsively, he forged across the field through the knee-deep snow towards the gate set close to the garage behind the house. Though it was easier to follow the road until it reached the Lund driveway, he took, as usual, the straightest route to his goal.

Halfway across the field, he heard the scream of the train's whistle but paid no attention to it. He was thinking of his last visit here at a dinner party for the high-school teachers. Despite his fluid disposition, he'd been ill at ease. Diane's aunt sat stiff and erect, and her smile, though frequent, was as mechanical and fitful as the whipping of a banner in the breeze. After dinner, at which everybody spoke softly and spasmodically, they'd gone to the living room. There she sat rigidly upon the sofa, like Queen Victoria herself. Her only sign of agitation came when he dropped a piece of cake on the floor. She rose and looked steadily at him with her light blue eyes. He'd dropped on his knees, saying, "I'll get it, Mrs. Lund. Clumsy of me." He was afraid he'd offended her, for he'd heard from Diane of how devoutly she kept her house clean.

It was then that his hand had moved the large window drape by the crumbled cake, and he'd seen, even in the dim light, the layer of greasy dirt against the base of the wall.

Thinking of that, he opened the gate and walked down the driveway towards the front of the house. At that moment the train roared over the crossing, and Diane appeared at the window and reached for the cord of the shade.

He paused. It was evident she'd just stepped from the tub. When he'd recovered from the shock, he did not think it wise to move. Perhaps, if he remained motionless, she'd pull the blind without seeing him. A move on his part would be sure to attract her attention.

He cursed the misfortune that had caused her to forget to close the shade and he cursed the storm window which prevented the inner window from steaming up. At the same time, he could not help admiring her. She'd always worn rather loose clothing which he now saw had concealed a tiny but exquisite shape. She did not at all have that somewhat flat and brittle appearance he'd mentally given her. His intimacies with her had been limited to a goodnight kiss on their last date, a week ago, the day before he'd conducted that survey. She'd been friendly enough to encourage him to think she preferred him to Redstag's other eligible men and might even love him but was too shy to say so. Physically, she'd been standoffish. The first few times he'd put his arm around her at a dance or show, she'd stiffened, though later she relaxed. All their contacts had subtly impressed upon him a false picture he'd not realized he had until this moment of revelation.

It seemed to him he stood just outside the square of light at his toes, unable to look away from her, until the cold drove up through his feet, crystallized his bones, and clotted his brain with ice. Why, why didn't she draw the shade? She was a marble statue, holding that pose, her left hand dangling by her side, her right stretched to the cord. Perhaps, he thought, suddenly knowing herself visible to the train's passengers had shocked her into immobility as a rabbit sometimes became when surprised by the hunter. Certainly, there was an expression on her face he'd never seen before.

Then, as the last of the coaches rattled by, she flowed out of her suspended animation and pulled on the shade. At the same time, she looked downwards, at him.

There was no jerky pause between the time she seized the cord and the time the light winked out, leaving the house once again dark and blind. Smoothly, she drew downwards, and her white features, as if sculptured from snow and ice, remained congealed.

McTyon at once came out of his paralysis. His heart thudded, and sweat poured from his armpits, just as they did before leaving a foxhole for an attack. Shaking, he walked around the corner of the porch, only to stop suddenly. The blinds were drawn across the large many-paned windows of the parlor, and no light showed beneath them. What if she were home alone? Should she hear the doorbell she might become frightened, might even—God forbid!—think he'd been spying and was now ready to take advantage of her solitude.

But there was the possibility that his silence might be taken for that of a peeper and coward. That was one thing he could not endure. He must face her and explain what had happened even if she would be very much embarrassed and pained.

Driven with the agony of the fear she might think him afraid, he walked swiftly onto the porch. There he opened the storm door and looked through the narrow diamond-shaped panes at the top of the inner door. He saw nothing but darkness.

Lightly, he touched the doorbell button but did not press it, for he was held by a new thought. Surely, if her folks were at home, Diane would have spoken to them by now, and her uncle, whose temper was well known, would have charged out to collar him. Since he had not, he must be gone, which made it doubtful if Diane would answer the bell.

He turned away, convinced he should go home and phone her from there. An explanation over the line would be less personal and less painful. Perhaps she'd accept his apology and would then agree with him that it'd be best if no one else knew of the incident.

Just as he reached the steps, he halted again. If he left a rabbit, he could later on point to it as evidence of his story and his good faith. He reached into his bag but stopped when he saw the flicker of a white face behind the little panes. A cold prickling ran up the back of his neck. Diane. He pressed his nose against the glass. There was nothing to see but darkness.

Deciding it was his imagination, he deposited the rabbit between the storm door and main door and walked the mile and a half into Redstag. Inside a phone booth in Katzen's Pharmacy, he asked the operator for the Lunds' line, only to be told that it was busy.

Four more calls made at fifteen-minute intervals from the hallway of his boarding house gave him the same angry and frustrating buzzing. He shrugged and went to bed, where he fell asleep only after plotting in detail just what he'd say to Diane when he saw her at church in the morning. The last thing he remembered was a far off barking which seemed, curiously, to get closer and closer the drowsier he became. The dogs were rallying around the moon.

In the morning, on arriving outside the church, McTyon was aware of the tight smiles or lack of smiles, the brief nods and curt good mornings, and the manner in which the older people skirted him as he stood by the side-entrance. Bob, the bartender, had been right. Resentment against him and his survey was more than a trickle. It was in high tide.

He fidgeted, wishing Diane would get there so he could snare her to make his explanations. Automatically, he groped in his pockets until, conscious of what he was doing, he dropped his hands. As a Sunday-school teacher, he wasn't allowed to smoke within a block of the church.

A young man of his own age, twenty-six, walked up to him. McTyon greeted him.

"Morning, Mac," replied Doctor Smith, smiling bucktoothedly and peering through thick hornrimmed glasses. Then he turned to look for his wife, who'd joined a group of women and was pointedly turning her back on McTyon.

McTyon said softly, "Why the general snub, Doc?"

"The phones were busy last night," answered Smith, smiling sadly. "But I doubt Diane's aunt. What's your story?"

"Wait a minute. I need a cigarette bad. Anybody who doesn't like it can lump it."

He held one to Smith, who unhesitatingly accepted it. While Smith listened to McTyon, he smoked, ignoring his wife's pleading looks that he join her.

Finally, he said, "My wife, who is—God forgive her—too easily swayed by public opinion, heard from her neighbor all the unpleasant details and fantastic surmises Mrs. Lund was spreading over the phone. She said that Diane was in hysterics."

He puffed on his cigarette, then said, "I find it rather significant, however, that her uncle did not call me to quiet her. Nor did he contact the sheriff."

Red-faced, McTyon spoke hoarsely, "Damn it, Doc! If Diane's uncle was there, why did he stay in the house?"

"He said it took him some time to get out of her the story of what had happened. When he did, he went outside, but there was no sign of you."

"What about the rabbit I left in the doorway?"

"He never mentioned it. And I don't think he will."

"What do you mean?"

"I can only give you speculations I can't prove. Old Chronoff was their doctor before I took over his practice. Before he died, he hinted to me during a casual conversation that their household was not as...He hesitated. "Well, you've noticed how hushed and chilly their house is and how clean. Too clean, I'd say. Too clean."

"There was dirt behind her aunt's drapes, dirt that'd been there a long time."

"Yes? Well, hmmmm. Well, the fact is that her uncle is overfond of her, too protective and restrictive. However, that's not important just now. What matters is that the Board will ask you Monday morning for a resignation. This I know."

"I'll refuse to resign," said McTyon loudly, not knowing he was crushing the cigarette in his hand.

"Then you'll be fired. And your career'll be ruined."

"I'll still fight."

Doctor Smith lowered his eyes, refusing to meet his friend's.

"I admire your courage, and my sense of justice is as outraged as yours. But you can't win. You can't! You've no witnesses on your side. And no money. Lund is president of the county bank, his word carries weight, and public opinion is against you."

"Thanks, Doc. I know you're my friend, but you're also a doctor and dependent on Redstag's good will, so you dare only go so far with me. And you think you're giving me good objective advice. Thanks a lot."

"What're you going to do?"

"I'm going to see Diane and her folks, because it's obvious they're not coming to church today. We're having it out. I'm in the right, and they must know it. Otherwise, they'd have called in the law or contacted me. And they wouldn't have hidden that rabbit.

"Will you tell the Bible Class supervisor to get a substitute for my kids? Good. Wish me luck."

"Good luck," said the doctor, shaking his hand. "And keep your temper."

Fifteen minutes later, McTyon pressed upon the Lunds' doorbell button. Bee bong! bee bong! bee bong! went the chimes within the house. He waited a minute, then pressed the button again. Bee bong! bee bong! bee bong!

He sensed rather than heard footsteps, ghosts of sound heralding the substance. A cold prickling ran up the back of his neck as it had the evening before when he thought he'd seen Diane's pale face behind the door panes. It was caused by the first sight of Mr. Lund's features, which convinced him he'd mistaken her uncle's face for hers. Not only was there a remarkable family resemblance with the black curly hair, classically Grecian nose, short upper lip, and very white skin, but he had the same curious indecipherable expression that she had had while gazing out the bathroom window.

The storm door banged against the side of the porch. Lund strode out, a tall thin man with wide dark grey eyes, the left one made of glass, replacing the eye lost in a hunting accident. It did not quite follow its living mate in its motions and gave him an unfocussed look that was at times comical but at this moment was sinister.

"Mr. Lund," McTyon began, and then stopped, for he saw the yellow-white knobby twisted stick in Lund's hand, the bull's pizzle used as a cane by his now-dead father and kept out of sight now in the umbrella stand but occasionally taken out by the banker and shown to male guests if no women were around.

McTyon raised his hands to defend himself, but the stick had gone up and come down, and the next he knew, he was lying on his back on the porch, confused, stammering desperately against the madness and injustice of what Lund was doing.

Through the cloudiness pressing in on him, he could make out only the twisted face, its glass eye staring not at him but a little to one side as if its owner disclaimed responsibility for his action. Then the cane struck for the last time that he knew about, and the clouds rolled in and met.

He woke to hear voices. A woman's said, "...claimed McTyon attacked him, so he used his cane, and..."

A man's: "That's what *Lund* said. Here. Hang on while I snip this off."

They were doing something to his head.

The bass of a bigbellied man boomed, "Lund says if he doesn't get out of town right away, he's going to sign a warrant against him."

"I'm the doctor, sheriff. If I say he can't move, he can't move."

"Yeah? Maybe so. But if I was him, I'd get out before Lund decides to crack down. Anyway, I'm going out to my car a spell. Call me if he comes to."

A door slammed. He winced and opened his eyes. Smith and his nurse, in their Sunday-best, were looking down at him.

"How'd I get here?"

"Walked," replied the doctor, gravely. "You were out on your feet, but you made it into town on your own power. The sheriff saw you outside my house and brought you in. You collapsed; you've been out for three hours."

"Is my head broken?"

"There was no blood from your ears or nose, and your eyes are unclouded. Feel sick at your stomach? No? Good! Look at this pencil. Hmm. You focus all right, which is more than I can say for most of the people around here. Are you drowsy? No? Good!"

McTyon tried to get up on one elbow, but Smith pushed him back.

"Stay there."

"Lord my head hurts. And I'm weak."

"Two stitches each in three different places," said Smith, mock-cheerfully. "Your head is wrapped like the Sheik of Araby's."

His voice became lower and more serious. "Mac, the sheriff'll be back soon. You'll have to make a decision then. If I were you, I'd resign for reasons of ill health. Lund says he'll let you do that so you may go some place else with a clean record. He says he wants no publicity if he can help it."

McTyon spoke through clenched teeth. "Doc, I'm sticking it out, and I'm suing Lund for assault and battery."

"For God's sakes!" cried Smith. Then, quickly, "Miss Nussen, I won't be needing you any more. Thank you."

After the nurse had closed the door, Smith said, "Look, Mac, you're that most dangerous of hunters, a hunter after the nocturnal creatures that lair in man's psyche. You want to explore the darkest of all continents, man himself, and capture the strange and furtive things that live there. But you've been stupid enough to ignore the fact that man resents the light of truth on himself because it shocks and humiliates him. The hunted turns on the hunter and tears him apart.

"The people of Redstag—and Lund, especially—resent you. If they can stop you or hurt you or do both, they'll do it. So far, it's only taken one of them to do a fine job of halting you dead in your tracks.

"That's not all. There's Diane. If she loved you, she'd have told you by now she didn't think you were peeping. Nor would she have allowed her uncle to attack you."

"Maybe he attacked me because she is in love with me," said McTyon.

"Perhaps. It would tie in with what I think is wrong with him. The point is, do you believe that?"

McTyon closed his eyes. Smith continued, "Diane is a lovely girl who should have grown up to be a warm, laughter-loving, life-embracing woman. She had the misfortune to be raised by a couple who've turned her into a shy and frightened creature who'd never make a good wife, especially for a brave and warm man like you, Mac. Too bad, but there it is."

There was a silence, punctuated by the ticking of the huge grandfather clock, heritage from dead Doctor Chronoff.

Suddenly, McTyon released a deep breath and said, "That clinched it. I'm leaving town."

Smith sighed. "It's a defeat. But it's also the saving of your career."

"Doc, you don't understand. I'm coming back tomorrow on the early train. When the school doors open, I'll be there to teach my classes."

Smith's lips opened briefly to show his buckteeth. He could not look his friend in the eyes.

"All right," said McTyon wearily. "You think I'm just blustering to save my face, don't you? You think I'll make a loud show of courage, get on the train, and never come back? Well, it's not so. I'm taking that train in order to do a little thinking."

"A railroad coach is no place for a man who may have a fractured skull."

"It is when you have in mind what I have."

"What do you mean?"

"Oh, there's a lawyer in Minnafield I want to talk to. But that's only one of my reasons for taking that train. Something you said a moment ago snared for me an idea that's been circling the fringe of my mind and bothering me ever since last night."

He would say nothing else about the subject. The rest of the day, when he wasn't staring at the ceiling, he talked of other things. At eight-thirty he rose and left the house, suitcase in hand. Smith had driven to the boarding-house and packed in it those few articles McTyon wanted to take. Then the two drove to the station, which was outside of town a mile. The sheriff's car followed them.

Just before McTyon boarded the rear coach, he was stopped by Smith who said, "Are you really planning on coming back?"

The teacher looked steadily at him from beneath the thick bandage around his head. "Don't give up faith in me so soon. It's going to be a long pull, and I need every friend I have. But if I do lose them, I'll still make my way alone.

"However," he said, smiling for the first time that day, "I expect to come back with ammunition for the fight, something that will convince you that you should stick by me."

Two minutes later, the train chuffed away. McTyon waved to Smith, then turned and chose the last seat upon the left side of the coach, though there were plenty of empties on the right. He sat behind two red faced salesmen from Minnafield, who, when they were convinced the conductor was not coming back for some time, produced a fifth and took deep swallows from it. McTyon glanced idly at them, then looked out the window. He could not see the moon, but its rays painted the fields of snow a bright silver-white. Redstag drifted by. It was not as white as the countryside, for smoke had lain a thin crust of dirt over the snow. But that was only for a few seconds, and they were back to where it was clean.

One of the salesmen sitting in front of McTyon leaned across the other to look out the window. He giggled and spoke loudly enough for McTyon to hear.

"There she is. Just like last night and the night before. What'd I tell you? Next time don't call *me* a liar." Slowly and reluctantly, the man with the bandage turned his head. The sickness in his stomach was not, he knew, caused by any possible fracture of his skull. No, it was from seeing what he had thought he would, yet had hoped he would not, even if it meant his cause was lost. He now had the key to her character and the reason why the uncle had not admitted finding the rabbit. Lund had known whose story was true, but he'd been afraid that McTyon would talk, so he'd tried to convince Redstag that McTyon was a peeper and a liar. And avoiding the printed publicity of a trial by running the teacher out of town was just what he'd desired.

McTyon was sure that Lund would now withdraw his version of the incident and would explain to the townspeople that a mistake had been made. Lund was beaten.

Even at that moment of vindication, he felt a sickness and a sense of defeat that had never come to him before.

No, he swore to himself, clenching his fists, he'd not admit that this could down him. He had to face the brutal fact that the break between Diane and himself was forever. Though he pitied her, he could not love her as a man should love his wife. He could love only a woman whom he thought was strong and was his equal. Diane was certainly not that.

At the same time, he did not despise or condemn her. Mingled with his sorrow was an anger at those who had taken her when she was very young and pliable and, because of their lack of love or because of their twisted love, had bent her into this. Not that they intended Diane to become this, for they would be horrified if they knew and would blame her. After all, hadn't they given her a roof and walls and food and education and taught her what was right and what was wrong?

He was angry with them, but he had no right to be. Weren't they as much the reflections of their parents as she was of them?

But he was angry. There was no use denying that.

And he was hurt by the knowledge that she needed his help desperately and that he alone could give it to her, for he was the only man who was not afraid to do so or who cared about her. He cared, not so much because she was Diane, though that had something to do with it, too, but because she was a human being who was suffering.

There, across the white and level field, black in the moon's radiance, had been the solitary house of the Lunds. Then, suddenly as a lid opening to reveal the living eye of a man thought blind, a windowshade had gone up. Displayed within the luminous chamber, like the image of a goddess fixed in a bright and transparent eye, was a woman. At that distance her features were a blank, but the lovely body just risen from the bath was undoubtedly Diane's.

The locomotive's whistle screamed at her; the coaches rattled on by, swaying towards her, swaying away from her.

Yet, though she could not help knowing she was being seen, she remained frozen, suspended in brightness and memory, her hand reaching halfway to the cord of the shade, almost as if she were saluting the onlookers.

McTyon, sitting in the last seat in the last coach, was the only one to witness the door to the bathroom swing open, violently, and somebody—whether her aunt or uncle, he could not determine—rush in and snatch at the string of the shade.

His own hand moved up to pull on the emergency cord. He was going back to the house, then and there.

The Rise Gotten

Previously unpublished.

Bette Farmer: "This piece was written for Bob Bloch for a collection he was doing. He'd asked for something unusual, but after he got it he told Phil he guessed he didn't make it plain to the authors what he wanted, because he didn't get it. So Phil put the story away, and forgot about it. I really never heard any more about the book, so don't know if it came out or not. Maybe the whole thing fell through. Bob was a very good friend of mine and then eventually Phil's. Bob said little about what he had published but his letters were hilarious. Somewhere I have a stack of them that I saved."

Twenty-four major humiliations every year for seven years.

Roger Briard, sixty-seven years old, had suffered many during his lifetime. The minor humiliations—forget them. They were too many to count, even though he remembered many.

His wife, Reynarda, fifty-seven years old, had caused all the major humiliations and at least half of the minor.

But if he had a different personality, he would not have put up with them. He would have defended himself from Rey by attacking her. Verbally, that is. He was incapable of physical violence. And, unfortunately, verbal violence.

So, why blame her? He was at fault. Partly, anyway. Knowing this, however, did not keep him from getting very angry at her. At the same time, he was almost as angry at himself.

Whatever the blame, here she was, regular as a laxative-taker, deeply shaming him again, causing another major stress. For some unknown psychological reason, she did this at or near the full moon and at or near the new moon. She was a sort of werewolf, and, at the same time, a sort of anti-werewolf.

Mainly, she was a loony. And he was a loony for tolerating her irrational behavior.

But, as she had said so many times that he was sick of hearing it, "A man nobody can get a rise from, can't express his anger, justified or not, is nuts. And he'll drive his wife nuts. Also, to drink."

Usually, the bimonthly humiliation happened after four in the afternoon. After her "cocktail hour." Which was followed, she had said more than once, by her getting no cock and his getting no tail.

During the "hour," she guzzled at least a pint of vodka or gin or scotch, though it was somewhat diluted by a low-sugar soft drink.

So now he was standing in front of the bed and trying to prove that he was a man, though what getting an erection had to do with manhood was beyond his understanding. He had also not succeeded, so far, in proving that encasing your penis with nitroglycerin tablets inevitably caused its blood vessels to swell.

Rey, as always, said that he did not love her. If he did, he would have no trouble getting a complete hard on. Or, considering his age and physical condition; one at least large and stiff enough to do the job. Never mind all that crap, that smokescreen, about his swollen prostate gland. He could not perform because he thought she was repulsive. He did not love her. He hated her guts, in fact, but was not man enough to admit it.

And so on in the same vein, then branching out to include other veins and all of the arteries.

Then—she seldom gave up, she could not admit being defeated—she started her dirty talk again. She insisted that that had to arouse him because it aroused her. (She never had been able to understand that other people did not necessarily feel as she did.)

"Give it to me! Ram that hard thing hard! Plunge, plunge as deep as you can! All the way to the muddy bottom of the sea! Fuck my brains out! Go, go, go! Split me apart!"

Great God Almighty! For the first twenty years of their marriage, she had been tender and soft-spoken and even a little shy during their lovemaking. Sex was part of the great romance of their marriage, and romance was a golden aura of love. She would not have said "shit" if she had fallen into a pile of it.

Now! Great God Almighty!

Neither tenderness nor coarseness would work.

He was turned off. If he had been turned on, he still would have been unable to do what she wanted. He was humiliated, shamed, and furious.

But he could not tell her that.

He wanted to do so. He was near to exploding with the desire to roar and scream at her. He burned. He shook. His mouth opened, and the words clogged his throat and choked him.

That was the trouble. He could not openly express his anger when he was face to face with the one who made him angry. He did not know why. He probably never would.

⤟⪼●⪻⤞

Though it was June, Roger Briard entered his home like March, roaring like a lion. At the same time, the big grandfather clock at the end of the short hall chimed, announcing three P.M. But it was no louder than the TV booming in the large room that did service as both living and family room in this small house. As the door slammed shut behind him, a crumpled Kleenex on the rug fluttered upward from the rush of air. It looked like a sick albino bat trying to fly.

Seeing the dirty tissue made him angrier. For God's sake! Rey would stand next to a trash barrel and drop her empty coke can on the ground next to it. He had seen her do it many times.

Grunting with the effort of bending over—he really had to diet and would soon—he placed the two heavy grocery bags on the floor. He picked up the Kleenex and stuffed it between a half-gallon container of skim milk and the side of the paper bag. If Rey was where she could see him, he would have ignored the Kleenex. When she saw him pick up anything off the floor, she accused him of silent criticism of her housekeeping.

When he straightened up with the bags in his arms, he said, loudly, "Jesus Christ! I'm not going out to the store again just because my dumbshit wife forgot something again. This is twice today. It's foggier than Reagan's mind out there, couldn't see past my headlights, half of those Neanderthals driving out there didn't have their lights on. I almost got clobbered!"

He knew that his wife could not hear him above the loud TV.

She must have heard the door slamming. Her words drifted into the hallway, riding on the surf of the TV.

"...get...dressing?"

"Yeah, I sure as hell did get it!"

He had spoken more loudly than he had intended or was good for him. He carried the bags, heavy, heavy, toward the room, the Holy of Holies with the great devil-god, the TV set, lording over it. Lamb-meek, March going out, he entered it. He hated himself for his withdrawal into Roger the Hen-Pecked, Roger the Pussy-Whipped. He wanted to hurl the bags across the room at her.

But "Character determines destiny," Heraclitus had written. The great ancient Greek philosopher whom Rey called "Hairy Clitoris" whenever she heard her husband mention him. Which he did no more. He got very irritated when she sneered at his classical references, his pseudo-intellectual talk, as she had called it too many times.

As always, his unspoken rebuttals bounced around in the echo chamber of his mind. He wished fiercely that he could utter them.

The old Greek had said, "What goes up must come down. You can't step into the same river twice. Character determines destiny."

What he had failed to mention because he knew nothing of them was that genes determine your character. The hapless human was born with a fixed personality, bound in triple brass, unchanged, predestined and predestinating. But what the human did, the peculiar direction of his actions, was influenced by the environment, of course. Roger would give environment that much credit.

Rey slumped in a big easy chair. Her legs were still great, Bette Grableish, Cyd Charisseish. But her once narrow hips were walled with fat. A Mae West of fat ringed her waist. Her breasts were two dirigibles hanging downwards. A sac of skin like that on the throat of a male frog when it bellowed its mating call swelled from under her chin.

Her hair was blonde; it had once been genuinely yellow. It was in the current messy style which only young women could get away with and not many of them. That face...her snaky hair style...the ancient Greeks had been misinformed. Perseus had not cut off Medusa's head. She resided in a small Midwestern city and was living off Social Security.

"Would that she would turn me to stone instead of this quivering inner jelly," he muttered.

"What did you say?"

"Nothing of any importance."

Her exceedingly light blue eyes had always lit up when she saw him, and they did now. But the light was that in the ice cubes in the refrigerator freezer. He walked by her and toward the kitchen door.

"You did get the ranch salad dressing?" she said loudly.

Stentor should have been a woman. Her voice, deep for a female, roared and rasped like a command from the Norns, the Viking Fates.

His voice dropped as he walked away from her.

"All the rest of the fucking stuff you fucking forgot the first time I went to the store," he said.

"What?"

"Nothing of any importance. Yes, I got it all."

He entered the kitchen, put the bags on the counter, and began putting the groceries on their destined shelves. Meanwhile, on the screen in the next room, Portia Pantage, played by Marsha Angelbrick, died as destined by the producers while the actors and actresses around her bed wept, moaned, and snuffled. Marsha's tears were genuine, he was sure. She was being pushed out of her twenty-year old role as the much suffering and too-goddam-saintly-to-be believed matriarch martyr of the highly Nielsen-rated *A Mother's Heart.*

Rey had told him—not that he cared—that Angelbrick had demanded too big a raise and too much control. So, she was out on her ass, which had grown big in the last two decades.

Having disposed of the groceries, he went into the tiny bathroom at its southern end. Here he emptied his bladder, though it took him some time. That chestnut-shaped organ known as the prostate gland was giving him trouble, more than just a little trouble. It was swelling and hence squeezing the urethral tube which passed through it. Inevitably, the gland would have to be removed or hollowed out.

He grimaced. Knives. Pain. More bills to pay than Medicare took care of. The company for which he had worked as an accountant had been taken over in a corporate raid, and, somehow, he had not only suddenly been out of a job, only two years from retirement, but he had lost his pension. That had added to the rage smoldering in him for the past ten years. He had many times tortured, mutilated, and killed the main criminal responsible for this—in his imagination—but it did not help cool the wrath.

When he was operated upon, then, maybe, Rey would quit complaining about his impotency and stop jeering at him. She refused to accept his reasonable and medically well-founded explanations for his inability. As always, she ignored the facts and the logic. Anything that happened to her she took personally. It was not his prostate, she claimed. The truth was—she knew it in her heart—that he thought that she was a fat, old, and disgusting woman. He no longer loved her. He hated and despised her and so on. Especially the and-so-on.

"You goddam wimp!" she would cry. "Why can't you come out with it, quit lying, tell me what you really think? What kind of coward are you?"

It was during these harangues and accusations that he envisioned a lion in a cage. It was angry and frustrated because it could not get past the thick steel bars. Its yellow eyes blazed, and it struck the bars again and again and even chewed on the steel, but it would be forever imprisoned. It smelled meat and mates and freedom to roam the veldt and, above all, the chance to kill, kill, kill. Kill those nasty creatures who had taunted it, jeered at it, degraded and humiliated it.

That image faded as he would say, "You're wrong, absolutely wrong. I do love you. I can't help it because I can't get a good hard on. You're unfair when you say the trouble is psychological."

Then she would fire her major weapon, the Big Bertha of the guns laying down her barrage.

"I've always suspected you were an unconscious homosexual!"

No matter how illogical, invalid, degrading, and unfair her insults, he never screamed back at her or struck her or even raised his fist threateningly. He smiled, and he kept smiling.

"Look at you!" she would scream. "You're enjoying this, you sadistic monster!"

Wrong. He was not enjoying it at all. He was sick. His guts were a ball of newly hatched snakes bristling with sharp quills, sliding over each other in the tangle, scraping each other as they writhed out of the mass, cutting, bleeding, and hurting each other, their individual pains making a whole of agony that was more than the sum of their parts.

Thinking of past scenes and mental images, trying to squeeze out the last drop, he saw another image. Someone had accidentally forgotten to lock the door to the iron cage. Now what? What if the angry lion could now get free? What if, then, it became afraid to escape?

"It ought to be shot!" he said aloud. "It's better off dead!"

He went to the washbowl and hand-scooped water over the glans. As he toweled it dry, he got a brief pleasure from imagining Rey drying her face with the same towel.

He thought, *What an asshole I am.*

The mirror showed him a being that did not look like a lion. It was more like a gorilla. It was jowly and bald. The eyes were a deep gray, but the whites were bloodshot. It had kangaroo pouches under the eyes. Two deep lines, scored by the knife of time, ran from the corners of the lips to his chin. Many shallower lines crossed his face to make a sort of shadowy fencing mask.

What could he expect? He was no longer the Golden Boy who had met the Golden Girl, Rey, in college. To be realistic, he had never been except during those four years. He had broken loose from his inhibitions, to a certain degree, anyway, and had capered like a satyr. But that had been with the aid of much cheap beer and wine and bad whiskey. Then, out of the unrealistically structured world of the campus, having to work, he had lapsed into his normal state. Nothing normal about it, compared to other people, that is. But they did not know it. He could be congenial when he had to do so, and he was a genius at not showing anger or aggressiveness, mainly because he was unable to do so.

Yet, the first two-thirds of the marriage had not been so bad. He and Rey had had a lot of fun, though not with his colleagues at work. Accountants, those he had known, anyway, were rather sobersided and diehard Republicans to boot. Rey's friends were different; they liked to whoop it up, drink it up, and put down the squares. But the occasional squalls with Rey, mostly caused by her anger at his "refusal" to express his love often enough, had increased. In the last decade, the calms were less frequent; the squalls had become hurricanes, monsoons, storms that seemed to last forever.

His friends had asked, "Why don't you get a divorce?"

"It's not all that bad," he would say. "We'll work it out. She's just temperamental. I can ride it out. Why get a divorce when we're so old?"

The implication of that last remark being that they could tolerate the marriage until one of them died.

Rey's friends, who knew much more about the Briards' marital troubles than his, asked her the same question. He had not told her about his friends' doubts, but she told him every detail of the conversation with her friends about her unhappiness.

"And I said to her that I'll get a divorce when I get a real rise out of you. But it won't be necessary then, I told her, because then you'll be a different person. More human."

By "rise," she meant a breakthrough, his genuinely showing anger or love or both. Good luck, he thought. God be with you and give that to you. And to me. But it won't happen. I was born this way, and I'll die this way.

"ROGER!"

He was startled. He had been standing in the doorway, wandering through the labyrinth of his mind, no way out until Rey, a screeching Ariadne, suddenly showed him where it was. That happened a lot lately. He seemed to be spending more time in his thoughts than in the outside world. He did not know which place was worse.

He went into the big room. Rey looked at him and said, "I thought you'd like to see this. It's so sad."

Tears were snaking down her cheeks. Caused, of course, by Mother Portia Pantage's swiftly approaching demise. It was almost time for another commercial and then there would be a few minutes for Portia's death rattles and final words and the last few whispered phrases of contrition from the children and grandchildren who had used and abused her. Everybody was weeping and sobbing as if the police had lobbed tear gas grenades through the window.

Roger would have liked to shoot the whole sorry crew.

"You know I don't like soap operas," he said.

He thought, only morons or neurotics or both watch them.

He stooped to pick up the newspapers Rey had scattered around her chair. Damn her! Was it so difficult to pile them neatly on the floor when she was through reading them.

"You have no heart," she said. "I thought that surely, somewhere, you'd find a spark of sympathy and compassion."

"For her?" he said as he put the folded stack of papers under his arm. "She's pathetic. She's put up with all that crap, lying, stealing, insults, betrayal, even forgiven her son for his attempt to rape her. She should have kicked them out years ago, turned half of them over to the cops, maybe shot them for what they did to her. She's got no guts."

Rey gestured with her hand, indicating that he was hopeless. That he had refused to agree with her, to stand up to her, did not register. But that was a trifling matter. He disagreed with her on many things, and that was all right as he did not get too sarcastic or insulting about it. She reacted strongly only when he got "personal," as she called it. Then she attacked him for opposing her. Yet, she wanted him to show anger.

Not until he had reached the hall did he realize his criticism of Portia Pantage had been a criticism of himself. Hell! He was Portia!

If he despised her, he had to despise himself.

So what? He did despise himself.

He started down the hall, then realized that Rey's glass of booze had not been on the table by her chair. And he had smelled no liquor when he came into the room. He went back to the doorway and stuck his head around it.

"Are you sick?" he said.

She turned the volume control down. A commercial was on, one of many before the next soap opera came on.

"No. Why?"

"You're not drinking."

"So, am I an alcoholic?"

"I'm not a doctor," he said. "Oh, oh! You're waiting for your sister! I forgot she was coming over today. You always wait for her so you can start even."

"I told you three times she was coming," Rey said. "Don't you ever listen? I might as well be living with a dummy."

"I am," he muttered, and he turned away.

The hall leading to the study at its end was narrow. It was dark because he had not gotten around to replacing the fluorescent lights in the ceiling. But it seemed much more murky than usual. Perhaps that was just a reflection—if darkness could reflect—of his state of mind. He went into the study, so-called, a small room with a rolltop desk, two chairs, a lamp, and bookshelves. Concealed under papers in a locked drawer in the desk was a pile of his own poems. Not even Rey, especially Rey, knew about them. No one even knew that he had written poetry for forty years or that not one had been accepted. Only one had been returned with a note from an editor, and that had suggested that he had no tal-ent for poetry and that the editor found his subject matter rather morbid.

Roger's vicarious revenge on the editors was to imagine them tied up while he glued their rejection slips to their balls and then set fire to them. The female editors were also tied up, but he had emptied a can of fire ants through a fun-nel into their vaginas. Such delightful visions cooled the anger somewhat. But second-hand revenge came cheap, and, like all cheap things, did not last long.

The clock chimed 3:30.

"For God's sake, Roger, are you afraid of Angie? Come here and give your sister-in-law the hug she deserves."

Reluctantly, he went down the hall. If he ignored Rey's command, he would pay for it after Angie left. Embracing her, he was enveloped in a power-ful reek. It was not true that vodka could not be smelled on a person's breath. When he freed himself, he said, "It really is too early to start drinking. For me, anyway. I have work to do."

He turned away and started down the hall. Angie called, "You're retired. What's the difference if you spend time having fun? You aren't going to live for-ever, you know."

"It's the quality of the time," he muttered.

When he was in the study, he read the paper. Bedlam and cigarette smoke from the main room filtered through the keyhole. The women were certainly having a good time. A noisy one too.

The *Journal Star* had very little in it about a good time. A shooting and a stabbing in a housing project. A woman's eye knocked out in a tavern brawl. Father accused of sexually abusing his eight-year old daughter. Sexually abusing? She had undoubtedly been fucked and buggered many times. Probably since she was four. Maybe earlier. Testimony from her six sisters and five brothers that their father had also abused them. A family of seven found living in an abandoned automobile. Seventy-eight-year-old woman raped by a burglar, her face slashed. *Savings and Loan* executive blows his head off just before arrest for embezzlement. Newborn dies of dehydration in a garbage can. Child shaken to death by its mother found rotting on kitchen shelf. Evangelical minister castrates himself. Social worker has nervous breakdown. Eighty-six-year-old woman dies of malnutrition. Three feet high pile of human waste in her kitchen. Fifteen thousand dollars found in her attic.

And this was just today's news in a city of 150,000 population. How many similar cases were unreported?

He put the paper down and looked at his almost complete collection of *Weird Tales* magazines on the bookshelves. They were near the books by the old and current masters of horror stories. But the real bone-chilling, blood-freezing, and gut-churning tales were those that actually happened every day over the whole world.

Consider the fantasies about Cthulhu the Unspeakable, Dracula, ghouls, demons, zombies, werewolves, animated cars, mummies of Pharaohs raised from the dead, severed crawling hands thirsting for defenseless necks to choke, the Fucking Fungi from Yuggoth, or the splatterpunk narratives. No matter how much they scared the shit out of you or made you want to vomit, they were not real and never would be. They could not compare with the terror and misery and madness that flesh-and-blood suffered from.

The sound of breaking glass startled him. That was followed by a shriek and Rey crying, "Oh, no, not the Drambuie!"

Those two were disgusting. But why should he blame them? They could no more help themselves than could the rapists and child abusers and addicts and all the other souls in this prep school for Inferno called Earth. They were born with their personalities and drives preset, programmed, fixed.

Knowing this, why did he hate the criminals and, at times, resent and loathe Rey and her sister? It was because his reactions were as fixed as theirs. Born to condemn others for what they could not help doing.

Another shriek jarred him again. He straightened up in the chair just as the chimes of the clock came through the door. It was now five-thirty. He must have fallen asleep.

He heard Rey's voice, stronger now that she was standing in the hallway. "Roger! Come out and say goodbye to Angie!"

Feeling sluggish, his mouth dry, he walked slowly to the front entrance. Angie, blowing great clouds of vodka and Drambuie, wrapped her arms around him and gave him a French kiss. Then she whispered, "For old times' sake, Roger."

Referring to their brief affair of more than thirty years ago.

Five minutes later, after the sisters has stood on the front porch chattering away, Rey closed the door. Roger expected her to scald his nerves with reproaches because he had not joined them in their drinking bout. But she grabbed him and thrust her tongue into his mouth and worked it over his.

"I won't take no for an answer," she said through the thick mist of booze. "We're going to bed, tra-la-la!"

When she was like this, she was irresistible. His heart thumped like a pile driver trying to hammer its way through solid rock. He turned away and started down the hall, saying over his shoulder, "I don't want a scene if nothing happens."

Rey darted ahead of him and walked backward, facing him, while she brandished a plastic prescription bottle. "Angie, God bless her drunken little heart, gave me something that's guaranteed to get a rise out of you! Which is more than I've been able to do! She made Simon use it, and it worked just fine!"

While she was undressing in the bedroom, she explained. The bottle contained some nitroglycerin tablets. Simon, Angie's husband, took them when needed for his mild angina. They expanded the arteries. So, Angie, the genius, had thought, if the tablets work on the heart, why not on the pecker?

"He has trouble, too," Rey said, "though not near as much as you, just my luck."

Simon had wrapped Kleenex over six tablets placed on his penis. And, lo and behold, oh, happy day, miracle of miracles! The skin had absorbed the nitroglycerin, and the results had been tremendous.

Roger, by now half-undressed, said, "For God's sake! What's all that extra nitro going to do to his heart? Doesn't Angie care that he might fall dead?"

"Simon says it's worth it."

"Ridiculous!"

"That's his worry. Anyway, you don't have any heart trouble. Mainly because you don't have a heart. You must try it. Simon says it works fine, though he does have a hell of a headache afterwards. So does Angie. The nitro affects her, too, would you believe it? It oozes from his thing right into her. But they both say it's more than worth the headache."

This was undignified, absurd, and humiliating. But Rey would argue that the end justified the means. And, if he summoned the courage to refuse to go through with this farce, and he would not, he would have to suffer screams, tears, and insults and dodge lamps, hairbrushes, curling irons, and whatever was handy for Rey to hurl at him.

By the time that he had wrapped the six tablets around his penis and had stood for two minutes waiting for the nitro to take effect, Rey was sprawled out in the bed. She was not at all the woman to heat up his groin. And he, he thought with distaste, was not a man to excite any woman except an old one who sure as hell was not going to excite him.

Roger thought, I'll try to act out this role even though I'm sick at my stomach and I'm worried that the nitro may give me a heart attack or, at the least, damage my heart. Who cares? Better to be dead than to live like this. Better off dead than to be caged within his own craven self.

"Give it to me! Ram that hard thing hard! Plunge, plunge as deep as you can! All the way to the muddy bottom of the sea! Fuck my brains out! Go, go, go! Split me apart!"

God Almighty! He wanted to do it. He wanted to prove himself and make her happy. In doing that he would make himself happy. Except that he would loathe himself for having given in to her. He wanted to do it, and he did not want to do it. He did not want to be forced; he wanted to do it for his own pleasure. Do it willingly and because of his own will.

No use. That thing had half-swelled, surprising him that it had succeeded in doing that. But it was not hard enough to penetrate.

Rey said, "Jesus Christ! You got it up that far! Put on some more nitro."

"No," he said. "I won't. I'm not going to kill myself just to satisfy you."

"Yes! You will! I'll die if you don't! What's two more? They won't hurt you! Look at me! I'm dying! I can't stand it if you can't do it! Come on, Roger! You can do it! Fuck my brains out."

"I always do what you want me to do," he said.

He was shaking. He felt hot all over. His face must be as red as blood because it was swelling with blood. A gyroscope inside him had started spinning. It hummed as it started up, then the humming became a scream. The whirling thing was starting to tear itself loose from its fastenings to the base of whatever secured it. It was shaking everything up that had been accumulating, piling up, sifting around in him, disorganized, and chaotic like a data file that had been glitched.

Now!

He knew that something had happened within him, something that he had thought could not happen. It had come now, and, if he did nothing about it, it would die. No. He could do nothing about it. It had seized him and was forcing him to do as it willed. He had no control over it, just as he had never been able to have control over anything. It was not a case of free will. Once more, he was acting out what his inborn persona told him to do.

"Fuck my brains out!" she cried. "You can do it, Roger, you can do it! Look at it! It's a miracle!"

Her voice reached him through the screaming in his mind. He looked down. There it was. A miracle indeed.

"But not for you!" he heard his own voice, as remote as Rey's. "You want your brains fucked out! You'll get it!"

"Roger! Where are you going?"

Her cry came faintly as he ran down the hall and to the door of the workroom where he kept the tools used for outdoor work. The cry sounded like the far-off squawk of some strange sea bird.

A minute later, he burst into the bedroom, the long-handled axe in his hands. Burst was the right word. He had burst loose from his cell—it was predestined, preset, ordained—and now he was going to do what he had wanted to do in his imagination but knew that he could never realize the fantasy.

There were two of him now. The Roger who was possessed and was ecstatic with what he meant to do, and the tiny Roger somewhere down there in him who was horrified. But who, at the same time, was delighted with the horror he was about to commit.

Rey screamed, then was silent as the axe knocked aside her hands and chunked into her forehead.

It was not easy to move her around so that she was at right angles to him, her head partly hanging over the edge of the bed. It required much more work to chop a more or less square hole in the top of her skull. He had to run down again to the workroom and bring back a screwdriver and a knife. Noting while he did so that his penis was as straight and stiff as when he had married Rey. Then he cut away the thick scalp and attached hair around and over the broken bone, dropped the bits on the carpet, and pried loose the area he had chopped out.

That left him panting. His heart slammed against his chest like a boxer hitting a punching bag. But he did not stop to catch his breath.

The thin but hard skin over the brain had to be cut away. The dura mater, he believed it was called.

Then he did what Rey had wanted him to do.

The jelly-like matter gave way easily and began oozing out of the opening.

Sobbing, he finished.

The clock chimed six P.M.

Immediately after, the doorbell rang.

Oh, God! he thought. The police already!

The gyroscope was no longer screaming inside him. Its whirling now gave off a loud hum.

He put on a dressing robe and wiped off the head of the axe and the bloodied part of the handle. Holding the axe, he went to the front door. He wished that he had had installed that peephole that Rey had been wanted for years. Too late now.

Whatever happened could not be helped by him or by anyone. Whatever the act to follow, it would be played out in accordance with a script no one could rewrite.

He put the axe beside the door and opened the door just enough to see who was on the porch.

Angie was standing there. Seeing him, she smiled and said, "I'm awfully sorry, Roger. But would you believe it, I forgot my purse!"

"I'll believe anything," he said. He swung the door open enough so that she could barely come in without having to turn to one side.

"We're not dressed, but what the hell?"

She grinned as she saw his dressing gown. "I hope I didn't interrupt anything."

"No. We're done. The nitro worked fine."

He reached behind the door and brought out the axe.

"As a matter of fact, it's still working."

The Good of the Land

First published in *RG Magazine,* Volume 10, Number 6, October/November 2002.

In September 1955, US President Eisenhower suffered a heart attack. At the time, Phil had been reading *The Golden Bough* by James George Frazer, which inspired him to write this short story. Under the circumstances, Frederik Pohl, then an editor at *Galaxy* magazine, felt that the story was in poor taste. Phil put it away.

For those that haven't come across it, *The Golden Bough* is a study in comparative folklore, magic and religion that shows parallels between the rites, beliefs, superstitions and taboos of early cultures and those of Christianity.

T he doctor had gone, taking his instruments of detection and bottles of power with him.

The President's wife readjusted the pillow behind his back so he could sit more comfortably in the wheelchair.

"Don't worry," she said. "The people love you."

"Loved," he said.

His once deep and resolute voice quavered. He raised a thinly fleshed hand to brush to one side the flap of hair which fell over his forehead. It was a gesture which had characterised him and at the same time endeared him to the people as being down to earth. Now, the salt and pepper hair was white, and the eyes which had once glared in denunciation of enemies or shone with such charm towards friends lacked either light. The eyes were sunken in the shadows of bony ridges and blue-black craters.

"Loved," he repeated, almost sobbing.

"The people still love you," said the President's secretary. But his eyes behind their thick lenses shifted away from the President's.

"How can they love me?" whispered the President. "I am sick, dying…"

"Please don't say that," said his wife. "Please, you're sick, yes. Dying, not at all. The doctor…"

"The doctor," said the President. "Didn't you see the doctor's face as he left? He was smiling, not because he could tell me I was going to get well, but because he had good news for the people waiting out in the street, standing by the fence, looking towards the White House, waiting for him to appear, to go into the death dance. The people will see him and they will be happy."

"No, no," said his wife. "That's not it at all. He smiled because he could tell the people that you were going to get well."

"Then why didn't he tell me so?"

"He did. He said that things would be much better in a very short time."

Suddenly, the President's wife gasped, and she paled. The President smiled grimly.

"There you are. He could have meant one of two things. And you know and I know what he meant. No. The people will not groan and weep because I am so loved. Love me? When I'm so sick? And the land is cursed? When millions are jobless and hungry? When storms roar across the land, burying whole cities and towns in snow and floods, leveling houses and trees, making millions homeless, destroying entire crops? When this mutated polio rides like the Fourth Horseman across the face of the country? When our enemies are threatening war and we must eat humble pie because they have superior weapons? When gloom and fear lie like a heavy blanket, stifling the breath of the people? No, they don't love me. I am sick and taking too long a time to die. If only I would die, now, so my successor, a young and healthy man..."

He stopped because he felt his wife's nails digging into his shoulder. He looked up at her face, contorted with grief, and said: "They're coming now? So soon?"

"Don't be afraid," said his secretary. "It is for the good of the land."

"I am not afraid," said the President. He straightened up, and his voice took on some of the resonance it had so long ago lost. "This is right and just and it is the law. The health of the nation is the health of its leader, and..."

The doors of his bedroom swung open. In strode the Chief Justice, the Speaker of the House, the head of the FBI and many important men of the Capitol and the reporters and the TV men, pushing their equipment in on soundless rubber-tired wheels. Those who had been wearing hats had taken them off, and all looked respectfully, but determinedly, at him. Some were weeping.

The group split into two. The doctor came forth, dressed in his ritual white surgical gown, reflector on his head and stethoscope dangling from his ears, the little black bag in his hands. Quickly, knowing what he would find, he made the ceremonial diagnosis.

After the doctor had disappeared into the crowd, the Congressional chaplain stepped forward and prayed.

Then the group parted once more. This time, the Vice-President walked towards his chief. The Vice-President was a tall, well-built man of 45, with hair red and bright as the morning sun and with a face sharp and fierce as a hawk's. He stopped in front of the President and lifted his hands so that all could see what he held in them.

The President looked at what he held. Then he smiled into the glare of the lights and the round eyes of the cameras and the tear-filled eyes of the men watching him. He smiled to show them that, come what might, he had not after all lost his courage or belief in the will of the people.

The eyes of the Vice-President were brimming; nevertheless he intoned loudly and firmly: "As it was in the old days, so it is now. In the old days, when the king was sick, the land was sick, too, and the people were afflicted with many plagues and troubles. Then, a young and healthy prince was chosen to do what he must to make the land well again."

The Vice-President paused. He raised the long thin cord with its three ritually correct strands of red, white and blue.

"For the good of the land!"

O'Brien and Obrenov

First published in *Adventure,* Volume 114, Number 5, March 1946.
Also published in *Farmerage,* Volume 1, Number 1, June 1978.
Also published in *Philcon 89 Convention Program Book,* 1989.

This is the first time Phil's first story has appeared in a collection.
"O'Brien and Obrenov" had first been submitted to the *Saturday Evening Post,* and the editor said he would buy it if the drunk scene was cut. *The Post* was a very prestigious publication and paid well. Despite being tempted, Phil refused. The story then went to *Argosy.* Its editor liked it very much but said that it was too long for *Argosy.* However, he did send it on to Ken White, the editor of *Adventure.* And he purchased it.

Phil: "This is my first story to sell, it was written in 1945. My next story, a tale about the historical Little Jack Horner, a real person, was bounced as being too crammed with action. So was my next story." (Editor's note: Neither was published.)

✥✦✧✦✥

Colonel O'Brien, of the Umpteenth Infantry Regiment, was about to step into a tub. There was a reason for this—the colonel stank. But the goatish odor was about to be washed away and replaced by the colonel's normal stench, one of soap and cologne. Remembering it was his first bath in eight weeks, he shivered with ecstasy and stuck a testing toe in the hot water.

The tub had once belonged to Herr Gruenz, ex-mayor of the town of Mautz. Herr Gruenz must have been fond of his enormous tub, modeled after Goering's famous one. It was while floating in warm water and black market soap suds that the mayor had decided to slash open his wrist-veins and die as pleasant a death as was possible under the circumstances. His decision was hastened by the news that the Americans from the west and the Russians from the east would soon meet in his town. He had reasons to believe it would be better to take a chance on his reception in the next world than to wait for a certain one in this.

In fact, the mayor's oyster-like lips had no sooner blubbered out his last breath than Colonel O'Brien skidded his jeep to a halt before the house, jumped out, kicked open the door, and strode in. The colonel was looking not so much for the mayor as he was for his famous bath-tub. He found both. It was an indication of his stubbornness that, having sworn to bathe in Herr Gruenz's tub, he wasn't balked by the mess that greeted him.

He ordered the ex-mayor to be buried in Potter's Field and the tub cleaned. The scouring of the tub was done by two of Herr Gruenz's cronies. They protested. The MP guarding them pulled out his pistol and remarked it was getting rusty from disuse. They got the idea, and began cleaning vigorously.

Glowing with happiness at the thought of the coming bath, O'Brien then drove to the town square where he met Colonel Obrenov of the Russian forces that were occupying the eastern half of Mautz. They talked under the shadow of the famed "Spirit of German Wrath" statue. It was a bronze figure of Goethe, dating from the last century, that had been set up by the burgomasters of Mautz to commemorate the fact he'd once lived here—perhaps a week or two. With the Nazis' rise, Goethe's stock had gone down. They couldn't stand that great artist's internationalism and broad-mindedness. An order was issued to tear down the statue, but the penny-pinching citizens of Mautz had what they thought was a brilliant idea. The bronze plate on which was inscribed the dates of Goethe's brief stay at Mautz had been ripped off and a new plaque titled "Spirit of German Wrath" had been installed at the pedestal's base.

More important, the iron pen in Goethe's right hand was removed to make place for a gigantic sword. The result was disconcerting. The cumbersome sword, besides being almost as long as the statue itself, that is, eight feet, was held in an unnatural position. Its edge was hard against the great man's face. Anybody but the fat-brained citizens of Mautz and Germany could have seen that the "Spirit" was engaged in a struggle, not to ward off the Reich's enemies, but to keep from cutting off its own nose.

The deep-graven lines of his forehead and mouth, once intended to portray the agonies of his soul while writing *Faust*, were now supposed to portray a bloodlust in battle. Nobody but an Aryan's Aryan would have thought so, or been able to overlook the fact that the former Goethe's eyes, instead of staring ahead at his foes, were cross-eyed, looking at the hand that once had held a pen.

The reconverted statue was grotesque enough to cause comment even from two men as ignorant of art as the Colonels O'Brien and Obrenov. What fixed the statue in O'Brien's mind, however, was the discussion he'd had with the Russian about removing it.

Shortly before the two armies had met in Mautz, the mayor, under pressure from the Nazi bigwigs, had ordered the statue pulled down as a contribution to the latest scrap drive. Halfway through its uprooting, the laborers, alarmed at the closeness of the Allies, had abandoned their work. The "Spirit of German Wrath" was left leaning forward to the south at a 110-degree angle.

The colonels agreed it was a public menace. O'Brien suggested his men pull it down, but Obrenov demurred; he wanted his soldiers to haul it away. The "Spirit" was a symbol; he liked knocking down Germans, whether they were actual or symbolic.

Finally it was agreed that both sides would pull it down at some future time.

After the colonels had drawn a chalk line down the exact middle of the town square, and set up guards on each side of the line, and made arrangements for a get-together that night, and decided the Americans would bring Scotch and the Russians vodka, O'Brien had gone back to his headquarters. He found his bath ready.

Now the colonel sat naked on the edge of the tub, a short, thin man of forty-two with close-cut, wiry, carroty hair, a snub nose and a long upper lip. He was preparing to slide into the warm water and finish the bath Herr Gruenz hadn't been able to live through.

O'Brien was thinking what a queer fish Colonel Obrenov was. A stickler—a stiff-backed, long-faced stickler. First, there'd been his insistence on having the honor of demolishing the statue. Second, he had demanded that one of his engineers survey the exact half of Mautz. He wanted no complications, no mistakes. And he'd invited O'Brien to check the line with an American engineer. Courteously, O'Brien had said he would trust Obrenov. The Russian had urged he check.

Annoyed, O'Brien had delegated the task to Major Razzuti of the Engineers. Razzuti had gone through the farce with a straight face, announced the line was correct, and congratulated Major Krassovsky, the Russian engineer, on his achievement. Krassovsky, who understood little English, had smiled and shaken Razzuti's hand.

Then the Yanks and the Russians had saluted each other and gone back to their respective headquarters with everything happily settled. O'Brien was now poised on the tub's marble brink for a descent into paradise.

———⟫◆⟪———

At that moment a knock sounded at the bathroom door. The colonel, as was the way of soldiers, cursed at the interruption.

"It's me, Lieutenant Tarpitch." Tarpitch sounded miserable.

"Anything you can't handle, Tarpitch?" O'Brien snapped.

"Yes sir. The colonel'd better speak to Sergeant Krautzenfelser. He's the one that wants the colonel. It's urgent, He says we got Schutzmiller."

There was a pause. Tarpitch coughed. "He also says we have not got Schutzmiller."

The colonel forgot about his bath. "What d'you mean—have and haven't?" he growled.

"I don't know, sir. Better speak to the sergeant."

The door swung open. Sergeant Krautzenfelser stuck his dark Choctaw face in.

"Close the door. What do I have to be to get any privacy—a four-star general?"

"Guess so, sir," grinned the sergeant. "Better hurry, sir. Urgent. Can't handle it. International complications."

"Well, what is it?"

"Can't say. See for the colonel's self. On the spot. Schutzmiller."

O'Brien coughed with exasperation, not for the first time during his three years' experience with the Indian. Mule-headed as he knew himself to be, he had met in Krautzenfelser an inflexible stubbornness that far surpassed his own. Krautzenfelser had inherited the German name from a Prussian grandfather who'd settled in Oklahoma shortly after the Civil War, but he was three-fourths Choctaw, and he showed it clearly.

He was a college graduate and had been, before volunteering for the Army, a professor of art at Kansoka University. In fact, he was now thriftily combining his wartime experiences with his profession by writing in his leisure hours, which were few, a monograph "On the Effects of the Fumes of Explosives on the Artistic Creativeness in the Period 1450-1920 A.D." The sergeant condescended at times to explain his thesis to the colonel. It irked O'Brien that he didn't know what Krautzenfelser was talking about.

Despite the Indian's brilliance, he had never been recommended by O'Brien for officer's training. "The first time he got mule-headed and did things his own way, instead of the Army's, he'd have his bars yanked off, or, worse, get shot. He'll be better off under my wing," the colonel had commented to his brother officers.

Still, he was a good man, intelligent enough not to burst in on the colonel unless the situation was too tough for anybody else to handle. He'd better haul hind-end—and fast. O'Brien gave up trying to dig a clear statement out of the sergeant. After one fond look at the tub he dressed quickly.

Schutzmiller! When you thought of atrocities, you thought of Schutzmiller. He was the SS colonel-general wanted badly by every one of the Allies. His name wasn't far below Hitler's on the War Criminal List.

As far as the Umpteenth Infantry Regiment was concerned, he was at the top of the list. They had been looking for him since the Battle of the Bulge, where, before his cold black eyes, over a hundred freshly-captured Americans had been lined up and machine-gunned. Half of them had been O'Brien's men.

When the sergeant spoke of Schutzmiller, he invoked the one name that had power to tear O'Brien away from his long-anticipated bath. As the colonel buckled on his pistol, he thought of this man to whom slaughter, rape, and torture were all in a day's work. Yet Schutzmiller raised love-birds and canaries, had once shot a man for kicking a dog, and was reputed to be a kind and loving husband and father.

Probably, thought the colonel, the dog had been Schutzmiller's personal property. The man he'd shot had been scheduled to be killed, and the dog was an excuse. Still, that didn't argue away the love-birds or the kids who thought their old man was the best in the world. Queer people, these Germans.

The colonel's jeep sped over to the town square. Krautzenfelser, who was driving, said, "See what I mean, sir?"

O'Brien saw. In the middle of the square was a knot of soldiers. They were pulling on something that was poised above the chalk-line dividing the square. That something was SS Colonel-General Schutzmiller.

When he was closer, O'Brien saw that two of his sergeants had a tight grip on the German's right hand and leg. Holding fast with an equally tight clutch on his left hand and leg were two Russian non-coms. The four were engaged in a tug-of-war with Schutzmiller's body as a rope.

His head was thrown back. His huge nose was pointed straight up; the bushy black eyebrows, supposedly the thickest in Europe, were writhing in agony. His mouth was as wide open as the beak of a worm-swallowing baby bird. Out of it streamed a gabble of curses and high-pitched commands to be let loose.

The sergeant said, "That's what I meant, sir. Those two and I were searching the houses. Our side of the square. We scared out this kraut. There."

He pointed to a hotel which dominated the south side of the square. "He bolted. Into the square. We knew it was Schutzmiller. We tried to take him alive.

"Those Russians. They spotted him. The kraut ran down the chalk-line. He tripped. We all piled on top of him. And the Russians wouldn't let go."

Colonel O'Brien threw his helmet off onto the cobbles. It bounced, landed on its rim, and rolled away. The colonel's orderly ran after it, not for the first time in his career as the colonel's orderly. The junior officers froze; the colonel was ready to blow his top.

Only Krautzenfelser ignored the colonel's anger. He grinned. "Well, sir. International complications. And on the first day here."

"Quiet, Sergeant! When I want your opinion, I'll ask for it." O'Brien's face was as red as his hair. What a thing to happen! On the surface of it, a comic-opera situation, something that could only happen on the stage.

But the complications! If he ordered his men to turn Schutzmiller over to the Russians, he would lose face both with his own men and with the Russians. Worse, there would be questions from GHQ, maybe from Washington. The brass hats would want to know why in thunder, why in the blankety-blank this and that, he allowed himself to get into such a predicament. And, secondly, once on it, why he hadn't immediately pulled himself out of it.

Worse and worse, Senator Applebroom, who was making a tour of Europe, would fly into Mautz tomorrow. There'd be senatorial fulminations, denunciations, philippics, cries for action, yelps to uphold the honor of the American public. The congressman would swing every ounce of his political weight in an effort to grab all the publicity he could. A spasm of disgust shook O'Brien. The fat Applebroom didn't like military men, and he would delight in spattering his muck on O'Brien; he would make him look like a fool and a heel.

The Colonel thought fast, but not fast enough. There was a screech of brakes as Colonel Obrenov's jeep shot into the square and came to a halt a few feet from Schutzmiller. Obrenov shouted at his chauffeur.

Tarpitch, standing at O'Brien's shoulder, translated. "He's cussing out his driver, a certain Sergeant Kublitch, for not running over Schutzmiller, purely by accident, of course, and solving the dilemma. He says Kublitch would have got a medal out of it. He says a Tartar never did have any brains. Kublitch is saying nothing."

"I don't need an interpreter to tell me when a man says nothing," snapped O'Brien. He looked at Obrenov's face, so startlingly like his own with its bright red hair, snub nose, and long upper lip. It was, as usual, grave.

O'Brien decided to waste no time. He stepped up to the line and said, with Tarpitch translating into Russian, "I say, Colonel, shall we settle this thing at once before our respective headquarters hear about it? It'll save our countries a great deal of embarrassment, not to mention ourselves."

Obrenov, instead of listening to Tarpitch, spoke to his own interpreter, who, in turn, spoke English, but addressed himself to Tarpitch, not O'Brien.

"The colonel would like to settle first which interpreter we're going to use. The colonel says that at our last meeting the American lieutenant translated. The colonel says that this time it is consonant with Russian dignity and might, not to mention fairness, that the Russian lieutenant, myself, interpret. The colonel insists."

O'Brien was for a second taken aback at the irrelevancy of the request. Then he saw that Obrenov was fighting for time. His brain, like O'Brien's, was spinning as rapidly as a cyclone and, like that greedy storm, seizing on everything he possibly could.

O'Brien said, "Tell the colonel the colonel may use the Russian interpreter, yourself, all the time. I don't care."

Tarpitch translated O'Brien's English into Russian, the Russian lieutenant listened gravely, then told Colonel Obrenov. He shrugged his shoulders, waved his hands, and borrowed a cigarette from one of his officers. While lighting it, his keen hazel eyes flickered a curse at Schutzmiller.

The German had ceased his ravings to listen to them, and he suddenly cried in English, "I surrender, I surrender, but to the Americans, not the Russians. Take me. This is no way to treat a colonel-general."

The Russian interpreter, Lieutenant Aramajian, quickly spoke to Obrenov. The colonel's body stiffened. His officers bridled and shot hostile glances across the border.

O'Brien said to Tarpitch, "Tell Schutzmiller he'll have to surrender to the Russians at the same time. According to treaty, we're bound to make no separate peaces."

Tarpitch spoke in German. The Russians, who understood it, unbent. Obrenov smiled, and said, Aramajian translating, "Now that that is understood, let us arrive swiftly at a solution. Apparently Schutzmiller is equally divided between the Americans and us. Apparently. But it may be he is a quarter of an inch more or less to one side. I suggest that we survey him, and whichever side has the most, gets him. That seems to be the only fair solution to an awkward situation, and that way, neither Moscow nor Washington will have a kick coming."

Aramajian smiled and dropped his role of interpreter for a moment. "A kick coming. Is not that a correct colloquialism?"

Tarpitch assured him it was.

O'Brien was astonished at Obrenov's proposal, simple enough to come from an imbecile, yet savoring of genius. He recovered quickly and agreed.

Razzuti and Krassovsky surveyed the prisoner. They turned long faces on their commanding officers. Razzuti said, "Major Krassovsky and I agree that the line splits him into two equal parts. Neither side has the advantage."

O'Brien suppressed a groan and suggested to Aramajian, "Tell the colonel that in America we often flip coins to decide issues."

Aramajian replied for Obrenov. "The colonel thanks the colonel for his suggestion and his cooperation, but the colonel doesn't think it would be consonant with the dignity and might of the Russian nation to settle issues in so flippant a manner."

Aramajian said, "Flippant, is that not good? It is a pun, is it not?"

Tarpitch congratulated him on his achievement.

Obrenov, who must have been aware by Aramajian's manner that he was ad libbing, pulled him up sharply. The lieutenant lost his grin.

Schutzmiller screamed, "This is no way to treat a German officer. It is not honorable."

Obrenov looked at Schutzmiller. The sight of the cruel hawk's face must have given him an idea. He produced a paper, scanned it, then spoke.

Aramajian said, "The colonel says the colonel has here a paper on which are enumerated in detail the crimes for which Schutzmiller is wanted by the Russian government. The colonel suggests the Russian and American list be compared. Whichever list is highest wins."

Schutzmiller screamed, "Let me up! Am I to have no chance to defend myself? Is this honorable? In front of these enlisted men, too. Is this honorable?"

O'Brien snorted, "Honorable? Where'd you get that word?" To Aramajian he said, "Tell the colonel, O.K." To himself he muttered, "Anything will do."

Lieutenant MacAngus, a giant with a red mustache and an even redder face, a lawyer in civilian life, compared his list with the one held by Captain Schmidt, the Russian representative. They stood at Schutzmiller's head, and the German threw his head back to stare up at them.

Fear now replaced arrogance on his face as the two read out his crimes.

"My colleague, Captain Schmidt and I," reported MacAngus, "find that whereas we, that is, the Americans, British, and French, I say we, that is Captain Schmidt and I, find that whereas we, that is, the Allies, and not Captain Schmidt and—"

"We know," said O'Brien. "Come on, Mac, the facts."

"We find the allies have 1,002 known executions of prisoners-of-war, 5,012 known starved prisoners-of-war, 300 known civilians tortured to death, 1,003 civilian hostages executed, all at Schutzmiller's orders. And 10 known women raped by Schutzmiller personally. The total on the Allied side is 7,327.

"On the other, the Russian, hand, we find they have 2,003 known executions of prisoners-of-war, 3,002 known starved prisoners-of-war, 1,102 known civilians tortured to death, 1,210 civilian hostages executed, and 11 known women raped by Schutzmiller personally. The Russian total is 7,328. They beat us by one.

"At first glance that would give the German to the Russians. But one of the raped women's names, Anna Pavlovna Krylov, appears twice. Either there are two Anna Pavlovnas or, more likely, she was raped twice. My colleague admits the truth cannot be ascertained immediately.

"Therefore, we have agreed that, for the time being, and until the affair of Anna Pavlovna is cleared up, the lists are to be considered equal."

O'Brien and Obrenov shrugged their shoulders and looked at each other. From the first they'd sized each other up and come to the conclusion it would do no good to pull any rough stuff. Both were stubborn, and eager to advance the interests of their countries, but they were equally anxious to thread their way out of the labyrinth into which the capture of Schutzmiller had thrown them. Not only was it a problem which might easily lead to strained, if not snapped, relations, it was a problem which might cost O'Brien his hide and Obrenov his head.

"Tell the colonel," said O'Brien, "that we seem to be stymied, but I have an idea. The colonel has refused a coin-flipping contest, and I think the colonel is correct—it leaves too much to chance and is undignified. But if the colonel will step to one side, I think I have a contest of another kind to interest him, one which should appeal to the sporting blood I know runs in Russian veins."

Obrenov hesitated and glanced at his fellow officers, doubtless wondering if a tête-à-tête with an American would be reported to his discredit back in Moscow.

O'Brien said, "Tell the colonel he may report what I say later on. There are those here, however, who shouldn't hear." He glanced meaningfully at the enlisted men.

Obrenov blushed at the reference to his fear of being turned in, but stepped off to one side. Aramajian followed. O'Brien whispered hurriedly, Aramajian whispered to Obrenov, Obrenov whispered back to Aramajian, who whispered to O'Brien. At the conclusion of the low-toned conference, Obrenov grinned and shook O'Brien's hand. Then they saluted each other and left.

Before going back to HQ, O'Brien put Sergeant Krautzenfelser in charge of the detail holding Schutzmiller's right arm and leg.

The sergeant protested, "Sir, couldn't we drive stakes between the cobblestones? Handcuff him to them? Hard on the men—squatting here, holding him."

"No. We're not allowed to manacle our prisoners."

"That's what those Russians are doing."

He pointed at Sergeant Kublitch, who was approaching with a pick, a hammer, stakes, and chains.

"I can't help that," replied the colonel testily. "Russia didn't sign the convention."

"But—"

"But, hell! Sergeant, you're presuming on our long and close acquaintanceship."

"Yes, sir." The Choctaw saluted.

"Oh, yes, Sergeant, it looks like rain. You'd better draw slickers for your squad."

O'Brien went back to the ex-mayor's house to resume his bath. While he undressed, the water was re-warmed. Just as he sat on the edge of the tub and stuck in his toe with a shudder of anticipatory ecstasy, he was disturbed by a knock on the bathroom door.

"Tarpitch, sir. It's about Schutzmiller's food."

"Give him what we eat. Do you think I'm a dietician?"

"No, sir!" Tarpitch was emphatic. "Schutzmiller won't eat Russian food, says it might be poisoned. And when we started to feed him, the Russians objected on the ground that he's half their prisoner, and they're entitled to give him half his food. They won't let us feed him unless we go halves, and the German won't touch their stuff."

O'Brien looked for his helmet to throw. Fortunately for Tarpitch, it hung on the outside of the door.

"Let him starve," he growled. "Tell him any time he wants food, he can have it, provided he'll eat half-Russian food."

"Yes, sir. Only he's making trouble by telling the Russians of alleged American atrocities and telling us of things the Russians have done to our boys."

"Now I know he won't eat! Tell him he either shuts up or starves. Personally, I hope he does."

"Yes, sir."

O'Brien listened to Tarpitch's departing footsteps. He sighed and slid into the water. He closed his eyes and let everything go. Ah, heavenly! The hot water was dissolving the sweat, dirt, and stink of eight weeks' accumulation. And unwinding a little the bowstring of tension that had drawn tighter and tighter since D-Day.

It must have been ten minutes later, though it seemed a second, that he was roused from his half-stupor by a knock on the door. He opened his eyes.

"Tarpitch, sir. It's raining."

"Good God, man. Do you think I can order it to stop?"

"No, sir. But Schutzmiller's hollering for shelter. He says we got to give it to him or else betray the Geneva Convention."

"Doesn't he know we can't move him?"

"Yes, sir. I've taken steps. We've put up a pup tent over him."

"Doesn't that satisfy him?"

"No, sir. The tent doesn't go any farther than the border, sir. And the Russ refuse to put one up on their side—they say they've got no orders about sheltering half-prisoners, just whole ones. The rain's coming in from the east side. Our tent is doing no good. He's drenched."

O'Brien grunted, "Too bad. My heart bleeds. Well, we've done what we could. You go and get ready for the party, Tarpitch, and don't bother me until it's time to go."

The colonel closed his eyes again. Was the world always to clamor at his bathroom door? A fist banging was his answer.

The colonel reached for a pistol that wasn't there. "You're lucky, Krautzenfelser," he cried, "if I don't have you shot at sunrise. What is it? And what're you doing away from your post?"

He knew it was the sergeant. Only one man had temerity enough to beat the colonel's door as if it were a gong.

"Sorry, sir," said the sergeant with no trace of sorrow, "Lieutenant Tarpitch sent me. It's the statue. It's going."

"Going?" repeated O'Brien testily. "Going? Where's it going? Since when does bronze walk?"

"Don't get me wrong, sir. It's falling, not running. When those heinies pulled it over, they loosened the bands that clamp it on its pedestal."

"Let it fall."

"It might hit Schutzmiller, sir."

O'Brien gave a chuckle which rumbled in the huge bathtub and echoed to the sergeant's ear like a ghoul slavering at the bottom of a meaty grave.

"Hagh! Hagh! Sergeant, when you have any tales of beauty and promise like that to tell, I'll forgive your bursting in on the sanctity of my bath. It's wonderful. Now, go. And don't come back unless Schutzmiller's dead."

"Yes, sir."

"Stop! Sergeant, does Schutzmiller know the 'Spirit' is coming down?"

"He's facing south, sir. But he heard it shift. By throwing his head back, he can see it. He knows it might fall on him."

"Agh, hagh! Sergeant, weren't some of your buddies lined up and shot by Schutzmiller's men?"

"Yes, sir."

"Sergeant, if you were Satan, and Schutzmiller had died and come under your jurisdiction, what torture would you think most appropriate?"

"Sir, I'd stretch him out on the ground, put over him a slowly toppling figure that might, or might not, dash out his brains. Then I'd let him sweat it out."

"Sergeant, you are a clever fiend."

"Yes, sir."

"Dismissed."

That evening, at 1900 hours, a group of American officers, guests of Colonel Obrenov, selected for a certain capability, got into their jeeps and drove off. O'Brien, in the lead car, stopped at the Russian border in the square. Krautzenfelser's big form strode through the heavy rain up to the colonel. He saluted.

Though he could see well enough for himself, O'Brien asked, "How's Schutzmiller taking it?"

"Sir, that kraut is tough. Here he is, drenched. Freezing. Maybe pneumonia coming on. And all he does is complain. Says it's an insult. To be guarded by a Jew."

The colonel blinked. "What Jew?"

"Me, sir. He thinks I'm a Jew. May I tell him, sir, I'm three-fourths Choctaw? Then maybe he'll shut up."

"Let him think you're a Jew. What do you care?" The colonel was enjoying the sergeant's discomfiture. "Isn't he scared of the 'Spirit' any more?"

Krautzenfelser looked downcast. "No, sir. It's falling slower than my arches, sir. I think it's gone as far as it's going to."

He jerked his thumb to indicate the "Spirit". The Germans had torn up the cobblestones and dug a pit on the south side down to the bottom of the slender marble pedestal. The cement ball which had anchored its end had been chipped away and thrown out. Ropes, attached to its neck and waist, had been used to jerk over the statue and the base, which wasn't much thicker than the figure, at the same time. The intention had been to drag it out in one piece.

But the work had been stopped halfway, and now the "Spirit" leaned forward, poised for a nose dive, deterred only by the bronze clamps which passed through its feet and curved tightly over the top of the pedestal. Half-broken through, the clamps still looked strong enough to hold for a few more decades. Schutzmiller seemed safe, and the hopes the colonel had pinned on its falling were blown away.

"Do you think he'll catch pneumonia, Sergeant?"

"He's too mean to die that way."

"If he does, give him prompt medical attention. No matter what our feelings, we've got to be humane."

"Yes, sir. But we can only treat half of him. Besides, sir, is it humane to leave him in the rain? With that statue hanging over him?"

"We can't move him unless the Russians consent. That's what tonight's conference is about. Besides, if we do let him die, though it wouldn't be humane, it would be humanitarian."

"I see what the colonel means."

Krautzenfelser suddenly leaned over and stared hard into O'Brien's eyes. He winked, and winked again.

"Sir, could I have the colonel's permission to measure the 'Spirit's' dimensions? Necessary information for my monograph 'On the Effects of the Fumes of Explosives'."

"Measure it? Monograph? Sergeant, how often do I have to tell you not to bother me with that stuff? This is war, man. Forget you were once a professor of art—and stay down off that statue."

Krautzenfelser shot O'Brien an indecipherable look. It made him feel the sergeant had been trying to tell him something without actually saying it, and that he had missed the train.

Then the sergeant grunted and twitched his shoulders as if he were shrugging off a disappointment. His face hardened into a mold the colonel had seen before; the times the sergeant had decided to bull along in his own way and to hell with the Army's!

It dwindled subtly into his usual happy grin. He smiled at the tarpaulin-concealed cases of Scotch on the jeep's back floor.

"Yes, sir. Happy conference, sir."

The colonel veiled his eyes and ordered Tarpitch to drive on.

The sergeant's buddy slouched up through the rain.

"The Old Man sure likes to gab with you, Krautzy, even if he does have to put you in your place now and then."

"Yeah," the sergeant grunted. He pointed at Schutzmiller. "What'll we do with that Thing? Do you realize the implications? He could be the cause of a serious quarrel. Between the Allies."

"Too bad we can't plug him and claim it was an accident."

"Thought of it. 'Twouldn't work. Courtmartial. Guess I'll go talk to that Kublitch. Looks like he's got Indian blood in him. Might not be a bad guy."

He walked to the chalk-line and spoke in German. The Tartar answered in the same language.

Did Kublitch know the brass hats were beating out their brains over Schutzmiller?...He did? Good...And did he know they hadn't come to a solution?...And that only a couple of good enlisted men, such as Kublitch and himself—used to simple ways—could cut the Gordian knot?...He did?...Well, here's what he thought ought to be done. He explained...

Schutzmiller, who had been listening, screamed a protest.

———⇒⋟⋞⇐———

Colonel Obrenov, welcoming his guests, seemed no longer the stiff and stubborn character he'd been on the chalk-border. His face, so much like O'Brien's except for the dignified, mournful lines into which it was usually cast, was now smiling. If it hadn't been for his uniform, he would have been indistinguishable from the American.

He shook hands with the Yanks and said, through Aramajian, "Welcome, friends, I have good news for you. In the cellar of this house, which you no doubt know once belonged to the late Baron Pfugelkluckensheimer, we have discovered an enormous amount of wine bottles, all, luckily, filled to the full with wine of rare vintage. I suggest we down those first, and then, if we're still thirsty, we can start in on the whiskey. It is a go, no?"

"It's a go, yes!" enthused the Americans.

Two high stools, much like those on which the umpires of a tennis match sit, were brought in and placed one on each side of the banquet table. Captain Pichegru, representing the Yanks, mounted one; Captain Ivantchenko, of the Russians, the other.

"Now, gentlemen," said Obrenov, "the ostensible purpose of this meeting is to break the Schutzmiller case. It is best, for all concerned, to find a way out before dawn. At that time a Senator Applebroom will land to make a tour of inspection on the American side. Undoubtedly, if he finds the German spread-eagled on the border, he will raise hell.

"To make it worse, a political commissar from Moscow is flying in tomorrow to investigate. I need not remind the Russian officers here that Moscow does not like unpleasant situations and often passes the buck with lead. In other words, painful words, the firing squad might remove us because we haven't removed Schutzmiller. We had hoped the 'Spirit' would fall and obliterate the kraut. But it isn't going to accommodate us.

"Colonel O'Brien and I have talked ways and means, but ended up stuck in the mud. So, we decided to hold a contest, a drinking race. Whichever country ends up at dawn with the most men on their feet gets the German. The rules are: Colonel O'Brien and I will start the toasting. If we fall silent, whoever has a good toast on his mind, let him stand up and get it off his chest. Should any officer feel full to the gills and turn down a toast, he is to be disqualified by the umpires. Is it clear as mud, gentlemen?"

The gentlemen agreed it was. Obrenov raised his glass.

"One moment, please," interrupted O'Brien. "Are the poor judges to go thirsty?"

A storm of protest broke out. Bottles were offered to the unreluctant Pichegru and Ivantchenko.

"A toast. To America!" cried Obrenov.

"A toast. To Russia!" proposed O'Brien.

"To the President...To Stalin...To Eisenhower...To Zhukov... To O'Brien...To Obrenov...To victory...To success...To the men of

Rooshia…To the men of the U.S…. To the women of Rooshia…To the women of America…To the women of the world…"

Toast followed toast so rapidly there was little chance to grab a bite between. No sooner had one torn off a strip of the delicious chicken or roast beef, mouth watering in anticipation, than one was forced to gulp a glass of wine. The system had an advantage; in a short time one felt lightning flashing through one's veins, not to mention the arteries, one felt glorious and dizzy, one ceased to remember that one had a belly crying for food. One lifted one's glass, emptied it down one's palpitating throat, and hurled it at the fireplace. One drank and drank.

"To the melting-pot of the nations, America," said O'Brien.

"This melting-pot, what means it?" asked Obrenov, through Aramajian.

"The U.S. is famed as a melting-pot, a mixture of different bloods, the sum total of which adds up to strength. For instance," O'Brien pointed down his side of the table at which sat his officers placed according to seniority, "there's Lieutenant Colonel Obisto, Major Razzuti, Captain Schmidt, and Lieutenants Tarpitch, Smith and MacAngus—all of widely different nationalities and creeds."

"Ah, yes," nodded Obrenov, "this Tarpitch is of Russian descent, no?"

"No, he is of English."

"But Tarpitch is a Russian name."

"Only seems to be. It is not derived from Tarpavitch, son of Tarpa. It is made up of tar, which means pitch, and pitch, which means tar."

"Ah, I see," said Obrenov with a puzzled expression. "This Smith, is of English descent, too?"

"No, he is of Hungarian. His parents, on coming to America, changed their name from Kovac, which means Smith, to Smith."

"Ah, I see. But your Captain Schmidt, like our Captain Schmidt—odd coincidence—is of German descent, no?"

"No, he is of Russian. Though if you were to go far enough back, you would find a kraut hanging from his ancestral tree."

Obrenov's expression became desperate. "But surely this MacAngus, he is Greek, yes? I say Greek because his name ends with a *u* and an *s*."

"No, MacAngus is an old and widespread Scotch name."

"Ah, but surely this Obisto is of Spanish descent, yes?"

"No, he is a Jew whose ancestors came from Portugal."

Obrenov sucked in his breath and blurted, "I will make one more guess. This Razzuti, he is of Italian descent, yes?"

"Yes."

"Ah, ha!" Obrenov was pleased. "Well, it is puzzling. One must get mixed up in your country. But so is Russia perplexing—we, too, are a big nation, a melting-pot. Lieutenant Colonel Efimitch is of Tartar origin, Major Krassovsky is a Jew, Captain Schmidt, of German ancestry, Lieutenants Riezun, Aramajian, and Stadquist of Ukrainian, Armenian and Swedish-Finnish grandparents, respectively."

He rose to his feet. "Gentlemen, to our ancestors, who—"

The rest of his speech was lost to the Americans, for at that moment Aramajian slid off his seat and disappeared under the table. He went early. But as the night thickened with darkness, so did tongues thicken and stumble, and other men, too, followed in Aramajian's footsteps.

These men who had all suffered and bled for their countries were now getting patriotically drunk. They gave their all. Some grew white as paper and dashed outside for air; the umpires disqualified them. Some laid down and quietly gave up the ghost of their reputations as topers; others were more noisy, but they, too, went the way of supersoaked flesh.

The umpires checked them off. Came the time when the umpires had deserted their posts. Pichegru had stumbled outside mumbling a sentence the words of which were too blurred for understanding, but the urgency of which impressed the officers. He didn't come back. Ivantchenko put too much trust in his equilibrium and crashed off his high stool on to the table. He made no effort to get up, at least none that could be seen; merely blinked at the chandelier's brightness a while, then, smiling happily, dozed off.

Obrenov and Riezun were left for the Russians; O'Brien, Tarpitch, and MacAngus for the Yanks. Even while O'Brien was counting his men he had to strike his interpreter off the list.

The survivors were degraded to speaking German, a language they had difficulty in understanding when sober.

"To the best man!" toasted O'Brien. They drank; Riezun accomplished the impossible feat of staggering while sitting down. O'Brien compared Riezun's condition with MacAngus's and smiled. He had faith in the big fellow's alcoholic impregnability. Mac came from a long line of whiskey-saturated ancestors; his corpuscles were Scotch in more ways than one.

Two more toasts, and Riezun foundered. Obrenov was left, as he muttered in thick German, left alone to bear on his shoulders the dignity, might, and honor of the Russian nation.

"To the bearer-er-gulp!—to the man who carries the honor of Rooshia," MacAngus managed to propose.

They hurled their glasses at the fireplace. During the course of the evening the empty goblets, which had at first unerringly crashed against the iron grates, had taken a tendency to wander far and wide. Many landed on the mantel or sailed through the open window by the fireplace.

O'Brien noticed that his and Obrenov's shattered close enough to count as near-hits, but Mac's wobbled off to one side, struck a portrait of the late Baron Pflugelkluckensheimer, and bounced back on the thick carpet, upright and unbroken.

"Come on, Mac, get up," croaked the colonel. "Don't leave me alone."

"Gawd, I can't!" groaned MacAngus. "So long, Colonel, I'm going. Dammit, I can outdrink anybody in whiskey—but not in that gawdforsaken wine. Who woulda thought it, an Irishman and a Rooshian, old buzzards at that, drinking me, a MacAngus, under the table? Da—sz, sz…"

The two stared at each other, reluctant to propose another toast. Slowly, O'Brien stood up.

"T' you and me. Two old buzzards, And t' whoever gets Schutzmiller."

They drank and stood, swaying, refusing to sit down for fear they might not be able to get up again. O'Brien suddenly felt sick, not from the wine, but from the realization he was a fool. Here was Schutzmiller breeding division between two great countries, a problem which needed unaddled wits and swift, firm hands, and here were two old drunken fools childishly engaged in a contest that was supposed to prove which was the better man. Yet, at the moment he'd proposed the toasting spree, he'd thought it was a good idea. His fantastic Irish imagination sometimes got the better of him. This was one of those times. Tears oozed from his eyes.

Obrenov was crying, too. "Instead of standing uselessly here, like a couple of stuffed owls, let's go down to the square and take things in our own hands. To hell with the consequences."

Arms around each other's shoulders they lurched outside. The heavy rain had been followed by a light drizzle; the north wind was blowing strong, strong enough to cool their superheated brains and sting some wits into them.

They passed through the dark streets. Now and then Obrenov barked the counterword to a challenging sentry. Presently they came to the edge of the square and paused to reconnoiter.

Searchlights, centering on the sprawled-out figure of Schutzmiller, were slowly weakening. Dawn was leadening the black clouds of the horizon.

O'Brien peered with bloodshot eyes. "What's Krautzenfelser doing on that statue?" he asked.

"I don't know. What's Kublitch up to?"

The Choctaw was hanging in the air with one arm wrapped around the "Spirit's" neck. With his free hand he held a tape-measure which he apparently was using to estimate the sword's length. His position was precarious; his legs dangled four or five feet above the cobblestones.

"Is that fool trying to break his neck?" muttered Obrenov.

"Why, I told him to stay off that thing. But no, the mule-headed ass has to go ahead and mix his artistic nonsense with business. Who cares what size that monstrosity is? I'll slap him in the jug. Where's an MP?"

He stepped out into the square. "You, Krautzenfelser! Get down! Consider yourself under arrest! You, Krautzy!"

He stopped. He ground his teeth in a convulsion of fear. The statue had suddenly shifted downward. The clamps around its feet, partially broken, were giving way under the sergeant's two hundred and thirty pounds.

"Hey, Krautzy! You'll break your fool neck!"

His voice wasn't heard. Schutzmiller, who'd been looking backwards with such wide eyes that even O'Brien could see the whites, began screaming, *"Nein! Nein! Nein!"*

The clamps squealed again. The statue lurched downwards an inch. Krautzenfelser lost his hold and fell backwards. He landed close to the German's head, and one of his buddies, seeing he was too hurt to get up, jumped forward and pulled him to one side.

He was in no danger—the "Spirit" had halted. It was suspended, sword in hand, giving birth in the bystanders' minds to the inevitable phrase—"like an avenging angel."

Schutzmiller must have thought so. He kept yelling his useless *"Neins"* until he saw the statue wasn't going to fall. His screams choked into a sob of relief.

O'Brien stood for a moment. Then he shrugged his shoulders. "There goes our last hope," he said to Obrenov. "Krautzy was trying to pull the 'Spirit' over on Schutzmiller under the guise of measuring it. It was a noble effort. I'll have to sentence him to a few days in jail for disobeying orders, but he'll eat caviar and drink champagne behind the bars. Too bad. Oh, well."

He walked up to the sergeant. He said, "Sprained your ankle disobeying orders, eh? Serves you right, Krautzenfelser."

The sergeant said, "I wouldn't mind the ankle if I'd succeeded in getting the measurements, sir. Anything in the cause of art, sir."

His eyes widened. He pointed up. O'Brien followed his finger and saw that the sword, slanting down in the statue's fist, was shaking.

The quivering ceased. The sword slipped out of the "Spirit's" loose grasp.

Schutzmiller gave a final scream. The tip of the sword halved his brains, and the left side of his head flopped neatly over the Russian border, while the right side of his head flopped neatly over the American border.

It was Obrenov who, in his simple Slavic way, pointed out what was obvious, but what he wanted to make sure all would see. "If it had been a pen in the 'Spirit's' hand, instead of a sword, it would have missed Schutzmiller."

Doc Savage

Writing Doc's Biography

Writing Doc's Biography

First published in *The Man Behind Doc Savage,* 1974.

Phil has had a life long passion for Doc Savage. In addition to writing a fictional biography *(Doc Savage: His Apocalyptic Life)*, Phil has the distinction of writing one of the few authorized Doc Savage novels, *Escape from Loki.*

Phil: "In my biography of the Man of Bronze, *Doc Savage: His Apocalyptic Life,* first published in 1973, I wrote of the day on which the very first Savage novel swam up in all its glory from the dozens of pulp magazines on racks in Schmidt's drugstore and hit me in the eye. That was on a Friday, February 15th, 1933.

That day radiated with a golden light.

ZAP!

But I prefer not to think of the golden light piercing through my skull as a beam from a ray gun. I prefer to think of it as the shower of gold which was the form taken by Zeus when he made the maiden princess of Argos, Danaë, pregnant. From this photonic or auriferous union was born Perseus, hero, rescuer of princesses, and slayer of dragons.

Doc Savage, though thoroughly modern and metropolitan, was a reincarnation of Perseus. Not to mention many other heroes of ancient and modern times."

Just as I sat down to start writing this article, the galley sheets of *Doc Savage: His Apocalyptic Life* arrived. That was the morning of April 19. Not until today, April 23, was I able to return to writing the galleys. Hopefully, all my corrections will be in the book. Such was not the case for *Tarzan Alive,* my biography of Lord Greystoke. For some reason, Doubleday did not incorporate my corrections, and I've never been able to get an explanation out of them why this omission occurred.

Things may be different this time, however. My title for the Tarzan biography was not used nor was I consulted about the dust jacket illustration. I didn't like either. But Doubleday is using my title for the Savage book and is following my suggestion that the "real," the "original," Doc be portrayed on the dust jacket. I had been afraid that the illustration would be based on those that Bama has been doing for the Bantam reprints.

As we all know, however striking Bama's covers are, his Doc Savage has little relation to that described by Dent and illustrated by Baumhofer or succeeding artists for the *Street and Smith* magazine originals. As a friend of mine, Jack Cordes, said, Bama portrays Doc as he would have looked like if Nazi Germany had won the war. (A cross between the Jolly Green Giant, and a Nazi Stormtrooper! . . RW[1].) In my opinion, Bama's Doc looks like a middle-aged, habitual criminal, or a 55-year old ex-Mr. Universe down on his luck.

When Ace Books published my Doc Savage pastiche, *The Mad Goblin*, I asked Don Wollheim, the editor, why Gray Morrow had not portrayed Doc, as described by Dent and myself. That is, as a man about thirty, handsome, and with straight bronze-red hair. Why was the cover illustration based on Bama's crewcut, widow-peaked, golden-haired monster?

Wollheim replied that the Bama was the only one most readers knew. The Bama-type cover would sell the Ace pastiche much better than a faithful picture of Doc. I replied that I was a purist and preferred the Baumhofer version. Besides, my Doc Caliban is not a Doc Savage imitation, but a pastiche, a continuation of the original. But when I write my next Doc Caliban, tentatively titled *Some Unspeakable Dweller*[2], Doc may be shown as he really was. Wollheim will be buying it, and he is now vice-president and editor of DAW Books, and so he can pick his own covers.

Bantam, by the way, sent a note to Ace after *The Mad Goblin* appeared. Bantam objected, not to the book, but to the cover because it was too Bamaish. Wollheim's comment on this was that Bantam did not have a copyright on a torn shirt.

Thus, I was pleased when Doubleday asked me to send them some copies of the *Street and Smith* Savage magazines, one of which would be used on the dust jacket. I made my choice from the Baumhofers. Baumhofer is, in my opinion, the best illustrator of Doc, though Emery Clarke is very good. Doubleday did have on hand the cover for *Quest of Qui* (July 1935), which is a head and shoulders portrait of Doc. I like this, but it has no action, and action is the essence of Doc. After consideration, I narrowed my choice to the covers for *Fear*

---

[1] Robert Weinberg, editor and publisher of *The Man Behind Doc Savage*.

[2] Although this book was never completed, Phil did write a chapter for the book and this was printed in the *World Fantasy Convention Program*, 1983 under the title *The Monster on Hold*. The piece appears later in this collection.

Cay (Sept. 1934) and *The Spook Legion* (April 1935). The former shows Patricia Savage, Doc, and (presumably) Renny caught in a net. Doc is tearing apart the thick ropes of the net, and we see lovely Pat full-face. *The Spook Legion* cover was my top choice because it shows Doc in a classical pose, riding a running board. Monk is at the wheel of the roadster; New York City buildings form a silhouette in the background. Diane Cleaver and the Doubleday artists agreed with me that this was the best. This made me happy, though I hated to omit Pat. As I say in the book, I fell in love with her when I was fifteen. (This explains why the chapter on Pat is twice as long as the chapters on the five assistant arch-enemies of evil. On the other hand, Monk Mayfair was my favorite character, perhaps because being so inhibited myself, I loved my opposite, the noisy, brawling, skirt-chasing, ungrammatical, vulgar, and violent Monk.)

The acceptance of my title and my choice of dust jacket illustration pleased me. I suspect, however, this came about because I was the only one involved in the book who knew anything at all about Doc. The Doubleday staff thought they knew about Tarzan, but Doc was an unknown quantity.

The full title, as it appears on the title page is:

DOC SAVAGE
His Apocalyptic Life

As the Archangel of Technopolis and Exotica
As the Golden-eyed Hero of 181 Supersagas
As the Bronze Knight of the Running Board
Including His Final Battle Against the Forces
of Hell Itself

The table of contents is as follows:

1. The Fourfold Vision
2. Lester Dent, the Revelator from Missouri
3. Son of Storm and Child of Destiny
4. The Bronze Hero of Technopolis and Exotica
5. The Skyscraper
6. The Eighty-Sixth Floor
7. The Hidalgo Trading Company and Its Craft
8. The Crime College
9. The Fortress of Solitude
10. Monk, the Ape in Wolf's Clothing

I give the table of contents so the reader may get some idea of the structure of the book. When I did *Tarzan Alive,* I modeled its structure somewhat after William S. Baring Gould's biography *Sherlock Holmes of Baker Street.* This demanded placing all of the stories in the sequence in which they happened, not in the publishing sequence. They were then summarized and the blanks left by Burroughs were filled in by me. I also tried to reconcile the discrepancies among the various stories and generated various theories or used those of various ERB scholars to explain certain difficult points.

But in writing Doc's life, I wasn't about to summarize all 181 of the supersagas. To do this would not only make the book about three times as long as it is, but it would appall and bore the general reader, who is no Savage specialist. So I structured Doc's biography on Baring Gould's *Nero Wolfe Of West Thirty-Fifth Street.* Even this summarized the forty-four Wolfe books published up to 1968. I knew that my summaries would be longer than Baring Gould's and would probably amount to about 181 typewritten pages if I kept restraints on myself.

But there are enough references to various stories throughout the book to give the nonspecialist the feel and color of the supersagas.

The first chapter, "The Fourfold Vision," is a comparison of four writers who have something in common: apocalypticism. These are Dr. E.E. Smith (author of the Skylark and Gray Lensman series), Henry Miller (author of *Tropic Of Capricorn),* William Burroughs (author of *Nova Express, The Soft Machine,* et al), and Lester Dent.

The second chapter, "Lester Dent, the Revelator from Missouri" is a biographical sketch of Dent. To get details of his life and to ensure accuracy, I twice visited Mrs. Dent in her home in La Plate, Missouri. She was very charming and helpful, and it was a thrill to see Dent's home, his studio, the Baumhofer originals, and the collection of manuscripts. He was a remarkable man.

Chapter 3, "Son of Storm and Child of Destiny," recounts Doc's immediate ancestry, his birth in a ship off Andros Island, his early training, his World War I experiences, and his deeds just before he moved into the Empire State Building.

(Yes, I know the actual 86th floor of the ESB is the observation floor and never was occupied by an individual, and I know that Dent never named Doc's skyscraper. But I explain this, satisfactorily, I hope, in the book.)

The fourth chapter, "The Bronze Hero of Technopolis and Exotica," sketches Doc and his activities and his character development during his adventures in the big cities and the Jungles and deserts.

Since "the skyscraper" and the 86th floor are as much characters as the living beings in the stories, chapters 5 and 6 are devoted to them. Chapter 5, "The Skyscraper," contains a line drawing of the ESB and the Hidalgo Trading Company. Floors prominent in the stories are called out, and the various secret express elevators, the subbasement garage, the giant under-ground pneumatic tube, the secret tunnel to the Broadway subway, and several other features are shown.

The sixth chapter contains a diagram of the 86th floor. This is to be referred to during the reading of the text of this chapter. This includes many, though by no means all, of the devices, furniture, lab equipment, secret wall panels, doors and various items (including the portrait of Doc's father and the mounted lion, etc.). It wasn't easy making the floor layout or placing many of the items. I had to reconcile the many discrepancies perpetrated by four writers trying to beat a deadline. But, in writing a biography of a "fictional" character, half the fun is in explaining away the discrepancies. It also generates much that wasn't in the originals, and it enables the biographer to fill in the blanks.

I put fictional in quotes because this book, like *Tarzan Alive, Sherlock Holmes of Baker Street, Nero Wolfe of Thirty-Fifth Street, The Life and Times of Horatio Hornblower, Sir Percy Blakenby: Fact or Fiction,* and *Yankee Lawyer: the Autobiography of Ephraim Tutt,* is based on the premise that Doc Savage was a living person. Of course, his exploits were considerably exaggerated and distorted, some of them being entirely fictional. Doc himself complained of the exaggerations in the memo he sent to Dent in *No Light to Die By* (May/June 1947).

The contents of the remaining chapters are self-evident by their titles, Addendum 1, subtitled "Another Excursion into Creative Mythography," is an extension of Addendum 2 of my *Tarzan Alive.* Doc's ancestry and relatives are described in this and end-paper genealogical charts are provided as aids for the reader of Addendum 1. This chart, unlike that in *Tarzan Alive,* spells out the names of the major characters and gives the initials of the minor people. The names initialed on the chart are spelled out in the text.

Perhaps some, reading this article, will be surprised to learn that Doc is a descendant of Solomon Kane, Captain Peter Blood, Raphael Hythloday (of More's *Utopia),* and Manuel of Poictesme (of James Branch Caball's *Figures Of Earth, Jurgen,* et al). And he/she may also be surprised to discover that Doc is related to Sam Spade, Richard Hannay, James Bond, Richard Bensen, Fu Manchu, Carl Peterson, Professor Moriarty, Captain Nemo, and Doctor Caber (of Dunsany's *The Fourth Book Of Jorkens).*

On the other hand, if the reader is acquainted with *Tarzan Alive,* he may not be surprised.

Addendum 2 is a chronology of the supersagas, an attempt to put the stories in the sequence in which they must have happened, which was not always by any means, the order in which they were published. I had a hell of a time with this. Some of the problems are described in the foreword to the chronology. Very few of the stories specify the dates or the day and the year of the particular event. A few specify both, and some of these presented additional problems because of this. Its axiomatic that an adventure has to occur before it can be written and published, and in some cases, the dates were too close to the publication date to be regarded as accurate.

Fear Cay enabled me to determine the year in which it took place because of the age of Dan Thunden. *The Squeaking Goblin* refers to a book published exactly one hundred years ago. Both of these adventures can thus be set in 1934, but both had to occur early in the year to have been written up and gone through the publishing process before appearing on the stands. *The Squeaking Goblin* (August 1934) appeared on the stands in July. Though Dent probably only took three or four days to write it, the editing and printing of it even at the speed with which pulp magazines put out issues, must have taken a minimum of a month and a half. I would have preferred to place the story in early spring, but *Goblin* definitely takes place during summer, during vacation time. I settled for the first seven days of June, when the rich could be vacationing early.

Many of the stories contain definite references to the season or seasonal data, and these enabled me to determine if the supersaga occurred in fall, winter, spring or summer.

Doc was often said to have just returned from one of his six month stints at the Fortress of Solitude. This stretched the chronology to impossible lengths, and I determined that only in 1933 could he have spent that much time at the Strange Blue Dome. He could have spent five months there in the first part of 1934.

Another problem was presented by the absence of the five aides on projects which required a very long time. These would also expand the chronology; the times of their absences had to be accounted for. I finally concluded that Doc's assistants couldn't have seen these projects through from beginning to end. Thus, when Renny is building a road or airport in China and Johnny is digging in Inca ruins, or Monk is rebuilding a chemical plant in post-war Germany, they were on these projects only as consultants. They flew in, looked around, straightened out the biggest problems, and flew back in time to join Doc in his latest exploit.

In the early years of the magazine, the stories often ended with a preview of the next adventure. These were supposed to follow immediately the story at hand. But this often just could not be. So I presumed that the editors wrote these previews to intrigue the reader. The facts were ignored. It was evident that Dent and his associates did not write the stories in the sequence in which they had actually happened. Not always, anyway.

It was necessary to classify some of the stories as all fiction. *World's Fair Goblin* was obviously written before the World's Fair at New York opened. And I classified *Land of Long Juju* (January 1937) as fiction, and abominable fiction at that, just as a story, it's ridiculous. But the description of and references to East African customs and peoples are absurd. Danberg knew nothing of this area, made up the whole thing, and committed an abomination. Why Bantam did not save this as the last to be printed in the series, why Bantam picked this one when there were so many better stories to publish, I don't know. But, I suspect that the editor of the Bantam stories does not read them before be chooses which one will be issued. More on this later.

The first three supersagas, *The Man of Bronze, The Land of Terror,* and *Quest of the Spider,* occurred in the published sequence. Doc was at the fortress, but only for two weeks, between *Land* and *Quest.* The fourth story in my chronology, *The Red Skull* (August 1933), was the sixth published, *The Polar Treasure* (June 1933) the fourth published, must have been the eighteenth in chronological sequence.

The Purple Dragon (Sept. 1940), one of my favorites, is definitely set in August, 1940 by the text. The "1940" has to be a typo of Dent's or the printer's, and so I put Dragon in the August 1-3 slot of 1939. This is a reasonable move, since the stories have many typos, and errors, including the names of characters who are not in the particular scene.

I suspect that some Savageologists will take issue with me on some of my chronology, or will want to know how I arrived at a certain decision. Don't write me about these, because I don't have time to answer such questions.

Write an article for *PULP* or some Savagezine and if I happen to have enough time, I might answer the article. Some of the slots into which I put certain stories were the result of many factors which had to be weighed against each other. Where discrepancies which existed were found, I favored that which had the most evidence on its side.

Addendum 3 is a list of the stories in published sequence. Date of publication, author, and Bantam reprint (if any) are given. The list of Bantams stop with the middle February, 1973 issue, *The Seven Agate Devils.*

I wrote the Bantam publishers to get their publication figures and also to find out what method was used to pick those stories published. In fact, I wrote three letters, none of which were answered. I mentioned in each that I wanted the information for the biography, which would be published in August by Doubleday. It was to Bantam's advantage to reply, since my book will give the Doc Savage stories some publicity.

It's my opinion that the editor of the Bantam Savage books has a very contemptuous attitude towards them. I doubt that he has ever read any of them, though somebody at Bantam has to have skimmed through them to get the blurbs which are on the back of the books.

This indifference seems to extend to the mail-order department. Some years ago, I ordered a batch of Savages through the mail. The package I received was lacking *Meteor Menace* and *The Monsters.* I wrote three letters asking for the books or a refund. No reply. I gave up.

Interim note relating to "biographies." I just strolled over to the Book Emporium on my lunch hour and looked for copies of the soft-cover *Tarzan Alive,* which appeared on most stands at least three weeks ago. (But, to my horror, Popular Library had omitted the end-paper charts, referred to in addendum 2 and essential to help the reader.) I could not understand why no copies had been received by the Emporium. Then, while strolling around, I passed the Biography section. And a certain cover caught my eyes. Yes, there it was, *Tarzan Alive,* nestled in with books on Hitler, Jennie Churchill, Hornblower, Einstein, Lincoln, Louis XIV, Dorothy Parker, et al.

I wonder what the fate of the Savage biography will be in this particular bookstore.

In conclusion, though the biography was hard work, it was also fun. I could have written three novels in the time I took to do it and could have made three times as much money. But, I'm glad I did it. I loved the Doc Savage stories when I was a kid. I still get a charge out of reading them, even if they're not great literature. And, I was finally able to fulfill a boyhood ambition, the writing of a book about my hero, Doctor Clark Savage, Jr.

Savage Shadow

Savage Shadow

First published in *Weird Heroes,* Volume 8, 1977.

The foreword published here initially appeared as an article in its own right in *Weird Heroes.* Here, it has been included as the intro to the main story, "Savage Shadow."
In "Savage Shadow," Phil engages in his trademark recursive fiction; What if the Doc Savage house name, Kenneth Robeson, was real and his own adventures were the source (suitably fictionalized) of the Doc Savage canon?

Foreword

Maxwell Grant is famous as the author whose by-line appeared on all but one of the *Shadow* novels. Kenneth Robeson is equally well known for his *Doc Savage* and the *Avenger* series.

The work at hand, Number One of *The Grant-Robeson Papers,* is the first new fiction by Grant since a softcover *Shadow* novel in 1967. "Savage Shadow," however, was written in 1935, four years after the appearance of the first *Shadow* novel. Kent Allard, sometimes known as Lamont Cranston, always known as the Shadow, is not Grant's hero in this tale. Ken Robeson is the protagonist.

In the story by Ken Robeson, to appear in the future, Maxwell Grant is the main character.

Why should these two writers use each other as their heroes? And why should these works, written in 1936, have been unprinted until 1977, forty-one years later?

These stories and others by Grant and Robeson have been in a small safe in a residence on Riverside Drive in Manhattan. Your editor was recently made aware of this when the estate of the late J***** D***, a wealthy manufacturer of safes, was inherited by a cousin, L***** C******. (The names are not revealed because of the wishes of the latter.)

It seems that Mr. D*** was an admirer of the works of Grant and Robeson. One reason for this was that Mr. D*** had been, in the early part of the twentieth century, a fighter against crime whose exploits pioneered the path for Doc Savage and the Shadow—not to mention the Spider.

Mr. D***, a collector in various fields, offered Grant and Robeson a tempting sum to write stories which would be unique items, so unique that only he, aside from the two authors, would know of their existence until after his death. Grant and Robeson were contractually obliged not to mention these stories until after Mr. D***'s death.

Though these two prolifics were busy, they had time enough to write sixteen short stories and novelettes for the eccentric collector. Being good friends, they decided, half-jestingly, half-seriously, to make each other the heroes (sometimes, the antiheroes) of their respective tales.

After the first four stories were written, Mr. D***, who was also a science-fiction buff, asked them if they would transfer the scene of their tales to the future—say, the late 1970s. He was interested in seeing, if he lived long enough, how close their fictions would come to reality.

The two responded to the challenge, but they retained their original heroes. In the stipulated decade, they would have been old men. But the writers arranged for both their protagonists—each other—to travel in time to the '70s. Thus, they were still young vigorous men, able to survive and adapt to the strange conditions of the future. They also agreed to depict a common milieu for their heroes, the same future world.

These "future" tales may appear in the heroic fantasy books of Byron Preiss Visual Publications from time to time. It should be interesting to note how closely these approximate reality while in other respects widely missing the mark.

Mr. D*** also asked that each writer attempt to write in the style of the other. This presented a problem. As the student of the *Savage, Shadow* and *Avenger* epics knows, both experimented with different styles during their careers. Even their concept of their heroes changed somewhat over the years.

The two sometimes wrote in one or another of the other's styles and sometimes tried entirely new styles. Mr. D*** apparently did not object.

Savage Shadow

By Maxwell Grant

—1—

There were no shadows here. Yet the white-haired man insisted he saw one. His own.

Kenneth Robeson, on this cold, cloudy December day of 1932, thought the tall, scholarly looking, middle-aged man must be crazy. He felt sorry for the daughter, a tall, beautiful, bronze-haired woman of about twenty-five. They were standing by the ramparts of the observation deck of the 86th floor of the Empire State Building. Robeson didn't know why they had come here to endure the bone-chilling wind. Aside from himself, they were the only people who'd stayed long out of the warm concession and display rooms.

He was up here to get an idea for a story. For a whole series, in fact. He'd spent one of the few coins in his pocket to take the elevator to this floor. He'd hoped that looking down on New York City might inspire him. But all he'd been able to think of was the Depression which gripped everybody except criminals.

The man and woman had come along about ten minutes later. He'd eyed them, especially the woman. She didn't look like a tourist or a newcomer, the only people who ever came up here. Her clothes were what he imagined the smart set would wear. A graduate of Vassar with money of her own. The man looked like a college teacher, since he wore tweeds and his hair was as wild as an orchestra conductor's. Or an absent-minded professor's.

They'd not been interested in the view. Instead, they gesticulated violently at each other. Thinking that something he might overhear could give a spark for a story idea, he'd edged close enough to hear them.

"You must go back, father!"

"Never! I tell you, they're doing evil things to me!"

That was enough. His mental ears were pricking up and Robeson moved even closer toward them. Writers had no shame about eavesdropping.

A minute later, as he tried to make sense out of their passionate, incoherent dialog, he saw the man jump to one side. He pointed down at the floor and said, "There it is! My shadow!"

His daughter spoke soothingly, though her face showed her distress.

"Now father, there's no shadow there! It's an hallucination. Admit it, you're sick!"

He saw her suddenly stiffen, and he turned to see what she was staring at. Three men had come onto the platform. Two were shorter by four or five inches than his own six-foot-three. They were chunky and dark-faced and wore long, black overcoats and dark fedoras. The third was almost as tall as he, slim, elegantly dressed, and blond. He was quite handsome, though a scar disfigured his left cheek. It could have been made by a knife. Or a saber.

The blond man smiled coldly on seeing the two by the rampart. He said something to his companions. Followed by them, he strode toward the couple.

A few seconds later, two more men came out. They wore dark overcoats, but the caps and the white trousers suggested they were ambulance personnel or hospital attendants. One of them carried a straitjacket.

The white-haired man tried to run. His daughter called out to him to stop. The tall blond gestured to the two thuggish looking men, and they ran after the fugitive.

Things happened fast after that. The white-haired man tripped and fell. The woman screamed. The blond grabbed the father, rolled him over, and tried to remove the father's coat. The two struggled. Then the thugs seized the elderly man and held him while the coat was taken off. One of them, struck by a flailing fist in the nose, howled. He hit the white-haired man in the belly.

Robeson started forward. The woman ran up to the man who'd hit her father and began beating on him with her fists. The blond pulled a hypodermic syringe out of his coat pocket. The woman staggered back, pushed by the man she'd attacked. He was yelling names at her which no gentleman would use in a lady's presence.

Robeson cut his speech off with an uppercut to his chin. Then he fell into a blackness, only vaguely aware that he'd been hit over the head from behind.

—2—

He awoke flat on his back on the cold concrete. The woman and a cop were looking down at him. His head hurt, but not so much he couldn't get to his feet without help. The father, his three attackers, and the two men with the straitjacket were gone. They'd been replaced by the curious from the 86th floor.

"Sure, me lad," the big cop said in a thick Irish brogue. "Are ye all right?"

"I don't think so," Robeson said. "Otherwise, I'd not have gotten into this mess in the first place."

"The blond gentleman said he's preferring no charges." The cop took a pencil from his pocket and held it, ready to write in his notebook. "I'll need your name, occupation, and address. And your version of the particulars."

Robeson gave it to him. The cop's eyebrows went up when he learned that Robeson was a writer. They ascended as far as they could go on hearing his residence.

"Bleeker Street, is it?" Indicating that anyone who lived in that area was of no consequence.

"Ye should go to a hospital and get checked out, me boy."

"I'll be okay," Ken said. He looked at the woman, whose makeup was smudged with tears. "How about you? Aren't you preferring charges against the man who hit you?"

She shook her head. "No. I'm not hurt. It wouldn't do any good, anyway. Father *had* escaped from a sanitarium. I shouldn't have interfered. But they were so *brutal!*"

"They shouldn't have hit a pretty colleen like you who was just showing a natural concern for her father," the cop said. He put away his notebook. "Ye both should go inside where it's warm and maybe drink a cup of coffee."

Robeson watched him walk away. He said, "I'm sorry about your father. It's none of my business, but...is there any way I could help?"

Looking utterly miserable and hopeless, she said, "No. No one can help."

"Well, at least you could tell me what it's all about. Maybe getting it off your chest will help."

He felt the blood rush to his face. Even with the coat on, she looked more than full bosomed.

"I mean..."

She began crying again. In a minute, they were inside, sitting at a table while the waitress was getting their coffee, and she was pouring out her troubles. Despite the pain in the back of his head and the feeling that he should be working out his series ideas, Robeson listened intently. Anyway, what she was telling him could eventually become the basis of a story, even if it didn't inspire him about the project at hand. All was grist for the writer's mill.

She was Patricia Burke. Her father was Professor Winston Burke, a teacher of chemistry and biology at a small upstate New York college. Her mother had died five years ago. Patricia, "Trish" for short, had taken care of the household duties for her father but had managed at the same time to attend classes at Kanyoto College, graduating in 1928. She'd gotten a job at a high school near Kanyoto, commuting to her father's home and taking care of him.

Then the Depression had come, and she lost her job. In 1930 she had gone to Manhattan to work as a bookkeeper for a friend who was managing a chain of beauty parlors. Her father had tried to make her stay at home, and this had led to a quarrel. Though they wrote to each other now and then, she hadn't visited him for a year. He felt that her duty was to be his housekeeper. Moreover, he strongly disapproved of her living alone in the big wicked city. Some of his letters even hinted that he did not believe that she was living alone.

"He's a very moral man," Trish said. "A real churchgoer. He just can't believe that I can resist the temptations of New York City. Which doesn't say much for his trust in me.

"Anyway, about a year ago I got a very excited letter from him. Instead of preaching to me, as he usually did, he told me that he had been experimenting with a chemical compound which, when injected into people, could force them to be moral. He didn't tell me the formula, of course, nor did he explain exactly how people could be made to act like saints.

"It was then that I began to have misgivings about his sanity.

"Six weeks later I got a letter saying that he had gone to see a big industrialist in Utica. This man, Mr. Bierstoss, was also very active in his church. In fact, he owns a radio station most of the programs of which are devoted to spreading the Gospel. You know, sermons, hymn songs, collecting money for missionaries. Stuff like that.

"Another letter followed. Father was in seventh heaven. Bierstoss was going to finance his experiments. I didn't hear anything from him until a month later. Actually, I didn't hear from him directly. I got a letter from a colleague, Professor Smithton, an old friend of the family. He said that my father had been acting peculiarly lately. I should come right away.

"I got a leave of absence and packed. But before I could get going, Smithton phoned. He said my father'd had a complete breakdown, and he was now in the Restful Meadows sanitarium. That's up in the Catskills. Mr. Bierstoss was paying for the treatment.

"I tried to phone Bierstoss, but I could never get through to him. His secretary said he'd call back, but he never did. So I drove up to the sanitarium.

"Doctor von Adlerdreck met me in his office. He was very nice but firm. My father, he said, was in no condition to have visitors. In fact, he probably wouldn't even recognize me. But he had great hopes that my father would recover completely in time. The doctor said he'd keep me advised. When it was okay for me to visit my father, he'd call me."

Kenneth Robeson gave no sign of his impatience. So far, there was nothing out of the usual in her story. Her father was undoubtedly crazy. He felt sorry for her, but he could do nothing for her. Still…maybe he could use her tale as a basis for the first in his series. It would make a socko beginning.

First, however, he had to get his characters outlined, establish their motives, their main purpose. Create a great villain for his hero and his sidekicks to combat.

The big shot at *Street & Smith* was waiting for him to come up with an idea that would excite him. If he could bring it in within the next three days, and set the big shot on fire with it, he'd be on easy street for a long while—if the series caught on with the public. A novel a month would bring five hundred dollars a month, big money. He could rap out a novel in a week and have plenty of time left to write other stuff, another novel, three or four short stories. Maybe he could bring in fifteen hundred dollars a month. Then, if the series continued to be popular, *S & S* would raise his rates, and in a year or so he'd be making three thousand a month.

Thirty-six thousand smackolas a year. Wow!

But if he couldn't get an advance within the next three days, he'd be kicked out of his sleazy, cockroach-ridden apartment. And he might have to sell apples on a corner like so many poor devils. Might, God forbid, be in such desperate straits he'd have to hock his typewriter.

He felt himself turn pale at the prospect.

No, he'd starve first.

He came back to his surroundings with a start. Trish Burke was looking at him peculiarly.

"Aren't you listening?"

"Sure. You were saying…?"

"Restful Meadows was supposed to be a high-class sanitarium. I was thankful that Mr. Bierstoss was footing the bills. If it'd been up to me to pay, poor father would have had to go into the county hospital, a real snake pit. But I didn't like the two men that lounged around the doctor's office, doing nothing except making rude remarks and drinking hooch from a flask.

"The doctor was a well-educated man; he'd attended the University of Berlin and a medical school in Vienna. I couldn't understand why those two thugs were around. I questioned him when we were alone for a moment, and he said they were his chief aides. He used them when a patient got violent.

"That seemed rather fishy to me. But I was in a state of grief and shock. So I left. What could I do?

"However, I had found out the names of the two attendants. When I got back, I phoned my cousin, Clyde Burke. He's a reporter for the *New York Classic.*"

"A real rag, a notorious example of yellow journalism," Kenneth said.

"Yes, I know. I don't know why Clyde works for it, since he is a very good reporter. Maybe because it doesn't demand much of his time, and he moonlights for other papers. It doesn't matter. Anyway, I asked him about the doctor and the two men with him.

"Clyde said the sanitarium had a good reputation. Von Adlerdreck was said to be a fine doctor, but at one time the FBI had investigated him about his rumored connections with the New York German-American Bunds. But they'd not been able to establish any link.

"However, Clyde was very surprised when I told him the names of the doctor's two associates. He said they were notorious criminals. Both Antonio 'Chips' Bufalo and Roberto 'Eggs' Ovarizi had been members of a Brooklyn mob. But they'd left town suddenly. Not because of the police. They were pro-Mussolini, and the Italian-American gangsters are violently anti-Mussolini. Il Duce had broken the power of Italian and Sicilian organized crime—what do they call it there, the Black Hand? The Italian gangsters here hate him.

"Clyde said that Bufalo and Ovarizi had taken off to keep from getting killed. They'd dropped out of sight. He was surprised to find that they'd holed up in the sanitarium. He said he'd like to find out why they were there, but his main source of information was in France at that time. Maybe he could find out something for me on his own."

Robeson stirred impatiently. "What about this shadow your father sees?"

"I'm getting to that. Late last night I got a phone call in my apartment. It was father. He'd escaped, and he…"

She stopped. Kenneth turned to see what she was staring at. Then he rose to his feet quickly, pushing the chair to one side.

Von Adlerdreck and his two swarthy companions had returned. The latter had their hands in their coats; it was evident that they held pistols.

—3—

Von Adlerdreck, his thin handsome features pressed into a smile, approached them. He stopped, bowed slightly, spoke in English with only a slight German accent.

"Your pardon, Miss Burke. Professor Burke has been taken in an ambulance to the sanitarium. But it occurred to me that I owed you an apology for the roughness of my men. I've reprimanded them, and they have promised never to act in such a hasty and rude manner again."

He looked at Robeson. "My sincerest apologies to you, too, young man. You were only being gallant when you interfered. I hope that your injuries are minimal."

Miss Burke said, "I don't think that it was necessary to be so rough. But then father was putting up a fight. I accept your apology."

Robeson said, "Which one of you hit me?"

Von Adlerdreck said, "My overzealous assistant, Mr. Bufalo."

He turned and pointed at the slightly taller of the two. Robeson strode past him. Bufalo growled, "Whatcha up to, punk?"

"This." And Robeson delivered a hard right-cross to the battleship-prow chin. Bufalo staggered back, his hands still in his overcoat pockets, and he fell to his knees. Trish said, loudly, "Oh, no!"

Robeson turned away. His fist hurt, and the blow had increased the pain in the back of his head. But he felt satisfied.

Trish screamed. Robeson whirled. Ovarizi had pulled out of his pocket a .45 automatic, a huge, ugly weapon which looked at that moment bigger than a cannon.

Von Adlerdreck shouted, "You fool! Put that away!"

There were about a dozen people in the room. All were silently staring at the group.

Bufalo was up on his feet by now, but he looked as if he still didn't know what had happened.

Ovarizi put the gun back into the pocket. The doctor said, "I suggest you leave now, Mr...?"

"Kenneth Robeson. And I'm not leaving until I know that Miss Burke is safe."

The German's mouth turned down. But he managed to bring it back up into a facsimile of a smile. "I assure you that I only returned to extend to Miss Burke my regrets for this unfortunate incident. Also to tell her that she can accompany us back to the sanitarium if she wishes. She can stay there with no expense for several days and observe her father. I wish to assure her that he is not being mistreated."

This fellow is too oily, Robeson thought. And he sure doesn't keep good company.

Trish Burke hesitated. She looked as if she wanted some advice from Robeson. Seeing that he wasn't giving any, she said, "Thank you very much, Doctor. I'll take you up on your offer in a couple of days. It'll be a weekend then, and I won't be working. I'm afraid I'd lose my job if I took any more time off."

She smiled. "You know how tough it is to get a job now."

He bowed slightly again, and said, "As you wish," turned on his heel like a soldier, and strode off. Bufalo's eyes had become unglazed then. He started toward Robeson, snarling silently. Von Adlerdreck said something Italian to him in a low voice.

Bufalo said, "I ain't gonna forget this, you punk." But he followed the other two to the elevator doors.

Robeson was shaking with the reaction. He said, "I'll bet those thugs don't have licenses to carry those guns."

He put a hand on her arm and looked into the wide blue eyes. "Listen. Take my advice. Don't go up there alone. There's something rotten about this. It isn't just a matter of a crazy old man."

Trish Burke said, "Why'd you hit him? Not that I mind. I'd like to do the same myself. But why…"

Robeson waved his hand. "I had to get my self-respect back. Or maybe I'm just angry at a lot of things, and I took it out on him. I had a good excuse. The thing is, this is too deep for you. You'd better go to the police. Fast."

Trish Burke said, "But I can't get the police interested unless I have something solid to tell them. Will you testify that Ovarizi pulled a gun on you?"

Reluctantly, Robeson said, "Yes. But he can claim it was in self-defense."

He frowned. She was right. The only thing on which the police might take action was the question of weapon licenses. They'd regard her as just a daughter overly concerned about her father, a patient at a respectable sanitarium. He was a penniless pulp-magazine writer—an unrespectable profession—and one who could be charged with battery and assault.

Time was speeding by. Monday morning's meeting with the big shot at *S & S* was getting nearer every minute. And he still had no series concepts worth considering. Why in hell had he come up here just in time to get involved with this woman, beautiful though she was?

He wanted to leave, but he couldn't. He'd feel like a heel, a coward, if he just walked away from her.

Besides…her father's nutty talk about a chemical that could control people's moral behavior! Wasn't that the type of thing he was trying to think of? And wasn't he in the midst of a situation that would make a rattling good story?

Trish said, "I'll call Myra and tell her I'm sick. She won't like it, but I can't just abandon my father because I'm afraid to lose my job."

"Then what?" he said.

She came close enough so he could smell her perfume. It was a very light odor, faint, but it did something powerful to him. Not to mention that beautiful face and huge, imploring blue eyes.

"I have a car. We can go up to Roosville now. They won't suspect we'll be there soon. We can scout around, try to find out what's going on up there."

She had no sense of reality. Maybe she had a touch of insanity, inherited, no doubt. But at the moment he felt as if he was, just by being close to her, receiving some of her determination, her unreasonable resolve to make this a quest of some sort. She was transmitting, and he was receiving. And of course he couldn't receive unless he was on her frequency. In other words, he was as unrealistically romantic as she.

He shrugged and said, "Okay. I'll go."

She didn't squeal with pleasure, but she looked as if she'd like to.

They took the elevators down to the ground floor. Robeson felt the change in his pocket and thought of the three dollars in his wallet. His worldly wealth. If she expected him to pay for her food and the gas for the car, she was going to be shocked. Gallantry only went so far.

They walked four blocks to her car, a rusty 1928 Model A coupe with a rumble seat. On the way he told her something about himself, his boyhood in the Midwest, his sudden resolve to come to New York and write for his living. She looked a little askance at his ambition. It was evident that she had no high opinion of pulp-magazine literature. But she confessed that she'd never read any.

"I suppose it is trash," he said. "Ephemeral stuff that'll be forgotten a month after it's published. But it's a living, and it's a stepping stone to the big league. However, it isn't easy to write for the pulps. You have to have a certain talent for it. Very few can do it. I've sold about a dozen stories, just enough to keep me alive. But I have a chance to make it big now. If I do, the money I make'll give me the leisure to write good stuff. After all, Balzac wrote thrillers in his early days, but he became one of the world's greatest writers."

He was angry with himself for having tried to justify himself.

Why should he appease her snobbery?

They got into the car and shivered in the cold until the motor was warmed up and the heater was going full blast. Trish drove the car down Thirty-Fifth to Broadway, then cut north toward the George Washington Bridge. They were silent during this time, he nursing his wounds over her remarks, she probably thinking about her father.

Then, as they took the highway toward the Catskills, he spoke for the first time. "We're being followed."

—4—

He was sure of it, when, five miles further, he told her to pull over onto the shoulder of the road. The big black car slowed, then stopped about four hundred and seventy yards behind them.

"Ten to one it's von Adlerdreck and his gatmen."

She drove back onto the highway again, keeping the beat-up Model A at its top speed, sixty miles an hour. Oil fumes began to fill the interior, and she eased the pressure on the pedal. "It needs a ring and a valve job bad," she said. "But I haven't been able to afford it."

"Who can afford anything nowadays? Keep going. Don't worry. I don't think they'll try anything until after dark, if then. Maybe they just want to see where we go."

"Just what are we going to do?" she said.

"Play it by ear. You're not tone-deaf, are you? Forget about them for the time being. Now, you said you got a phone call from your father. He'd escaped."

"Yes. He wanted me to meet him. He said that von Adlerdreck would be looking for him to go to my place. So I suggested the 86th floor of the Empire State Building. I suppose because I'd been reading an article on its construction when he called. The talk was very short. He was very nervous, he said he'd give me all the details when we got together.

"When I saw him in the restaurant, he insisted that we go outside. He said he didn't want anyone to overhear us. He seemed to think the place was full of spies. And he kept talking about his shadow. Then..."

"Just what did he say about the shadow?"

"He said that it was menacing. Savage. It threatened him."

"How could a shadow threaten him?"

"By making terrible faces at him. It had a mouth, and though it couldn't speak, he could lip-read what it said. It said awful things to him. Most of them unspeakable. I mean, they were so bad he couldn't even tell me what they were. Obscene and profane things. So bad they were driving him crazy."

Robeson thought that the professor had the cart before the horse.

"When did this shadow appear?"

"I don't know. Dad was all right one day, and the next day he went crazy. He woke up and there it was, dancing in front of him, grimacing, mouthing those awful words, leaping at him but never touching him. He went to Mr. Bierstoss, who suggested he go to a sanitarium. Dad refused, but Mr. Bierstoss phoned Doctor von Adlerdreck anyway. That evening the doctor and those two yeggs showed up and took him away in a straitjacket."

"Yeggs?" Robeson said. "A yegg is a safecracker."

"Oh? Well, gorillas. What's the difference?"

"Bierstoss must've known the doctor," Kenneth said. "I'd say there's a link between the two. But it may not be sinister. Maybe von Adlerdreck was recommended by Bierstoss's doctor."

"Maybe, but I don't believe that's all. Do you?"

"No. What do you know about Bierstoss? Aside from his being an industrialist. What does his company manufacture? What's his background?"

"I don't know much except what father told me in his letter. He came over from Germany in 1920 at the age of thirty. He seems to have had some money then. He purchased a garage and a used-car business. After he'd set up a whole chain of these, he sold it and bought a partnership in a small pharmaceutical firm. He also bought a small publishing house that dealt in religious books. His rise was phenomenal. Five years later he was president of a chain of pharmaceutical stores and some more publishing houses. Even the stock market crash didn't affect his businesses too much."

"What about his politics? And his attitude toward Germany?"

"Dad didn't say anything about those."

They stopped to eat lunch and to gas up. Trish insisted on paying for the food. Robeson didn't object. The big black car had dropped out of sight. That meant nothing. If the doctor was in that car, he knew by now where they were headed. Robeson studied the road map he'd taken from the glove compartment. The doctor could have taken a country road a half a mile back and come back out on the highway two miles northwest of them.

Just before dusk, they pulled into Roosville. This was a village which, according to a sign, had fifty-nine friendly citizens. There was no hotel, but the service-station attendant directed them to Mrs. Doorn's boarding house. Trish turned off the ignition and looked steadily at him. He felt his cheeks flushing.

"I have all my small savings in my purse," she said. "I took it out so I could give it to Dad if I decided to help him hide. I have enough to pay for two rooms—if Mrs. Doorn's charges aren't outrageous—for a couple of days. But I'd like to save as much as I can. So...I propose we share a room. We'll tell Mrs. Doorn we're married.

"But I want your word you won't make a pass. I'll tell you now that I'll say no. Maybe, if I'd known you longer, if I were in love...I'm no prude but I am sensible. I don't give myself away. You understand?"

He hesitated, looked away, then said, "I'll be honest with you. I don't think I could stand it. It's been a long time, and you're so beautiful."

"Thanks. Okay. If I can manage it, I'll get us separate rooms. We'll say we're brother and sister. Which makes me Patricia Robeson. Here, take the money. It wouldn't look right if I paid."

Mrs. Doorn, a tall, fat, red-faced woman of fifty, accepted their story. She gave Trish a room on the top floor of the three-story house, built when Queen Victoria was still living. Kenneth took a small room in the basement, the cheapest available.

"I go to bed at ten," Mrs. Doorn said. "The key is under the doormat if you intend to stay out late. There isn't anything to do here at night except listen to the radio."

Robeson thought it best not to say that they had business at the Restful Meadows. His feeling that he was on an absurd quest got even stronger. What, after all, could the two of them do? And why should they be doing anything?

Though they weren't very hungry, they ate dinner at Mrs. Doorn's well-laden table. Kenneth, after his meager diet of hamburgers, hot dogs, and french fries for the last three months, decided that he had an appetite after all. A big thick steak, mashed potatoes with gravy, cranberry sauce, a salad, and a big slice of Dutch apple pie left him feeling happy but logy. It was worth the trip just to eat here. Especially since he wasn't paying for it.

Well, he was footing the bill in a sense. He was giving Trish his time, a commodity a writer couldn't afford to waste. He thought of the typewriter in his crappy apartment, sitting mute and inglorious on a table, waiting for its master's fingers to type out a pulp masterpiece.

While the landlady was cleaning off the table, most of the boarders went into the parlor to listen to the radio. Robeson went to his room for a moment to go to the toilet. He came up into the hallway expecting to meet Trish there. Instead, he found two of the diners. It was evident that they wanted to speak to him.

—5—

One was a very tall, very skinny man about forty named Bill Homer Smalljack. His long thin nose was very red. He wore very thick spectacles, one lens of which was a supernumerary. Behind it was an obviously glass eye, not even matching the hazel of the good eye.

The other was a middle-aged giant, towering, well muscled, his face as long, narrow, and gloomy as the stereotyped Puritan's. His hawk nose was as red as his companion's. His hands looked as big as quart jugs. In fact, one of them held a jug. He'd been introduced at the table as Hans van Rijnwijk.

Smalljack's profession was digging holes in the ground. Wells, graves, basements, postholes. Van Rijnwijk was a mechanic for the local garage, but he also repaired agricultural machinery, clocks, anything mechanical. Nowadays, a person had to quit specializing to survive.

Smalljack said, "Hans and me run a little business on the side. Give him a sample of the wares, big boy."

Hans, who didn't like to talk, silently removed the cork and handed the jug to Kenneth. He smelled the odor rising from the open neck. His eyes watered.

"Good stuff," Smalljack said. "The best white lightning in New York. I should know. I've tasted it all. Guaranteed, too. And cheap. Go ahead, take a snifter."

"I can't do that," Robeson said. "I don't have much money. I couldn't afford this."

"Sure you can. It's only two-fifty a quart. Even if you don't drink, you can resell it in the city. That'll bring you three times as much on Broadway."

The prospect of making a profit interested Robeson. God knew, he needed the money. But if the car was by some chance inspected by the police...oh, what the hell! So he forked over the money to Smalljack, thanked them, and took the jug, wrapped in his coat, to the car. He put it in the rumble seat. While he was doing this, the bootleggers came out of the house. Smalljack winked at him as the two got into a 1932 Packard. Business must be good if they could afford that.

He started back to the house but stopped as Trish Burke came out. After they'd gotten in the Ford, he told her what he'd just done.

"I know it was your money, but it's a good investment."

"Investment, hell," she said. "We'll invest it in our tummies, right now. I need a shot of Dutch courage."

Robeson was pleased, since he had expected her to blow up about it. But he told her to wait until they got out of town. They mustn't be seen by the local sheriff. She drove onto the gravel road that led to Restful Meadows, then stopped on the other side of a wooden covered bridge spanning a wide creek. Robeson got the jug out and offered her the first drink. Though her hands and arms were slender, she handled the heavy jug well, holding it horizontally across her upper right arm.

"Wow! That makes you see stars!"

Kenneth took his turn. The stuff burned his mouth, his tongue, his gullet, his stomach. But it wasn't rotgut. It was just powerful.

Trish took another long draught, then said, "I'm ready to tackle a tiger now."

Robeson decided he'd pass up seconds. His brain was already beginning to feel numb.

Then they froze. Headlights struck across the bridge, and they could hear a motor. The black-and-white car slowed as it went by them, and they could see a tall-hatted man, Sheriff Huisman, looking at them. But the car speeded up and disappeared around a bend.

Robeson felt his heart resume beating. "We were lucky. He's out after bigger game. Our two dispensers of tabu juice of the corn, I'll bet. You want me to drive?"

"I never feel comfortable when someone else is driving," she said. "I'm just as good as any man behind the wheel and better than most. And I can drink nine out of ten under the table." She added, "In case you were figuring on taking advantage of my drunken condition."

He chuckled. She sure was a pistol. One of those modern liberated women. Maybe he should have registered them as man and wife. No wonder her father didn't want her to go to New York. Even a permissive parent would have worried about her.

The road was dark, the sky being cloudy. The headlight beams showed patches of snow, dry weeds, tall bare trees, ruined choirs. About halfway to the sanitarium, a car passed them going in the opposite direction. It was the sheriff's, going too fast for the road.

"He might be back," Robeson said. "So we ought to park this buggy where it can't be seen."

"Give me some credit for brains."

She was no longer the seemingly helpless woman he'd met on top of the skyscraper. He doubted it was the liquor causing the change. She played roles, and when she was in Rome she did as the Romans did. Or were supposed to do. This tough capable character of hers, though, was probably her real one.

They saw the sanitarium about five minutes before they got there. Lights blazed from and around it. It was obviously set on top of a high hill. When they got to the entrance, they found a pair of iron gates set in a high stone wall. A ditch ran along the walls paralleling the road. A stone bridge crossed the ditch, on the bottom of which was half-frozen water.

Trish stopped the car but left the motor running. "Maybe we should just breeze on in and ask to see my father."

"Then we'd see what they want us to see. That'd be no more than you saw on your last visit. I think we ought to scout around. Maybe we could even get inside the building and waltz off with your father. But if we're caught, we could be charged with kidnapping. Or illegal entry. It isn't that I'm afraid. It's just that I think Falstaff had something when he said discretion is the better part of valor."

"I really have no right to ask you to stick your neck out," she said. "But you did volunteer, and you know there's something rotten about von Adlerdreck and his two mobsters. Why don't we just walk around outside, get the lay of the land, maybe do a Peeping Tom act? Then we can come back to the car for a powwow. After all, we don't necessarily have to take any action tonight."

Robeson agreed. She drove the car into a road which was more two rutted tracks than anything. This cut through a farm across the road from the sanitarium. Trees and bushes lined the wire fence along the acreage. They could conceal the Ford behind them.

Trish drove the car across the muddy field in low gear. Robeson said, "Oh, oh!" He indicated a long black Packard parked by the cover they'd picked out. There seemed to be no one in it.

"It's the bootleggers!"

"The sheriff didn't see it, so it must be invisible from the road," she said.

They left the Ford behind the Packard. They found that the wire fence had been bent open enough to allow them to crawl through.

"Evidently they use this a lot," Kenneth said. "Well, we'll have to be careful we don't run into them."

They jumped across the watery area of the ditch, scrambled up the bank with muddy shoes, went across the road and the stone bridge. As he'd expected, Robeson found that the padlock enclosing two links of the chain around the gates was open. He removed the lock, opened the gates, and the two went inside. He reached in through the steel bars and put the chain back into the large links. A passerby in the dark would think that the lock was shut.

On second thought, he removed the lock and threw it into the darkness alongside the wall. He didn't want to be trapped if the bootleggers closed the lock when they left.

The gravel road wound around the estate, climbed the hill corkscrewlike, and emerged at the front of the huge cubical building. They started down it, then halted.

"Voices! Over there!" Trish said.

—6—

Somewhere deep in a grove of leafless trees a match was struck. It went out, but the ends of two cigarettes glowed like fireflies.

He took her hand, and they walked into the trees. It was easy to take cover, though the unmelted snow under the branches made slushing sounds. When within earshot, they stopped behind a broad-trunked sycamore.

He counted seven dim figures, all standing close together. There was just enough light to see the silhouette of a jug being passed around.

From the conversation it wasn't difficult to know what was happening. Smalljack and Rijnwijk had come here to sell some of the patients their white mule. The latter had sneaked out of the building to rendezvous here so they could get the forbidden liquor.

If people could get out, unobserved, then they could get back in. Which meant that he and Trish might also enter.

There had been enough time for the exchange of whiskey and money. But the bootleggers were hanging around for the party, accepting the drinks from the people they'd just sold the liquor to. Or, perhaps, the patients had urged them to stay because they wanted the company of outsiders. Whatever the reason, all seven soon moved on, one of them complaining about the cold. This was a woman called "Pat," the only female in the group.

Robeson's face became warm when he heard some of the remarks. They were certainly risqué. Trish didn't seem bothered. On the contrary, she giggled.

Robeson considered going up to the building and trying the doors. He presumed that the patients had left by a ground floor exit. It didn't seem likely that they would have come from an upper story window down a string of bed sheets tied together. But the more he listened to them, the less sure he was. They sounded like a crazy bunch.

Which, he told himself, was just what they were. Otherwise, they wouldn't be here.

Trish said, "Shouldn't we be moving on. I'm frozen."

"I don't know. Maybe we ought to follow them. We might overhear something we can use. Also…maybe we ought to declare ourselves. They won't turn us in. They can't without exposing their little setup. They might even be willing to help us. In any event, they could tell us something about your father."

Trish didn't think that was a good idea. He argued for a minute, and she finally agreed.

They followed them to a clearing near the wall. In its center was a summerhouse, a rather large round edifice with a platform extending from the front. Possibly a band played here in warmer weather. A concrete path led from it toward the hill on which the sanitarium stood.

One of the group must have had a key. The door swung open, they trooped in, and the door was shut. Presently he could see a thread of light between a drawn blind and the window ledge. A few minutes later, wood smoke poured from a metal chimney sticking from the side of the house.

He and Trish crept up on the porch, and he placed his ear against the door. There were sounds of low revelry: roars of laughter, fast-talking, a sudden scream of delight, or maybe it was protest, from the woman. A radio started blaring the *Maple Leaf Rag*.

Trish was crouching, peeking under the shade. Robeson joined her.

There were Smalljack and van Rijnwijk, still dressed in their overalls and checked shirts. They were consuming their own booze, a testimony to its excellence. Or perhaps they would drink anything.

One of the revelers was even taller than van Rijnwijk. He was about fifty, a hard fifty, broad-shouldered, and he looked as if he might have had an outstanding physique in his youth. He also could have been very handsome once. But dissipation had lined his face, bagged his eyes, and fattened throat and waist. It had also coarsened and reddened his nose. His skin was a sickly yellow and his hair was that sort of brown which youthful red turns into as middle age creeps up. He was chugalugging a jug as the others clapped and cheered him on. Robeson was in awe at this feat. Anybody who could drink that fiery stuff down gulp after gulp, pint after pint, and not burst into flames, was a phenomenon.

The next to catch his eye was probably the most extraordinary looking person there. He was very short, not more than an inch or two over five feet. In fact, he looked almost as broad as he was tall. His arms hung down almost to his knees, and the face was that of a chimpanzee's: low forehead, the most prominent supraorbital ridges he'd ever seen—they would have put an Australian aborigine's to shame—under which were small rusty eyes, a long upper lip, a receding chin. Though he was about fifty, his shock of hair was rusty red, and a tuft of curly red hair spilled out from the top of his open shirt.

He was engaged in drinking and in arguing with a tall, slim, hawk-faced fellow of the same age, dressed as if for a formal dinner. Robeson couldn't believe it. A tuxedo and an opera hat! He carried a cane, no doubt because of his limp. However, it had another purpose. Robeson saw him twist the gold-colored knot at its top and remove it. He upended the cane, out of which slid three glass vials. While talking loudly and angrily to the apelike man, he uncorked the vials, filled them with corn whiskey, corked them, and slid them into the hollow interior of the cane.

The sixth was an anemic-looking, skinny little fellow with a sour expression. His hair was of a peculiar indeterminate color which Robeson could only describe as "pale." He sat in a corner on a bare wooden folding chair, drinking steadily from a glass.

The last member was the woman, a tall, long-legged woman in a tight, red low-cut dress and very tall high heels. Her stockings were fishnet. She looked as if she were fifty but she could have been younger. Robeson guessed that the lines in her face had been put there, not by the natural aging of Mother Nature, but by hard living. Nevertheless, the bone structure showed that she had been a very good-looking woman in her prime. Her long hair was peroxided. Her bosom was huge, in startling contrast to her waist, which, though ringed by puffy fat, still looked narrow.

When she walked, she had the long stride of the professional burlesque queen. The eyes of the men followed her legs and the swaying hips when she walked—except those of the pale runt. And the fact that he looked everywhere except where she was showed that he was intensely interested in her. But he didn't want anyone, including himself, to know it.

Ken Robeson, wondering if his plan to question these people was right, despaired. Obviously, they were alcoholics who'd been sent to Restful Meadows by relatives or the lawyers who managed their estates. They'd managed to circumvent the watchdogs of the sanitarium and gotten into contact with the local bootleggers.

They probably wouldn't even know what was going on in the place.

Yet...they had to be sober most of the time, even if they didn't like it.

He watched and listened while he tried to make up his mind what to do. The very tall man, whom the others called "Doc," seemed to be of French origin. Though he spoke excellent English, he had a slight Gallic accent. It was obvious that his companions regarded him as a sort of leader. He might be the person to concentrate on.

"Listen, Trish," Robeson said. "These drunks could help us. Or they might think we're just intruders who'll make so much trouble for them that their source of alcohol could be cut off. What do you think?"

Her face was close to his. Her perfume, mixed with the white lightning breathed on him, was intoxicating.

He thought, How lovely she is!

She said, "They can't tell on us without exposing what they've been doing. But maybe von Adlerdreck doesn't care. Maybe he's just running this sanitarium as a cover-up, and he could care less if his patients are drinking themselves to death.

"Maybe I'm paranoid. But...what he's been doing to my father...I think he's more than just a doctor who's concerned about a crazy old man. I don't have any real evidence to back up my feelings. But I'm a pretty good reader of character. I could detect nuances in a voice, in an expression. I know von Adlerdreck's concealing something sinister behind that oily smile. Don't smile. It isn't woman's intuition. It's a fine-honed ability to tell what a man is really thinking. A lot of women have it because they had to develop the ability in order to survive in this man's world."

"I'm crazy to go on just a feeling," he said. "But there is something wrong. I..."

He should have been looking into the room instead of at her. The door was flung open, and a man stepped outside.

—7—

Robeson started to rise. The man, the near giant, reeled toward him, grabbed his wrist, and started shouting. Robeson tried to back away, but he was held in a grip like a loan shark's. He quit struggling. There was no use antagonizing him and the others.

"We'll go in with you," he said. "If you keep yelling, they'll hear you up there." He gestured at the building on the hill.

For a minute, it was impossible to enter. The apelike man and the slim fellow in the tux tried to get through the doorway at the same time. Jammed together, cursing, they writhed and wriggled, then both fell through together. The big man, still holding on to Robeson, stepped over them into the house. Trish followed them.

Inside, he released his hold and closed the door in the faces of the two. They howled and beat on the door until van Rijnwijk opened it for them. And they fell again, sprawling on the floor.

The woman named Pat screeched with laughter. The others stared silently.

"All right," Doc said, his nose almost meeting Robeson's as he stooped down. "What in hell were you doing? Spying on us?"

Robeson felt the concentration of whiskey in his veins soar as he breathed the man's breath. You could get drunk just by being near this man. His eyes were a peculiar yellow color. Jaundice. This man was dying of liver disease, and yet he was hastening the process by consuming enormous quantities of alcohol.

The two clowns got up from the floor and dusted themselves off. They kept up a firecracker series of insults and curses.

Robeson said, "No, we're not spies. If you'll listen without interruption, I'll tell you who we are and why we're here."

Nothing was to be gained by lying. The truth might be of some help, though these people didn't look as if they would be much help for anybody. Including themselves.

After he'd finished, there was a long silence. Then the big man said, "Whash, whash..." He paused, struggled to get control of his tongue, and spoke more slowly. "What do you want from us? Help against that..."

He paused, swallowed the word he'd been about to use, no doubt in deference to Trish, and continued. "Against that medical Attila the Hun, Herr Doktor von Adlerdreck?"

The apish man exploded. "I'm all for it! I tell you, that so-and-so is involved in something crooked! Otherwise, why would he hire two gangsters?"

The lady called Pat said, "Yeah, and I'll tell you something else that's fishy. Eiderduck gets a lot of mail from overseas and from Washington, D.C. Only the letters don't come in envelopes from overseas or Washington. They come inside other envelopes from a New York address."

"Eiderduck?" Robeson said.

"She means Addledrake," the apish man said.

"We call von Adlerdreck a lot of things," the big, dark, yellow-eyed man said. "Some of which ain't fit for young ladies to hear."

He introduced himself as Doctor Marcel Sebastien LeClerc du Bronce du Fauve. He was, he said, a French Canadian of aristocratic descent.

"He ain't a real doctor," Pat said. "He's a chiropractor, a bone bender. He got into trouble because he was too much a ladies' man with his female patients. So he ducked out and hid here. Not that he shouldn't be here. He's a real rummy, just like the rest of us."

"You got a big mouth, Pat," Doc said. "A healer is a doctor, and I healed bodies and broken hearts. Is it my fault that I am temperamentally unable to resist beauty?"

He bowed to Trish and smiled dazzlingly. She backed away, dizzy with the heavy fumes of fermented corn.

The others were introduced. Pat Coningway was just what Ken had guessed. An ex-stripper. But she'd married an old millionaire who'd died a year ago. "He was vigorous for his age, but his heart couldn't take it," she said, looking smug.

The apish man was Anderson Maypole Blidgett, but everyone called him "Jocko." The man in the tux was Ted Scrooch Creeks, Ted to everyone but Jocko, who called him "Oinks."

Jocko said, grinning at the outraged Creeks, "Oinks is a shyster, an ambulance chaser who got drummed out of the New York Bar Association. I calls him Oinks because he defended a pig rustler in his last case. But he was so bombed the judge threw him in the slammer for contempt of court."

"An out-and-out lie!" Oinks said, waving his cane so close to Jocko's nose he had to step back. "I suffer from diabetes and that morning I had neglected my dosage of insulin. This left me somewhat confused, and the judge refused to accept my defense. He himself was a heavy drinker who had no mercy for those defendants in a similar plight."

"Yeah, tell that to the Marines," Jocko said.

Jocko, it turned out, was a wealthy pharmacist who owned a chain of drugstores. But, as he cheerfully admitted, booze got to be a bigger problem than he could handle. So he'd committed himself to Restful Meadows to dry out. So far, without success.

The anemic squirt with the two bootleggers was Bob Thomas. He'd once been a telephone lineman, but he'd gone into full-time whiskey making with the other two. He lived in the basement of a private house where he worked on his inventions in his spare time.

"When he's sober, that is," Jocko gleefully said. "Maybe if Lunger Tom laid off the juice, his inventions might work."

Thomas, his colorless eyes blazing, said, "Yeah, you throwback to the missing link, you'd drink too if you'd got caught in a mustard gas attack. What's your excuse?" He began coughing violently but got over the fit when he swallowed more of the white lightning.

"That stuff'll cure what ails you," Smalljack said.

Robeson said, "Well, what about it? Miss Burke and I would like to get her father out of here. But it'll be risky for you, since we don't have a legal leg to stand on."

Doc Fauve lowered his huge bulk into a folding chair, and he took another gargantuan swallow from a jug. Smacking his lips, blinking owlishly, he said, "I don't like that arrogant son of a...gun. I'd like to stick it to him. Especially since there is some evidence that he's up to no good."

"Evidence which wouldn't stand up in court," Oinks said, swaying slightly. "But, if we were to capture those letters and we could find someone who could read German and Italian, we might find that he and his two thugs are engaged in illicit, perhaps even treasonable, activities."

"Treasonable!" Jocko said. "How do you figure that out, Blackstone?"

Oinks hiccupped, then said, "Anyone but a low-browed facsimile of an orangutan would deduce from what has been reported that von Adlerdreck is an agent of, or at least a sympathizer, with, the Germans. And Ovarizi and Bufalo are agents of, or at least sympathizers with, that strutting jackanapes, Mussolini. It's only a suspicion, I'll admit, a hypothesis, but it certainly warrants investigation. In a sense, though civilians, we are soldiers for our country. All of us here, except for our two young visitors, are veterans who fought in the Big One. I even include Pat, since, as I understand it, she was something of a camp follower and materially contributed to the morale of the doughboys, not to mention any number of officers."

Pat growled, "How'd you like this jug jammed up your...?"

Doc Fauve interrupted sharply. "Hold it, Pat! There's a lady present!"

"Why, you drunken, lecherous quack, you mean I ain't no lady? It'll be a cold day in hell before I let you sweet-talk me again into..."

Robeson said, "Please! No quarreling! Now, how about it? Will you help us? If you agree to, then we should make some plans now. And act quickly."

"That a boy, young feller!" Jocko said. "I ain't been in a good brawl since just before I committed myself."

"He doesn't mean we'll bust into the place like a band of Comanches, you microcephalic," the lawyer said. "This will take subtlety, silence, organization."

Doc Fauve said that they should take a vote. Everybody held his hand up. Robeson was surprised that the three bootleggers wanted to join in.

The beanpole, Smalljack, said, "Us three fought against the Kaiser, you know. I was a corporal, Van and Lunger Tom was sergeants. If this Kraut is a spy or something, we'd like to get our mitts on him. Ain't that right, boys?"

"Yeah," van Rijnwijk boomed. "Here we fought and got wounded so we could save the world for democracy. And here's the Boche up and back on his feet and making noises again. This time, he ought to be kicked silly so he'll think twice the next time before he goes out to conquer the world."

"I say," said Jocko, "let's storm on up there, kick hell out of the Kraut and them two Sicilians, get the letters, and turn the whole lot over to the Feds. Meanwhile, Robeson and the lovely Miss Burke—you're a real peach, kid—can hustle her old man out of here."

This was voted down, since the gangsters were armed and, for all they knew, some of the attendants might be, too.

Everybody downed some more white lightning, including Robeson and Burke. Then the lights were turned out, and they walked toward the big house on the hill. Before they could get out of the trees, they heard automobile motors to their right. They hid behind trees and waited for the cars to come by on the road. But the cars seemed to be staying at the gateway.

Robeson said, "I'll sneak down there and find out what's going on."

Doc, Jocko, and van Rijnwijk said they'd go with him.

"Maybe it's Sheriff Huisman," the latter said. "He's been out looking for us. He's mad at us because we won't kick in more money for protection."

"You mean…?"

"Sure. You think we could operate like we do if we didn't have some official warning us when the Internal Revenue guys are pussyfooting around? I guess we'll have to up the ante to him pretty soon. But we're making him sweat it out."

His three companions kept bumping into trees and crashing through bushes and falling down when they stepped into depressions. Robeson finally called a halt. "You're all too loaded. They'll hear you a mile off. I'll go ahead. You stay here."

"I'll drink to that," Doc said, and he pulled a flask from his coat pocket.

When Ken Robeson got close to the gateway, he saw two long black limousines on the road just inside the walls. The headlights were turned off, and several men were standing by the front right-hand door of the lead automobile. They were looking up at a telephone pole outside the gateway. A man was up there, faintly silhouetted against the light gray sky. Even as Robeson watched, the last of the wires fell away. The man who'd cut them began to climb down.

Robeson tried to count the number of the party. It was too dark to be accurate, but he estimated that there were twelve.

And then, as someone lit a match to light a cigar, he saw a tough face beneath the brim of a hat. And a tommy gun in the hands of the man standing nearby.

Combining stealth with speed, he turned and made his way back to where the three were. Just as he got to them, he heard the acceleration of motors and the shifting of gears. Through the trees he could see the two vehicles, their lights still out, moving along the road.

"We got company," he said. "Heavily armed troops of some sort. I don't know if they're mobsters or G-men."

They went back to the rest of the group. By then the two limousines had passed the hidden watchers and were climbing the winding road. Robeson told the others what he'd seen.

Trish Burke said, "Then that means we don't have a chance. Unless they're government people making a raid."

"We can only wait here and see what happens," Ken said. "But cheer up. Who knows but this may mean that your father'll be sprung very soon?"

At that moment there was a yell. It came from a distance, but even its faintness could not filter out the despair in it.

—8—

Robeson looked at the building. In its blazing light was a tiny figure running down the hill. Behind it came three others, all shouting.

By now the two limousines were out of sight beyond the curve of the hill.

Trish started forward, crying, "Father!"

Robeson grabbed her arm and swung her around. "Don't let them know we're down here!" He turned to the others. "Duck behind the trees! Get ready to jump Adlerdreck and the Gold Dust Twins. But be careful! They're armed. Rijnwijk, why don't one of you get the car? Have it ready for us."

Van Rijnwijk, swaying, said, "Well, I dunno. We can't all gesh...get in our car. Need another."

Robeson said, "Trish, you take off with him and bring your car, too!"

"What! And leave my father! I can't, I have to find out what's going to happen to him!"

He could understand her reluctance, though he thought it was ill advised. He said, "Jocko, what about you? Would you take her keys and drive the car to the gateway entrance?"

"Not me, kid! I ain't gonna run away when there's a good fight coming up! Oh, boy!" He rubbed his big, hairy-backed hands together and hopped up and down like a chimpanzee working himself into a battle frenzy.

Robeson got Trish to open her handbag so he could remove the keys. He offered them to the lawyer, Creeks, who shook his head. "Not me. I like a brawl as much as that monkey there. Anyway, he'd say I was chicken if I took off."

All the men refused on the grounds that they'd be thought cowardly if they left now. Besides, as Doc said, they were spoiling to get their hands on Adlerdreck.

Then van Rijnwijk refused to go on the same grounds.

"Whyn't you go?"

"I will, but I can't drive more than one car at a time!" Robeson cried. "Don't any of you have any sense at all!"

"I do!" the ex-stripper cried. "Theshe dimb bozosh ain't go' the shenshe they was born with—if any. Gi'…give me the keysh!"

Robeson doubted that she could even find the car, let alone drive it. But she was a last hope. He handed her the keys to the Ford. She immediately dropped them and was then down on all fours groping for them. Lunger Tom, the pale, sour runt, said, "Okay. I'll bring the…hic!…limouzhine. I got some shenshe, and nobody'sh gonna call me chicken. No'…not after I got gashed…gassed…in the Big One. Gi' muh the keysh to Trish'sh…Triss's…car."

But he began coughing violently, and Doc Fauve and Smalljack jumped on him, covering his mouth so the approaching quartet wouldn't hear them. He kicked out, catching Rijnwijk in the groin. The big man howled in pain, let loose of Thomas, and writhed on the ground. Jocko leaped upon him and clamped his hand over Rijnwijk's mouth. Then he howled and danced around holding his hand which the big man had bitten.

Robeson threw his hands up in the air.

Doc Fauve said, "Shomebody's gotta shtraighten em out. All thish noise."

His big right fist cracked three times, and Thomas, van Rijnwijk, and Blidgett were laid out and snoring. Robeson almost went amok then. They needed every man available to overwhelm the three pursuers of Burke, and all of a sudden they were reduced to six, two of them women.

He looked up the hill. The professor was still going strong, almost at the road at the foot of the hill. The others were about ninety feet behind him.

Then he saw the first of the big black limousines come around the corner of the house and pull to a stop in front of it. Men with tommy guns and shotguns piled out of it while the second vehicle stopped behind the first. One of the men must have looked down the hill. He pointed, and the others turned to look. One had a flashlight which he directed toward the four running men.

One of the men from the limousines, evidently the leader, waved his arms and screamed orders. Four men ran into the building, their guns ready. The others plunged on down the hill.

By then Professor Burke was heading toward the woods, wheezing like an asthmatic mule.

"Quick! Drag these guys under the trees!" Ken Robeson said. "Then get ready to jump on the Doc and his buddies!"

"Doc?" Fauve said, swaying. "Whash you wanna jump on me and my buddiesh for?"

"Doctor von Altereddrake!" Robeson said. "Holy cow! You got me doing it! I mean, Adlerdreck and his thugs!"

"Oh! Well, okay. Lishen, Robeshon, don' worry. I'm a chiropractor. I may be deshpished in the medical profeshion, but I know what I'm doing. Thoshe quacksh are jealoush of ush chiropractorsh. Don' worry about me taking care of thoshe guysh! I know all about presshure pointsh on the human body!"

Robeson had already dragged van Rijnwijk's heavy bulk under the branches of a nearby tree. Pat and Trish, he saw, were carrying off the light body of Lunger Tom. He straightened and said, "What do you mean? Pressure points?"

Doc's gigantic body loomed above him, swaying like the Empire State Building in a high wind. A big hand came down and its thumb pressed on his neck.

"Like thish, shee? I probe, I find the nekshush—nexus—of nerve shentersh here, I pressh, and…"

—9—

Kenneth Robeson wasn't unconscious very long. But in the short period Professor Burke had reached them. He must have been startled to find a body—Robeson's—on the cold ground and above it a gigantic menacing figure weaving back and forth. Probably mumbling about the prejudices and persecutions of the medical profession and the pressure points of the human nervous system.

Though he didn't know what had happened while he was out, Robeson could reconstruct it. Burke had veered to one side, but von Adlerdreck and his two colleagues, following him closely, had rammed into Doc Fauve. All three had fallen.

He supposed this was so—he was still in the supposing stage because his wits hadn't all rallied to him yet—since the sanitarium head and Bufalo and Ovarizi were just getting up off the ground.

Then two figures—Pat and Trish—flew out of the darkness. Trish's handbag thudded against Ovarizi's temple. He went down. The long-legged, high-stepping, high-kicking Patricia Coningway—she must have thought she was on the stage—kicked high. The point of her shoe caught Bufalo under the chin. He emitted a glugging sound, and went down.

The tall blond von Adlerdreck didn't even see what had occurred behind him. He was running off into the darkness, shouting something unintelligible.

Robeson got to his feet. Doc Fauve rose a few seconds later. Very dignifiedly, he said, "Offisher, I wassh jusht crosshing the shtreet, with the light, mind you, when thish truck..."

He stopped, took a quick look around, and said, somewhat embarrassedly, "What happened?"

At that moment Jocko, muttering something about "Mabel," got up. He stood for a few seconds, crouching, his knuckles on the ground, exactly like a gorilla aroused from sleep. He growled, "Where are they? I'll kill 'em!"

Robeson, restraining his anger, said, "Drag them under the trees!"

Too late. Ovarizi and Bufalo leaped up and staggered off. It was evident from the way they kept running into the trees that they were still dazed. Since they were armed, Robeson decided not to go after them.

Van Rijnwijk, Thomas, and Jocko, all groaning, got to their feet. At that moment, Robeson heard feet thudding. There were so many, it sounded like a buffalo stampede. Before he and the others could hide, they were invaded. Men poked guns at them in the illumination of two flashlights.

Robeson could not see for a moment or so. Then the blinding beam was directed toward the surrounding trees. The two women were not visible. Either they'd fled or were concealed behind tree trunks.

Now he could see the leader. He was medium-sized though muscular, clad in a gray cloth coat with a gray fur collar. His head was bare, allowing Robeson to see a shock of polar-bear white hair and a middle-aged face that would have been handsome if it weren't for its total lack of expression. It looked like the mask of a dead man. Or the features of a man playing dead. Since Robeson was very close to the man, he could distinguish the color of the eyes. The gray of Arctic ice fields. But under the pale, washed-out flatness was a blaze as if a natural-gas leak has caught fire under the polar icecap.

Robeson recognized him from the photographs and the descriptions in many newspaper and magazine articles.

"Ricardo Bensoni!" he gasped.

"You said it, punk!"

The dead lips didn't move. It was as if Bensoni were a ventriloquist who projected his voice. In fact, the words seemed to come from the open, but still, mouth of a huge guy standing like a wooden dummy by him.

So this was "Il Vendicativo." "The Avengeful." The story was that his wife and daughter had disappeared, and Dito "Finger" Sporcizio's mob was blamed. Dito's protests of his innocence did him no good. Bensoni and his gang had wiped out every member of Sporcizio's organization, including some kids who ran numbers. Then Bensoni had taken over the dead ganglord's territory.

A few months later, a juvenile street gang had made the mistake of stealing the hubcaps from Bensoni's armored Cadillac. Bensoni had burned them out of their basement headquarters and machine-gunned the survivors as, their clothes on fire, they ran into the street. The next day, crime dropped 86 percent in Brooklyn.

One of Bensoni's uncles, who ran a grocery store in the Bronx, was beaten up because he refused to pay for "protection" by Affamato Porco's thugs. Bensoni wiped that gang out.

The police knew who had committed these crimes but couldn't prove it. Only last month Bensoni had been shocked to find out that Sporcizio had been innocent after all. Bensoni's wife had run off with a used-car salesman, taking her child with her. They were last seen boarding a ship in Los Angeles bound for Brazil.

The huge man was Hidtkot Schmidt, chiefly noted for his ability to get past electrical security systems. And now Robeson saw another infamous member of the mob, McMurdoro, "The Murderer." He was a tall Scot with hands almost as big as van Rijnwijk's.

Bensoni did not have the prejudice of Sicilian mobsters against non-Sicilians. He hired only the best help, and if the man wasn't from the Old Country, he did not care.

Il Vendicativo spoke softly to Robeson, asking him who he was and what he was doing here. Robeson was too deep in a state of shock to think of a lie. He told Bensoni the truth.

"If you're giving it to me straight, you have nothing to worry about," the wax-mask-faced man said. "Some people say I got a mean streak, but that's a lie. I'm not vengeful. I just see to it that justice is done."

He turned to Schmidt and McMurdoro. "Get Burke. Don't hurt him. Don't knock off Ovarizi and Bufalo if you can help it. I want to put some questions to them."

A chill ran over Robeson at these words. He could imagine Bensoni's type of inquisition.

All of the gang except a tall, skinny colored man ran into the woods to do Bensoni's bidding. The Negro held a tommy on the prisoners.

Bensoni started to say something but stopped. A wild yell came from the woods, followed by the booming of .45 automatics and the chatter of submachine guns.

—10—

"You bums stay here!" Bensoni snarled without moving his lips. "Otherwise, I blow your heads off!"

He and the Negro ran off into the trees. Robeson called softly, "Trish! Pat! You out there?"

A scream soared above him and through the branches, riding even over the gunfire. It was a woman's voice filled with terror. And it seemed to come from the direction where all the noisy action was.

Robeson ran toward it, shouting, "Where are you, Trish?" Behind him was a thunder of feet, the others stumbling after him. He went perhaps a hundred yards, then dived into the cold, hard ground as streaks of fire shot off the night and bullets wheeling above his head, smacked into tree trunks, and pattered in the soil around him. Behind him was a heavy thump, his followers hitting the dirt at the same time as if they were a trained ballet group.

The firing stopped. A car motor roared, and tires squealed. Raising his head, he got a glimpse of headlights moving away from him. They flashed on the steel gates and then they disappeared. From the sound of the motor, the car was going full speed toward Roosville.

There was some loud cursing near the gate. Then Bensoni's voice rose. "That does it! #%$&**! Burke got kidnapped! Right in front of our eyes, under our noses! †=%&*@¢#!"

Robeson called out. "Hey, Bensoni! Are the women okay?"

"Yeah! It was on account of them we quit shooting! That #$%&@¢†=&!X Bierstoss used them as shields!"

Bierstoss! Who…? Then Robeson remembered what Trish Burke had told him. Bierstoss was the industrialist who'd financed the professor's experiments. The man who'd paid von Adlerdreck to take care of him. He must've driven up just in time to get the professor. What was he doing here?

"Can we come in?" Robeson called.

"Okay. But with your hands up and slowly."

Evidently Bensoni didn't trust anybody. Robeson didn't blame him. The kind of life he led, he couldn't afford to trust his own wife. *Especially* her.

He got up, then stood still as Bufalo's voice cut through the night. "Hey, Bensoni! A truce! We…"

The rest was cut off as the second limousine, occupied by the four men who'd entered the building, roared up. Il Vendicativo told them to hold their fire, and he said, "Okay, what is it, Chips?"

"I was just wondering if we ain't after the same thing. For the same people. How about a truce so's we can talk?"

At that moment someone touched Robeson on the shoulder. Startled, he whirled, ready to strike out. But it was Trish Burke.

She said, her voice trembling, "Oh, Ken! That man drove off with my father! Where's he taking him?"

Robeson didn't know. He shushed her so that he could hear the powwow. However, there wasn't going to be any.

Bensoni ordered his men into the two cars. As he got in, he called, "Chips! You and Eggs! You keep out of this if you know what's healthy for you! Got me?"

The lead car started out with the wheels turning in the gravel, firing stones right and left. The second car followed, tommy barrels bristling from the windows.

Robeson figured that the gangsters were going after Bierstoss and his captive—if Burke had been taken along involuntarily.

Von Adlerdreck and his two attendants suddenly emerged from the bushes on the far side of the driveway. They ran up the hill, evidently making for the garage by the big building.

Ken Robeson grabbed Trish's hand and pulled her after him as he ran for their car. Behind them came the sound of stampede again, the patients and the moonshiners taking off after them, none probably knowing why. When, breathless, he and Trish got to the Model A in the farmer's field, the rest piled into the big Packard. All but Doc Fauve. He got onto the running board of the Ford and shouted through the closed window.

"There isn't any room for me in there! I'll ride here so I can be your lookout! We're not going to miss out on the excitement! Tally ho!"

Robeson thought he was nuts, but if Doc wanted to stand out there and freeze, it was okay with him. The cold should sober him up, though he'd be lucky if he didn't get pneumonia.

Then, as Trish backed the car toward the farmer's road, a figure ran toward them. Crouching, its long arms dangling, bounding in a curious run, it looked like a chimpanzee. Trish straightened the car out on the road and started forward. Shouting, Jocko leaped on the running board, opened the door, and got in.

"They threw me out!" he said bitterly. "That lewd shyster Oinks got kind of familiar with Pat, and he blamed it on me. Wait until I get my mitts on him. I'll tear the wings off that legal eagle!"

There was an explosion, and everybody tried to duck. Robeson banged his head on the dashboard, and the pain in it, which had disappeared during the recent frenzy, came back. Trish said, "That wasn't a shot! My right front tire blew!"

The car was stuck in the gateway to the wire fence. The Packard stopped behind them, and everybody tumbled out. There wasn't time to put on the spare, which was, in any event, as bald as the one just punctured. Smalljack said he'd push the Ford out of the way with his car. Then they should all get into his car. There was some argument between Pat Coningway and Jocko while Robeson and Trish danced with impatience. Finally, Jocko, unable to convince Pat that he wasn't the culprit, said he'd promise to keep his paws off her. By then the Ford had been pushed over into the ditch on the other side of the highway. They started to get into the Packard. Jocko took advantage of Oinks's unprotected rear and kicked it hard.

That started another brawl. The lawyer swung his cane at Jocko, missed, and slammed it across van Rijnwijk's shoulder. The huge fellow struck Oinks on the shoulder with his great fist.

By the time peace had been restored, and they were all jammed uncomfortably into the car, some on top of others, they saw headlights coming out of the sanitarium driveway. They'd wasted so much time, the doctor and his cohorts had gotten a head start.

Within forty seconds, they were rocketing down the road, the rear lights of von Adlerdreck's car about a quarter-mile ahead. Robeson was never to forget that wild, reckless, dangerous, stomach-squeezing, tire-screeching ride. Smalljack drove like a drunken maniac. Maybe he wasn't crazy, but he certainly was intoxicated. He took the Packard at the sharp turn into Roosville beautifully, however. It only turned around three times while negotiating the curve, it didn't roll over once, and it ended up pointing in the right direction.

It tore through the village of dark houses with rustic sleepers inside. Robeson wondered where Sheriff Huisman was. Fifteen minutes later, he found out. By then their car was only a few yards behind the doctor's. And less than a quarter-mile ahead of it was a red flashing light on the roof of the sheriff's car and the faint wail of a siren lifted toward them.

"Huisman must be chasing Bensoni's gang!" Smalljack said. Holding on to the wheel with one hand, he lifted a jug with the other and drank. Then he passed it through the window to Doc Fauve, who was standing now on the running board of the Packard. Doc drank deeply and passed the jug back to Smalljack, who passed it to the ex-stripper.

She began to drink, then stopped, and, swearing, rammed the bottom of the jug hard against Jocko's forehead.

"You keep your hands off me!"

The pharmacist said, indignantly, "Honest to God, Pat, I never touched you. It's that sneaky ambulance-chaser."

"I can vouch for that," said Trish, who was sitting on Robeson's lap. "I know it wasn't Oinks because Jocko's been trying to feel my leg!"

Jocko swore that he was innocent. He claimed it was Lunger Tom, who was seated next to Trish. Lunger Tom got mad and took a poke at Jocko. Oinks began laughing but Jocko's hand closed around his throat. Van Rijnwijk, in the front seat, turned and roared, "No more of that! How in hell can Homer here drive with you bunch of stupid jerks rousting around back there?"

Smalljack said, icily, "I told you never to call me Homer, Van. It's Bill, and don't you forget that!"

For a while there was comparative peace. For some minutes, Robeson could even close his eyes and enjoy having Trish Burke on his lap. Would that this were so in a less disturbing situation. Would he ever get her on his lap again?

The big question, though, was: Would they survive this ride? A dozen times, swinging around sharp curves, the right wheels had gone off onto the shoulder. Once, they skidded sidewise, and this time Robeson was sure they'd turn over. But Smalljack straightened the vehicle out.

Robeson wanted to ask how fast they were going, but he was afraid to.

After an hour and a half, which seemed like five hours, they roared through a police roadblock. This had been set up at the junction of the county road with the state highway. But Bierstoss had taken the narrow opening between two cars and thundered on through. So did Bensoni's limousines, the sheriff's Plymouth, and von Adlerdreck's. And, emulating them, so did Smalljack.

Presently, there were five State Police cars, lights flashing, sirens screaming, behind them.

After Robeson got his breath back—it had been caught somewhere below his lungs—he shouted, "Why don't we stop and explain the situation to the police?"

"Are you crazy?" Lunger Tom squeaked. "We got all this moonshine, and there's distilling equipment in the trunk, not to mention two rifles, a sawed-off shotgun, and a couple of hot gats."

Robeson shut his eyes again. He couldn't bear to look. He could hear Jocko and Oinks quarreling again. The lawyer was angry because he'd just found out that his swing at Jocko with the cane had broken the glass vials inside it. When he'd unscrewed the gold knob, the liquor had run over his arm and his shirtfront and soaked his pants. Jocko was laughing like crazy, then a sharp sound exploded in Robeson's ears.

He opened his eyes. Jocko was howling with pain and holding his cheek. Trish said, "Keep your hairy paws off of me!"

"It was an accident, an accident, I swear!" Jocko said.

He hunkered down on the floor, jammed between Thomas's legs.

"See! I'll keep my hands in my pockets!"

"Good!" Oinks said, and he poured the rest of the booze in the cane over Jocko's head.

Robeson expected that the police would set up a roadblock at the George Washington Bridge. But there wasn't any. And the crazy caravan continued at seventy miles an hour down Broadway, then over to Fifth Avenue, with whistles blowing, tires screaming, horns blaring, pedestrians and angry car drivers shouting. And violent bumps as the Packard sometimes detoured traffic and went over curbs and down the sidewalk, Smalljack pushing in on the horn button, it blaring, and Doc Fauve, on the running board, waving wildly with one hand for the pedestrians to dive out of the way.

Then, a block from Thirty-fourth, what Robeson had been praying for happened. The gas tank ran dry.

Smalljack smoothly put the gear into neutral and the car rolled for another block.

Robeson looked out the window. They were right back where they'd started from: the Empire State Building.

—11—

Bierstoss's Lincoln was parked with its left wheels on the sidewalk. Just behind were Bensoni's two Cadillacs. And entirely on the sidewalk, its front smashed against the side of the restaurant at the corner, was von Adlerdreck's Cadillac. He never did see the sheriff.

All the vehicles were unoccupied.

Doc Fauve, his yellow complexion blue from the cold, was running up—no, shambling—toward the entrance to the building. Trish opened the door and slid out from Robeson's lap.

In the distance came the dismal sound of sirens. The State Police, and the city police who'd joined them, would arrive inside a minute.

Robeson got out. He wanted to tell Trish they should stay here and tell the police what had happened. Otherwise, they were as likely to be shot by the cops as by the gangsters. But Trish was running toward the doors to the skyscraper. He found himself also running, though he told himself that the smart thing to do was to stay put. However, he couldn't let her venture by herself into that place which would soon be no-man's-land.

The lobby was brightly lit. Some kind of festivity was being held; big signs, ribbons, decorations, booths all over the place. The attendants, however, were not in a festive mood at the moment. They were running this way and that, screaming, yelling, diving under the counters of the booths, heading toward the exits, taking protection behind the many stone pillars.

A stench of cordite hung in the air, and one pillar was chipped where bullets had struck. No one seemed to be hurt, though.

Robeson saw Trish going into an elevator. He ran after her but the doors closed in front of him. Trish didn't seem to hear his pleas to keep the doors open.

He grabbed a man by the arm. "Those guys who were shooting? Where'd they go?"

The man, pale, trembling pointed upward. Robeson took another elevator.

But only to the second floor. Swearing at himself for not keeping a cooler head, he watched the dials over the doors. Trish's elevator was one of the two expresses, already past the 52nd floor. She didn't know any more than he did about Bierstoss's destination. She was just going up in a frantic, desperate search. But maybe she wasn't so foolish. Maybe she thought that Bierstoss would, in his panic, go as high as possible. He could be operating on the fugitive's instinct, one inherited from ape ancestors. Get as high on the tree as possible.

He went down the stairs to the lobby. By then it was full of state troopers and New York's finest. They didn't seem to know what to do; they were milling around or questioning people. He took the other express elevator which fortunately wasn't being used. It would go to the 80th floor, as high as any elevator could go in one stretch. When he got out, he went down the hall and hopped over the chain put up to keep visitors out. Then he took the elevator that would carry him all the way to the 86th floor. Nobody stopped it because nobody was around.

But plenty of people had been here recently. There were cigar butts, cigarette stubs, a chewing gum wrapper, and a broken whiskey jug just outside the elevator doors.

When the doors opened, Robeson started to stick his head cautiously out of the exit, He didn't hear anything, but that meant nothing. There might be many men lying silently in wait for all hell to bust loose.

Then, a screaming, arm-flailing, leg-kicking, wild-eyed tousle-haired apparition appeared. It seemed to come from nowhere, but its destination was certain. It struck Robeson, drove him back against the back of the cage, and almost bore him under. He grabbed the crazed man—Professor Burke—and he tried to shout sense into him. No use. The man kept on attacking him, at the same time screaming, "My shadow! My shadow! Keep it away from me!"

His face was scratched and his nose was hurting where it had been struck and Robeson angrily picked up the thin man and shook him. "Pipe down! There isn't any shadow!"

Then he hurled the professor against the wall, and the man, sobbing and moaning, crumpled. Robeson stepped forward to punch the button. He'd take this maniac down to the ground floor, tell the police his story, and let them handle it from there on. Much as he wanted to find out where Trish was, he knew that the logical way was to let the cops do it.

But Doc Fauve's big dissipatedly handsome face, its normal, if unhealthy, yellow hue restored, appeared. He seemed to have sobered up somewhat.

"Robeson? You got him, huh? Listen, von Eiderduck and his Gold Dust Twins're cornered by Bensoni's men. The former are outside on the observation platform. The latter're inside, waiting until they can get a shot at the former. Or is it the former is the latter and vice versa?"

He frowned, then said, "Never mind. What does matter is that Bierstoss has got the young lady, and he's in the top room of the dirigible mooring mast."

"Where are your buddies?" Robeson said.

"We're in the hallway outside the elevators and behind the concession counters. We got Bensoni's men at a standstill."

"With what?"

"With our weapons, of course. Didn't you see Lunger Tom and Smalljack get them out of the trunk?"

"No. How'd Professor Burke get here?"

The near-giant scratched his head. "I don't know. Must've broken loose and nobody shot him because he's the key to the whole mess. One thing he's good at. That's escaping."

"How'd Bierstoss get hold of Trish?"

"Who knows? Somehow, during the confusion, he got hold of her but the professor took off."

Robeson said, "Is Bierstoss armed?"

"Is Roosevelt a Democrat? Sure he is. I got a glimpse of him. He's got two .45 automatics."

"I'm going to take this poor devil down," Robeson said. "The cops can handle it from there."

Doc Fauve came into the cage. He was carrying a gallon jug, and he proceeded to lighten its weight with four or five swallows.

"Yeah? Well, me and the boys, we're going up the elevator into the mooring mast. And we're going to rescue the damsel from the dragon."

"You'll get her killed!" Robeson said. "You guys are too bombed to know what you're doing. You can't go charging in there. He'll open fire the moment the elevator doors open! You'll be massacred!"

Doc Fauve offered the jug to Robeson, who shook his head.

"Yeah? Maybe so! But we're going to do it anyway. Listen, buddy, there's none of us worth a damn. We all had good prospects; we could have been something. Decent, respectable, giving something to others, our relatives, families, the community. Instead, we peed it all away. We're all drunks, von Addledrake's patients and the moonshiners. And up there is someone who might be something, a real nice girl who got into a situation she isn't responsible for. We've talked about this among us, and we figure we can atone for what we've done, our wasted life, if we can rescue the girl from that villain, Bierstoss!"

Doc Fauve sat down on the floor and drank some more moonshine. Robeson said, "It's alcohol that's talking. It got you into this mess. One final act of redemption, huh? Nonsense! You'll get slaughtered, and Trish will get killed, and all because your booze-soaked brains and your whiskey-rotten conscience have told you you're no good, but you can redeem yourselves by throwing yourselves away. You understand?"

Doc Fauve began weeping. "You don't understand! We're trying to make up for what we've done!"

"If you were sober and aching for drink, you wouldn't be doing this," Robeson said. "It's strange how alcohol carries the seeds of its own..."

At that moment a voice bellowed out. Bensoni's.

"Von Adlerdreck! Ovarizi! Bufalo! We know who you are! We got the goods on you! Listen! This has gone far enough! We've been working at cross-purposes! I didn't want to have to tell you this, but there's no way out!

"Listen, I just found out about you last night. I mean, I found out who you and your buddies were and what you were up to! So come on in, you three, and we'll put our heads together and see if we can work something out without these civilians making trouble! How about it?"

Robeson could hear a voice muffled by the glass windows on the 86th floor. But he thought he heard von Adlerdreck say something about not knowing if Bensoni was lying to him.

Doc Fauve got up. He was no longer crying. He said, "What's that gangster talking about?"

The professor quit whimpering, and he tried to get up on his feet. Robeson pressed him back down.

"I don't know. This has been a very confusing night."

Doc Fauve bellowed, "You guys! Come here! We're going on up and rescue Miss Burke!"

The others appeared and crowded into the cage. Robeson wanted to get out; but the press of bodies prevented him. He said, "Damn it! All right! I'll go with you! But this is idiotic! Bierstoss will murder us!"

"He can't get us all!" Jocko shouted. He punched the button and the cage shot up. "One of us'll get him! Here, Robeson, you look scared! Have a shot of Dutch courage!"

Ken Robeson shook his head. "You damn fools! If you start blazing away the moment the doors open, you're just as likely to shoot Trish!"

"Yes," the lawyer said. "But at least we'll have vengeance! Bierstoss isn't going to escape!"

The cage stopped. The doors, whispering, began to open.

The tall, skinny Smalljack and the apelike Jocko held revolvers. Van Rijnwijk had the sawed-off shotgun. Little Thomas, who was coughing, waved the deer rifle around. Pat Coningway had a knife in her hand.

Robeson said, "Where'd you get that?"

"I keep it in a garter sheath," she said, smiling. "That's to defend my virtue."

"Yeah," Jocko said. "This is the only time she ever pulled it out. And her virtue ain't at stake. How about that?"

"How'd you like this shoved up between your glutei maximi?" Pat said. Jocko broke up, bending over with uncontrollable laughter, slapping his knee, and then "accidentally" ramming his elbow into Oinks's ribs.

Oinks yelled with wrath and grabbed Jocko by the throat. "You Pithecanthropus not-so-erectus! I'll squeeze your throat until your brains pop out! If, that is, you have anything in your skull except a vacuum to squeeze out!"

The doors opened. Smalljack's revolver exploded. Van Rijnwijk's shotgun boomed. Pat, screaming like a Valkyrie, tried to dash forward, her little blade extended. Unfortunately, Doc Fauve was in her path, and the point sank into his back. He yelled and threw his hands out, one knocking Thomas out and the other rendering van Rijnwijk half-unconscious. Jocko's revolver went boom!-boom!-boom! as his eyes popped under the pressure of Oinks's fingers. Fortunately, it was pointed upward, and its bullets smashed harmlessly through the ceiling of the cage.

Later, Robeson was to think how extremely fortuitous it was that Trish Burke wasn't standing before the elevator doors. But she was off to one side, looking down at Bierstoss. He was a short, pudgy man lying on his back, his mouth open, his eyes closed.

His forehead was streaked with red. Trish held a .45 automatic pistol by the butt. She was waiting for him to recover consciousness.

But for the moment, she was frozen with shock at the bellow of shotgun and crack of revolver.

The cage was emptied, its occupants spilling out, most of them falling flat on their faces. Robeson went to Trish. "Are you all right?"

"Yes," she said, lowering the hand holding the Luger. "I grabbed him where…" She seemed reluctant to say the exact words. After all, she was a lady. "I mean,…you know…and while he was writhing on the floor, I grabbed his gun from the floor…he'd dropped it because he was in such pain, and I hit him on the head with it."

Swaying, pale, she looked at him with enormous blue eyes. "How's father? Is he safe?"

Robeson jerked a thumb at the elevator cage. "I think so."

Trish's eyes got even wider, a feat he would not have thought possible.

"But…the elevator! It's gone!"

Robeson turned. The doors were closed. Somebody, maybe the professor, maybe a person on the 86th floor, had punched its button.

As he stared, too stupefied from all that had happened to react swiftly, the doors opened. And there, in the cage, was the white-haired, expressionless Bensoni. With him were von Adlerdreck, Ovarizi, Bufalo, Schmidt, McMurdoro, the colored man, and a dozen others. All had weapons, tommies, .45 automatics, some revolvers. One man was even holding a grenade.

Bensoni stepped out into the room. He said, in his emotionless, robotlike voice, "Well, this is quite a mess, isn't it?"

He put his hand inside his gray flannel jacket and pulled out a gray wallet. He flipped it open. Robeson got a flash of a badge.

"You're all under arrest!"

—12—

Kenneth Robeson sat typing in his one-room apartment. He'd been writing since morning, stopping only for obligations of Nature, including a three-hour sleep. By now he not only had the continuing characters, themes, and permanent locales of the series worked out in detail, he had half-written the first novel.

His fingers were flying, the keys spewing out golden words of high adventure and low comedy, when someone banged at his door. Impatiently, he rose and went to the door. He didn't want to be interrupted by anybody, not even by Trish Burke.

He flung the door open and looked up at the yellow face and eyes of Doc Fauve. The near giant looked even sicker. In his hand was a quart bottle, not of moonshine, but of Duggan's Dew of Kirkintilloch. At sight of that Robeson lost his cross expression. He was only a moderate drinker, but this brand of scotch was his favorite liquor. He hadn't been able to afford it for a long time.

"I know you're busy," Doc said. "But I'd like to have a few minutes. This is a sort of farewell visit. A couple of snorts, and I'll be off. But I'll leave the bottle behind as a memento mori."

Ken felt a shock travel through him. Fauve didn't expect to live much longer, and he'd come here so Ken Robeson could pay his premortem respects. And he was paying his way with the gift of scotch.

"Come on in," Robeson said. "Sit down."

He got two chipped coffee mugs and half-filled each. Doc, sitting on the worn and torn overstuffed chair, raised his mug. "Here's success to you in your career. And a wish that you and the young lady hit it off well."

Ken sipped at the delicious, heady liquor. Doc Fauve said, "Our bootlegger friends have had to close down their local stills. Sheriff Huisman is mad because Bensoni and Bufalo and the feds and God knows how many other agencies put the lid on everything. The word is mum. Nothing ever happened. He can't even talk about the affair, let alone arrest anybody. But he did find and destroy our friends' booze-making equipment. So they're bringing in stuff from Canada until the heat dies off. Lunger Tom slipped me a couple of cases of Duggan's yesterday."

He hadn't taken his greatcoat off. Now he opened it and revealed two more bottles of the priceless stuff in specially made pockets. He removed these and put them on the floor.

"These are yours, too. Whenever you take a drink, think of me. And the other guys, including Pat."

Robeson felt a little embarrassed at the references to Doc's coming demise. He said, "Listen, I'll think of you, of the whole bunch, every time I write a story in the series."

"Yeah. I'm glad you told me about it. I'm tickled. All the boys, and Pat, too, are tickled. It's a sort of immortality, you know.

"But whoever would have thought the other night that things'd turn out the way they did? Bierstoss was a German agent, planted years ago so he could operate as a respectable manufacturer and pillar of the church. And so here comes Professor Burke and his secret chemical formula. Burke thinks the chemical can force people to act morally. Bierstoss sees it as a great thing to make people sort of brain slaves. The formula could be modified, he hopes, to make people think as the German state wants them to think. Of course, he doesn't tell Burke this.

"But Burke goes crazy, poor old devil. The chemical injection brings up all the evil thoughts and repressed desires that are in even the most moral of people. So he sees his subconscious projected as a savage shadow which threatens his inner being. He can't endure it, and he goes insane.

"Bierstoss is upset by this. But he figures that maybe the effect can be used after all. All it needs is experimentation. There's plenty of human guinea pigs available to the Germans. So he sends Burke to Adlerdreck, who's a federal agent posing as a German sympathizer. Bierstoss thinks von Adlerdreck can get the formula out of Burke. Burke hadn't told Bierstoss what it was; he carried it in his head. But that head was all mixed up. So von Adlerdreck was supposed to catch Burke in a sane moment and get it from him, even if he had to use torture.

"Von Adlerdreck pretended to go along with Bierstoss so he could get a line on everybody in Bierstoss's organization. Including his tie-ups with the secret Italian Fascist cells. He used Ovarizi and Bufalo, who were also double agents."

Robeson laughed. "And Bensoni was another double agent working for another secret federal agency. Like Ovarizi and Bufalo, he'd established himself as a genuine gangster. But he didn't know the doctor and his two cronies were also Uncle Sam's employees."

Doc Fauve lost his smile for a moment. He shook his head. "Yeah. That Bensoni! He got lost in his role. It's all right to knock off rival gangs. But to murder a juvenile street gang just because they stole the hubcaps off his car. The man's a psychopath."

"That he is," Robeson said. "Still, that gang was mugging old ladies and beating up store owners if they didn't come across with protection money."

"I heard he's locked up in a mental hospital now," Doc Fauve said. "Though that may be just a story to account for his disappearance. He had to drop out of sight once his cover was blown."

Robeson nodded. Bensoni had been furious, but he had to tell everybody involved just who he was and what he'd been doing. First, he'd extracted a promise of silence from the people in the mooring-mast floor. Everybody agreed, especially after Bensoni had threatened to throw them in jail on trumped-up charges if they didn't keep their mouths shut. Then, while the elevator was kept from operating, so the police would be held off for a few minutes, Bensoni had revealed all that needed to be known.

Robeson had asked him if the story of his wife's running off with a used-car salesman was a fake, too. Bensoni had looked as if he were going to strike Robeson, and he'd told him that was none of his business.

Doc Fauve emptied his cup and poured in an even more generous portion. "Ah, the stuff that kills!" he said. "I'm glad to see you don't overindulge, my boy. Don't ever do it. It wrecks the brain, the belly, the kidneys, the liver, and isn't too good for the heart. And it causes financial distress, breaks up marriages and friendships, strews its golden path with cripples and corpses. Demon Rum and John Barleycorn! Thy names are Satan! Thy grip is legion! I campaigned for Prohibition, I know, and I'm a member of the WCTU. So much for a weak will and a lust to commit slow suicide!"

Robeson didn't want to get into a long drunken-maudlin scene. He said, "I'll have to get back to work soon. But first, let me tell you what I've done. I got a great concept for the series. It's about a sort of superman who, with his five aides, battles the forces of evil. He's one of the richest men in the world, young and handsome, absurdly knowledgeable, moral, and dedicated. He's been raised by scientists who've taught him all they know, which is about everything except women. He invents all sorts of things to benefit mankind and a lot of gadgets to help him in his battle against crime.

"His headquarters are on the 86th floor of a mid-Manhattan skyscraper."

Fauve raised his eyebrows. "There's only one building high enough to have an 86th floor. And that's the observation floor. Nobody lives there."

"Sure. But how many, including native New Yorkers, know that? Anyway, this is fiction, and I take poetic license."

"So, what's the name of our superhero?"

"Doc Savage. Fauve means a wild beast in French. That made me think of Savage. Catchy, isn't it? Has a nice ring—and Savage is also known as the Man of Bronze. In fact, that's the title of the story I'm writing. Doc is called this because his skin is a golden-bronze derived from long exposure to tropical suns. His hair is bronze, too."

Fauve laughed. "Unlike my yellow pigment, huh?"

"Well, one of your family names is du Bronce. That gave me the idea for the bronze aspect."

"And Doc Savage's eyes?"

"Yellow. No, don't laugh. Not bilious yellow, begging your pardon, but golden. Magnetic whirlpools of molten gold."

"You could have named your hero Sauvage. French for savage."

"No offense, Doc, but all the major leads in this series will have to have English names. The big boy at *S & S* says the readers don't like the good guys to have foreign names. It's okay to use Irish or Scottish names, but English names are surefire. It's the Anglo-Saxon complex.

"So, Hans van Rijnwijk becomes John Renwick. He was only a sergeant in real life, but in this series he's a colonel. The same with the other aides of Doc. They're brigadier-generals, majors, et cetera. And van Rijnwijk is promoted from a garage mechanic to one of the world's greatest engineers.

"Anderson Maypole Blidgett, 'Jocko,' a pharmacist, becomes Andrew Blodgett Mayfair, 'Monk,' one of the world's greatest industrial chemists. And so on with the others. You get the idea."

"What models do Patricia Coningway and Patricia Burke provide?"

"Well, I'll combine them, an ex-stripper and a bookkeeper for a beauty salon chain, into Patricia Savage, Doc's lovely young cousin. She'll come into the series later. She'll own and operate her own very posh beauty salon, and she'll be a scrapper who's always getting into trouble. A real Amazon but feminine. She ought to appeal to the adolescents who'll constitute the bulk of the readers.

"There'll be a lot of science in the series. Pseudo-science, rather. And the stories and the characters'll be bigger than life. A lot of the locales will be in far-off, exotic places. This is the Depression, Doc. The readers don't want grim stuff that'll just remind them of their sorry lot. If they're going to part with a hard-earned dime for a story, they'll only do it for something that takes them into the golden realms of fantasy. Where they can identify for a couple of hours with men and women who're rich, who fight successfully against the evils which make so many people feel helpless, powerless to battle."

"Sounds like a splendid idea," Doc Fauve said. "I wish I was going to be around long enough to see for myself! Oh, well, the others ought to live long enough to read some of the series. If they can stay sober long enough to read them.

"But what about this Ricardo Bensoni, Il Vendicativo? Since you've turned sick alcoholics and small-time rural moonshiners into heroes, what about Bensoni? You could use your inside-out magic on him and his associates, transmute their lead into gold."

"I've thought about that. If this series peters out eventually, I could start a new one. The hero could be Richard Benson, the Avenger. Gangsters do away with his wife and daughter in a vast, malevolent plot. Benson's hair turns white and his facial muscles become paralyzed from the shock. He vows to avenge the deaths of his loved ones, and he does. This gets him into the business of fighting crime—he's independently wealthy—and he forms *Justice, Incorporated,* an illegal but highly effective tool for laying low the great criminals of this nation.

"I might even use that Negro aide of Bensoni's as a model. But he won't be the type you usually find in pulp fiction, the 'hush ma mouf, feets-get-going' comical type. He'll be college-educated, speak excellent English, and be a genuine contributor to *Justice, Inc.* I don't know if the reader will accept this type of black, but by the time I get the Avenger series going, maybe readers' attitudes will've changed. We'll see."

Doc Fauve raised his mug. "I like your transmutations."

"They're such stuff as dreams are made on."

Doc drank, then said, "A slight paraphrase of Shakespeare's *The Tempest,* a line from Shakespeare's *The Tempest,* act four."

He refilled the mug and raised it again.

"And this is such drams as stiffs are made on."

Ken Robeson winced, and said, "Well, it's time for you to go back to your world and me to mine."

Doc Savage and the Cult of the Blue God

A Screen Treatment by Philip José Farmer Based on The Doc Savage Books

By Kenneth Robeson

Previously unpublished. Originally titled *Doc Savage: Archenemy of Evil.*

Whether one is shocked, repelled, or fascinated by Farmer's Doc Caliban stories, they are certainly hard to forget. In these pastiches of the 1930s and '40s pulp hero Doc Savage, Farmer lets loose his muse and delves unrestrained into the darker side of the character.

Doc Savage and the Cult of the Blue God is a straight portrayal of Doc and his aides. Invited by producer George Pal to write a screen treatment for the sequel to the 1975 film *Doc Savage: The Man of Bronze,* Farmer—with a biography and pastiches of Doc Savage on his resumé—was the perfect choice to pen a new Doc Savage adventure. But as Pal's first Savage movie tanked, plans for a sequel evaporated (though if one looks carefully at the end of Pal's film, a tag for *Doc Savage: Archenemy of Evil* may briefly be glimpsed).

While Farmer wrote of his anticipation for Pal's film in *Doc Savage: His Apocalyptic Life,* he has since expressed dissatisfaction with the finished product. In Farmer's opinion, Pal made camp of what was essentially already camp. Many Doc Savage fans have echoed this sentiment. Therefore it is even more interesting to see how Philip José Farmer would translate the bronze man onto the silver screen. Based loosely on the 1936 pulp novel *Murder Mirage,* Farmer's previously unpublished treatment is an action-packed adventure with more than one Wold Newton ancestor thrown in for fun.

Cast of Characters

DOC SAVAGE (Clark Savage, Jr.)—The man of bronze—A mental and physical superman. Trained from birth in science, the martial arts, and criminal detection. A wealthy man, he devotes his life to doing good and to battling evil.

THE FABULOUS FIVE—Doc's aides. These are:

> **MONK**—One of the world's greatest industrial chemists. Short, squat, aggressive, deliberately vulgar and ungrammatical. Seldom unaccompanied by his pet pig, HABEAS CORPUS.

> **HAM**—Monk's pal, though you'd never know it except in moments of peril. Tall, slim, one of the ten best-dressed men in the U.S. A distinguished Harvard law school graduate. Never seen without his sword cane.

> **RENNY**—One of the world's top civil engineers. A giant who likes to smash his huge fists through doors, just for fun.

> **LONG TOM**—An electronics wizard. Pale and skinny but he can lick nine men out of ten and the tenth will think he's tangled with a wildcat.

> **JOHNNY**—One of the world's foremost archaeologists and geologists. Two men tall and a half a man wide. Likes to use big words, mainly to bug his pals.

PATRICIA "PAT" SAVAGE—Doc's beautiful cousin. His lady auxiliary and a bronze knockout.

LADY CYNTHIA CLAYTON—A young blonde English explorer. An early victim of the Horrible Humpback.

RANYON CARTHERIS—Lady Cynthia's brother.

THE ALL-WISE ONE (The Horrible Humpback)—A hideous creature, leader of the Cult of the Blue God.

MARIAN LE DENE—Tall, beautiful, and bad. Ex-actress who plays several roles.

HADITH THE HATEFUL—A giant Arab who looks like a very dark, shaven-headed, earless Sidney Greenstreet. The All-Wise One's right-hand man.

MUSA THE TOAD—Hadith's brother. Looks like a very dark Peter Lorre, has the same voice and sneaky ways. Addicted to eating popcorn.

CAPTAIN GRIFFEPLUIS—French police chief in the North African state of Maghreb. Looks like Claude Rains.

A shabby street in lower Manhattan. Midnight, Christmas week, 1936. It's deserted except for a patrolman checking the doors of the grimy shops. He strolls out of view, around the corner to the right a model A Ford put-puts across the background.

The roar of an accelerating automobile engine comes from the left. Suddenly, tires screech. A sedan hurtles around the corner, left, foreground, on two wheels. It rolls over onto its top and stops with a crash against the right-hand curb.

A beautiful woman, Lady Cynthia Clayton, crawls out of the window on the driver's side. She rises shakily as a long black limousine squeals around the corner and screeches to a halt. Wild-eyed with terror, bloody, she limps painfully down the street.

Two cars swing around the corner at the other end of the street, cutting off her escape route. They contain Arabs, dressed in blue native robes, men from the state of Maghreb, near Morocco. The woman turns back and tries to open doors without success. In the front seat of the limousine is Hadith the Hateful, a giant Arab, a dark Sidney Greenstreet. The driver is Musa the Toad, his younger brother, a black Peter Lorre. Musa dips his hand into his ever-present bag of popcorn while his brother turns to the curtained rear.

"The woman is cornered, All-Wise One," Hadith says. "What should we do now?"

The curtains part, and a hideous face stares out. Below its shapeless blue hat, long greasy locks stream out. The face is a travesty of the Wicked Witch of The Wizard of Oz.

Gloved hands thrust from the curtains. They hold a round object, football-sized, wrapped in lead foil. Hadith and Musa stare at it with religious awe.

Musa opens his mouth, and the popcorn he'd tossed at it misses.

HADITH: "Praise be to the Blue God and his priest, the All-Wise One! The son of the Blue God is to be born again!"

He makes a religious sign, adding: "Glory to us, his worshippers! And the shadow death to his enemies!"

The woman, now quiet, cowers in a doorway, staring horrified as Hadith gets out of the car, the lead-foil object in his gloved hands. Hadith places it on the sidewalk, removes the lead foil, and reveals an object shaped like a blue brain. It pulses slightly, emanating a blue glow.

Seeing it, the woman screams. She limps up the street away from the object. The men in the cars duck down so that the metal bodies protect them.

Hadith picks up the blue ball and throws it with one hand. It lands about thirty feet from the screaming woman. Hadith runs back to the car and joins Musa, who had ducked down against the seat.

The curtains in the limousine's rear part again. The gloved hands hold a small metal box from the front of which a flanged cone projects. The cone points at the blue ball. A finger flicks a toggle switch, marked 'activate,' on the back end of the box. A weird pulsing sound is heard, a frequency obviously directed at the blue ball. The blue ball becomes brighter; its pulsings increase their rate of speed. The box's sound frequencies have stimulated the blue ball, and the glows are building up to something ominous.

The box is withdrawn; the curtains close. The blue ball glows brighter and brighter, faster and faster. The woman comes out of her paralysis and hobbles desperately away.

Suddenly, a blinding blue flash.

The woman stops, frozen, her head bent back, one arm stretched out as if clutching for safety. Between the pulsing blinding flashes, a black silhouette is visible. She has completely disappeared, but the silhouette—the shadow-print—remains, burned into the plate-glass front of a store. Metal objects hanging in the air fall onto the sidewalk, and we see that these are her shoe nails, garter clips, a diamond ring, bra clips. Everything of flesh and bone, and her woolen dress, silk stockings and underwear, cotton bra, felt hat, have been disintegrated by the climaxing blue flash.

The All-Wise One, the humpback, sticks the cone of the metal box through the curtains. His finger flicks the deactivate switch. An equally weird, but different, sound sings through the street. The glows slow down, become less bright. And then the ball is in its normal state, pulsing slightly and slowly.

Around the corner, two blocks away, a patrolman has seen the blue flashes. Blowing his whistle, he runs toward the flashes. Police car sirens begin to scream nearby.

The four cars are in a group now. Hadith returns the ball, wrapped in foil, to the Horrible Humpback. He orders the metal objects picked up and the shadowprint destroyed. As an Arab raises his automatic to shoot the glass shadowprint, the cop comes around the corner. He and the Arab shoot each other. The police sirens are very close now. The Humpback orders the gang to clear out at once. They can destroy the glass silhouette later; they can't take a chance on being caught by the police.

HADITH: "But, All-Wise One, she did succeed in sending a telegram to Doc Savage. What…"

THE ALL-WISE ONE, interrupting, snarls: "We'll take care of Savage! Now, get out of here! Quickly! Quickly!"

Cut to an exterior view of Doc's fabulous 86th floor penthouse. This is followed by the final scenes from the first movie, *Doc Savage: The Man of Bronze*. Scenes 464 through 468A show the penthouse interior (the library), the elevator stopping at the 86th floor, Doc leaving it, Doc entering the library, Doc listening to the voice on his robot Record-O-Phone.

The unidentified man, speaking with a Brooklyn accent, tells him that millions are in danger. He must get down to the Warfield Drug Store at once.

Cut to the phone booth outside the Warfield Drug Store. We see the back of what seems to be a man's head and hear the same voice Doc is listening to.

Cut back to Doc. Suddenly, the voice is choked off, as if hands had grabbed the speaker's throat. Doc runs out of the library, headed toward the drug store.

Cut to the phone booth. The man hangs the phone up, and he turns. But he is a woman, Marian Le Dene. She grins evilly at Hadith and Musa, who are standing outside the booth.

MARIAN: "Doc Savage fell for it, hook, line, and sinker!"

HADITH, grinning: "You're a great mimic, Mrs. Le Dene."

During this dialog, Musa has dropped some popcorn by the half-open phone-booth door. He also throws the empty sack on the sidewalk.

Renny is in his office, studying blueprints. A model suspension bridge is on the table before him. Superimposed: RENNY. IF HE CAN'T BUILD IT, NO ONE CAN. The big ring on Renny's finger suddenly flashes pulses of light and emits audible dots and dashes. Hearing—and seeing—the message from Doc, Renny says, "Holy Cow!" and he dashes off.

Johnny is in an office of an archaeological museum, working late. Superimposed: JOHNNY. HE DIGS UP DINOSAUR BONES AND BURIED CITIES. He is gluing the final pieces onto a reconstruction of an ancient piece of pottery. Johnny looks at it, puzzled, and scratches his head. Something is wrong. The ceramic has the exact shape of a modern toilet stool. Doc's message comes via his ring, and he leaves.

Long Tom is in his electrical laboratory. Superimposed: LONG TOM. HE MAKES ELECTRONS SAY UNCLE. He is working on a model of a machine—the Mancatcher Robot—we will see in Doc's laboratory later on. It has four wheels, a tubular body, a piston on top, a round opening in front, and a long wire-mesh bag attached to its rear. A tiny dummy of a man stands in front of it. Long Tom sprinkles a yellow powder on the miniature dummy, and he flicks a switch—"Dust Act"—on the model. It roars like a tiny vacuum cleaner, moves up to the dummy, sucks it into the front opening, and expels it into the rear bag. At this moment, Long Tom gets Doc's message and races away.

Ham is asleep in his apartment in the Midas Club. Superimposed: HAM. A LEGAL EAGLE. He is evidently having a bad dream. Doc's message issues from the big gold watch on the bedside table. It half-wakes him, and he sits up, muttering, "Your Honor, I never promised to marry Mabel." Then, fully awake, he grabs his clothes.

Monk is sleeping in his garishly furnished penthouse apartment. The bedroom door, open, shows his chemical laboratory. His ring emits the pulsing lights and the audible dot-dashes. He sleeps on. Suddenly, from under the covers, a baby pig, Habeas Corpus, erupts. It nuzzles Monk, oinks, but fails to rouse him. Finally, it nips his ear, bringing him upright, yelling, "Ham, keep your mitts off my girl!"

Montage of all five aides racing in their cars toward the Warfield Drug Store. Monk and Ham are in Monk's garish car "like a combination of sunset and earthquake."

Doc's bronzed Cord speeds by the sidestreet where the woman was shadowprinted. He sees the flashing red lights of police cars and an ambulance. He goes on to the phone booth, two blocks away around the corner. His car screeches to a halt a few feet beyond the booth. He leaps out and crosses before the Cord's headlights. The villains, in their cars a block away, see his silhouette.

The humpback points the sound-projector at the booth and flicks the activate switch. The weird pulsing noise begins. Doc, who notes everything, sees the popcorn and the sack left by Musa.

The blue light begins to build up its pulsations. Doc stops, utters the peculiar trilling sound he makes when he makes an unexpected discovery or has a brainstorm. Swift as a tiger, he whirls and dives away, toward the curb, behind his car.

A blinding blue flash fills the street. The humpback presses the deactivation switch. Presently, Hadith and Musa come out from the car. They approach the booth warily, look around.

HADITH: "Musa! He escaped the blue death! There is no shadowprint! He must be as cunning as the desert fox!"

MUSA, whining like Peter Lorre: "Then he may be hiding somewhere close by! I do not like this, Hadith! They say the man of bronze is a combination of tiger and ghost! Even in Africa they tell tales about him that freeze the blood!"

Hadith picks up the blue ball, and both run away.

Doc's face appears in the opening of a storm sewer just behind the Cord. He crawls out and sees the shadowprints of the popcorn and paper sack dropped by Musa. Again, he utters the weird trill. Now he knows what the blue ball does to objects of vegetable and animal origin, what fate was planned for him.

The two plug-uglies return to the humpback's car. Trembling, they confess that the man of bronze has somehow eluded the trap. The humpback curses—in Arabic—with such violence that the gang cringes.

Then, calming down somewhat, the All-Wise One says that it is time to prepare another trap. If the male hyena refuses to eat poisoned meat, he may be lured by the scent of a female hyena.

Doc hears a woman running desperately down the street. He fades back into the fog. The Cord's door slams. The woman is sitting in his car, panting hard. Doc suddenly appears behind her, startling her so that she opens her mouth to scream. At that moment, Doc's five aides appear in their cars. They swarm around him, but he tells them to follow him. And he drives with Marian Le Dene, posing as Lady Cynthia Clayton, to the scene of the shadowprint.

MARIAN LE DENE: "Thank God, you somehow escaped that blue death! I followed them after Marian and I escaped from them. I...I," she starts to weep, "I saw what happened to poor Marian. It was horrible. And, and I was afraid you'd die, too!"

DOC: "Slow down and back up. First, the identification. I'm Doc Savage..."

MARIAN, nodding: "Of course. I've seen your photos in the *Archaeological Journal*. And elsewhere. I'm Lady Cynthia Clayton. I..."

Doc hands her the telegram. "I got it. But almost too late. Why didn't you just phone me?"

MARIAN: "Because after I got away from them, they were too close. I ran into a Western Union office, sent the telegram, and went out the back way."

DOC: "Why didn't you call the police?"

MARIAN: "For the same reason. No time. Besides, everybody knows you can do things the police can't do."

DOC: "All right. I'd read in the archaeological periodicals that you and your brother, Ranyon Cartheris, were on an expedition to find the mythical city of Tasunan in the Sahara Desert."

MARIAN: "It is no myth. Ranyon and I, and my secretary, Marian Le Dene, did locate the ruins of Tasunan. We discovered that the legends are true. There *is* a strange mineral under the ruins. It's like no other radioactive substance ever discovered. It's a terrible thing, and it's being used by a strange sect of natives. They're not Moslems. They call themselves the Cult of the Blue God. And they conduct rites…"

Doc swings the car around the corner. He parks by the police cars and approaches the officers gathered by the shadowprint. They greet him warmly, since he has an honorary commission in the NYPD. He looks at the shadowprint and the metal objects on the sidewalk. He utters his strange trill.

MONK: "What is it, Doc?"

DOC: "It's too early to say anything definite."

An ambulance draws up. Two attendants get out; one looks at the silhouette burned into the glass. He whistles, and he says, "The coroner is going to have a hell of a time performing an autopsy on *that.*"

Marian (posing as Lady Cynthia) bursts into tears. Then she tells Doc that she recognizes the profile of her employee, Marian Le Dene. Evidently, the All-Wise One, the priest of the Cult of the Blue God, caught up with the poor woman.

Johnny has been moving a radiation counter (a pre-Geiger invented by Doc) around the area.

JOHNNY: "The count is high, Doc. But it's not at the danger level. And it's weakening at a very fast rate. Whatever caused it, it's not radium."

DOC: "Ham, call the Commissioner. Ask him if I can remove the silhouette. I want to study it."

HAM: "O.K. Doc. I see no problems."

Monk, an excellent ventriloquist, throws his voice so that his pig seems to be speaking. "You shyster! The only thing you could ever see is a well-turned ankle!"

RENNY: "Holy cow! Pipe down, you two clowns! This is no time to be horsing around! Can't you see that Lady Cynthia's had an awful shock?"

DOC: "You're right. Monk, Ham, you two take her to Pat's apartment. Pat can take care of her."

MONK: "But Doc! You know Pat! She'll want to get in on this! There's no talking her out of it once she gets wind of something adventurous. And I just can't say no to her."

DOC, aside to Ham: "Get the full story from Lady Cynthia on the way to Pat's. Then report back here."

Monk and Ham drive off with Marian in Monk's car.

Patricia Savage is asleep in bed. She is a beautiful bronze-haired woman, about thirty, with features resembling Doc's. Monk knocks on the door. Pat sits up, wide-awake, and pulls out a drawer in a bedside table. She removes a huge old-fashioned six-shooter, a family heirloom. With it in her hand, she approaches the living room door.

Superimposed: PAT SAVAGE, DOC'S COUSIN, LADY AUXILIARY AND BRONZE KNOCKOUT.

PAT: "Who is it?"

MONK, singing hoarsely: "Oh, it's only me from across the sea, Barnacle Bill, the Sailor! Open the door, or I'll huff and puff…"

PAT, smiling: "Oh, it's the miniature Gargantus. Come on in, you hairy throwback."

MONK, opening the door: "Thanks for the kind words, Pat." He stares at her. She is clad only in a low-cut filmy nightgown. (This is the only thing she wears, aside from a pair of high-heeled shoes, throughout the picture.)

MONK: "Wow! You're a pippin, Pat, a real peach! I ain't seen a doll that could stack up against you, not even at Minsky's."

HAM: "I'll say one thing for Monk, Pat. He is tops in vulgarity."

PAT, looking at Marian Le Dene: "Who is this?"

HAM, hesitantly: "Lady Cynthia, Pat Savage. Listen, Pat, Lady Cynthia's told us her whole story. She can fill you in. We have to get back to Doc."

PAT, her voice rising: "I *knew* it! You have the guts to wake me at this hour just to be a baby-sitter? You're on an interesting case, and you want me for the usual boring job, riding herd on the usual dizzy blonde?"

PAT, to Marian Le Dene: "Sorry, milady. No offense. It's just that I'm as good a man as any of Doc's gang, and just because I'm a woman I'm shut out of all the fun. I'm as hooked on excitement as Doc, but…"

Cut back to the shadowprint scene. The cops and ambulance attendants have gone. Doc is finishing the removal of the silhouette with a diamond glass-cutter. Doc and Johnny carry the glass shape between them toward the Cord. Renny and Long Tom are standing guard by the car. They carry superpistols, Doc's invention, rapid-firing guns shooting mercy bullets. The magazines are shaped like ram's horns.

DOC: "Careful, Johnny. If we break it, we'll lose our only clue."

JOHNNY: "This personage is bathically supersensitive to the frangibility potentialities of this vitrine megaphenomenon."

Long Tom, standing nearby in the doorway, rolls his eyes at Johnny's long words. Suddenly, around the corner in the foreground, out of the fog, tires screaming, hurtles a car. It holds five Arabs, all armed. The two on the side near Doc open fire. Renny and Long Tom shoot back, and the two Arabs collapse.

The driver, however, is determined to smash the glass shadow. He bounces it over the curb, heads it toward the shadowprint between Doc and Johnny. Doc snatches the glass shape from Johnny with one hand. Holding it high, he whirls like a matador, the fender almost scraping him. But the glass-shadow is safe. The car smashes into the storefront, and the Arabs are badly hurt, hors de combat.

Pat sits sleeping on a chair in the living room of her apartment. The six-shooter, handed down from Grandpa Savage, is in her lap. A wall-clock indicates 2:10 a.m. Background: a half-opened door reveals part of a bedroom. Presumably, Marian Le Dene (posing as Lady Cynthia) is in the bedroom. The door to the hallway opens quietly. A pair of bolt cutters snip the door chains. Pat starts, sits up. The door slams open, and Hadith and Musa enter, running. Pat is knocked down, her pistol sent flying. She gets to her feet and struggles with Hadith the Hateful. Tearing at him, she snatches off his blue headdress. She freezes in horror, staring at his earless head. Musa, holding a .45 automatic, goes toward the bedroom.

The fabulous five and Doc are in the vast 86th floor laboratory. Its tile floor is covered with alternating black, white, and red squares. Tables with chemical and electrical equipment are here and there. There are other items: a radiation chamber, deGraaf generators, etc. In the center is a gigantic circular glass fish tank, five feet high, twenty feet across. At its base is a sign: WARNING! PIRANHA AND POISON FISH! flanked by skulls and crossbones. Some yards away from it is a strange machine. This is the full-size mancatcher robot, model of which we saw in Long Tom's laboratory. The metal-mesh bag trailing from it is twenty feet long; the round opening in its mouth is large enough to swallow any invader.

Johnny comes from the reception room. He holds a photostat just delivered by the lobby pneumatic tube. He explains that it is a copy of the only known Tasunan tablet. It was brought out by an explorer in 1882. Johnny, the expert on ancient Semitic languages, shows it to them. It bears what is obviously a drawing of a shadowprint and letters in square Hebrew-looking script.

JOHNNY: "I had to wake up Professor Lovecraft, but he rushed a copy over by messenger. Irrefutably and indubitably, these are archaic Occidental pre-Punic alphabetical scrivenings."

MONK, irritably: "Fine! So you've shown off, you long-winded long-worded longshanks! What do those chicken scratches *mean*? In plain English?"

JOHNNY: "Divert your nasal appendage from non-personal phenomenosities or be prepared to experience the deprivation of a personal third dimension."

MONK, exploding: "You and your hundred-dollar words! What's he saying, Doc?"

DOC: "Don't stick your nose into business which doesn't concern you. Or you'll die the shadow death!"

JOHNNY: "Aside from this inscription, and what I've heard from superstitious natives, I know little about the lost city of Tasunan."

DOC: "The man who taught me the art of criminal detection has written a monograph about Tasunan legends. He knows more about that fabled civilization than anyone else on earth—except Lady Cynthia, of course. She's been there."

MONK: "She told Ham and me what happened. She and her brother, and her secretary, Marian Le Dene, found this ruined city in a valley in the very heart of the Sahara desert. The original Tasunanians have died out. But their religion still survives among the tribes that live in the mountains nearby. They worship the Blue God, whatever that is. The chief priest is called the All-Wise One. He's the horrible humpback Lady Cynthia told us about at Pat's apartment. The cult of the Blue God cornered the explorers and their Arab helpers in a building in the ruins. But Lady Cynthia and Marian Le Dene snuck out one night and got away. They got to a seaport and traveled to New York. The humpback and his gang followed them and caught them. Then the two women escaped. Lady Cynthia went one way, and Marian the other. The thugs caught up with poor Marian, and, well, how do you explain what they did to her, Doc?"

DOC: "I can't—as yet. Evidently the cultists have access to a mineral unknown to modern science. The legends indicate that this mineral is in a mine underneath the ruins of Tasunan. The Blue God is also supposed to be located there—in a temple of some sort. From what Lady Cynthia told you, Monk, I'd say that the radioactive element—let's call it *tasunite*—can be stimulated by a certain sound frequency. It can also be deactivated by another sound frequency."

RENNY: "So what do we do now, Doc? Go to North Africa, find Tasunan? Or what?"

DOC: "I think…" He pauses, holds up his hand. "Quiet!"

They listen intensely. The noise of an autogyro motor and thrash of vanes comes through the ceiling of the laboratory. Renny leaves the lab, goes down a short corridor, and enters the library. He sees an autogyro about to land on the glass roof of the library.

The autogyro, holding six armed Arabs, crashes through the glass roof. Its vanes bend up, and it falls a short distance onto the floor of the library. Renny ducks back, trying to avoid the falling glass.

In the laboratory, a section of wall explodes. Smoke pours in as Doc and his four aides lie stunned on the floor.

Arabs pour through the hole blown in the wall between the laboratory and the elevator corridor.

The door of the reception room has also been blown open. More armed Arabs rush through that into the reception room. It's a three-pronged attack by the All-Wise One and his gang!

Doc rolls over as dynamite smoke momentarily fills the laboratory. He stands up and opens a wall panel. He punches buttons and pulls a switch on a control panel. The many defenses and traps he's installed in his HQ are now set.

The Arabs in the laboratory level their tommies, rifles, and pistols, waiting for the smoke to clear. But, as Doc throws the switch, the metal weapons are torn out of the Arabs' hands, fly through the air, and cling to the wall. These have been seized by the giant magnets concealed in the walls.

The same thing happens to the weapons of the Arabs in the library.

Outside, in the corridor, the horrible humpback, the All-Wise One, looks worried as he hears the screams of fright from his followers.

The Arabs are deprived of their firearms. But they outnumber Doc and pals four to one. Now they seize anything that can be used as weapons. They break off glass bottles to use the jagged edges on the faces of the defenders. Some pick up jugs of acid from the supply shelves. Others remove their sashes to use as strangling cords. A few wield the lightweight wire chairs to use as clubs. And then they advance.

The great, 86th floor battle of the century had begun!

In the reception room, as seven men go toward the door to the lab, they leap back. A sheet of hot blue flame fills the doorway, burning gas from jets, one of Doc's traps.

Renny, in the library, throws a huge lamp at the six men advancing from the crashed autogyro. It intercepts a heavy metal ashtray hurled by an Arab. Renny charges them behind a chair raised before him. He knocks down two men with it before the others pile on top of him.

Doc catches a jug of acid thrown at him, whirls, tosses it back. The man catches it, but falls backward over Habeas Corpus behind him. The man screams, throws the jug away, and it breaks by two men grappling Long Tom. Yelling, their robes burning, they run off.

Three men swinging jagged glass bottles advance on Doc. Doc stamps on a black square, and two lines of red squares snap up, closing like wolf-trap jaws on one man's leg. Doc runs, leaps, kicks both men at the same time in the chests.

Musa the Toad and two burly men charge skinny Johnny. He stomps on a black square. It sinks in a little, and a glass partition drops from the ceiling before them. They run full tilt into it and fall, temporarily stunned.

Monk, bellowing, head down, charges two men. A thunder of hooves, a fanfare of trumpets, a crowd shouting, "El Toro! El Toro!" Monk slams into the two men, picking them up, carrying them backward against a wall, dropping their senseless bodies, shaking his head, glaring, as we hear cries of "Olé! Olé!"

In the library, the men on top of Renny rise up and out, petals from an exploding flower. Renny picks up one of the men to slug him but is hit with a leather strap over his head. Reeling, he makes for a revolving bookcase, two men behind him. He jumps onto the bookcase's side, clings, shoves it around with a foot. For a moment, he is out of sight. As it whirls him into view again, Renny, holding to the side with one hand, slugs a villain with the other. The second man stands back, waits to smash Renny with a lamp base. The case turns a second time: *no Renny*. The man looks behind the case; there is only a blank wall. He's joined by two more puzzled villains. Renny steps out from a wall-panel and attacks them from behind, plowing his monster fists into the necks of two before he's grabbed by three.

Hadith the Hateful, as big as Doc, grapples with the man of Bronze. They strain, facing each other, their hands interlocked. Hadith tries to bite Doc's nose off. Doc squeezes the Nubian's hands, bones crack, Hadith howls with pain and jumps back, his hands momentarily paralyzed.

Long Tom has been whirling like a dervish, throwing glowing dust from a vial on various villains, usually in their faces, blinding them. Now he flicks the 'Dust Act' control-panel switch on the giant suction-robot. It roars into action, its piston thumping, trailing the long bag behind it, its rotable eye seeking men covered by the dust. A glowing thug runs from it, trips, and is sucked into the big vent. Expelled out of the rear vent, he finds himself in the bag. He screams and struggles as he's dragged along. In a short time, the robot has drawn in four men, yelling, bumped and banged as the robot whips around, swinging them out like the end of a lash, knocking over tables and battlers.

Two Arabs charge Ham. He forgets about the magnetic fields radiating from devices behind the walls. He releases the blade from the end of his cane. The field snatches it from his hand and it sticks to the wall. Grinning, the two villains advance. Ham jumps forward, coming down on a black square. It sinks a little, obviously activating the two white squares on which the men stand. The squares slam horizontally back into the floor section. The two drop into the holes; the squares slam back, pinning the men across the chests.

Doc hurls a man away. The villain slides backward on his seat, stopping in a puddle of smoking acid. He leaps up, screaming, his rear end burning, and he jumps into the huge fish tank to wash the acid off. Even more quickly, he jumps out when the fish attack him.

Doc thrusts an Arab away, leans down, flicks a switch at the base of the fish tank. Its water level sinks a few inches, revealing the top of a wide glass tube in the center of the tank.

A villain, yelling, is hanging on to the leg of a massive table laden with chemical equipment. The robot's suction pulls him and the table steadily toward the intake. The man's boots and robe are whisked into the vent. The table tilts over, spilling its retorts and racks of vials of fluid. Fireworks! Smoke! Into the intake goes the Arab and out into the bag, exploding chemicals following him.

Suddenly, the gas supply exhausted, the flames shooting across the door go out. The men in the reception room charge through the doorway. The foremost is given two fingers in the eyes, the Arab dances around until he's grabbed by Doc. Gripping the man by his shirt and the seat of his pants, Doc hurls him through the air. The man's flying body bowls over four men at the doorway.

Renny, in the library, knocks down an Arab with his fist. As he half-turns, he sees an Arab opening the door from the corridor to the library. He slams the door-panel with his huge fist, closing the door but also driving his fist through the panel. His fist rams into the Arab's face, on the other side of the door. The Arab drops.

Renny turns to face four Arabs, all bloody and tattered but determined. They back him up against the fireplace.

In the laboratory, Long Tom is knocked down. His out-flung hand accidentally flicks the robot's switch from "Dust Act" to "Nondust Act." The machine wheels, its detector now set on those who don't have dust on them. Long Tom is sucked into the machine and vented out into its bag.

Monk, battling two men, sees this. He cries out for someone to reset the switch to "Dust Act." But the robot turns toward Monk its body-laden bag whipping around and knocking down Ham and two Arabs. The robot sucks in the pig, and we see him shot into the bag. He then bites a fellow-captive, a villain, on the nose.

Pursued by the machine, Monk runs through the doorway into the corridor to the library. It right-angles, enabling Monk to roll to one side. Carried by its great momentum, the robot bursts the doorway, bringing down the lab wall around it. It goes across the hall, and smashes through the wall into the library before stopping.

Renny, half-senseless, is being slugged by two Arabs when the front end of the robot explodes the fireplace. All the fighters are knocked out and half-buried by debris. Then the bricks, plaster, mantelpiece, etc., start to disappear, sucked into the bag.

In the bag, Long Tom cries out that the debris will squeeze the occupants of the bag to death. Monk turns the robot off, steps through the doorway into the lab, and is knocked out with a huge dictionary by an Arab.

Ham stuns an Arab with an attaché case. But an Arab rabbit punches him, and Ham sags.

Doc and Johnny and the eleven Arabs left pause. They catch their breath while smoke from spilled chemicals and acid swirls through the lab. They cough, their eyes water, while they estimate their chances. This is too large a group for even Doc and Johnny to handle. As the Arabs move toward them, Doc cries out for Johnny to run. Johnny objects; Doc says it's an order. Johnny runs for the toilet door, gets through it just before a flying jug breaks against it, spilling its acid.

Inside the toilet, Johnny locks the door, throws a switch on a wall, and a panel opens. Johnny goes through it as six pipes lower through holes in the ceiling.

Doc backs toward the fish tank as the Arabs warily advance on him. Two big Arabs charge the toilet door and slam into it. It flies a little way inward, then out, forced by a roomful of water. Johnny has activated the mechanism which rapidly fills the toilet to the ceiling with water. The flood knocks over the two Arabs and comes roaring out, scaring the others.

Taking advantage of the confusion, Doc wheels, runs, and leaps onto the rim of the tank. He jumps out into the air and straight down the transparent tube in the center of the tank. A villain tosses a jug down the shaft. A crash, and acrid fumes rise out of the tube.

Doc dives out of the door into a room in the floor below. The splashed acid almost gets him. He goes out of the room into the corridor of the 85th floor. He runs up the steps and into the corridor leading to the reception room. The Arabs still able to walk are limping into the elevators. They've had more than enough. The humpback, who has been standing guard in the corridor all this time, shoots his Tommy gun at Doc. Doc ducks back around the corner.

Dawn. Arabs are stretched unconscious on the laboratory floor. Long Tom and the pig are being pulled from the Mancatcher Robot's bag. Some men in bronze uniforms (bearing the label: DOC SAVAGE'S REHABILITATION CENTER) are carrying Arabs out on stretchers.

ATTENDANT FROM THE CENTER: "Doc, this is the biggest haul of crooks you've ever made."

DOC: "Yes. When I have time, I'll come up to the Rehabilitation Center. But it may be a month before I can perform the operation that will turn them into honest men."

ATTENDANT: "There's no hurry, Doc. These bimbos will be in the hospital ward for a month at least."

Doc gives a truth serum hypo to an Arab. He quickly questions him. He's shocked when told that the women (Pat and Lady Cynthia) will be flown to the North African nation of Maghreb and then to Tasunan.

JOHNNY: "You're wanted on the phone, Doc. I'm afraid it's bad news."

Doc answers. He hears a low gravelly voice, the humpback's (All-Wise One's) voice. Pat and Lady Cynthia are in the humpback's hands. Unless Doc drops the case, the two women will be tortured and then killed. And Arabs are masters of torture techniques.

Doc tells the humpback that he'll track down the whole gang and kill them if Pat and the woman are harmed. The humpback hangs up. Doc tells the five the situation. Agony. What to do?

LONG TOM: "The way I see it, there's only one thing to do. Go after them! You know as well as I do, Doc, that they're not going to release Pat and Lady Cynthia. They'll be killed, anyway."

RENNY: "Besides, when did we ever let danger to a hostage stop us! Once you give in to that kind of hellish blackmail you open the way for more of the same. I agree with Long Tom, Doc, that we cannot sit down and fold our hands because of possible harm to hostages. We go after the murderers, and if the women get killed, it'll be a terrible thing. But…"

DOC: "You're right. It's like the Arab that felt sorry for his camel during a sandstorm. He let the camel stick his nose in the tent. Before it was over, the camel was all the way in the tent and had crowded the Arab out. And the Arab died in the storm!"

Decision: Tally-ho!

They go into the pneumatic tube room. This houses the 86th floor terminus of a giant pneumatic tube. The great pipe goes straight down through the skyscraper into the Manhattan bedrock, curves, becomes horizontal, and curves up again to end in the Hidalgo Trading Company. The vehicle shot through the tube by air pressure is bullet-shaped, large enough to hold six men. They jam into it and put on acceleration harnesses. Doc presses a button on the panel in the vehicle (which Monk calls the 'flea run' or 'go-devil'). The port seals the vehicle, and then the massive cap of the pipe swings shut.

There's a whoosh of air. The go-devil travels at a hundred miles an hour.

About twenty seconds later, the go-devil stops at the other terminus. This is inside the Hidalgo Trading Company, a huge warehouse building on the Hudson River near 35th Street. It also houses Doc's dirigible, amphibian planes, a yacht, and his submarine.

Inside the padded car, Monk starts to open the door. Doc says: "Wait, Monk!" He points to a flashing red light on the instrument board.

Four Arabs, armed, are waiting for Doc and crew to get out of the go-devil. But body capacity alarms have warned Doc of the presence of intruders.

Directly above the go-devil is Doc's fabulous futuristic-looking airship: the DSD-1. Its bronze skin shines in the bright floodlights. It's about four hundred feet long, porpoise-shaped, streamlined. The control room is inside the nose. Its diesel motors are mounted in two tunnels on each side, creating a jet effect during flight.

DOC: "It's a trap! But we're not going to spring it!" He punches a control board button.

Cables with magnetic clamps at their ends descend from the airship. At the same time, the roof opens into two wide sections. As the frustrated Arabs shoot at the bulletproof go-devil, the clamps lift it. Mooring cables fall from the airship. It rises straight up, winches inside it pulling the go-devil up inside an opening on its bottom.

When the DSD-1 is out at sea, the go-devil is released. It falls into the ocean.

Later, inside the bridge of the DSD-1, Renny is at the steering wheel. Ahead is a black stormfront. Long Tom turns from the radio set. He tells Doc, who's working at the navigator's table, that he's sent the radiogram to England.

Inside a little villa on the English Sussex Coast. Two aged men, obviously Sherlock Holmes and Dr. Watson in retirement, are in the front room. Through the window we see rows of beehives.

Watson, puffing his pipe, rises when the doorbell rings, and he takes a telegram from a uniformed boy. Holmes puts down the violin he's been playing and takes the message from Watson. After scanning it, he says, "It's from my most brilliant pupil, Doc Savage. You remember him, of course. And his father, the young man who was implicated when the duke's son was kidnapped? In Hallamshire?"

WATSON: "Harrumph! Of course I do, old friend. I'm not so old that I can't remember *that* case! The brutal accomplice of Savage, Senior, murdered a man, though Savage, Senior had nothing to do with that terrible deed. But he was so horrified that he fled to the States and there..."

HOLMES (interrupting): "And there decided to dedicate his life to making recompense. In a sort of magnificent obsession, he would battle evil wherever he found it: But it was his goal to *rehabilitate* the criminal, not to kill or punish him. He brought up his son with the same ideals. To this end he saw to it that Savage Junior was tutored by the world's greatest scientists and criminologists. Doc and his gallant band of specialists go everywhere, all over the world, fighting men of evil against whom both the police and decent citizens are helpless. If I were not so old, my dear fellow, I would be with them on this quest. Even so, I am still of some help to Doc."

He looks along a shelf of reference books. "Doc wants to know everything available about the fabled Saharan city of Tasunan. I am, I must confess, the foremost—ahem!—authority on the subject. Ah, here it is!"

He takes out a book and begins reading.

The Ford trimotor airplane in which the villains flew from a Long Island airport comes down for a landing. Below it is the glittering white city of Abyad, capital of the North African state of Maghreb. The primitive landing strip is about a mile from the city. By it wait four cars to pick up the trimotor's passengers. The humpback has radioed ahead to his colleagues in Abyad to get them away before the police find out about them.

In the plane are Arabs, Pat, and Lady Cynthia (Marian Le Dene). Pat's hands are tied. Lady Cynthia is in the seat behind Pat. We can't see her hands so we don't know if she's tied or not. A curtained compartment in the rear indicates that the Horrible Humpback must be sitting there. As the plane comes in for a landing, Pat tries a desperate trick. This is her only chance to escape, and she may be killed. She rubs the heels of her shoes together. The friction causes the chemicals impregnating the heels (one of Doc's inventions) to explode. She has shut her eyes, and the glare blinds everybody else aboard. The pilot, startled, unable to see, slews the plane around. It crashes on one wing, swings around, and overturns.

But Pat is seized by the men in the cars as she crawls out. The villains and the captives ride furiously toward the city. One of the cars is a limousine with a curtained rear compartment.

The storm has overtaken the DSD-1. The crew strap themselves down in the violently buffeted airship. Thunder bellows, and lightning strikes around the ship. Suddenly, the craft is struck with an especially savage gust.

Monk reports via intercom that the starboard horizontal surface is damaged by the wind. The elevator framework is twisted upward, and the plastic skin has been stripped off much of the surface and the elevator.

Renny, at the wheel, says he knows this; he can't get the starboard elevator to respond.

Doc runs out of the bridge and along the lower catwalk inside the airship to the stern. As he arrives, he sees smoke pouring out of the motor controlling the cables to the elevator. The cables snap under the strain, one narrowly missing Doc. The airship is pointed upward now; Renny reports that they're gaining altitude and there's nothing he can do about it.

Long Tom and Johnny hand out oxygen masks. If they keep on rising, their limited oxygen supply will run out, and they'll strangle in the too-thin air. Monk asks why they don't valve out helium to bring the ship to a lower altitude. Renny tells him he's released all the gas he can safely lose. After a certain amount is gone, the ship will lose its dynamic lift, and it will fall into the ocean.

At a port by the horizontal surface, Monk and Ham pay out a rope attached to Doc's waist. He is climbing out onto the surface, hanging on to the naked skeleton of the surface while the ship bucks and lightning cracks around him. Fortunately, the elevator has retained its skin (or most of it). Otherwise, the air would just whistle through the framework, affecting the elevator not at all. Doc makes his perilous way to the middle of the main horizontal member. He kicks through some skin on it, hangs upside down for a moment, then swings his body upward. Gripping the strut of the elevator, which is at right-angles to the main strut, he pulls downward on it. While lightning illumines him, he exerts a power only the mighty man of bronze possesses. Slowly, protesting metallically, the elevator comes down.

Another violent blast, rolling the ship to port and almost wrenching Doc loose. Monk yells through the wind that the port elevator has been stripped of its skin. The only way they can go downward now is by use of the starboard elevator. Doc, his swelling muscles tearing his shirt, pulls down again. The elevator reluctantly responds.

Emerging from the stormfront into the sunlight, comes the DSD-1. It is headed at a slant toward the coast of North Africa. Ahead is the shining white, walled, and minareted city of Abyad, capital of Maghreb. Doc is still gripping the elevator, holding it down so that the ship can land.

Near the landing strip (where the wrecked trimotor is) is the dirigible. Its nose is tied to an abandoned minaret. Mooring cables are tied to rocks. Renny and Long Tom are already repairing the elevator structure. Doc is talking to Captain Griffepluis who looks like Claude Rains. Griffepluis is the French chief of police of Abyad.

GRIFFEPLUIS: "Of course, Doc, I will cooperate fully. But the All-Wise One and his gang fled into the Kasbah before I was even aware that they were here. If I should ever get my hands on *that* monster, and his co-murderers, Hadith and Musa, I'll make sure that they end up beneath the guillotine."

DOC: "I thank you for your offer. But I think that one man, alone, in disguise, of course, might be more effective than a horde of policemen!"

GRIFFEPLUIS, shrugging: "Perhaps. But you say that Marian Le Dene, Lady Cynthia's secretary, has met a horrible death. You may be sure that these worshippers of the Blue God will not hesitate to kill your cousin and Lady Cynthia if you press them too hard.

"I was horrified when I heard about Le Dene. Quel beauté! What a woman! She was an actress, you know. Her traveling troupe folded while in Abyad, and she was left penniless. Lady Cynthia felt sorry for her and hired her as a companion and secretary. Poor woman! She would have been better off if she had remained here, instead of going on that ill-fated expedition.

Better hungry than dead. Though I doubt, my dear Doc, that she would have had to go hungry long. I myself, well, never mind that. I am a married man…"

A late afternoon sun rides over a street in the Kasbah. Through the crowd passes a giant figure, Doc in native clothes. Under a sash around his waist is a ticking radiation counter. As he nears a five-story building, higher than its neighbors, a man crosses the street in front of Doc. He looks remarkably like Charles Boyer as Pepe Le Moko.

The counter suddenly chatters wildly. Doc steps up to the Bedouin standing guard in the doorway. He squeezes the neck nerves of the guard, paralyzing him, and drags the man inside.

Doc goes to the fifth story, passing a room full of villains. He sees two armed Bedouins outside a door around the corner. Doc takes two glass balls from beneath his robes and tosses them down the hall. The balls shatter, releasing a gas. The guards fall asleep. Doc tries the door, finds it locked, searches the guard but fails to find a key.

Doc raps softly on the door, and Pat replies. Lady Cynthia is with her. She has been kept elsewhere, but some minutes ago she was put with Pat. Pat doesn't know why.

Doc looks wise. (Later, we find out that Doc has suspected that Lady Cynthia is really Marian Le Dene.)

Doc shoots the lock off with a guard's rifle. The two women run out while Doc fires, driving Hadith and his men back into their room. A horde of Bedouins charges up the steps from the fourth floor. Doc upsets a giant vase on the landing, crushing many below. But they are too numerous. He and the women retreat up steps onto the rooftop.

DOC: "Why are you limping, Pat? Did they hurt you?"

PAT: "Doc, I have a bone to pick with you. I tried to wreck the plane when it landed so I could get away. I rubbed the heels of my shoes together, and the chemicals exploded alright! They darn near blew my foot off!"

DOC: "Sorry about that, Pat. But you knew you weren't supposed to be wearing the shoes when you set the chemicals off."

PAT: "My hands were tied, Doc I couldn't take my shoes off with my *teeth*!"

Doc and the women are trapped on the rooftop. The neighboring houses are three stories lower, too low to jump down onto. Doc shoots near the villains' heads whenever they try to get on the roof. When his ammunition is exhausted, the Arabs boil out, and a battle follows. Doc's robe is torn off, revealing a thin square pack attached to his back by a belt and shoulder straps.

Pat is carried off. Unable to get to her, menaced by knives, Doc seizes Lady Cynthia (Marian Le Dene). He leaps off the roof over the street. An explosion sounds as a gas cartridge blows the small parachute to instant fullness.

Doc and the woman land on a camel, which gallops crazily down the street, carrying them to safety.

Monk and Ham enter an Abyad night club with their dates, two French peaches. The club looks exactly like that in the movie, *Casablanca.* In the background, by a piano played by a black man (Sam) stands a Humphrey Bogart-like character. He's listening to "As Time Goes By."

Ham is furious. Monk is carrying the pig in one arm, and it's dressed exactly like Ham. A top hat, dark glasses, white shirt, dark tie, tails, gloves, shoes. They sit down at a table. Monk tells the staring waiter that it's Ham's child, and he orders a high chair for it.

Monk goes to the Men's room. Ham takes one shoe off and plays footsie with Monk's date. (Ham and Monk are always trying to steal each other's girlfriend.)

Monk comes out of the Men's Room and sees what Ham's doing. He returns to the table, sets Habeas Corpus on the floor, and points at Ham's unshod foot. The pig bites down hard on Ham's toe. Yelling, holding his toe, Ham hops around on one foot.

The pig runs out on the floor, squealing, losing its hat and glasses. The waiters and the Moslem customers become furious. By the beard of Allah! The Ferengi have brought in a pig, a religiously unclean beast!

A riot follows.

A corridor in the Abyad jail. Monk and Ham are behind bars listening to Doc ream them out. Captain Griffepluis stands by grimly.

DOC: "Here you are, the world's greatest industrial chemist and Harvard's most distinguished law graduate, acting like fifteen year old kids! And not very bright kids at that. I told you how Moslems feel about pigs. Disgraceful! I'm sorry, but we're in a foreign country, and we have to obey its laws. You'll just have to serve out your sentences while the rest of us go looking for Pat."

The Terrible Twain raise a howl, but Doc and the captain walk away.

In the jail's admittance room, Doc, smiling, tells the captain to let the two Katzenjammer Kids sweat it out for a few hours. Maybe it'll teach them a lesson, though he doubts it. The captain winks.

The airship, repaired, is on its way to Tasunan. High above, a blazing Saharan sun. The Fabulous Five are in the "bridge," the control room. In the distance, the white city of Abyad. Long Tom and Johnny search the desert with binoculars.

MONK: "See anything yet, gents?"

LONG TOM: "Not a caravan in sight. But they could be hidden behind those high hills or in a dry riverbed."

HAM: "We know they're not in the city. Captain Griffepluis went through the Kasbah like a monkey looking for fleas. They must have sneaked out right after Doc rescued Lady Cynthia."

MONK: "They got three days' head start on us. But they can't have gotten too far. We'll find them. Say! Where are Doc and Lady Cynthia?"

RENNY: "Doc's doing his daily two-hour exercise in the stern observation room. I guess she's with him."

LONG TOM: "Resting, I suppose. She was pretty shaken up. She had Doc take her to the airship right after he rescued her. She wouldn't even see Captain Griffepluis. Said she only felt safe here."

MONK: "Poor woman! She must be lonely. I think I'll go aft and keep her company."

HAM: "You sad-sack skirt-chaser! You don't have a chance with her! Why would a beautiful cultured English aristocrat give you a tumble? A swineherder"—he looks at the pig—"who looks like an ape!"

MONK: "Yeah? Well, I've sunk pretty low sometimes, mainly from associating with you. But I never was so degenerate I was an ambulance chaser. That's about as near the bottom as you can get!"

He leaves through the door. Ham follows him, remarking that he intends to protect Lady Cynthia from apes, pigs, and other repulsive creatures.

A second later, they are back in the control room, their arms up in the air.

Doc is in the stern observation room, exercising. As a radio plays Arabic music, he ripples his muscles in tune with the weird ululations. Lady Cynthia (Marian Le Dene) enters. She stops, stares with admiration at his magnificent figure, clothed only in bathing trunks. She licks her lips.

Doc turns and is startled to see her. She has removed her blouse and skirt and is wearing only a bra and panties. Belly-dancing, she moves toward him. He reaches over and turns off the radio, but she puts her arms around his neck.

MARIAN (as Lady Cynthia), huskily: "You're a magnificent man, Doc. Ever since you held me in your arms when you jumped off the roof in the Kasbah, I've had this...this feeling! This yearning!"

DOC: "I don't want to hurt your feelings, Lady Cynthia. But what you're thinking of just can't be."

MARIAN: "Why not? This is the twentieth-century; we're not living in the Victorian age. Women have just as strong desires as men. Why should men be able to cat around all they want, yet we women have to be so chaste, so virtuous. Goddesses on a pedestal and all that sort of nonsense.

"I'm a passionate woman, Doc, and I've not had...been with...a man for almost a year."

DOC: "You misunderstand me, Lady Cynthia."

MARIAN: "Why so formal? Call me Cynthia. All my close friends do. And I certainly feel friendly. And I am close. Though I'd like to be even closer."

DOC, gently disengaging her arms, but he's breathing hard: "You still don't understand. I can't allow myself to become emotionally involved with a woman. I have many enemies, and they'd be only too glad to grab any woman with whom I was...close. They'd use her against me."

MARIAN, scornfully: "I wasn't asking you to *marry* me!"

DOC: "Put your clothes on. I know you weren't. But even if I am inclined to do what you suggest...and I am tempted...after all, I am human...I wouldn't.

This is neither the time nor place. All hell might break loose any moment. And my friends might walk in at any moment.

"But those are not the compelling factors. I have a code, Lady Cynthia. It might seem simple and corny to you, too idealistic…"

MARIAN: "I know all about your code! Monk recited it to me! I thought I was at a Boy Scouts' meeting!"

She laughs scornfully.

DOC: "Do you remember the last line of the code?"

MARIAN: "I thought I'd break up. Of course, I do." She recites: "Let me do right to all, and wrong no man."

DOC: "I should have added, *nor wrong any woman, either!*"

Furious, the woman grabs her clothes and stalks out, leaving the door open. Doc puts on his shirt and pants. As he is tying his shoes, an Arab enters. Doc straightens up, his back to the Arab. The Arab crashes the butt of his .45 automatic on top of Doc's head. Doc reels under a blow that should have fractured his skull. But he remains half-conscious.

Doc leans against the open window, shaking his head. The Arab, grinning evilly, rushes him and forces him halfway out the window. Doc catches hold of the window ledge with one hand. With the other, he grabs his own hair. And he pulls from his head a wig, a thin hard metal wig! It is this that softened the blow of the gun!

Using its edge, he slams the Arab in the neck. The man falls unconscious.

Doc runs out onto the bottom catwalk. The woman has disappeared. Knowing that there must be other villains stowed away, Doc runs down the catwalk, headed for the control room. As he does so, he suddenly stops. Some pieces of popcorn have fallen from above onto the catwalk before him.

He looks up through the maze of girders, wires, and giant gas cells. And he sees an Arab and Musa, both wearing parachutes, on the structure above a gas cell. The Arab is finishing attaching a bomb to the metal just above the helium bag. Musa, holding a handful of the popcorn he carries in a huge pocket of his robe, is frozen at the sight of Doc.

In the control room, Ham and Monk back up. An Arab, wearing a parachute, herds them in with a pistol. Renny stays at the wheel; Long Tom and Johnny raise their hands.

MONK: "We're being highjacked!"

HAM: "We're going to list heavily to port, gentlemen."

THE ARAB: "No talking. Or I kill you!"

Monk whistles softly. The pig cocks its ears. Evidently, this is a signal for it. It runs behind the Arab, who steps away to avoid contact with the religiously unclean beast. Renny spins the wheel, and the dirigible heels to the left. The Arab is pitched to one side. Long Tom and Johnny, expecting the maneuver, leap on him. The Arab recovers, backs up, waving the gun. He trips backward over Habeas Corpus, and four of the aides pile on him.

The four aides boil out of the control room.

Doc points upward, and they see the two with the bomb. Doc begins climbing up through the maze. Monk also starts climbing. Doc pauses to yell at the others to put on their chutes. If the bomb goes off now, they've had it.

Monk keeps on climbing. The others obey. The two Arabs work frantically. Monk and Doc climb up near the Arabs. They straighten up, having set the bomb to go off. Musa jumps, falls through the maze and breaks through the thin fabric of the hull.

The other Arab watches, then jumps. As he does so, Monk thrusts a knife into his chute. He falls through the hull, unable to open the chute. Monk looks down through the hole watching him. As Doc arrives, he shakes his head.

MONK: "He bounced so high, he musta been made of rubber"

DOC, reproachfully: "You're too bloodthirsty, Monk. You didn't have to do that."

MONK: "Gee, Doc, you know how impulsive I am!"

Doc gives the bomb one quick look. It's no use trying to defuse it. Any tampering will blow it that much sooner.

The five chute out several cases of supplies and devices. Then they start to put on their parachutes. They're short one chute, since Doc insists on giving one to the captured Arab in the control room.

DOC: "Have any of you seen Lady Cynthia?"

The others reply that they haven't. Doc looks puzzled.

DOC: "There are some extra chutes in the observation room. Lady Cynthia and I can use them. But where could she have gone to?"

MONK, finishing strapping his chute: "Maybe them Arabs got her, Doc."

DOC: "I hope not. But she disappeared so suddenly..."

He runs out of the control room and along the catwalk, calling her name. No answer. In the observation room, he picks up a parachute.

By then his men and the cases are in the air, their chutes open. The men look up at the DSD-1, wondering when Doc will leap.

The airship explodes violently. Close-up. Doc, his chute in one hand, is blown out of the window of the observation room.

The dirigible, torn in half, falls burning.

Doc, unconscious, but still gripping the chute, falls, falls. His men yell with horror.

Doc wakes up and straps on the chute, though with difficulty. He pulls the ripcord just in time. The chute snaps open very close to the ground.

The group are trudging on foot, carrying the cases, through the desert. They enter a native village.

The group, on camels purchased from the natives, leaves the village. Ham gets seasick. Monk laughs at Ham, then also turns green.

The group is camped out in the desert. A sandstorm sweeps up, enveloping them, blowing the tents over. The camels run off into the storm.

The group, thirsty, hungry, are on foot again.

Suddenly, on the ridge before them, two Arabs riding horses appear. A moment later, fifty riders face them. They are dressed in blue, and Monk thinks they must be the Horrible Humpback's gang. The nomads charge, yelling, waving their long flintlock rifles, firing some. As they get closer, the group sees that the riders are wearing veils.

DOC: "They may be dangerous, but they're not the All-Wise One's men. They are Touaregs. Touareg men wear veils but their women leave the face exposed. Just the opposite of the custom of Arabs!"

MONK: "What's the difference if they kill us?"

The fifty riders pull up short, horses rearing. Then, a moment of silence as the five and Doc get ready to battle hopeless odds, to sell their lives dearly.

The chief gets down from his horse, his hand on his scimitar. He strides up to Doc, stares at him from behind the sinister veil. Doc says nothing, waits. Suddenly, the man opens the veil; he's smiling.

DOC: "Abu ben Adhem!"

TOUAREG CHIEF: "My old friend and savior of my only son." And he steps forward and embraces Doc.

Doc, it seems, once performed an operation that saved the chief's son.

There is joy and jubilation. The chief gives the group horses. Unfortunately, he doesn't have quite enough. But one of the five can ride an ass.

Ham and Monk toss a coin to decide who'll get the horse. Ham knows that Monk always calls tails; he flips a coin with two heads. Unfortunately, he accidentally drops it (or it slips through a hole in his pocket). Monk picks it up. Instead of taking immediate revenge, he waits until Ham has mounted his horse.

Monk gets on the ass.

HAM, grinning: "Monk, how does it feel to be riding your *brother*?"

Monk tosses firecrackers under the horse's tail. It rears, tumbling Ham, while Monk roars with laughter.

Doc and the five are riding down a mountain pass in early morning. They are on a narrow stone ledge which curves around the cliff. Opposite is another cliff, and five hundred feet below, at the bottom of the canyon, is a mountain stream.

Through a break in the mountains they see spread below the Valley Of Tasunan. In its middle is a pile of ruins, though some buildings still stand here and there. It's a blue city, its stones composed of something like blue jade.

The tents of the villains are pitched outside the city on sand dunes. From the city rises the black smoke of gunpowder.

Cut to an ancient blue building, covered with a greenish moss, forming part of the wall. Its lower part is a gigantic doorway, and in this we see Ranyon Cartheris, Lady Clayton's brother. With him are some of his men, Arabs. They shoot at the Arabs in other buildings. Obviously, they are very low on ammunition. A shot zings off a wall, chipping pieces of stone, which cut Hadith the Hateful. He curses in Arabic.

Zoom across to the camp. We catch a glimpse of the All-Wise One, the Horrible Humpback, in his blue tent.

Back to the ledge on the mountain. As the group rides single file around a corner of the cliff, they are confronted by ten Arabs. These are on a broadening of the path and are armed with rifles and one machine gun.

Doc, near the rear, looks behind him. More Arabs! They've hidden behind an outcropping of the cliff behind them. The five and Doc are cornered!

DOC dismounts and whispers: "I hate to desert you! But somebody has to be free to get you out of this when the chance comes!"

MONK: "That's O.K., Doc. It's the only logical thing to do. But just how in jumping blue blazes do you plan to leave this place? You ain't gonna try and dive, are you? Doc even *you* couldn't make it!"

DOC: "Don't worry, Monk. But a little prayer for me wouldn't hurt."

He presses a button on the long case borne by the horse beside him. The top of the case flies open, and a long flat bundle flies out. Doc grabs it, twists a dial on its side, and leaps into the air, clutching it.

The Arabs yell with surprise, then watch Doc falling. After a descent of fifty feet, the bundle spreads out. It's become a hang glider! Doc climbs into the strap beneath it, tilts it, and he's gliding along the canyon wall. The Arabs fire their rifles; the machine gun is depressed and begins shooting at him.

Doc is going too fast; the bullets are uncomfortably near. Taking evasive action, he turns the glider and volplanes back and forth between the narrow canyon walls.

Bullets zing by. A wing tip scrapes against the cliff. He turns again, heading against the wind. The water rushes up. Too swiftly. He skims across the water, drawing up his feet. Impact at this speed, even in water, could be fatal. He brings the hang glider up, stalls, losing much speed and drops into the water.

The narrow stream carries him swiftly away. He clings to the glider, turns a dial on its shaping mechanism. It refolds itself into a canoe. Doc gets aboard, detaches a portion for a paddle, and paddles away.

His men cheer. But a bullet strikes the shaping-mechanism. The canoe folds up, forming a tent around Doc, and it sinks, trapping him.

The five groan? Is Doc drowned? Or will he somehow struggle free?

The Arabs, grinning now, force the five away from the scene.

The mid-afternoon sun is over the camp of the All-Wise One.

Inside a blue tent are the Fabulous Five and Pat Savage. Faraway explosions and yells drift to them from the battle between Cartheris' gang and the villains in the blue city of Tasunan.

PAT is saying: "…shortly after I saw the dirigible fall, Lady Cynthia was brought in by Musa and Hadith. Apparently, she did manage to get a parachute and jump to safety. I never got a chance to speak to her, though. We were bundled off right away, and for some reason I was blindfolded during the entire trip. I did see her once, when a guard opened my tent flap. She was standing inside a tent, looking out. But her guard turned around and said something to her, and she closed the flap."

MONK: "And to think we were only a few miles from you when the dirigible blew up. If only we'd known…!"

Johnny holds up his hand for silence. They listen. The sounds of battle are gone. Aside from the wind, there is quiet.

Cut to the building by the wall. Ranyon Cartheris is fighting with an empty rifle as Hadith and Musa and a score of Arabs close in on him. Cartheris' men are dead, lying where they fell. Cartheris slams the rifle stock over an Arab's head, and then he is knocked out by the giant Hadith.

Cut to the tent of the prisoners. Suddenly, the tent flaps are pushed aside. Hadith and Musa, bloody, grinning, storm in.

MUSA: "Praise be to the Blue God and his high priest, the All-Wise One! All the defenders, except the white devil, have been slain!"

HADITH: "And the All-Wise One orders that you be taken to the temple of the Blue God!"

He leers at Pat. "All the *men* that is!"

PAT, bravely but with a shaky voice: "And what about me?"

HADITH: "It is not the custom of the Bedouin to waste swift camels and beautiful women! The All-Wise One is saving you for the delight of all of us!"

MONK, yelling: "I'll kill you, you filthy camel pusher!" rushes at Hadith. But Musa sticks the muzzle of his rifle against Monk's chest.

Just outside the wide mouth of the blue building are several scores of Arabs and the prisoners. The Five and Cartheris are gang-chained. Iron shackles are latched around their necks, all connected by a single chain running through the latches of the collars. Monk is holding his pig.

MONK mutters to Cartheris: "I'm worried about Pat! And your sister, too! I don't even wanta think about what that monster is going to do to them. But all ain't hopeless, Cartheris. Doc Savage is around here, somewhere, you can bet on that. He's gotten us out of situations just as bad as this."

HADITH THE HATEFUL, who has eavesdropped: "You fool! *Never fear, Doc Savage is here!* Is that what you hope! You're as stupid as a camel! Savage is dead, drowned! You saw him drown, yet you still think he'll rise from the dead, like a god!"

And he spits in Monk's face. Monk lunges at him but is brought up short by the chain.

The All-Wise One, carrying his sound-projector box, appears with several Arabs. The villains, some of whom carry torches, and the good guys enter the building and go down a steep stairway cut from stone. This comes out into a large tunnel through which a river runs. The long line, the chained prisoners in the middle, proceeds along a narrow walk raised a few feet above the river. Then they turn into a series of tunnels for a while. This is the underground complex of the ancient Tasunans. Cases holding mummies line the walls. Here and there is a vein of faintly glowing blue tasunite ore. There are also many shadowprints on the walls, the floors, the cases, and other places. These are the relics of invaders who met the shadow-death, anywhere from 2000 to 3000 years ago. Their silhouettes look like those of Biblical Assyrians, armed with spears, swords, and battle-axes.

The procession comes out again on the walk alongside the underground river. And they enter a vast underground dome.

The ceiling of the dome is so high it is lost in darkness. The river widens to fill its base, forming a small lake. In the center of the lake is a flat round stone islet. A narrow arching stone bridge, in need of repair, connects the walk and the islet.

The only illumination is provided by the torches and a pulsing blue glow from a gigantic, monstrously shaped idol in the center of the island. This is the

Blue God, carved from a block of tasunite.

The captives are led over the bridge through the pulsing blueness and in a silence that is ominous, spooky. Opposite the idol, near the southern edge of the island, are an oblong stone wall and a shield-like structure.

The shield is made of lead but has a long mica window through which observers may see the fate of the prisoners without themselves being affected. On each side of the tall curving shield is a gong. These are suspended from metal poles. The gongs themselves are crescent-shaped and of a thin quartz-glass material. Near them, behind the shield, lie long metal poles bearing large metal knobs.

Monk looks at the stone wall, which is slanted at an angle so that the people behind the shield may witness the shadowdeath of the sacrifices. He groans: "Oh, no!" and he looks around as if expecting Doc to appear. But the walk is empty of men, and the blue-black waters around the island flow sullenly, not a ripple on their surface.

The Horrible Humpback places the sound-projector box on the edge of the island, behind the shield. He's not going to need it, since the ancient Tasunans used the gongs to stimulate and to inhibit the tasunite idol. But he's brought it along, just in case.

The prisoners are led to the wall and backed up in a line against it. Their feet are enclosed in a long metal stock at the base of the wall. This is essentially a single bar which can be opened and closed with one movement. Its end is secured by a latch.

The captives are secured. The villains genuflect while the All-Wise One chants in Arabic (or perhaps in the ancient Tasunan language, preserved only in this ritual). Incense burns in tripods. Then the villains retire behind the shield and look through the mica window.

The All-Wise One gives an order. Hadith the Hateful picks up a gong-stick and strikes the right-hand gong from behind the protection of the shield. The quartz-glass gong emits a weird pulsing sound exactly like that projected by the sound-box.

Hadith taps the gong seven times in all. At each tap, the sounds build up, becoming shriller. And the Blue God responds, pulsing more swiftly and brightly. The sounds echo back from the walls and the ceiling with a blood-chilling effect.

The prisoners are scared, no doubt about that. Their death will be painless, but there's something horrible about disintegrating leaving behind only their burned-in shadows. Monk speaks to Cartheris: "How long have we got?"

CARTHERIS: "About two minutes. The idol is so big it takes longer."

The smaller the amount of tasunite, the quicker it reaches climax.

Behind the shield, the All-Wise One nods to Musa. He picks up the stick for the left-hand (the deactivating) gong.

MONK: "Ham! It looks like curtains for us! Doc ain't going to show! Listen, Ham, I know I played a lot of dirty tricks on you. But I love you, Ham! I love all you guys! And Doc…" He weeps.

A bronze hand reaches up from the blue-black waters on the island's edge. It snatches the sound box, and we see Doc, up to his shoulders in water, open the lid of the box. He deftly removes the de-activation circuit and tosses it away into the water.

Then, as he treads water, he removes a false tooth from his mouth. He uncaps it, and he drops a small pellet from it. He licks it (water detonates powerful *quinmolite* explosive five seconds after contact). And he throws it at the stop gong.

Explosion! Quartz glass flying, cutting some villains. All are knocked down by the blast.

Doc comes up out of the water behind the wall holding the captives. He looks blue now in the increasingly swift and bright pulsations. He unlatches the stocks while the Five and Cartheris cry out in jubilation. But Doc knows there is very little time; it may yet be too late.

"Get out of here!" he yells. "There's nothing to stop it now! It'll build up until it reaches critical mass!"

Meanwhile, the villains have gotten to their feet. The humpback looks for his sound box to stop the pulsations, realizes it's gone, and screams. Suddenly, the villains panic. Pell-mell, they pour over the bridge after the captives, who lead them. They jam in the bridge, and several are forced over the edge.

They run through the tunnels.

Then they are back on the walk, screaming, yelling, shoving.

In the deserted dome, the Blue God is pulsing ever more swiftly, brightly. Now the upper part of the dome is illuminated, and we see that the ceiling is covered with carvings. The hideous, leering, demonic faces spring out of darkness, glow bluely, seem to melt, to reform. They're the embodiments of all the evil that ever existed.

On the walk, Hadith grabs Long Tom, last in the chain gang, and hurls him into the river. Though he is little, Long Tom's weight is enough to pull in Renny after him. Yelling despairingly, the entire six fall. Doc, hearing them shout, turns. Hadith runs at him to push him, too, out of the way.

Doc throws him into the river. The hunchback stops but is knocked down by the panicked men behind him. Doc dives into the river, swims under, and finds the six, weighed down by the heavy iron collars and the chain, writhing on the bottom.

He grabs Ham's collar and strains, his biceps swelling, his face agonized. The latch breaks, and he slides the chain out through the latches of the other collars. They are free to swim back to the walk now. But is it too late?

In the dome, the Blue God pulses, pulses. Then: climax!

The dome disappears in a hot blue expansion!

The ruins of Tasunan, on the surface, tremble, shake, some buildings collapsing, parts of walls tumbling.

A vast hole suddenly opens in the center of the ruins. A colossal blue beam shoots from the hole, seeming to reach to the skies.

The buildings and the earth fall in around the hole, form a whirlpool of stone blocks and trees and idols, pour down, and fill the hole. The blue beam is shut off, blocked by the enormous amount of material stopping it.

The few Arabs left in camp flee in horror.

Doc and his pals, now back on the walk, see a great wave of river water, lifted and expelled by the explosion, sweep down on them. They are sure to be drowned, to be smashed into bits of pulp against the stone walls of the tunnel.

But the water roars out of the wide mouth of the blue building in which is the underground entrance. Bodies: Arabs, Cartheris' dead men, the humpback, Hadith, Musa, and Doc and gang, are carried out on the crest of the water. It splashes on the ground, depositing them violently. Then the wave subsides with a long hollow roar back into the building. But the building, weakened, collapses, and some huge blocks of stone almost crush Doc and Ham.

Silence. Then, a few moans. The humpback recovers first. He runs wobbly toward the camp. Doc and the five, with Cartheris, recover almost immediately after. Hadith and Musa are still unconscious. All the others are dead.

Doc and all except Ham and Monk are outside the tent in which Pat was imprisoned. Pat is with them now. Doc has opened one of the long flat cases chuted from the DSD-1. He's putting together some thin dark pieces of glass taken from the case. The others watch interestedly.

Ham and Monk return.

MONK: "Doc, we've looked all over the camp. Everybody's gone, including the Horrible Humpback. We couldn't find the blue ball he used. I don't know why he took it along. He doesn't have a sound-projector."

DOC: "I think I know where the blue ball is. And I suspect that he had an extra sound-projector."

He stands up, having fitted together the jigsaw puzzle. It's the shadowprint cut from the plate glass storefront.

RANYON CARTHERIS looks at it and cries: "Oh, my God! No! No!"

DOC, quietly: "Yes. It's your sister, Lady Cynthia."

PAT, startled: "But, Doc! Lady Cynthia was with us! She's not…Oh! I see!"

DOC, nodding: "Yes. It was poor Lady Cynthia who was caught by the shadow-death. It was Marian Le Dene who pretended to be Lady Cynthia. And I suspect that it was she who imitated that man's voice on the Record-O-Phone. She was an actress, you know."

"We'll track her and the humpback down, Cartheris," Renny says. "They can't have gotten too far."

At that moment, they hear a faint thump. And the brainshaped ball, glowing bluely, rolls into their midst.

They look up the side of the steep sand dune down which the ball was rolled. Through the air flies a false hump! It lands near the blue ball, and they see that it's made of metal, its bottom section is open, and leather straps hang from it.

The All-Wise One, no longer crook-backed, stands tall and straight on the dune's crest. His hands grip a sound-projector, and one finger is bent to flick the start switch.

Monk and Ham look at the rifles stacked nearby. Doc mutters: "Don't try it, men. He can start the ball pulsing and duck down behind the dune for shelter before you could get the guns."

The All-Wise One utters a low gravelly laugh.

Then he stoops, sets the sound-box down.

MONK: "Now, Doc?"

Doc shakes his head.

Shouting, "See what fools you are!" the All-Wise One grips his robe around the waist. He jerks it upward, and as it rises we see long white feminine legs, black lace panties, then a skimpy black lace bra over large female breasts.

The robe is raised above the woman's head and then ripped off. With it comes the woman's facemask, in effect, *pulling her face off.* The robe and the mask have formed one piece, a unit.

CARTHERIS cries: "Marian Le Dene!"

"Yes, Marian Le Dene, your sister's secretary!" she shouts. "Marian Le Dene, ex-actress, Lady Cynthia's slave! And then the All-Wise One! You're all fools, fools!"

She stoops swiftly, lifts up the sound box, and places a finger on the start switch.

"Of all you fools, the biggest one is you, Doc Savage! You stupid lump of bronze! You deliberately destroyed the greatest source of power in the world! I could have sold the tasunite for millions, billions, to the highest bidder! Can you imagine what a weapon it would make!

"But no, Savage, you destroyed it! And why? Because of your puritan ideals! Your stupid ideals?"

Scornfully: "*Let me do right to all and wrong no man!*

"Imbecile! I had the world and all its wealth and all its power in my hands! No more making a fool of myself on the stage for low-browed rubes! No more half-starving in cockroach havens, freezing in winter, roasting in summer! No more sneaking out the back door, leaving the luggage behind, fearing every policeman I saw! No more cheap hotel rooms letting stinking fat-bellied cigar-smoking salesmen make love to me!

"And I had the world by the throat!

"And I was ready to share it with you, Doc. I could have used your scientific knowledge to develop the tasunite into truly awesome weapons! And I wanted you as I've never wanted another man! When we were in that room in the airship, when I put my arms around you, I was ready to offer you both me and the world! All in one package, Doc, yours for the taking. But you...you..."

She chokes with emotion, then recovers.

"I knew you would never agree with me. You think you're a knight in bronze armor. So, you had to die!"

A pause. The only sound is the desert wind, shifting the sand on the sides of the dunes.

DOC, quietly: "You only had me fooled part of the time, Marian. I compared the voice of the man who called me from the Warfield Drug Store phone booth with your voice. The wave frequencies on the voiceprints showed that you were the same speaker. I played along with you so that I could find Pat and also the source of the tasunite. I wanted to destroy the tasunite. It has, as far as I can determine, no beneficial uses whatever. It's evil, and so it had to be kept from falling into the wrong hands!"

MARIAN: "Much good that did you, Savage! You'll die and your men and your cousin and Cartheris will die with you. There's nothing you can do to stop me, nothing!"

She flicks the start toggle switch. The weird pulsations of the projector stimulate the ball of tasunite. It begins to flash more brightly and with greater speed. Marian Le Dene stands on the sand dune crest, laughing triumphantly, ready to drop behind the crest before the climaxing blue flash.

Doc shouts to the others: "Run!"

They obey, but he remains. He snatches Ham's cane as Ham runs by, clicks out its sword point, and drives the blade into the tasunite ball. Then, with a quick powerful sidewise movement, he lifts up the ball on the point, jerks it, and the ball flies off the blade point like a piece of meat off a skewer. It soars through the air, tumbling, glowing, toward Marian Le Dene.

She screams as she sees it flying toward her, propelled up the dune with a force only Doc Savage is capable of.

She drops the sound box which rolls down the dune toward Doc. She throws up her hands to ward off the ball. But it strikes her in the chest, she falls backward on the other side of the dune and disappears.

Doc throws his hands over his eyes as a blinding blue glare soars up from the other side of the dune.

A moment later, after Doc has stopped the ball pulsations with the sound box, all seven climb up to the top of the dune. They look down the opposite slope. The ball glows at the bottom of the dune. But halfway down is the black silhouette of Marian Le Dene. One arm is outflung, her head thrown back, much like the shadowprint of the ill-fated Lady Cynthia on the storefront.

The sand shifts under the desert wind. The shadow-picture trickles, turns into rags of blackness. The sand continues to move. Presently, there are only a few patches of black sand. Then, only brown sand.

In an operating room in Doc's Rehabilitation Center, Hadith lies anesthetized on a table while Doc sews on plastic ears over the ugly orifices.

Later, in the same room Doc performs the evil-eradicating acupuncture operation on Hadith. On a table nearby, waiting his turn, is Musa.

Doc says goodbye to the two at the gate outside the Rehabilitation Center, wishing them good luck.

Exterior of a wrestling arena, the poster announcing, HADITH THE HATEFUL VERSUS THE MURDEROUS MONGOLIAN.

In the ring, Hadith's opponent grabs the giant's ears, steps back, looking horrified at the ripped-off ears in his hands. Hadith grabs him and throws him out of the ring.

Doc is on a New York street corner, about to cross to his skyscraper. He sees Musa, now operating a mobile popcorn stand. Musa grins and waves at him.

Heavy black clouds dim a spring day. Doc and the Five, including the pig, are getting into his big bronze limousine by a street-curb. The gang, with the exception of Doc and the sartorially sensitive Ham, are wearing bright conical birthday hats and most are carrying recently opened cardboard boxes. Pat stands before her beauty establishment, waving to them. The plate glass window beside her bears the legend: PAT'S POSH PARK AVENUE PALACE, *Take The Fat Off & Put on a New Face, Try Pat's Special Tasunan Clay Facial Pack.*

PAT: "Happy Birthday again Doc, may you have many more! But don't call me for your next case! I'm tired of getting kidnapped"

The limousine drives down the street, and we see the license plate:

DOC-4, New York State, 1936.

Inside the limousine, as it drives down the street, Monk slips the pig a piece of chewing tobacco. Ham, sitting beside him in the rear seat, is too busy talking to notice. Renny interrupts to ask Doc if he's got any new cases lined up. Doc says he doesn't. He intends to fly up to his Fortress of Solitude, his place in the remote Arctic, and do some experimenting.

At this moment Habeas Corpus spits tobacco juice into Ham's pocket while Monk stares innocently ahead. Ham blows his top, swearing he'll jam his sword cane down the pig's throat and up whatever happens to be handy in Monk's case.

MONK: "It ain't my fault, Ham. I gave him strict orders to spit only on the floor." He breaks into laughter.

The carphone rings, and Doc holds up a hand for silence. Doc flicks a switch so they can all hear the phone. A woman's voice, desperate, issues from the speaker. "Doc! This is Wendy Finnegan! Remember me? I was in your Rehabilitation Center two years ago! Listen, Doc, I don't have much time! I'm at Hoskowitz's Nautical Supply Store on Ashcroft near Third! Come quick, Doc! They're breathing hard down my neck! Org's men! New York is in terrible danger! Thousands, maybe millions, might die! And the whole city's gonna be destroyed. Org's..."

A scream. Then: "Watch out for the deadly rain, Doc"

Glass breaks and another scream shrills through the car. Afterwards: silence.

The limousine screeches in a U-turn while a cop blows his whistle at them. Suddenly, it is raining heavily. Renny cries out, "Holy Cow!" as the drops strike the windshield and explode. The glass is criss-crossed with stars. If it weren't bulletproof, it would have shattered.

In the street, the raindrops blow up with tiny electrical flashes as they hit cars, the pavement, and a few pedestrians. A storefront window falls into a hundred pieces. Ahead, a fire hydrant soars into the air like a rocket, the water spurting from its open end crackling like a thousand Fourth of July sparklers. The waterspout from the main rises up, falls, explodes on the sidewalk and street.

JOHNNY, pale, staring: "I'll be superflabgastamated!"

MONK: "Doc, what is it? It just ain't possible!"

The blood had drained from the faces of all except Doc, who looks grimly determined.

At this moment, FREEZE THE FRAME. The "Doc Savage March" plays as the credits roll. When THE END is announced, a fade out. Then, a quick fade in. A title:

Watch for Doc Savage's
Next Thrilling Adventure!
DOC SAVAGE
in the
Supersaga of
Death in Silver

FINAL FADE OUT

NOTE: In this version, the audience knows (or thinks) that Marian Le Dene is working for the Horrible Humpback and is posing as Lady Cynthia. It might be more startling and dramatic if the audience does not know this. Her identities could be revealed suddenly (in a one-two punch sequence) as both Le Dene posing as Lady Cynthia and the Humpback. In which case, Le Dene's face won't be shown in the phone booth scene.

The Monster On Hold

The Monster On Hold

(a chapter from a projected novel in the Lord Grandrith/Doc Caliban series)

First published in the *World Fantasy Convention Program,* 1983.

The 1983 World Fantasy Convention was held at Chicago in October 1983 with Phil in attendance.

In this fascinating snippet, Phil gives us an overview of the entire novel—the improbable merging of the pulp stylings of a Doc Savage story with the disturbing horror of Lovecraft's Cthulhu mythology. The excerpt presents an engrossing scene where Caliban encounters the truly supernatural for the first time since his frightening encounter with the 'Devil' in the last recorded chronological adventure of Doc Savage *(Up from Earth's Centre).*

The story following this introduction is a chapter in a projected novel originally titled *The Unspeakable Threshold* (now titled *The Monster On Hold*). This will be a "Doc Caliban" story and the latest in the series beginning with *A Feast Unknown* and continued in the *Lord of the Trees* and *The Mad Goblin. Feast* started in east Africa and is told in first person by James Cloamby, Viscount Grandrith (pronounced Grunith), an Englishman raised by a subhuman species (a variant of Australopithecus) in west Africa. Grandrith, while still a youth, became one of the high-echelon agents of the Council of Nine. The Nine are the secret rulers of earth, most of whom were born circa 30,000-20,000 B.C. though they looked as if their age is only a hundred.

The Nine have considerably slowed their aging with a longevity "elixir" which they share with certain agents who have earned it. Grandrith is one of the very few so privileged. Though eighty-three he looks and feels like a twenty-five year old man.

In *A Feast Unknown,* Grandrith is suffering unforeseen side effects of the elixir. These make it impossible for him to get an erection unless, and to avoid one if, violence is involved. He finds this out when he is attacked by Jomo

Kenyatta's forces. Then he discovers that an American agent for the Nine is out to kill him. Doc Caliban believes (wrongly) that Grandrith has killed Caliban's cousin, Patricia Wilde, also an agent of the Nine. Caliban is suffering from the same side effects of the elixir.

Just as the two have what should be a final confrontation, they are summoned to a meeting of the Nine in a subterranean area in east Africa. The oldest man of the Council, XauXaz, has died, and Caliban and Grandrith are the top two candidates to replace him. One must kill the other to get a seat on the Council. In the end of *A Feast Unknown,* after many adventures, the two almost kill each other, but they then unite to fight against the Nine.

In *Lord of the Trees,* Grandrith manages to kill Mubaniga, the proto-Bantu member of the Nine. In *The Mad Goblin,* Jiinfan, a proto-Mongolian member and Iwaldi, an ancient Germanic member, are killed during a night battle at Stonehenge. Four of the Nine are dead, leaving as head of the Council Anana, the withered hag born about thirty thousand years ago in the area which would become Sumeria. Other living members are Tilatoc (an ancient Amerindian), Ing (the patronymic leader of the early English tribes when they were living in Denmark), Yeshua (a Hebrew born circa 3 B.C.), and Shaumbim (a proto-Mongolian).

The three novels above took place in the late 1960s. The events of *The Monster on Hold* begin in the late 1970s when Doc Caliban penetrates Tilatoc's supposedly impregnable fortress hideout in northern Canada. I won't describe the result because I don't want to reveal too much about the novel. But Caliban goes into hiding again. He hears that Anana has decreed that whoever kills Grandrith and Caliban will become Council members even if they are not candidates. (Caliban almost loses his life when he gains this piece of information.) When the second section of the novel begins (in 1984), Caliban is in Los Angeles and disguised as an old wino. Tired of running, he's decided to attack, but, first, he needs a lead. One night, a juvenile gang jumps him, thinking he's easy prey. He disposes of them quite bloodily, but he spots a man observing the fight. Later, he sees the man shadowing him. After trapping him, Caliban questions him, using a truth drug he invented in the 1930s. As Caliban suspects, the man is an agent of the Nine. Caliban allows him to escape and then trails him. This leads to a series of adventures I'll omit in this outline.

During these, Caliban begins to suffer from a recurring nightmare and has dreams alternating with these in which he sees himself or somebody like himself. However, this man, whom he calls The Other, also at times in Caliban's dreams seems to be dreaming of Caliban.

Caliban thinks he has shaken himself loose of the Nine's agents, but then another appears. Caliban catches him and then recognizes him as a man he last saw in 1948.

He's shaken. The man, now calling himself Scott Free, figured prominently in an adventure which Caliban recalls with horror and much puzzlement. That is, when he does think about it, which is as seldom as he can help.

Caliban and his aides and some others had ventured deep into a labyrinthine cavern complex in New England. There they had encountered things which Mr. Free (one of the party) had said were the metamorphosed spirits of the dead. "Devils." Free claimed to be a lower-echelon devil who had escaped from Hades. Caliban, a rationalist and agnostic, did not believe Free's explanation. Yet, some of the events had no acceptable explanations. Whatever the truth, Caliban had escaped something very horrible. He had had no desire to explore the caverns again. At the same time his scientific curiosity about them had tormented him from time to time.

The adventure had been thirty-six years ago, and here is Mr. Free looking as young as then and trying to make him his prisoner. By whose orders?

That of the thing which Free had implied was Satan? That of the Nine? Or was he trying to get Caliban on his own?

Doc gets into contact with his two aides, "Pauncho" Van Veelar and Barney Banks. They're living under assumed names in upper New York but come at once when Doc summons them.

The truth drug fails to work on Free, but Caliban forces a story out of him which seems to be true. At least, the instruments that Doc used indicate this. Free confesses that the story about the cavern being Hades and its inhabitants being doomed souls is false. But he was born in the middle of the eighteenth century, and he had worked for the Nine. Too ambitious, he double-crossed the Nine to gain a vast fortune. Caught, he expected to be tortured and killed. Instead he was condemned to be one of the guards in the cavern complex in New England.

There he discovered that he was to help guard some thing that he could only describe as "the monster in abeyance" or "the monster on hold." But it did have a name, Shrassk, meaning "She-Who-Eats-Her-Children." Free has never seen the monster. He says that in the eighteenth century the Nine were faced with a situation similar to that of Grandrith's and Caliban's revolt. Then, three candidates had tried to overthrow the Nine. They had so disrupted the organization, slain so many agents and candidates, come so close to killing some of the Nine, that the Council, in desperation, had summoned a thing from another dimension or perhaps from a parallel universe.

(Not too parallel, Free says. Caliban says that things are either parallel or they're not. Free says that the other universe is, then, asymptotic. Which explains why the area in which the monster is contained in the cave is partly in this world, partly out of it. Or, from what he's heard, it may be suspended between two universes, acting as a sort of bridge.)

Shrassk, Free says, has the power, perhaps uncontrolled by it, a wild talent, to touch the subconscious of some sensitive human receptors and cause nightmares. God only knows what else.

Its touching may have been what caused Lovecraft to form his Cthulhu mythos, a dimly perceived and mostly fictional concept but based on the real horror.

In any event, Shrassk was not to be released directly upon the world in an effort to get the three rebels of the eighteenth century. While Shrassk was held in abeyance, it would reproduce after some mysterious mating and conception, and its "children" would be loosed to seek out and destroy the three without fail. Some children, that is.

Before that happened, the three rebels were caught, tortured, and then fed to Shrassk. It would not, however, go back to where it had come from. The Nine had to maintain the guards for the children and the forces that held it back from entering this world. Meanwhile, Shrassk was breeding, though very slowly, more of the children. Free says that Shrassk is imprisoned by geometry but, if it escapes, will do so by algebra. He is unable to clarify this enigmatic remark.

In 1948, Free had escaped from the cavern but had been forced to re-enter the cavern by Caliban and his aides. After they had gotten out of the cave, Free had teleported himself from jail. But teleportation is a power not always on tap. After a few "discharges," as Free puts it, the user has to recharge his battery.

Doc doesn't believe the story about TP. He thinks Free is lying and that he's just a superb escape artist.

Now, Free says, the Nine are so desperate that they are considering letting loose a "child" to destroy Grandrith, Caliban, Caliban's cousin, Pat Wilde, and Van Veelar and Banks. If that "child" doesn't succeed, another will be released.

Doc wonders if the truth drug isn't ineffective on Free and if Free hasn't been planted by the Nine to allure Caliban to go back to the cave. Nevertheless, he decides that he will attack. He gets into contact with Van Veelar and Banks and, after some difficulty, with his cousin, Pat. After taking the small stone fortress at the opening of the cave, the four descend into the many-leveled subterranean complex. This time, they penetrate much deeper than in 1948. They encounter a greater variety of denizens than the first time, including one which Doc thinks for a while is Shrassk. Doc becomes separated from his companions and has to go on alone.

The following is the first draft of a chapter of the proposed novel.

Free had said that the "children" were born out of flame by Shrassk.

Why then, as Caliban had proved so many times in the past twelve hours, were they terrified by fire? Was it fire itself, the reality, or the idea of fire that panicked them? Or both? Or something else?

He crouched behind the seven-foot-high cone of dark brown stuff oozing from the wide crack in the rock floor. Its rotten-onion stink and his knowledge of its origin sickened him. That the cone was building up at the rate of a quart every five minutes meant that monsters like the one he had just killed were in the neighborhood. Unless, that is, the dead thing was excreting after death and its wastes were flowing through the undersurface fissure complex. No. This cone was too far from the carcass.

Others of its kind must be nearby.

Soft noises came from the other side of the cone. Whisperings, chitterings. Nonhuman. He moved slowly along the edge of the cone. The gray-green light seemed to be dimming somewhat. Was the chocolate-brown goo absorbing the light? Nonsense. Or was it? He could not know here what was or was not nonsense. Anyway, calling something nonsense meant only that you did not understand it.

He looked around the cone. In the half-light he could see the rear of a creature he had not encountered so far. It had a tail two feet long, about an inch in diameter, hairless, studded with dark warts, and exuding slime. The tail was switching back and forth much like that of a cat thinking whatever sphinxlike thoughts a cat thought.

He moved slowly further around the edge of the cone, prepared to duck back if the thing should turn its eyes—if it had any—toward him. Then he saw that he had been wrong in assuming that the creature had a posterior part. It was two feet in diameter and a foot high. There was no head, hence, no rear, just an armored dome from which four tails - some kind of flexible members, anyway—extended. If the tail he had first seen came from the south of the round body, the others extended from the north, west, and east. The end of the west tail was stuck into the brown cone and was, since it was twice as large in diameter as the others, swollen with the sucking-in of the excrement.

Because the thing seemed to be eyeless, Caliban stepped forward two paces. Beyond the creature were four others, all feeding with the tail-like "west" organs.

Beyond them, its back to him—he supposed it was the back—was a bipedal creature. It was almost as tall as he and was unclothed. Though human in form, its skin was a dull blue. Black ridges ran both vertically and horizontally over its legs and body and hairless head. The ridges formed squares in the center of which was a livid red circle the size of a silver dollar. One hand, quite human, held a shepherd's staff.

The whisperings and chitterings came from the "shepherd."

The creature began to turn around. Caliban backed away around the cone. He looked around. No living thing in sight—as far as he knew. Here, he could not be sure what was or was not living. The rock floor slanted upwards at a ten-degree angle to the horizontal. At least, what he thought was the horizontal. The only relief to the smoothness and emptiness were some tall rock spirals, huge boulders, and brown cones here and there. The warm thick air passed slowly over his sweating skin.

He walked in the opposite direction so that he could watch the shepherd while it was facing the other way. And then the flickerings began again—flickerings he knew now were not phenomena outside him—and he saw The Other, his near-double.

For a moment he was frightened. Shrassk was touching his mind again. But, he reassured himself, that did not mean that Shrassk knew where he was. On the other hand...

He slid that possibility into a drawer in his mind and watched the vision with inner eyes while the outer watched the cone. If that shepherd strolled around the cone, it would have him at a disadvantage. He should go ahead with his plan. But he could not move.

The man who looked so much like him was walking through a rock tunnel filled with the same light as this cavern, the gray-green of an old bone spotted with lichen. He, too, wore a backpack and a harness to which was attached many containers for instruments and weapons. Suddenly, The Other, stopped. His expression shifted from intense wariness to fright. That quickly passed and he stared straight ahead as if he were seeing something puzzling.

Caliban relaxed a trifle. The other man was probably also touched by Shrassk. He was seeing Caliban as Caliban was seeing him.

Caliban anticipated that they might soon do more than just see one another. It seemed to him that The Other was not perhaps in the same universe as Caliban's. Not yet. Perhaps never. But Shrassk was in the third universe which was a bridge between Caliban's and The Other's. A crossroads. And Caliban and The Other could leave their two worlds to meet in the third, Shrassk's.

This anticipation was based on Free's explanation, which meant that neither was grounded in reality.

Doc forced himself to move. With the first step, the little glowing stage and its single performer vanished. It was as if his connection with the vision had been switched off by muscular action. By the time that he came to the other side of the cone, he was running and his mind was completely wrapped around his intent. A big knife was in one hand and the gas-powered pistol was in the other.

The shepherd had its back to him. It was turning one of the round things with its staff so that the tail on the south side could be inserted into the cone. Caliban slowed down just a little because he was astonished. The crook at the end of the shepherd's staff was straight now. Its end had split into two, and these were clamped around the lower edge of the dome-shaped cone-eater. Using these, the shepherd was turning the thing so that it could insert another tail into the goo.

The checkerboard-skinned thing must have heard him or have felt the vibrations of Caliban's boots through the rock floor and its bare soles. It yanked the staff from the edge of the round tailed thing and whirled. The ends of the staff merged together.

Caliban noted this and also the sex of the shepherd. It had no testicles, but a thin orange-prepuced penis reached to its knees.

The shepherd grinned, exposing four beaverlike teeth. Its face was human except for the black squares and red spots. It raised the staff as if it were going to throw it at Doc. The end nearest Doc swelled, the shaft shrinking in length and diameter as substance flowed into the end, and the end became a thin pointed two-edged blade.

Doc raised the gas-pistol and squeezed the trigger. There was a hiss. The projectile appeared, its needlepoint buried in the blue chest. The thing staggered back two steps. It should have been unconscious in four seconds, but, screaming, it ran at Doc, the staff held as if it were a spear. Which it now was. The thing's arm came down; the spear flashed at Doc. He ducked. The spear missed, but the lower back end sagged, became supple, and whipped around Doc's arm.

Still holding the pistol, Doc sawed with his knife at the creature squeezing on his arm. Its body seemed to be as hard as hickory though it was as flexible as rubber.

By then the shepherd was upon him. Doc brought the knife up from the snake-shaft and down into the shepherd's thigh. The blade sank halfway into the flesh, but Doc was knocked down by the impact of its body. He rolled away and started to get up. The snake-shaft coiled the rest of its body around Doc's neck. He fell on his back, dropped the knife and pistol, and, while the thing cut his breath off, got his fingers between it and his neck, though not without cutting his skin with his fingernails, and, with a mighty yank, uncoiled it and cast it away.

Few men would have had the power to do that, but Doc had no time to congratulate himself on that. The shaft was writhing on the floor in an effort to reach him. Lacking the belly plates of the true snake, it was making little progress. The shepherd, however, screaming, blood gushing from its wound, was hobbling towards him. Doc rolled away until his right hand was within reach of the snake-shaft. His fingers closed around it just back of the head, which was swelling—toward what shape?—and he rose to his feet and threw the thing at the shepherd in one fluid movement. He had taken the chance that the staff might be so quick that it would whip itself around his wrist or even, perhaps, around his neck again. But, cracking it like a whip, he had avoided that. Now the shaft fell around the shepherd's head, chittered something, and the shaft fell off it.

Doc had hurled himself against the shepherd then, and he had knocked it down. It started to get up, but Doc's boot caught it under its rounded and cleft chin. It fell back, unconscious.

Panting, Doc bent over the shepherd. Since he wanted no witness left behind, no one to tell—whom?—that he had been this way, he intended to drag the shepherd to a nearby deep fissure and drop it in. He screamed and straightened up and grabbed at his crotch. Something had wrapped itself around his penis and was squeezing it. For a few seconds, he was so taken by shock and surprise that he did not recognize what it was that had seized him. Now he saw that the proboscislike sex organ of the shepherd—if it was a sex organ—had coiled itself around his penis. It was yanking at it as if it was trying to tear his organ off. Fortunately, the cloth of Doc's pants was interfering with the effort.

The shepherd seemed to be still knocked out. The drug from the hypodermic and its wound had surely done their work. But they should also have made its sex organ, or whatever it was, flaccid. Knocked it out, too. Unless it was partially independent of the blood supply of the main body.

No time to think. Gritting his teeth, Doc backed away, the shepherd's body dragging behind, pulled by the proboscis attached to Doc's penis. The pain became worse. He had a vision of his organ being torn out by the roots, but he kept backing until he was by the knife. He fell to his knees, grabbed it, and sliced away the blue length and orange prepuce with one motion. Blood, almost black in the dim light, geysered out from the shepherd.

"God Almighty!"

Doc staggered to the gas gun, picked it up, sheathed it and the knife, and ran. The pain faded away but not the memory. After a few yards, he slowed to a walk. A glance showed him the shepherd's still body, the shaft writhing, and the five round things. What next? When he reached the far wall of the cavern, he went along it for perhaps a quarter of a mile and found in the shadows the entrance of a smooth downslanting tunnel. With both arms outspread, he could touch its walls. The top was a foot higher than his six feet and seven inches.

The tunnel, after a half a mile, ended with a flaring out as if it were a trumpet. Before him was silence and the biggest cavern yet. The walls opposite him were draped in blackness which, for a second, he thought moved. The ceiling soared into darkness. The floor, far below, was bathed in a brighter light than that which he had gone through and was now green-yellow. Its source, however, was still unknown.

A ledge extended from the tunnel exit. Two feet wide, it ran more or less horizontally from both sides of the tunnel mouth as far as he could see. The straight drop from the ledge to the floor was, he estimated, about a mile. From here, the floor seemed to be smooth among the ridges, hillocks, and curious shapes, some of which looked human. Vaguely. They could not be, however. For one thing, they did not move. For another, they would have to be far larger than elephants for him to make out their shapes at this distance and in this twilight.

For the first time, he saw water in large quantity. A river wound through a rock channel, its surface dark, smooth, and oily. Perhaps it wasn't water.

Something darker than the river and the stone banks moved slowly on the surface. Doc removed his backpack and took out the night-vision subsonic-transmitter. He lay down on the ledge, his elbows propped near the edge, put the viewscreen to his eyes, swept the area that had attracted his attention, adjusted the dials, moved the instrument back and forth, and held it steady.

The slowly floating mass was a rowboat with an unmoving figure seated in it. The figure seemed to have its back to him. But something extended from its front out over the water. A fishing rod? What kind of creatures could live in the barren river. There was no food for them. Unless...there were cracks in the riverbottom and the chocolatey onion-stinking stuff oozed up from them. Maybe the "fish" ate that stuff.

Doc moved the line of sight over the boat. It was white, though that may not have been its color. Objects on which the instrument focused looked white; objects near the edge of the screen and in the background were dark. He did not think that the boat was made of wood since wood was absent in this world. The boat had probably been carved from stone.

The fisherman could be stone, too. He certainly had not moved any more than a granite statue would. If that were so, then the monk's cloak and hood on him were of stone, too.

Doc had to keep moving the instrument slowly because the boat, like the river, was moving sluggishly. Then he started, and he lost the boat for a moment. The fisherman had shifted. By the time that he was in the screen again, he was on his feet and holding the pole with both hands. The line from the pole was too thin for Doc's instrument to reflect, but Doc knew that there was a line. Proof of its existence was climbing out of the river on the line.

The thing ascending the line hand over hand had a ghostly-white face with enormous eyes. A snub human nose. Thick pale lips. A rounded chin. Under which hung a loose bladder of skin. The thing had a high and bulging forehead. If it had a head of hair, it was not visible. It had no ears or ear openings that Doc could see. The neck was fat, and the body was a baby's, the arms and legs very short. It stood swaying, its nonhuman round feet with long webbed toes spread out on the stone bottom of the boat. The fingers were also long and webbed.

Doc widened the field of vision. The fisherman was three times as tall as the catch. If the former was six feet high, then the catch was two feet tall.

Doc's muscles tightened, and the back of his neck chilled. The fisherman had turned so that Doc could see the profile under the hood. It was human and familiar. The big hooked nose could be Dante Alighieri's.

Stop thinking like this, Doc told himself. That is not the centuries dead Florentine poet. He—or it—is probably, no, certainly, not even human. Free's claim that the dead were reincarnated here was ridiculous.

Now the fisherman had put the pole down in the boat. Now he was picking up the large but slim fishhook at the end of the line and was walking carefully—didn't want to rock the boat—toward the creature that looked like a hybrid of baby and frog. Now he had grabbed its neck—the creature was not struggling—and had savagely driven the end of the hook through one side of the bladder below the neck and out through the other side.

Even then the creature was passive. Perhaps it was in shock, though Doc did not think so. Something in its attitude indicated that it was fully co-operating. And now the fisherman had tossed the creature into the water. He walked back to the pole, lifted it, and sat down, becoming again a stone-still Izaak Walton. The pole did not move, which meant that the thing on the hook was not struggling.

What was the prey for which the baby-frog would be bait? Anything big enough to swallow it would be too big for the simple Tom Sawyer fishing tackle to handle.

Getting answers here is secondary, Doc thought. I shouldn't be wasting time lying here and watching. I must be moving on. Besides, in this place, what I see from a distance, even with the viewer, may be quite different from what I'd see close up.

Nevertheless, he did not get up at once. The fisherman maintained his unhuman lack of movement, no wriggling, no looking around, no scratching of nose or hair. Only the boat and the river moved, and they did so very slowly. Nor had anything else moved except some shadows seen out of the corners of his eyes. When he looked directly at where the shadows had been, he saw only the pale dead-looking light.

Though he kept the viewer on the boat, with occasional sweeps across the floor, he could not help but think of other things. For instance, what was the ecosystem of this place? There had to be some kind of order here despite all the appearances of illogic and chaos. Everything he had seen had to be obeying or acting in accordance with a "law," a "principle." Everything had to be interconnected here as much as everything above it was. The "laws" of entropy, of energy input and output, conception, reproduction, growth, aging, and death had to operate in this deep underground. There had to be a system and an interdependent network.

What?

Doc vowed that, before he left here—if he did leave—he would at least have an inkling of the system. He would have some data on which he could theorize.

Finally he rose. He was ready to go on. But, lacking a parachute or enough rope, he could not get down or along the glass-smooth wall below the ledge. He could go to the right or the left on the ledge. One direction had to lead down to the cave floor. There was traffic from the lower levels to the upper, and, thus, this ledge was the highway. Perhaps both the left and right were used. He could not, however, afford the time to take one and find out that it petered out somewhere on the side of the immense bowl.

Take the left. Why? Because that was the sinister side. It seemed to him that the sinister would always be the right direction in this place. Chuckling feebly at his feeble pun, he began walking faster than caution recommended, his left shoulder brushing against the wall now and then.

After a quarter of a mile, the ledge began sloping gently downward. In an hour, he was halfway to the floor and above a roughly three-cornered opening in the wall into which the dark river flowed. By then the fisherman had inserted his pole into a socket in the corner of the boat and was rowing back up the river. Were his oars also made of stone?

The ledge took Caliban to the other side of the cavern before it reached the floor. He stood there for a while and listened to the total silence, which was a ringing in his ears. The fear bell ringing, he thought. Someone is at the front door and pressing on the button.

Though he had no reason to think so, he felt that he was getting close to his goal. Which perhaps explained why his fear had come back and was moving closer to that sheer hysterical horror he had suffered during an incident in his first venture into the cave so many years ago.

Caliban, your hindbrain is trying to take over, he told himself. Use your forebrain. Don't use it to rationalize and justify what your hindbrain is telling you. Don't turn and run away. Don't walk away, either. Push on ahead. If you flee now when you are so close, after you've gone through so much, you'll

474 PHILIP JOSÉ FARMER

despise yourself forever afterwards. You might as well kill yourself. In which case, if you're going to die if you run away or die if you go ahead, you might as well, no, it'll be much better, if you die because you went ahead.

Despite this, the fire of panic was burning away his reason and courage. It might have caught hold of him and turned him around. He would never know because the vision of The Other sprang into light in some place in his mind. And, as fire lights fire, a cliché but sometimes true, the vision swept away the fear.

The Other was standing at the entrance to a cave. He was smiling and holding up one huge bronze-skinned hand, two fingers forming a V. Then the scene widened, and Doc saw that The Other was about three hundred feet from a great circle of stone symbols brightly lit by burning gas jets at their bases. There were nine: a Greek cross, a hexagon, a crescent, a five-pointed star, a triangle with an eye at its top, a Celtic cross, an O with an X inside it, a snake with its tail in its mouth, and a winged horseshoe. They enclosed a shallow bowl-shaped depression in the rock about three hundred feet in diameter. In the center was another circle of stone symbols, smaller than those that formed the outer circle and unfamiliar to Caliban. Inside the smaller circle was a platform shaped like an 8 on its side. The upper side of the 8 had holes which projected to the far ceiling bright violet-colored rays.

Where the two Os that formed the 8 met, a strip of stone about ten feet wide, was a high-backed chair cut from a blood-red stone. The chair was not empty.

Caliban felt as if every cell in his body had turned over.

The being on the chair, surely Shrassk, She-Who-Eats-Her-Young, was not at all whom or what he had expected.

The fear surged back in; the vision dimmed. But he forced himself to push it back down, though it was like pressing down on a lid over a kettle of cockroaches breeding so furiously that the lid kept rising. For a moment, the vision became brighter and clearer. Doc saw that *his* Other was making signs in deaf-and-dumb language, indicating that his *Other*, Caliban, must hasten to aid him. Alone, each would go down quickly. Together, they might have a chance.

Caliban began running in a land where it was not good to run.

—>•<—

Thus ends this chapter. Will Caliban and The Other kill Shrassk?

Or will they be lucky to get away with life and limb? Will both survive? Will Doc Caliban ever analyze the ecosystem of what might or might not be Hell?

You will find out when *The Monster On Hold* is published.

Tarzan and ERB

The Princess of Terra

The Princess of Terra

by Charlotte Corday-Marat

Previously unpublished.

The writer and French revolutionist Jean-Paul Marat was born into a well-bred, middle class family. He had a skin condition that caused him enormous discomfort. The only relief he got was soaking in his specially designed bathtub with a warm towel wrapped around his head. He had a table designed for himself so that he could do his work, keep up his correspondence, and receive visitors there. One such visitor (Charlotte Corday) claimed to have a grievance to discuss with him, entered his room and stabbed him. She justified her actions with the claim that Marat was responsible for the civil war engulfing France.

Phil: "Why the pseudonym? Just for fun."

NOTE: The following is extracted from the book-review section of the Martian science-fiction and fact magazine, *Parallel,* formerly *Supersincere Science Stickler Stories* and still referred to by fandom as the Big S. The review was written by the prominent SF author and critic, Remlil Esspee, and was published in Vol. 69, dated (Martian style) *Day of the Devout Data Digger, Week of the Witching Wands, Month of the Muttering Mountebank, Year of the Yearning Yo-Yo, Cycle of the Psionic Seersucker.*

Here we have a reprint of another book by a writer once regarded as a master of science fiction, Erb of Anazrat. *The Princess of Terra* was the first of a series written about the third planet from the sun and needs no introduction for those who read the original when it appeared fifty-one years ago. But, for the third generation of readers, who may never have heard of Erb of Anazrat or may know him only through the movies based on his character Nazrat of Sepa, the story must be reviewed.

The novel begins over a hundred years ago, shortly after the end of The War Between The Estates. The hero, Noj Notrak, is an ex-officer of the gallant but defeated Short Stick Army. While prospecting for gold in the Great South and Sandy Wastes, he is forced to run for his life from a band of wild Painted Bottoms (pretty wild in those days but now mainly concerned with operating resort areas).

He takes refuge in a cave. There, he is put under a spell by an old witch of the Painted Bottoms. Through the spell or some means (Erb is vague about this), Noj Notrak, or his astral body, or something, is released from his corpse. He soars through space and lands on the surface of Terra, the native name for the planet we call Gongoos. Notrak has a very strong affinity for this world, the pagan god of war, and it is this affinity that attracts him like a nail to a magnet.

Presumably, on this principle, if Notrak had been a great lover instead of a great warrior, he would have gone to the second planet from the sun. Notrak, however, is rather shy with women and only feels at ease when impaling somebody on his trusty and never rusty blade (a phallic substitute?).

Why Erb chose this method of transporting his hero to Gongoos, or Terra, is a matter of speculation, if not of extreme wonder. Fifty-one years ago, it would have been scientifically valid to extrapolate interplanetary rockets. However, to be fair, rockets were not feasible in the period in which this story takes place. Perhaps, Erb was justified in using the unorthodox, even mystical, method of transportation. If it is considered as a form of teleportation, it even becomes credible. After all, many SF people, including the editor of this magazine, believe in this and other types of ESP.

Anyway, Erb wanted to get his hero quickly and without too much fuss to the third planet, and he certainly did that.

The reader who swallows the astral-corporeal method of space travel has only begun to choke. Erb paints a picture of a world based on the insufficient and sometimes incorrect data of his day. For one thing, though he correctly assumes a denser atmosphere for Gongoos than for that of our planet, he does not make the air as thin as scientists now know it to be. Actually, the gases are so heavy that beings with lungs just simply could not operate them efficiently enough to maintain life.

Erb also assumes vegetation, which probably does exist on Gongoos, but his vegetation has an incredible variety and abundance. Given the known conditions of extreme humidity and heat, only a very primitive and hardy type of flora (such as our own ubiquitous ancient sea-bottom moss) could live. Fauna, if any, would be limited to the colder polar regions.

But Erb is only out to tell a rousing good tale and to exercise the imaginations of his readers. This he does, although the present generation, accustomed to the modern "staccato" school of writing founded by Yawgnimmeh, will find Erb's style rather old fashioned, and, indeed, bad. It is far inferior to the splendid literary offerings of the authors you read every month in *Parallel*. (Note especially the current serial, "Errand Of Levity," by Lah Tnemelk.)

Noj Notrak finds that he must move slowly and with some effort because of the great gravity of Terra. This is, however, no real handicap. Terran beings, though fast, are very lightly constructed and fragile. They have to be so in order to move at all against the gravity and heavy air. Attacked by a large beast of prey (four-legged!), the sturdy Notrak smashed it with his fist. The beast's porous muscles and hollow bones crumple at the first impact.

However, Notrak is taken prisoner by a tribe of black men with only two arms when they overcome him by sheer numbers. In an effort to be colorful, Erb ignored, or was ignorant of, the fact that beings with heavily pigmented skin just could not survive on Terra. The intensity of the sun would cause a very dark skin to absorb so much radiant energy that the internal temperature of a body would be raised to a fatal level.

Be that as it may, Noj Notrak is taken to the camp of the black nomads (who ride a beast called *nag*, also four-legged). There he finds a fellow prisoner, a beautiful woman called Siroth Hajed. She resembles us Martians, but she is pink-skinned and belongs to a species that bears its young alive. Despite her eggless method of reproduction (disgusting if you think about it long enough but only lightly touched on in Erb's narrative), she is soon loved by Notrak.

Siroth Hajed is a princess of Ingillan, a country entirely surrounded by water. (The astronomers of our planet designate Erb's Ingillan as Maraba, after the ancient stargazer who first saw it during one of those rare moments when its cloud cover dissipated.) She was captured by the blacks when the flying vehicle on which she was a passenger was forced to land because of engine trouble.

The vehicle does not use lighter-than-air gas. It depends on lift from extended surfaces and is driven forward by propellers turned by engines of great power. While it is true that the dense air of Gongoos, or Terra, would provide greater support than ours, it is also true that the energy required to force such a craft through the very dense air would make this method of flight mechanically and economically unfeasible.

Notrak and Hajed escape from the black men. Several chapters are then devoted to their ordeals on the surface of the vast expanse of waters on Terra's surface. Erb describes these as being of great depth. (Scientists have evidence that they cannot be more than neckdeep.) The waters swarm with huge ferocious creatures which not only live in but *breathe* the water. He does not bother to explain the biological mechanisms that would make this possible. Perhaps, this is for the better, since there is enough to strain the reader's sense of credulity without adding this.

There is, however, a very good scene (considering Erb's prose) about the terror that Notrak feels when he is suspended in a watercraft over this abyss of liquid. Every reader will respond as Erb intended, but Erb could hardly fail with such a horrible idea.

The two finally get to London. (Perhaps, Erb chose the name of a gas as the nomenclature of a city because the element London had just been discovered in his day and was being used in dirigibles.) It is interesting to note Erb's explanation for the large splotches of light seen by our astronomers on the third planet's night surface. Notrak finds that the cities are so large and so well illuminated that their light is visible even to us.

At one time, this was a popular speculation not easily refuted. However, in the past twenty years, we have developed instruments able to detect radioactivity at a distance of over 40 million miles. In view of the sporadically high radioactivity emanating from Gongoos (Terra), it is very likely that the many glows of light are heavy concentrations of radium or similar materials spilled out onto the surface by volcanic eruptions. This, in itself, would make a profusion of animal life very improbable.

Aside from the above objection, the proximity of cities such as London to so much water would overstimulate the growth of fungus and other vegetable life. The cities would be buried under the plants.

The Londoners have no such problem. Instead, they are on the verge of defeat in their war with the sinister Hoons of Jirmani. Led by Notrak, who slays the leader of the Hoons, the Kighzar, the Ingillaners defeat and invade Jirmani. Notrak then marries Siroth Hajed.

Suddenly, the air becomes too thick. People begin to die of oxygen richness. The whole planet is doomed. Notrak, however, during one of his adventures, found the secret entrance to the supposedly impregnable air-burning plant of Terra. This building has been built as a joint effort by all nations to oxidize part of the atmosphere. If it were not for this measure, the atmosphere would become fatally dense. Now the operator of the oxidizing plant has gone mad and turned off the equipment. Notrak gets into the building, kills the insane operator, and turns the air-burners back on.

Terra is saved, but it is too late for Noj Notrak. He dies and is hurled through space and finds himself in his original body (uncorrupted) in the cave on our planet. However, those who care to do so may read the sequels, *The Gods of Terra* and *The Warlord of Terra*, and discover how Notrak gets back to the third planet and wins his beauteous pink-skinned princess.

I fear that only those of my own generation who read Erb in their boyhood and want to experience a nostalgia, or those too young to have read much modern science fiction or to know much of modern science, or the incurable romantics, will want to own these reprints.

The Golden Age
and the Brass

First published in *The Burroughs Bulletin,* Number 12, 1956.

This article is a perfect example of the ironic old saying "The cobbler's children have no shoes." Phil has introduced legions of science fiction fans to Edgar Rice Burrough's Tarzan (as opposed to the movie and television version of Tarzan), and other pulp heroes such as Doc Savage. He's even inspired his readers to pick up such classics as *Moby Dick, Around the World in 80 Days* and Homer's *The Odyssey;* he had less luck at home with his own son.

⁂

When I was ten, I built my personal pantheon of heroes. There were many stalwart and crafty and bold men and demi-gods among them. Hercules and Autoyous (the Greek Shadow) and Manabozho and Thor were in the front ranks. A little ahead of them stood broadshouldered Odysseus. Him I often imagined myself to be; a dug-out along the creek-bank became Polyphemus' cave, and I escaped the blind Cyclops' hands by throwing a sheep-skin (an old burlap sack) over my back and crawling out on all fours, baaing like mad.

Bright as these Greeks and Norse and Algonquins were, however, they were outshone by others, men and demi-gods who sprang, like Athena from Zeus' brow, full-grown from the mind of an American.

This man was a modern. He was Edgar Rice Burroughs, a man as fertile in the making of modern myths as his middle name indicates. From his brow and nimble fingers—some say *too* nimble—sprang tall heroes and divine heroines. They were, though created by a man of our times, not the characters you would expect in latter-day myths. There was nothing of the whining, brooding, and introspective protagonist who haunts and shadows so many present day novels and whom so many novelists would have you believe bodies forth the zeitgeist of the twentieth century. Not these mighty-hewed and utterly courageous giants! These men had no qualms about what they were doing;

their only concern about their destination was removing those who stood in their way. Their normal code, if rather simple and stiff-necked—even, if I dare say it, unrealistic—was still one that they did not doubt, one that did not throw them into throes of agonies over whether or not they were doing the right thing. These mighty-muscled gorilla-grapplers and sizzling swordmen were pitted against forces that they knew were *evil.* There were no greys or other shades in their universe; you were either black or white. The moral issues involved were few but were simple: the oppression of the good by the vicious and brutal, the forcing of good and clean and faithful women by lustful and foul men. All was very simple, and all was, after the encountering of many novel and very interesting and heart-pounding dangers, simply solved. Alexander cuts the Gordian knot; John Carter cuts down the villainous Jeddak, Tarzan breaks the Arab slaver's neck.

This, it must be admitted from a viewpoint that has now been aged and matured in the wood of time, was not an altogether admirable outlook on the universe. But for its time and for its readers it was good enough. The hero did not toss off drinks right and left and leap into buxom blondes' beds—or anybody's for that matter—nor did he take a vicious and bestial delight in shooting women in the belly. Indeed, he adhered to the code that you must not harm a woman with fist or weapon. And even though the hero was as likely as not to take justice and vengeance in his own hands instead of leaving it to the legally constituted authorities, he was not so tarred with the same brush as the villains' that it was hard to see the difference between them—especially in a dim light.

As I was saying before I got off on a slight tangent, I had my personal pantheon when I was ten. Some were heroes and demigods of the Golden Age; others were not. The latter existed in a sort of auriferous limbo which, while it did not have the antiquity and prestige of the legendary men, had a glow all its own and one, indeed, that shined rather more brightly than the more legitimate Valhallas and Olympuses.

Be that as it may, I spent far more time playing John Carter that I did anything else. I "was" John Carter, late of the C.S.A., and the woods and creekbanks not too far from my house was the dying planet Mars. Armed with a lath for a rapier, I slashed through hordes of big green "dumb Warhoons" and rescued the lovely red-skinned Dejah Thoris (whom I thought of as being literally, scarlet-skinned) from various lustful Jeddaks.

When I had exhausted Mars for the time being, I shifted into Tarzan's "valence," swung through the trees and dropped in on lions and mad gorillas and Ay-rabs and broke their necks or slit their gullets. So proficient did I become in this, I was soon called "Tarzan" by all my classmates. And, incidentally, I built muscles during my arboreal activities that helped me later in my athletic career.

My really favorite character, David of Pellucidar, was, for some unknown reason, neglected in my play. I preferred to sit around and dream about what Dian and he were doing. Usually, they were being chased by some dinosaur—which dinosaur, by the way, I imagined them as being, in some way, fond of. Dinosaurs, I think, dwell in an affectionate part of every science fiction and fantasy lover's heart—albeit slightly fearsome beasts. Just so, I think, did the knights of old love their dragons, and they must have been very sorry when the last dragons died.

What has the above got to do with today or even with the admitted subject for this project? Briefly, it is this. I read the Oz books and the Raggedy Anne stories, Grimm's Fairy Tales, the Mark Tidd books, Jules Verne, a series about some world-traveling, animal-collecting juveniles whose author I can't recall, and, climax, Edgar Rice Burroughs. All glowed golden, but Burroughs' books gave me the deepest and most lasting thrills. I read each one of his series at least twenty times. To get them I had to visit the local libraries, reserve them, and then, after waiting a few weeks, seize them, fondle them, and dream over them during the two weeks I was allowed to keep them out.

I saved money from my allowance, and, one by one, built up an almost complete Edgar Rice Burroughs library. My father wasn't interested in fantasy or SF, but he indulgently allowed me to purchase such with my own money. On birthdays and Christmas I would ask for, and get, at least one ERB, usually a John Carter or Tarzan, but occasionally there would be *The Moon Maid* or *The Monster Men*.

The point is, if my father had had the ERB collection I now possess, I would have blithered with joy, blown a tender young blood vessel with ecstasy. But my son is being raised in the heyday of the comics. He, in common with most of his kind in this neo-Noachian age, is being flooded beneath a deluge of crud that will last longer than forty days because there seems to be no end to paper, whereas even rain can last only so long.

(Lest I be accused of being partial, I hasten to add that some comics are quite good.)

My son, instead of living in the golden age, is surrounded by brass. Brass is notoriously easier to get than gold and is far noisier. Not that I mind the presence of brass. I can ignore it and reach for the gold.

Unfortunately, most people don't. And most can't see the gold—which they would naturally prefer—because brass glitters in their eyes and they can't see beyond it. My son looks at the John Carter, the David Innes, the *Moon Maid*, the *Land That Time Forgot*, the Tarzan books. There is an interested but dubious expression on his face. Then, after leafing through their pages—which contains so *many* words—he turns to the comics—full of pictures and their swiftly-read balloons. I am somewhat impatient, because I want him to know the joys I knew, because he does have the type of imagination that revels in the things that throng in ERB.

Yet, I can't force them on him, and I wouldn't want to.

Time passed, as it always did and does. I resigned myself to letting dust gather and dim the golden treasury of Burroughs.

Then one bright day in the midst of many grey, I noticed one thing that gives me hope. Among all the hundreds, perhaps the thousands, of the comics he has read, he remembers none over six months old. Except two, which he read at least eight months ago. Both these are John Carter comics, ERB transliterated. He still talks of these, and I am gently guiding him back to those dusty volumes, gently, gently, for I hope his interest leads to the day when he, too, knows the delights, raptures, and terrors that I, as a child and budding adolescent, found in the mythmaker Edgar Rice Burroughs.

An Appreciation
of Edgar Rice Burroughs

First published in *20th Century Fiction*, 1985.

W hen almost 36 years old, with a wife and three children, disappointed in his military and various business careers, Edgar Rice
Burroughs decided to try fiction writing. His first sale, later printed in hard-
covers as *A Princess of Mars*, was serialized in *All-Story Magazine* in 1912. The
first of a series still immensely popular, the novel illustrates most of the
strengths and weaknesses of his works. Fast-paced, colorful, and often strikingly imaginative, it stimulates the sense of wonder, especially of children and
juveniles. The one-dimensional characters as either evil or good, and the use of
coincidence, is abused. Though his "Barsoomian" cultures are vividly presented, they are not developed in depth. The historical novel that he next wrote,
The Outlaw of Torn, and his "realistic" stories, notably those of crime and corruption in Chicago and Hollywood, illustrate his failure to be convincing at
anything other than fantasy. Tales set on Mars, in darkest Africa, or in earth's
center, worlds which he nor his readers knew much about, were never-never
lands that he could deal with.

Burroughs is best known as the creator of Tarzan, son of an English nobleman, Lord Greystoke, raised from the age of one in the African jungle by lan-
guage-using great apes. Critics have maintained that Burroughs wrote *Tarzan
of the Apes* to demonstrate his belief in the superiority of heredity over environment, and especially of the superior heredity of the British nobility. In one
sense they are correct. Tarzan's human genes gave him an intelligence superior
to the apes'; they gave him an innate curiosity and drive which would have
taken him out of any ghetto or other underprivileged community he had been
born into. But in the final analysis it was the environment which molded
Tarzan's character. Raised as a feral child, he is a classic example of the outsider,
one who has an objective view of human society because he has not imbibed
its irrationalities along with his mother's milk. Through Tarzan's eyes,

Burroughs satirizes Homo sapiens, as he did through some of his other heroes, notably Carson Napier of the "Venus" series.

However, Burroughs' ape-man is more than a Voltairean observer or noble savage. Though he regards pre-literates as superior in their way of life to civilized peoples, he is never quite human. He is, when in the jungle, free of the mundane, drab, wearing, and often tragic restrictions of tribal or civilized life. It is his being a law unto himself, and his extreme closeness to nature which have been part of his appeal. But Burroughs, though unconsciously, also gave him most of the attributes of the pre-literate and classical hero of fairy tale, legend, and mythology, including the Trickster. He is the last of the Golden Age heroes, a literary character who reflects the archetypal images and feelings of the unconscious mind noted by Carl Jung and Joseph Campbell.

Like Arthur Conan Doyle, Burroughs had the gift of writing adventure stories with an indefinable quality that made them endure while thousands of similar novels dropped into oblivion. Like Doyle he created a classical fictional character of whom he wearied. The later Tarzan novels, in fact all of his works written in the latter part of his career, show a flagging invention, repetitiveness of plot and incident, excess of coincidences and improbabilities, and failure to develop fully promised themes.

He never thought of himself as anything but a commercial writer of romances. His works betray the biases, conservatisms, and timidities of his social class and times, and his style is old-fashioned. With the exception of Tarzan and a few others, his characters are cardboard. His genius was in the creation of the archetypal feral Tarzan and the writing of many pseudo-scientific romances which have enthralled generations of young readers, many of whom have remained loyal to him through their middle age.

The Arms of Tarzan

(The English Nobleman whom Edgar Rice Burroughs
called John Clayton, Lord Greystoke)

Originally presented as a speech at the Dum-Dum banquet
on Burrough's day, 1970.
First published in *The Burroughs Bulletin*, Number 22,
Summer 1971.

A scholarly piece typical of Phil's investigative nature. Who
else would go to such lengths to establish the heraldry of a supposedly fictional character?
The original artwork for the Coat of Arms was generously
donated by Phil to the Edgar Rice Burroughs Memorial Collection
in Louisville, Kentucky.
Please note that the book referred to as *The Private Life of
Tarzan* was actually published as *Tarzan Alive*.

⚜

NOTE FROM PHILIP JOSÉ FARMER: The speech published here is not quite
that given during the Dum-Dum banquet on Burroughs' Day, September 5, 1970,
in Detroit, Michigan. Some changes have been made and insertions and additions
worked in due to corrections of errors on my part and a failure to resist the temptation to gild the lily. It is, however, in the main, the same speech.

L adies and gentlemen, mangani, tarmangani, gomangani, and bolgani.
I'm happy to be here. Whether or not you will be happy remains to
be seen. I warn you that what I am going to say has little "relevance." I'm all
for relevancy to the problems of our time. I belong to the ZPG (Zero
Population Growth), have worked in the Write For Your Life campaign, and
have consistently tried to combat prejudice and inhumane thinking in my
writings. I've been working for some time on a book concerning the need for
an Economy of Abundance. I've just finished two short stories about pollution
in our times. I'm writing a novel, *Death's Dumb Trumpet*, about the effects of
pollution twenty years from now.

But you won't be getting any of that today. Men must have hobbies, otherwise they go mad. The works of Edgar Rice Burroughs (ERB) are, to me, a gate into parallel worlds where there are problems, but none that my hero, and, therefore, me as the hero, can't handle. There I can relax and forget, for the time being, the noisy, stinking, dusty, and hostile world that exists outside my window. And, too often, inside the window.

It's not my purpose today to justify my love for ERB's worlds. You know why I love them, otherwise you wouldn't be here.

I propose today to inspect a very small segment of the world of Tarzan, one that has been left entirely unexplored, as far as I know. For that purpose, I've had some transparencies of the subject for today, the Greystoke coat-of-arms, prepared. You can observe it in widescreen color on this wall while I lecture.

THE ARMS OF TARZAN *491*

I furnished the original research for these arms, the first rough sketches, and the blazoning. But Bjo Trimble did the actual execution, which I consider to be superb. She took a keen interest in the project and put in much time she could ill afford in research of her own and in the actual calculations and drawings. The result exceeded my expectations; her visualizations surpassed my own.

NOTE: This illustration is at present, September, 1971, scheduled to be part of the jacket illustration of my *The Private Life of Tarzan*. This is a biography of Lord Greystoke along the lines of W. S. Baring-Gould's *Sherlock Holmes of Baker Street* and *Nero Wolfe of West Thirty-Fifth Street*, and also of C. Northcote Parkinson's *The Life And Times Of Horatio Hornblower*. The latter was issued after the Ms for the Tarzan life had been turned in to the publisher, Doubleday.

The Tarzan books describe, or hint at, many things. But in none is there any reference to the coat-of-arms of the "Greystoke" family. There is a reference in *Tarzan Of The Apes* to the family crest on the great ring which Tarzan's father wore. But the crest is not described. Greystoke, as you know, is not the actual title of the noble family that engendered the immortal ape-man. Greystoke is a pseudonym used by ERB to cover the real identity of a line of English peers. I intend to speculate about the real title. But Greystoke has been associated too long with Tarzan for any of us to be at ease in using any other title. This is the way it should be, and this is why I have placed the legend, GREYSTOKE, under the arms.

However, though Greystoke is not Tarzan's real title, he is descended from the de Greystocks, the ancient and distinguished barons of Greystoke, Cumberland, England. I refer you to Burke's *Extinct Peerage*, Nicolas' *A Synopsis of the Peerage*, and Cokayne's *The Complete Peerage* for their history. This descent of Tarzan through several lines of this family is one of the reasons ERB chose Greystoke for a pseudonym.

Now—the blazoning, I'll give it to you as it would be in Burke's *Genealogical and Heraldic History of the Peerage, Baronetage, And Knightage*. Burke's *Peerage* (to use its short title) has over 2475 pages of very small, closely set print devoted to genealogy.

After the blazoning, I'll explain the technical terms I used. Then I'll go into the history of each family represented here. I'll demonstrate that Tarzan, king of the tribe of Kerchak, chief of the Waziri, a member of the English peerage, lord of the jungle, demigod of the forest, has a noble genealogy indeed. In fact, no one in Europe, not even Queen Elizabeth of Great Britain, can boast of a more ancient and varied lineage.

The Blazoning:

ARMS—Quarterly of six: 1st, GREBSON OF GREBSON, *argent*, on a saltire *azure* drinking horns in triskele *gules*; 2nd, DRUMMOND, *or*, three bars wavy *gules*; 3rd, O'BRIEN, *gules*, three lions passant guardant in pale, per pale *or* and *argent*; 4th, CALDWELL, *sable*, a torn *or*; 5th, RUTHERFORD, *gules*, a wild bull's head cabossed, eyes of the first, otherwise of its own kind, between the horns a wild man's head affrontée, eyes of the first; 6th, GREYSTOCK, barry of six, *argent* and *azure*, over all three chaplets of roses *gules*. CRESTS—A sleuth-hound *argent*, collared and leashed *gules*, for DRUMMOND; issuing from a cloud *azure* an arm embowed brandishing a sword *gules*, pommel and hilt *sable*, for GREBSON; a spear *or* transfixing a Saracen's head *gules*, for GREBSON. SUPPORTERS—Dexter, a savage wreathed about the middle with oak leaves, in the dexter hand a bow, with a quiver of arrows over his shoulder, all *vert*, and a lion's skin or hanging behind his back; sinister, a female great ape guardant, all proper. MOTTOES—"Je Suys Encore Vyvant"; "Kreeg-ah!"

The explanation of the technical terms:

Quarterly of six. Quarterly originally meant the four equal parts into which the shield was divided for showing four arms. But some people added even more, and the family of Dent, the Baronage of Furnivall, has a quarterly of ten. The Greystokes could add a hundred, if they wished, since they are descended from that many different noble families. But the shields generally are restricted to a reasonable number.

Argent is a heraldic term for silver or white. Azure is blue. A saltire, or St. Andrew's cross, is a cross in the form of an X. The St. Andrew's cross is usually found in the field of a Scots family but not always. Gules is red. In triskele indicates a figure composed of three usually curved or bent branches radiating from a center. Triskele, or triskelion, is from a Greek word meaning three-legged.

Or is gold. A bar is a horizontal division of the shield occupying one-fifth thereof. Wavy means undulating. Passant is a term for beasts in a walking position with the right forepaw raised, although I've seen the left front paw raised, for instance, in the lion passant of the crest of a branch of the English family of Farmer.

Guardant is front or full-faced. In pale indicates that the charges, in this case, the lions, are arranged beneath one another. Per pale indicates the particular manner in which a shield or field or a charge is divided by a partition line. Thus, the lions, in pale, per pale *or* and *argent* are arranged in a vertical column and each is half-gold and half-silver, as you see.

Sable is black. A torn is a heraldic spinning wheel. Torn was an archaic English word for the early type of spinning wheel used in the late 13th century.

A wild bull's head cabossed. Cabossed, or caboshed, indicates the head of any beast looking full-faced with nothing of the neck visible. "Of the first" means that the color is the first one mentioned in the blazoning. In this case, of the first means gules. The eyes of the bull and the wild man are bright red, giving the Rutherford charges a fierce and sinister look. Making the eyes red was Bjo's idea, a stroke of genius on her part, as far as I'm concerned. Of its own kind, or proper, are terms applicable to animals, trees, vegetables, etc., when they are their natural color.

A wild man's head affrontée. Affrontée is a term applied to full-faced human heads.

Barry describes the field or charge divided by horizontal lines. Thus, GREYSTOCK, barry of six, *argent* and *azure*, means six horizontal bars alternately silver and blue.

Crests over coats-of-arms were originally derived from the actual crests of helmets worn by the nobles. The only term used for the crests so far not explained is *embowed.* (Pointing to the center crest.) An arm embowed. Embowed means bent or bowed.

The Saracen's head originally indicated an ancestor who went to the Holy Land on one of the crusades. The head is gules, instead of a proper or natural color, because of a story associated with Tarzan's crusader ancestor. The story will be told in the genealogy of Tarzan in *The Private Life of Tarzan.*
Regard the two supporters, the figures holding the shield up. One is dexter; the other, sinister. Dexter means the right-hand supporter. Right and left,

in heraldry, are as seen by the man behind the shield. Sinister, of course, has no evil meaning in heraldry; it merely indicates the left-hand position.

The savage, or woodman, or wildman, is all *vert*, that is, green.

The upper motto is French in archaic spelling. *Je Suys Encore Vyvant.* Translation: *I Still Live.* Or *I am Still Living.* Or *I Yet Live.*

Tarzan, as you no doubt recall, said these words more than once in seemingly hopeless situations. In *Tarzan the Untamed,* Bertha Kircher, the supposed German spy, and Tarzan are about to be caught by the insane Xujans and their hunting lions. She says to Tarzan, "You think there is some hope, then?"

"We are still alive," was his only answer.

And in *Tarzan the Terrible,* when Jane and Tarzan are soon to be sacrificed, Jane asks, "You still have hope?"

"I am still alive," he said, as though that were sufficient answer.

Thus Tarzan echoed the motto of his ancient family, the old war cry his fighting ancestors used to rally their men around them when the battle seemed to have turned against them.

I probably don't need to point out that "*I still live*" is also the motto of another great fighter, John Carter of Mars.

The lower motto, "Kreeg-ah!" is, of course, the warning cry of the great ape. (As an aside, I'd like to suggest that it's long past time for the great ape to be given a scientific classification. And since Tarzan's father was the first European to describe the great ape—in his diary, of course—I propose that we honor him by terming this new genus *Megapithecus greystoki*. This would also honor his son, who knows more of the great ape than anyone in the world, civilized or uncivilized.)

The lower motto, "Kreeg-ah!", was added by Tarzan to the family arms when he assumed the title in late 1910 (according to my reckoning). The great ape supporter is also Tarzan's idea. The original supporter was a heraldic Sagittarius, a centaur with a bow. But Tarzan wanted to honor his foster mother, Kala, and so he replaced the Sagittarius with a female mangani. This changing of supporters in a coat-of-arms for personal reasons is not unprecedented. The 10th Duke of Marlborough, for instance, replaced both supporters on his family's arms. However, this type of arms is usually regarded as a personal coat-of-arms, a variation on the family's, and other members of the family may use the older type if they desire. I would imagine that Korak would keep his father's arms, inasmuch as he was also closely associated with the mangani.

While I'm at it, I might as well say that these arms are not complete or even accurate from the strict viewpoint of the College of Heraldry. All of the quarters except the first and fourth should have little symbols, such as a crescent or mullet (a five-pointed star) or others to indicate that these are different branches from the main Drummond, O'Brien, Rutherford, and Greystock lines. However, the symbols for difference are not always used, and Tarzan's noble forebears never got around to conforming to strict usage.

Also, the Drummond crest, the sleuthhound (that must be Sherlock Holmes' crest, too) should be on the sinister side. The crests of the primary family, the Grebsons, should occupy the dexter place of honor and the center. But these crests entered the Greystoke arms a long time before heraldry became regulated by a college of heralds or by royal authority. The crests should be somewhat smaller and all placed above the shield, but, again, they were drawn thus in the distant old days, and the Greystoke family has never seen fit to change them.

The headpiece you see on top of the shield is the coronet of a duke, not to be confused with the ducal or crest coronet. It has a circle, or coronet, of gold surmounted by eight golden strawberry leaves, of which only five are visible, and by the red golden-tasselled cap with the ermine under-rim you see. I know that some of you are thinking: Why the coronet of a duke? Tarzan, according to his own statement in *Tarzan, Lord of The Jungle*, is a viscount. And several other Tarzan books assert that he is a viscount.

Is he? My own theory is that he may have been a duke, a marquess, earl, baron, or baronet (a baronet is not a noble but a sort of hereditary knight), or any combination of these. But he would not be a viscount. Or, if he were, it would be only one of his titles. ERB took great pains to conceal the true identity of "Lord Greystoke." He would have altered the reply Tarzan really made when asked (by Sir Bertram of the city of Nimmir) what his rank was. ERB knew that Tarzanic scholars would search through the some 120-plus viscounts listed in Burke's *Peerage* for evidence that one was Tarzan. So he directed them down a blind alley.

I don't want to go into this theory in detail at this time, but the feudal society Tarzan found in a lost valley in Ethiopia was supposed to be descended from two shiploads of Englishmen who had set out with Richard I on the First Crusade. This was in 1191, but viscount, as an English title, was not used until 1440. If Tarzan had "truly" said he was a viscount, Sir Bertram wouldn't have known what he meant. Obviously, Tarzan did not say that. Or, if he did, seeing that Sir Bertram did not understand him, he went on to his other titles. Sir Bertam would have heard of "earl" and "baron", since these were the only English titles of nobility extant in Richard's time.

From the above argument, we can assume, with a good amount of reasonableness, that Tarzan is an earl or baron. Given the ancientness and honourableness of his line (stressed by ERB in the first Tarzan book), the chances are that he is both.

On the other hand, very few Englishmen, that is, men of Old English descent, actually accompanied Richard. Most of his crusaders were Normans, and it is doubtful that Richard had enough Englishmen to fill one ship, let alone two. (Accounting at least 60 knights per ship as a shipload.)

This would mean that the people of the valley were descended from Normans and so spoke an evolved Norman. This leads to developments that I don't have time for here but will lay out for the interested reader in *The Private Life of Tarzan.*

It is, however, incredible that the man we know as Lord Greystoke would not be a duke. If Peter Wimsey's father was Duke of Denver and Lord John Roxton's father was Duke of Pomfret, then surely Tarzan must be a duke, regardless of how many other titles he holds. Don't forget that Tarzan is referred to as a "dook" twice, once in *Tarzan and the Foreign Legion.* I do have more solid reasons than this for placing him in the highest rank of nobility. But I have to expound these elsewhere, due to lack of time here.

To arms. The first, first. GREBSON OF GREBSON. Am I revealing, for the first time by anyone anywhere, the true name and title of Tarzan's family?

Not exactly.

The present Lord Greystoke wishes to have his identity stay hidden, and I respect his reasons. (Besides, I would not think of offending the Lord of the Jungle.) So I have picked a title and a coat-of-arms which reveal certain facts about him, or come close to the facts, without disclosing his genuine identity. The title and the arms are analogs. They are not the real title and arms. But they are near enough to give an idea of what the genuine items are.

Some of you know that ERB, in the original Ms of *Tarzan of the Apes*, used Bloomstoke as Tarzan's title. Then he changed it. Why? For one thing, Greystoke sounds more aristocratic than Bloomstoke. Also, Tarzan *is* descended from the Greystokes. (So is half of the peerage of England as you may ascertain if you care to take the trouble to trace them through Burke.) But the Grey in Greystoke was also provided by ERB as a clue for some scholar who might want to tackle the formidable hunt for the real Tarzan. (We know that ERB was fond of codes and sometimes used them in making up names or disguising real names for his characters and places.)

Following this coded lead (among many others), I hunted down and identified the real-world Tarzan. The project took me two and a half years and involved reading every word of the lineages in 2,475 pages of Burke's *Peerage*. However, all the work I put in would not have led me to the real Tarzan if I had not stumbled across a certain clue through sheer good fortune. Only a highly improbable sequence of events could permit another to follow the trail I followed. I am sorry, but I cannot supply the necessary clue, since "Lord Greystoke" himself has asked me not to. Therefore, I am compelled to suppress everything I know for sure and behave as if I were as ignorant as everybody else in the matter. I have to proceed by analogy, and if you choose to dispute my theses, you have a perfect right to do so.

I will tell you one thing. Tarzan's real title does not start with GR (as in Greystoke or Grebson). That initial letter cluster will, however, lead you to some of his ancestors and relatives in Burke's *Peerage*. Nor does his title contain the word *grey*. It does contain an archaic word implying grey. I won't tell you if the word is of Germanic, Latin, Pictish, or Celtic origin, however.

Grebson, our analog family name and title, comes from the Old English Graegbeardssunu. This means The Son of the Grey-Bearded One. And who was the Grey-Bearded One? He was Woden, the chief god of the Anglo-Saxons or Old English, the same as the Othinn of the Old Norse or the Wuotan of the Old High Germans or Othinus of the continental Saxons. According to the Norse *Edda*, the great god had many epithets. To read off all his titles would take several minutes, so I resist the temptation.

Tarzan's real title contains an epithet for Woden, though not the one I give here, which is an analogous epithet.

Note the argent field and azure saltire of Grebson's arms. Argent and azure are Woden's colors. Note the three drinking horns with interlocking tips. This ancient sign for Woden (or Odin) is found carved on rocks in many places in Scandinavia and a number of places in the British Isles. In Old English it would be called the *waelcnotta* and in Old Norse is the *valknutr*. It means the "knot of the slain" and stands for Woden (or Odin) in his aspect as the god of the warriors who've died in battle. Hence the gules, or red, color of the drinking horns.

You won't find this symbol on Tarzan's real shield. But you will find something analogous, if you are persistent enough and wildly lucky.

Apparently, the founder of Tarzan's family, the original Grebson, claimed to be descended from the god Woden. The Queen of England makes exactly the same claim, as you can find out by reading "The Royal Lineage" section of

Burke's *Peerage*. She is descended from Egbert, King of Wessex (died 839 A.D.). Egbert, like the other kings of English states at that time, Mercia, Deira, Kent, Eastanglia, etc., had a traditional genealogy which went unbroken back to Denmark of circa 300 A.D. and to the great god Woden.

Those interested can refer to page 165, Vol. 1, of Jacob Grimm's *Teutonic Mythology*, Dover Books.

I submit that a human being can't have a more highly placed or illustrious ancestor.

That Tarzan's arms bear the ancient symbol of Woden indicates that his ancestors clung to the old religion long after their neighbors were Christianized. Originally, their shields bore only the drinking horns gules in triskele on an argent and azure field. Then the saltire was added to convince others that the family was truly of the new faith. History tells us of the tenacity with which parts of rural England held on to the ancient faiths. And ERB, in *The Outlaw of Torn*, says of the peasants' love for the outlaw, "Few...had seen his face and fewer still had spoken with him, but they loved his name and his prowess and in secret they prayed for him to their ancient god Wodin and the lesser gods of the forest and the meadow and the chase..."

Second, DRUMMOND. Drummond comes from the Gaelic *druim mon-adh*, meaning *back of the mountain*. This Scots family is presently represented by the Earl of Ancaster and the Earl of Perth. The family was founded by Maurice, the son of George, a young son of Andreas, King of Hungary. Maurice came to Scotland in 1066 and settled there. He, in turn, could trace his ancestry unbroken back to Arpad, the Magyar chief who conquered Hungary (died 907 A.D.).

Third, O'BRIEN. A prominent member of this ancient Irish family is the Baron of Inchiquin. In an unbroken line it descends from Brian Boroimhe, chief Irish monarch in 1002 A. D. and victor of the battle of Clontarf, though he himself was killed by the Danes. This line can actually trace itself back to Cormac Cas, son of Olliol Olum, King of Ireland, circa 200 A. D.

Fourth, CALDWELL, *sable* a torn *or*. Some of you pricked up your ears when I first blazoned these arms. You remembered that Tarzan, in *The Return of Tarzan*, used the pseudonym of John Caldwell when he was a French secret agent traveling on a liner from Algiers to Cape Town.

Why would he use that pseudonym? Obviously, he picked the first name that came to mind, that of his illustrious ancestor, John Caldwell. No doubt, Tarzan had been reading in Burke's *Peerage* about the Greystoke lineage and the story of John Caldwell was fresh in his mind.

Another reason you pricked up your ears was the mention of the torn, the heraldic spinning wheel. You recalled Richard Plantagenet, son of Henry III, he who would later be called Norman of Torn or the Outlaw of Torn. You probably asked yourself, "What does Farmer mean by that? The Outlaw of Torn is Tarzan's ancestor? But Norman killed one of Tarzan's ancestors, a Greystoke!"

Did he? ERB did not say that this particular Greystoke was an ancestor of Tarzan. That's an assumption by some of his readers. Perhaps the slain Greystoke was a member of the genuine de Grestocks of Greystoke Castle, Cumberland. He may or may not have been Tarzan's forefather, but I'm inclined to believe that Norman of Torn certainly was. Tarzan would certainly have the greatest warrior of the Middle Ages in his family line.

The Outlaw was born in 1240 A.D. and was 15 years old when he slew Greystoke. This would be in 1255, the 39th year of Henry III's reign. So the Greystoke whom Norman killed was probably the son of Baron Robert de Greystock (died before 1253) and the younger brother of William de Greystock. William's son, John, was the first Greystoke summoned as a baron *by writ* to Parliament. This was in 1295 A. D. in Edward I's time. This, by the way, was the first regular parliament, recognized as such.

We know that Henry III finally became aware that the famous, or infamous, outlaw was his long-lost son, Richard. But Henry died in 1272, and his son, Edward I, called Long Shanks, was, though a very good king for those days, proud, jealous, and suspicious. His younger brother Richard, too popular with the common people, would have been forced to flee on a trumped-up charge of treason (nothing rare in those days). By then Bertrade de Montfort, his wife, had died, probably in childbirth or of disease, very common causes of fatality then. Richard would have taken a pseudonym again, that of John Caldwell, landless warrior. In the North of England he met old Baron Grebson. The baron had no male issue, and so, when his daughter fell in love with the stranger knight, he adopted him. This was nothing unusual; you will find similar examples throughout Burke's *Peerage*. The family name became Caldwell-Grebson, though the Caldwell was later dropped. Similar examples of this also abound in Burke.

John Caldwell could not use the same arms as the Outlaw of Torn, of course. So, instead of *argent* a falcon's wing *sable*, he used *sable* a torn *or*. That he chose the torn showed he could not resist an example of "canting arms," a heraldic pun. One, indeed, that proved as dangerous as might be expected. Edward I heard of the appearance from nowhere of a knight who bore a torn on his shield, and he investigated. The king's men ambushed John Caldwell, and though he slew five of them, he, too, died.

How can we be sure of this?

An obscure book on medieval witchcraft, published in the middle 1600's, describes the case of a knight who was, for reasons unknown to the writer, slain by Edward I's men in a northern county. When his body was laid out to be washed, his left breast was found to bear a violet lily-shaped birthmark. This was thought to be the mark of the devil. But we readers of *The Outlaw of Torn* will recognize the true identity of the man suspected of witchcraft.

This theory could be wrong, of course. I propose an alternate to consider. You may have noticed the remarkable resemblance between the Outlaw and Tarzan. Both were tall, splendidly built, and extremely powerful men. (Anybody who can drive the point of a broadsword through chain mail into his opponent's heart is strong enough to crack the neck of a bull ape.) Both men had grey eyes. Both wore their hair in bangs across their foreheads. Neither knew the meaning of fear.

But the description of the Outlaw could also apply, except for a few minor points, to John Carter of Mars. What if the Outlaw did not die, as I first speculated, but had somehow defeated the aging process? What if, like Tarzan, he had stumbled across an elixir for immortality? During his wanderings in rural England, he came across a wizard or witch, actually a member of the old faith, who had a recipe for preventing degeneration of the body. If a witch doctor in modern Africa could have such, and give it to Tarzan, then a priest of an outlawed religion in the Middle Ages could give such to the Outlaw of Torn.

Sometime during the following six centuries, the Outlaw suffered amnesia. This was either from a blow on the head (again recalling Tarzan, who suffered amnesia many times from blows on the head) or because loss of memory of early years is an unfortunate by-product of the elixir. Thus, on March 4, 1866, the Outlaw, a long-time resident of Virginia, an admitted victim of amnesia, left a cave in Arizona for the planet Mars. ERB called this man John Carter. Notice the J. C. I suggest that he may have been Richard Plantagenet, Norman of Torn, John Caldwell, and, finally, John Carter.

It is possible that John Caldwell was not killed, that he slew all of Edward's men, who actually numbered six, mangled the face of one tall corpse, and stained a violet lily mark on the corpse's left breast. And, once again, he disappeared into pseudonymity but gained immortality as the Warlord of Mars.

It's true that the Outlaw's hair was brown and Carter's was black. But hair gets darker as one ages (until it starts to grey), and 626 years are long enough for anybody's hair to get black.

If this theory is correct, the Outlaw of Torn is not only John Carter of Mars but Tarzan's ancestor by about 600 years. But John Carter may have been the ancestor of Tarzan many times over. He may have followed the fortunes of his descendants with keen interest and, every now and then, remarried into the line and begat more powerful, quick thinking, fearless, grey-eyed men and fearless grey-eyed beautiful daughters. I wouldn't be surprised if he were not only the ancestor of Tarzan's father but of Tarzan's mother, Alice Rutherford. Perhaps this regular insertion of Carter's genes into the line is why ERB insists so strongly on the influence of heredity in Tarzan' s behavior.

And I point out, as something for you to chew on, that Sherlock Holmes, Professor Challenger, Raffles, Richard Wentworth, Lord Peter Wimsey, and Denis Nayland Smith were all grey-eyed. And, though some were slim, all had very powerful muscles. Could these, together with Tarzan, be descendants of John Carter of Mars?

Their relationship, with those of Doc Savage, Kent Allard, Korak, Lord John Roxton, Nero Wolfe, and The Scarlet Pimpernel, will be described in a separate essay. Oh, yes, I almost forgot Bulldog Drummond.

Fifth, RUTHERFORD.

As we know, Tarzan's mother was the Honourable Alice Rutherford. The *Honourable* indicates that she was the daughter of a baron or a viscount, though ERB does not tell us what the title of her father was. The Rutherfords are an ancient and once-powerful Scots border family. Its name comes from the

Old English *hrythera ford*, meaning *wild cattle of the ford*. The arms you see here, the wild bull cabossed and the wildman's head between the horns, are the arms of the lords of Tennington. Internal evidence in *The Return Of Tarzan* convinces me that Tarzan's mother was the aunt of the Lord Tennington who married Hazel Strong, Jane Porter's best friend. The reasons for this conclusion will be given in a separate essay.

Sixth, GREYSTOCK.

Tarzan is descended through at least half a dozen lines from the barons of Greystoke. At present, the barony is in abeyance, the last male heir having died in 1569. The Earl of Carlisle, the Baron of Petre, and the Baron of Mowbray, Segrave, and Stourton are co-heirs. The Earl of Carlisle bears the Greystoke arms on his shield, and a cousin of the Duke of Norfolk resides in Greystoke Castle. I have a letter from the cousin in which he says that he was very fond of the Tarzan books when he was young. But, he adds, "...as you know, I am not Tarzan."

What he doesn't say is that he is a relative of Tarzan's.

(Please put the first slide back on.)

About all that remains to explain in the arms is the dexter supporter. Aside from it being green, it looks like the usual savage or woodman supporter. Actually, it represents the son of John Caldwell. After his father's supposed death, the son had to flee into the wilds of northern England to escape the King's officers. There he adopted a green costume and used a green-painted bow and green arrows. Because of these, he was known as The Green Archer or, sometimes, as The Green Baron. His legend was combined with that of Robert Fitz-ooth to create the Robin Hood legend.

The golden lion skin which he wears here was added by Tarzan to honor Jad-bal-ja.

So you can see that the baby born in a little log cabin on the West African coast, raised by apes, naked until twenty and then wearing second-hand clothes, yet came from a lineage few can match and eventually inherited the golden coronet and crimson miniver-edged mantle of a peer of the realm.

Before I close, let me summarize the illustrious ancestors of Tarzan.

First, the nonhuman founder of his line, Woden, chief god of the Old English tribes.

Henry III and through him William the Conqueror and Rolf the Ganger (the Viking who conquered Normandy). Through Henry III's wife, Alfred the Great, Egbert, and Charlemagne, Charlemagne could trace his ancestry back to Pepin the Short, died 768 A.D.

Also, through Henry III, the Outlaw of Torn and his son, The Green Archer, one of the two men whose exploits contributed to the Robin Hood legend.

And possibly, many times over, the genes of the Outlaw of Torn, later known as John Carter of Barsoom.

Through the Scots Drummond family, Tarzan is descended from Arpad, the Magyar conqueror of Hungary.

Through the O'Briens, from Olliol Olum, Irish King, early 200's.

I don't have time to go into the many other famous ancestors of Tarzan, such as Sir Nigel Loring (whose story is told in Doyle's *The White Company* and *Sir Nigel*). Or such as William Marshal, the Earl of Pembroke, who served Richard I and King John and was undoubtedly the greatest warrior of his time and probably of the entire Middle Ages (outside of the Outlaw of Torn). These will be described in detail in the lineage of Tarzan, which will be in my, *The Private Life Of Tarzan*.

I hope you have enjoyed this visitation into Tarzan's ancestry via his coat-of-arms.

I thank you.

The Two Lord Ruftons

First published in *The Baker Street Journal,* Volume 21, Number 4, December 1971.

Farmer made his debut in the scholarly Sherlockian publication *The Baker Street Journal* with "The Two Lord Ruftons" (published December 1971). For those unaware, it is quite an honor to be selected to appear in the hallowed pages of *The Baker Street Journal,* an indication that the writer has contributed something original to the study of the Great Detective. In this study, Farmer illustrates the genealogical connections between Doyle's Holmes story "The Disappearance of Lady Carfax" and his non-Holmes works narrating the life of Brigadier Gerard.

Holmes, in *The Disappearance of Lady Frances Carfax,* notes that Lady Frances is the unmarried daughter of the late Lord Rufton. The famous Napoleonic soldier, Brigadier Étienne Gerard, also writes in his memoirs of a Lord Rufton. (Gerard's literary agent and editor, A. Conan Doyle, was also Watson's.) Lord Rufton, in Gerard's "How He Triumphed in England" (title by Doyle), was the English nobleman who, in 1811, was the host of Gerard while he was waiting to be exchanged for an English prisoner. In his autobiography, the Frenchman gives an account of his adventures which are, as usual, highly self-revealing and amusing. We need concern ourselves here only with the relationship of Gerard's host to Lady Frances, though we won't ignore certain implications or suggestions.

Holmes's case occurred 1 July to 18 July 1902, according to W.S. Baring-Gould in his *The Annotated Sherlock Holmes.* However, he admits that others have a good case for 1897. For our purposes any time between 1897 and 1902 is acceptable. Holmes says that Lady Frances was "still in fresh middle age," which would mean anywhere between 40 and 43 by late Victorian (or early Edwardian) standards. If she was 42 at the time of the case, she would have been born in 1855 or 1860.

Gerard's Lord Rufton seems to have been anywhere between 25 and 30, though he could have been older. Gerard does not mention any wife or child of his, and, while Gerard was one to stick to the essentials of his story, he surely would have said something about Rufton's wife if she had existed. The brigadier was too conscious of the fair sex not to have done so.

Gerard says that Lord Rufton came to Paris five years afterwards (in 1816) to see him, and Gerard does not mention any Lady Rufton in connection with this visit. Thus, it seems likely that Lord Rufton did not get married until after the visit, though he would have gotten a wife within a year or two if he were the ancestor of Lady Frances Carfax.

It's pleasing to think that Lord Rufton met and married Gerard's sister while in Paris, but we may be sure that this event would have been commented on at length by the Brigadier.

Holmes said that Lady Frances was "the last derelict of what only twenty years ago was a goodly fleet." He also said that she was the only survivor of the direct family of the late earl. Thus, a number of the earl's children, and perhaps the earl himself, still lived in 1882 (or 1877). Any sons the earl may have had had predeceased him. Lady Frances apparently did not begin her wanderings in Europe until four years before the case began. This would indicate that the last tie to her ancestral home had died at that time and that this tie was a sister or her father. I opt for the earl himself, since the money and, presumably, the ancestral seat, went to the distant male relatives. Lady Frances would have been forced to leave home sooner than four years before if the earl had died much earlier.

If Gerard's Rufton was the ancestor of Watson's,[1] he would have been Lady Frances's grandfather. Her father would have been born circa 1817-1840, and his father would have been born circa 1785.

An objection to the theory of the Ruftons' being of the same family is Gerard's reference to the lord's sister. He called her Lady Jane Rufton, whereas he should have said Lady Jane Carfax, if she was of the same family as Lady

---

[1]There was a typo in the original publication of this article, which has been corrected here. Here is Phil's letter on the subject.

From Philip Jose Farmer, of Peoria, Illinois to the Baker Street Journal March 1972

The December issue was, as always, very entertaining and highly informative. I was pleased to find my article, "The Two Lord Ruftons," in it. However, there is an unfortunate typo which makes it appear that I said that Gerard's Lord Rufton was the ancestor of Watson's. But I am sure that the readers are perceptive enough to see that an apostrophe and an "s" were dropped (On page 222, line 12, "If Gerard's Rufton was the ancestor of Watson…" should be "of Watson's.") otherwise, I may have to write another article proving that Gerard's Rufton was indeed Watson's ancestor.

Frances. But Gerard consistently shows in "How He Triumphed in England" and in other chapters of his memoirs, a deep ignorance of British titles. Indeed he displays a deep ignorance of other things British, especially British sports. It would not have occurred to him that the earl's sister would be called by her family name, not her brother's title. And it is likely that he had never heard Lord Rufton's family name.

Gerard's account and Watson's illuminate each other so that what one lacks in data the other supplies. Thus, combining the data, we know that Lord Rufton was an earl, that the ancestral seat was High Combe, located near the north edge of Dartmoor, and that it was near enough to Tavistock to get there on the north-south highway in an hour or two on a fast horse. High Combe is close to Baskerville Hall, and it is possible that Lady Frances's grandfather (or father or both) had married a daughter of the Baskervilles.

Of course, neither "Rufton" nor "Carfax" is genuine. Gerard doubtless gave the real title of his house in his memoirs, but his editor, Doyle, changed it to avoid embarrassing an old and highly placed family. Later, as literary agent for Watson (and, undoubtedly, a collaborator on some occasions), he recognised that Lady Frances was a descendant of Gerard's lord. Doyle had changed the name of Rufton in editing the memoirs, and now he could not resist changing Watson's original pseudonym for Lady Frances's father to Rufton also. (No doubts he did so with Watson's permission.)

Doyle (or Watson) chose Carfax as the fictitious family name because of association with another name or object. I suggest that Doyle derived Carfax from the actual family's coat-of-arms, probably through a reverse use of canting, or punning, arms. The family's shield may have borne a *quadriga* (a Roman two-wheeled chariot with a team of four) and a fox, hence, *car* plus *fax*. Or perhaps, knowing that Carfax Square in Oxford is believed to be an Anglicisation of the ancient Roman *quadrifurcus*, and knowing that the shield bore four shakeforks (or pitchforks or eel spears), or even a cross moline voided, Doyle chose the family name. At this moment I am going through Burke's *Peerage* for such arms in an effort to identify the real Carfaxes.

We know that the issue of the Carfax case was successful and even happy, since Lady Frances and the Hon. Philip Green were reunited. Apparently, they got married and had issue. Watson does not take the story far along. But he may have referred to it, with typical Victorian obliquity, when he put into Holmes's mouth the comment that Lady Frances's middle age was "fresh." This would be another example of Watson's humour.

A Reply to
"The Red Herring"

First published in *Erbania*, Number 28, December 1971.

D. Peter Ogden's "The Red Herring" (published in *Erbania*, 27) is part of an on-going debate among Burroughs scholars as to how to interpret seeming inconsistencies in the Tarzan novels. Farmer's reply, written just after the completion of *Tarzan Alive*, is a solid rebuttal of Ogden's position that Burroughs deliberately altered Tarzan's birth date in order to protect his identity. What is perhaps more fascinating than the debate itself is Farmer's description of the process used to differentiate between fact and fiction when studying fictional works as biography.

I've re-read your article on Tarzan's and Korak's age ("The Red Herring"— *Erbania 27)* a number of times and also studied Harwood's and Starr's, which I knew fairly well before your article came to me.

It looks like a tossup, as far as validity goes. Either you accept Harwood and Starr's adopted-relative theory to explain Korak or you push the date of Tarzan's birth back to 1872. Whichever theory you choose, you do violation. You have to change a number of things in the novels and say, "No, ERB didn't present the truth here. But, of course, he had good reason. Now, here is what we believe is the truth…"

You make a good case, and if I had thought about it more, I might have used 1872 and proceeded from there. I would have satisfied very few people, the various schools of thought would all have jumped on me. Not that I mind that. But it was too late to rewrite the book—from the 1872 viewpoint; the work I did on the version now in Doubleday's hands was enormous and changing it to start from 1872 would have required an equal amount. Just about every page would have to be rewritten, many cast out and entirely new ones written. And I would still have felt that I was departing from the truth.

Yet—would ERB have given the true date of Tarzan's birth? Would it not have been simple then to look into the records of that year, including the sailing dates of ships from Dover in May, 1888, and locate the young nobleman and his wife who sailed out, never again to return?

No, the answer is, it would not be simple. Because I wrote to the Dover Port Authority two years ago to ascertain this point, and I was told that the records are not available. I deduced that they had been destroyed in the bombings (WWII), though the Authority didn't say so. BUT—what if money and influence has been used by—guess whom?—to make sure that these records are not available? Or no longer available, I should say.

I wrote two letters to the Freetown, Sierra Leone, Port Authority, inquiring about ships that put out in the May-July, 1888, period, especially those sailing ships that went southwards along the coast with the intention of setting a young English nobleman and his wife on shore on the west coast. Or, I said, I'd be satisfied with just the lists, let me do the searching. But the Freetown Authority never bothered to reply or else the mail is such that it didn't get my letters.

But it must be remembered that ERB could have shoved the true date of sailing from England a year or two ahead or behind. More probably behind, because the exploitation of the Congo by Leopold had really not begun yet. Also, from what British colony were the Belgians seducing the natives for their armies? Look at the map of Africa, 1888. I believe that the truth is that Greystoke was sent to investigate what the Germans were doing on the Kamerun-Oil Rivers. This is the only thing he could have been sent to investigate at that time. ERB knew this, of course, but deliberately misled the reader about the true destination and mission of Greystoke.

If you take 1872 as the true date, then you have to think up an entirely new reason for the Greystokes going to Africa. You would end up by theorizing that the two were really just taking a trip to South Africa, or that Greystoke was an amateur explorer and injudiciously took his wife along, or that he was sent to investigate the illegal slave trade but first meant to accompany his wife to S. Africa and leave her there to visit relatives while he returned to the tropics. Or he may even have gone to Gabon, with his wife, because she wanted to find out what had happened to her uncle. (It's my contention that Trader Horn's George T—was Alice Rutherford's uncle. The reasoning for this you will read in *The Private Life of Tarzan*.)

As you know, I have gone through Burke's vast *Peerage* in an effort to find a candidate for Tarzan. I think I know who the real Tarzan was, but I can't reveal that at this moment. To make sure I'm not in error, I'm going to have to go through Burke several times more and search the records of births from 1872 on. Inasmuch as Burke contains over 1250 pages of small close-set type of genealogy, I won't be finished with my study for some time to come.

Another point. Besides the wrong date of sailing, ERB might have given the wrong port.

And perhaps Tarzan's parental ancestors weren't nobility after all but just baronets. ERB made the Greystokes even more distinguished than they were, made them viscounts. (Though, as you know from my Detroit speech*, Tarzan couldn't have been a viscount, or, at least, if he were, he must also have been either an earl or a baron or both.)

The possibility that Tarzan's ancestors may have been baronets extends the search through Burke, extends it very much, since baronets take up much of the space therein. The chances are that his ancestors were of the lesser nobility or of the baronetage, since it would have been difficult to hide from the press the fact that a long-lost heir to a dukeship or marquessate or even an earlship had been found in the jungles of Africa. On the other hand, if enough money were spent in the right places, it might be done. But not very easily.

You say that the idea that Korak might be adopted, not Tarzan's real son, spoils *The Son of Tarzan* for you. This book is one of my favorites; I've read it many times and it doesn't spoil it for me to think that Korak is adopted. The way I look at it, there are two Tarzans, the real Tarzan and the fictional Tarzan. The fictional Tarzan is based on the real Tarzan that ERB knew, and, undoubtedly, ERB drew the longbow now and then in his "biography," added some things, left others out, and even wrote several Tarzan books that were total fiction, such as *Tarzan at the Earth's Core*, or only partly true, such as *Tarzan and the Ant Men*. Knowing this doesn't spoil them for me. When I read them, I read them as I would any other book of fiction and enjoy them as they are.

When I study them as biography, then I differentiate to the best of my ability and knowledge between the fact and the fiction. This is not always easy to do, but it's a lot of fun and rewarding in many ways. Thus, when I read *The Son of Tarzan*, I know that Korak is adopted (or I should say, I believe he is). My own theory is that he is the younger brother of Bulldog Drummond, reasons for which theory I give in *Life*[1]. I believe that Korak's career in the jungle did not last more than a year, or two years at most. A proper chronology of Tarzan's life demands this. But this doesn't bother me. In the first place, Korak was an extraordinarily strong and adaptive individual, but he wasn't Tarzan, as he was the first to admit. There is only one Tarzan, and Korak, mighty though he was, was not his equal. Undoubtedly, John Drummond was an unusually strong person, like his older brother, who, as you may remember, in his first recorded adventure, snapped the neck of a half-grown gorilla with

---

* "The Arms of Tarzan," published earlier in this collection.

only his fingers. (I think it was a gorilla. On the same page, the beast is called a gorilla, a baboon, and a monkey. McNeile wasn't very strong on zoology.)

Anyway, when I read *Son*, I forget the facts behind this story and read it as ERB wrote it, knowing that he had to fictionize the true story and that, as you suggest, he did want it to be regarded as fiction.

By the way, what are your thoughts regarding ERB's killing of Jane in the magazine version of *Tarzan the Untamed*? Was she really killed but ERB realized that an investigator could find out her identity and thus Tarzan's, by looking into the deaths of plantation owners' wives killed in western Kenya in 1914, and so brought her back to life in the book version to throw any such investigator off the trail?

As far as I know, your idea that the person who first told ERB about Tarzan was D'Arnot is original. It seemed a likely one, but there are problems about it.

In the first place, the "I" of the first few pages of *Tarzan of the Apes* could not have been ERB. ERB was never in England. What happened, I think, is that the "I" was a man, or woman, who got the story from the "convivial host" and then told it to ERB who was, I believe, living in Chicago in 1911. ERB was inclined to give the narrator his own identity, as you will recall from *A Princess of Mars*, where the "I" could not possibly be ERB. (I mean, of course, not the "I" of John Carter but the "I" of his supposed nephew.) Besides, ERB couldn't read French and so wouldn't have been able to read the elder John Clayton's diary.

Was D'Arnot the person who told the story to the "I" of *TOTA*? If he were, he must have been in England, since he and "I" went to the Colonial Office to dig through the "musty manuscript, and dry official records". And why did he have access to British Colonial Office records? He was neither British nor a member of any secret agency which might have gotten permission to look into the records. Especially since, it seems to me, the Clayton family would have made sure that the records were not accessible to anyone except the highest authority.

But there is the matter of Clayton's diary. The last we see it is in Chapter XXVI of *TOTA*, in which the police official is reading it. Did he give it back to Tarzan or to D'Arnot? Tarzan left for America the next day, so I think it likely that D'Arnot kept it for further perusal while he waited for M. Desquerc, the fingerprint expert, to arrive. The "I" of *TOTA* read the diary, so he must have gotten it from D'Arnot or his "convivial host,"whoever he was.

Would D'Arnot reveal to anybody, without authorization from the Claytons, the story of Tarzan? Undoubtedly not. What happened, as I reconstruct it, was that Tarzan, or a member of the Colonial Office, placed the diary with the records of Clayton's mission to West Africa. The "musty manuscript" must have been the summary of the story of the Claytons and their son. It was written by a Colonial Office clerk. The "I" was a visiting American who got loaded over a bottle with a British official who was one of the few who knew the story. The official must have been a very vain man to have insisted on "I" seeing the Greystoke material just so he could prove he wasn't lying. And he must have been unethical, too. I suspect that "I" may have used a bribe to get the official to show him the records. What the nature of the bribe was I don't have the slightest idea, of course.

Fortunately, the "I" told ERB the story and then either forgot about it or was prevailed upon not to disclose the truth after the first book about Tarzan came out and was such a hit. Perhaps, "I" died shortly after revealing to ERB what he had learned about the "Greystoke" case. ERB, of course, took care to conceal the true identities of the "principal characters", though there is evidence (as H. W. Starr has pointed out) that ERB only changed the titles of the noble persons concerned and retained the family names. Clayton and Rutherford are, after all, not unusual names in Burke's *Peerage and Landed Gentry*.

The reconstruction, based on the above: Tarzan never picked up the diary again, though he made sure that he could see it whenever he wished. The diary was transferred to the Colonial Office for keeping with the records pertinent to the Greystoke case. A clerk made a summary, in handwriting, of the story. (Unless "I" means that the "musty manuscript" is also the diary, since a diary is written, or was in those days, in handwriting.) The manuscript was never, for some reason, typed out. Perhaps because it was a summary for the eyes of some high authority only. (The French Naval Intelligence would also have a report, you may be sure of that. D'Arnot was Tarzan's best friend, but he would have been required, as a matter of duty, to report on the "incident." His report, plus those of other personnel of the cruiser, and the policemen's report about the fingerprints, would have been put in the secret files of the French Navy, where, no doubt, they still are.)

The "I" of *TOTA* then learned about the British records and the diary and got his egotistical and probably corrupt host to let him see whatever he wished to see concerning the Greystoke case.

---

[1] *The Private Life of Tarzan*, by Philip José Farmer, due from Doubleday April 1972. (The title of the book, when published, was *Tarzan Alive*.)

The Great Korak Time Discrepancy

First published in *ERB-dom,* Number 57, April 1972.

The chapter in *Tarzan Alive* which deals with the novel *The Son of Tarzan* is befittingly entitled "Problems." Once again, in "The Great Korak-Time Discrepancy" (first published in *ERB-dom* in April 1972), Farmer delineates the questions left inadvertently by Burroughs in this novel. Was Tarzan born in 1872 or 1888? Is Korak the adopted son of Tarzan? How could Tarzan's friend d'Arnot be a French naval lieutenant in 1909 and yet an admiral in 1914? The answers may not please all scholars of Burroughsiana, but Farmer's love and enthusiasm for these stories and characters will.

Some Problems in writing a Tarzan biography

"THE SON OF TARZAN"

Tarzan is a living person.

This is the basic premise of my *Tarzan Alive, A Definitive Biography of Lord Greystoke* (Doubleday, 1972).

This premise that Tarzan is not a fictional character makes inadmissible any speculation about the literary origin of Tarzan. Romulus and Remus, Kipling's Mowgli, Prentice's *Captured by Apes* and the dozen or so other sources so far advanced as the sources from which Burroughs derived his idea of Tarzan have no relevance to reality.

Since this premise removes Tarzan from the realm of fantasy it requires that the stories about him be examined for their fidelity to fact. Or to what we can classify as fact, admitting that evidence may be uncovered in the future which will force us to reclassify.

With this in mind, we can reread the Tarzan epics by Burroughs. And we can place some in the category of largely fictitious, some in the half-true, and some in the nearly all true. Few, for instance, would deny that almost all of *Tarzan at the Earth's Core* and most of *Tarzan and the Ant Men* is fiction. The reasons for these conclusions will, however, be dealt with in separate essays.

This essay is devoted to the epic about which the most controversy has raged in the world of Tarzanic scholarship: *The Son Of Tarzan*. This storm is not due to ambiguous or obscure statements by Burroughs or lack of pertinent data. No, certain facts are clear enough. But certain scholars have refused to admit these facts, and they have done so because of emotional factors.

These people cannot admit that Jack Clayton, or Korak, cannot be Tarzan's son.

The Great Korak Time Discrepancy Controversy must be old ground for most of the readers of this publication. For the benefit of the new, I'll go over the familiar material. However, I'll introduce some aspects not considered before. And I'll then go on to an examination of other features of the book. (My textual source is the 1918 A. L. Burt reprint edition.)

The Son of Tarzan, written in 1915, is a sequel to *The Beasts Of Tarzan*. In *Beasts*, Tarzan's and Jane's son is a babe in arms, and, from all internal evidence, is less than a year old. Burroughs does not say so, but it is evident that Jane is nursing the baby she carries with her in her flight from Rokoff. This baby is the same age as little Jack.

The events in *Beasts* must take place in 1911 or, at the earliest, in late 1910. In *Son*, Sabrov, a Russian, is rescued after ten years as a captive in an African cannibal village. Burroughs says that his real name was Paulvitch, though he does not say how he could have known that. Sabrov never told anyone that his real name was not Sabrov. Thus, if Burroughs is writing a novel based on certain events which did, in fact, happen, he had no way of knowing that Sabrov was Tarzan's old enemy. But it would make for a fine dramatic point to have Sabrov be Paulvitch, and Burroughs, first and foremost a storyteller, would not be likely to let such drama go by.

Burroughs does state that it is ten years since the events in *Beasts*. This means that Sabrov is rescued from the cannibals circa 1921.

In *Son*, Jack (Korak) must be ten or eleven years old. He is a remarkably powerful youth, since he can subdue his young male tutor with ease. A few months after this, he strangles to death with his bare hands an adult black savage. This man is presumably much more powerful than the tutor and is fighting for his life.

A year later, Korak, himself only eleven or twelve years old, throws the eleven-year old Meriem across his shoulder and leaps nimbly into the lower branches of a tree. A year or two later (Burroughs is vague about the exact time), Korak fights a mighty mangani male with his bare hands and teeth and rips open the great bull's jugular vein. Immediately after follows a scene in which it is obvious that both Korak and Meriem are well into puberty. This is succeeded by a scene in which Korak uses fists to beat another giant bull into near-unconsciousness.

All of the above except one are just barely credible. It's possible that Korak could carry Meriem as easily as Burroughs says, that Korak and Meriem were coming into sexual maturity, and that Korak was skilled enough and powerful enough to hammer a bull great ape into submission. But it is difficult to believe that any human's teeth, let alone a twelve year old male's, could bite through the hair and thick skin and jugular vein of a massively muscled anthropoid the size of a gorilla. Especially while the anthropoid was tearing away with his hands at Korak. The great apes are described by Burroughs as being equal to a gorilla in strength, and a gorilla's strength has been estimated as equal to at least ten men's strength.

I don't doubt that Korak did win in his fights. But I think it's likely that Burroughs was gilding the lily for story purposes and that Korak used his knife and may even have had some help from Meriem and her spear. Even so, these feats would be remarkable and would need no exaggerating to get our admiration and respect.

Meriem, or Jeanne Jacot, is ten years old when Korak is forced to flee London with Akut, the great ape. When the book ends, she is sixteen. Thus Korak would have been in the jungle for almost six years. He was also sixteen. It would not be discreet to ask why Korak's parents permitted their son to marry at such an early age.

It is permissible to wonder about the Honourable Morison Baynes. He must have been at least 21 years old and was probably at least 25, judging from his considerable hedonistic experience on the Continent and his sophistication. Yet he estimates that Korak was his own age or possibly older. This can be explained as due to Korak's unusual large size, an accelerated maturity due to the rigors of jungle living, and the possibility of a beard. Burroughs says nothing about Korak shaving, so we can at least speculate that he could have had facial hair. Some youths do get rather heavy beards at sixteen. Tarzan didn't; he does not seem to have had to shave until he was about twenty.

In *Tarzan The Terrible*, Korak is old enough to fight during the Meuse-Argonne operation (Sept-Nov, 1918).

Peter Ogden, editor of *ERBANIA*, has published a theory to account for the Korak Time Discrepancy. He says that Burroughs could have given the wrong date for Tarzan's birth in *Tarzan Of The Apes*. He would have done this as one more cover for the true identity of Lord Greystoke. And, working backwards from 1914, so that the chronology of *Son* will be consistent with reality, Ogden figures that Tarzan was probably born in 1872.

(It's not relevant, but is interesting, to note that 1872 was the year of Phileas Fogg's amazing dash around the world and of the mysterious case of the *Marie Celeste*. I am presently working on a book which will tie the two together.[1])

Thus, Tarzan could have met Jane by 1893 and married her in 1895. Korak would have been born in 1895 and would be ten years old in 1905. He and Meriem would've married in 1911.

Ogden's theory raises more problems than it solves, and these will be dealt with in my essay on *Tarzan Of The Apes*. However, after all the evidence for the 1888 or 1872 theories is in, neither can be "proved." The reader is free to choose whichever he prefers. What he is not free to choose as the truth, if he insists on being logical, is Burroughs' version of *Son* in its entirety.

The central insurmountable fact that *Son* was written in 1915 means that all events in *Son* have to have taken place before Burroughs started writing it. Korak married Meriem before 1915, when both were sixteen. If Korak was sixteen in 1914, he would have been born in 1898. Tarzan did not meet Jane until Feb. 1909 (See *Tarzan Of The Apes*).

The Burroughsian has two choices. Believe Ogden's theory or believe Harwood-Starr's. If you choose the latter, then you must accept as a fact the adoption of a boy born about 1898 by Tarzan and Jane. Probably, he would have been a close relative who had been orphaned. In my book *Tarzan Alive*, I opt for Bulldog Drummond's younger brother, John. (That is, for the younger brother of the man on whom the fictional character of Bulldog Drummond was based. Do not, however, be misled by the statement of McNeile that this man was Gerard Fairlie.) My reasons for this are developed in *Tarzan Alive*; to present them here would expand this essay to too great a length. But the reader may examine the evidence presented in my biography and say yea or nay to it.

Harwood and Starr also suggest that Tarzan's son really was the baby who died in *Beasts* and that Burroughs suppressed this and distorted other facts to give the book the happy ending which he knew his readers would demand. I reject this. Otherwise, how do you account for the "youthful Jack" in *The Eternal Lover*?

I believe that Tarzan's real son lived but that we shall never know anything about him except what Burroughs tells us in *Beasts* and *Lover*. Because of having

---

[1] Editor's note—This was published by Tor in 1982 as *The Other Log Of Phileas Fogg*

presented Korak as Tarzan's true son in *Son*, Burroughs was obliged to leave out any reference to the true son thereafter in the novels. At the time, Burroughs may have thought that this was a small price to pay, since Jackie was a baby and it would be many years before he, too, could have adventures and so become a worthy subject of Burroughs' fictionalized biographies. But I wonder if, around the time of World War II, he did not regret this. Surely, the real Jack Clayton III, first in line to the title of Greystoke, must have been a remarkable man in his own right. Nor do we have to suppose that Tarzan and Jane had no other children after him just because Burroughs does not mention them. If the Claytons had daughters, for instance, we may be sure that they would have been tall, lovely, and grey-eyed and very capable of taking care of themselves.

The Son of Tarzan has to end in 1914, before August of that year. From August on, Tarzan was looking for Jane until after the end of World War I. The chronology of *The Eternal Lover* indicates clearly that the Custers were visiting the Greystokes at their plantation in 1914 not too long before WWI broke out. Tarzan's baby son and Esmeralda were present then; Korak and Meriem, if present, are not mentioned by Burroughs. But they were undoubtedly still in Europe, visiting Meriem's parents. Tarzan and Jane would have accompanied them to England first, as indicated at the end of *Son*, and then would have returned to Africa, where they were visited by the Custers. For some reason, Esmeralda took young Jackie to England, since the two were not at the plantation when it was destroyed by the Germans (in *Tarzan the Untamed*). Perhaps the "business" which Tarzan was attending to in Nairobi when *Untamed* opened was sending Esmeralda and Jackie away to England or France.

Beasts seems to have ended about the middle of 1912. Since *Son* would have started not too many months later, it is obvious that Paulvitch could not have been a prisoner of the cannibals for ten years. And it is obvious that Sabrov is not Paulvitch. Harwood-Starr's surmise that Burroughs identified Sabrov as Paulvitch for dramatic reasons is the only reasonable theory so far advanced. Even if Paulvitch had disguised his appearance, he would not have been able to conceal his individual body odor, and Tarzan would have identified him immediately.

What did happen to Paulvitch?

We'll never know. If his name had been Pyotrvitch (Peterson), I'd be inclined to think that he had made his way back to Europe, had become a master at disguise, no doubt to ensure that Tarzan would never hear of him, had become as powerful as the late Professor Moriarty, and died (supposedly) in a flaming dirigible in 1927 after he'd tangled once too often with Korak's older brother.

Paulvitch, by the way, is not a standard Russian name. It should be Pavlovitch or Pavlitch. However, it is possible that Paulvitch's grandfather was a Frenchman, perhaps a captured French soldier who settled down in Russia after Napoleon's defeat, and Paulvitch was his hybrid Gall-Russian name.

Many opponents of the "adopted relative" theory point to the numerous references in *Son* to Korak's inheritance of his father's traits. But Burroughs would have made these up and inserted them in the novel to strengthen the premise that Korak was Tarzan's issue. The novel is consistent within its own framework, though there are some curious things to consider.

Captain Jacot, Meriem's father, is a grey-haired general at the end of the book, an "old man." In nine years he has gone from a seemingly vigorous young man and captain to an aging general. And d'Arnot, a naval lieutenant in *Apes*, which ended in 1909, is, in 1914, an admiral.

John F. Roy, in *ERB-dom* #18, has explained the latter promotion. He says that Admiral d'Arnot could be the father of Tarzan's good friend. As for Jacot, it is true that Burroughs does not specify his age at the time when Meriem (Jeanne) was kidnapped. He could have been a vigorous fifty or so. And that he could see further than his men, that they called him for this reason the Hawk, may have been due to the long-sightedness brought on by middle age. And it is possible that a combination of fortunate events, good connections, and his outstanding military record, did advance him to a generalship.

Another problem. How did Korak, who was only ten, when *Son* began, according to Burroughs (but fourteen according to my estimate) manage in one day to get false passports for himself and Akut? He had the money to flee England, but how did he make the necessary connections with the criminal world?

Also, Burroughs says that Tarzan would not tell Korak the location of his African plantation? Would not a boy with Korak's driving interest in such matters have found out?

The *Marjorie W.*, which picked Sabrov up, was chartered by a scientific expedition. Why would the scientists aboard have permitted Sabrov to walk off with Akut, obviously a specimen of a hitherto unknown genus of great ape? (Or, if my theory is right that the mangani were hominids akin to *Australopithecus robustus*, the uniqueness of Akut would have been even more apparent.)

It is probable, however, that the scientists were botanists and chemists so unqualified in anthropoid identification. And Sabrov's claims to Akut as his property could easily have prevented any attempt by the scientists to obtain Akut for their uses. But Sabrov and his property did have considerable publicity after getting to London. It is difficult to understand why scientists there would not have known that Akut was something new in the zoological world. Perhaps they did, but, again, Sabrov refused to recognize anything but the jurisdiction of private property.

This matter can be cleared up by examining the London *Times* of this period (say, from 1911 through 1913 to cover a broad enough area). If no such case is mentioned in the papers, then the next step is to admit that perhaps Ogden's theory of Tarzan's birth in 1872 is right. The *Times* for the period of 1893 through 1896 should be covered for items about Akut or a reasonable facsimile thereof.

Would anyone, even in the slums of London, have taken in such a lodger as Akut? Especially when Akut does not seem to have been locked up in a manner to satisfy the public as to its safety? Would not the police have been called in by the terrified tenants of the house where Sabrov and his "pet" lived?

Perhaps not, if Sabrov had greased enough palms. And it is possible that Akut was much more restrained during transit between the East End lodgings and the theater than Burroughs implies. It was only during the theater shows and in Sabrov's room that Akut had any comparative freedom.

Another problem is Jane's concern about Korak's clothes after hearing that he has been found. She wants Tarzan to take to Korak one of his "little suits" that she has saved. This would indicate that a long time has elapsed, since Tarzan says that Korak has grown so big that he would fit only into one of Tarzan's own suits. But this little scene is, again, one of the fictions of Burroughs to make the novel consistent in its own framework. Even so, it's doubtful that Korak, big enough at the age of ten to overpower his tutor would have been wearing a *little* suit when he disappeared.

The ability of the monkeys and the baboons (who are really monkeys and not apes) to speak should be examined. But this will be taken up in a separate essay.

There are some problems about the location of the Greystoke plantation, but this will be dealt with in the essay on *Tarzan The Untamed*.

Meriem, at ten, is the Sheikh's prisoner in a small native village "hidden away upon the banks of a small unexplored tributary of a large river that empties into the Atlantic not so far from the equator..." (*Son*, p. 63). Here the Sheikh's tribe collects goods and twice a year carries them on camels to Timbuktu. An examination of the (Michelin) maps of Africa fails to locate any river which will fill the above requirements. The only large river near the equator which empties into the Atlantic is the Congo. Any small tributary of the Congo which emptied into the Atlantic would be about 1800 miles on a straight line from Timbuktu. A caravan route would cover two or three times that distance, perhaps four times 1800 miles. Moreover, no camels could traverse the thousands of miles of heavy jungle, rugged hills, and many rivers between the tributary and Timbuktu (which is in the present nation of Mali). Burroughs could not have meant that the tributary was one of the Congo's inland rivers, because Korak found Meriem in a village near the coast. The text clearly indicates this.

However, about 1500 miles from the equator (northwards), in the German Kamerun (the Cameroons), ibn Khatour's tribe *might* have had a headquarters. They would have been fairly close to Korak, who probably disembarked at Douala. Even so, the tribe still would have had to travel through considerable jungle and it would have been about 1200 miles (in a straight line) from Timbuktu. A year later, both Meriem and Korak were on the other side of Africa, near the Greystoke plantation. To get there, they had to round the great lake of Victoria and cross steep mountains. What ibn Khatour's tribe was doing in this area is not explained. Probably it had been driven out of western African because of its criminal activities and was headed for fresh opportunities for ivory poaching and slave raiding.

But on page 325 of *Son* is a phrase which seems to indicate that the tribe and Meriem, after a few days' march, are back at the village on the tributary of the Congo, back on the west coast. Meriem is brought back "to the familiar scenes of her childhood…"

Obviously, this is impossible. Burroughs must have meant for the reader to interpret this as the people and type of buildings with which she had been familiar during her childhood. But it could not have been the same location.

Why did not Tarzan recognize Malbihn when he showed up as Hanson? Meriem might have failed to recognize him because Malbihn had changed his appearance. But Tarzan should have recognized his odor. On the other hand, his contact with the Swede had been very brief. And no doubt Malbihn as Hanson not only bathed frequently when he was to be with Greystoke, he used a strong cologne.

The river on which Meriem escaped and on which Malbihn was wounded could be the Mara river of lower western Kenya and upper western Tanganyika. It is not, however, "a great African" river (p. 333) nor is it in jungle territory. But inasmuch as it seems the only candidate reasonably near the Greystoke plantation and since *Untamed* indicates the plantation is in southwestern Kenya, then the river should be the Mara. That it is a jungle river in *Son* can be due to Burroughs' tendency to romanticize. Also, Burroughs often deliberately confuses locations so that the true site of the Greystoke plantation cannot be found from a reading of the novels.

In conclusion, I sympathize with the fundamentalists' desire that Korak be Tarzan's real son. But I do not find that the Harwood-Starr theory of an adopted relative spoils *The Son Of Tarzan* for me. It is one of my favorites, and it contains several scenes which still bring tears. Such as Meriem's joy on finding a mother's love again in My Dear's arms or in Korak's reunion with Jane. When

I am not reading *Son* to analyze it, I read it as a novel. And I accept, for the time being, the internal premises of the story.

No reader should be disappointed that Korak is not Tarzan's real son. After all, as Korak himself says,

"THERE IS BUT ONE TARZAN...THERE CAN NEVER BE ANOTHER."

The Lord Mountford Mystery

First published in *ERB-dom,* Number 65, December 1972.

Farmer, with his "literary genealogies," utilises inscrutable attention to detail and connective creativity to form a unified field theory of fictional characters. What is special about Farmer's forays into literary genealogy is the way in which an old story suddenly comes alive when viewed from a different angle. "The Lord Mountford Mystery" is a prime example of the seamless logic with which Farmer makes his case. Here he ties together the family history of two generations of "Mountfords" by his research into the works of H. Rider Haggard and Edgar Rice Burroughs. Burroughs' *Tarzan the Magnificent* may now be seen as a sequel of sorts to Haggard's novel *Finished.*

⚜

As almost everybody knows, Tarzan does live, and most of the stories told about him by Edgar Rice Burroughs (ERB) are true. However, ERB did mix some fiction in his biographies of the immortal apeman. H. Rider Haggard (HRH) was also not above falsifying some accounts of Allan Quatermain. Unlike ERB, though, he never concocted a story. His deviations from reality were confined to giving some of his real-life people fictional names or falsely locating the fabled cities which the great hunter and explorer of Africa found. Just as ERB used pseudonyms to protect some persons from unwanted publicity and gave hopelessly confused directions for finding Opar, so HRH used fake names and made it impossible to track down Kor, Zuvendis, and Waloo by following clues in *She, She and Allan, Allan Quatermain* and *Heu-Heu.*

The American, ERB, and the Englishman, HRH, never met. HRH probably heard of ERB as they both had stories in *New Story Magazine* in late 1913. It's highly likely that ERB had read some of Haggard's very popular works, and he probably did research on one of HRH's minor protagonists before writing one of his Tarzan tales.

It's the purpose of this essay to show just where a work by each intersected in a certain English noble family.

"The Lord of the Jungle is abroad" in *Tarzan the Magnificent*. He's far north of Lake Rudolf (which is near the northern border of Kenya) on a mission for Haile Selassie I, King of Kings, Lion of Judah, and emperor of Ethiopia (Abyssinia). (As an aside, Tarzan, like Selassie, is descended from King Solomon, as may be seen by referring to addendum 3 of my *Tarzan Alive*. Greystoke, however, is lord of far more than Selassie can claim, since all Africa is his domain.)

Tarzan finds a skeleton of a black message-bearer and in the runner's cleft stick, a nineteen-year-old letter. Since *Tarzan the Magnificent* occurred in 1934, the letter was written in 1915. Its writer, Lord Mountford, and his wife had disappeared twenty years before while exploring this vast arid, and mountainous area. Mountford says that he and his wife were captured by a tribe of white women who live on the plateau of Kaji. Kaji, ERB says, is not far from where the Mafa River empties into the Neubari River. A study of detailed maps of Ethiopia and several encyclopedias and atlases fails to locate these. We can assume that ERB is using fictional names for real rivers. The only large river in the area northwest of Lake Rudolf is the Omo (sometimes spelled Umu). The Omo forms the eastern border of the northwest area. The only town of any consequence in this area is Maji, which has an airport now. The similarity of Kaji to Maji is no doubt a coincidence.

Possibly, the confluence of two rivers which ERB described may be, in reality, the point where the Akobo River branches into two streams. Certainly, this territory is rugged and unpopulated enough to still conceal the cliff dwellings of the Kaji and the small village and two-story building of the Zuli, the enemies of the Kaji.

Lord Mountford says in his letter that his wife bore a daughter a year after they were captured. His wife was killed by the Kaji because she had not delivered a son. The Kaji amazons needed white males to keep the "white blood" in the tribal veins. This murder seems to be illogically motivated. Why not allow Lady Mountford to have more babies, some of which might be male? However, as we know, all societies, literate or preliterate, often proceed on illogical and nonsurvival grounds, and this seems to have been the case with the Kaji.

A little later, Tarzan finds a refugee from the Kaji. He is Stanley Wood, a travel writer who has capitalized on his "natural worthlessness, which often finds its expression and its excuse in wanderlust."

It may be that ERB put these words into Wood's mouth. Every now and then, in his books, ERB pokes fun at his own profession.

Wood and a friend had led a small safari to search for the long-lost Mountfords. On the way, Wood finds Mountford, who has just escaped from the amazons and their chief, a male witch doctor. After some delirious statements, Mountford dies. He is a man well under fifty, and so, if he's in his early forties, would have been born circa 1892. This point is made here because it's relevant to the chronology of my theory.

Tarzan later encounters Mountford's daughter, a beautiful nineteen-year-old blonde. She is known only as Gonfala. After many adventures, aided by Tarzan, Gonfala and Wood escape to civilization and are, presumably, married there. They'll be wealthy, since Tarzan is going to give them the enormous emerald of the Zulis or some share of it.

Tarzan the Magnificent does not give many details about the Mountfords. It says nothing, for instance, of their family background or history before their disappearance. Nor are the Mountfords mentioned in the other Tarzan epics.

But Allan Quatermain, in *Finished,* Haggard's 1917 novel, meets a member of the Mountford family in 1877. And from this story, we can fill in the background which ERB left blank.

Quatermain, while in Pretoria, then a frontier town, runs into a Maurice Anscombe. He is a younger son of Lord Mountford, one of the richest peers in England. He is tall and loosely built and between thirty and thirty-five years old. He has steady blue eyes with a humorous twinkle. His face is attractive, though the features are too irregular and his nose is too long for good looks. He served in a crack cavalry regiment, resigned, and went to South Africa to hunt big game. He is brave, but a bad shot.

Anscombe has inherited much money from his recently dead mother. His father is also dead. An older brother is the present Lord Mountford. None of his brothers have any children.

Anscombe goes to the Kashmir in India to hunt wild sheep but returns on October 1, 1878 to hunt with Quatermain. While they're tracking a wounded gnu, they run into the alcoholic and terrible-tempered Marnham and his sinister partner, Doctor Rodd. These recruit native labor for the Kimberley mines but get most of their money from smuggling diamonds and running guns for rebellious natives. Marnham once served with Anscombe's father in the Coldstream Guards but was cashiered for striking a superior officer during a card game. He had married a beautiful Hungarian, but she died a year after giving birth to a daughter, Hedda.

The daughter is almost twenty-one, is tall and slender, and has auburn hair and large dark-grey eyes. Rodd is in love with her but is killed while trying to do away with Anscombe and Quatermain.

A weird black dwarf, the wizard Zikali, the Opener-of-Roads, the Thing-that-should-never-have-been-born, predicts that Hedda will have five children. Two will die, and one will give her so much trouble she'll wish it had died, too. Inasmuch as all of Zikali's prophecies come true in other Quatermain tales, it can be assumed that this one is valid.

Zikali then makes a strange statement. "But who their father will be I will not say."

Whatever this means, Anscombe and Hedda do get married. After many years, Quatermain hears they're still alive and spend most of their time in Hungary, where Hedda has inherited property.

"Lord Mountford" is as fictional a title as "Lord Greystoke." Mountford, to the best of my knowledge, is not to be found in any book on extant or extinct peerages. The real title is a matter for future research.

But ERB, when writing of the peers who figure in *Tarzan the Magnificent*, decided to use HRH's title, since they were both writing of the same family.

Since Maurice Anscombe's brothers would have died childless, he would have inherited the title, perhaps late in life. One of Hedda's sons, born when she was about thirty-four, would have become Lord Mountford when Maurice Anscombe died. It was this son who was the Lord Mountford of *Tarzan the Magnificent.*

It is possible that, since he was raised in Hungary a good part of this time, he married a girl of that country. Their daughter, Gonfala, could be one of the beautiful Hungarian blondes typified by the Gabors. Probably, Gonfala's mother was of that ancient aristocracy which, like Baroness Orczy, biographer of *The Scarlet Pimpernel,* traces its ancestry back to Arpad, the Magyar conqueror of that area to be called Hungary. (Lord Greystoke himself, as shown in *Tarzan Alive,* could do the same through the founder of the Scots family of Drummond, a Maurice by the way.)

Whether or not Gonfala could lay claim to the title is not known. When her father disappeared into Africa, the title may have gone to a male relative, a brother, a nephew, or cousin. If there were no male relatives, the title may have become extinct. If, however, the patent permitted a female in the direct line of descent to inherit the title, as some English patents do, Gonfala could have become a peeress.

If this were not the case, she probably went to the USA as just Mrs. Stanley Wood. The latter seems more likely, since there is nothing in the various chronicles of the years circa 1934 indicating that the daughter of a long-lost peer suddenly appeared out of Africa.

In any event, there is evidence that Henry Rider Haggard did write the story of the parents of Edgar Rice Burroughs' Lord Mountford.

From ERB to Ygg

First published in *ERBivore,* Numbers 6 and 7, August 1973.

This article was originally printed in two "consecutive" issues of *ERBivore,* published as a double issue.

What do Norman of Torn, Alice in Wonderland, Robert the Devil, and the Norse All-Father god Odin all have in common? Farmer answers the question with his usual thoroughness in "From ERB to Ygg."

All persons of North European ancestry, and the majority of those of South European extraction, are descended from Charlemagne. Charlemagne, or Karl the Great (742-814 A.D.), was the king of the Franks and emperor of the West (Holy Roman Empire). Most American blacks can also claim the distinction of descent from this famous monarch, since very few lack white ancestors. Furthermore, those belonging to Indian tribes whose original habitat was east of the Mississippi can make a similar claim. Further, anybody whose forebears were of old British stock also has as ancestor in Alfred the Great (849-899 A.D.), king of the West Saxons. This includes many Dutchmen, Belgians, French, and Germans, since the British, in their many, many wars and travels, have left a trail of babies behind them in western Europe and elsewhere.

Unfortunately, few of us in the United States know who our great-grandfathers were. We can only show that Alfred and Charlemagne are in our lineage by arithmetic. Suppose you were born in 1950 A.D. Assuming 25 years per generation, you had sixteen ancestors living in 1850. Doubling each generation as you go backwards, you had 256 ancestors living in 1750. By the time you get to 1040 A.D., you have 23,873,978,368 ancestors.

The world population today is about 3.4 billion, the highest by far that it has been since the human species began. The world population in 1 A.D. was somewhere between 200 and 300 million. Obviously, you could not have had over 23 billion ancestors living in 1040 A.D. Marriage between cousins, near and far, is the only explanation of this discrepancy. The world is, and has been, a hotbed of incest.

It's no exaggeration to say that we're all related and that all of us have noble and royal ancestors. The difference between the majority of us and a small minority is that the latter can offer documentary proof of their descent from kings and nobility. They can give the names, step by step, ancestor by ancestor, of those in their lineage.

Edgar Rice Burroughs (ERB) belongs to this minority. His lineage is distinguished indeed. In fact, it can be traced back to the great Germanic God Woden, known in various languages as Odin, Wuodan, Wodan, Wuotan, etc. One of his epithets in Old Norse was Ygg, hence the name in the title of this essay. Ygg means "The Terrible One," and Yggdrasil, the great ashtree or worldtree of the Old Norse, means "Odin's Steed."

But let's go to a son of Odin, the man whose lineage is the subject of this article. He was born in Chicago on the first of September, 1875. Neither his environment nor his immediate ancestry smacked remotely of the divine. Yet this man, Edgar Rice Burroughs, had an imagination which would carry his readers further than Woden ruled, to the center of the Earth and beyond Earth itself, faster than Odin's eight-legged steed, Sleipnir, could travel.

His parents were George Tyler Burroughs (1833-1913) and Mary Evaline Zieger, married 23rd February, 1863. George was a major in the U.S. Army during the Civil War and a successful businessman afterwards. He was the son of Abner Tyler Burroughs (1805-1897) and Mary Rice, married 16th December, 1827.

Abner Tyler Burroughs was the son of Tyler Burroughs (1771-1845) and Anna Pratt. The ancestors of Tyler Burroughs are not known to me, though Mr. Porges, in his biography of ERB (published 1975—*ERBivore* Editor) may extend the genealogy in the Burroughs line.

However, it is the purpose of this article to trace ERB's lineage through the Rices. The genealogy of ERB's other American ancestors, the Ziegers, Colemans, McCullochs and Innskeeps, is not covered here.

Mary Rice (see above), ERB's paternal grandmother, was born in 1802 at Warren, Mass., and died 1889 in Chicago, Ill.

Her parents were Thomas Rice (1767-1847) and Sally Makepeace, both of Brookfield, Mass.

Thomas' parents were Tilly Rice and Mary (Baxter) Buckminster of Brookfield.

Tilly Rice was the son of Obadiah Rice (born in Marlboro, Mass.) and Esther Merrick.

Obadiah was the son of Jacob Rice (born in Marlboro) and Mary—[1]

Jacob Rice (died 1746) was the son of Edward Rice, born in Sudbury, Mass. Mary Evaline Zieger, ERB's mother, says in her booklet on the family, *Memoirs of a War Bride* (1914), that Jacob Rice married Mary—. *Burke's Landed Gentry*, 1939, states that his wife was Mary, daughter of Christopher Bannister of Marlboro.

Edward Rice (died 1712) married Anna —, according to *Memoirs of a War Bride*. Burke says that Edward's wife was Agnes, daughter of John Bent of Marlboro.

Edmund, called Deacon Rice, father of Edward, was born about 1594 in Berkhampstead, Hertfordshire, England. He emigrated to the colonies and settled in Sudbury, Mass., in 1639. Edmund was one of the founders of Sudbury, a proprietor and selectman, a freeman and a deputy to the General Court. He had a twin brother, Robert, who followed him to America.

Edmund's father was Thomas Rice of Boemer, county of Buckinghamshire. There seems to be no record available of Edmund's mother.

Thomas' father was William Rice, born 1522 in the same town as Thomas. William was important enough to be granted a coat of arms in 1522. These arms are illustrated in color in *Burke's Landed Gentry* of 1939. Their blazoning: Argent on a chevron engrailed sable between three reindeers' heads erased gules as many cinquefoils ermine. As descendants of William Rice, ERB and his posterity are entitled to bear these arms.

William Rice was a younger son of Rice ap Griffith FitzUryan and Katherine, daughter of Thomas Howard, 2nd Duke of Norfolk. It is through these two that noble and royal blood enters the Rice family. Let's consider the Welsh line before we go to the English line.

First, though, it must be admitted that William Rice is a weak link in the genealogical chain. *Burke's Peerage* in the section on *Dynevor* gives only a son, Griffith ap Rice FitzUryan, and a daughter, Agnes, as the children of Katherine Howard and Rice ap Griffith FitzUryan. *Burke's Landed Gentry* states that it is said that William Rice was a younger son of Katherine and Rice. Dr. Charles Rice of Alliance, Ohio, a genealogical writer, indicates that there is no doubt about William Rice being their son. Since Burke often does not mention children who founded "unimportant" lines, the omission in the *Peerage* may be due to this. This may also account for the omission of Obadiah Rice in *Landed Gentry*. Obadiah (ERB's great-great-great-grandfather was "unimportant" to *Landed Gentry*. This is ironic, since *Gentry* lists in detail the accomplishments and novels of two of the descendants of Edmund Rice; but who today has ever heard of Cale Young Rice and Alexander Hamilton Rice? Yet, in 1939, Edgar

[1] Old records often use a dash to indicate an unknown name

Rice Burroughs was a world-famous writer and the creator of a character, Tarzan, whose only close rival in literary stature is Sherlock Holmes. I have no hesitation in saying that these are immortal characters, literarily speaking—the best known in the 20th century, and undiminished by time. As the years go by, they grow bigger.

Again, the family of Doyle is not even listed in *Landed Gentry*, though A. Conan Doyle came of ancient and distinguished stock from both sides. But then, neither Doyle nor Burroughs were considered to be "respectable" writers. And they are still vastly underrated by the literati.

The Welsh line of ERB's ancestry is studded with knights, princes and gentlemen. Those who are interested can refer to the section on the barons of Dynevor in *Burke's Peerage*. This begins the Rice lineage with Uryan Rheged, Lord of Kidwelly, Carunllou, and Iskennen in South Wales. He married Margaret La Faye, daughter of Gerlois, Duke of Cornwall, and he built the castle of Carrey Cermin in Carmathenshire, Wales. He had originally been a prince of the North Britons, but was expelled by the Saxons in the 6th century and fled to Wales.

His great-grandfather's sister was supposed to be Helena, mother of Constantine the Great. However, Helena's origin as a Briton is based on legends which are not backed by records contemporary to Constantine.

Uryan Rheged's great-great-grandfather was Coel Codevog, King of the Britons. Coel, who lived in the 3rd century A.D., seems to be the original of the nursery song, "Old King Cole." (See *The Annotated Mother Goose*, William S. and Ceil Baring-Gould, Clarkson N. Potter, 1962.)

Let's return now to the English line of ERB's family tree. Katherine Howard, William Rice's mother, came of a line which had many kings in its pedigree. The present head of the family, the Duke of Norfolk, is the Earl Marshal of England and the premier noble. Katherine was the daughter of Thomas Howard, 2nd Duke of Norfolk, and of Agnes, daughter of Hugh Tilney. Thomas led the English to their great victory over the Scots at Flodden Field, 9th September, 1513.

Thomas' father, Sir John Howard, 1st Duke of Norfolk, married Katherine, daughter of William, Lord Moleyns, and died fighting for Richard III on Bosworth Field.

The 1st duke was the son of Margaret, eldest daughter of Thomas, Lord Mowbray, and of Sir Robert Howard.

Sir Robert's lineage started with a John Howard of Wiggenhall St. Peter, 1267, who married a Lucy—. Sir Robert was also descended from King John of England, Duke of Normandy, through Joan, daughter of Sir Richard de Cornwall, a bastard of Richard Cornwall, second son of King John.

Margaret, Sir Robert's wife, was the eldest daughter of Thomas, Lord Mowbray, and of Elizabeth FitzAllen, daughter of the Earl of Arundel. Her brother, be it noted, was the ancestor of Isabel Arundell, the wife of the great explorer, writer and anthropologist, Sir Richard Francis Burton. Another item of interest is that some of the present branches of the Howard family are descendants of the barons of Greystoke. (See Burke, *Extinct Peerage*.) The de Greystock blood, alas, entered the Howard veins too late for ERB to claim them as forefathers. Captain Stafford Vaughan Stepney Howard-Stepney is the present Lord of Greystoke Manor in Cumberland and a distant relative of ERB.

Thomas, Lord Mowbray, was the son of John, Lord Mowbray, and of Elizabeth Segrave.

Elizabeth Segrave was the daughter of John, Lord Segrave, and of Margaret Plantagenet.

Margaret was the daughter and heiress of Thomas de Brotherton, Earl of Norfolk and Earl Marshal of England.

Thomas was the eldest son of King Edward I by Margaret, daughter of Philip the Hardy, King of France. Philip's dynasty will be described in Part II, along with other ancestors of ERB, the rulers of Scotland, Normandy, Norway, Hungary, and the Swedish Norsemen rulers of medieval Russia.

Edward I was the son of Henry III and of Eleanor, daughter of Raymond Berengaris, Count of Provence. Edward, be it noted, was the brother of Richard, also called Norman of Torn or the Outlaw of Torn. ERB says that Richard was a legitimate son, but there is plenty of evidence that *The Outlaw of Torn* is a semi-fictionalized account. Richard was probably one of Henry III's "natural" children. The identity of the mother is a subject for a separate article. I may also mention that Alice Pleasance Liddell, the real-life model for Lewis Carroll's Alice, was a descendant of Edward I. Her line came through John of Gaunt, Edward I's grandson. But she, along with Old King Cole, is a relative of ERB's.

Henry III's father was King John, who's had such a bad press that no king of England has ever been named John since. Actually, John was no worse than any of the medieval monarchs and a lot better than many. His brother, Richard the Lion-Hearted, was a thorough rotter who probably couldn't even speak English, but writers (until recently) made a hero out of him.

John married Isabel, daughter and heiress of Aymer, count of the French province of Angouleme. John's parents were Henry II and Eleanor, daughter of William, Duke of Aquitaine.

Henry II's father was Geoffrey, Count of Anjou and son of John, King of Jerusalem. Henry's mother was the empress dowager of England and daughter of Henry I.

Henry I married Maud, daughter of the king of the Scots, Malcolm III, surnamed Caennmor. Maud, also called Matilda, was directly descended from Alfred the Great.

The father of Henry I was William (1027-1087), called the Bastard or the Conqueror. He and his Normans defeated King Harold of England at Hastings in 1066 and so won the rulership of England. William was the illegitimate son of Robert I, Duke of Normandy, also known as Robert the Devil. His mother was Arletta, daughter of a tanner of Falaise, and the story is that she caught the Devil's eye while he was riding past a brook where she was washing clothes. Robert dismounted and mounted. And thus was created another link in the blood-chain which resulted in ERB. Little William was raised in Robert's house and, since Robert had no surviving legitimate sons, became Robert's heir. In those days, the upper crust often took in their natural children to rear as their own. There was no stigma attached to bastardry.

What if Robert the Devil had not happened to be riding by that particular spot on that particular day? Quite probably the Norman conquest of England would not have occurred. The world, especially the English-speaking world, would be different in many respects. The English speech would not quite be what it is today, nor would our political and social institutions. Most of us (North American and European readers) would not exist. Our places would be taken by entirely different individuals. The works of Edgar Rice Burroughs would not exist, and this article would not have been written.

William the Conqueror was the descendant of Rollo, or Hrolf, the Norseman who conquered that part of France which became Normandy. Rollo was called the Ganger, or Walker, because he was so huge that no horse could bear his weight.

William married Maud, or Matilda, daughter of Baldwin, Count of Flanders. She was descended from Alfred the Great and Charlemagne.

Skipping a few Old English kings, we come to Alfred the Great. He was the son of King Ethelwulf (died 857) and of a lady named Osburh. Ethelwulf was the son of Egbert, King of Wessex, also titled Bretwalda, "ruler of Britain," deceased in 839.

The line of descent from Offa (reigned 757-796), King of the Mercians and of all England, is uncertain. But since there was much giving in marriage of sons and daughters among all the early Old English kings, it's highly probable that Egbert was descended from Offa.

Offa, according to a traditional genealogy, was a descendant of Penda, a king of Mercia. Penda's ancestral line consisted of Wibba, Creoda, Cynewald, Cnebba, Icel, Eomaer, Angetheow, Offa, Waremund, Wihtlaeg, and the great god Woden.

(The latter Offa is quite likely the Offa mentioned in *Beowulf.*)

No one today is claiming that a god actually begat Wihtlaeg. This founding of a royal line by a deity was traditional and common to all the kings of Kent, Eastanglia, Essex, Mercia, Deira, Bernicia, Wessex and Lindesfaran. But, according to some modern authorities (Jacob Grim, among others), Woden was probably a hero of the early Germanic peoples who became deified after his death.

He would have lived, however, somewhere between 1000 B.C. and 800 B.C., not the 4th century A.D.

This early date means that the majority of those who read this article are also the many times great grandchildren of that ancient proto-Germanic speaking hero.

The descendants of ERB are living today, but the scope of this article ends with ERB. As it is, it's been a long journey from Woden to Tarzan.

From Woden to Edgar Rice Burroughs
– a pictorial family tree

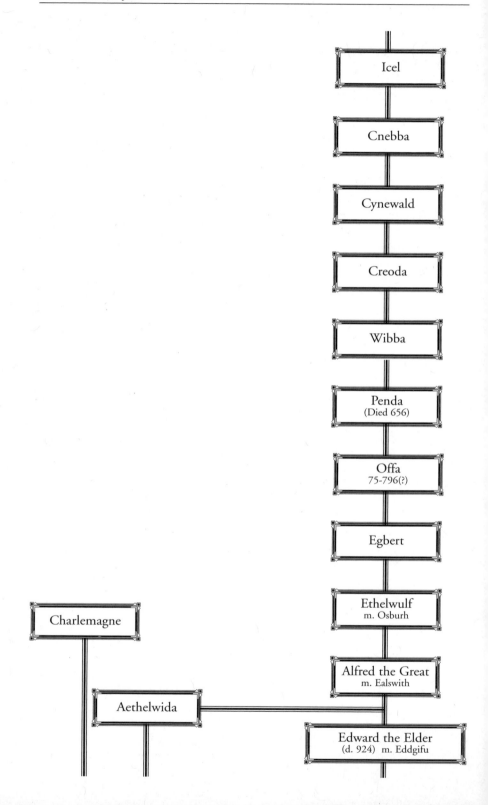

Icel

Cnebba

Cynewald

Creoda

Wibba

Penda
(Died 656)

Offa
75-796(?)

Egbert

Ethelwulf
m. Osburh

Charlemagne

Alfred the Great
m. Ealswith

Aethelwida

Edward the Elder
(d. 924) m. Eddgifu

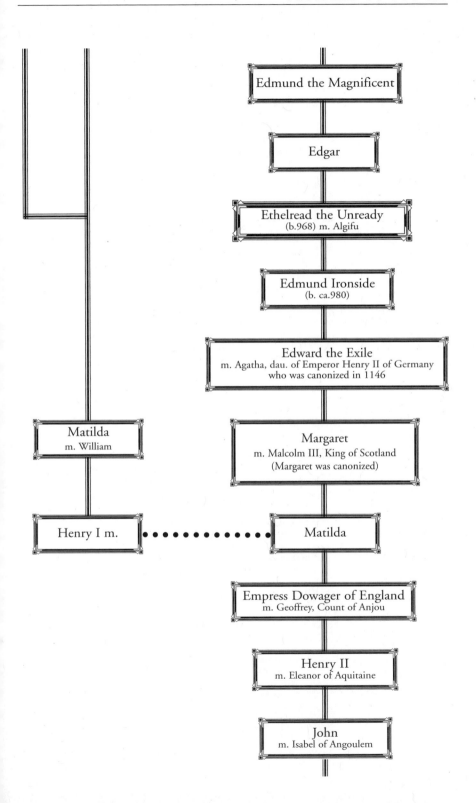

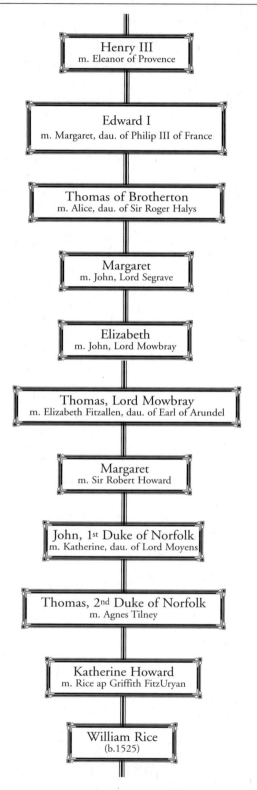

Henry III
m. Eleanor of Provence

Edward I
m. Margaret, dau. of Philip III of France

Thomas of Brotherton
m. Alice, dau. of Sir Roger Halys

Margaret
m. John, Lord Segrave

Elizabeth
m. John, Lord Mowbray

Thomas, Lord Mowbray
m. Elizabeth Fitzallen, dau. of Earl of Arundel

Margaret
m. Sir Robert Howard

John, 1st Duke of Norfolk
m. Katherine, dau. of Lord Moyens

Thomas, 2nd Duke of Norfolk
m. Agnes Tilney

Katherine Howard
m. Rice ap Griffith FitzUryan

William Rice
(b.1525)

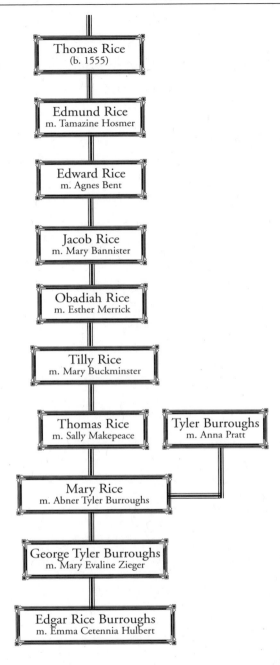

Thomas Rice
(b. 1555)

Edmund Rice
m. Tamazine Hosmer

Edward Rice
m. Agnes Bent

Jacob Rice
m. Mary Bannister

Obadiah Rice
m. Esther Merrick

Tilly Rice
m. Mary Buckminster

Thomas Rice
m. Sally Makepeace

Tyler Burroughs
m. Anna Pratt

Mary Rice
m. Abner Tyler Burroughs

George Tyler Burroughs
m. Mary Evaline Zieger

Edgar Rice Burroughs
m. Emma Cetennia Hulbert

A Language for Opar

First published in *ERB-dom*, 75, 1974.

Opar, the lost city of Edgar Rice Burroughs' Tarzan novels, was the springboard for two novels by Farmer, *Hadon of Ancient Opar* and *Flight to Opar*. These adventures detailed the cultural changes which stirred the African outposts of Atlantis approximately twelve thousand years ago, at the end of the last Ice Age. In previous articles, the author used genealogy to explain the connections between the novels of Burroughs and Haggard. However, in "A Language for Opar" he uses anthropology—physical, cultural, and linguistic—to draw his conclusions.

In *The Return of Tarzan,* Tarzan is captured the first time he enters the city of Opar. He is placed on an altar to be sacrificed, and the high priestess, La, recites a "long and tiresome prayer." At least, Tarzan presumes it's a prayer, since the language is unknown to him. Later, La addresses him. Tarzan replies in five languages, none of which she understands. The last is "the mongrel tongue of the West Coast," a beche-de-mer or pidgin spoken in the ports and along the shoreline of West Africa.

So far, I've been unable to identify this pidgin, though no doubt it exists and my research has not been extensive enough. The surprising thing is that Tarzan knows it. He's had the time to learn French, English, Arabic, and Waziri (to some extent, anyway). But when and where did he have opportunity and leisure to learn the West Coast pidgin? During the events of *Tarzan of the Apes* and *The Return of Tarzan,* he has been very busy and had very little contact with the natives of the West Coast.

But seek and ye shall find. Tarzan must have learned at least its rudiments while he and d'Arnot were in the port-town they found at the end of their wanderings in *Tarzan of the Apes.* Tarzan, always a magnificent linguist, could have picked up the beche-de-mer very quickly.

During the ceremony at the altar of this lost outpost of Atlantis, Tha, an Oparian priest, makes a complaint. Tarzan is surprised to hear him speak "his own mother tongue." This is the speech of the Mangani—"the low guttural barking of the tribe of great anthropoids." La answers Tha in the same tongue.

Burroughs could not have meant that the two Oparians were emitting dog-like barks. Possibly, a language could consist of clusters of long and short barks, a barking Morse code, in other words. But humans would never adopt such a speech.

Besides, Burroughs makes it evident throughout the Tarzan books that the Mangani speech has definite words with consonants and vowels and that these are arranged in syntactical order. Intonation also plays an important part in the meaning. It determines whether "kagoda" means, "Do you surrender?" or "I do surrender." And intonation in a barking language is impossible.

The only way to reconcile Burroughs' two contradictory descriptions of the Mangani speech is to assume that he meant something that did not accord with the conventional definition of "barking." Perhaps the force with which the words were uttered suggested to him the "barking" metaphor. Thus, in English, a drill sergeant can "bark" orders.

Burroughs' use of the adjective "guttural" must mean that the Mangani used sounds not found in English and seldom found in other languages. I believe that he meant by this one of the definitions of "guttural" given by Webster: "being or marked by utterance that is strange, unpleasant, or disagreeable." Burroughs was no linguist and hence did not use "guttural" in a truly linguistic sense.

Note that the original language is "a grunting monosyllabic" tongue. What Burroughs means by "grunting" is open to speculation. He does not define the term. "Opar" and "Oah" (Cadj's fellow conspirator) are not monosyllables. But Opar must be a heritage of the period in which the language was not monosyllabic. Oah, instead of being O-ah, could be a diphthong, pronounced as our English "aw" or "oy." Burroughs doesn't tell us its pronunciation.

Whatever the sounds of the Mangani language, they are not out of the range of human speech. Apparently, the Mangani have teeth, oral cavities, larynxes and pharynxes much like those of human beings. And this tells us that the Mangani are not as ape-like as Burroughs depicts them. But that's the subject of another article to be in *ERB-dom* soon: "The Reconstruction of the Mangani."

After Tarzan kills the madman Tha, he and La have a long conversation in Mangani. La tells him of the origin of Opar and summarizes its history. And we're confronted by a problem at once.

Both La and Tarzan use many words which the Mangani tongue just would not have. In the paragraph beginning "You are a wonderful man..." La uses "city" and "civilization." Tarzan, in his reply, uses "religion" and "creed." Some of the other non-Mangani words in the following dialog are "priestess," "temple," "ten thousand," "gold," "ships," "mines," "slaves," "soldiers," "sailed," "fortress," "galley," "rituals," "sacrilegious," and "God."

It is probable that La used these words. But they would have been loanwords from the Oparian tongue and hence unintelligible to Tarzan. He knew only the Mangani of the west coast of Africa. This, as chapter IV, "The God Of Tarzan," of *Jungle Tales of Tarzan* indicates, had no concepts of, or words for, any words to do with religion. And what would the Mangani among whom Tarzan had been raised know of gold, galley, mines, slaves, civilization, etc? Doubtless, the Oparian language had a word for "ten thousand." But the preliterate Mangani would not. For most preliterates, a word signifying "many" has to represent numbers above twenty. Some can count above that, but not very far.

How Was Tarzan Able to Understand La?

One explanation is that he interpreted the unfamiliar words from the context. Another, the most likely, is that he interrupted La many times to ask her for the definition of a word. This would not have been easy for La, since she would have had to use the limited Mangani vocabulary to make the definition. Apparently, she was successful. Tarzan's acquaintance with the vocabulary of several civilized peoples enabled him to grasp her meaning quickly.

In any event, the dialog did not proceed as reported by Burroughs.

This linguistic difficulty may have been described to Burroughs. In this case, Burroughs just ignored the facts and described the dialog as if it had gone smoothly. He did this for the benefit of the reader, whom he thought (rightly or not) wouldn't be interested in the mechanics of the conversation. Burroughs discarded realism for the sake of speed of narration. The essential thing was to communicate the basics of La's history of Opar.

Since the humans and the Mangani of Opar were in such close linguistic contact, it is likely that some of the personal names of the humans were borrowed from the Mangani. La doesn't seem to be one of these. Since she is the inheritor of a priestesshood and queenship many thousands of years old, it is probable that "La" came from the other tongue. It might have originally been a title. Perhaps every chief priestess was named La. On the other hand, Oah, during her brief tenure as the chief priestess, did not adopt the name of La. Or perhaps Burroughs did not tell us that she did because he did not want to confuse the reader with two La's.

Some ERB scholars have speculated that La might mean, simply, She. That is, The She, Ayesha, the immortal queen and high priestess of the city of Kor (see H. Rider Haggard's *She*, *She and Allan*, and *Ayesha*) is addressed as "She" or "She-who-must-be-obeyed."

It's my theory that the city of Kor was founded by refugees from the same great civilization which gave birth to Opar. After the cataclysm which destroyed the mother-culture, survivors fled to various parts of Africa and founded their own tributary cultures. The cities of Athne and Cathne, Xuja, and Tuen-Baka may have been built by the refugees, and the wild Kavuru may also have been descendants of the refugees.

John Harwood and Frank Brueckel have originated this latter thesis, and it will be expounded in their forthcoming article, "Heritage of the Flaming God, an essay on the History of Opar and its Relationship to Other Ancient Cultures." This will be published by Vernell Coriell in a *Burroughs Bibliophiles*. Harwood and Brueckel originated the idea that the lost cities of the Tarzan books may have been built by survivors of the destroyed mother-state. It is my own idea that Kor (and the civilization of the Zu-vendis, see Haggard's novel *Allan Quatermain*) were also founded by refugees.

One final speculation. The religion of Opar seems to have been monotheistic. This means that it was the end-product of thousands of years of civilization. It has gone through the polytheism which is an inevitable stage of early cultures and now has one deity, the sun, the Flaming God.

The Flaming God is a male, and yet the head of the theocracy is, and apparently always has been, a woman, La.

There was a typo in the original publication of this article, which has been corrected here. Here is Phil's letter on the subject.

From Philip Jose Farmer, of Peoria, Illinois to the Baker Street Journal March 1972

The December issue was, as always, very entertaining and highly informative. I was pleased to find my article, "The Two Lord Ruftons," in it. However, there is an unfortunate typo which makes it appear that I said that Gerard's Lord Rufton was the ancestor of Watson's. But I am sure that the readers are perceptive enough to see that an apostrophe and an "s" were dropped (On page 222, line 12, "If Gerard's Rufton was the ancestor of Watson..." should be "of Watson's.") Otherwise, I may have to write another article proving that Gerard's Rufton was indeed Watson's ancestor.#

Yet, in Opar, a woman is the head of the state and the chief of a religion which worships a male god. Does this singular situation reflect a long struggle between the priestesses of a mother-god and the priests of a father-god in ancient Opar? Was the sun-god originally a son of the Great Goddess, and did he finally rise from the rank of a secondary deity to that of the primary and, finally, that of the only deity? Such seems to have been the case with the male gods in Greece and other Mediterranean countries.

And was the struggle in Opar solved by a compromise? Did the son-sun become the only deity but the priestesses retained their position as the head of the religion?

This seems the only explanation to account for the unique Oparian religion. And this indicates that the mother-state, the mighty empire stretching from sea to sea, was a matriarchy, and its chief deity at that time was an earth-goddess.

However, it is possible that she was the sun in the beginning, and that in the end the sun had to become masculinized.

In Kor (according to *She and Allan*), the struggle was still going on. She, priestess of the moon, had long been challenged by Resu, priest of the sun. Only because of the intervention of Allan Quatermain and his mighty Zulu ally, Umslopogaas, were the worshippers of the moon (a female deity) able to triumph.

The question of the ancientness of religious sacrifice of human beings in Opar is not answered in the Oparian novels of Burroughs. Apparently, it had been going on for a long time. But this does not mean that human sacrifices were a part of the religion of the mother-state at the time of the cataclysm. In ten thousand years much will change, and the Oparians had degenerated in many respects.

The Purple Distance
A Foreword

Previously unpublished.

This was to be a foreword to an edition of *Hiawatha* that would have been published by Fokker D-LXIX Press, 1973
    Although ostensibly an introduction to Hiawatha, Phil quickly reverts to discussing his primary interest, Tarzan.

᠅᠅᠅᠅᠅᠅

This is an edition of Longfellow's *The Song of Hiawatha* with illustrations by J. Allen St. John.

At first thought, it might seem that the illustrations are the only thing about this book to attract Burroughsphiles. St. John is the supreme portraitist of the Tarzan, Barsoom, and Pellucidar series and many other books by Edgar Rice Burroughs. Therefore, any book illustrated by St. John is of interest to the Burroughs fan.

However, a study of *Hiawatha* and of various Burroughs novels, particularly the Tarzan books, reveals that this assumption is false. There are many striking parallels and similarities between Burroughs and Longfellow, between Tarzan and Hiawatha, and, in one respect, between *Hiawatha* and the early Barsoom books.

While rereading *Hiawatha* recently, I was struck by two passages in a verse near the end of the poem. Hiawatha is in his magic canoe, heading into the setting sun, his destination is the kingdom of Ponemah, the land of the Hereafter. He has said farewell to his people, though he promises that he will someday (like King Arthur and the meso-American god-hero Quetzalcoatl) return. (The italics are mine.)

And the people from the margin
Watched him floating, rising, sinking,
Till the birch canoe seemed lifted
High into that *sea of splendor*,

Till it sank into the vapors
Like the new moon slowly, slowly
Sinking in *the purple distance.*

It seems to me that Burroughs and St. John together placed Tarzan, Barsoom, and Pellucidar in a sea of splendor. Both the writer and the artist wrought magic, magic of a sea of splendor with a purple distance of heroic romanticism between the reader and the novels. The purple distance is that spell of unique sorcery cast over us by the collaboration of these two, of the combination of word and picture.

Admittedly, Burroughs would be as famous today even if St. John had never existed. But those of us raised on the St. John-illustrated Burroughs books know that the artist helped cast that purple distance beyond which was the sun of splendor. Other great artists have illustrated Burroughs, Frazetta, for one, and the Czech, Burian. Artistically, Burian may be the greatest of all. His illustrations of Tarzan are indeed both realistic and romantic. But for us who knew St. John in our childhood and youth, St. John is the only one who will ever limn Tarzan and John Carter against that sun beyond the purple.

Hiawatha and Tarzan have many things in common. Some of these I've described in chapter 24, "Tarzan and the Monomyth," in *Tarzan Alive.* There is no need to recapitulate these here. But there are many more similarities which were omitted in that biography and which should be brought to the reader's attention. Also, there are similarities in the attitudes and methods of Burroughs and Longfellow in dealing with their heroes.

The tales of both the Amerind and the African hero were based on actual human beings. Both Longfellow and Burroughs treated these historical persons in a purely literary manner. They regarded them as material to be used in the creation of romantic epics, not as the stuff of biography. When they thought it necessary, they exaggerated, falsified, and distorted, added elements from unconnected stories, legends, and myths, and often deleted elements which did not suit their purposes.

Longfellow did extensive research into eastern and Midwest Amerind customs, history, mythology, song, and language before starting to write *The Song of Hiawatha.* But one of his authorities, Henry Rowe Schoolcraft, had confused an Iroquois hero, Hiawatha, with Nanabozho, an Algonquin myth-figure. The Iroquois not only spoke an entirely different language from the Ojibway (Chippewa) Indians, but the former lived in upper New York while the latter were located in the Lake Superior region. What was worse, if possible, Hiawatha married a Dakota (Sioux) woman, Minnehaha.

However, it is possible that even if Longfellow had not been confused, he might have done exactly what he did. He was writing a poem, not history or a historical drama, and his combining disparate elements of the Amerinds would have furthered the theme of the poem, that of a dream of universal peace.

Burroughs seems to have done little research before writing the first Tarzan novel, *Tarzan of the Apes*. This resulted in some ludicrous errors. The basis of his story, that of an English nobleman who had been raised in Africa by great apes, was true. But, lacking the true details and background, Burroughs filled these in with imagination. Hence, his error in placing tigers in Africa, an animal found only (outside of zoos) in Asia.

The readers of Burroughs were as quick to point out this error as Longfellow's had pounced on his error. The tiger was in the initial appearance of *Tarzan of the Apes* in *The All-Story Magazine* of October, 1912. When the hardcover edition appeared, Sabor the tiger had become Sabor the lioness. Burroughs was stuck with this, which is why Panthera leo is the only species in the Tarzan series which has different names for the male and female. All the others have generic names, regardless of sex. Manu the monkey, Sheetah the leopard, Tantor the elephant, Gimla the crocodile, and so on are so named whether male or female.

Burroughs also called the leopard the panther, but there is some excuse for this, since the leopard is called this in some areas of Africa. St. John failed to do some research on his own, and he portrayed Sheetah as the American panther, cougar, or mountain lion, Felis concolor. Thus, when the reader sees the St. John illustration of Tarzan and crew sailing away from the island in *The Beasts of Tarzan*, he sees the North American big cat sitting in the prow.

It doesn't matter. The story itself is true in its basic elements. And if the storyteller Burroughs had not written of Tarzan, we would never have heard of him. Likewise, if the poet Longfellow had not composed his erroneous epic, who today would ever have heard of Hiawatha? Only scholars.

Both Tarzan and Hiawatha "talked" with animals. In Hiawatha's case we are sure this ability is sheer poeticising by Longfellow. Many heroes of myth and legend have had the gift of conversing with beast, and Hiawatha is one of these. In Tarzan's case, however, Burroughs is not exaggerating, or, at least, not much. The immortal apeman could communicate with them on a far higher level than any other known human being was, or is, able to do. Just how he does this, Burroughs doesn't say. However, it is only with the animals that are in the upper spectrum of intelligence, the apes, monkeys, elephants, and lions, that Tarzan can "talk." Hiawatha, on the other hand, speaks to, and is answered by, all types of animals and, in addition, birds and fish. This gift is clearly deep within the realms of fairy tale or myth.

The historical Hiawatha seems to have been either a Mohawk or Onondaga statesman whom tradition says flourished circa 1570. Longfellow has him establishing a league of peace, though it was in fact Dekanawida who was the prime mover. Hiawatha was Dekanawida's disciple and most active colleague in forming the confederation of the five Iroquois nations (later, six). This was not in any way intended to promote universal peace. Its primary reason was to introduce intratribal reforms, one of which was a law against blood feuds. The League eventually evolved into an instrument of warfare against the Algonquin Indians, though it didn't begin to be effective until about 1630. At this time, the Iroquois were making a desperate effort to control the fur trade with the French and Dutch. It was economics, not a desire for peace, that brought the Iroquois together. Even then, they did not present a united front against their enemies; there was much rivalry and dissension among the Six Nations.

Schoolcraft gave Hiawatha's real name as Hayóó-went'ha, meaning "very wise man." Later authorities give it as Haionhwa'tha, meaning "he makes rivers." The Manabozho (or Nanbozho) with whom Schoolcraft confused Hiawatha was a purely mythical character, a sort of demigod of the Ojibways. In fact, Longfellow started writing his famous poem with Manabozho as his chief protagonist's name. A short time later he decided to use Hiawatha's name because it was more euphonious. Hiawatha is really a highly idealized Manabozho and, aside from the name, has nothing to do with the Hiawatha of Iroquois fact or legend. Manabozho was, in the Ojibways religion, a benefactor. He taught the Ojibways how to hunt and trap, how to make stone weapons and tools, and how to cure diseases.

But he was also a trickster, often mischievous, conceited, treacherous, and malignant. He also performed prodigious sexual feats. Longfellow strained out these elements, which did not bother the Indians but would have been unacceptable to the white readers of that day. Moreover, Longfellow wanted to paint a consistent picture of a noble man of peace, and so esthetics demanded that he eliminate all incongruous elements. He was not an anthropologist; he was a poet.

Tarzan was a trickster. Burroughs doesn't hesitate to tell us this and to show many examples of his tricksterism. He admits that Tarzan was often needlessly cruel in his youth. This was, however, due to the thoughtless cruelty of the young and not to a deeply ingrained flaw in his character. He grew out of this trait, though he continued to be a trickster when dealing with vicious men until late manhood.

Tarzan was also a benefactor to his people, the mangani. He invented the running noose, the full nelson, storing food, and a system of sentinels. His people were too unintelligent or too conservative to adopt any of these except the guard system. In time, they seemed to have abandoned that.

Tarzan also acted as peacemaker many times during his wanderings. He never officiously strove to do this, but he often got into situations where he had to assume that role if he was going to get out alive or rescue people in whose fate he was interested. And he was too observant of human nature to believe that the peace would be maintained long after he had left the area.

Longfellow used the meter of the Finnish *Kalevala* for his poem. The *Kalevala* has often been called an epic, but it is not one in the same sense as *The Iliad, The Odyssey, The Aeneid,* and *The Song of Roland.* It is actually a string of loosely connected lays and legends and myths sung by Finnish bards and collected and arranged by Elias Löönnrot, a Finnish physician and philologist. The meter is trochaic tetrameter, a line of four feet, each foot beginning with a primary accent on the first syllable followed by one (or often two) syllable(s) lightly accented. This meter is not natural to English poetry, but Longfellow, despite much criticism for using it, chose it well. It is peculiarly fitted for this tale of a primitive hero of the American Indian and its mythic and often supernatural setting. Though many critics have jeered at it, and the poem is the most parodied in the English language, Longfellow's poetic instinct was right. The meter, and the many parallelisms of image, evoke the sound of Indian tom-toms, of the structure and the chanting of Indian songs, and a dreamy "purple distance" of primeval forests and talking animals, of evil spirits and heroic men.

Longfellow's *Hiawatha*, however, has nothing of the gigantic or the amorphous superhumanity of Lemminkainen or Vainamoinen, the brawling, lecherous, treacherous, lusty heroes of the *Kalevala.* In these respects, they resemble the Manabozho of the Ojibway. As Newton Arvin, in his *Longfellow: His Life and Work*, points out, Hiawatha does have something of the primitive and the elemental in him. But he is not the savage as devil (that of the Puritans) nor the noble savage of Cooper or the heroic savage of Melville. He is the gentle savage. He is, as Arvin Says, "a poetically stylized but a falsified version of the American Indian." He means that the Amerind was all of the above—much like civilized whites—but the devilish, the noble, and the heroic had been too much stressed by writers before Longfellow. The poet added the gentle savage to the others to make a rounded figure.

Tarzan was the gentle savage, too. He was, in fact, a gentleman, though raised in the jungle, more of a gentleman than most of the English nobility. This characteristic is seen throughout the novels but is especially strong in the last in chronological sequence, *Tarzan and the Foreign Legion.*

In the end, Hiawatha sails his canoe into the setting sun. (Yes, sailed, not paddled, since it was a magic canoe.) He is leaving his people, the world, in fact, to voyage into the Hereafter. Just so, old Vainamoinen of the *Kalevala* leaves this world in a magic boat. Indeed, the verses describing this in the Finnish poem are remarkably similar in spirit to Longfellow's description of the departure of Hiawatha. Vernell Coriell has pointed out that Hiawatha's final voyage is reminiscent of the final trip the Barsoomians took down the river Issus. Like Hiawatha, the Barsoomians longed for a world of peace and love, and so they voluntarily left the living world to voyage down the dark river.

This thought leads to the speculation that Burroughs might have derived this custom, not from the floating of corpses down the Ganges, as some suggest, but from a reading of Hiawatha. Let us hope that Hiawatha truly found his isles of the Blest, his kingdom of Ponemah and was not, like the Barsoomians, doomed to a hideous revelation.

Tarzan would never voluntarily go to the Hereafter. Though he doesn't fear death, he doesn't love it. This may not be the best of worlds, but it is the only one he has. He will fight to stay in it until his last breath. "I still live!" is his motto, as it is of John Carter of Barsoom.

PJF On SF

"I've been reading and writing SF for almost 86 years,
give or take a decade. And I still can't define SF satisfactorily.
It's like talking about God. Not that I worship SF, but it's
a huge concept, bigger than my brain or yours and as
ungraspable as a shadow. What is it? Indefinable yet there."
—Philip José Farmer.

The Source of the River

The Source of the River

First published in *Moebius Trip Library's SF Echo,* Number 22, April 1975 where it was titled "Some Comments."

Sufism pervades much of Philip José Farmer's best work. *The Unreasoning Mask,* named one of the top one hundred novels of the science fiction genre *(Science Fiction, The 100 Best Novels* by David Pringle), chronicles Captain Ramstan's quest to save the pluriverse from the entity known as the *bolg,* as he revisits his lost Sufi faith. "Coda," a gem of a short story crowning the Riverworld series, narrates Alfred Jarry's maturation through the help of his Sufi teacher Rabi'a. Farmer also goes as far as revealing in *Escape from Loki* that one of Doc Savage's mentors is Hâjî Abdû El-Yezdî, the fictional narrator of Sir Richard Burton's The Kasîdah. But it is in the Riverworld series that Sufism first takes root in Farmer's writings.

"The Source of the River" is Farmer's response to Randy Hagan's article (also printed in *Moebius 22)* claiming the substantial influence of Burton's *The Kasîdah* in *To Your Scattered Bodies Go.* As a mystic tradition well aware of psychology before its "discovery" in the West, Hagan makes a good point. In the author's reply we see a deepening of respect and understanding of Sufism as the Riverworld concept evolved.

After 25 years, it's difficult for me to remember exactly what the genesis of the Riverworld series was. But Mr. Hagan's article caused me to probe back to 1952, when I first conceived and wrote the original, *Owe for a River* (also tentatively titled *Owe for the Flesh*—Editor). This was 150,000 words long, written in a month to make the deadline for the Shasta Pocket Books Fantasy Award Contest (or something like that). The story of what happened to it is much like that of the novel Frigate wrote for Sharkko's contest in *To Your Scattered Bodies Go.*

Actually, though "Sharkko" did not mean to do so, he did me a great favor by ripping me off. I put the novel aside since, in those days, there seemed to be no market for it. Years later, I sent it to Fred Pohl, editor of *Galaxy, If,*

Worlds of Wonder, and he suggested that the theme was too big to put into one book. So I started to rewrite it as a series. I'd changed considerably during the interim, and so the Riverworld concept had also changed somewhat. And the direction it's been taking has changed while I've been rewriting it.

As I remember it, I got the basic idea while reading John Kendrick Bangs' *A Houseboat on the Styx* (1895, Harper). This takes place in the afterworld; most of the action occurs on a houseboat in which a number of famous people live: Shakespeare, Homer, Ben Jonson, Sam Johnson, Nero et al. Mark Twain, however, has his own boat, a paddlewheeler. He also has it made. As he travels along, the river is literally created in front of him, so that he has a never-ending continuously new Mississippi before him. He can't run out of river.

Houseboat is sheer fantasy. But the idea sparked a science-fiction novel. I constructed a world on which a ten or twenty million-mile river covered an entire earth-sized planet. Not only that, it supported all of humanity and sub-humanity from about 2,000,000 B.C. through A.D. 2008. Or at least, it seemed to do so. I drew a number of maps of the Riverworld, some of which are still in my files.

At this time, I had started reading books about and by Burton (I have a pretty good collection of Burton, though it's not complete). I'd read the *Kasîdah*, of course, and this, as I remember it, was my second spark of inspiration. The two, Bangs' description of Twain and his never-ending river and the *Kasîdah*, fused together and I was off. Not for long. I was called back to the starting blocks and the gun didn't sound the signal again until about 1965.

It's not easy now to separate my own philosophy and Burton's in the writing of the original novel. I may have directly used some of the *Kasîdah's* concepts and attitudes of mind. Or I may just have found some of my own concepts and attitudes reinforced when I read the poem.

What I do know is that I was far from fully understanding the poem. It's Sufistic, and at that time I didn't know much about Sufism. Very little, in fact. There wasn't much available about it, not to me, anyway.

It seemed then like a poem influenced by Fitzgerald's translation of Khayyam's *Rubiyat*. And inferior. Of course, I knew that Burton had written it years before Fitzgerald did his translation. But it still sounded like an imitation.

I did not know then that Fitzgerald's work was a perversion of the original, that he misunderstood completely its esoteric references, that he was far from being fluent in Persian. What he did was to force a 12th-century Iranian mystic's poetry into a mid-Victorian agnostic form.

Burton, in addition to being well versed in the Persian language, history, and customs, was also a Sufi. At least, he claimed to be, though I have doubts that he was a genuine Sufi. But, intellectually, he knew the history of the Sufis, what they stood for, what their goals were. And he undoubtedly had come into frequent and intimate contact with many of The Woollen Ones. He may have passed through the early stages on the road to the final stage.

In recent years, many books on Sufism have become available, and I know more about it than I did in 1952. I've become very interested in it, though my appreciation of it is mostly intellectual, and that's far from being enough. I've reread the *Kasîdah* with much more understanding of it. This will be reflected in the third of the series, *Alice on the Riverworld*. (For those interested, this should come out sometime in 1976[1].)

To conclude, Randy Hagan has an interesting theory. I can't remember accurately what the influences of the *Kasîdah* were; too long a time has passed for me to be able to sift the unconscious from the conscious inspirations. What I do know is that the next Riverworld novel will be based on conscious influences. Or will it?

(If anyone would like to read a good book on Sufism, try *The Sufis*, Idries Shah, Anchor Books Edition, paperback.)

---

[1] Published as *The Dark Design*

A Rough Knight
for the Queen

Previously unpublished.

"Rough Knight for the Queen" was written in 1953. It is a colourful depiction of Richard Burton's earthly life before going on to play a central role in the Riverworld series.

In Gods of Riverworld, Peter Frigate (Phil Farmer's fictional alter ego) claims that he had written a biography of Richard Burton but that Fawn Brodie's biography of Burton came out before Frigate could get his published. Phil says "I was going to write a biography of Burton but Fawn's biography came out (1967). It seemed to be pretty definitive so I decided not to write more."

The original Riverworld novel *(River of Eternity)*, written in 1952—published 1983—featured Richard Black, a pseudonym for Richard Burton.

Phil: "This was written for what was called 'A Man's Magazine.' I think the magazine was titled *Gonads*, but I am probably wrong. Anyway, for reasons unknown, the article was rejected and so went into the proverbial trunk."

Storms were always blowing up in Richard Burton's path and changing or frustrating his plans. Sometimes, the storms were raised by mediocre men who blew hot in their jealous efforts to thwart him. Other times, Nature did her best to trip him up. She it was who was now stalling Burton's expedition into East Africa to search for the unknown headwaters of the Nile. And it was men who would put the finishing touch to that old bitch Mother Nature's interference.

Richard Francis Burton, captain in the Bombay Army of the East India Company, landed at Berberah on April 7, 1855. Berberah was located on the northern shore of the east horn of Africa, on the Gulf of Aden. Burton had just come back from Aden, situated across the Gulf in southwest Arabia. Only a short time before, he had plunged into the Ethiopian wilderness with a few natives and had become the first European to visit the forbidden city of Harar.

Thirty explorers had tried to enter its walls and had died; he alone had met and had outbluffed the all-powerful and murderous Amir of Harar. Now, he and three English lieutenants were to set out from Berberah, would revisit Harar, and then go into the jungle to find the source of the Nile.

Everything went well at first, ominously so. Fifty-six camels were purchased, and a small army of mercenaries, armed with sabers and flintlock muskets, were hired. Instead of starting at once, the unfortunate decision was taken to wait for the mid-April mail from England, which was to contain surveying and navigating instruments. But on the ninth of April, the monsoons began with a storm. The next day the city of Berberah was almost deserted, for the Bedawin preferred to travel in the rainy season, when they could find water easily. Eleven days later a gunboat from Aden landed a dozen Somali who wanted to go with Burton as far as Ogadayn. Though Burton asked the boat to stay, it left. However, a native ship anchored, and though it meant to leave that same evening, Burton, fortunately, ordered a rice and date feast for the crew and captain. They decided to stay over.

At sundown, Burton inspected the camp. As he strode about, swaggering, he made an impressive figure. He was a broad muscular man about six feet tall with jet-black hair and eyes. He carried himself proudly and moved abruptly, like a startled panther. His eyes were unusual, described by friends and enemies alike as being piercing, stinging, hypnotic, unfriendly, savage. He sported a dragoon's thick moustache, and his jaw looked hard and strong enough to bite an iron bar in two. He radiated strength and authority, so that any visiting native would have had no trouble in picking out the leader from the four white men.

All seemed to be well. The camp had been pitched on a rocky ridge close to a creek, about three-quarters of a mile from the city. Lt. Stroyan's tent was on the extreme right, Lt. Speke's on the left, and in the middle was the *rowtie*, a sepoy's tent, supported by two uprights and a transverse and open at both ends. Burton and Lt. Herne slept there. The horses and mules were tethered in the rear, and the camels in the front. At night, two sentries were posted, and these were kept from sleeping by regular visits from the native and English officers.

Suddenly, shots were heard from behind the tents. Burton raced to find the cause of the commotion and was told by the guards that they had fired over the heads of three horsemen. They were afraid that these were the scouts of a raiding party, and they'd wanted to scare them off.

Sharply, Burton said, "From now on, don't do any bloody shooting unless you know it's absolutely necessary. And then don't shoot over them. Shoot their bloody heads off!"

After giving this characteristic order, he questioned the three Bedawin. They replied that the local sheik of the Abban tribe was in a neighboring port with four ships. He intended to occupy Berberah when it was deserted and build a fort there. The three had come to see if the ship in the harbor carried building materials. Laughingly, they asked if Burton feared danger from them. All believed their story and went to bed without any uneasiness.

Sometime between two and three in the morning, the Balyuz, the native commander, ran into the tent, shouting that the enemy was on them. Burton leaped out of bed and listened for just a second. The rush of men outside sounded like a stormy wind; it was evident that they were outnumbered. He called for his saber and ordered Herne to find out just how many the attackers were. Then, with a Colt in one hand, Herne ran to the rear and left of camp, where the most noise seemed to be. He looked for the mercenaries and found a few. The others had leaped from bed and run off into the darkness, not even waiting to pick up their weapons. Herne fired twice into the assailants, without being able to see if he'd struck anybody. Finding himself alone, he ran back to the tent. Something hard struck his legs and sent him sprawling on the ground. The tent's pegrope. As he started to rise, a Somali leaped from the darkness, his warclub lifted. Lt. Hems fired, and the man crumpled. When he burst into Burton's tent again, he found Speke also there, for the captain had aroused him. Stroyan was nowhere to be seen. Speke had been awakened by the musket fire, but he thought it was the normal false alarm, warning thieves away, and tried to go back to sleep. Then, hearing clubs beating on the sides of his tent and the shuffle of naked feet, he ran into Burton's tent.

The Somali, three hundred and fifty strong, attacked the three Englishmen and the Balyuz, the only native who had not run away. They swarmed outside the tent, trying to nerve themselves with fierce screams. Javelins flew into the opening of the tent, and long heavy daggers were cast at the occupants' legs. Burton, armed only with his saber, ordered Herne to his right and Speke to his left. Each had one pistol, which they fired until their ammunition was gone. So close were the spearsmen, a man fell at every shot. Herne rose to search for his powder horn in the rear of the tent. "Damn, I can't find it," he called out. Then, "There's usually some spears tied to the centerpole." He ran back to Burton. "One of those bloody blacks is slashing through the rear of our tent. They'll be on our backs in a moment."

Just as he ran out, the tent sagged, for its ropes had been cut in the hope that the English *Roumi* would be caught within, where they could be stabbed like fish in a net. Burton, knowing this trick, had ordered them out. He led them straight into the whole mob. Just outside the entrance were about twenty Somali, kneeling and crouching behind their shields, their spears held out before them. They looked like black-faced ghosts, with their ostrich feathers atop their bleached yellow-white hair, and their white robes edged with scarlet.

Burton rushed into the twenty, his saber swinging. Clubs swung at him and seemingly bounced off his hard muscles or else were turned aside by the steel blade. He smashed through canvas-covered shields, then, unexpectedly, drove the point into their throats. These savages had never heard of thrusting with a sword; they were dead before they had caught on. And many of them suddenly found their spears and clubs had dropped out of useless hands. Burton used the *manchette*, a trick of swordplay which had helped earn him the title of *maitre d'armes* from the French. A cut at the forearm, then an unexpected backhand drawing, the sharpened backedge of the saber slicing the nerves and tendons of the enemy's wrist.

Speke and Herne were swallowed in the horde. Burton was left alone. Thinking that he saw Stroyan's body lying on the sand, he cut his way towards it. Meanwhile, the Balyuz, who would not use his spear because of a sore right thumb, was trying to help Burton out. His efforts were limited to pushing him along. Burton, thinking he was an enemy, turned to cut him down.

"For the sake of Allah, it is I, your friend!" cried the Balyuz.

Burton halted the sword at the top of his swing. Instantly, a Somali who had been lurking at the edge of the fight for just such a chance, stepped forward and drove his broadheaded spear through Burton's cheeks. Then he turned and fled, escaping the avenging cut at him.

Though the blade had knocked out four of his back teeth and driven into his palate, Burton fought on, the spear hanging from the side of his face. The savages, though wild to gain the glory of killing this great warrior and of soaking their ostrich crests in his blood, could not stand before his fury. Within a minute he was in the darkness, where some of his mercenaries and servants offered to go back with him. But as he approached the enemy once again, they faded off into the night, leaving him alone. Meanwhile, Balyuz reappeared. Burton ordered him to go to the native boat in the harbor and tell it to wait for them. The rest of the time before dawn he spent in wandering about looking for his three companions, the spear still sticking through both cheeks. Finally, his pain and fatigue were so great that he had to lie down.

At dawn he rose, and went to the head of the creek, where an armed party from the boat found him and carried him to safety. Fate, that so often had and would cast events to trip him up, had this time saved him, for had the boat left the night before, as they intended, he would have been slaughtered by the Somali in the daylight.

Stroyan's badly mutilated corpse was later found. Except for some bruises from warclubs, Hems was uninjured. Speke was captured and stabbed many times in the chest and thigh, but he escaped.

It would have been better for Burton if Speke had died there, for it was the lieutenant who was to rob Burton, on a second expedition, of the glory of having discovered the Nile headwaters, after Burton had borne the burden of the safari and fallen sick. Later he spread lies about the whole incident at Berberah, making it out that he, Speke, was the leader, was the first to turn out, and only he had the courage to defend himself. Moreover, Burton, instead of getting credit for the exploration into East Africa and a commendation for his magnificent fight at Berberah, was actually rebuked by the government, as if it had been his fault, and was also made a scapegoat for international political complications which arose from the incident. Burton had broad shoulders, but there were times when they would sag a little under the many misrepresentations and malicious lies made against him. Some of this persecution was his own fault, however, due to a total lack of tact and a brutal outspokenness. However mean and ornery his enemies, Ruffian Dick, as he was sometimes called, was meaner and ornerier.

Almost from the first, Richard Burton showed his famous streak of contrariness and self-contradiction. Born in Barham House, England, on March 19, 1821, he was a beautiful blue-eyed and redheaded baby of distinguished ancestors. One of them was Louis XIV, the Sun King of France, who had had a bastard son by the beautiful Countess de Montmorency. From them he probably got his black hair and eyes. Another famous ancestor was Rob Roy, the Scottish outlaw. From him he probably got his red hair and blue eyes. He did not, of course, get both sets of colors at the same time. He was born with the light coloring, and his maternal grandfather, old Mr. Baker, was so overjoyed that he decided to will to little Richard his fortune of 80,000 pounds. That is good money today, and was worth more than six times as much in those days. Apparently, redheaded Richard had been born with a silver spoon in his mouth.

But his mother, the very person who might have been thought to have guarded this windfall for her first child, was the very one who cheated her son out of it. She had a passionate attachment to her wastrel half-brother, in whose favor the will had originally been made out. For three years she argued with her father against changing the will. Finally, the old man said that it was his money, and he'd do what he wanted to with it. He drove in a carriage to his lawyers to carry out the change. And dropped dead of a heart attack at the door. Richard's uncle got the money, was at once swindled out of 60,000 pounds in Paris, and later lost it all.

Meanwhile, Richard's red hair and blue eyes, as if to demonstrate his contrariness and to show that he was captain of his own body, if not of his grandfather's money, changed to a jet black. And so they remained the rest of his life.

Afterwards, his childhood was spent in being dragged over France and Italy while his hypochondriac father searched for relief for his asthma. His mother, not to be outdone by her husband, also developed her professional illness. The boys had a succession of drunken and brutal tutors and of governesses who could not keep them in hand. Mr. Burton, a retired Lt. Colonel on half-pay, took up boar hunting and developed the unfortunate habit of riding head on into trees. Many times he was brought home unconscious, leading the neighbors to think he was dead drunk. Richard and his brother and sister grew up rather wild; very early, his talents for exploring, his daredevilry, his love of swordsmanship and fast women, his facility with languages, and his quick temper, began to show. At three he began to learn Latin; at four, Greek.

In Sorrento, Italy, there was a great natural arch which the peasants told him could not be climbed. He and his brother did so, anyway, though the crumbling stone and great height made it very dangerous. And when Mt. Vesuvius erupted, the boys ran across a lava stream in smoking boots and dared the Italians to follow them. No one did. There were many deep vents which gave off poisonous gases; at the Grotto Del Cane a dog was lowered in a basket half a dozen times a day for visitors to watch its asphyxiation. Burton had himself lowered, and was pulled up just in time to keep from being completely overcome. Meanwhile, Col. Burton was making their houses chokingly unbearable with his stinking experiments at soapmaking. Burton and his brother Edward became drunk for the first time and visited a cathouse, though only as sightseers, being too young for anything else. Burton broke his violin over his teacher's head, which effectively ended his forced lessons. At Naples, the cholera plague struck. The dead were hauled away at nights in carts. They were dumped into huge pits above which hung a blue flame, gases from the festering bodies piled below. Dick and Edward stole out at night, masked like the deathwatch, and helped load the corpses. Neither caught the plague, and it was during this time that both became interested in medicine. Later, Edward became a doctor, and Dick was always very good at amateur doctoring, both for animals and men.

At this very early age Burton took fencing lessons from Cavalli, the most famous rapiersman of the time. Even then he began his idea of combining the best points of the French and Italian schools into one system. Meanwhile, the two boys disdained masks until the day Dick drove his foil into Edward's uvula, almost destroying it.

Burton's early days were spent in just such pranks, all calculated to relieve his boredom and drive his parents frantic. His father, however, persisted in his desire that both his boys go into the Church, so he sent them to Oxford with that idea in his mind. Not theirs, for Edward speedily managed to annoy the dons until they 'rusticated' him, or, in plain words, kicked him out. Richard took a little longer. He became very interested in the Near East and decided to learn Arabic and Hindustani. Unable to find a teacher who knew much of either subject, he began to teach himself Arabic and soon perfected a system whereby he could learn a language in two months. It was then that he met Don Pascual de Gayangos, a Spanish Arabist. This fellow burst into laughter when he saw Richard's self-taught method of writing Arabic letters, for they were written from left to right, that is, the wrong way. But he admired Richard's daring and ability in tackling such an obstacle by himself.

Burton soon came to the conclusion that he cared neither to become a minister nor teacher. Bored with college, he began easing himself out. He played a hundred students' pranks. Once he had himself lowered by a rope into the garden of an old don, and there removed many of the choicest flowers by the roots and replanted huge marigolds in their place. He liked to shoot birds with an air gun as they flew over the heads of the teachers, out playing lawn bowls. The dons would pick up the birds and theorize as to how they died, only to find out when blood dripped on their clean clothes.

He gambled, being unusually lucky at public game houses though not so much at private card parties, got drunk, drove tandems, forbidden to the students, went on a visit to Heidelberg, where he and his brother scared hell out of the roistering, swaggering, bragging German saber-dueling students. Unmasked, the two gave a display of their skill and then challenged any comers. They got no takers. Finally, Richard deliberately went to a horse race when he was supposed to be at a lecture. Summoned before the college dignitaries, he boldly though unsuccessfully defended himself, and the next day Richard drove off in a tandem over the flower beds of the dons, kissing his hand to all the pretty shopgirls be knew—and he knew too many of them for his own good. He left college forever.

The Afghan War was raging, and Richard thought he'd like to get in it; there was a good chance for rapid promotion during wartime when soldiering for the East India Company, the officers died like flies, though more from disease than bullets. Too poor to afford the Guards or other crack regiments, he bought a commission in the Bombay Army, and setout for India on the *John Knox*. The skipper, a tall Scotchman, wished to establish his reputation as a hard man to deal with and by way of doing so he challenged the young recruit with the black and burning eyes to a boxing match. Burton tore like a young Dempsey into him, beat him backward around the ring, punched him in the middle until he was sucking wind for breath, then knocked him down for good. Afterwards, he practiced upon the flageolet until his passengers and crew were driven crazy by the horrible squeaking, but nobody dared take this handy fellow with his fists to task. Finally, Burton found three Hindustani servants and set them to teaching him the language, much to the relief of everybody.

Full of eagerness, Burton landed at Bombay, only to find that the war was over. It would not be the last time that he arrived upon a scene of action just a bit too late.

Now that the chance for rapid promotion was over, there was only one way to rise in John Company's service. That was through the slower and harder way of languages. Skilled interpreters were in demand, so Burton set himself to studying twelve hours a day, and in the seven years he served in India became a master of Hindustani, Gujarati, Persian, Maharati, Sindi, Punjabi, Arabic, Telugu, Pushtu, and also learned Turkish and Armenian. His first teacher told him that he was a man who could learn a language running, and he was later given the Brahminicial thread by the Hindu wise men, an honor few people got. Burton noticed that the *Bibi* or white woman was rare at that time in India and that most of the officers solaced themselves with a *Bubu*, a native woman. He was not above living with some of these "walking dictionaries" as he called them; besides providing him with the comforts a man needs at home or away, the *Bubu* was an easy way to learning a language and the customs. She kept house for him, managed the servants and the money, nursed him when sick, and had a neverfailing recipe for preventing motherhood, if the man so desired.

Tired for a while of living with either man or woman, Burton set up a household with forty monkeys. He taught them to eat from plates while servants waited on them and he talked to them. He claimed that he could converse with them and that he had compiled a dictionary of sixty of their words. Unfortunately, the book was later lost in a fire.

There were other amusements. He learned the fine art of falconry from a Baloch chief and mastered it so well that they accused him of being a Moslem. He wrote a book on it, *Falconry In The Valley Of The Indus*, which is still a fine work consulted by those who want to learn something of the native art.

He had a horror of snakes. To overcome it, he took lessons from snake charmers, so well that he soon was petting cobras.

At Karachi in the Sind, Burton and his friends used to visit a pool of sacred crocodiles. While the keeper was kept occupied with a bottle of cognac, they blasphemed the sacred beasts by teasing them. One fellow skipped across the pond by leaping from one scaly back to another. Burton, using a chicken for bait, hooked a monster reptile. After landing it, he tied its jaws together with a rope, then leaped on its back and rode it as it raced towards the pool. When the swiftly running reptile was about to slide into the water again, he jumped into the air to one side, high enough to avoid a blow from its tail that would have broken every bone in his body.

About this time all his boyish playing came to an end. He met Captain Walter Scott, a nephew of the famous author of Ivanhoe. The captain was looking for a good man to help him in surveying the Sind canals for their possible improvement. As Burton was not only regimental interpreter but had taught himself the use of compass, theodolite, and level, Scott picked him. His duties were to wander over the districts, leveling the beds of canals and making preparatory sketches for a grand survey. Since he was thrown so much among natives, he came to depend upon them for society. He began a systematic study of them. To get to know them better he decided to pass himself off as one of them. After trying several disguises he settled on that of a half-Arab, half-Persian from the shores of the Persian Gulf. Thus he could explain his imperfect accent to the Sindi people. About this time his fellow officers, who did not understand why he should hang around the natives, began to call him 'the white nigger'. Burton, as usual, on hearing of insults, laughed. He gloried in them, and, besides, no one would have called him that to his face. There were few if any swordsmen or pistol shots the caliber of Burton in all India.

One day a certain Mirza Abdullah of Bushiri, a *bazzazz* or seller of fine linens, calicos and muslins, stepped out of a tent into which Sahib Burton had gone. Long hair fell to his shoulders, his beard was long, and his face, hands and feet were very brown—with henna. Only one who had known it was he could have detected Burton. This Mirza wandered over the countryside with a single native servant and seemed to spend more time talking than selling. Occasionally he would open a shop and sell figs, dates, tobacco, molasses, and strong-smelling sweetmeats. He was very popular, for besides being a good looking fellow, he liked to pass gossip around, could tell wonderful tales, and always gave the ladies, especially the good looking ones, heavy weights for their money. Added to all this was a repertoire of magical tricks. In no time at all everybody came to look forward to his visits, he was welcome at private homes, in the market, and the mosque. Sometimes he even gained entrance to a harem, and several times proud papas offered their daughters' hands to him.

He came through every experience unrecognized; this adventure was to prove the prelude to the far more important time when he would pose as a dervish and make the pilgrimage to the city of Mecca. As a matter of fact, the seven years he spent in India, though seemingly wasted at the time, were to prove wonderful tune-ups for his later, more famous trips to forbidden cities and lost lakes.

Some people think that it was upon Burton that Rudyard Kipling based his famous character of Strickland, the Englishman who could so successfully pass himself off as any of a dozen different kinds of natives. Burton's wife said that Strickland even talked like Burton.

Then came the Sikh War which was to add the Punjab to British possessions. A chance for glory again, and for swifter promotion. Burton, though a hardworking scholar, was essentially a man of action who thirsted to lead. He had trained his native troops as best he could in the use of the saber, teaching them to do more than slash, to cut and parry, to use the point, if need be. He marched with the 18th Bombay Regiment from Rohri on the 23rd of February. April 2nd, he was back, miserable and deflated and tired. The war was over.

Tempers were soured among the young officers who had been waiting for a chance at combat. Burton began making doggerel rhymes on men's names at mess, but knowing something of his commanding officer's touchiness, passed him over. The hot-tempered Colonel, ordered him to write one on him. Burton, never one to resist a dare and also resenting the order, wrote:

"Here lieth the body of Colonel Corsellis;
The rest of the fellow, I fancy, in hell is."

The Sikh war might be over, but war with his C.O. was now officially declared. There was little he could do against him, but he would go disguised as a native and, riding a camel through the gates of Hyderabad, pass Corsellis, who never once knew his impertinent subaltern under the turban and beard.

Burton's adeptness at disguises got him into very bad trouble with the East India Company and the Foreign Office. Sir Charles Rapier, the governor, wishing to know more of the native vice in the sinkholes of the cities of the Bind, asked Burton to investigate them. Burton joyfully accepted this very dangerous mission. If there had been the slightest suspicion at any time of his true identity, he would have died on the spot, for these bhang-smokers and homosexuals did not wish any white man to be nosing around them. So it was a tribute to his mastery of language and knowledge of custom that he came out alive. Of course, Burton overextended himself and surpassed his orders. As Frank Harris was to say of him many years later, "It was the abnormalities and not the divinities of men that fascinated him." So detailed and shocking was his report that it was hidden away in the files, presumably there never to see publication. But when a new administration entered, the papers came to light. The governor was hostile to any friend of his predecessor and when these papers, so offensive to the Victorian prudery of those days, were drawn to his attention, he put a black mark against Burton's name. It was totally unfair, thus listing him to be passed over for promotions and to be gotten rid of at the first excuse. It was almost as if they'd suspected Burton of having taken part in the perversions and orgies that he had witnessed. Some of the evil rubbed off on him, and he was never to get rid of it, in their eyes, at least.

An honest and dangerous job that would in another age or with another type of brass have gotten him a medal or a citation, had ruined his chances of success. Indeed, his very detailedness was praiseworthy, for Burton was the forerunner of the scientifically trained anthropologist of today; his books were to be used as reliable textbooks by a later generation of Ph.D.s. But his name was mud on John Company's list.

He was not permitted to take part in the Mooltan campaign. The interpreter's position was given to an officer who could only speak one native tongue, and that not nearly as well as Burton.

Stricken with a recurrence of a painful eye disease, almost blind, discouraged, thinking he was an utter failure, his seven years of hardships and constant study wasted, Burton applied for sick leave and left for Europe. Yet he had an understanding of India and an ability that should have made his superiors consider him as its viceroy. And he was on the verge of the greatest exploit of his life.

Burton was twenty-nine when he went to France in 1850. There he went through a typical rest cure for him, which consisted of furious practice with the rapier and saber. So good was he that he became one of the very few Englishmen awarded the *brevet de pointe* by the French, thus making him a *Maitre d'armes*. He favored the *manchette*, which was a cut at the opponent's forearm, made in *tierce* or outside and vertically, followed by one in *carte* or inside, horizontally. He developed the devilish trick of sharpening the false or dull back edge of his saber, so that when he withdrew the blade during a manchette, it would cut the nerves, perhaps the tendons, and cause his enemy's sword to drop.

During this time he began writing his *Complete Book of Bayonet Exercise,* intended for the British Army. Instead of being thanked for this valuable work, he was rebuked by his friend, Colonel Sykes. "Relying on the bayonet will make the men in the ranks unsteady," said Sykes. This was a time when every other army in the world except England's recognized the value of the bayonet in close fighting. Burton knew that the lack of it was the weak point in their military system. Later, the Crimean War demonstrated to the high command that the English soldier was very much in need of training with the bayonet. So Burton's pamphlet was taken out of the pigeonhole, its dust blown off, and a few modifications, not improvements, made in it. For this he got not one word of thanks or congratulations from the Commander-in-Chief. One day he received a huge letter from the Treasury, informing him that he could draw from it the immense sum of one shilling. This was all he was to get.

Burton laughed grimly and set out for the War Office. If they owed him a shilling, by God, he'd collect it. Even that was not easily done, however, for he ran into red tape that could not have been more tangled if he'd come to collect a million shillings. After forty-five minutes of very hard arguing with a dozen clerks and visits to as many different offices, he drew the one shilling. And as he stepped out of the War Office, he saw a beggar with his hand out. At once, he gave it to the man.

"Lord love yer, sir."

"No," said Burton, "I don't expect him to do that. But I dare say you want a drink?" And he jauntily strode away. If the Empire could sneer at him, he could repay it in the same coin.

While still on sick leave Burton decided to carry out the project which first brought fame to him, if not fortune. He wished to study thoroughly the "inner life of the Moslem," and to make a pilgrimage to the holy city of Mecca, which was to the Mohammedan world what Rome is to the Roman Catholic. With this difference; that all roads go to Rome, whereas infidels were strictly forbidden, on pain of torture and death, to visit Mecca.

Research showed Burton that he would not be the first European to penetrate the forbidden walls. Several Italian and English converts, beginning with William Pitts of Exeter in the seventeenth century, had gone into Mecca. The Swiss Burckhardt, in 1814, had made a famous pilgrimage in native disguise. But he'd been too nervous to take notes or make sketches. Whereas Richard proposed to take his usual detailed notes and make many sketches.

His first step was to apply to the Royal Geographic Society, asking that they back him. He would take three years leave and then fill out that huge white spot on the map, the Rub Al Khali desert in southeastern Arabia. The Society voted him funds, but the East India Company refused to give him more than a year, which was to be for the purpose of studying Arabic, wherever he found fit. Probably, they hoped the troublesome lieutenant would come to grief, but if he did, they weren't going to pay his survivors a pension.

The evening of April 3rd, 1853, two Bombay officers walked into a rundown London house. A little later, one of them, Captain Grindlay, walked out. With him was a longbearded Persian, one Mirza Abdullah of Bushiri. Both hopped into a cab, whose shades were drawn as it hurried to the train waiting to take them to Southampton. At the port, the captain, acting as the Persian's interpreter, led him to their cabin.

It was absolutely necessary that Burton adopt the disguise so far from his destination. If the mysterious grapevine of the Near East had had enough warning of Burton's disguise, he would undoubtedly have ended up with a knife in his ribs long before he got to Arabia.

As it was, the other Moslem passengers had no suspicions of his true identity, with the exception of one. Burton took the chance of practicing on them; there were a hundred things he had to perform exactly right. When Abdullah drank a glass of water, he could not carelessly toss it off. He clutched the tumbler as if it were the throat of a foe and called out, "In the name of Allah, the Compassionate, the Merciful!" Then he swallowed it all at once, and ended with a satisfied grunt. Before setting down the cup, he sighed, "Praise be to Allah!" an expression of thanks which meant much when said in the waterless desert. And when a friend said, "Pleasurably and in health," he must reply, "May Allah make it pleasant to thee!" Moreover, he could not drink while standing, unless it was water from the holy well of Zemzem, water given in charity, or that which remained after Wuzu, the lesser rite of washing. And he must use his right hand when he stroked his beard or ate, leaving the left or unclean hand for ignoble duties.

As the days passed and the *S.S. Bengal* drew closer to Alexandria in Egypt, Burton became more and more the character he'd adopted. This throwing himself headlong into his role was one of the reasons for his success. Like all born actors, he was the identity he'd assumed. Circumcised at the age of thirty-two, the better to pass as a Moslem, he found himself now actually regarding the uncircumcised dogs of infidels with contempt. His fierce eyes glared at them, and he avoided the company of all the *Roumi*, except for his interpreter's, of course.

But once while he was pressing his face against his prayer rug on deck, he looked up into the eyes of a Turk who was curious to see this devout Moslem. Burton paled a little under his henna-stained skin, for it was Turabi, a friend of his, and from Turabi's burst of laughter there was no doubt he recognized him. Frantically, Burton made signs to him not to give him away. The Turk, after keeping Burton in an awful suspense for a few minutes, turned and walked away, still grinning. Later, he and Turabi met in private, where Burton disclosed to him what he was going to do. The little Turk was not displeased, for he knew the Englishman would be making the pilgrimage devoutly enough, not with the intention of mocking Mohammed's faith. He advised Burton on several points.

At Alexandria he stayed with John Wingfield Larking, in a little house to one side of the main villa. Here he hired a local wise man and got him to coach him in memorizing the Koran, and in the various forms of prayers. He decided to drop the Mirza, or Mister, and became Shaykh Abdullah, the dervish. A dervish was almost a licensed vagabond, he could go anywhere without questions being asked. And in an hour of danger he had only to act insane, and he could go untouched, for the East respected the mad, as being the favorite sons of Allah, the "touched of God." Also, since he knew a little medicine, he set himself up as a *hakim* or doctor. When not studying, he visited the baths and the coffeehouses, hung around the bazaars and shopped. His fame as a good doctor and a magician—for he brought along his bag of tricks—spread rapidly. In a short time, men and women were hammering on his door. Again, he had access to harems, though he was always careful while there to act as a holy man should. One old patriarch offered him his daughter's hand in marriage.

At last he felt that he must leave Alexandria and move on. To do so, he had to ask for a passport. After being pushed around by many minor officials and roundly cursed, he got it at the British consulate, where he used very broken English. He almost came to grief when a native police officer tried to run him off. "Rukh ya Kalb! (Go, O dog!)" said the official, swishing a whip of hippopotamus hide in his hands as if he intended to use it. Burton, fighting hard to control his famous temper, threw away the plea he had meant to give about their being true brothers of the Moslem faith and replied with a curse. Then he turned away slowly, fists clenched. If the officer had struck him, he would have gone down beneath the hard Burton fists, and he could not afford to ruin his chances in such a manner.

A few days later, he was sworn at again, this time by an English officer because he had brushed up against him in his filthy coat and dirty blue baggy trousers. This was while he was boarding the *Little Asthmatic*, a Nile steamer bound for Cairo. With all his possessions wrapped into a roll on his back, and fingering a rosary which was large enough to be used as a flail if he was caught in a brawl, he went aboard. The canal was at its worst, with the water level very low. Instead of thirty hours, the boat took three days and nights to reach Cairo, and they grounded four or five times every day. As an impoverished dervish, he'd taken third class deck passage. A roasting sun cut through the canvas awning as if it hadn't been there. At night cold dews settled on him like a Scotch fog. The ship's cook was the world's worst, and he could not touch the better food of the infidels. With the rest of the natives, he drank muddy water drawn out of the canal in a bucket, and he munched his bread and garlic. A group of French housepainters going to paint the Pasha's palace at Shoobra offered him a drink of strong wine. He thirsted, for though he preferred whiskey, he would have been glad of any alcoholic drink at that time to help pass the boredom of the voyage. Sadly, he had to turn it down, because his role as a holy man demanded he not touch the drink forbidden by the Prophet. He sat and smoked and spent most of his time fingering his rosary or else stared at the one pretty woman on board, a Spanish girl, and cursed inwardly again because she would be even more forbidden than the alcohol.

He met two destined to play big parts in his stay at Cairo. One, Miyan Khudabakhsh Namdar, was a short fat man who appeared too late to catch the steamer, yet would not give up because he would have lost his fare. For a long time he ran alongside the canal, stumbling, calling, praying, cursing, falling into hollows, puffing as he clambered uphill, stopping now and then to turn back and hurry his donkey-boy, who was carrying his carpet bag. Finally, the captain, after laughing himself sick, stopped the boat. A few minutes later Khudabakhsh, exhausted, lay down and slept on the deck. When he woke up, he introduced himself to the false Abdullah. He'd been a shawl merchant in London and Paris. Attracted to Burton's style of conversation, he invited him to stay at his house at Bulak. And though Burton disliked the fat overdressed fellow with his Indian manner of fawning and frowning at the same time, he accepted.

The other, Haji Wali, was to become a good friend.

At Bulak he found that the caravanserais were full, so he was forced to stay with the shawl merchant for ten days. The man became rather tiresome, because he was so full of Western ways of acting. But Burton's time was not, he thought, wasted. Not long after he had met him, the merchant whispered to him that the native troops in India, the Sepoys, were plotting a great uprising. Burton had no chance then to warn the authorities, but he was to do so later. And of course, as usual, he was ignored and his reports pigeonholed. If the War Office had paid some attention to him, heeded the warnings of a man who knew India, and had followed his advice, the bloody revolt of the Sepoys, the Black Hole of Calcutta, and the equally bloody and vicious reprisals of the British might all have been avoided. But Burton was always to play the role of a bearded Cassandra to the Empire.

In Cairo, Burton found lodgings so scarce that he was forced to take a room in the Jemaliyah, the dirty brawling Greek quarter. In one way this was fortunate, for he ran again into Haji Wali. Together, they smoked the forbidden and highly intoxicating weed, hashish. Burton told him who he really was. Wali had been born in Russia, had traveled a great deal, and had discarded most of the superstitions and prejudices of the Moslems. "I believe in Allah and his Prophet, and nothing else," he said. He advised Burton to throw away the dervish's gown, large blue pantaloons, and short shirt.

"Get rid of everything that connects you with Persia. If you insist on being an *Ajemi,* you will get into trouble. In Egypt you will be cursed, in Arabia you will be beaten as a heretic, you'll pay three times what other travelers do, and if you fall sick you will die by the roadside, while those who would otherwise help you will spit on you."

Burton considered. It was true. The Persians belonged to the Shia sect. They had rejected the first three caliphs who had succeeded Mohammed as spiritual heads of the Moslems after his death. They claimed that Ali, the Prophet's son-in-law, was the rightful claimant, and they did not acknowledge the Sunna, orthodox theory and practice. They added five extra words to the prayer and did other heretical things that made the Sunni Arabs despise them.

So Burton became a Pathan, born in India of Afghan parents. To spread his reputation as a doctor, he began by treating the porter of the place where he stayed. This fellow, like most poor Egyptians, had a disease of the eyes. Burton poured silver nitrate into them, meanwhile announcing loudly that he never took a fee from the poor. Naturally, after the porter's eyes improved, he spread the good word. The poor flocked around, talked of this great and generous doctor, and soon the rich began drifting his way. Burton did not care whether he was paid or not. This was just as well, because there was no word for gratitude in any Oriental language that he knew. The natives would kiss your hand as long as they were sick. Cured, they would have nothing to do with you, especially when it came to paying the bill. But his reputation spread. Though he used some Western medicines, he also took advantage of the Eastern. The natives liked the huge bread pills, dipped in a solution of cinnamon water, flavored with assafoetida, and they enjoyed painful remedies, such as rubbing themselves with a horse brush until they were scarred.

Burton would administer the medicine with his own hand saying, "In the name of Allah, the compassionate, the merciful." After the patient had choked down the huge pills, Burton would intone, "Praise be to Allah, the curer, the healer."

He had fun playing the doctor. He would have liked to use hypnotism in his practice, for he was a pioneer in this, as he was in other things. But Wali advised against it, saying that it would detract from his reputation as a holy man. People would noise it abroad that he was using demons, and he would soon find the better class of patients steering clear of him. Burton took his advice; the Haji then built up Burton's reputation by praising him wherever he went. Across the way lived an Arab slave dealer, whose Ethiopian slaves were always sick. Burton cured half a dozen girls of the price-lowering habit of snoring. The grateful trader spread Burton's fame and talked of his devoutness.

Pilgrims wanting to go to Mecca began gathering around Burton. He hired two servants, Nur, a thieving East Indian youth, and Mohammed. The latter was from Mecca, was fat, humorous, loved women and wine at too early an age, and was too curious to suit his master. He'd known Englishmen in India, and this made Burton fear his disguise would be penetrated. He did buy from Mohammed his *kafan* or shroud, which every pilgrim takes with him to be buried in if he should fall by the roadside.

Others were Omar, a chubby Circassian youth who had run away from home; Saad the Devil, a giant and ugly black slave sent by Omar's parents to bring him home. These, with many more waited for the Shaykh Abdullah to make up his mind to start, but he was having too much fun to wish to start the dangerous trip at once.

Then, one afternoon, a burly Albanian captain of Irregulars swaggered into Burton's rooms. After a few choice insults, he grabbed a pistol from the doctor's bag. Burton, his black eyes blazing, and itching with a desire to blow off some steam collected during the fasts of Ramazam, snatched the pistol back. Fortunately, the mustachioed Albanian had forgotten to bring along his pistol, otherwise he would have gone for his own pistol, and Burton would have had a charge of murder on his hands—and possible exposure.

He glared into Burton's eye, trying to make the other drop his. But of all men, he had chosen the least likely. Every man who met Burton and wrote of him mentioned his eyes. Stinging, like a sullen serpent's. Compelling, hypnotic. Wild. Fierce. A caged leopard's. Burton's face revealed "a tremendous animalism, an air of repressed ferocity…"

The captain received the full impact of those eyes and dropped his own. His head whirling, he stumbled out. But in a few hours he was back to find out what kind of man this supposedly quiet Indian doctor was.

"By Allah, thou art stalwart for a *hakim* and a shaykh!" he bellowed. "Wrestle with me so that we may see who is the better man." He was bigger than Burton, but the Englishman never refused a dare. He grappled with the Captain, and they stood upright, breathing garlic and wine in each other's faces, straining to upset the other. Everywhere Burton had gone, he had taken pains to learn the local secrets of self-defense, and now he used his strength, kept in shape by exercise with foil and boxing gloves, to aid his wrestling lore. He shifted his weight suddenly and followed it with a cross-buttock that sent the Albanian flying to the floor. For a minute the captain lay there, half-stunned. Then he jumped up, bellowing, not with rage but with delight. "By

Allah, you are the kind of *hakim* I love! Let's have a drink on your victory, and another to our eternal friendship!"

Burton knew better than to touch the forbidden alcohol, but the terrible demands of the Ramazam, the Moslem Lent, had left him drier than a camel's hoof. When the captain came staggering into the room, his arms burdened with bottles of the fiery *araki*, Burton did not refuse him. The stuff burned his veins and loosened his brain; soon he and the captain were singing songs and telling dirty jokes. One thing led to another; finally, the Albanian insisted they go out to look for some pretty girls to help them celebrate. They roared into the next room, where Haji Wali was trying to take a siesta. When he threw up his hands in horror at the idea of alcohol, they poured his slippers full of *araki*. And they charged out after the girls, only to stagger into a room kept by two old women. Scandalized, the sharp-tongued harpies scolded them so viciously that Burton became half sobered and dragged the captain home to his bed.

Next morning, the scandal was all over Cairo. The devout hakim's reputation was badly bent, if not broken.

Haji Wali, grinning, said, "You had better start on your pilgrimage at once."

Burton agreed, and took leave of his friends. But he was cautious enough to tell them that he was going to Mecca by way of Jeddah, whereas he really meant to go there by way of Yambu. If word of his plans should fall into a robber's ears—and it was very possible, almost certain—then he would wait in vain on the wrong road.

Burton had wondered how much four years of comparatively soft living in Europe had affected his endurance. There could hardly be a better test than riding eighty-four miles in the hot midsummer desert sun, on a bad wooden saddle on a vicious camel. He was right; his bones were to ache, and his skin would be burned black and raw by the sun beating through his thick robes. But the moment he was in the desert, he felt his spirits rise. The heat like a lion's breath, the pitiless and naked sky, the vast desolation and ever-present sense of insecurity and of death, these stimulated and sharpened Burton, so that, like a true Bedawin, he felt at home. Here, the keen air and the exercise were wine enough. In the desert, liquor only disgusted you. A man dropped the hypocrisies of civilization, became open-spoken, hospitable, and resolute. He loved the desert, and there were times when he thought of living the life of a Bedawin, among whom he would have been a chief.

A little later, he ran into Mohammed El Basyuni, the boy from whom he'd bought his pilgrim-clothes in Cairo. They traveled together, with Burton amused at the way this city Arab abused his desert kin. The next day they stopped under a mimosa tree to rest, and here Burton had his first trouble with a bunch of Maghrabi pilgrims. These were hungry and thirsty, and Burton, who really had a tender heart under his fierceness, gave each a pint of his water and some bread. The Maghrabis asked for more, which Burton could not spare. Then they cried out that they would take money instead. Burton thought that a few pence wouldn't hurt, but when they began demanding them and hinting that their knives might come out to enforce their demands, he took his pistols out. The pilgrims subsided.

At Suez Burton loaned money to his companions: Omar the Circassian, Saad the Devil, a Turk, Salih Sakkar and a Shaykh Hamid. Here Burton almost came to grief, for his boy Mohammed, in pawing thru his luggage, came across the sextant which Burton intended to use in making meteorological notes. When Burton was out of his room, Mohammed announced that this instrument proved that Abdullah was an infidel from India. The others, however, objected. Omar replied that Abdullah must be a very learned and devout Moslem, because he had several times answered questions about minute points of the faith which Omar himself did not know. Shaykh Hamid, thinking of the money he intended to borrow from Burton after they reached Mecca, cursed Mohammed for a pauper, an owl, an excommunicate, a stranger, and a savage. Everybody heaped ashes on his head, but when Burton returned and found out what had gone on, he decided, sorrowfully, that the sextant had better remain behind. He could not afford even the slightest suspicion.

The pilgrims boarded the *Golden Wire*. This was a two masted *sambuk*, of about fifty tons, undecked, except upon the poop, which was high enough to act as a sail in a very strong wind. The captain had no means of reefing, nor a compass, log, sounding line, or chart. It was by guess and by Allah that he navigated.

On climbing aboard, Burton's heart sank. Ali Murad, the owner, had promised to allow only sixty passengers in the hold. And here were packed ninety-seven. Boxes and luggage were piled from stem to stern, and a group had established themselves on the poop, which was reserved for Burton and his friends. Saad the Devil, the giant negro slave, began clearing the deck in his simple forthright manner. He would pick up men by the scruff of their necks and toss them down into the hole below, along with their luggage, not caring whether a man landed on a box or a box on a man. There were still eighteen people on the poop, which was ten feet by eight. And the cabin was stuffed with fifteen men, women, and children. Down in the hold the same Maghrabis who had given Burton trouble were already scrapping with some Turks for elbowroom. One of Burton's party, a Syrian, jumped down to restore order. At once he sank from view into the living sea. When fished out, his forehead was cut open, someone had snatched away half his beard, and sharp toothmarks were in the calf of his leg.

Daggers were drawn, and in a few minutes five men were seriously wounded. The fighting stopped. A delegation was sent ashore for Ali Murad to tell him the vessel was overcrowded. After three hours, he deigned to appear in a rowboat, and, staying well out of reach of any missile, said that anybody who wanted could leave and get his fare back. No one would go, so, after telling his passengers to trust in Allah and all would go well, Ali rowed off. At once, another brawl started. The Maghrabis demanded that the poop "aristocracy" relieve the pressure by taking a half a dozen from the hold.

Saad the Devil rose, cursed, and threw to his friends a bundle of *nebut*, thick ash staves, six feet long, well greased.

"Defend yourselves, if you don't wish to be the meat of the Maghrabis!" And to the savages, "Dogs and sons of dogs, now you shall see what the children of the Arab are!" His friends joined in. "I am Omar of Daghistan!" "I am Abdullah, the son of Joseph!"

The Maghrabi were not daunted by this naming of names; they swarmed like hornets towards the poop, shouting, "Allah Akbar!"

But the poop aristocracy had the advantage of being about four feet above them and their staves were longer than the enemies' palm sticks and short daggers. They began banging the savages on the heads; many reeled back with broken skulls.

Nevertheless, it took many hard blows to put a dent in those hard heads, and those who fell were trampled by their brothers, eager to get at the poop. Burton saw that they would shortly be overcome; looking around for something to help them his eyes lit on a large earthen jar full of drinking water, standing in its heavy wooden frame on the very edge of the poop. The whole contrivance must have weighed about a hundred pounds. Edging his way towards it so he wouldn't give away his plan, he suddenly shouldered it over the deck, and it rolled over on the heads below. Shrieks of pain and panic arose, for many were knocked down, and others were cut by the broken potshards or flooded in the water which burst forth. The Maghrabis withdrew to the other end of the ship.

Soon a delegation arrived from them suing for peace. Burton and his men agreed, on the condition that the Maghrabis take solemn vows not to make a disturbance again.

At Yambu they were told that the Hazimi tribe was harassing travelers. Burton decided to go on, anyway. He hired a litter, because it was easier to take notes in it than on a saddle on camelback. Besides, he had his sore foot as excuse for this woman's way of travel. This foot gave him much trouble the rest of the pilgrimage.

Every pilgrim carried a *hamail* or pocket Koran. It was hung in a red morocco case from silk cords hanging from the left shoulder. To conceal the fact he was taking notes and making sketches, Burton substituted an article that looked on the outside like a hamail. Inside were three compartments. One, for his watch and compass. The second, for money. The third, for penknife, pencils, and slips of paper, which he could hold concealed in the hollow of his hand. These were for drawing. He could always be writing his diary in the presence of the others by pretending to the illiterate that he was casting a horoscope for them or writing out a charm or that he was taking notes for a book of genealogy. To the curious Bedawin he would say, "And you, sons of Harb, on what ancestor do you pride yourselves?" And while they went into excruciating detail about their grandfather's ninth cousin, he would be writing on some other subject.

The caravan picked up other pilgrims. It had two hundred camels carrying grain, and an escort of seven Irregular Turkish cavalry. Thieves attacked and were repelled with a few shots.

Later, they picked up an escort of two hundred men from a fort, but these returned when a band of Bedawin refused to allow the pilgrims to pass unless the soldiers left them. Later, another troop of Albanian soldiers joined the caravan, and they had a running fight with a band that fired on them from high rocks. Twelve soldiers were killed and many camels.

At Medinah, Burton visited Mohammed's supposed tomb and noted the legend that there is an empty place therein, reserved for Jesus after his second coming. According to the Moslem belief, Jesus will come again to announce the resurrection of Mohammed.

At a monument on Mountain Ohod, which commemorated the place where the Prophet lost some front teeth by stoning from infidels, Burton, like any gawking tourist, wrote on the wall, "Abdullah, the servant of Allah," and beneath it the date according to Arabic numbering.

When the time came to go on, his friends urged him to stay and open a shop. He replied that he must make the pilgrimage required of every Moslem at least once in his life. "Goodbye O Father of Moustachios," they said. "Peace be with you." Burton smiled at the nickname, for in Arabia everybody must be a father of something, and it was better to be the father of long whiskers than of a cooking-pot or a bad smell.

The Shaykh Hamid came to him one morning after a visit at the bazaar, and said, "You must make ready at once, Effendi. All Hajis start tomorrow.

Allah will make it easy for you. Are your waterskins in order? You are to travel dawn the Darb El Sharki, where you will not see water for three days!"

Hamid was horror stricken, but Burton was happy. No European had ever traveled over the eastern road; besides, this was the path that the caliph famous in the Arabian Nights, Harun al Rashid, had taken in company with the Lady Zubaydah, his wife.

Amid wild confusion, the caravan of seven thousand followers of the prophet plunged into the hellish desert. The rich rode on expensive saddles; the poor trudged barefooted. The camels, ponies, and asses began to drop under the terrific heat. Every mile seemed to add another carcass. The half-baked Takruri pilgrims, the poorest of the lot, would quickly cut the beast's throat to bleed it so that it would be religiously correct to eat it and then would cut out huge steaks which they would carry with them. Sometimes, the ever-hovering vultures beat them to the carcass and so defiled it.

The sun became hotter and hotter; the scorching wind of the simoom struck; thin whirling columns of sand danced among them. Men would suddenly quiver and fall in their tracks and die and would be buried in a hastily scooped out shallow grave. Burton noticed that the Bedawin, though used to the desert, did not endure thirst any better than the others. Yet, though they often called out "*Ya Latif!* (O merciful Lord!)" they bore their tortures like men and drank spoonfuls of clarified butter. Burton had the water-camel placed out in front so no one could steal water. Meanwhile, he observed that the more you drank under this sun, the more you wanted; your thirst just could not be satisfied. But if you could control the desire for the first two hours, you had won the battle, and to refrain from then on was easy.

Tempers grew exceedingly short. A Turk who could not speak a word of Arabic argued violently with an Arab who knew no Turkish. The Turk wished to add a few dry sticks to the camel's load; the Arab threw them off. Suddenly, the Turk struck the Arab. That night his stomach was ripped open with a dagger. Still living, he was wrapped in his shroud and placed in a half-dug grave. Burton did not see this interment, but he commented that it was a horrible way to die, for the sun would beat on the poor man's head all day, and at night the vultures and jackals would begin eating without bothering if he were still alive or not.

At El Zaribah the pilgrims bathed and put on ceremonial white robes with narrow red stripes, shaved their heads, trimmed their moustaches, and cut their nails. This latter was done so that they would not accidentally kill vermin while scratching themselves. And they were to leave their bald heads free of any covering from the hot sun, though they might form shade with their upraised hands.

Leaving El Zaribah, the caravan fell in with another from Baghdad. This was accompanied by about four hundred Wahahbis, all screaming, "Here I am!" and guided by a large loud kettledrum, marching in double file behind the standard bearer, whose green flag bore in white letters their creed. These mountaineers were wild and fierce looking, with hair twisted into thin plaits and carrying spears, matchlocks, and daggers. Their women despised veils and looked as tough as the men. When either sex saw a man smoking, they cursed him out as an infidel. Their camels were as wild as they and would dash through the caravan, creating confusion everywhere.

They plunged into a deep and stony valley. Everybody fell silent, as if expecting something gloomy. Suddenly, a small curl of smoke rose from a precipice to the right, and the dromedary just in front of Burton's fell dead, throwing his rider. There was a frightening confusion; men and animals jammed the narrow passage, all trying to get through. Bullets fell like rain into the solid mass. The irregulars tried to force their way through to attack. And the pasha in command, seeing that nothing could be done for the moment, spread his carpet at the foot of a cliff and argued with his officers about their strategy.

Then it was that Burton thought better of the Wahhabis, for, while one group fired on the Utaybah robbers, another charged up the hills. Presently the robbers fled, but panic overtook the caravan, and the wounded and dead were left behind, with many dead camels and much abandoned baggage.

At the beginning of the skirmish, Burton had primed his pistols and then calmly waited to see what he could do. Finding that there nothing, he called out loudly for his supper.

The people around him exclaimed, "By Allah, he eats." Shaykh Abdullah, a man of better stuff, asked, "Are these Afghan manners?" Burton replied, "Yes, in my country we always dine before an attack of robbers, because those gentlemen are in the habit of sending men to bed supperless." The shaykh laughed, but the others looked offended. Burton thought that perhaps his bravado, typical of him, was too much for these people. But his words had made him a reputation and helped calm those around him.

After leaving the pass, the survivors hurried on. A day and a night passed with the tension mounting as they neared their goal. Then, at one a.m., Burton was awakened by cries of "Mecca! Mecca!" Screaming for joy, weeping, the pilgrims passed through the *Bab El Salam*, the Gate of Security. From Medinah to Mecca, the journey of two hundred forty eight English miles had been accomplished in eleven marches.

Burton stopped off briefly at the home of Mohammed. Then he hurried towards the last step of his pilgrimage: the House of Allah, a towering cubical building, in one corner of which was the holy black stone of the Ka'abah. He said the prayer for the unity of Allah, then made the seven circuits around the stone. Afterwards, the tremendous mob all rushed towards the stone to kiss it. Burton was in despair, because he could not get through them to study it. Finally, his boy Mohammed came to his rescue. Mohammed had been demonstrating his zeal by cursing every Persian in his path because they belonged to the heretical Shia sect. Besides, in 1674 A.D. some wretch had smeared the sacred stone with fecal matter so that those who rushed in to kiss it left with dirtied beards, and the Persians, unjustly, were accused of being defilers of the Ka'abah.

He now formed a flying wedge of six Meccans, and they bowled everybody out of their way. The Bedawin reached for their daggers, which they weren't allowed to carry in the holy city, and were knocked down. Burton took advantage of his husky guards to study the stone for at least ten minutes. If at this time he had been exposed for what he was, or even had there existed a bare suspicion, he would have been torn into bits by the crowd, pitched to the highest extreme of religious frenzy. Mohammed could have gained eternal glory by shouting out his suspicions that his master was the wicked white man who had disguised himself in India, "Ruffian Dick."

But the boy was either satisfied with Burton's disguise or else was thinking of the money he hoped to get from his master's stay. He never said a word and, for a while, at least, cooperated.

Burton, though studying the Ka'abah scientifically, at the same time shared in the same feelings as the most devout Moslem. To him it was as if the legend were true that the waving wings of angels were blowing the black curtains hung over the shrine. He thrilled with ecstasy. But, as he later confessed, part of the ecstasy was gratified pride at being the first infidel to have closely studied the holy black stone. Always the explorer, the man who wants to be first, he could not help being proud.

While kissing and rubbing his forehead on it, he narrowly examined the stone and concluded that it was a meteorite. It had fallen from the skies, been shattered, put together, and become a holy object long before Mohammed was born. The legend was that it had once been white but had become black because the sins of those who kissed it passed into it. Burton passed on to the holy well of Zem Zem and was drenched in foul-smelling water. Later that night he sneaked back to tear off a piece of the Ka'abah's curtain, but too many eyes were on him. However, with a coolness that some might have considered foolhardy, he took out a tape and measured the size of everything in which he was interested.

Burton went religiously through the other ceremonies: the stoning of the devil, the hearing of a sermon on Mount Arafat, where Eve was first supposed to have set foot on earth. During the latter, he began a flirtation with a very nicely shaped girl whose eyes looked beautiful through her mask of muslin. She made signs favorable to him; her chaperone seemed unaware; all was going fine; then she became lost in the crowd.

The next day, word came to him to appear at the Ka'abah. Bareheaded, barefooted, he appeared in the square. A crowd was there, but at the cry, "Open a path for the Haji who would enter the House," they made way. Two sturdy Meccans lifted him up to a third, who drew him into the building. He was questioned very sternly about his name, nation, and other particulars. Though apprehensive, Burton answered correctly, and the boy Mohammed was told to conduct him around the building and say the prayers. Burton, looking at the windowless walls, the officials at the door, and the crowd below, felt like a trapped rat. Any unorthodox action, a misjudged prayer or bow, and he'd have been crucified or perhaps impaled in a peculiarly painful manner. Nevertheless, he made careful observations and penciled a rough sketch on his white robe. Then he passed from the big black house like a cubical coffin, having done that which many who made the pilgrimage had not. For the majority could not afford it, since those who walked the holy floor could never again tell lies, and lying was the breath of life to the Oriental.

There were other visits and ceremonies which he made; but he was impatient to get out of Mecca. His purse was almost empty, and his room was hot as an oven. He took a caravan to Jeddah, where he appeared at the British Consulate. He was left to cool his heels for a long time. He heard someone say, "Let the dirty nigger wait." When he finally did get in, he gave the Consul a piece of paper, supposed to be a money order. He had written on it, "Don't recognize me. I am Dick Burton, but I am safe yet. Give me some money, which will be returned from London. Don't take any notice of me."

Burton went back to Egypt. Worldwide fame waited for him because of his exploit. His book, *A Pilgrimage to El-Medinah and Meccah*, was to become one of the greatest books of travel. Not only the West praised him, but the East too, because he had performed the pilgrimage with devoutness, and was a true Haji. He could have seized the chance to make money and become a social and literary lion. Any other man would have done it, but Burton had a fatal sense of mistiming. Time and again he was to be on the brink of his dreams; only to refuse to appear to gather his rewards or else to go off on another expedition. At this time he could have made a huge success in England with lectures and interviews. All kinds of wild stories about him were circulating; it was said he had stabbed a Moslem who had penetrated his disguise.

But he had a peculiar and fierce pride. His discoveries could speak for themselves. He would stay in Egypt to write his book. He would also brood over his *Kasîdah* a long philosophical poem setting forth his dark and pessimistic views on life and death and chance and God. It sounds much like the *Rubaiyat* of Omar Khayyam and was written, though not published, years before Fitzgerald's famous translation.

His leave was up. He went back to his regiment at Bombay. Again, he became restless and unhappy. There was the city of Harar in the eastern horn of Africa, behind whose walls no infidel had ever been. What lay behind them?

The Royal Geographical society, also interested, backed the now famous captain. The East India Company, more than ever suspicious of Nigger Dick, gave him permission, provided he went as a private traveler and asked them for no funds. Perhaps the directors hoped he would end up on a spear this time and finish their troublemaker for good.

Burton didn't care. All he wanted was cooperation; he would provide the brains and the guts. And, of course, he wasn't even to get a minimum of help. Only misunderstanding and deliberate fouling-up from his inferiors.

"The city of Harar will fall when a Frank (European) enters it," ran one proverb. And another: "As soon enter a crocodile's mouth as the walls of Harar."

Despite this, thirty Europeans had from time to time tried to go into Harar; all had died. Richard Burton would be the thirty-first to try; death and proverbs were a challenge to him.

The East India Company had long wanted to explore eastern Ethiopia. Berberah, the chief port of Somaliland, was the safest and best harbor on the western side of the Indian Ocean, much better than Aden, across the Gulf. When Richard offered to fill out the big blank area on their maps, they eagerly agreed. But cautiously. He could go as a private traveler and would get no protection from the government. Agreed. He selected three men, Lts. Herne and Speke of the army, Lt. Stroyan of the Indian Navy. But as usual, he ran into obstacles from the first. Not from the natives but from his fellow Englishmen. Sir James Outram, the political resident at Aden, opposed the expedition because he thought it would stir up the Somalis, and he told Buist, the editor of the *Bombay Times*, to run down the project.

Burton had to change his plans because of the continued vehemence of the resident against his plans. The original route was to have been from Berberah westward to Harar, and then southeast to Zanzibar. Instead Speke was told to land in the harbor of Bunder Garay, where he would trace the watershed of the Wadi Nogal, buy horses and camels, and collect red earth that might contain gold. Unfortunately, his guide proved treacherous, so Speke's plans failed. Herne was to go to Berberah, where he would meet Stroyan.

Burton chose the most dangerous mission—although the most glorious if it succeeded. Disguised as an Arab merchant, he would go to Harar. Bad news came at once. On landing at Zayla, he was told that the friendship between the Amir of Harar and the governor of Zayla had broken up. The road through the Easa tribe had been closed up because of the murder of Masud, the governor's adopted son. All strangers had been thrown out of Harar because one of them had misbehaved. And smallpox was raging so furiously in the city that the Galla peasants around it would allow no one in or out.

Nevertheless, Burton went ahead. Though the governor, Sharmarkay, knew who Burton was, he pretended to accept him as an Arab. For twenty-six days he stayed at Sharmarkay's home, while be lived religiously as a devout Moslem and also chose his caravan retinue. These might have stepped out of the Thousand and One Nights. They were El Hammal, or The Porter, a bull-necked, lamp-black sergeant of the Aden police. Guled, called the Long, a tall living skeleton of a policeman. Abdy Abokr, the End of Time, a catlike, long-backed hedge priest with a villainous grin and close-set eyes. His title came from the prophecy that the end of the world would find every Moslem priest totally corrupt, and he seemed to fit that description.

With his servants and some mules and camels, he set out on November 27th, 1854. Every person there was a character, even the camels had individuality; one was so mean and noisy that he at once was called El Harami, the Ruffian. Raghe, their Easa guide, strode first, bearing in one hand a spear and in the other a round leather shield. Behind him waddled the two female cooks, each large as three average women rolled into one, muscular and enormously hipped. They were stronger than the men, and did the work of four. Once they got over their first shyness with Burton, they began making jokes with him that would have made a camel-driver blush. When they became tired at the end of the day, one would lie down and the other would walk barefooted on her back, kneading with her toes. Then she would rise, refreshed.

Their attendant, Yusuf, was one-eyed, and nicknamed the Kalendar, after the cyclopean porter in the Arabian Nights. He was highly moral and wished to discipline the two cooks with sticks. Only Burton's harsh orders kept him from beating them to death; they hated Yusuf's guts, and waited for a chance to revenge themselves.

Behind them, the camels, then the three policemen on horses, with their greased frizzled wigs, new spears and shields. No guns for them, for here in Somaliland they would be laughed at for such outlandish weapons.

Behind them, Burton, on a fine white mule, a double-barreled gun across his lap, and two pair of holsters, holding his Colt six-shooters.

They traveled due south along the coast through a hard stoneless plain, now muddy, now dry, and through flats of black mold powdered with salt. The second day, they came to a village where the Bedawin gathered around and muttered, "Faranj!" (Frank) and laughed at their weapons. Burton waited his chance; then, when a large vulture settled on the ground, he shot it. Loading his gun with swan-shot, he shot another as it flew over. Screams of admiration rose; a graybeard, putting his finger in his mouth, called, "Praise Allah! May he defend me from such a calamity!"

Pleased with the effect he'd made, Burton decided that from then on one barrel would always be loaded with shot. Next day, the old man asked for a charm to cure his sick camel. Burton gave it to him and had to listen to a speech of thanks that took half an hour. Afterwards, the old man spit on everybody in the caravan to give them good luck. Burton endured this, for it was well in this country to get along with the old men, who were looked up to by their tribesmen.

A few days later they fell in with a tribe that was migrating. One of the Somali fell in love with the huge cook Sheherezade, and asked her to marry him. She delayed saying no, but didn't dare come out with a flat refusal for fear of angering him and his fellows, one hundred and fifty spearsmen. The suitor then suggested that the marriage ceremony was really unimportant. The others grew sulky because Burton had not passed out enough tobacco to suit them. Just before leaving, he sent the mules out to water, and when they did not come back, he thought the Bedawin had seized them. He sat on a cow's hide in the sun and ordered his men to load their guns. Loudly, he threatened the culprits with death by witchcraft if they were bothered. The old man then declared that it was not good to detain these strangers; the mules came back, but the escort Burton had asked for was not forthcoming. He pushed on without them.

The footprints of a large Habr Awal cavalcade lay in the dust before them. The servants huddled together, silent; the End of Time spoke hollowly, "Verily, O pilgrim, who so seeth the track, seeth the foe!" Though despising their cowardice, Burton felt uneasy, for they were nine against two hundred horsemen. Fortunately, they soon came to very rough country, where the natives would not care to endanger their horses.

The plain faded behind them; the mountains lay before them, and the jujube began growing tall. They met some wild Gudabirsi, and from them Burton learned how fast the grapevine worked even in these far-off hills. They talked of the latest battles of the Russian war, and he heard of a storm which had wrecked ships in the Bombay harbor, only a few weeks after it happened.

Later, some Gudabirsi tried to seize Raghe, declaring he owed them a cow. Burton fired a pistol over their heads, and they cringed like dogs. Poor Raghe was in a bad spot because he was in a country with whose people his had a blood feud. He feared to sleep in their villages, yet he could not sleep outside because of the lions.

They met some Abbands, and having heard from them that they knew of a place where elephants were thick as sand, he went hunting. The End of Time rode with them, but he lagged behind. And he looked so miserable on hearing that a mule cannot outrun an elephant that Burton sent him back to their kraal.

"Do you believe me to be a coward, O Pilgrim?" said the hedge priest.

"Of a truth I do," replied Burton.

The End of Time rode away, saying, "What has a man but a single life? And he who throws it away, what is he but a fool?"

Burton found no elephants and returned to camp disappointed.

They rode on. The Bedawin they met repeatedly said, "They will spoil that white skin of yours at Harar."

On the 23rd of December they descended to the Marar prairie. This the Eesa, Berteri, and Habr Awal made a happy hunting grounds for robbers. A traveler burst in on the caravan. Naked, he had escaped from the savages with nothing but his life. Late at dusk, Burton riding as rear guard, noticed his mule prick up its ears. Looking back, he saw a large animal, following stealthily. His companions would not fire, because they thought it might be a man, but he shot—missing because of the new moon's weak light—and scared off a huge lion. He got another chance to notice the cowardice of his friends, for they ran about, tossing their hands in the air, and talked of nothing but the lion the rest of the night.

At Wilensi, Burton was busy settling arguments between El Hammal and The End of Time. The latter was getting bigheaded because he'd been made ambassador to the Girhi chief by the governor of Zaylah. He wanted to command the whole caravan. The two buxom cooks begged to be left behind. They were afraid that the smallpox raging at Harar might make them ugly. Burton, though thinking that they could not become any uglier than they were, ordered the one-eyed Kalendar to remain behind to guard them. He marched on to the village of Gerad Adan, a chief. Here he came down with the colic and thought that he would die. For five days he lay, while the Gerad went off to Harar for millet beer as medicine. This powerful drink would surely have killed him, for it was mixed with a poisonous bark, and affected even the hardened natives with splitting headaches. The Gerad's daughters sacrificed a sheep for his recovery; the Galla Christians crowded around him and wept for him because he was going to die far from his fatherland, under a tree.

Nothing would have been easier, but Burton could not endure the thought of such an ignoble death. To go down under a charge of savage spearsmen was one thing; to perish of colic, ridiculous.

He rose, dressed in his Arab best, and prepared to push on. Five strangers appeared; they took the Gerad aside and advised him that Burton was a spy and should be sent as prisoner to the Amir of Harar. The Gerad replied that he did not betray his friends.

Nevertheless, the Gerad was afraid of his Harari kinsmen and refused to escort Burton. The End of Time, almost fainting with fright, begged to remain behind; Burton granted permission.

He then made a speech to his two faithful soldiers, boldness was the word from now on. He would take off his Arab disguise and openly proclaim his true identity. They would ride into Harar behind no false faces. He would present a letter which he had written himself, but which purported to be from the English resident at Aden. He mounted and rode forward, while the villagers recited the prayer of the Fatihah for the dead.

When they mounted the crest of a hill and saw Harar, his companions looked at each other in wonder. Were they facing death for this somber pile of stones? But Burton was exultant, for none of those who had gone before him had succeeded in entering. And he was sure that he would at least get in.

They did, and there the warder of the gate told them to dismount and to follow him at a trot. Burton refused, because he would look undignified. After a delay, during which he declined to part with his dagger and revolver, he marched through a double line of tall scowling Gallas, each holding a spear with a blade broad as a shovel. He went through a curtain and stood before the feared chief.

The Amir sat in a dark room on whose whitewashed walls hung rusty matchlocks and polished fetters. He was a young, small man with a yellow complexion, frowning forehead, and bulging eyes.

Burton entered, loudly saying, "Peace be upon you!"

The Amir answered graciously enough and held out a bony hand, like a kite's claw. Two men grabbed Burton's arms and bowed him over the hand. But he would not kiss it, and, after a minute, he was released. His two servants then kissed the chief's hand twice.

"What is your errand?" asked the Amir. He glanced briefly at the letter and demanded further explanation. Burton said that he had come to Harar with the compliments of the governor of Aden and also to see the light of the Amir's countenance.

There was a pause. Burton scarcely breathed, though he kept his face composed. The many relatives and courtiers watched the chief's face to see how they should react. The matchlock men held their burning fuses in their hands; let the Amir command, and they would tear the Frank apart with their huge musketballs. And if, inconceivable thought, they should miss, the Galla spearsmen gathered behind Burton would plunge their blades into his back. But Burton resolved that if he had to, he would run up to the throne and hold his pistol against the Amir's head.

Suddenly, the Amir smiled. Burton relaxed a little, and soon he was in the second palace, which would be his home as long as he lived in Harar. Where there had been frowns, there were now smiles, but he knew that they could as swiftly change back. Burton sent a revolver as a present to the chief, and began making himself comfortable.

He was to spend ten days in Harar, largely monotonous, except for the overtones of fear and insecurity. At any time the Amir could have changed his mind, and as he was notoriously fickle even among a fickle people, there was never any assurance that the next day would find Burton alive.

He examined the city, found it to be one mile long by a half a mile wide. The wall had many holes in it, through which wild beasts sometimes crept at night. He could not make even a single note, because he was so closely watched. Afterwards, he compiled from memory a grammar of the Harari language. It was, he noted, spoken only within the walls and was not Arabic but was related to the Amharic. The citizens hated all foreigners with a holy zeal, Moslems as well as Christians. Both men and women were very loose in their morals, and everybody was drunk as often as they could get their hands on alcohol of any kind.

Some Habr Awals came to the Vizier and told him that spies were waiting at Berberah for the return of their brother from Harar. These were, of course, Speke, Herne, and Stroyan. Summoned to the Vizier's house to answer these charges, Burton found the old man sick with bronchitis. He at once made him feel better by burning under his nose brown paper matches steeped in saltpeter. He also promised to send him enough medicine from Aden to last his life. Won by this, the Vizier promised to intercede with the Amir for Burton, even though he might lose his own head. He had his chance in a short time, for the Amir sent for him. Not long after, Burton was also called. They had a long conversation about what the English were doing in Arabia. Reassured as to their own intentions towards him, the Amir smiled his rare smile and gave Burton permission to leave. Perhaps he thought that Burton might send down a doctor to him, too, for he suffered from tuberculosis.

The Englishman had been hearing too much recently about the dungeon beneath the palace, where a man went down alive but never came up so. He said a short prayer for the Amir, and retired. At the palace, he whispered to his two comrades, "Achcha! (All right)"

A few days later, he rode away. But on the road back to Berberah, they lost their way, following their incompetent guide. The sun beat on them; they dared not drink from their almost empty water bags. Burton became delirious with visions of water bubbling icily over the rocks. Half-conscious, he realized that he had ridden twenty-four hours without water. Even twelve hours in the desert without water was generally enough to kill a man. A few more hours, and they would drop in their tracks, food for the vultures and hyenas. Thirty-six hours passed without water. The twilight of the tropics rushed towards them. Then he saw a *katta*, a sand grouse, flying towards the hills. These birds had to drink at least once a day; this one must be making for water. The party, hearing Burton's cry, took heart and followed the bird. A hundred yards away was a spring, which they would surely have missed. All plunged their heads into the water, too mad with thirst to pay any attention to the swarm or insects and tadpoles, and drank till they were likely to burst. Burton never again shot a katta.

When they reached Berberah, the natives swore aloud that they could not have ridden from Harar in five days. Such a thing was impossible.

Though the weather was bad, Burton got upon a native boat and ordered in loud voice that the sail be set for Aden.

The crew and passengers raised a hubbub. "He surely will not sail in a sea like this?" asked the captain.

"He will." replied El Hamal.

"It blows wind," protested the captain.

"And if it blew fire?" said the Arab, meaning that the Frank was crazy enough to sail into anything.

The captain and a soldier invaded Burton's cabin, still protesting. He grabbed the former by his beard and pants' seat and threw him out on the deck.

At Aden he picked up men for another expedition to Harar and returned to Berberah, where he was attacked by the Somali and speared through the jaw. On sick leave again, he returned to England in 1855. Now was his chance to get into the limelight, the chance he had thrown away when he had stayed in Egypt after the Mecca pilgrimage. The Harar expedition was an even greater feat, and the fight outside Berberah, attested to by the two scars on his face, would have been a crashing climax to his lecture.

But fate, the ironical bitch who seemed to have it in for Burton, chose that time to drown out everything else of interest with the Crimean War. Nobody had ear for anything personal; it must be on the grand scale and on the Russian-British front. He finished his book, *First Footsteps in East Africa*, and then volunteered. Not being able to get the commission he wanted from the War Office, he took ship to Constantinople. There he got an appointment as chief of staff of the Bashi-Bazouks, Turkish irregular cavalry. The four thousand wild Albanians knew nothing of discipline, of morning roll calls or drilling. Their favorite amusement was dueling, in which the contestant would stand with a glass of araki in one hand and a pistol in the other. He who first emptied his glass banged away at the other. Not only that, but the British officers knew nothing of the use of the sword they carried. He could do little about the duels except ensure fair play, but he did teach the English saber play and he soon had organized the troopers into a fairly well disciplined and dependable outfit.

At that time the city of Kars, held by the Turks, was being besieged by the Russians. Despite famine and light numbers, they were holding out bravely. Burton conceived the plan of galloping to the city's relief with his Bashi-Bazouks. Inspired, he rode to Constantinople, where he laid his brilliant idea before the English Ambassador.

Lord Stratford grew purple-faced. "By God, sir, you are the most impudent man in the Bombay army!" he roared.

That was the only answer he got. Bewildered, Burton left. Months later, he discovered that the high statesmen of England and France had decided that Kars should be allowed to fall, a sort of peace offering to Russia, salve for her loss of Sebastopol. And he, only a captain, had almost upset some very delicate undercover work of the great men.

Nevertheless, Stratford must have been impressed, for he commissioned Burton to visit Schamyl. Schamyl was the Circassian who was leading his mountain country in a revolt against Russia. This was just the sort of mission to appeal to Burton, for he would have to disguise himself and ride through Russian territory to get to Circassia. But there was one problem. What would he say to Schamyl?

"Oh, say you are sent to report to me," replied Stratford.

"But, my lord, Schamyl will expect money, arms, and possibly troops. What am I to reply if he asks me about it? Otherwise, he might take me for a spy, and my chance of returning to Constantinople will be uncommonly small."

Lord Stratford could promise nothing, so Burton regretfully refused the useless mission. Schamyl and his country would later be crushed, a victim of high-powered diplomacy, as Kars had been. Given English support, Circassia might have held Russia for a long time, perhaps remained independent. Years later, a young man was to come out of this area and become ruler of Russia. If Circassia had been free, he might have stayed there. In his native mountains he was called Djugashvil. Russians knew him as Stalin.

As usual, Burton's talents were wasted; he would never fight on a battle-front. All his actions would be personal, confined to his superiors.

Burton resigned and went back to London, where he dreamed again of tearing aside the veil of Isis, of discovering the true source of the Nile. Many men had tried and failed, but, he noted, they had started at the end of the river and worked up to its beginning. Characteristically, he would ignore the common route and would slash through from the side. Inland from the coast of East Africa would be his path. Did not the Arabs talk of a Sea of Ujiji? Might not this fabled great lake give birth to the Nile in the hot heart of the Dark Continent?

The Royal Geographical Society talked the Foreign office and the East India Company into granting him a thousand pounds and two years leave of absence. With Speke, now a captain, he landed on the island of Zanzibar at the end of 1856. There was little reason why he should have chosen Speke, for the man knew no Arabic nor Swahili, and he was not a scientist. He was brave, but from all indications he would be more of a hindrance than a help, in a country where Burton would need all the aid he could get. It was almost as if Burton had taken steps to defeat himself.

But beneath his roaring voice, iron face, and fierce black eyes, Burton was kind and fair-minded. He knew that Speke had suffered in East Africa, and that he wanted a chance to explore again. What he did not know was that Speke secretly resented him, nursing the inevitable hatred of the mediocrity.

They were to take along his old friend, Doctor Steinhauser. This man loved Burton and his medical knowledge would help them through the fevers they knew they'd catch. Unfortunately, it was the doctor who fell too sick to go along, not Speke. Unable to wait past the middle of May for him to recover, the two set out.

From the beginning, he had trouble. His Balochi mercenaries and native porters were rogues, thieves, and cowards to the last man. The porters would carry only the lightest of loads, leaving the heavy on the ground. Burton used threats, pleas, and a whip; it was the latter that decided them; they could carry their loads after all. But many were scared by the tales of the dangers they would run across; poisoned arrows of the bush negroes, the deadly long horned rhinoceros, mad elephants. One hundred and seventy carriers had been hired, but only thirty-six were brave enough to show up for work. The others fled into the jungle with their advance pay. Burton had to hire others.

Lack of money troubled him from the very start. If he had had five thousand pounds, he could have hired a hundred matchlock men and had enough to pay the tribute that every chief they met would expect. They could even have marched through the country of the Masai, now on the warpath. But the kind of safari he wanted would have cost at least a hundred pounds a week; six weeks, and his money would be gone.

To add to his handicaps, he received a letter from the East India Company, ordering him to return to London, where he would be a witness in a court martial. Though he knew that a court martial might be his own fate if he disobeyed, he decided to ignore the command. No matter what the consequences, he could not abandon the expedition now, would not be thwarted a second time. On June 26th, 1857, he gave the signal. Their guide raised his blood red flag, which always marched in the front of a Zanzibar caravan, kettledrums and cowbells boomed and clanged, porters yelled with excitement, and the procession lurched into the jungle like a drunken and monstrous land-serpent.

In eighteen days they marched one hundred and eighteen miles. Their Zanzibar asses, too delicate for this climate, died. They were forced to use the half-wild Wamyamwezi beasts. Many of these were killed by hyenas, so bold they would bite off the faces of the men as they slept at night. Always, every chief they met assumed he would be given gleaming beads and bolts of precious cloth. Everywhere lay clean-picked skeletons and the swollen corpses of porters who had starved to death. Smallpox, famine and slavers stalked the land; one place had so many graves that it was called the Valley of Death and the Home of Hunger. Sick natives died where they fell, abandoned by their families to the vulture and the fox. Witch-hunts were terrorizing every village. Men and women were burnt at stakes, and their children, guilty by association, were also cast onto the flames.

At Dut'humi, one chief had kidnapped five subjects of another chief. Though sick, Burton organized a counter raiding party and brought the unhappy ones back home.

Malaria brought Richard down for twenty days. Delirious, he saw himself as two men, each fighting against the other, forever scheming against and tripping the other up. This strong sense of a divided personality attacked him during his fever fits throughout his life. It was not just wild dreams but a real clue to his true character. Burton *was* two; he was forever defeating himself when just on the verge of victory.

And he must have cursed during this time of weakness and feverish hallucinations. He was a cursing man; it is probable that the malaria released his inhibitions and that during this time, Speke heard much of what caused this splitting of personality and Speke learned the true source of his psychological injury. Just as later, Speke would become sick and in his ravings reveal his secret hatred for Burton.

Burton must have cursed many times during his life because of what his mother had done to him. If she had not so hatefully and stubbornly resisted his grandfather's changing his will, he would have been a rich man. Wealthy, he could have organized expeditions that would not have been crippled from the start. The time would come when Stanley and Baker and Grant and Cameron would be famous names on everybody's lips. Yet Burton was the greatest of all nineteenth century explorers and stands at the very top of list of the greatest of all time. Where the other men of his day had plenty of money to hire supplies and soldiers and tribute goods, he had to forge practically alone. Given the fortune that should have been his, he could have mapped most of the huge white blank in Africa's dark heart years before anybody else. Even so, what he did was magnificent. For instance, his chartings of routes in East Africa and Arabia were used by World War I soldiers. Stanley took one book along in his travels. Not the Bible, as reported, but Burton's *Lake Regions of Central Africa*. And Lawrence of Arabia declared that Burton's description of the pilgrim's route from Medina to Mecca was correct to the least detail.

Moreover, as money talks, his fortune would have influenced the snobs of the Foreign Office to give him the consular posts that he deserved, instead of the third rate ones to be tendered him. There is little doubt that with the proper sort of backing his money would have brought him, he would have gotten the viceroyship of India or the general-governership of Egypt. If he'd had the latter post, England's relations with her province of the Nile might have been different. No Khartoum, no massacre of 'Chinese' Gordon.

All this was *if*…He did not have the great fortune; his mother had preferred to cheat her son so that her adored half-brother might gamble it away and give it to confidence men.

It is strange that none of his biographers have noted such an obvious breeding ground for mental wounds or for the birth of some of his twisted attitudes. Nobody, not even his wife in her two-volume *Life* mentioned that possibility. It is probable he never spoke of it to anyone, but there must have been times when he felt how keenly his poverty had robbed him of the success he deserved; an angry man, he could not have repressed into total unconsciousness the tide of fury against his mother.

In his fever-deliriums, hags pursued him. Were these symbols of how he really felt about her? In waking life, he was always flirting with pretty women; his tremendous masculinity and overpowering personality assured him success with the fair sex wherever he went. But his contempt for them was well known. He thought they were, by and large, a brainless silly deceptive backbiting lot. Never once did he see that this view exactly described his male enemies, who were always opposing him. Whereas he never considered that most women, except for his mother, helped him.

All old women, he stated, looked like apes. And when the ladies asked him to autograph one of his books, he would write in Arabic: "I stood before the gates of Paradise, and lo! most of its inmates were the poor; and I stood before the gate of Hell, and lo! most of its inmates were women!"

There is a good chance that when he was expressing his sarcasms towards the generality of womankind, he had his mother in mind. Burton, though no gentleman in the conventional meaning of the term, preferred pretty blue-eyed blondes with birdbrains. His mother's likeness? It matches her description. The fact that he had a passion for blondes, instead of hating them, does not disprove this theory. What a man's unconscious mind hates, his conscious often loves. And vise versa. A pioneer in hypnotism, he liked to put them under the spell of his gleaming black eyes and make them do ridiculous things. He forced his wife to be his favorite subject. She was herself one of the pretty yellow-haired types, though no dimwit. And she gave him what he had lacked in his real mother, an all-worshiping hovering slave-like love. Too much so, in fact, for Burton, the man of extremes, had picked out a woman who almost smothered him with devotion.

It was shortly after his grandfather had dropped dead on his way to change the will that Richard's red hair and blue eyes became gypsy-black. Chameleonlike, he was two persons: the man he showed to intimates, the soft-spoken, gay, tender, warm fellow, and the man he showed to the outside world, the loud, swaggering, bragging, monstrously lying, almost savage fellow. He was split right down the middle; he dreaded snakes but forced himself to play with cobras and like it; he had a horror of graveyards and corpses, yet he could collect cholera-ridden carcasses in a cart and help pile them in a dump; he could face one hundred and fifty howling spearsmen with only a saber, but he could not stand to say "goodby," the word was so taboo to him that even when he thought of saying it he broke out into a trembling and a cold sweat; he could get so dangerously drunk that he would stagger home with a revolver clutched in his hand, frightening all in his path, yet he nursed the famous explorer Lovett-Cameron, and the poet Swinburne with such loving care that they declared him the gentlest and kindest of men and worshipped him as a superman. He believed absolutely in nothing spiritual, was deeply pessimistic, yet he spent half his life becoming more adept in various religions than any except the most fanatic.

His very face betrayed his character. As Swinburne was to say, he had the "brow of a god and the jaw of a devil."

All of this was shown by the delirium-images when he came down with twenty-two bouts of malaria during this expedition. But he survived the one at Dut'humi and rose to go on.

Speke suffered sunstroke. Yet they rode on, so weak they could hardly sit on their saddles. Then a stay at the Usagara Mountains helped them recover their strength. They continued. Burton became sick again. He sent Speke on ahead to a village to get a hammock for him. Speke failed to send it back, so Burton remounted. The caravan had been held up by an attack of wild bees. They passed through villages destroyed by slavers and found two who had escaped the man-hunters lurking in the jungles. Horse-ants bit them so they danced like the chorus of a comic opera; then tsetse flies, which could bite through a hammock. At Rubeho, the third range of the Usagara, they met a caravan of Arabs. These, like all their countrymen, hailed Burton as one of their own and fed him milk and honey.

Up the mountains they went, Speke so weak three men had to hold him up. Burton, the stronger, only needed one. Suddenly, the war cry rang out, and long files of savage Wahumbas appeared. The two white men were too weak to rise, and their soldiers and porters crouched, ready to run off. But for some unknown reason, the Wahumba ignored them, probably intent on their blood-feud with the Inengé, dwellers in the plains.

At Great Rubeho, Speke became so violent that Burton had to take his guns away from him. The tawny-haired Englishman appeared to have suffered permanent brain damage from this attack.

Reports came that some half-caste Arabs were preceding them with tales that the whites were wizards come to ruin the land. The chiefs became more hostile and bolder, demanding more tribute. Though an attack on their part would have crumpled the weak caravan, Burton packed his animals and ordered them to stand to one side. They cringed.

The hundredth and thirty-fourth day after leaving the coast, they entered Kazeh. Here they stayed for a long time, while Burton felt at home among the Moslems stationed there. Speke, who knew none of the languages, became soured at this isolation and also aggressive, probably because he felt guilty about his own increasing incompetency. A fresh gang of porters were hired, but these were as lazy, cowardly, and dishonest as the others. Again, they set out. And Burton had to watch every man, for there was not a one who did not, sooner or later, try to desert.

Nevertheless, they admired Burton. He was muzungu mbaya, "the wicked white man." To have been called the "good white man" was to be considered a weak fool, one ripe for the plucking.

"We will follow muzungu mbaya," they sang.

"Puti! puti! (Grub! grub!)

As long as he gives us good food.

Puti! puti!
We will cross the hill and the stream,
Puti! puti!
With the caravan of this great *mundewa* (merchant).
"Puti! puti!"
A partial paralysis took hold of him, creeping upward from his feet. His ribs felt as if they were caving in, then the attack stopped. In ten days the numbness had passed from hands and feet, but it would be over a year before he could walk a long distance.

They passed quickly and quietly through a land laid waste by the fierce Watuta. On the 13th of February, Burton saw his *fundi* or leader change their direction. They went up a hill so steep Speke's ass, the only good one they had, dropped dead, and the other beasts were too tired to follow. "What is that streak of light below?" he said to Sidi Bombay.

"I think it is *the* water you are looking for," replied Bombay.

Burton's heart sank. Was this little lake the Ujiji that the Arabs said was so great a sea? He cursed them for liars and thought of returning at once to explore the Nyanza.

But he walked a few yards further, and on his half-blinded eyes burst a glorious vision, the immensity and beauty of Lake Tanganika. Suddenly, he thrilled with the knowledge that all their hardships had been worth it, and that he was the first European to have reached the headwaters of the Nile. Isis lay unveiled before him in all her beauty.

The whole caravan joined in his ecstasy. Only Speke, blind, grumbled he could see nothing because of the mist and glare. On a dhow hired from an Arab merchant, they set out on the fabled sea. His triumph disappeared under new sicknesses brought on by the cold damp, and the fish and vegetables, which they ate too much of. Speke had an affliction which made him chew sideways, like a cow with her cud. Too ill even to talk, Burton sent Speke to the northern end of the lake, from which a large river was supposed to flow northwards. There he was to hire a dhow for a month's cruise. Twenty-seven days later, Speke returned, with rusty guns, wet powder, and nothing but a promise that after three months they could get the boat for five hundred dollars. This was the same dhow whose owner had previously promised Burton he could have it as soon as he wanted it. Though disgusted with him, Burton helped him write out his diaries. He was surprised to see that Speke had traced a vast horseshoe shaped range of mountains in a place which he knew had only a thin ridge of hills. Later Speke published the map in Blackwood's magazine and stated the little hills were the true Mountains of the Moon.

Burton bribed Kannena, a chief, and got two canoes and fifty-five men. With these he sailed for a month up and down the two hundred and fifty mile long Tanganyika. His tongue got an ulceration which made him unable to speak for a long time. But the end of the trip found him far healthier than the beginning. The rainy monsoon broke up; at the same time, though, Burton had to begin digging into his own pocket to pay his men. A caravan arrived with letters from Europe. Now he first learned of the Indian mutiny against which he had vainly warned the authorities years before.

He had planned on exploring the southern end of Lake Tanganyika, then returning to Zanzibar by Nyassa Lake and Kilwa. But the goods sent by his agent via the caravan were too poor for him to hire porters for that long trip. Nevertheless, he was happy to leave on the back trail, May 26, 1858.

When they halted at Kazeh again, Burton had fallen sick once more. Speke felt better, because the burden of the expedition had fallen on his leader. During their stay at Kazeh, they had heard from Arabs of a large lake lying sixteen marches to the north. Burton decided to send Speke to investigate. There was no need for both of them to go, and he did not want to leave him behind, for Speke could not talk to any of the natives. Moreover, there were other preparations only Burton could make before they started their journey homeward.

On the 25th of August Speke came back, bursting with the news that the lake was much larger than expected. And, much more important, that he had discovered the *true* source of the White Nile!

Again Fate, that yellow-haired and smiling bitchgoddess, had struck Burton when he was on the verge of success. She had handed the prize, won through such sufferings and effort, to a man who had ridden as a parasite on his back all the way from Zanzibar.

Burton would not, could not, believe it. He listened to Speke's story. The geography given by Speke did not ring true, and part of the man's belief was based on the testimony of Arabs not known for their reliability. It was too much to swallow. He made up his mind that Speke was wrong, and he never changed it to the end of his days.

But Speke was right.

On the way back, they spoke only when they must. Once again, disease struck. Speke was attacked by the *kichyomachyoma*, the "little irons," so called because it felt like many knives sticking into a man's sides. Wild beasts and lion-headed demons seemed to attack him; he foamed at the mouth and barked like a dog, cramps made him rigid as wood, spasm after spasm shook him. Burton did not leave his bedside for days, nursing him tenderly. All this despite the fact that the delirious man raved his secret hatred for Burton. Nor was he grateful to his leader when he recovered. When they reached Zanzibar, where Burton fell sick, Speke would not wait for him to recover, though Burton asked him to. Instead, he hurried home to England, where he began spreading lies about Burton and claiming all the credit for the expedition. Though he had promised Burton he would not speak before the Royal Geographical Society until he was with him, he began arrangements at once for another expedition, leaving his chief out in the cold. The Society, believing his stories about Burton's incompetency and his cheating of his porters—an out-and-out lie—sent him in company with Captain Grant to visit Lake Victoria Nyanza. Even so, Speke failed to make a thorough exploration, which was not done until 1874, when Stanley circumnavigated it.

Burton was not to get a chance to defend himself for five years.

He applied to Lord Russell for a consular post. Russell replied that the best he could do was Fernando Po. This best was the worst, for the post, known as the Foreign Office Grave, was a low hot fever-ridden island in the bight of Biafra, off West Africa. The very year Burton was to come there a yellow fever epidemic would kill off in two months seventy-eight out of two hundred and fifty white men. He would be paid the sum of seven hundred pounds a year for the chance of losing his life. This man whose knowledge of the East and whose abilities fitted him for the highest posts in India or Egypt, including the viceroyship, was given the lowest rung on the ladder of diplomatic service. Nevertheless, Burton, who had a new and young wife, had to have some sort of salary. And it was a step.

"They would like me to die," he said, "but I don't mean to."

As if that were not enough, the East India Company, whose army had now come under the Crown, took advantage of this chance to strike his name off their half-pay lists. The rule was that no Indian officer could take another appointment and keep his pay. It was generally ignored, but 'John Company' wanted to get rid of their troublesome and too-outspoken Ruffian Dick. Off came his name, and he was left with no money at all.

When he first appeared at Nanny Po, he was watched curiously by everybody. The whites there had allowed the negroes to gain the upper hand, partly because English law so protected the blacks they could sue a white man for practically anything. British prestige was suffering; the natives were becoming arrogant.

A few days after Burton arrived, a large black man, dressed like a dandy, walked into the Consulate. He slapped Burton on the back, laughing loudly. "How do, Consul," he said, holding out his hand. "Come to shake hands—how do?"

Some Englishmen standing around watched Burton, for he would set the attitude of the whites for some time to come. Burton fixed upon the intruder his fierce glare, then shouted to his Kru boys to throw the uninvited guest out. Whooping with joy, his canoe boys leaped upon the big man and bodily tossed him out the window, which fortunately was only four feet from the ground. The cast-out one landed with a thud, got to his feet. and ran off. And there was no doubt from then on as to who was master in Fernando Po.

Nor was he soft with the whites who disputed with him. The rule was that every ship that stopped there should wait eighteen hours so that the merchants could have a chance to receive and answer their letters of business. Otherwise, so rare were boats, they might have to wait for a long time. But the captains had gotten into the custom of ignoring this and of sailing as soon as they had discharged their cargo. The first captain who tried that ran up against an iron wall. Burton pointed out that the delay was part of the ship's contract. The captain replied that none of the other consuls had tried to enforce the rule.

"Ha!" replied Richard. "More shame to them! Now, are you going to stay?"

"No, sir, not I."

"Very well then. I am going up to the Governor's, and I am going to load two cannons. If you go out *one minute* before your eighteen hours expires, I'll send the first shot across your bows and the second slap into you. I'm a man of my word. Good morning!"

Stunned, the captain left, and he was so sure of Richard's word that he did not leave until half an hour after his time was up. And every other captain from then on made certain that he too stayed the lawful limit.

Meanwhile, Burton visited every place along the coast, was the first man to scale the Pico Grands, the highest peak of the Cameroon mountains, hunted gorillas, unsuccessfully, and investigated cannibalism. He reported that the Pang tribesmen, so famous for eating their prisoners of war, did not seem to have their hearts in it.

One of the places he wished to visit was the land of Dahomey. Lord Russell, hearing of this, appointed Burton as a commissioner. He was to protest to King Gelele against the great slave trade and also to ask that the Customs of the country be abandoned. The Customs in this case meant the slaughter of hundreds, perhaps thousands, of prisoners of war and of criminals. The land was a cruel and bloody one, where the king cut a man's throat every time he wanted to send a messenger to the ghosts of his dead ancestors. Animals were tied up in the most agonizing positions; the King had had pregnant women cut open while alive so that he might see what it was like.

And there was an army of Amazons there, genuine women-warriors.

Of course, the Foreign Office did their best to cripple his chances of success. Burton knew the King would only listen to a man who brought pleasing gifts.

Yet the Office sent only a few, and these largely useless. And they did not send what the King had very much wanted; an English carriage and horses. Their feeble excuse was that the horses could not stand the climate. Burton swore, because it should have been left up to him to get the horses to Agbomey, the capital, alive. But, handicapped as he was, he must go ahead and see what he could do.

Their progress was slow. Every half mile they had to stop to endure a ceremonial dancing and drinking, given by every chief of a village, which often consisted only of a half a dozen huts. And every chief expected a gift.

But they did make up songs about him.

"Batunu (Burton) he has seen the world with its kings and caboceers,

He now comes to Dahomey, and he shall see everything here."

They halted finally at Kana, the king's winter quarters. Buko-no Uro, Gelele's doctor and chief wizard, came to tell them that Gelele would receive them in the morning. Burton knew from bitter experience that the African liked to hurry up the white man, then to make him sit in the hot sun in full uniform for hours in front of a mud wall, and let him sweat until the potentate put in a leisurely appearance. So, though he was supposed to be at the so-called English house at ten a.m., he did not go until one in the afternoon. And then he was an hour early.

Here he met various dignitaries. One was Yevogan, the viceroy of Whydah. He was used to white men who cringed before him because of his power. He tried, jokingly, but really in earnest, to pull Burton and his companions off their stools. Under orders from the Consul, they firmly resisted him. It would undoubtedly ruin their mission if they were to lose face at the very outset. Besides, Burton was not the kind to allow any man to unseat him. They reviewed a parade of warriors, then went to the palace.

They passed the King's sleeping room, which was paved with the skulls of neighboring princes, so that he might walk on them.

The King, Gelele, finally appeared. He was a tall man, well built, between forty and forty-five, his nails long as a Chinese mandarin's, his teeth blackened by tobacco. His eyes were red, bleared, inflamed. It was not bloodlust that caused this, but the glare of the sun during the long reception hours, the harsh winds, too much smoking, and too much time in bed with his many wives. Under the law, every woman in the country was his wife, and if one pleased his eye, he could take her. And often did. Nor could the husband protest, for he, like every man, was the king's legal slave.

There were women everywhere, unarmed women as well as the many Amazons. All were as ugly as they were black; all made up for this with their intense devotion to His Majesty. If he sweated, they at once wiped off his brow; if he wished to spit, a royal wife offered him a gold spittoon; if he sneezed, everyone touched the ground with their heads; if he drank, all gave a blessing.

Burton saw at once that conversation was going to be tedious, for the King had to address the Meu, or chief general and tax gatherer, who spoke to the interpreter, who spoke to Burton. He determined to attack the language, which he did, and before he left Agbomey, he could understand most conversations in Efon and could carry on a simple dialog.

Healths were drunk, but the King, after touching their glasses, had a white calico screen put up before him, so he could drink in privacy. At this, guns were fired, Amazons tinkled bells, ministers bent to the ground, clapping their hands, and the commoners, cowering to avoid the sight, turned their backs, if sitting, or danced, if standing, and made paddling motions with their hands.

Afterwards, salutes were fired. The first was for the King; then, eleven for Commodore Wilton who had once made a mission to Gelele, and nine for the Consul. Burton insisted that he be given the same number as his predecessor. Beecham, one of their native interpreters, turned blue with fear because of the Consul's boldness in dealing with the savage monarch; nevertheless, he interpreted. The King at once apologized, saying it had been a mistake, and two more shots were fired. Then Burton's party retired.

The Amazons, Burton noted, were all big strapping women, so masculine they could usually be distinguished from the men only by their great buttocks. On the other hand, the men were somewhat effeminate. Even at that moment a party of warrior women were off attacking a village in the country of the Makhis, whose king had insulted Gelele.

This was truly a country of women, for they took precedence over men everywhere. Even the women slaves of the Amazons wore bells that warned men to get out of the way and not to dare to look at them. Burton had been very much annoyed on the way up to Agbomey because his pace had been cut down to half a mile an hour, his men had been so busy throwing down their burdens and taking off for the bush at every tinkle.

A grand review was given in his honor. Past him filed in barbaric—and often ragged and dirty—splendor, battalions of full-breasted soldiery. The She-Mingan led the first brigade, flags and umbrellas on every side of her. After her came the She-Nens and the royal bodyguard, the Fanti, big-muscled women who danced as they marched and swung blades eighteen inches long, shaped exactly like a razor. These whistled through the air as the women demonstrated how they would cut off their enemies' heads. Behind them, the blunderbuss women, then the ammunition bearers; the elephant huntresses, musketeers, bow women, scouts, and stretcher-bearers.

Men applauded but did not crowd close. It was high treason and death or exile even to touch an Amazon by accident. As the King's wives, they were vowed to chastity. Despite this, the King had just discovered that one hundred and fifty of his virgins were pregnant. Most of the men pointed out as guilty were punished, but most of the females were pardoned.

"After all," the King remarked to the Consul, "women will be women."

After the review, the King stalked off, while men ran ahead of him, pointing out every stick and stone with finger-snappings and smoothing out every roughness so he might not stumble.

The English went to their unpleasant quarters, where they would be kept for two months while the endless talking and feasts of the African would go on. The Buko-No Uro came and asked to see the presents for the King. Burton refused, saying that the King himself must first see them. Burton then insisted strongly that if anybody were to be put to death in his presence, he would leave at once for Whydab and not come back.

Late in the morning Burton appeared with his gifts, passed through the Gate of Tears, and went on into the inner court. Here women sold provisions on one side, while on the other was dead King Gezo's huge war drum, hung with wreaths of skulls. Burton showed with a sinking heart the things that the Foreign Office had sent. Gelele reacted as he had expected; there was not even one word of thanks from the sullen King. The tent was far too small, and its pegs, instead of being of silver, were of wood, which would last not very long in this land of wood-eating insects. The heavy silver pipe was never used, Gelele preferring his lighter clay with the wood stem. The silver belts were also rejected, because Gelele had specifically asked for bracelets. Like all Africans, he took it as a personal slight if his wishes were not carried out to the letter. The coat of mail was too heavy and hot, so the King hung it up as a target to shoot at. Only the silver trays were admired, but the King had to ask what they were for.

"What about the carriages and the horses?" said Gelele, still looking around him as if he expected Burton to produce them from a hat.

Burton, concealing his exasperation, answered for the twelfth time that the Queen had feared that the horses might die and that it was very difficult to transport carriages.

"But carriages have been brought before," said Gelele, "and if the horses died even on the beach of Whydah, I would at least have known that the white Queen thought enough of Gelele to send them." He was very cold and haughty, but evidently seething inside.

Though he knew that now was not the time, Burton then asked if Gelele would do anything about stopping the slave trade and also abandoning or at least greatly reducing the slaughter and torture of prisoners.

Gelele did not reply.

Dismissed, Burton returned to his house, where his landlord, the old Buko-no, told him of his trouble with his latest wife, a young one. As he was married to eighty women, the Buko-no was having trouble in keeping them happy. Would Batunu have in his medicine bag a charm that would pep up the Buko-no? Burton replied that he was sorry but he did not. Not only was the old man disappointed, but his wives later heard of it and scolded him soundly for having asked for an aphrodisiac, as it reflected on their own stimulating abilities.

On St. John's Day, the war chiefs were seen coming in from out-stations and parading before the palace. Burton was sick at this news, for this meant the Customs would soon begin.

The rites were to supply the late father of Gelele with fresh attendants in ghostland. Some idea of how they were carried out could be told from the people's name for them, the *Khwe-ta-nun*, or Yearly Head Thing. It was not true, however, that the King paddled about a pool of human blood in a canoe. The two pits used to collect blood were only about two feet deep and four in diameter, not large enough for a boat.

Burton was stunned for days by the constant procession of soldiers, male and Amazon, the booming and barking of guns, the singing, the dancing, the drinking, the gaudy flashing display of colors and arms, the speeches, the drums forever beating. Once the King threw money into the crowd; and in the frantic scramble men were killed and had eyes gouged out and noses bitten off. Even Burton and his party had to submit to scrambling for the cowrie shells which passed as currency, but the fight was strictly among themselves, with no bloodshed.

The King then walked up to the shed where the victims-to-be sat on stools. He threw cowrie shells among them, which were placed by attendants upon the prisoners' caps. Then Gelele snapped his fingers at Burton—the Dahomean version of the handshake—and the interpreter said that if Burton cared to plead, some of the victims might be pardoned.

This was not a way of making Burton lose face, but was part of the Customs formula, whereby the King might show his big heart. Burton replied that mercy well becomes great kings. So half of the prisoners were released, and heard their pardon while they crouched on all fours. Another speech; a clash of cymbals, a drinking of rum, and Burton's party was given permission to leave the royal presence.

The Evil Nights came, when no man except officials could stir outside without being beheaded. Burton chafed because he would get no chance to learn what really happened. On the other hand, he had himself told the King that he would not witness any executions. He believed that the victims were all made drunk with rum and that the King began by bringing his sharp blade down on the neck of a kneeling criminal. Afterwards, the high officials would also cut off heads.

He knew that every time the King thought a report should be sent to his father's ghost, he would charge a man or woman with a message and then send them off via the decapitation route. Such trivial things as making a new drum, being visited by a white man, or even moving from one place to another, required the services of another victim. He estimated that not less than five hundred were slaughtered at the yearly Customs, nor less than one thousand during the year of the Grand Customs, held when a king died. Whenever the King fell ill, many were also killed on suspicion of witchcraft.

It was plain to Burton that abolishing human sacrifice would be the same thing as abolishing Dahomey. The practice rose from the idea of honoring one's father and had been in long usage. The powerful priesthood supported it. Not only that, if the King did try to get rid of the Customs, he might end up being a sacrifice himself. Despite their groveling before the King, the captains and courtiers really held the power, and it was rumored that they had poisoned Gelele's grandfather because he had seemed to favor Christianity.

However, Burton noted this was the first time that no lives had been taken publicly, so he knew that his visit had driven the first small wedge into the eventual death of the Customs.

On the night of the fifth day, the deep boom of the death-drum and the firing of a musket told them that someone had died. In the morning, they rose to go to the palace. On their way they saw four corpses, dressed in white shirts and nightcaps, sitting on stools. Three men, naked, dangled head downwards from gallows. They had been beaten to death, and their genitals were cut off so as not to offend the King's wives with the sight.

Outside the Komasi house lay a dozen heads, face downward. Within the palace gate were two more. At least twenty-three men had died during the Evil Night.

More parading, dancing and speeches followed. Burton sat through the late morning and most of the afternoon, making detailed notes about the barbaric spectacle. At last it came to an end, and Burton asked the King that he be allowed to rest the following day. Permission granted, he spent Sunday trying to drive out the noise from his ears and the dazzle and glitter from his eyes. All that day another phantom parade passed before him.

Burton watched the big black Amazons carefully and noted that they were fiercer than the men. Part of this might be laid at their enforced continency, which he thought made them so irritable they wanted to fight. But the celibacy was hard to enforce; he noted that all the passions are sisters, and that bloodshed caused these women to remember love, not to forget it. They were more savage than wounded gorillas, far more cruel than their brothers-in-arms.

However, their very existence was a drain upon the kingdom. The female troops, numbering twenty-five hundred, would produce about seventy-five hundred children. But they were forbidden issue, so that Dahomey, which had already lost many in their numerous wars, was fast sinking in population. Not only that, but Dahomey was constantly weakened by her export slave trade. She was no longer as feared by her neighbors as she had been, and the Egbas had twice repulsed Gelele with heavy losses. He was to try again to take Abeokuta, their capital, where his army would be crushed.

Monday, Burton passed through the city gate, where he saw the corpses, now being eaten by turkey buzzards. Upon meeting Gelele, he was told that he ought to fight again for the cowries. Burton refused, as he wished to see how the King would take it. Besides, he had sprained a wrist in the last scramble. The King graciously excused him, then said that he must dance for him later on.

Burton had been putting off this honor, but the time came when he could no longer do so. One day the King announced that he must, so the Consul gave the right timing to the band, then threw himself headlong into a violent Hindustani single step. Loud cheers, even from the King. Burton danced again. More cheers. Firing of guns and presenting of arms. Burton was a big success, and he was made an honorary Brigadier-General of the Amazons.

The days and nights went on, with the King putting off the official reading of the message from Lord Russell. The drums beat, and the cymbals clashed to hide the cries of the victims, and every morning there would be fresh bodies for him to see, while the buzzards waited on nearby calabash trees. And for every male corpse displayed, Burton know, there was a female to match it within the palace walls, where the women were slain.

Burton had spent six weeks in Agbomey, and now he received word that a cruiser was waiting off of Whydah to take him to the Oil Rivers region. It could not stay too long, so he must get his business over, one way or the other. He ordered his bags to be openly packed in the house's compound, knowing that word of this would reach the King. He also sent two men to tell Gelele that the thirty porters he had asked for had not been delivered, and that he was setting out the next day, regardless.

The King flew into a rage because his ministers had neglected to deliver the porters, and had his Amazons drive them out of the palace with blows from bamboo sticks. Then the King sent an apology to Burton, saying that he could not at once attend to the Consul's affairs because he was too angry. Two days later, the Customs came to an end. Typically violent, they finished with a wild drunken feast and the breaking of all the glass and the smashing of the furniture.

Two days later the King condescended to receive them to hear the message. "I hear that you have been complaining about me, O Batunu, and this after we have been the best of friends, dancing and drinking together."

"I have no grievance against you," replied Burton cautiously, "but it has not been well to hold up for two months such an important message."

"I have been busy," said Gelele. "Besides, you have already told me the substance of your message."

Burton then complained of having been kept practically a prisoner for two months in his house, that the Buko-no had subjected them to many small annoyances, and that they had been kept from hunting in the Makhi mountains to the north. The King passed these off with evasive answers. Burton became heated, and asked Gelele if he knew that they had been kept that afternoon for hours in the sun before the gate, a custom not followed in civilized countries. The King said he had not; then, to get off a disagreeable subject, joked with Burton about his having kept the house slaves in order with a light beating. Burton's frown disappeared; whereupon the King asked him to read his message.

Burton knew enough about the language by now to know if the interpreter was translating correctly, so he checked him. He suspected that during the first days of his visit his words had changed somewhat when going through the middleman. The interpreter had not cared to offend his King, for he might be exiled or even killed. Now, however, he told Gelele in straightforward words that the British government intended to put a stop to the slave traffic and that the United States would no longer let her ships carry slaves. As for the sacrifices, the less of them, the better Her Majesty's men would feel.

Burton felt hopeless, for it was evident from the King's face that he might as well be talking to the wind.

"The ruler of England and I are like my finger," said Gelele, "but your men-of-war are now capturing slavers near my beaches, and I cannot allow that."

Burton explained that in civilized countries the right of a nation extended no farther than three miles off shore, and the English ships had not come inside that. As for the King's excuses for not being able to end the Customs, the people would always follow the example of their ruler. Moreover, unless the spectacle of nude and mutilated corpses left to hang in the sun were spared visitors, Burton would advise all Englishmen to avoid the court during the time of the Customs.

Never before had anybody dared to speak up to the King in such a blunt fashion. He scowled, and his ministers shifted uneasily, perhaps wondering if they would have to call in the Amazons with their beheading knives.

Burton was in a tight spot, but he did not betray a lack of confidence. Gelele, of course, had no real idea of what Great Britain was; he thought of it as a slightly larger and richer Dahomey, surrounded by water and inhabited by white men. Nevertheless, if he were calm, he would never consider going to war with England. He was having enough trouble with his war against the Egbas.

But he was a totally arrogant man whose slightest wish was instantly carried out, and he did not like being rebuked before his ministers and wives. A moment's anger, and he might give the order that would send his savage women to drag Burton off. Also, there was always the temptation of the glory the King would have if he owned the skull of the great Batunu for his drinking cup. No other West Coast monarch could boast such a splendid possession.

Gelele's bloodshot eyes gleamed, while Burton waited for his reply. Then, slowly, a smile replaced the scowl, and the Consul breathed easier.

There was more talk. Nothing came of it, except that Burton knew he would have to report that there was little Her Majesty's government could do about the slave trade or the sacrifices except to allow them to die out. At eight p.m. the King said he was tired of talking.

"If you are not still angry, Batunu, we will drink together."

Burton diplomatically replied that he had never felt personally displeased with Gelele, just with his ministers, who had given him a hard time. They stood up and drank gin. No noise was made at this time; the ministers, not wishing to draw the King's attention to them, were happy just to kiss the ground as he left. At the doorway which was too narrow for two abreast, Burton fell back. The King asked why he had done that. Burton said that crowned heads always walked first. Pleased, Gelele shook hands with him.

"You are a good man but," he added, rolling his head, "you are too angry."

Nor would Burton promise to come back for another visit. Though the King might pardon him this time for his anger because of the novelty, the next incident might find him in a less pleasant mood. And there would be no restraining the famous Burton temper, if he were pushed too far.

He went back to Fernando Po, where he was granted a leave to England. Lord Russell wrote to thank him, saying he had carried out the mission to his "entire satisfaction." This was in a personal note to Mrs. Burton, however. As usual, Burton received no official recommendation.

On his return from Dahomey, Burton found that Speke and Grant had come back from their central African expedition and were receiving a tremendous ovation. Despite the injuries done him, Burton was the first to praise their work. Then, on hearing Speke's account, he changed his mind, for it was apparent to him that the two had spent much time in accomplishing little, that their story was full of errors. Others found this out; Speke's reputation fell as Burton's rose. And he could take pride in the fact that it was his labor that had made the road easy for them. He had opened the way for Englishmen; they had only to follow him.

Burton challenged his former friend to discuss the sources of the Nile with him before the Royal Society at Bath. Speke agreed. At the same time, Burton was told that Speke had said that if Burton appeared at Bath, Speke would kick him.

"Well, that settles it!" roared Burton. "By God, he shall kick me!"

When the day came for the debate, excitement had reached a high pitch all over England. Ruffian Dick was boiling mad, so went the rumor, and anything could happen. Though broken in health by his travels and no longer a young man, he could challenge Speke to a secret duel. If so, the money would be on him. People still remembered his exhibition duel with a French hussar in which he had struck the man's saber so hard he'd knocked it out of his hand seven times in a row. And the Frenchman had had to beg off, saying his arm was numbed by the terrific force.

The first day there was to be no discussion about Africa, but the two sat on the same platform. Speke looked at Burton, then at Mrs. Burton, who had talked to him in an effort at reconciliation. His face was sad and yearning and perplexed. Then it hardened. As the speeches went on, he began to fidget. Presently, he rose, muttering "Oh, I cannot stand this any longer." Burton remained.

The next day, a larger crowd than ever assembled. Burton and his wife stood on the platform, alone. His notes were in his hand, held like a pistol ready to fire. But Speke did not appear, and they waited in a gathering tension for twenty-five minutes. Suddenly, the council and the speakers filed in. The president arose and announced that Speke had been shot while hunting that morning. His friends had heard the gun and seen him stagger. Running up, they had found him wounded, close to the heart. Within a few minutes, he was dead.

Burton sank into his chair, his face pale and working. Called on to speak, he talked briefly of other matters. When he got home, he wept long and hard, and Mrs. Burton spent days trying to soften his grief.

Whether Speke had been the victim of an accident, or whether he committed suicide because he could not face the man about whom he had lied, was never known. The jury said that it was accidental death.

Unable to kill him off at Fernando Po, the Ministry now gave him the consulship at Santos, Brazil. Though not as unhealthy as his first post, it was not far behind. However, it was a step up the ladder, and he beat the heat, fever, and plague as he had done in Africa, by establishing residence at a place high in the hills, further inland. He traveled much, hunted for diamonds and sea serpents, and finally, while home on sick leave, was appointed to the consulship of Damascus. Both of the posts were gotten through the efforts of his wife. During her lifetime she wrote, literally, thousands of letters to the high statesmen, pointing out that they were ignoring her Richard's great talents and accomplishments in favor of lesser men. She cornered officials and drove them to desperation with her praises of her husband. However, Lord Derby, held a high opinion of Richard and was pleased to get him Damascus, a high post.

No less joyed were the Burtons, for he would be home once again in his beloved East. But there he ran afoul of a combination of several cliques. One was represented by the Turkish governor of Syria, a fat and, corrupt beast. Another was his jealous superior, the Consul-General at Beirout. A third, the Christian missionaries, who resented Burton's free thinking philosophy and his close connections with Mohammedanism. A fourth were the Greek Orthodox. And a fifth were the Jewish moneylenders.

Burton narrowly prevented a wholesale slaughter of Christians by Moslems aroused by the too-ardent preaching of a British missionary. He browbeat the Turkish governor into sending his Moslem soldiers out to stop the riot. But the Consul-General wrote home that the danger was imaginary. The missionary who had been saved a martyr's death wrote letters home, accusing Burton of hostility to Christians. Rashid Pasha, the viceroy of Syria, laid an ambush for Burton with three hundred Bedawins. Isabel found out about it and warned him so that he slipped away. But she got him into trouble herself by getting him to protect the Shazli sect, which was thinking about wholesale conversion to Roman Catholicism. Rashid warned Burton that he was taking onto himself too much authority. Burton had many Jews as friends but the Damascus moneylenders were not among them. It was a fact that they were charging many poor peasants interest even higher than sixty percent; the natives who fell into their clutches could not get out of them. Burton could not stop the practices, but he did refuse to help the moneylenders collect their debts. Offended, these wrote to the wealthy and influential Jews in England, claiming to represent 'all the Jews of Damascus' and complaining falsely of persecution. The English Jews, of course, had no way of checking up on the stories. He earned more hate from Rashid because he warned the Druze Arabs that the Turk was trying to use them as a cat's paw by stirring up revolt among them.

While visiting Nazareth, Isabel Burton had a thieving Copt thrown out of her tent. He threw stones at her servants; they beat him. Just then, a crowd of Greeks came out of a church close by. They hated Burton because he had defended the Jews when they had protested against the Turks selling a synagogue of theirs to the Greek bishop. Now they seized their chance and stoned Burton and his party. Many struck him; one hurt his sword arm so badly he was crippled for two years afterward. He stood his ground, calmly picking out the ringleaders among the raving mob of one hundred and fifty. But when three of his servants were badly hurt, he grabbed a revolver from the belt of a man and shot over the heads of the crowd. Isabel ran off for help, and ten Americans and Germans, armed, came running. The mob fled in panic.

The storm of wrath broke, Burton with his self-defeating sense of timing, delayed sending the report on the incident. Meanwhile, every party and sect he had offended, forgetting the many good things he had done for them, clamored for his recall. A cool investigation on the part of the government would have disclosed their Consul's innocence of the charges made against him. But, fearing to offend Turkey, the Foreign Office listened to the flood of complaints. One day, as Burton was getting ready for one of his long rides into the desert, he was handed a note. It had been sent by his successor, the first notice he had of what had happened.

Too proud to appeal, he left at once. But he had the satisfaction of seeing hundreds of the people gather in a popular demonstration of their love and respect for him. Later, Rashid and the Greek bishop would be disgraced, and the ringleaders of the moneylenders would go bankrupt.

His friends at home came to his rescue too late. The best they could get him was the third rate consulship at Trieste. He could not afford to refuse it as he still clung to the hope that someday he would get the post at Morocco. Isabel kept up her agitation for him, but Lord Salisbury put her off with the half-joking remark that if he were put in charge of some attachable country, England might have to take it over before she was ready for the job. Even so, he might have gotten Morocco had not Salisbury's party gone out of power.

For thirty years he had been thinking of making a translation of the *Thousand Nights and a Night*, better known as the *Arabian Nights*. He knew well this great collection of Oriental fairy stories, for in his disguises he had often entertained the crowds in the marketplace and coffee shops with them. Now he set himself to his task, one for which he was fitted better than anybody else in the world. Not especially inspired as a prose writer or a poet, he was a magnificent interpreter. Not only that, but he refused to issue a castrated version. Mrs. Grundy could go to hell if she objected to the many spicy tales and utterly frank language of the characters. What was dirty in England was not necessarily so in the mouths of Ali Baba and Aladdin and the naughty ladies kept under lock and key by the genies. Another attraction were his many footnotes, containing vast knowledge of Eastern lore, including many curious bits of sexology. His readers ate up the first issue and clamored for more. He pocketed twelve thousand pounds and calmly accepted alike the bitter denunciations of outraged prudes and the compliments of scholars and statesmen. "Now I know the tastes of England," he said to Isabel, "we never need be without money."

But what his explorations had not done, his pen had. One day there came a telegram addressed to Sir Richard Burton. Thinking it a practical joke, Burton refused it at first, but when he opened it, found that Queen Victoria had made him a Knight Commander of St. Michael and St. George. It was not the wished-for K.C.B., the Knight Commander of the Bath, but it was enough of an honor to make him happy for some time and to send his wife into an ecstasy.

The thrill passed. An American journalist, Frank Harris, visiting Burton at Trieste, called him a desert lion dying in the cage. He was dying of disappointment and boredom and lack of outlet for his great abilities. In spite of literary talents and great gift of speech, he was fundamentally a man of action, a leader.

Harris, who worshipped Burton, asked if he would have preferred to be viceroy of India or consul-general of Egypt.

"Egypt! Egypt!" cried the old man. "In India I should have had the English civil servants to deal with—Jangali, or savages, as their Hindu fellow-subjects call them—and English prejudices, formalities, stupidity, ignorance. They would have killed me in India, thwarted me, intrigued against me, murdered me. But in Egypt I could have made my own civil servants, trained them. I could have had natives, too, to help. Ah, what a chance!

"...I know the Arab nature. The Mahdi business could have been settled without a blow," he exploded, speaking of the revolt that had killed his friend, 'Chinese' Gordon. "What did Dufferin know of Egypt? Poor Dufferin, what did he even know of Dufferin?"

He told how he had come back from Africa and offered all East Africa to Lord Salisbury. He'd made treaties with all the chiefs, and no other nation was interested enough to object. But Salisbury asked if East Africa was worth anything. Twenty years afterwards, the Germans had moved in to take over colonies which England was to buy with blood during the First World War.

He ended up, "England...makes me an office-boy."

So he finished his days at Trieste, literally eating himself into the grave. Gout and gas around the heart, brought on by the tremendous appetite of the disappointed, steadily crippled him. He grew too weak to handle the iron cane that he always carried to keep his sword arm strong. The night of the 19th of October, 1891 as Isabel was saying her night prayers to him, a dog howled. Richard took that as an omen of death, as he had done the tapping of a bird at his window three days before. He went to bed, became sick at midnight, and at four in the morning, crying out, "Oh, puss—chloroform—ether—or I am a dead man!" he died in his wife's arms.

At his funeral at Trieste, the entire population of one hundred and fifty thousand turned out to say farewell to the beloved Consul. His body was then shipped to Mortlake, in England, where he was buried in a tomb built in the form of the Arabian tent he had loved so well.

Justin M'Carthy and Swinburne wrote poems about him, but the finest tribute is undoubtedly that given by Walter Phelps Dodge in his book on Burton.

"Who can doubt that he faced the crossing of the Styx with the same coolness and courage he had ever shown! or that his hail of Charon bore the right accent!"

The Journey as the Revelation of the Unknown

First published in *The New Encyclopedia of Science Fiction*, 1988.

Curious for the fact that Phil refers to himself in the third person, presumably to maintain his independence as an introduction writer.

❧❧❀❧❧

The journey is one of the basic themes in ancient and classical literature as well as in modern science fiction. The mystery of what lies beyond the horizon—or the planet—has always lured people; even stay-at-homes have been eager to hear, read, or see tales of the distant unknown and the exotic unknowable. But the purpose of the journey in literature is not simply to arrive somewhere; the trip itself is fraught with peril, uncertainty, and adventure, as much in ancient times as in prospect.

The pattern of the literary journey—a lone adventurer or a band carefully assembled who by accident or design sally beyond the ken—was fixed in the earliest fiction: Gilgamesh, the Sumerian hero (ca. 2000 B.C.), goes on a long journey to discover immortality, and Odysseus's troubled travels home from Troy (ca. eighth century B.C.) were so influential as the model for later works that odyssey became an alternate term for the journey of adventure and discovery. The point of Homer's story, like that of so many journeys, is not so much what Odysseus discovers when he finally gets home to Ithaca but what happens to him along the way. Journeys are learning and testing experiences.

The pattern of SF journeys that cross space or time instead of seas has changed only in the addition of scientific or pseudoscientific rationales for the means of travel and sometimes in the stress on self-discovery over the discovery of other beings and places. In the process the best tales set forth the writer's philosophy through the hero's goals: to return home, to defeat an enemy threatening the hero's life or world, to rescue a friend or lover, to achieve immortality for oneself or for humanity, to gain godlike powers or keep the villain from attaining them, to make the world better, or just to survive.

Gilgamesh and Odysseus, to be sure, arrive home wiser men, but the earliest known physical journey that ends specifically in self-knowledge may be the biblical Book of Jonah (ca. 300 B.C.). After being swallowed by a big fish, Jonah is spat out upon a beach, goes to Nineveh, that great and wicked city Jonah wishes God to destroy, and discovers that he is not as righteous as he thought and that Gentiles too are children of God. Twentieth-century SF journeys, such as Alexei Panshin's *Rite of Passage* (1968) and David Lindsay's *A Voyage to Arcturus* (1920), also focus on self-revelation; it is worth noting that their methods of travel, interstellar spaceship and "crystal torpedo," are no more scientifically possible than Jonah's whale.

Lucian of Samosata, surnamed The Blasphemer, wrote two satiric proto-SF works: *Icaromenippus*, which tells of a philosopher who straps on one wing from a vulture and one from an eagle and flies to the Moon; and *A True Story*, which satirizes the travel stories of his predecessors (including Homer) by having the ship of a band of adventurers caught up in a storm and carried to the Moon, where the characters fight for the King of the Moon against the armies of the Sun King for the right to colonize Venus.

Utopias, beginning with Thomas More's eponymous 1516 work, used the journey as a means of making their ideal states more plausible—explaining why the world has not heard of the utopia in question as well as describing how perfection can exist in a corrupt world—and utopias such as Campanella's *The City of the Sun* (1623) and Francis Bacon's *The New Atlantis* (1627) are similar to *A True Story* in that their journeys are more entertaining than the dialogues and descriptions that follow.

The means of travel has, for many writers of SF, been as important as the journey itself; the genre continues to be fascinated with the mechanics of things. Johannes Kepler's *Somnium* (1634) is about a dream voyage to the Moon (by demon), but the hero of Bishop Francis Godwin's *The Man in the Moone* (1638) is lifted by a bird-drawn chariot. Cyrano de Bergerac, in his satiric and still lively *States and Empires of the Moon* (1657) and *Comic History of the States of the Sun* (1662), described several methods of levitation, including dew in glass bottles that are drawn up by the Sun and rockets. *Travels into Several Remote Nations of the World: Four Parts* (1726)—better known as *Gulliver's Travels*—is still a widely read example of proto-SF, enjoyed by both children and adults, though for different reasons. Jonathan Swift's journeys, however, are only the means to launch Gulliver into new satiric situations. *The Consolidator* (1705) by Daniel Defoe is a social satire in which the hero uses an alcohol-burning machine to get to the Moon; Defoe's *Robinson Crusoe* (1719), though not SF, does involve a journey and influenced a great deal of later SF, particularly Jules Verne's *The Mysterious Island* (1875), which begins with a journey via a balloon caught up in a storm, like that of Lucian's characters.

Most of these early journeys aimed at the Moon, and the Moon continued to be the most prominent off-Earth destination in the eighteenth and early nineteenth centuries. Samuel Brunt's satiric *A Voyage to Cacklogallinia* (1728), Murtagh McDermot's *A Trip to the Moon* (1728), and Ralph Morris's *The Life and Astonishing Transactions of John Daniel* (1751) are about journeys to the lunar world. The protagonist of Baron Ludvig Holberg's satiric *Journey to the World Underground* (1741) goes to the center of the Earth. But Joseph Atterley's *A Voyage to the Moon* (1827) and Edgar Allan Poe's "Hans Pfaall" (1835), in which his hero ascends to the Moon in a balloon, reverted to the favorite far-off place of contemporary satire-romancers. Poe's *The Narrative of Arthur Gordon Pym* (1838) is almost all voyage (and not remotely SF) until Pym arrives near Antarctica.

In the later nineteenth century, as proto-SF began evolving into science fiction, writers started to extrapolate from the new ideas, discoveries, and techniques created by the accelerating Industrial Revolution and the burgeoning of science and technology, pushing their fiction out into the Solar System and beyond through travel. But the worlds at journey's end were usually no more realistic than those of their predecessors. Jules Verne's *From the Earth to the Moon* (1865) and *Around the Moon* (1870) were the first true hard-core SF stories because they represented the attempt by an SF writer to adhere strictly to contemporary scientific knowledge—although Verne failed as a prophet by using an enormous cannon, rather than the rocket proposed by his fellow Frenchman, de Bergerac, to launch his spaceship.

John Jacob Astor's spaceship in *A Journey to Other Worlds* (1894) is propelled by an antigravity source called apergy, derived from Percy Greg's *Across the Zodiac* (1880). Astor also may have been influenced by Marie Corelli's *A Romance of Two Worlds* (1886), in which interstellar travel is achieved by "personal electricity," and Robert Cromie's *A Plunge into Space* (1890), which uses an antigravity device and touches on some of the harsh realities of space voyaging. William R. Bradshaw, whose *The Goddess of Atvatabar* (1892) is a grandiose tale of a voyage to the center of the Earth, exemplifies writers who choose to go inward instead of outward. Gustavus W. Pope's *Journey to Mars* (1894) was followed by his *Romance of the Planets, No.2: Journey to Venus* (1895). John Munro's *A Trip to Venus* (1897) was the first story to use the modern method of multistage rockets for propulsion.

H.G. Wells, in *The First Men in the Moon* (1901), used an antigravity metal named Cavorite; he knew the metal was scientifically impossible, but he was more interested in depicting possible societies than means of travel. The same may be said for his *The Time Machine* (1895), which is confined to a small geographic area but journeys far in time.

Around the turn of the century George Griffith, Ellsworth Douglas, Fenton Ash, John Mastin, Garrett P. Serviss, and Edwin L. Arnold all wrote novels about journeys in space. The most influential use of another planet began with Edgar Rice Burroughs's "Under the Moons of Mars" (1912; as *A Princess of Mars*, 1917). Its hero, John Carter, and a later character named Ulysses Paxton shuttle by astral projection between Earth and Mars in this novel and its sequels; their process may have anticipated *Star Trek's* method of beaming matter without a receiver to re-form the dissociated molecules because Carter and Paxton were able to form flesh around their projected "souls" after arriving at their destinations.

Astral voyages in space and time also are made by the hero of Jack London's *The Star Rover* (1915), while the unnamed hero of London's *Before Adam* (1906) achieves the similar experience of reincarnation by racial memory. Journeys are common in the gadget-oriented dime novels about Frank Reade, Jr., as they are in almost, all of Verne's *voyages extraordinaires*; several series of adventure stories for boys, particularly the Tom Swift series by Victor Appleton (house name) and the Great Marvel series by Roy Rockwood (house name), were constructed around journeys, although their focus, as in Verne's work, usually is a novel vehicle or method of propulsion, for instance, in Rockwood's *Through Space to Mars* (1910), which uses waves pushed against the ether by an "Etherium motor."

Arthur Conan Doyle's *The Lost World* (1912) followed the pattern of the earlier lost-race romances launched by H. Rider Haggard's *She* (1887) in locating the plateau that has sheltered dinosaurs in the remotest corner of Brazil, where it must be reached by an arduous journey.

Perhaps the best example of rigorous but inventive extrapolation from given scientific premises is Hal Clement's *Mission of Gravity* (1953/1954). The trip across a high-gravity planet, Meskelin, by the centipedelike natives, aided from a distance by Earth dwellers, is a journey of self-discovery that can truly be called an odyssey in which the journey itself is the focus. Murray Leinster in "Proxima Centauri" (1935) and Don Wilcox in "The Voyage That Lasted 600 Years" (1940) were the first to deal with the concept of the generation starship, in which only the descendants of the original passengers will reach their destinations. But Robert A. Heinlein's "Universe" (1941) and its sequel "Common

Sense" (1941; as *Orphans of the Sky*, 1963) achieve the journey's most complete realization as a theme: the real history and purpose of the voyage are lost after a mutiny, and myths develop that consider the spaceship the entire universe and the voyage as the journey between creation and the final end of life.

Aniara (1956), an epic poem about a starship by the Swede Harry Martinson, became the basis for the first true space opera, performed in 1959. Other noteworthy treatments of starships are Judith Merril's "Wish upon a Star" (1958), Brian W. Aldiss's *Non-Stop* (1958; as *Starship*, 1959), Edmund Cooper's *Seed of Light* (1959), J. T. McIntosh's *200 Years to Christmas* (1961), A. E. van Vogt's *Rogue Ship* (1965), Samuel R. Delany's *The Ballad of Beta-2* (1965), Harry Harrison's *Captive Universe* (1969), Damien Broderick's "The Star Mutants" (1970), and Brian M. Stableford's *Promised Land* (1974). Perhaps the most mind-expanding version is Poul Anderson's *Tau Zero* (1970), in which a starship accelerates uncontrollably and slows down the rate of time passage for its crew, which witnesses the death of the universe and the rebirth of a new one. Larry Niven's *Ringworld* (1970) describes not only the difficulties in getting to a distant star but the adventures of the characters as they attempt to explore this magnificent piece of engineering with its enormous surface area: two journeys for the price of one.

Other space voyage works not about starships are "Shadow of Space" (1967) by Philip José Farmer, in which a faster-than-light vessel expands to become larger than the universe and is trapped in hyperspace (a crew member lights his cigar on a dying galaxy); Richard A. Lupoff's *Into the Aether* (1974), a satire on Roy Rockwood-type SF; Farmer's comic *Venus on the Half-Shell* (1975, as Kilgore Trout), in which the antihero seeks the origin of the universe and the cause of pain and death; his *The Unreasoning Mask* (1981), in which the hero discovers that intra-universe spaceships cause the collapse of the "walls" between universes, which are in reality the cells in the body of an infant God; Piers Anthony's *Macroscope* (1969), another mind bender in which the journey through the universe is accomplished by shrinking Neptune and using its superdense matter to punch holes in the fabric of space-matter, thus giving the travelers shortcuts to their destinations; and George Zebrowski's *Macrolife* (1979), which makes the journey the permanent and ideal state for the human species as it establishes its future home not by settling on distant planets but by traveling in space itself.

In any period the method of SF travel reflects what writers are able, given the state of contemporary technology, to imagine. But the purposes of the journey are always the same: to allow the characters, and through them the readers, to undergo the concept-changing, character-shaping experience of travel and to reach the enlightenment and revelations of the unknown.

The Josés from Rio

First published *Luna 6,* 1969 as "Report."

As this book shows, Phil has written so many articles for so many different magazines and fanzines it is very hard to find them all. While several nearly complete bibliographies of Farmer's works were compiled in the 1970s and 1980s, this piece went unnoticed for over 30 years. Published in 1969, it wasn't until a Farmer collector bought an entire collection of *Luna* in 2002, and then read them cover to cover, that it was rediscovered.

The photo above was taken at the second International Film Festival, Rio de Janeiro, March 23-31, 1969. Phil is over Forrest J Ackerman's right shoulder, about a third in from the left. Forry is facing the camera, holding a magazine cover up.

The Rio airport is hot, sticky, and noisy. We're standing in line, waiting to board the plane for New York, wondering if this evening, a nightmare (though comic at times), will ever end. Brazilians crowd around Jonathan Harris, the Mr. Smith of Lost in Space to worship and to get his autograph. Behind the worshippers are Bester, Clarke, Ellison, Farmer, Harrison, Moskowitz, and Van Vogt, none of whom are recognized.

So people do knot themselves around the lead character in a silly-ass space opera. This is natural, I tell myself. One picture worth ten thousand words.

Harris is a friendly likeable person, we find out later, and I wish him continuing good fortune. Moreover, I wonder what would happen if SF were as big as TV and we were the ones being surrounded? I find it inconceivable that the majority of the population would ever dig "good" SF. If they did, then you'd have a different kind of human being. In fact, mankind's history would have been slightly different. I don't say it would have been for the better. It would have been different.

What does this have to do with my impressions of the trip to Rio as a guest of the International Film Festival?

Everything. If I must write a travelog, I'll write one of the mind.

Finally, we board the Argentinean Airlines plane. It takes a hell of a long time getting off the ground, as if it were overloaded. I have a fantasy that the plane never does manage to get into the air. It keeps on going. The lights of Rio have wheeled away. We're in darkness tunneled out by the plane's lights. We keep going and at last the pilot comes out of his numbness (which, it turns out, is not internally generated). The plane stops, after a while, we get out. The ground is wet and grassy. The time for sunrise comes. No sun. Sentients riding animals glowing with biological light appear, and we know we're in another world.

But the plane does take off. Harry passes me his quart of Scotch. The stewardess brings drinks. I think of what Ziva Sheckley said when we were on a trip to the Corcovado, on top of which is the Stoned Christ of Rio, and we had stopped at a restaurant hanging out over a cliff. Ziva is from New York City and everything Midwest is funny anyway. But she rings the changes on my middle name, speaking of Bob José Bloch and Bob José Sheckley and Brian José Aldiss and J. José Ballard, who were with us. There was more of that later on, but now I see that Ziva spoke true even in her joking. I've always had the feeling that SF people are a community with a peculiar simpatico, that, in one sense, I am merged with the others and they with me. Their middle names are José, even when they don't come up to my ideals and even when they have a deep antipathy towards me. Thus, John W. José Juggernaut and Jim José Kaltfisch and Robert José Zounds and Ted José Blanko, although they've disliked me from the first, still are, in an underground sense, me.

And, at this moment, after our seat belts are unstrapped, I feel more than ever that the writers aboard are more than brothers (since my own brothers would only read SF at the point of a gun and wouldn't understand it if their lives depended on it). The aisle explodes with voices, most of them happy. Maybe they're happy because they're going home, but I like to think it's also because we're together, having a little convention. Behind me, two mortal enemies (in print) Harry José Harrison and Sam José Minostentor are talking, bellowing rather. They seem so polite, yet what invectives and nasty put-downs they've been hurling at each other in fanzines!

Sam, standing in the aisle, is leaning far over the tray of the person in the aisle seat so he can talk to Harry. He feels he has to get close to Harry, though God knows why. That roar can be heard the length of the plane and possibly even in the pilots' compartment. (I see them frantically testing controls, lights flashing, buzzers zinging, CRTs jumping with sine and square waves and dots as the crew probe for the sudden and fearful noise the jets have developed.)

Beside Harry is a small brown-skinned, brown-eyed, dark-haired, bespectacled little girl, fifteen years old, from Austria. Her sandwich is on a plate on the snap-down table before her. She eyes the sandwich and the toothpick skewering it. Sam Minostentor's massive codpiece hangs an inch above it; no wonder she looks as if she's lost her appetite. I'm worried, Sam is like a big zeppelin lowering to land, the pouch containing his genitals is the gondola, and if he doesn't maneuver better, the anchor tower of the toothpick is going to drive up through the gondola.

I think about calling his wife, Jacqueline José the Ripper, to carry him off to safety under her arm, but she is Indian wrestling with Jonathan Harris and winning. Sam is bellowing something about the New Wave pricks at Harry. The conversation is taking a nasty turn, or do my ears deceive me? Sam lifts his zeppelin body and the gondola and floats back to his seat. The young Austrian looks at her untouched sandwich and when the stewardess comes by tells her to take it away.

We settle down. A Spanish movie is shown, despite the efforts of Sam and wife to get up a petition to cancel it. Harry passes the bottle to me a few more times. Good Scotch. In Rio, imported hard liquor is very expensive, which is why I usually drank the beer. The beer is better than most U.S. beers and comes in a 24-oz. bottle and costs about a quarter or 20,000 cruzeiros. I think of the article I promised to write. What were the highlights? Getting away from Rio into the heights above the city was one. Being in the poison-green jungle, close to the clouds, in the quiet, was delightful. But part of the delight came from being with people I liked. Bob Bloch, the Sheckleys, Ballard, Aldiss, Souto, Gasca, our girl guide, Monica Leib, Mrs. Bester.

The cable car ride to Sugar Loaf was even more exciting and memorable. From there you get a view of the bays and the jungle or the steep mountains in the middle of Rio. A haze hangs over the waters and the islands. You can understand how awed the first white men felt when they sailed their dirty, rickety vessels into these magnificent waters. It is hard to believe that the beautiful white-towered city below is a hell of streets filled with fender-raking, bumper touching, gas-belching, noise-farting, out-to-kill cars, mostly Volkswagens.

Up here it's serene and cool and beautiful, I hate to go back down. But I do.

Although I don't love the city, I don't hate it. It has a hustling driving air with an overlay of good humor or congeniality which American cities lack. The young generation, the under 25s, are taller than their elders. Apparently they've been well fed and are following the trend for tallness which prevails in the youth of the world. The girls are pretty and sometimes even beautiful, ranging from German type blondes to Sicilian brunettes. They dress quite mod, wear microskirts, and an air of sex hangs over the city, like an invisible cobweb.

At New York, we split. Van Vogt, Leigh Chapman, and myself go on to LA. Howlin José Hellzapoppinson says goodbye sadly. It has not been a pleasant or rewarding trip for him, for several reasons, and I'm sad because I love Howlin and wish him happiness. Success he has, but there's always a storm raging around him because there's always one raging inside him. He's like a rocket that would like to go into a parking orbit but can't turn off the fuel and so must keep going, on into extra-solar space.

I say goodbye to Harry José Harrierson, whom I also love. Harry is speaking at the University of Chicago. Subject: science fiction. You've come a long way baby. Guest lecturer at great universities and guest of the International Film Festival in Rio. We've all come a long long way, baby. I sigh. I'm happy for him and the others, but the pleasure of being in a ghetto is slowly fading away.

The customs held us up so long, we missed our plane. We stand by and get one with no trouble. The beautiful Leigh sits by herself and Van Vogt and I are side by side again and continue our conversation.

Again, I find myself revising my opinion of him. I am always doing this with Van. It seems that I come to wrong conclusions, although they're based on what he says or what he's written. He is one of SF's greats, whatever you think of his work, and he's also one of the great offbeats, the originals, a unique, and, to some, a weirdo. Personally, I've always found him very charming, amusing, educational, and rational. I remember what Daimon José Knight, whom I met at Rio for the first time, said about Van Vogt.

Daimon once wrote a long article which should have destroyed Van utterly but seems to have affected his career or the esteem of the general public not one whit. Daimon gets a wry joy out of this, because, despite his big-bertha blasting, he likes Van's stories. There is, Daimon says, something vast and slimy and intriguing going on down below, way below, in the substructure of the universes of Van's stories. This analysis catches my attention and delight. Something slimy. Now I've always thought Van's stories were based on the philosophy that this universe is founded on nothing, absolutely nothing. Except Maya perhaps.

However, at one of the negative feedback lectures held during the festival in the mornings in an almost empty theater, Van made some statements which rotated me like Charlie Brown catching a ball. Van said he was one of the few men left who believe in a worldwide Communist plot to take over Earth. Also, he stated that we're all golden fruits on a cosmic tree. In addition, he upheld Lysenko's genetics.

At that point in the speech, I said to Howlin, "Van's out of his fucking mind."

So here I am, homeward bound, finding out that I am wrong again. Van says nothing of the Communist plot, though he speaks of the other matters in his lecture. No matter. The Communists have never been backward about admitting they are out for world conquest. But there is also a capitalist plot, although the master blueprint lies scattered in a hundred thousand fragmentary phrases in a thousand books. And the Communists are fighting among themselves, as any student of human nature knew would happen.

Van explains that his statements about the golden fruits of the tree of the cosmos and about Lysenko are only statements that his (Van's) behavior and thinking are based on an as-if philosophy. In other words, he follows Vaihinger; he acts "as if" Lysenkoism were true but he would not deny that it could be false. I don't say anything about Vaihinger to Van. I remember him vaguely from my college days, when I loved philosophers, before I found out that most of them were suffering from syphilis of the psyche.

Once again, I am charmed into believing that Van is right, though I wonder if he isn't playing the flute to my cobra.

The movie begins. Bullitt. I decide to watch it. I'm crazy about private eyes or rugged policemen who fight the mafia and their own corrupted or stupid colleagues. The movie is exciting, fast, and bloody, but illogical. More illogical than the typical comic book or cartoon, but I don't fully realize this until I see it again on the broad screen, a few weeks later.

Just after the tremendously exciting—and dumb—chase through San Francisco, lightning streaks through my head. It's as if a switch had been thrown. And this, in a way, is just what happened.

I've long held that the creators, composers, painters, inventors, poets, philosophers, psychoanalysts, writers, etc., are born with their vivid imaginations. That is, in the casting of the lots, which is what, essentially, genetics is, the creative brain cells come up. Rather, the combination of cells which result in the configuration of heightened imagination. The brain cells have a peculiar hookup which enables them to perceive connections between things thought unrelated.

This happy configuration of cells may die or be repressed and, in our society, often does and is. But if the configuration is nourished, it grows, and new nerve networks grow and grow. And every once in a while, one configuration grows into another, and inspiration, revelation, comes like current when a circuit is completed. The nerves creep out like tentacles and when they touch: Light.

This sudden light in my head was the result of going to Brazil. The experience in a far country, in a strange land, opened doors of perception.

What shall I call it, the result of this light? We seem to have a need to categorize, to label, to tag. I don't want to label, but if I don't, somebody else will.

Subjectivity? Interiority?

These terms are not accurate and have too many carryovers from long usage. In-with-ness?

That's good enough for the time being.

I won't know what it really means until after digging down, layer after layer, until I get to the core, break through into my personal Pellucidar. Down there may be nothing or something vast and slimy or a fire bed of crushed protons.

In-with-ness.

What it means is writing that has little reliance on latitude or longitude, on chronometers or barometers, photographs and tape recordings, histories and newspapers, or word of mouth. In short, it's a writing which won't be concerned with accuracy about the so-called objective world. It won't rely on indications from instruments or instrument-interpreters. In-with-ness will interpret the world as it sees and remembers it. In-with-ness is a system of logic, an internal logic, just as a language does not conform to the rules of classical or symbolic logic but has its own peculiar logic. Thus English has its system and Iroquois its own and Macri its own. Each works within its own enclosed rules and yet each can be translated with more or less exactness into the other.

There is some foreshadowing, a tentativeness, a nuclear cell in the yolk, in this report on the Rio trip. For instance, my statement that the Rio beer bottles are 24-oz. bottles. I don't know that this is objectively valid, instrument-true. It seemed to me that it was. Thus I report it.

I don't know if the Sugar Loaf was east, west, or south of Rio. It seemed to me that it was east, but the next time I think of it, it may be south. It will be south, according to my internal compass.

I don't know that I'm reporting Van's speech correctly. Or as he would report it. A copy of it lies in a nearby desk; I can refer to it. But I prefer to report the impression of the speech, its conversion into the system of my logic.

But in-with-ness is not subjectivism. Subjectivism is too occupied with personal imagery. The reader does not understand the references because he is not the writer. In-with-ness is concerned with the inner latitude and longitude but is also concerned with communication. Its goal is communication. It interprets. There may be something lost in the interpretation but better a loss than impenetrability.

In-with-ness will not experiment with style in that sense that Joyce and William Burroughs did. The English will be straight enough (most of the time), but the difference is in the translation. Joyce and Burroughs and Ballard, for instance, are also translators, but the first two are experimenters in style, as if they were trying to create new languages. Ballard uses the conventional language in conventional syntax, but he seems to be trying to speak Iroquois with an English vocabulary.

Joyce is like bits of wreckage floating up from the bottom of the mind-dark sea. Burroughs is fluid and shifting and nonsequential, like bits of a horror film spliced at random. Ballard is a somnambulist carving images out of a quartz landscape.

In-with-ness won't show up immediately in my work. I will brood on it and with it and let it brood on me. For the present, I'll finish up the novels and short stories I've already started in the same style I began them. To rework them would spoil the stories and also the concept of in-with-ness. And I will use the old styles and approaches in series I've been publishing for some time: the Riverworld and Wolff-Kickaha series.

This is what going to Brazil means to me, this is the travelog of the mind.

NOTE: A friend to whom I showed this said, "You're one of the nuts on the cosmic tree Van talked about!"

So be it.

Getting A-Long
with Heinlein

First published in *Moebius Trip Library's SF Echo*, Number 19, January 1974.

In 1961 Heinlein dedicated *Stranger in a Strange Land* to Phil and two others (Fredric Brown and Robert Cronog). Phil was the first author to treat sex overtly in the SF genre. Since Heinlein had wanted for a while to be able to publish material dealing with sexual themes, he may have felt that Farmer had helped pave the way for him to be able to write a book like *Stranger in a Strange Land.*

Farmer's very in-depth analysis of *Time Enough for Love* and where Heinlein was at this stage of his career shows that Phil honestly liked the book in contrast to other, less favourable, reviews.

A long time ago, the summer of 1941, I first read Heinlein's *Methuselah's Children* as a serial in *Astounding.* Though many of the readers of *Moebius Trip* probably were not born then, all must by now have read this story in hardcover or softcover. And all must be aware of Heinlein's Future History series, of the Grand Plan of the future into which a number of his works fit. *Methuselah's Children* was one of the earliest, one of the few demanding a sequel, and the one for which we may be thankful Heinlein was in no hurry to write the sequel. If *Time Enough for Love (TEFL)* had been written in, say, 1951, it would not have been the same book. Not by any means. Heinlein was then still in his first "phase" or "period," his so-called "juvenile" stage. I'd prefer to call it his Classical 1 or Nonsexual Phase. Never mind the labels. Or, if we must have them, call Phase 1 his "Caterpillar" stage. Call Phase 2, the present one, the "Late Pupal" stage. What comes next? Hopefully, the Imago, the full-blown butterfly, stage. I say this because I don't think that *TEFL* is Heinlein's final word by any means. He is always the paradoxical, the surprising, and his works of the Pupal Stage contain contradictory elements.

Maybe a better analogy would be one based on Hegel's thesis, antithesis, and synthesis. Heinlein's Stage One, the early, the Astounding-juvenile, stage is thesis. The present one is antithesis. The next is synthesis, where he'll quit fucking around about fucking, take sexual attitudes for granted, and describe them only *en passant*. The verbiage necessary to set forth all the details of his safari into darkest sex will no longer be needed; we should have then a third Heinlein, one who is actually a melding of the best of the "old" and the "new" or present Heinlein.

I once commented to an editor that Heinlein was writing for therapeutic reasons. This was reported in a fanzine, and the report gave the wrong impression. What was lacking was my follow-up comment that all writers write for therapeutic reasons.

I don't mean by this that writers write only for therapy. That statement would be nonsense. Misleading, anyway. Most writers have a talent which they use to make money, just as engineers and claims adjusters and Mafia killers have talents which they use to make money. But the latter do not feel the need to project their internal conflicts, their personal Angst and Weltsicht, as fiction. They may concretize objectively their subjective secretions—excrete as it were—but these are "real" phenomena. And, be it noted, ephemeral. Buildings and bridges and cars, settled claims, and murders take place in the real world, but their effects vanish after some passage of time. Or at least are not obvious. Bridges and cars rust and disappear, settled claims result in the exchange of paper and direction of actions but these do not endure, and though a murder is a permanent act, both victims and killer are forgotten after a while.

But a work of fiction, if it has any merit, endures. An unreal thing, it lasts long after real things have vanished into the past.

And in this sense, the production of unreal things via very real but invisible feelings, writers are writing for therapy. Even the most commercial, the ultimate of hacks, the formula writer, casts his formulae into personal form. Their shape is not quite like anybody else's. But they are too much like many others, and so they are not memorable. Their impression on the reader is slight.

Heinlein's works, whatever their faults, whatever the scorn and excoriations they bring out in various readers and critics, are memorable. He is denounced as a "right-winger," a "Fascist," an "old-time robber capitalist," etc., but the denouncers are very much aware of the story and the characters and the plot, and they won't forget what they scorn with such vehemence. It is true that memorableness is not necessarily equated with merit or a high value. You can read a story in your youth, be tremendously impressed with it, in fact, never forget it, not even if you live to be a hundred. Yet rereading it as an adult you see that it has very little merit; it struck you because you were young and somewhat of a tabula rasa. This is not the case with Heinlein's stories. When I reread the early ones, I find them as good as when I first read them. And even if I had not reread them in recent years, I would remember them.

The point is that, whether you love or hate Heinlein's works, you don't forget them. He is a great individualistic writer; though he has no distinct style, he is as distinctive a writer as the very self-conscious stylists Ballard, W. Burroughs and Lafferty. And he sometimes manages, though mostly in his earlier works, to create a character who lives and breathes and whose death can evoke tears. At least, that is my reaction. Whereas none of the three mentioned above, despite their great writing skill (or even genius, if you will), have so far been able to create three-dimensional, flesh and blood, people. Their characters are as flat as, no, flatter than, those in the Doc Savage stories. This is heresy, I know, and if it is, so be it.

Yes, I know that Ballard, Burroughs, and Lafferty are not concerned with showing real human beings. They are out to show their peculiar world-pictures, and they do so very effectively. But, at the same time, I believe that they would give you real human beings in their works if they were capable of doing so. I don't think they are capable. They are geniuses but stunted geniuses. Or is "stunted" too harsh? I don't really think so. Edgar Allen Poe was a genius, but a stunted genius in comparison with, say, Fielding or Dickens or Tolstoy or Dostoyevsky.

What does this have to do with *Time Enough for Love*? And what's all this talk about real human beings? Surely Farmer isn't saying that Heinlein's protagonists are real human beings? Do they really exist? Does anyone anywhere know even one such person as Lazarus Long? Has there ever existed such a man, one so quick, so wise, so crafty-cunning, so horny, so healthy, so "survival-fraught," to coin a phrase? Consider this description of Woodrow Wilson Smith, known also as Lazarus Long (not to mention a hundred other aliases).

He has a heart which is unusually large and beats slowly. He has only 28 teeth, no caries, and is immune to infection. He has never needed surgery except for wounds or rejuvenation treatment. His reflexes are almost superhumanly fast. His eyesight is perfect; he can hear into the subsonic and supersonic further than other human beings. His color vision takes in indigo. And he was born with no vermiform appendix and without a foreskin. Also, Heinlein adds, "without a conscience." All these desirable and rare characteristics are due to genetic mutation.

In addition, just about everybody he runs across in *TEFL* (including a thing, a computer) wants Long to lay her, him, it.

And, though he can be killed, he isn't going to be. He is, in effect, immortal, that is, unless he just gets tired of living and gives up the ghost.

Know anybody like that? Perhaps you do. I have one candidate, but you wouldn't believe me if I identified him, so I won't. The point is that it doesn't matter whether or not there are such people. Is Lazarus Long believable while you're reading *TEFL*? He was for me; to me he seemed a flesh and blood person and *TEFL* was a genuine biography. If he also seemed to be a gabby old man, and there were times when I wished he would shut up and do something, that only added to the realism. Besides, it was worth the often too-long dialog (or monolog) to get to the juicy parts. And Heinlein's extrapolative powers (always superb) have not diminished in this novel. Not by any means.

Of course, people will say that Long is just an extension or variation of Heinlein's heroes and that Long is also Heinlein. Or Heinlein as he would like to be. And they'll be right. And so what?

Let's look at the other side of the coin, in this case, Ballard. His protagonists (or antiheros, I should say) are extensions of the previous ones. In other words, all alike. And they are also Ballard. (Admittedly, not Ballard as he would like to be but Ballard as he is or Ballard as he conceives Everyman to be.) And if Heinlein's heroes are examples of what Aldiss calls "the power fantasy," Ballard's are examples of "the powerless or castrated fantasy." Ineffectual and too weary and pooped even to whimper.

Your real person, Everyman and Everywoman, is somewhere between the two poles of Heinlein's Wolfman and Ballard's Slugman. Some are closer to one than to the other, and some are very close to one or the other. The Wolfman is at least operating, he's alive, he's doing something for himself (though often doing it to others), but the Slugman has just given up.

NOTE: Pause to consider that I am not glorifying Heinlein or downing Ballard as far as their overall merits go. I'm just talking about their type of (anti-) heroes. I like to read Ballard because of the structure of his stories, the peculiar geometric Weltsicht they project, and the occasional poetry. And I also like W. Burroughs because he gives me a deeper glimpse into hell than Dante can.

I think that one of the best ways to see that Heinlein can't be neatly labeled or categorized or stuffed and mounted is to look at a recent review of *TEFL*. Richard Lupoff wrote about *TEFL* in the November, 1973 issue of *ALGOL*. Lupoff hates the book, says it's the worst novel of 1973, and at the same time he admits he *loves* it, and it is the only book he reviews that infuses life into his reviewer's voice. The only one he gets genuinely enthusiastic about, though in a negative fashion. Much of what he says in his anti-Heinleining is true, but what he says proves that you can tell the truth and yet lie if you only tell part of the truth.

To prove that Heinlein's hero Long is a pseudo-Mao, an egotistic dimwit, he quotes one of Long's maxims from his Notebooks. This is: "Masturbation is cheap, clean, convenient, and free of any possibility of wrongdoing—and you don't have to go home in the cold. But it's lonely."

If all the maxims were of this level, Lupoff would be correct in scorning Long's "wisdom." But they are not. In fact, about two-thirds of them are novel or amusing and well worth quoting. Yet Lupoff picks the worst, one which, by the way, did not originate with Long. It's a variation on an old folk phrase which has been around for several centuries and which I first heard when I was sixteen and carrying water for a streetcar line repair crew.

Let me quote you a few maxims which will show you that Lupoff was distorting the notebooks of Lazarus Long with a sin of omission.

"One man's theology is another man's belly laugh." (A variation of that could be: One man's ideology is another man's bellyache, but let it pass.)

"It's amazing how much 'mature wisdom' resembles being too tired."

"Your enemy is never a villain in his own eyes. Keep this in mind; it may offer a way to make him your friend. If not, you can kill him without hate—and quickly."

"A brute kills for pleasure, a fool for hate."

"A woman is not property, and husbands who think otherwise are living in a dreamworld."

"All men are created unequal."

"Yield to temptation; it may not pass your way again."

"All cats are *not* gray after midnight. Endless variety—."

"Secrecy is the beginning of tyranny."

"...Keep your children short on pocket money—but long on hugs."

I could go on and would like to. But let the reader take them all in himself. And then judge if this is a dyed-in-the-wool, misogynist, warmongering, capitalistic ultrafascist.

Lupoff says that Heinlein has a patronizing attitude towards women and that it makes his blood boil. He'd love to see a militant feminist have a go at the book. Well, so would I. But I'd want a perceptive militant feminist to do the critique, and she (or he) might not agree with Lupoff.

After all, Long admits (laughing the meanwhile) that he has been cuckolded a number of times nor does he blame the woman for having put the horns on him. He may be a superstud (though he never says so himself), but he's had plenty of wives who got tired of him. And vice versa.

The prime maxim of a society should be, Long says, women and children first. If it isn't, the society does not survive and wasn't worth saving while it did live. Anybody going to argue with that? And how many societies are actually based on this? Is ours?

Lupoff criticizes Heinlein because the universe (galaxy, anyway) in *TEFL* is inhabited only by man (Earth's colonists) and one race which agreeably keeps to itself. Lupoff cites this as an example of Heinlein's human chauvinism. In the first place, it's evident from *Methuselah's Children* that there is more than one nonhuman species in the galaxy. In the second place, for literary reasons, there is no reason the author can't assume that most planets are uninhabited by sentients. I don't believe that this is true; statistically, there should be at least a million inhabited worlds in this galaxy alone. But I don't think Heinlein believes this either. If he did, why has he presented so many nonhumans in his previous novels?

It seems to be true that Heinlein cannot conceive of any desirable economy other than capitalism. I say *seems* because a close study of his novels might upset this notion. And also he isn't through writing, and so you don't know what this surprising man is going to come up with. My own viewpoint, which I've made elsewhere in some detail, is that all three present systems of economy, capitalism, socialism, and communism are obsolete and brutal and wasteful and should be done away with posthaste. But I don't expect them to be so treated. I expect that all three will evolve slowly into something quite different from their present state, perhaps meld into one. That is, if we don't collapse first and go back to a primitive agricultural and barter system—after a billion or so casualties.

Lupoff says that the politics of the book are "violently and blatantly anti-democratic."

Read the notebooks again, Richard.

Still, Lupoff does have a good point when he says that "everything is expressed with a kind of snide superiority that brooks no disagreement or even discussion beyond the level of 'Please tell us more, Lazarus dear.'"

On the other hand, consider that Long is an ancient ancestor of practically the whole human race and can exercise his right to be Chairman of the Galaxy if he wishes. Thus, the depiction of everybody as being awed by him and eager to please him is valid.

Let me backtrack for a minute. One of the things that I disagree most vehemently with is Heinlein's attitude towards prostitution. The Notebook says: "A whore should be judged by the same criteria as other professionals offering services for pay—such as dentists, lawyers, hair dressers, physicians, plumbers, etc." Well, yes, except that I don't think that any sane humane society would have, or need to have, prostitutes. I think that Heinlein thinks that they're a natural product of society. And a quite acceptable part. Or does he? There is some evidence that he equates them with lawyers or perhaps places them on a higher level. It's hard to say what his exact attitude towards prostitutes, and the men who use them, is. I get the impression that he believes that they're inevitable and that the attitude towards them should change. Instead of being pariahs, necessary evils, exploited by pimps and courts and, of course, their customers, they should become an honorable profession. I'll go along with that—if prostitution is inevitable. But I don't think it is; I think that it's a grim grisly exploitation which no healthy society would endure for a minute. *TEFL*, like many of Heinlein's works, contains, or seems to contain, contradictions in philosophy and economy and psychology and all the other -ologies. Read *TEFL* and judge for yourself. But don't leap to conclusions; think, instead of reacting with conditioned reflexes.

———————

(The above is essentially a "first draft". However, such a situation was brought about more by Phil's having to enter the hospital for tests, etc., than by his pressing writing schedule. Due to the time lost, the latter must take precedence over whatever polishing—and lengthening—might have been done on this critique.

Fortunately, Phil got out of the hospital without losing any of his permanent attachments.—Ed Connor, a fellow Peorian and Editor of *Moebius Trip*.)

God's Hat

First published in *Heavy Metal,* Number 54, September 1981.

This piece was originally titled "Farmer on Wilson" and sat alongside a piece by Wilson titled (appropriately enough) "Wilson on Farmer." Wilson's article was a review/discussion of the Riverworld series.

Robert Anton Wilson (RAW) is the Kilgore Trout of Quantum-Cum-Cthulhu universes. A rereading of his books always turns up something you'd not apprehended the first time. Also, he's very quotable, a true poet: that is, a master or testersterstoned mistress who (or which) is inspired by the muse, who sometimes looks like a moose and who dwells in the mews (labyrinthal or feline or both), a Krazy Kat bammed by the photonic Brick of Ignatz Mouse (read: Ignites Muse).

Though I'd heard much about the *Illuminatus Triology* (which RAW wrote with Robert Shea), it wasn't until five months ago that I read it. I was at once bewitched by this "paranoid" *Gulliver's Travels.* I also thought perhaps RAW had been somewhat influenced by me—which was only fair since I was, in turn, being influenced by him in a helicoidal or helicoital feedback. (But, as I and he maintain, every quantum that's rubbed elbows influences every other, though they're twenty-three billion light-years apart.)

Shea and RAW parted company, though not quantum influence, and RAW wrote *The Cosmic Trigger*, which unexplained the trilogy. He then went on with *Masks of the Illuminati* and *Schrödinger's Cat*, a three-volume *Allah's in Wonderland.* These books are vital for your health, though the recommendation carries more weight in this universe than in the one next door. Or is it vice versa?

RAW's works, though he may not know it, are codes. Work them out, and you'll know the secret of the universes. The codes are not sent by people/things from Sirius. RAW is confused. The messages do come through the area of Sirius, but they are from a "place" a googol-plex of light-years and several universes beyond Sirius. Really? Not really. The source transceiver is here in

Peoria, but the bending of the medium caused by SMUT (Space-Matter-Uber-Time) makes the codes come from way behind but along the line of sight of Sirius. (Dirty time is slower than clean time. And who dirtied it?)

I had a vision eight years ago. (Consider the octave and its temporality of significance.) The vision meant nothing until I read *Schrödinger's Cat.* Then I realized what I thought it meant. And now RAW will translate for me the meaning of this vision (from Peoria round-about the line of sight of Sirius), and then I'll translate his translation for him. And so on. Feedback.

Though Melville omitted it, Captain Ahab said. "In one sense, Aleister Crowley is lower than whale shit. In another, he's as high as God's hat. The true shaman knows that God's hat is made out of dried whale shit."

To Forry Ackerman, the Wizard of Sci-Fi

First published in *LUNACON '74 Convention Program Book*, 1974.

Phil and Forrest J Ackerman are well acquainted. To the point where, in *Image of the Beast*, the character Woolston Heepish is a parody of Forry. In its sequel, *Blown*, Forrest J Ackerman appears as himself.

Bette Farmer: "We spent many pleasant evenings at Forry's and Wendy's home. Around the holidays they would divide their friends into groups of 6 or 8 and have about 4 parties, one on each Saturday night for about 4 weeks. Everyone was always asking, "Are you going to the 3rd party or the 4th or what?" They were always lovely, fun parties with wonderful food. One time Forry didn't show up until half way thru the meal. He was in the basement working on his wonderful collection. It was a wonderful world—'The Ackermansion,' and a privilege to be a part of it."

I knew Forry Ackerman years before I met him.

Our first audiovisual contact was in 1953 at the World Science Fiction Convention hosted by the Philadelphia fans. But I had been very much aware of Forry Ackerman since 1929. That was the year I started to read science fiction magazines, in this case, Hugo Gernsback's *Air Wonder* and *Science Wonder*. It seemed to me then that every issue contained a letter from Forry in "The Reader Speaks" column. These were all signed quite formally: Forrest J. Ackerman.

Note the punctuation after the J. In those days Forry had periods.

Though I had not the slightest idea what he looked like, I envisioned a man about six feet six inches tall, very wide-shouldered, black-haired, and having a huge battleship-prow chin and piercing gray eyes. (All heroes had gray eyes in those days.) This image of a Tarzan-like superman was based on the extreme militance and excessive vigor of his letters. Never had I read such prose!

Of course, in these days, when we have become accustomed to such as Harlan Ellison, the language seems mild. But at that time it was considered not very nice.

Here's an example from an early *Amazing Stories*. This was, by the way, edited by T. O'Conor Sloane, Ph.D. Sloane was remarkable, or perhaps strange would be a better word, for two characteristics. One, he stated flatly that space travel was impossible. Two, he took so long to make up his mind about the stories submitted to him that many writers were convinced he went into hibernation in early November and did not emerge from his hole until late March. He took two years to decide on a novel submitted by Charlie Tanner, which provoked Charlie to write a letter of enquiry in which the editor was addressed as "To, Oh, Come On, Slow One!"

However, Sloane did print promptly the letters from his readers, and I reproduce a typical letter from Forry. This appeared in the Discussions section of the January 1932 issue of *Amazing Stories*. Forry's address at that time was 530 Staples Avenue, San Francisco, California. Here it is, verbatim and entire, so you may get some idea of the Forry Ackerman of that day, the Forry then generally considered the Demosthenes, the William Pitt, the J. J. Pierce, of SF letterhacks.

Preceding the letter, in big black letters, was the customary prefatory comment by T. O'Conor Sloane himself.

A CORRESPONDENT WHO SAYS WE DON'T KNOW OUR SHIRT FROM SHINOLA, BUT LIKES OUR STUFF ANYWAY.

Editor, Amazing Stories:

I beg of you to print this. You've been publishing stories lately containing brickbats so you surely should print this.

Where are the great illustrations and the great stories of yester-year? Gone, gone with the (censored, Ed.)-ing snows. What's happened? Where did you go wrong? Good Heavens! I once thought you were the greatest, but I now think you're a (censored, Ed.)-head. You used to make me cream in my jeans once a month, make me swoon with ecstasy, when your rag hit the stands. But lately you've been feeding me and the long-suffering public a pile of (censored, Ed.).

Where are the incredible artists and the sense of wonder of the *Amazing Stories* I once knew? Gone, gone down the (censored, Ed.)-ing drain. What happened to the incomparable Paul, Wesso, Morey? Where are the giants of purple prose: Ed Earl Repp, G. Peyton

Wertenbaker, Captain S. P. Meek, Hendrik Dahl Juve, J. Lewis Burtt, B.Sc., Miles J. Breuer, M.D., and Wood Jackson? These are all immortal names, destined to go down through the ages as classics, read as long as the English language lasts.

Your rivals, the twin magazines (censored, Ed.) have illustrations by these great artists and these great authors. So what's wrong with you, you (censored, Ed.)hole? Get these giants back and quit publishing tired old reprints of Verne and Wells and Rousseau, you cheap (censored, Ed.).

Otherwise, your rag isn't bad at all, and if it ceased publication I'd just die.

After Forry's letter, the editor added his usual comment. Or perhaps it wasn't so usual.

(Up yours, too, Forrest J. Ackerman. And in reply to your letter of October 20th, 1931, why should we pay you a cent a word for your letters? That's more than our authors get, when they get it.)

I hope I'm not shocking any of the thousands of Forry's admirers by exposing his youthful vitriolics or, as some might claim with some justification, lack of self-control. I quote this letter merely to show the contrast between the impetuous juvenile Jeremiah of the early 1930s and the Forry that we have known for so many years: the mild-mannered owner and occupant of stately Ackermansion. I was surprised when I first met Forry. I had expected a fiery stentorian-voiced eat-em-up-alive juggernaut. Instead, I found a pleasant gentle-voiced man of about my own age, one remarkably well informed on SF and fantasy and movies. (I didn't know about his colossal collection then.) I was also to discover, through the years, that here was a man with about the biggest heart going, one without a trace of that vindictiveness and malice that most human beings have, whatever other good qualities they possess. Time and again, I've been amazed and touched at his generosity, his idealism, his gentleness, his constant kindnesses, and his thoughtfulnesses.

To keep from being accused of oversentimentality, I'll say here that Forry is not perfect. But then who is? And he has peccadilloes but no true sins.

One of the things about him that sticks in my mind, and there are many, is the yellow brick road he had in back of his house on Sherbourne Drive. Yes, Forry did have a yellow brick road in his backyard, hence the title of this encomium. I first saw it when I took my six-year-old granddaughter to show her the Ackermansion, its objets d'art, and its lord and master. Forry conducted her through every room, explaining what this and that was and where it came from. Then he led us out to the backyard, and we saw the yellow brick road. It started out just like the road in the movie, spiraled, and then, alas, disappeared. But my granddaughter Kim was delighted, entranced, I should say. She has never forgotten that, never will, I suppose. There really *is* a yellow brick road of Oz, and though she has her suspicions about the authenticity of Santa Claus, she doesn't have the slightest doubt about the existence of the yellow brick road.

Neither do I, and I suspect that Forry's faith is as deep as mine.

Forry, you see, is the man who built the yellow brick road. From fantasy, he constructed reality. And this is what he's been doing all his life. He fell in love with SF, and he took what was basically fantasy and built a real world out of it. He put together the fantastic Ackercollection in his Ackermansion, and he built his own life at the same time in accordance with the blueprints of SF. As SF grew, he grew, and vice versa.

So, Forrest J Ackerman, here's a *salud,* a toast, to you. I won't be at the Lunacon to lift a glass in your presence. But I'll be doing it here at home the night the attendees are honoring you. Here's to the Old Master Painter of Future Vistas, the Preserver and Advancer of Sci-fi, the Contractor Who Built the Yellow Brick Road.

Pornograms and Supercomputers

First published in the *New York Times Book Review*, September 2, 1984.

This is a review of Lem's *Imaginary Magnitude*, 1984.

Phil: "'Some things do not bear looking into.' Perhaps that can be said about the whole universe, about everything."

⚜

Stanislaw Lem, the Polish author, has been praised as the world's greatest writer of science-fiction. Those who know the field know that there is not a "greatest" in this peculiar genre. It's a democracy of monarchs, each ruling his or her own province of talent, each unique. Theodore Sturgeon and Thomas Pynchon, for instance, exceed Mr. Lem in depicting "real" people and are just as "idea-inventive." Mr. Lem, however, has no equal in his literary explorations of machines and their physical and philosophical potentialities.

This is not surprising. Mr. Lem has stated that he is more interested in things and objects than in human beings. The theme he stresses in most of his work is that machines will someday be as human as Homo sapiens and perhaps superior to him. Mr. Lem has an almost Dickensian genius for vividly realizing the tragedy and comedy of future machines; the death of one of his androids or computers actually wrings sorrow from the reader.

Since Mr. Lem is a world class author, comparisons between the great Polish author Joseph Conrad (who wrote in English) and Mr. Lem (who writes in Polish) are pertinent. Both are deeply pessimistic, but Mr. Lem (like Mark Twain) uses humor as an instrument to deal with the tragic and the inevitable. Conrad, through one of his characters, Mrs. Verloc in *The Secret Agent*, expresses one of his final conclusions about life: Some things do not bear looking into.

Mr. Lem not only does not mind the unbearable, he delights in it, plunging headlong into agony. Highly trained in science, he knows that, in a sense, there is no good or evil and that the universe is indifferent to us, also that it is inexhaustible in entities that Homo sapiens will never comprehend. Although our end is puzzlement and death, Mr. Lem dances with Pan, and we enjoy his dancing.

Imaginary Magnitude is not a novel but a collection of imaginary introductions to books that do not yet exist. It is a sequel to his *Perfect Vacuum*, which was made up of reviews of nonexistent books. Here, the first introduction is Mr. Lem's introduction to introductions, after which comes the introduction to the imaginary Cezary Strzybisz's *Necrobes*. This introduction, like those that follow, require readers to have more than a smattering of classical literature, Latin, formal logic, mathematics, physics, chemistry, philosophy, linguistics, history, computer lore, and cybernetics.

On the other hand, where else can you read about Pornograms, the new art of taking X-ray photographs of people during group sex? Where else, as in the introduction to Reginald Gulliver's *Eruntics*, can you read about a scientist who teaches bacteria to write English? Who else could make you believe that this is possible?

Juan Rambellais's introduction to *A History of Bitic Literature* is even more amusing and intellectually stimulating and could be a gold mine for science-fiction writers who have trouble finding new ideas. In this, Mr. Lem (as elsewhere) sneers at "sci-fi" as trivial literature. Or is he satirizing those obtuse academics, miseducated fossils who themselves scorn science-fiction?

Among the riches in this collection are an encyclopedia that gives its readers future knowledge and a supercomputer that rebels against its intended misuse by the American military—not for moral reasons, since machines, even though sentient, know nothing of human morality; it just wants to be its own "man," a being that humans cannot understand. Though the "Golem" sections are, among many other things, a satire on United States politics and the Pentagon, they also satirize the Soviets but without actually naming them. Mr. Lem, who now lives in Vienna, walks a tightrope as far as Poland is concerned, but he manages to semaphore his revulsion for the inhumane regime there.

Mr. Lem, a science-fiction Bach, plays in this book a googolplex (the figure 1 followed by a staggering number of zeroes) of variations on his basic themes. That is, we will never comprehend all of the non-Homo sapiens world, and machines will someday be equal or superior to their maker.

A few words of praise for Marc Heine, the translator, who deserves more than a few words. Mr. Lem's works are Carrollian in their puns and portmanteau words. Most of them cannot be translated literally into English. Yet Mr. Heine finds equivalents or approximations, and brilliantly transposes the sprightliness and intellectual leap-frogging that so distinguishes Mr. Lem's writing.

A Review of *Chrysalis*

First published in *Algol,* Spring 1978.

Another book review by Phil which, again, shows to best advantage his extensive reading habits and his ability to not take things at face value.

⚜

"...ALL ORIGINAL...ALL UNFORGETABLE..."
"NEW WORLDS UNFOLD FROM THE PENS OF THE MOST TALENTED SCIENCE FICTION WRITERS OF THIS GENERATION"

Over the years, pressure, fueled by irritation and sometimes anger, has been building up in my boiler. So, though this is supposed to be a review of, not a critical article about, *Chrysalis,* I'm taking this opportunity to vent a little steam. Not about the anthology but about blurbs and covers.

The stories herein have not been printed before. No argument there. But are they all unforgettable? That, I think, depends upon whether or not the reader has a photographic or Asimovian memory. If you're of a lesser breed, you will soon forget some of the works, though I hasten to add that they're all excellent.

Are these tales really from the pens or typewriters of *the most talented science fiction writers of this generation?* The contributors are all talented. But the blurb states the stories are by the most talented SF writers. So, where are Lafferty, Le Guin, Lem, Aldiss, Ballard, Heinlein, and a slew of others?

It's the omission of "some of" just before *the most* that irks me. Where is the truth in advertising?

And what does *this generation* mean? Ted Sturgeon has been writing SF fantasy since 1939. Lupoff and Ellison, though not hoary old men, have been around a long time, the latter since the 50's.

Blurb writers get me down and send me up. For instance, the inner dust jacket of a recent novel of mine states that Leslie Fiedler has called me "the greatest writer of science fiction." That makes me cringe and blush. Fiedler never said or even intimated such a thing nor does he believe that. Nor would I commend such a statement if it had been made. It seems that every time I pick up an SF book it's been written by the greatest SF writer. Hyperbole, thy name is Blurbwretch.

The cover art for *Chrysalis* is adequate: I've nothing against it. But I've seen so many illustrations that have nothing to do with the story. I'm not talking about symbolic art. But why do the illustrators of so many naturalistic or realistic covers depict scenes not in the text? Why, when the writer has gone to such pains to describe the characters, the artifacts, the situations, does the illustrator ignore these and make up his own?

Why put birds on and a moon above a planet which the text clearly says does not have them? Why give the hero a moustache when it's been stated that he's clean-shaven? Why a cover depicting the hero leading a horse on which the heroine rides when there are no horses in the story and, in fact, one of the premises is that no horses exist in the maritime empire? Why, if the author describes one as a rigid, one as a semi-rigid, and one as a blimp, does the artist draw three rigids on the cover? None of which look like the ships described in any detail.

These examples are from three books of mine. There are many other examples from my books and mucho from works by others.

Having gotten some gripes out of the way (admirably restraining myself), on to the text.

"Discovery of the Ghooric Zone - March 15, 2337" by Richard Lupoff is a satire on Lovecraft and various forms of purple-prose fantasy/SF. It's also much more. Though it doesn't have the impact, the socko, which unforgettable stories are supposed to have, it is very clever and, in a way, unforgettable. It's so curious that a reader may remember it years from now.

Spider Robinson's "The Magnificent Conspiracy" is a very warm and human story, up to his usual high level. It should stick in my memory, and it's my favorite of the anthology. Read. Enjoy.

Chelsea Quinn Yarbro's "Allies" and Thomas Monteleone's "The Curandeiro" would distinguish any anthology. Both have the trappings of hardcore SF but are human-oriented psychological stories. Yarbro's has a gimmick which is interesting but irrelevant to her tale. It's written so that the reader won't know the sex of the characters. If the editor hadn't told me about it, I'd never have noticed.

Here's Sturgeon's first new story in five years, according to the editor, the poignant "Harry's Note." It's an intellectually stimulating but emotionally saddening story about the unknown, possibly dying because unused, potentiality of the human brain. A recurring Sturgeon theme. Ted means it to be optimistic, but I don't come to the same conclusions he does.

Elizabeth A. Lynn, a fine and up-and-coming writer, is represented by two very short works, "Mindseye" and "The Man Who Was Pregnant." If The New Yorker took SF, it might buy these.

"The Dark of Legends, The Light of Lies" by Charles L. Grant is about the tyranny and waste of rigid conformity and its legalized enforcement. It's also about writers. It's told very well, but Grant has written better. (I shouldn't have said that but must. After all, is every story of a writer expected to be his best? Hopefully, yes, but it just ain't possible. Should writers write only when their biorhythm charts tell them it's O.K.? Nonsense. Some of the greatest stories have come from writers who, at the time of writing, were feeling sad, lonely, angry, bitter, generally down.)

Last on the list is Harlan Ellison's "How's the Night Life on Cissalda?" Ellison is among the ten top writers in SF, in my list at least, but this offering is a finger exercise. It really isn't fair to compare it to "The Deathbird" or "Pretty Maggie Moneyes." It's amusing, and it's not the weakest in the book. But a more judicious editor shouldn't have made it the final story, not if he wanted the book to end on a strong, perhaps even unforgettable, note.

Though I'm a book collector, I'm not a magpie. If I don't intend to reread a book, I give it away. Chrysalis, however will stay on my shelves.

Review of
The Prometheus Project

First published in *Science Fiction Review*, Number 39, August 1970.

A review of *The Prometheus Project; mankind's search for long-range goals* by Gerald Feinberg, 1969.

This article illustrates that genetic engineering was as much a topic for discussion and concern over 30 years ago, as it is today.

⁂

"This book is intended, quite literally, to change the world," the dust jacket blurb says. Indeed it is, and in a constructive sense, which is pleasant news. Many books are intended to change the world but not always for a goal of which men of good will can approve.

The author, a young man with a Ph.D. in physics, is concerned about man's long-range goals, of which, so far, man has none, barring the religious. Dr. Feinberg fears that certain decisions about the use of certain scientific devices will automatically eliminate other decisions and devices. Once a road is taken, it may be impossible to retrace your steps and take another road. Thus, the decision to use atomic energy was made without any consideration for anything other than an immediate goal.

Dr. Feinberg believes that mankind should ask, first, what kind of questions mankind should ask. Then mankind should look for answers. And the question-asking and decision-making should not be left up to the state governments. They should be done on as democratic a basis as possible, since everybody will be affected for generations to come.

For instance, what directions should molecular engineering take? How much changing of man's genes will be permitted? If mankind transforms himself through biological manipulations, he will produce a man with a different set of interests and potentialities. And, once having started down one biological highway, he may regret having taken that irreversible route.

Dr. Feinberg suggests many long-range goals in many fields; biological, economic, social, psychological, astronautic, and religiophilosophical. He describes the dangers and the attractions and benefits of personal immortality, one goal that almost everyone will want to study.

Feinberg goes through the many problems of long-range goals very methodically and coolly, yet he gives the impression of being, at the same time, very concerned. He believes that mankind doesn't have the time now to wait for some gifted individual to appear and formulate goals for mankind. Moses, Jesus, Mahmet, Guatama, and others have done this in the past. But their goals, and their systems to attain these, were irrational and are irrelevant for these times (as I interpret his comments). Now is the time—past time, perhaps—for the Prometheus (that is, Forethought) Project. And all of man should take part in the process of formulating the goals.

Very good. Very stimulating. The book rings true, and I recommend it. I hope that enough people get interested in this book to form Prometheus Project groups and initiate Feinberg's proposals.

But it took me a long time to finish the book. The style is fairly easy and clear, and the ideas are stimulating, as I said. But when I began to read, I came across a passage which threw me. And it stopped me for considerable stretches of time whenever I started the book again.

On page 23 of the hardcover edition I read: "My own concern with more remote problems is based on the optimistic estimate that *most of our immediate problems will be solved in a relatively short time by the march of technology and the worldwide spread of those aspects of Western culture responsible for our high living standards*...Since I regard such problems as relatively short term, I will not deal with them in any detail here." (Italics are mine)

Is a man who believes this far too naïve and idealistic to be taken seriously? Does his blindness, or ignoring, of current problems discredit what he has to say about our long-range goals and their attainability? If we don't solve the problems of overpopulation, war, urban decay, civil rights, and pollution (and especially pollution) we won't be here to ponder long-range goals.

Dr. Feinberg's attitude towards present problems put me off again and again. But I finally forced myself to break through the blindness barrier. And I found a book that I recommend and commend. Science-fiction fans should like it, since Dr. Feinberg refers to a number of SF books, and the Prometheus Project sounds as if it could be the basic idea of a book by Dr. Asimov or Piers Anthony.

But we had better start a project to have our world (not just our nation) cleaned up very soon. Otherwise, Prometheus will die, not from a vulture's beak but by strangulation in garbage solid, liquid, and gaseous.

Review of
How the Wizard Came to Oz

First published in *Locus,* Number 380, September 1992.

A review of *How the Wizard Came to Oz* by Donald Abbott, 1991.

✦✦✦

At the age of seven (1925), I read the first book in the Oz series, *The Wonderful Wizard of Oz* (first published in 1900). It was indeed wonderful. Since then, I've read and frequently reread all of L. Frank Baum's Oz books and many by other writers. Thus, I was glad to review the Abbott novella.

As the title indicates, it's an "origins" story about how O. Z. Diggs, a goodhearted circus ventriloquist and balloonist was blown to the Land of Oz. It also tells how this gifted conman became Oz, the Great and Terrible, and the builder of the Emerald City. Herein the reader is introduced to the Cowardly Lion, the Tin Woodman, the Scarecrow, and many other characters whom Dorothy was to encounter when she landed among the Munchkins.

The prose and style is closely modeled on Baum's. Abbott's illustrations are in the style of W.W. Denslow, the artist for Baum's first Oz novel. I can't tell the difference between their works.

Abbott's narrative goes swiftly and keeps your attention just as Baum did in the 14 novels, except for the boring *The Road to Oz.*

How the Wizard Came to Oz should be a fun trip for all Oz fans and for fantasy fans who still retain their childhood sense of wonder.

Oft Have I Travelled

Oft Have I Travelled

First published in *The Pontine Dossier,* April 1969.

This piece is an appreciation of August Derleth, who is perhaps, now, best known for his association with HP Lovecraft. August Derleth founded Arkham House with the stated intention of furthering the works of great gothic writers such as HP Lovecraft, Lord Dunsany and Algernon Blackwood. One of Phil's own stories, the Lovecraft inspired "The Freshman," appeared in *Tales of the Cthulhu Mythos* by Arkham House.

Phil is a Solar Pons fan and this piece brings out his fond memories of August's character.

There are many worlds in which I have roamed for a long time. Other worlds have opened their doors to admit me only briefly. Some I have put behind me forever. Some I re-enter now and then to breathe an almost forgotten air and see a sun with a unique light. The world of Solar Pons and of Parker is a world in which I dwelt briefly but passionately.

"The game is afoot!" cries Pons, and into the London fogs plunge the two divers after pearls of mystery and murder. And I plunge with them, the unseen and shadowy third. I watch them; I listen to them; I rejoice when they find the pearl of light and the seas around are momentarily illuminated.

As we know, these two are derivative and perhaps are pale shadows of the two great originals. But they burn with a flame of their own, tiny but bright enough and intense enough so that I wish August Derleth could find the desire and time to present more. Many more. I believe that others—many others—share this wish to read of the further adventures of the peregrine of Praed Street.

Indeed, Mr. Derleth may, in presenting these pastiches of Sherlock Holmes, have unwittingly become a pastiche of A. Conan Doyle. Doyle came to regret having visited Baker Street, because he had written much better books, more literarily worthy novels, such as *The White Company*, for instance.

Yet his noncanonical works are far less appreciated, and, to the public, Doyle means Holmes, not Sir Nigel Loring or even Professor Challenger.

In the same way, Mr. Derleth may be remembered for his association with Praed Street despite having written many other novels. And he has written superb poetry which should, rightfully, survive and be much more widely known than it is.

The result of the love for the creations of another man is an ironic quirk, indeed. But enough of these speculations about literary values and literary longevity. The fog closes in like a grey fist, and the clipclop of hooves resounds in the murky swirlings. The only light in the fog is Solar; may its brightness be august, and may it long bridge the gap between the reality of Praed Street and the fantasy of this our mundane world.

White Whales, Raintrees, Flying Saucers...

First published in *Fantastic Universe,* Volume 2, Number 1, July 1954.

In a time when science fiction, especially magazine science fiction, was considered the poorest of literary ghettos, Farmer makes a good case for its being taken seriously and standing next to main stream fiction.

Phil: "Damon Knight told me that I must have been half-assed with drinking beer when I wrote this. No. Not at all. I was alcohol free but perhaps half-stoned with a fine frenzy, the lift that imagination gives me."

✦

Parables travel in parabolas. And science-fantasy, being in essence a parabolic form, can shoot over barriers which often stop the flight of earthbound straight fiction. It adopts certain modes of presentation forbidden to the mainstream of literature and thus strikes us harder with its insight.

Any good story, science-fantasy or not, creates order out of the chaos of this universe, and invests it with a meaning we the readers had not noticed before. Entertainment, always a necessary element in any good story, comes from the slight and pleasant shock of having our awareness-threshold raised by the author's skill in shaping new patterns of value for us.

Our problem is, can SF fit the definition of good fiction, as given in the above paragraph? Can SF wave its magic wand and conjure from chaos a meaningful, value-laden picture?

Answer: yes...Any bad fiction, no matter the genre, is a wild exercise of the imagination which explodes in the night of our minds, makes garish pyrotechnics, then dies, leaving the night blacker than before. But good fiction is a steady light even if sometimes a small one. By it we walk without stumbling, and we may return at any time to see under its flare other topographical features we did not understand the first trip.

Thus, a story that deals with unicorns and virgins, demons and wizards, rockets to Mars, self-conscious robots, or other mythical creatures and creations is not necessarily bad fiction because it uses devices that we know do not exist. If the story clenches a hard core of truth or flashes a facet of life not realized before, it is good. And its magical paraphernalia, far from obscuring its goodness and truth, is the very thing that brings them out. It makes it more than just a jag of fancy. It demonstrates beyond disproof that we are mad if we pursue the White Whale to our destruction; that even if we do find the lost raintree we'll lose it at once unless we keep our innocence; that flying saucers may equate the remoteness of stars with the abyss of loneliness between each human; that if you do not put a perfect trust in the one you love you will make her less than human and in the end kill her; and that even if you can't possess the moon yourself you can have no greater love than to break your heart getting it for others.

And, always, a good story, SF or not, shows you a hero with whom you can identify. Win or lose, he wrestles with a giant whose mask, no matter how fantastic, conceals our arch-friend or arch-fiend, our recognizable universe.

IF R.I.P.

First published in *Worlds of If: A Retrospective Anthology,* 1986.

Startling Stories, where Phil launched his SF career and *The Magazine of Fantasy & Science Fiction,* where much of his output from the 1950s to the 1970s was printed, including his John Carmody and "fictional author" series, are the first publications that come to mind when you consider where Phil has been published. But, seven stories that have been printed in previous Farmer collections, including the very often reprinted little gem, "The King of the Beasts," all appeared in three magazines under Fred Pohl's editorship; *Galaxy, Worlds of If,* (usually just called *If),* and *Worlds of Tomorrow.* Throw in "Seventy Years of Decpop," which is in this book, and the six serial installments of the first two Riverworld novels, which we should all be grateful to Fred Pohl for printing, and suddenly you realize just how different Phil's career might have been without them.

NB. The seven stories mentioned above are: "The Blasphemers," "King of the Beasts," "Heel," "A Bowl Bigger than Earth," "Down in the Black Gang," "The Shadow of Space" and "Riverworld."

⚓

Alas! Poor *If* is dead!

I wish that I could also say, as Hamlet said of Yorick, that I knew him (it) well. But I did not know it well except during the late sixties. At least, that's what I thought when I started writing this. Then I read a short history of *If* in a science-fiction encyclopedia. And I found that the magazine started in 1952. I just don't remember its inauguration. I do, however, vividly remember picking up from a bookstand an *If* containing Blish's now classic "A Case of Conscience." I wanted to buy it but didn't because I was short of money. I preferred to invest what little I had in *Astounding* or *Galaxy* or the *Magazine of Fantasy & Science Fiction.*

This occurred, according to the history, in 1953. I made a mistake then. Blish's story was, as I discovered much later when I read it in the unabridged book, the best thing published in that year. Even though *If* was regarded as

Galaxy's little sister and paid lesser rates than its big sister, it often had stories better than those in the more prestigious publications.

My first story to appear in *If* was "Heel" (May 1960 issue), a very minor tale. When it came out, I read it and the other stories in that issue, and that started me reading *If* more or less faithfully. Some of the stories were stimulating.

Then I took out of the "trunk" the manuscript of the original Riverworld novel. *Owe for the Flesh,* written in late 1952. It seemed to me that perhaps there might be a market for it. I decided to send it to Fred Pohl with the suggestion that if he liked it he could serialize it in *Galaxy.* (I bypassed John Campbell of *Astounding,* since he never liked *any* of my submissions.) Pohl wrote back that the concept of the Riverworld was too vast and had too many potentialities to be published even in a 150,000-word novel. He proposed that I should rewrite it as a series of novelettes. Thus, I could take my time and use all the space I'd need in developing the many ideas inherent in the concept. And I could also write as many of the story lines as I cared to.

This seemed to be a good idea. It was one which I'd have proposed myself if I'd thought that there was any chance that an editor would accept it. As it turned out, owing to Fred's keen perception and his willingness to turn me loose, the Riverworld series was a far better story than the original.

Pohl also purchased a number of short stories from me for *If* during the later sixties. Some of these I've thought good enough to reprint in my 1971 collection, *Down in the Black Gang.* I became even more interested in *If* and so had the pleasure of reading such classics as Harlan Ellison's "I Have No Mouth, and I Must Scream" and Larry Niven's "Neutron Star."

However, Fred did not run the Riverworld series in *Galaxy.* He started it in another little sister, *Worlds of Tomorrow.* But when *WOT* folded, Fred transferred the series to *If.* I don't know if he'd have transferred the series to *Galaxy* when *If* was canceled. By then I'd decided not to write any more novelettes but to compose future Riverworld novels as complete books for issuance by book publishers.

Fred Pohl did a great job with *If,* and it wasn't his fault, but that of the shrinking market at that time, that the magazine was forced to fold. Though he couldn't pay the contributors to *If* as much as he paid contributors to *Galaxy,* his editorial thaumaturgy acquired Hugos for *If* as the best SF magazine for 1966, 1967, and 1968. On a shoestring and near-genius.

"Down in the Black Gang" was commissioned by Fred. He wanted a story from me for a special issue of *If* containing only works by Hugo winners. At the time (late 1968 or early 1969), I was a technical writer for the space industry segment of McDonnell-Douglas. Shortly before I got Fred's invitation, I was standing near a group of engineers. One of them said, loudly, "What about the bleedoff?"

He was talking about rocket motors, of course, but that question, over-heard by chance, sparked something in my mind. Relays began clicking. Lights blinked. My unconscious, whom I now image as a demon named Abysmas, plugged in hitherto unconnected circuits and, for all I know, grew some new circuits. The she-demon Abysmas, in partnership with my conscious, named Wabasso, developed the story.

The story is at least one-half autobiographical and wholly therapeutic. For me, anyway. The Bonder family (Bonder comes from the Old Norse and means the same thing as a farmer or peasant) is based on the Farmer family. We were living in a Beverly Hills apartment just like that described here. The people directly below us were as presented here; nothing about them is exaggerated. And I was the minor but pivotal character, Tom Bonder, caught in that cosmic human comedy which Tom unwittingly transformed into a tragedy and thus aided in providing more thrust for the universe, which is actually a spaceship driving towards some unknown port.

I don't know where we're going, but it's sure hell getting there. On the other hand, there are many joyous moments and some great rewards for some of us. Does that make the trip worthwhile? Only journey's end will tell us.

The Tin Woodman Slams the Door

First published in *Destiny*, Number 10, Summer 1954.
Also published in *Oz-Story*, 6, 2000.

Phil: "Looking back, long after I wrote this I see that I was really hurting because I'd lost part of my soul. But I'd gained much more, so this wasn't just a pouring out of grief or regret."

<hr>

The Tin Woodman it was who first opened the door for me. He took me around and introduced me so that, in time, I knew them all, Tik-Tok and the Ragged Man and Ozma and the Cowardly Lion and I could go on and use up the rest of this space with just a list of the marvelous citizens.

After many adventures, some of which I untiringly lived through a dozen times through a curious type of time-traveling called rereading, I began to see things in a slightly polarized light. The Woodman's movements began to be a little jerky, the Cowardly Lion had no real reason to be afraid, the Gingerbread Man was just a little too sugary, and the final blow came when I wondered if Dorothy would object if I gave her a kiss. She did object, and so the Tin Woodman, metal jaw cranked to a grim angle, shook his shining axe at me and slammed the door in my face.

I said, "But, but, I didn't really mean any harm!"

No, of course I didn't, but I wasn't aware that if you want a thing to grow up with you it may—quite rightly—refuse, preferring to remain timeless within the walls of the archaic and innocent garden.

During the years after that, I tried many times to sneak back through the door. Always, I was confronted by that shining axe.

Not too long after this deportalization, I was blinded by the garish gateway of Gernsbackis, a wondrous land indeed. I quit sighing over that other lost door. Came the day when that portal was closed, too, when Treemainia, Campbellis, and others beckoned me to ever more fascinating odysseys. Yet, travelling there did not give me the sense of wonder that the yellowbricked highway had. True, I waited with eagerness for what next month's saga would offer in some strange place and puzzling time, but gone was the pristine breathlessness I'd known when knocking on the door to the Emerald City.

And then, one day, when I wasn't even looking for it, a gate swung open, and there he was.

"You?" I said.

"Not exactly. I am his grandson."

It took me a minute. Then I said, "Ike Positronic!"

He grinned tinnily and introduced me to the citizens of this not-quite-verdant metropolis, and I saw the Cowardly Lion's grandsons, which, if you've read *Gratitude Guaranteed*, you have, too, and I saw ten raggedy men with firewater bottles, and quite a few wizards, some mad and some mules, and some writing articles on scientology, and I saw Dorothy, but she was tall and had filled out here and there and didn't seem at all averse to a kiss, and there were also the evil gnomes, though they were bald and psychopathic, and I could go on.

But I think you get the idea, and you'll be no more surprised than I when the Tin Woodman, in answer to my complaint that this was all very nice but didn't give me the good old-time sense of wonder, replied, "Well, do you think that cybernetic brains and antigravity machines and psionic powers belong more to the world of reality than sawdust brains and flying powders and magic mirrors? It's all just a matter of sounding more adult, you know. Besides, you grew up and gained some things and lost others, and you wouldn't give up all this for that little door you used to knock at, now, would you?"

I answered, "I suppose not," and I really don't think I would, do I?

Witches and Gnomes and Talking Animals, Oh My

First published in *20th Century Fiction*, 1985 as an appreciation of L. Frank Baum

For those of you wondering, this title is a corruption of "Lions and Tigers and Bears, oh my" from that wonderful musical *The Wizard of Oz.*

⚜

L. Frank Baum's *The Wonderful Wizard of Oz*, illustrated by W. W. Denslow, is his masterpiece. It made him famous and, with its 13 sequels, has established him as a classic writer of children's stories.

The Wonderful Wizard of Oz was a novelty in children's books at the time it was published, lacking the didactic, moralizing, and stilted tone so common. Its characters spoke the American vernacular; its plot was simple but intriguing and well structured. Moreover, Baum created five characters worthy to stand with Lewis Carroll's. Dorothy and the Wizard, and the three non-human characters (the Tin Woodman, the Scarecrow, and the Cowardly Lion), are all archetypes yet sharply distinguished individuals. The quest of the Scarecrow for brains, the Woodman for a heart, and the Lion for courage, qualities they already possessed but did not know how to use, is the stuff of which classics are made. All have become literary figures as instantly recognizable as Alice and Peter Pan.

The Wizard was also Baum's most successful, though not his best, example of what he called the American or modernized fairy tale. Responding to ideas expressed by Hamlin Garland and others, he intended to write fantasies which would be distinct from the European and New England tradition. They would recognize the existence and importance of the industry, technology, and social concepts of the dawning 20th century. He did incorporate mechanical gadgets (particularly electricity, which fascinated him) into his works—*The Master Key: An Electrical Fairy Tale* is the best example—and dealt with such modern concepts as Populism. But in general his ambition to create a new genre was only partly successful. Though the visitors to Oz were American, the country itself was as foreign as James Branch Cabell's Poictesme or Swift's Lilliput. Furthermore, he often used such traditional fairy tale paraphernalia as witches, gnomes, talking animals, and wishing caps. What many consider to be his best book, *Queen Zixi of Ix*, is entirely derived from European children's literature, though it contains many imaginative novelties.

Baum tired of his Oz series. But just as public demand kept Doyle writing his Sherlock Holmes stories when he would have preferred to concentrate on more "serious" works, so it kept Baum at his Oz tales, though he did write many other children's books, few of them fantasies. Though written "to please a child" (Baum's phrase), the Oz books have also been popular with adults, who recognize subtleties which escaped them as children. *The Wonderful Wizard of Oz* is still popular, and now seems to have passed the judgment of time.

Suffer a Witch to Live

First published as in introduction to *The Ultimate Witch,* 1992.

Phil had already provided stories to three books in the Ultimate series (all reprinted in this collection) and decided he didn't want to write another. What he did, instead, was to pen a perceptive essay on hypocrisy and literary censorship.

They flourished in the Old Stone Age, and they are still with us. But, whereas they were the only game in town in the Paleolithic, they are, today, up against stiff competition. Their rivals, believers in different religions, far outnumber them. Moreover, these do not play fair. They loathe and detest witches as evil heretics and would like to kill them.

"Thou shalt not suffer a witch to live," the Old Testament declares. Ever obedient to Biblical precept, the ancient and medieval Jews stoned them to death. The medieval Christians hanged or burned them. Until the early nineteenth century, a witch could be executed after due process of law in many countries. Only because many enlightened people ceased to believe in magic as a reality did the legal persecution of witches cease.

However, despite the myth that we are a civilized and nonsuperstitious nation, many in the United States (and elsewhere in the world) believe that magic does exist and that its "laws" are as valid as those of physics. They also believe that magic can be used only for evil purposes. There is no such thing as a good witch, the Christian literalists declare. (This would be news to Glinda the Good.) Though fear of punishment by the law restrains the Christian fundamentalists (of the fanatic branches) from murdering witches (or those they think are witches), they do persecute them to the extent that law allows. Sometimes, they go beyond the law.

By coincidence, the day after I was asked to write an introduction to this anthology, the *Chicago Tribune* published a full-page article on early and modern witches in its Women News section. One of those cited is a self-declared witch who has lived in Salem, Massachusetts for eight years. Some of its citizens still cross the street to prevent closeness to her and, thus, contamination by evil. Some also call her names such as "Child of Hell" and "Satan's daughter." Another witch, who lives in Medford, a Boston suburb, was ousted from her apartment along with her family when her landlord found out that she was a witch.

The Salem witch mentioned above is a graphic artist and a Girl Scout troop leader. Her aerospace engineer husband, who is no witch, has been asked by fellow workers to get his wife to cast spells for them. She refuses to do this because she never uses her magic on others without their permission. When she does so, she only uses her magic for good.

This witch and many others claim that they are neopagans and that their religion must not be confused with Satanism or any form of devil worship. She states that she and her "sisters" base their religion on spirituality and environmentalism. Earth is sacred; Earth must not be polluted. Men and women should be allies and symbiotes of our planet, not exploiters and ravagers. Also, these witches' spells are more like prayers than curses, like benedictions, not harmful works of evil.

Witches, genuine witches, would like to overthrow the patriarchal system for one based on the true equality of men and women.

It is no coincidence that Salem is a magnet for witches and that many live in its area. Salem became famous, or, rather, infamous, because of the witch trials of 1692. Twenty citizens, mostly women, were hanged, and over one hundred were put in prison. Then good sense triumphed, shame replaced the hatred, and the hysteria died out. But the laws against witchcraft stayed on the books long after the unfortunate victims of Salem had died.

I have stated above that the fear of witches ceased when the majority of people lost its belief in magic. I'll have to modify that. Here we are, the twenty-first century on the horizon, supposedly a rational people, surrounded by an ever-burgeoning technology which is itself a magic of the mind. Superstition should be an evil which flourished only in the barbaric past. It should have been cast into the dustheap of the long-ago. But this has not happened. Far from it.

Many people still believe that magic is viable. They also believe that certain men and women can use its principles and powers as scientists use science. Witches can cast spells, don't have to use airplanes to fly, can summon up storms, can kill or cure you at a distance with a spell, can make people fall in love with you, can give you good fortune or ill fortune, and can bring up demons from hell. They can ensure good crops or blight them, and they can make women fertile or cause stillbirths.

In olden times, they could make your cow's milk turn sour in the udder. Nowadays, I suppose, they can put a spell on your new car so that it doesn't run.

Those who believe in the witchly powers include both witches and non-witches. Many among the latter are certain, as I've said, that magic can only be wielded for evil. But the nonwitches are ignorant of the very long history of and lore about witches. They don't know that many legends and folktales in many areas of the world are about good witches. That is, white witches. And, in certain areas, such as in Dartmoor, Devonshire, England, gray or "double-ways" witches figure in many folktales. These use their magic for good or for bad, depending upon whether or not they like the person who is the target of their powers. This belief was not confined to Devon by any means. Among many tribes in North America, the shaman could cure you or put an evil spell upon you.

Then there's the Devil, Satan, Auld Hornie, Old Nick, The Black Man, the ancient fallen angel Lucifer. Many envision this supreme evil spirit as having the form of a man with horns, hooves, and a tail. They also affirm that he commands a horde of lesser demons. They name his worshipers "Satanists," and are one hundred percent certain that all witches are servants of the Devil. This belief is, however, chiefly held by Christian literalists, that is, those who insist that the letter of the bible is to be taken as expressed. No part of it, except for the obviously poetic, is symbolic or allegorical. Thus, God really did take one of Adam's ribs and transform it into the first woman, Eve. There really was a worldwide flood brought about by God because of the general wickedness of mankind then. Only Noah, his family, and specimens of every animal in the world survived by riding out the deluge in a huge boat, the Ark. Also true according to the literalists is the Old Testament story that King Saul got the Witch of Endor to evoke the ghost of Samuel, a prophet.

Thus, the literalists, also called fundamentalists, believe that magic is an evil science. It was created by the Devil, and witches, devotees of the Devil, have been taught by him to wield their evil upon the worshippers of God. Since magic is a creation of the Devil, all witches have to be evil. No such thing as a white witch exists.

This belief has driven the literalists to some strange conclusions and even stranger behavior. They object to the Oz books because they depict witches. It's not just that one of the characters is a good witch. They don't want their children—or any adults, for that matter—to read books depicting witches, good or bad. They object to TV or movie shows about witches. They have made efforts in several cities to ban the Oz books in public libraries.

Just why they have this attitude about witches in books and movies is incomprehensible. It may be that they fear that the supposed evil of the witches will rub off onto the reader. But, if the literalists were logical, their efforts to repress all such books would lead them to ban the Bible. After all, witches and demons are described in it.

Pathetic. But dangerous. The most absurd case of this of which I know is a book written by Jane Yolen, one of the contributors to the book at hand. It's titled *The Devil's Arithmetic*. But it's not about the Devil or devils, unless you consider the Nazi's to be fiends incarnate, as the cliché phrase goes. It's a time-travel story in which a modern Jewish girl, one who doesn't take much interest in her religion or traditions, is carried back in time to the Holocaust. Not through magic but, seemingly, by a slip in time. Her experiences make her realize the horror and inhumanity of the Holocaust.

Only the title has anything to do with the Devil. Yet, a fundamentalist in a city protested publicly against the book. She had not read the book and assumed that it was about witches and Satanists. So vehement were her protests and so strong was the adverse publicity she generated, she succeeded in making the publisher withdraw Yolen's book from the stores.

Absurdity plus. Ad nauseam.

Jane Yolen has been living in Scotland off and on for some time. Scotland used to be overrun with witches, which means that some are still around. If I were Jane, I'd hire a Celtic witch in the Fife area to make the house of the woman who's given Jane so much trouble burn down. Or cause the woman to bear sextuplets, all horned and hooved.

Hiring the witch would at least be a test to determine if witches do indeed have such powers. And I'm sure Jane could use the hire-money as an exemption on her income tax.

I cite Jane Yolen's situation to show the moronicity of anti-Satanists and the power they have. Also, to demonstrate that there are people, well-organized though, I hope, not numerous, who firmly believe in witches and the Devil. Yet, the woman who is so fanatical and irrational that she objected to the "Devil" in the title obviously knows very little about his genesis, history, and evolution. But she does embody the beliefs of many people, whether they are Christians or not.

Where do Satan's horns, hooves, and tail come from?

He has these because he derives directly from sorcerers of the tribes of the Old Stone Age. The earliest known image of him is found in the Caverne des Trois Fréres in Ariege, southern France. It's dated as being in the late Paleolithic (Old Stone Age). Thus, sometime between 40,000 B.C and 10,000 B.C., the image of the half-man, half-animal was painted deep within the cave. Other paintings of animals appear with it. But the Horned Man is a misnomer for this magic-evoking figure painted on a wall deep within a cave. The sorcerer bore stag antlers.

The wordage limit in this foreword forbids an extensive survey of the evolution of the truly ancient, cave-dwelling, man-stag witch into the horned Devil of a later era. Suffice it here that later witches formed groups of thirteen, a coven, and that the male leaders of these groups were known as the Horned Man. The witches' religion of western Europe derived from those of the Old Stone Age and maintained an unbroken (though not undistorted) continuity in time.

When Christianity became the state-supported religion of Europe, a fierce warfare against the pagans began. It continued up to approximately the middle of the seventeenth century. Since the Christian priests have written the records about this warfare, they give the impression that complete conversion to Christianity occurred. But this is not true. Much of the rural populations continued to cling to the Old Religion, though many pretended to be Christians.

There is evidence to show that even the nobility and the monarchs were secret Old Religionists up through the medieval and Reformation times. *The God of the Witches* by Margaret Murray, for instance, states that such kings and well-known people as Rufus, son of William the Conqueror, Gilles de Rais, Marshal of France, Joan of Arc, the maiden savior of France, and Thomas à Becket were voluntary ritual sacrifices of the Old Religion.

In any event, much larger numbers of pagans continued to believe in their faith than the Church historians would like you to believe. The Old Faith was never stamped out, and it flourishes in this somewhat tolerant late twentieth century in Europe and the Americas.

But the old gods become the demons of the new religion. Thus, the Church identified the Horned Man as Satan, the Devil. His worshipers were said to do evil through their magic, and the Church sought to eliminate them entirely by burning and hanging. Many genuine witches, that is, Old Faith believers, and many innocents were killed. During this period, Satan acquired in the popular mind the horns (once antlers), hooves, and tail (though deer don't have much of a tail) of the ancient sorcerer. However, the more enlightened Christians did not believe in this image of Satan. The Bible does not describe Satan as such any more than it portrays angels as winged.

Despite the Horned Man as the leader of the coven, the Old Faith also had female goddesses, higher in the deity level than men, the most important being the fertility goddesses. Much of this lingers in present-day witchly belief. In fact, many witches have stated that their supreme deity is Mother Earth and that the Horned Man (under various names) is secondary to Her. Some don't even acknowledge his existence in their religion.

Now, having dealt with Old Faith from the rational viewpoint, I'll write briefly of it from the irrational viewpoint. By irrational, I don't mean "insane" or "crazy." I mean the Irrational, those supernatural things and beings which science rejects as impossible or highly unlikely. I am human, therefore both rational and irrational. There is in me as in all humans, a feeling, often subconscious, that the Irrational: God, spirits, demons, and ghosts may exist. The Old Stone Age savage lives in all of us, no matter how vehemently we deny it. Perhaps, just perhaps, I think, there may be genuine witches here and there. Magic does exist; its practitioners exist. I like to think of myself as open-minded. Thus, I don't finally and forever reject the possibility. After all, I've twice seen ghosts and twice had mystical experiences. The latter convinced me, however briefly, that the universe does have meaning and that all is well in God's world despite its never-ending horrors.

These intimations of the Irrational (or were they emotional hallucinations?) and those of other people I know demonstrate that there are two worlds within our seeming physical limits. They occasionally touch each other at points where humans happen to be. Perhaps, just perhaps…

Whatever the truth, I've loved stories and movies about witches since my childhood. Not all of them are Grimm; many are fun. But the more threatening stories always strum a fear-filled chord deep within me. The Old Stone Age caveman still lives.

Whether or not you believe in the magic of witchcraft, you do believe in the magic of the written word. Read the stories at hand, and shiver a little or enjoy. Or both.

Poems

Phil's poems have never been collected previously
and for the most part appeared in extremely hard to find
publications. It was only at the eleventh hour that the
text for "In Common" was found and along the way
two previously unknown works by Phil were discovered;
"Black Squirrel on Cottonwood Limb's Tip" and
"Good But Not Good Enough."

Imagination

First published in *America Sings,* 1949.
Also published in *Thrilling Wonder Stories,* Summer 1954.

America Sings was an anthology of College poetry.

Can imagination act
Perpendicular to fact?
Can it be a kite that flies
Till the Earth, umbrella-wise,
Folds and drops away from sight?

Miles above the Earth we know,
Fancy's rocket roars. Below,
Here and Now are needles which
Sew a pattern black as pitch,
Waiting for the rocket's light.

Poet, steer your rocket down.
Lights are useless, though they crown
Half of space with glory, yet
Leave this hard old globe in jet.
Earth's the start, the end of flight.

Good But Not Good Enough

First published in *Bradley Quarterly,* August 1949.

*T*he thing that ran and screamed and fell a pace
From me was he whom I had never thought
To see in Hell, where none like him were brought
To flee the blackish glare of Satan's grace.
He scrambled up and clutched my hand to brace
Himself against what he on Earth had wrought
And now, no matter where he ran, was caught
By it before he had begun the race.

I dropped his hand, for what is there to do
For one whose gift from Satan is a tail
Whose tip is fastened to an angel's head
With fiery lips that shriek, "It is too late to rue
The man you might have been, too late to veil
My face—your face—the horror you would shed!"

The Pterodactyl

First published in *Skyhook*, Number 16, Winter 1952-3.
Also published in *The Magazine of Fantasy & Science Fiction*,
July 1965.
Also published in *Burning With a Vision*, 1984.

*F*ar pre-father of feathers, you are flying
Through cerebral Jurassics in a spasm
Of leathery vanes, afraid to sound the chasm
Where saurian trades of tooth and loin are plying.
Wing-fingered feeder on metaphysics, signing
From withering bowels denotes enthusiasm
Wasted chasing toothsome ectoplasm
And omens a skeleton decease while trying.

Sawbeaked epitome of bodiless
Idea, tossed by gusts of ether, dive
Through abstract mists and raid the sea of fact.
Eat rich strange fish, grow long bright feathers, press
Form's flesh around thought's rib, and so derive
From the act of beauty, beauty of the act.

Sestina of
the Space Rocket

First published in *Startling Stories,* February 1953.

*O*ne thing is sure, O comrades, that the love
That fights to keep us rooted in the earth,
But also urges us to dare the stars,
This irresistible, this ancient power
Wedged in the soul, unshakable, is the light
That burns our roots and leaves us free for Space.

The way is open, comrades, free as Space
Alone is free. The only gold is love,
A coin that we have minted from the light
Of others who have cared for us on Earth
And who have deposited in us the power
That nerves our nerves to seize the burning stars.

Courage, comrades! Let the fire of stars
Reflect their flames in your hearts till men lack space
To say enough of the inexpressible power
That gives the strength to sever us from love
Of beautiful women, strength which makes large Earth,
Once so close, now only a spurt of light.

Eyes forward! Sing a paean to the light
That God gives us to net the distant stars
In eyes that once were blinded with black earth.
Man had no time for aught but toil, no space
For aught but war. Yet God, in His great love,
Has cleared our eyes and given a hint of Power.

Now we have lit a candle to the power
Of atoms; now we know we're heirs of light
Itself and know no more that fleck whose love
And hates are far from us, as far as stars
Once were, now let us swear to leave no space
Unconquered till we find a better earth.

Yes, we hope to seed a new, rich earth.
We hope to breed a race of men whose power
Dwells in hearts as open as all Space
Itself, who ask for nothing but the light
That rinses the heart of hate so that the stars
Above will be below when man has Love.

God, Whose hand holds stars, as we lump earth
In our fingers, give us power, give us light
To hold all love within our breast's small space.

Beauty in This Iron Age

First published in *Starlanes,* Number 11, 1953.

Beauty in this Iron Age must turn
From fluid living rainbow shapes to torn
And sootened fragments, ashes in an urn
On whose gray surface runes are traced by a Norn
Who hopes to wake the Future to arise
In Phoenix-fashion, and to shine with rays
To blast the sight of modern men whose dyes
Of selfishness and lust have stained our days
With acid blotches, days that should be white
With other Helens' sea-foam breasts, with wheat
Of Deirdres' hair be rippling, days whose flight
From Timo is hand in hand with Beauty fleet.

Reader, pray that soon this Iron Age
Will crumble, and Beauty escape the rusting cage.

In Common

First published in *Starlanes,* Number 14, April 1954.

Prometheus, I have no Titan's might,
Yet I, too, must each dusk renew my heart,
For daytime's vulture talons tear apart
The tender alcoves built by love at night.

Black Squirrel on Cottonwood Limb's Tip

First published in *Skyhook*, Number 23, Winter 1954-55

Bright-eyed surmise on a grey twist like my mind:
Flirt-tailed punctuation, fluid sign
That branches, like phrases and mazes,
Never end but link
In aerial conjunction, I'd think
You're a luciferous nuciferous
Metaphysics that I'd like to swallow
Whole. Not for your flesh. To fill a hollow
Lust to interpret me through you, but can see
You know no me nor you, only fear food frenzy;
That tipping your tiny skull as cup, grey bead
Of brain as exquisite shot will bring no readback
Trick of using your eyes in fusing feedback.

Oh, I'd reach beyond the comma of you
To the invisible phrase, the dangling Omega! No use. No act
Of mine or mind denies the ante-cerebellum fact
Of furry you, poised fleetingly, bright flex,
Black reflex, too leaping for me to ink and fix
As period to end what has no period, no, no
End, just quo vadis? Quid nunc? Cui bono?
Myself am quo quid cui — quit
Of that big black question mark on branch
Of brain only when Death'll crack me, crunch
Me, chattering quo quid cui

cui
cui?

We too. No wisdom to utter.
You've beauty, flux, and terror
To tell. So've I. And they're
Very hard to mutter
Through so much chatter and stutter.

Job's Leviathan

First published in *JD Argassy*, Number 58, 1961.
Also published in *First Fandom Magazine*, Number 4, June 1961.

A Jungian Analysis

Job as Simple Simon, soul as pail,
And Beauty, Leviathan: the king of deep
On deep, unbribed guard of the sunken keep
Where primal gods deman expensive bail.
Let those who think the soul is shallow rail,
They must be warned before they dare to leap
They'll plunge into the twilight depths where sweep
In ceaseless thirst great teeth too swift to fail.

Job's Word is bait; the big fish strikes; the line
Grows taut; vast treadings crush abysmal grapes;
Drowned idols swirl like seeds in chaos' wine.
Look, Job! Caught Beauty, held to light, now apes
A good, now evil, thing—the shifting sign
And spectrum of archaic, psychic shapes.

PJF on PJF

Maps and Spasms

Maps and Spasms

First appeared in *Fantastic Lives,* 1981.
Also published in *Mystery Scene,* Issue 28, January 1991

In this autobiographical article Phil mentions a story he wrote about a conservative woman who exposed herself to passing trains. This sounds remarkably like "Hunter's Moon" which is published for the first time in this collection.

Phil also talks about Horace Gold and the rejection of "The Lovers." The story here is at slight odds with that contained in "Lovers and Otherwise" where Phil takes a much more conciliatory line to Gold's reaction.

The article takes us from Phil's birth (and covers a significant period of time before) to the acceptance of "The Lovers" for publication in 1952. The promised part II was never written, to our loss.

Phil: "I was in an ecstatic but mellow mood when I wrote this autographical bit. It all sounds much more poetic than it really was. But that's the way I remember it."

<hr>

"Other maps are such shapes, with their islands and capes!
But we've got our brave Captain to thank:
(So the crew would protest) "that he's bought us the best—
A perfect and absolute blank!"

The Hunting of the Snark, Fit the Second, the Bellman's Speech

The Bellman's map is the future. Science fiction writers try to anticipate the course of the ship, this Earth, instead of waiting to fill out the map as islands and capes do show up. Kooky Columbuses, balmy Bellmans, they venture fearlessly into the unknown even if they do sometimes get the bowsprit mixed up with the rudder.

Another type of blank map is the newborn. An infant is usually considered to be an empty sheet of paper on which the world will scrawl its often unintelligible pictures and writings. But—the world has more buts than people—but I believe that a newborn is a palimpsest. The moving pen of the environment is going to write upon the sheet, but it's not blank. It bears texts and pictures only partly rubbed out.

Heredity, the chance mingling of genes and an occasional mutation, plays as powerful a part as environment. Sometimes, it is stronger in that it determines the choice of environment in the adult. People are born reactors or nonreactors, born leaders or followers, born with certain tendencies and leanings and temperaments. Many have argued with me about this thesis, but the accumulating evidences from psychology and genetics in the past ten years back up my thesis.

I don't mean that a person is just a sort of protein robot programmed by heredity and reacting in ways shaped by his genes and environment. Mark Twain and Vonnegut are wrong about this "chemical determinism," to use a phrase from Theodore Dreiser. (He, by the way, was born a few miles from my birthplace.) Humans have freewill, the ability to raise themselves (or lower themselves) by psychic bootstraps. Often, however, this free will may be unconsciously used by a person to determine that he won't use his free will. That's the final act of free will in this type of person. Free will is a third force, the weakest and strongest of the trinity, the other two being heredity and environment. Having stated that I believe that a human is tripartite, I'll proceed with the autobiography.

I was born under the sign of Aquarius in a house in North Terre Haute, Indiana. Many ghosts of ancestors crowded around to assist in the delivery. The Good Fairy blessed me with one gift, and the Evil Witch laid on me some curses and geases. St. Francis of Assisi and Jack the Ripper telegrammed their regards. World War I was still raging, and Fimbulwinter had gripped the Midwest. My father had to walk hip deep in the snow to get the doctor that night. By the time they arrived, the bloodied and shocked infant had been spanked, cut, and washed. I don't remember the event, though I've fantasized it during dianetic and Scientological sessions. My earliest memory in reality is of my first haircut at the age of one and a half.

My father, George Farmer, was then in his first year at Rose Polytechnic Institute in Terre Haute. My birth interrupted his plans to get a degree in civil and electrical engineering. He had to quit school at the end of his freshman year to support his wife and child. On the other hand, I saved him from the draft. His broken college education foreshadowed my own. He didn't give up, though. Through the years he took International Correspondence School courses and eventually got the equivalent of a college degree. His father,

William Albert Park, had been given at the age of two to a distant relative, George Farmer. William's father, Dr. Park, had just died, and William's mother had left the child with the Farmers and taken off for Texas with her two older daughters. Dr. Lida Park would there become the first woman osteopath in the world. (Her father was a medical doctor.)

William's father's death and his desertion by his mother must have savagely wounded William's psyche. The direct though seemingly circuitous result of this was that I wasn't raised in Terre Haute as the scion of a wealthy family. William was reputed to be the best mechanic and machinist in Indiana, and he owned a big machine shop, many farms, and several houses. But he was a self-destroyer, exceedingly eccentric, a boozer, womanizer (hence, a womanhater), and reckless gambler. Before I was born, he'd blown most of his money, and deserted his wife, in tenuous revenge, I suppose, because his mother had deserted him. He fled for parts unknown, leaving his wife, Josephine Dooley, with ten thousand dollars, a big sum in 1912. Foolishly, she gave the money to a gambler who claimed that William owed it to him. She was forced to live with a relative and take in ironing to support herself and her two younger children.

A few years later, a gasoline-heated iron exploded while she was pressing clothes, and she died from burns. My father never forgave his father. In his old age, young sinner Bill (Park) Farmer became a fanatic fundamentalist, so Bible-rigid that he wouldn't let my aunt eat ice cream on Sunday when she visited him.

Why do I go into such detail about my ancestors? Because their lives have affected me and my writings. The effects are both psychic and physical. Certain themes in my fiction can be traced back to my reactions to these ancestral voices and deeds.

My mother's father, John Jacob Jackson, was supposed to be part Cherokee, though my mother denies it. Born in Arkansas (maybe), he homesteaded near the Rio Grande in Texas but left because of the many raids by Mexican bandits. He was a rather sinister character, if what my relatives said was true. His death certificate gives his trade as teamster. It omits, however, that he was a "honeydipper," a man who cleaned out outdoor toilets and hauled the excrement away in his wagon. I can see various hostile critics now, greeting this news with, "Yes. Heredity will tell."

J. J. J.'s second wife (he may have drowned his first in the Red River) was Marie Reich, more than twenty years younger than he. When ten years old (1881), she'd come from Germany to Kansas City. Her family had been persecuted by their Lutheran neighbors because it had converted to the Baptist faith, and it sought religious freedom in the United States. My mother's grandfather, like my father's father, had owned a machine shop.

When I gave Sam Moskowitz information about my ancestors for his *Seekers of Tomorrow*, I didn't know as much about them as I do now. Moreover, some data was wrong. My father's mother was a Dooley, but not of Irish descent, as I thought then. The first Dooley of whom we have record so far was of Welsh descent. Moses Dooley left Bedford County, Virginia, in 1781 (the year Herschel discovered Uranus) with his five children and his wife, Mary Boyd, of Irish descent. The family walked five hundred miles into Kentucky. Mary carried the youngest child all the way. For a while they lived in a stockaded fort because of the Shawnee wars then going on.

Twenty-three years later, Moses and Mary and their children (seven by then) moved to what would become Preble County in southwest Ohio. Moses was, besides being a farmer, a circuit-riding minister in Ohio and Indiana, a justice of the peace, and an overseer of the poor. A son, Silas, cleared the land for what would be the town of Camden, Ohio, some day. The Dooleys had troubles with the Indians there, too, though the local Indians were friendly. Reuben Dooley, another son, my direct ancestor, helped build the local Christian (Disciples of Christ) church near Eaton and several others. He was a minister, too, a mighty savior of the backslider and pagan during camp revivalist meetings.

Reuben's son, Martin Luther, was born in 1812. Martin went to Parke County, Indiana and became a well-to-do farmer and pillar of the Christian church. His son, Jerome Bonaparte, my great-grandfather, was a Civil War veteran who fought at Kennesaw Mountain and was with Sherman up to the siege of Atlanta. After getting too old to farm, he became a rural mail carrier.

I remember him and his wife well, having visited them several times before they died. Her father was Jacob Oldshue, a captain in the Mexican War and of Pennsylvania Dutch ancestry. Great-grandpa Dooley told me many stories about his Civil War experiences. Including when, during his first hitch, he'd been captured by the Confederates near Uniontown, Kentucky, but was later exchanged. He also told me that, when he was a juvenile, he'd met a veteran of the Revolution, a very old French-speaking Swiss who'd known Voltaire. Ten years old when told this, I didn't, of course, have the faintest idea who Voltaire was. But my great-grandfather seemed to think I should be impressed. I was—later on.

Maybe it was this which gave me a strong sense of and interest in historical continuity. I knew a man who'd known a man who'd known Voltaire. And Voltaire was to be one of my early and lasting literary influences. The human species is a web of flesh spun by some vast spider. The shaking of the web in a distant time and a distant place trembles us.

My middle name, José, derives from my father's mother, Josephine Dooley. She was called Jose for short. When I took Spanish in junior high school, I masculinized and hispanicized my middle name by adding the accent mark. Besides, I thought that a Spanish name would add glamour to an otherwise undistinguished handle. I'd always hated the name of Farmer with its rustic and hickish connotations. Certainly, José is an eye-catcher.

My father claimed that he was descended from Mungo Park (1771-1806), the famous Scots explorer of Africa. But research so far indicates that his claim was one of his many flights of fancy. Actually, the Parks are descended from the founders of Jamestown, Virginia, the first permanent settlement by the English in North America.

So...the infant P. J. F. was a palimpsest, not the Bellman's blank map. His ancestors, direct and collateral, had been hardworking adventurers, and many had been pioneers, land-clearers, wild-game hunters, farmers, school-teachers, preachers, physicians, mechanics, and engineers. Some of them were rather eccentric, too. Nowhere in the recorded line was a fiction writer. The genetic slot machine came up with three cherries. Or maybe it was three lemons. I haven't decided yet.

As for environmental influences, my parents encouraged me to read and often purchased books for me. I didn't need the encouragement, though. My parents also encouraged my three brothers (all younger) to read, but they failed to respond. My sister, the youngest sibling, did become a great reader. The environment for all five of us children was somewhat the same. But it was the genetic disposition that took only two of us, the oldest and the youngest, toward the fabulous world of literature.

Here's a strange thing. My brothers regard my writings, indeed all science fiction, as shit. They may be right, though not in the sense they mean. However, their children like science fiction and are proud of Uncle Phil.

Back to Terre Haute, named by the French voyageurs High Land because it was on a plateau above the banks of the Wabash River. Shortly after I began talking, my mother and I went to live on Great-grandmother Farmer's farm-house (in an area now quite suburbanized). My father had a job in Indianapolis but he didn't want us to come live with him until the job was permanent. I remember Mrs. Farmer quite well as an incredibly ancient woman, which she was, having been born in 1835. And I remember the old grandfather clock on the staircase landing, keeping me awake at night, reminding me, though I didn't know it then, of the irresistible and merciless passage of time.

I was about two years old then, and the world seemed to me what Wordsworth describes in his "Ode, Intimations of Immorality from Recollections of Early Childhood." And even more from his "On the Beach at Calais." "Listen! the mighty Being is awake,/And doth with his eternal motion make/A sound like thunder—everlastingly." There was a light from the horizon and faint voices, mysteries which most children forget but which I still remember. Wordsworth doesn't mention that he saw rags of evil and fear among the trailing clouds. He may not have seen them, though I find that hard to believe.

Somewhere on the horizon of the Indiana farm, somewhere in the golden aura, were slight but detectible tentacles of evil and fear. The worm was just beyond the curve, evident only as a faint odor, molecules staining the glory. Every wonder is smirched.

Sixty years later, I can recapture something of those visions streaming auroralike from over the horizon. And now and then, not often, the voices call from the edge of the visible world as they did when I was an infant. They call my name, though I don't know why. And, perhaps strangely, perhaps not, the voices do not now have the slightest suggestion in them of evil and fear. They are not voices of my ancestors, as I once thought, though they may be the same voices that my remote ancestors (and yours) heard. Perhaps the Old Stone Agers, Ab and Og, not only heard these voices but talked to their owners, just as they may have talked to animals and trees then. Perhaps then there was no hint of the worm in the light or the voices. And perhaps there was, since life seems meaningless unless it contains corruption and death. But it also seems meaningless unless it promises immortality. Perhaps "meaning" is just an inevitable epiphenomenon of sentiency.

When we moved to Indianapolis, we lived in an apartment building. It was here that I encountered my first ghost and the works of Homer, which I couldn't read then, of course. The latter meeting is described in my foreword to the Phantasia Press edition of my *Maker of the Universes*.

Then we moved to Greenwood, some miles south of the Hoosier capital. My brother, Eugene Avon, was born here, and I missed by the fraction of a second being killed by an automobile. It ran over me while I was lying under a pile of autumn leaves, and, if I'd raised my head, it would have been knocked off.

When I was about four we moved to a farmhouse outside of the little village of Mexico, Missouri. My brother Jerome William was born in this house. Here I got a terrible shock when I saw a rooster swallow a dead mouse. For the first time, I realized that creatures ate other creatures. And a short time later I saw my father wring off a chicken's head and watched it as it ran around headless for a few seconds. Until then I hadn't connected the chicken on the plate with the fowl in the barnyard. Other children see such things and worse and are unaffected by them or easily get over the shock. I didn't.

I remember looking across the country road in front of our house at the meadows on the other side. Something was bellowing beyond the low hills beyond the meadows, and I wondered if it could be a new voice among those I sometimes heard calling from the horizon. I asked my father about the bellowing, and he said that it was made by a giant. If I didn't stay in the yard, if I crossed the road to the meadows, the giant would "get" me. My child's imagination pictured a hairy ogre twenty feet tall whose favorite delicacy was infants.

When I was five, we moved to Peoria, a small mid-Illinois city by the Illinois River. Founded by French traders and soldiers, it's the oldest white settlement west of the Appalachians in the United States. The river was pure then and citizened by mighty fish. The valley was a hunter's paradise with, believe it or not, parakeets providing colorful grace notes. Alan Ginsberg, in his poem "Howl," calls Peoria a holy city, a Benares by the Kickapoo Creek. Holy it was for me and still is, though I now know that what Sir Richard Francis Burton said about holy cities is true. They are also the most corrupt. Peoria was once exceedingly corrupt and may still be for all I know. But it could never hold a candle to Chicago.

Ghosts of the Peoria Indians still haunt its car-choked streets. Especially, Withihakaka, the trickster. (The name of Kickaha, the trickster of the World of Tiers series, is not based on the Peoria trickster. I made up Kickaha long before I read about Withihakaka.)

Our first home there was a small run-down house with an outdoor toilet in the backyard. My father worked as a draftsman for Illinois Power and Light, the streetcar company, though he would eventually become an engineer and supervisor. The house on New Street was on the South Side, then and now a section for the poor. It was integrated, and I walked to school and back with a little black girl, Dorothy. Once, my father, seeing me walking hand in hand with her, made fun of me. This is my first remembered experience with color prejudice, though doubtless I'd heard racial slurs before then. A short time later, the girl failed to show up at school. My mother told me she'd gotten sick and died. I didn't cry, but I was disturbed that my walking mate could suddenly disappear; it was as if the Boojum had snatched her. Nor did I weep when my puppy died of distemper, though I was shocked when my father threw the carcass into the garbage can. It seemed such a callous way to dispose of a being I'd loved. Thirty-three years later, suddenly and unexpectedly, I wept over the puppy. I'd been holding the grief and anger within me all that time.

It was in 1924 that I happened to look up while playing on the sidewalk and saw a silvery dirigible flying west. It had to be either the *Shenandoah* (lovely Amerind name!) or the *Los Angeles*. This was the moment I became hung up on lighter-than-air craft, but my passion wouldn't be evidenced in literary form until many decades later.

Five or six blocks away from our house was a silent movie rerun theater, the Grand. Here I saw my first movie, Douglas Fairbanks in *The Three Musketeers*. This was made in 1921, but I couldn't have seen it until 1924 or 1925. I remember many scenes from it just as I do from *Robin Hood*, *The Thief of Baghdad*, and *The Black Pirate*. I saw these at least three times (an old lady played mood music on the piano in the orchestra pit while the film flickered) as I did *The Deerslayer*, *The Iron Horse*, and that fabulous serial, *The Green Archer*. Lon Chaney in *The Phantom of the Opera* almost scared the piss out of me. *Peter Pan* and *The Lost World* entranced me, and Tom Mix was a semidivine being. These movies, seen before or during first grade at Webster, influenced me as much as the books I was to read a few years later.

Our neighborhood was the slums of Peoria then, but it was safe for a youngster to walk the streets at night. Nowadays no nocturnal street anywhere is safe, and girls are raped in daylight in the suburban areas.

In 1926 we moved to Reservoir Heights, a village bordering Peoria and on the bluffs above the river. My brother George was born in the house on London Street. It was a happy time for me, as I remember it, though I sleepwalked a lot. A few blocks away was a hilly forest with a creek and a swamp and a real-live hermit who lived in an old shack. (Believe it or not, his name was Savage, and his nickname was Doc. He was said to be a doctor who'd become an alcoholic bum.) Two blocks away was a narrow road with very infrequent traffic. Now it's a heavily traveled boulevard, and where the forest and swamp were are a graveyard, industrial buildings, and houses. The swamp was a big place where dragonflies and crows flew and big frogs jumped and turtles swam and someone had built a raft which my playmates and I poled through the green-scummy waters and giant lilypads. It was a primeval swamp, and I scared my brother Gene by telling him that at its bottom in the thick mud lay the great serpent Kenabeek. (I lifted Kenabeek from an illustrated *Song of Hiawatha*.)

It was also in this forest that Doc Savage interrupted our inspection of the not-so-private parts of a female collie. This incident was to become, fifty-three years later, the genesis of my *Playboy* magazine story, "The Leaser of Two Evils."

Foul and fallow may be cognate words in the mind.

I remember well when the news came that Lindbergh had crossed the Atlantic. The houses were emptied, and people stood around in the muddy streets of Reservoir Heights marveling over this great exploit.

How many science fiction authors went to a one-room school? I did at Reservoir Heights. And I paid for it when we moved in the fall of 1927 to a house on Hanssler Place in Peoria. Columbia Grade School was more advanced, and I had a very hard time with arithmetic. My father threatened to whip me if I got another F on my report card, so I ran away with two other equally unhappy boys. One gave up when we were two miles north of the city and went home. The other boy (Fred Hopkins, now dead) and I decided that we'd go to Cripple Creek, Colorado and be gold miners. (We thought Cripple Creek couldn't be more than fifty miles due west.) But we needed supplies, tools, and a grubstake. So we went back, following Dry Run Creek to Kickapoo Creek for some reason, then went east into the downtown area. We were going to break into a big department store there and get all we needed to dig out and pan gold.

But my father, who'd been cruising around looking for us, spotted us. Though we ran into a junkyard to hide, we were found, taken to a police station to scare us, then taken home where our respective fathers whaled us with a strap. That was the start and end of my criminal career and prospecting life. It was also the third and last whipping my father gave me.

It seemed that every time we moved, another baby was added to the family. George was born at Reservoir Heights; Joan Delores, at Hanssler Place. Then my mother had a hysterectomy, and that was the end of the deluge. But even so there were five children crowded into a very small house. Which, by the way, had once been a rural one-room schoolhouse. By the time we got to it, it was near the edge of the city. It was also the first house I lived in that had an indoor toilet. And it was here that we got our first radio.

I'd first encountered science fiction in the fifth grade when I read E. R. Burroughs's stories, Roy Rockwood's Great Marvel Series, and many others in the excellent branch library near Columbia. In fifth grade I wrote a story, for a class assignment, which took place during the Civil War. But I assumed that science had developed somewhat faster than it really had, and the Blue and the Gray were using airships and airplanes like those in 1914. In the sixth grade I wrote a very long story about gladiatorial combats in ancient Rome, all based on my reading of our history textbook and a great deal of bloody-minded imagination. My teacher accused me of plagiarizing, but she was wrong.

And then in 1929 I came across the first issues of Gernsback's *Air Wonder* and *Science Wonder* magazines. Hooked! How marvelous were Paul's illustrations, how the stories made my mind soar. I've forgotten most of the fiction, but the Pauls were forever burned into my brain.

Before this great day, though, I'd read and reread many times *Gulliver's Travels*, Carroll's *Alice* books, various books of the Bible, Bunyan's *Pilgrim's Progress*, much of Mark Twain, the *Iliad* and *Odyssey*, *The Arabian Nights*, the *Oz* books, *Robinson Crusoe*, Olive Schreiner's strange little fantasies, *Treasure*

Island, much of Jack London, Greek and Norse mythology, Lang, Andersen, Grimm, Crump's *Og* novels, an abridged Malory, *Robin Hood,* Doyle's *The Lost World* and *Sherlock Holmes* stories, A. Hyatt Verrill, *The Rime of the Ancient Mariner, Peter Pan,* several books on Amerind mythology, and had even skipped through *The Book of Mormon.* These were the books that shone a golden light on my childhood; their influence has never waned.

Many of these I first encountered in a library of little red pseudoleather books my father purchased for me. Therein I also found outlines of some novels such as Behn's *Oroonoko* and *Frankenstein.* Of the Bible books, I relished and reread most Genesis, Exodus, Jonah, Job, the four Gospels, and Revelation.

Even as a child, I could see that, though God was a hell of a good poet, He could give no satisfactory answers to Job's questions. I also could never really believe, though I tried, the story of how the snake lost its legs in the Garden of Eden. That tale seemed to me to be on a par with Kipling's story of how the elephant got its long trunk. The trouble was, though, that I both believed and didn't believe. This crosscurrent state set up tensions in me which came out in some dramatic dreams.

Along about the time I started to talk, my parents became Christian Scientists. I was sent to C. S. Sunday schools where I learned very little about the religion. My parents explained the tenets to me, but I never understood them. Nor did I when, much later, I read Mary Baker Eddy. I couldn't make head or tail out of the mishmash of pseudoscience, Buddhism, Hinduism, and Boston balminess. Moreover, Twain's comments on Eddy had prejudiced me against her. (My parents wouldn't have been so ready to buy Twain's books for me if they'd known his attitude toward her.) Finally, I began to see what C. S. was supposed to be all about, though I still didn't grasp its techniques. Then my parents had a fit of religious apathy—backslid for a while—and I was sent to a Presbyterian Sunday school and forced to attend services afterward. The main reason I was sent there was that I could walk to the church, whereas the First Galvanized Church of Jesus Christ Scientist was almost downtown. It was in the Presbyterian domain that I first heard to my astonishment and dismay, the doctrine of predestination. And came across it soon after in Twain's *What Is Man?,* which had a secular version of predestination and which seemed to my uncritical mind clear proof that there was no such thing as free will.

Despite this, I still didn't believe in Presbyterian or Twainian predetermin-ism. But then I knew that Twain would claim that I believed in free will because I'd been predetermined to do so. It was, like most theories and argu-ments unbased on science, based on circular reasoning. So I went around in circles like the hen whose head my father had twisted off.

The early stages of puberty had me in the grip of metamorphosis then, and it set up tensions, conflicts, with my semi-Puritanical conditioning and my Bible reading and the opposition between free will and determinism. I don't suppose anybody watching me then would have realized the internal battles. I was studying hard, clowning around in class and on the playground, playing football and basketball and hiking or climbing trees and behaving and talking like a normal boy without a serious thought in his head. But hair was sprouting on the pubes and I'd be embarrassed by uncontrollable erections in class. Many a time I was called upon to stand up and recite and would do so red-faced, sure that everybody could see my fly bulging out. Some of the more daring boys were even boasting about masturbating, but I found that disgusting and immoral. My father had told me that masturbation resulted in idiocy, and I also had read what happened to Onan. In those days the unenlightened (most of the population) thought that self-abuse, as it was so quaintly called, led to acne, impotence, degeneration of the brain, and perhaps socialism. Two generations before my time, the medical doctors believed that it could lead to (I quote an 1864 text) "Nervousness, general weakness, constipation, dejection of spirit, despondency, dislike of female society…&c., and, if allowed to run on, chorea, epilepsy, insanity, mania, consumption, &c."

I would have been more skeptical if it hadn't been for the example of Erlking Curning (long dead now). He not only loved to jerk off in the back of street cars, he would, if dared, and he often was, eat horse manure. To me this was proof that onanism (another quaint word) did result in a fungal mentality. However, years later, some of the biggest masturbators I knew became excellent scholars, war heroes, and wealthy businessmen.

This brief lecture from my father on the evils of self-abuse was very embarrassing to both of us. The subject of sex wouldn't be brought up again by him until I was nineteen. But he contrived a circuitous method of instruction when I was in high school. He purchased a book on sex, and, after he and my mother had read it, left it lying on a table in their bedroom so that I'd be sure to find it. (Everybody used the bedroom as a short cut from the bathroom to the front room.)

My brother Gene and I devoured the book but found it lacking in the more interesting details of actual copulation. It wasn't short in descriptions of the horrors of gonorrhea and syphilis, however. And it stressed the unnaturalness of fellatio and cunnilingus.

When I was nineteen my father suggested that I go to whorehouses if I was suffering from sexual tension. I thought this advice morally schizophrenic, though I wasn't surprised at it. By then I'd concluded that most of mankind was insane in many respects though not hopelessly so. Young idealist that I was, I thought that there were ways in which Homo sapiens could be cured of the vast social ills and psychological fuckups which had cursed it since record-ed time and probably before it. It took me thirty-one years to abandon this belief that mankind could find a cure or cures for what ailed it. At that time I still shared the beliefs of most science fiction readers that Science would show us the way out from our madness to a near-Utopia.

The last spasm of this belief was the speech, titled "Reap," which I gave in 1968 at the World Convention in Oakland, California.

Afterwards, Robert Silverberg told me he thought that it was rather naive, and he was right. It took me several years, however, before I reluctantly agreed with him. During that time I found out that both the conservatives and liber-als rejected my theses and that it would take a Robert Owen, a Bakunin, or a Karl Marx, or a combination thereof, to launch and to push the organization I'd proposed founding. Since I wasn't a fanatic and since I realized that I might do more harm than good if I persisted, I abandoned my plans for action. However, I am both a pessimist and an optimist, and the two take turns possessing me.

During my early juvenile years, I had two recurring dreams which I'll describe because they show my character then and foreshadow themes in my fiction.

One was a nightmare out of Revelation in which the end of the world and final judgment had come. On a wide bare plain were upright poles from the tops of which soldiers hung from ropes tied around their ankles. They wore the uniforms of American doughboys and carried rifles with bayonets, pointing downward, of course. By the bases of the poles were wide dark circular holes. The whole scene was illumined in a ghastly light from the far horizon. Then a mighty voice spoke from the light, and the ropes untied themselves. The sol-diers dropped head-down into the holes, which seemed to me to be shafts to hell, which was in the center of the earth.

I'd wake then, moaning, sweating, and shaking with terror. Were the sol-diers myself? Probably. And almost undoubtedly the nightmare was a dramat-ic Cocteau-like presentation of the conflict between my morally rigid upbring-ing and my burgeoning sex. My unconscious was wasting its time, however, because I was too young and uneducated to know what the dream meant. It would be some years before my sexual dreams abandoned symbolism and became quite direct and literal.

In another recurring dream I was lying on a big meadow and looking up at a cloudless starry sky. Suddenly, a prominent constellation would begin changing shape; the stars composing it would slowly drift to new locations. I knew that the stars, when they stopped, would form another constellation, and this would be a code. If I could decipher the code, I would know all the Great

Secrets, the hitherto impenetrable Mysteries: finity and infinity, time and eternity, death and immortality, the Creator's nature. Almost, almost, I grasped the meaning of the code. But I always awoke just before I comprehended All.

Codes. Pictographs. Hieroglyphs. Runes. Exotic alphabets, syllabaries, and ideograms. Mnemonic knots. They all seemed to me, or to my unconscious, anyway, to contain secrets. And so they did and do, though not the secrets I was looking for, not the revelations I desired. It was this hopeless hope that led me to linguistics and to the reading of so many grammars of non-English languages, to the study of words which might lead me to the Word.

The Word is in no language, written or unwritten. But a study of languages, especially the exotic, especially the Amerind tongues, gives you different worldviews and makes supple the muscles of the imagination. It may also subtly bend the shape of your mind and enable you to touch the oversoul (or undersoul) of all human beings.

Strangely, or perhaps not so strangely, the above paragraph summons from the deeps of forgetfulness the very first dream I remember. It hadn't been available to my consciousness for many years, and then the magic key, the fey wand, disclosed it again. I was between two and three years old and living in the apartment in Indianapolis when I dreamed this. It seemed to me that the doorbell rang and then a furious knocking came up the steps to my bedchamber. I rose and walked (or climbed) down to the front door, and I reached up and turned the knob and opened the door. It was night outside, but a single streetlamp outlined a tall thin man with a high hat of curious shape. He held in one hand a bulky shapeless case. He said, "I can come in or you can come out." And that was the end of the dream of the mysterious stranger.

Later, I dreamed of this dream, knowing that I was dreaming a dream. I forgot it for some years, but when I read Twain's *The Mysterious Stranger,* I remembered it. What does it mean? I don't know. But ten years ago I wrote a note in my ragged journal about this. I asked myself what I would see if I drew on a map a line connecting all the places I'd lived in. Would the line reveal the outline of a continent of the mind, a continent which would also be a hieroglyph? And would this hieroglyph, if readable, reveal a mystery or the Mystery? I never attempted to draw the line, and that is probably significant.

At this time I also noted that there wasn't much psychological difference between me and Gilgamesh, the legendary and perhaps historical king and founder of the ancient Sumerian city of Uruk. Both of us were searching for the same thing, the secret of immortality, and a snake had snatched the secret from both of us. Our snakes were not the same. At least, I didn't think they were. I hadn't seen mine, couldn't even name it. But then perhaps Gilgamesh hadn't seen his either or been able to name it. He was in very murky waters when the snake robbed him.

It was also at this time (when I was fifty-two) that I became convinced that everything was interrelated and connected. Or else nothing was related and connected. So I made a choice of the former belief, a choice determined by temperament, not by logic. This assumption is one of the underpinning themes of my fiction, but so far it's only been commented on rather briefly in my works. (Mostly in "Riders of the Purple Wage" and *Venus On The Half-Shell*.) I expect to make the theme the basis of some stories some day, however.

Back to Columbia Grade School. In the early grades I'd been rather gregarious, open, talkative, and athletic. But as I advanced into puberty, I became rather shy and retiring except in athletics. In Peoria Central High School, I'd blush if a girl whom I'd not known at grade school spoke to me. I was extremely self-conscious and what is called "a nervous pisser." I had to urinate every half-hour or so. The result of this imperative, painful to me but comical to others, was that I had to dash for the boys' room between every class. Some years later I found out that this was partly due to an exceptionally small bladder, a condition inherited from my mother. The other part was due to tension.

I also had what is called a "bashful kidney." I couldn't urinate if someone was watching me. I told my father about this some years later, and he said that he'd been afflicted with one, too, until he was thirty. Then he suddenly and unexplainably was free of the inhibition. Though I got over some of the effects of this, I was in both a mental and physical agony when I was in the army air force. This was the main reason I washed out as an aviation cadet. (Hmm. Washed out. Is there some curious perverse connection in my unconscious between this phrase and the kidney neurosis?)

I did well in my studies in high school, however, except for geometry, in which I got a C average, and in a shop course, which I dropped after a few weeks. Though my father and uncle were engineers and I came from a long line of people with high mechanical aptitudes, I had trouble with inanimate objects. (Which, I'm convinced, are not as inanimate and will-less as most people think.) The required course in speech was agony for me, though I got a good grade and even played the role of a villainous Roman centurion in a Christmas stage play in the auditorium. And during an assembly period I did an impromptu dance on the stage.

Despite studying hard and earning letters in football and track, I managed to read many books and magazines not on the curriculum. The science fiction magazines, *The Shadow, Doc Savage, Weird Tales, Argosy, Blue Book,* and dozens of other pulp periodicals. Doyle, London, every Twain book available, Dumas,

Dickens, poetry, Haggard, Cooper, Wren, Wells, Reeve, Sabatini, Zane Grey, Curwood, Smollett, Fielding, Cervantes, Buchan, Wallace (both Lew and Edgar), Chesterton, G. B. Shaw, Thackeray, rereadings of E. R. Burroughs, Verne, Bunyan, Swift, and Stevenson. I also read the slicks: *Saturday Evening Post, Collier's, Liberty*, and the women's magazines. I even read *True Confessions* for a while.

It's true, as some critics have said, that I was raised on the pulp tradition. But at the same time I was reading classics, and in high school I read the unabridged adult versions of Homer. And at sixty-two I'm still reading him.

In my senior year (1936), I discovered Dunsany. He so inspired me that I made notes and sketches for a story in which a single planet, shaped like a Tower of Babel and having not-quite Terran laws of gravity, occupied the center of a parallel pocket universe. The only other celestial objects were a sun and a moon. An Amerind named Kickaha roamed this exotic planet and had many adventures.

These scribblings and crude drawings were the basis for the World of Tiers series. I didn't do anything about them until 1964, however. Then the tiered-planet universe became only one of many artificial worlds, and Kickaha became a Hoosier Caucasian (though with some Amerind genes) modeled on the type of person I sometimes think I'd like to be. Some people have noticed that the Lords in the second in the series, *Gates of Creation*, have names out of William Blake. The reason for this will be revealed in the sixth or seventh (final) book in the series.

"Little did I know" (as the heroine says in Gothics) that I would one day become the second-best-known graduate of Peoria Central. The best known would be a girl who was a sophomore when I was a senior. She was Betty Goldstein then, later to be Betty Friedan and a world-famous feminist. I knew her name and saw her frequently in the halls or at assemblies. But we never exchanged words. Like me, she was a lonely somewhat alienated kid, though for different reasons. She went out into the world to change it, and I went out to create new worlds. It took both of us a long time.

I was a bookworm, yet active in sports. Introverted, yet bursting at times into dramatics. Almost pathologically shy and afraid of physical or verbal violence (except in athletics), yet once challenging to a fistfight a football player who'd been unmercifully riding me. (He backed down and apologized though he was much larger than I.) A Puritan with a Gargantua deep within me. A voracious reader who enjoyed knocking down football players, the hardest hitter on the team. I was also insanely idealistic and far more naive than most of my peers. I loathed having to work summers because it reduced my reading time, but I enjoyed the physical exertion. I was overly respectful of and obedient to authority, yet was aware of the irrationality, hypocrisy, and greed motivating the authorities. I was patriotic but had done enough reading even then to know something of the vast evils existing in our nation.

It was a fucked-up kid, a raw callow youth who left Peoria Central and had to pick out a college to go to. I wanted to work for a couple of years before going on to higher education, but my father insisted that I go now. He was afraid that I'd end up like him, be without a degree. I said that I'd like to go to Bradley College, which was in Peoria. But he knew that I wanted to be close to home, to safety and security. Only by getting away from it, by being on my own, could I cut the silver cord. So I entered the University of Missouri with the intention of becoming a journalism major.

The Great Depression was still going on. Though the Farmer family didn't suffer much from it, it didn't have much money. Sending me to Missouri instead of Bradley completely decanted my father's bank account. I did pay for part of the expenses by working summers as a groundman for the line crew of the streetcar company, but in the second semester we had to borrow money from my uncle to see me through that period. Moreover, I was so busy adjusting to this new life that I didn't study as hard as I had in high school. (Where I'd been one of the five lettermen elected to the National Senior Honor Society.)

One of my father's friends, an alumnus of Old Mizzou, had given me a letter of introduction to his fraternity, Lambda Chi Alpha. I lived in its house and eventually became an active, but only after a crisis-ridden pledgeship. While I was a pledge the actives tried to scourge me of my social ungraces, my shyness, my sometimes rebellious attitude, and what seemed to them my cynicism about society and politics. They forced me to get dates and encouraged me to drink, and I proved to be too apt a student. I acquired a taste for whiskey though it had nauseated me when I first tried it.

In those days, there were weekly "bitch" sessions where the actives told you what was wrong with you. You also had to bend over and get whacked by a paddle if you deviated from the behavior prescribed by the active members. Despite many anxieties and miseries, my freshman year was a lot of fun and, in the end, good for me. (No pun intended.)

I was still reading *Doc Savage*, science fiction, and other pulplit, but I'd discovered Hemingway, Faulkner, Goethe, Marlowe, the Restoration dramatists. And while prowling through the university library I found two fascinating books, one on comparative Germanic and a bilingual Prose Edda.

The freshman year ended. I went home. During the summer I worked with the line crew repairing electrical lines, replacing line poles, and sometimes repairing high-tension wires in the country. Being with them was as educational as being in a university, though in a different way. The linemen had little formal schooling, but they knew the ways of the world and were independent, individualistic, rough-and-ready, full of folklore and superstition, bigoted but fair according to their own lights, essentially kindhearted, and very hardworking. The crew had one asshole, of course. Any group with more than two members somehow usually includes one asshole. I'd noticed that while living in the frat house. But even he had his good points.

When we had especially big jobs, an itinerant lineman would usually be hired to help us. These were always wild mavericks, real "characters," working tramps, men whose crazy but true tales gave me an insight into the "real" world. And especially into the conditions of the workers in the United States in the 1910s and 1920s. I was shocked, and I later got into some hot heavy arguments with my father, a staunch Republican, about the working class and the exploiter class. These always ended when he told me to shut up because I was too young and ignorant to know the truth.

Because we worked in the streets, we came across many of the street people, especially in the South Side, where I'd once lived. Perhaps the most flamboyant and memorable was a punch-drunk Negro. He was short but massive and built like an ape with his short legs and extraordinarily long arms. He had cauliflower ears and much scar tissue about his eyes. His eyeballs were deep yellow with jaundice. He always wore castoff gymnasium warm-up clothes, torn tennis shoes, and a dirty visored cap. His English was right out of *Uncle Remus*. Every once in a while, when we were repairing the lines, he would appear, rolling sailorlike toward us, his arms swinging, his huge yellow teeth shining wetly. The others in the crew knew him well and had a great time kidding him. And sometimes one would slip him a dollar.

From what the crew said, he lived in a packing box behind a tavern in the summer and only God knew where in the winter. He made his living as a swamper in some taverns and as a fighter in the ring, usually in the mass battle called "tank fights." Though a real down-and-outer, a stumblebum, he had a flair for original (to me, anyway) phraseology. He was a skidrow poet. I never forgot him, and years later I used him for the model of Old Man Paley, the junkheap garbage-dump Neanderthal of "The Alley Man." The dump where Paley lived actually existed. It was in the land by the Kickapoo Creek between Peoria and Bartonville. There were also in Old Man Paley traces of Crump's Og and of the nameless ape-man of London's *Before Adam*.

A month before I was to go back to Missouri for my sophomore year, I got bad news from my father. To have money to put me through college, he'd started a business, a garage which checked out autos on dynamometers. This was a side project since he was still working for Illinois Power and Light. He'd borrowed heavily to launch the business, and it had failed. Now he had to declare bankruptcy. This meant that I not only could not continue my college education, I had to work to help him repay his debts. Though he was not now legally obligated to do so, he intended to pay back his creditors every cent on the dollar. I agreed with him that this was the only honorable course. After all, hadn't Sam Clemens done the same thing when he'd gone bankrupt?

So, from July, 1937, to February, 1939, I stayed out of college and worked on the line crew. My father satisfied his creditors, and I earned some money toward going back to school. In this interim I read a lot, so much in fact that when I returned to college I had read much of the curriculum in English literature and much more than was required in other fields. I also did a lot of dating and running around with former classmates at Central. During this time I sent some short stories to *Weird Tales* and *Astounding*. All were rightly rejected. I also wrote the first third of a novel, some of which is salvageable today if rewritten. And I started but never completed a mystery novel.

In 1938 (as I remember it), the first softcover editions of hardback books started appearing. While in a drugstore near the downtown library, I came across Fairfax Downey's biography of Sir Richard Francis Burton. This so fascinated me that I went to the library and found out that it had an almost complete collection of Burton's works and all the works about him. (Donated by a wealthy Peoria citizen.) I read these and was captured. Thus was planted one large seed of the Riverworld series. Another seed, of course, was my very early acquaintance with Mark Twain.

One of my friends, whom I'd known since fourth grade at Columbia, formed with me and a few others a sort of village atheist group. But when his parents died of cancer, he couldn't endure the thought that they were forever dead, that they would be dust and less than that and nothing more. He converted to the type of Fundamentalism in which he'd been raised. Worse, he wouldn't rest until he'd also converted me. I'd read much biblical criticism and was also able to detect discrepancies in the Bible myself. We argued much, I at least having a good time at it. But I accepted his invitation to go to a revival meeting, and all of a sudden, found myself at the altar and accepting Christ as my savior. Unfortunately, or fortunately, a week later I'd gotten over the emotional pressure and enthusiasm and had backslid into Ye Compleat Atheist.

This incident shows in private life what became of one of my minor but always present themes in most of my writings. That is, that despite a person's rational attitude, he is never free of the early conditioning, of the attitudes, concepts, prejudices, and images, pressed deep into him when very young. Or not so young. The emotional factor is always waging war with the rational. Or, if the emotional, the deeply neural, has made peace with the rational, then it uses the rational to justify the emotional.

This theme was one of the two major ones in my mainstream novel, *Fire and the Night*. In this the protagonist, Danny Alliger, was aware of the conflict between his conditioning in racial terms and his enlightenment by reason. I suppose that most readers are aware of the too-obvious resemblance between the names of the hero and Dante Alighieri. Which also explains why the name of the black couple in the novel was Virgil. What the reader may not know is that Dante's family name was German in origin and was Alliger.

At this time I was drifting, though I had vague plans to go back to college when my father's debts were paid. I'd also determined that I didn't want to be a newspaper reporter. I lacked the aggressiveness required, and it seemed to me that a reporter's writings were too ephemeral. Vague also were my plans to be a fiction writer. But I thought that if I did become a fictionist, I'd write mainstream. The reason that I'd only written science fiction or fantasy (and not much of that then) was that these seemed to come easier. I was very ignorant then; I had no knowledge of the extremely low rates paid to science fiction or fantasy writers or what a dog's life it would be to support myself even minimally in this field. I didn't even know there was such a phenomenon as the fan world. Now of course I'm thoroughly aware of the fans, though the rates paid in the science fiction magazines are still extremely low.

In 1938 I discovered Dostoyevsky and I was stunned. This man, I thought, is the greatest. Do I have the potential to be a Dostoyevsky? An American Dostoyevsky or Melville? Or combination thereof? A few years later I told myself that I might have the potential, but it would never be actualized unless I lived as fully as Dostoyevsky or traveled as extensively as Melville. What I ask myself *now* is whether or not I can realize the potential of Philip José Farmer.

When I was at Missouri, I had several sessions with a faculty psychologist and freshman advisor. He told me after forty-five minutes that I had a drive for self-defeat, an unconscious desire to fail. A psychoanalyst in 1966 was to tell me the same thing, though it took the Beverly Hills doctor ten hours to see this. What both didn't see or didn't tell me was that I also had a drive to succeed. And that this conflict set up one more of the many tensions operating within me. I wish I could say with certainty what set up these wrangling drives. I wish I could say it with only some uncertainty. Or even with much uncertainty. But I don't have the slightest idea of the causes. I only know that these opposing compulsions are within me and that I must be on my guard against them.

During this drifting period, I quit reading all pulp magazines except *Astounding*. Aside from this, only modern fiction and classical mainstream or fantasy in hardbound books interested me. Nonfiction, history, biography, anthropology, and psychology were my chief interests. And, like most Midwesterners of my age group, I was only vaguely aware of the rising Hitler menace. I didn't get out of Peoria much except for some trips to the Wisconsin Dells, Hannibal, Missouri, the Mammoth Cave, and the New York World's Fair. I did think seriously for a while of going to Africa when I got enough money to do so (Africa had always fascinated me) instead of returning to college. But that would have bitterly disappointed my father. Besides, it was easier just to fantasize the trip.

In late 1938 a friend introduced me to a woman whom I shall call Felicia. She was three years older than I and had an M.A. in psychology from a large state university in the East. She was very attractive, superbly built, pixy-faced, and husky-voiced. She introduced me to Freud, Jung, Adler, and the depths of contemporary psychology. She also knew more than I did about literature, in fact, she knew more than I did about most things.

However, she was interested in the stuff I'd written and read it with what I now see was great perception. She said that I showed some promise and had a vivid imagination but that I had a long way to go before I became a good writer. She also said that she wondered if I would become a writer. Here I was, almost twenty-one, and yet I'd produced very little. Did I have the drive and self-discipline needed to succeed? We had long talks and went for long walks in the country. After some time, she admitted that she was engaged to a man she'd met in the university and who lived in an eastern city. But since they didn't see each other much they dated others.

Despite this, my relationship with Felicia wasn't Platonic. Within a month we were doing what was called then, quaint phrase, light petting. That progressed to heavy petting, an even quainter phrase. And then to copulation in the missionary position. After a few times of this, she told me that she was also screwing her fiancé (I'd guessed that), but that he was rather prejudiced against unconventional sexual practices. In fact, the idea of them disgusted him; he thought people who practiced them were perverts. She didn't think so, but she was convinced that her fiancé would never get over his revulsion. Though she'd never been in to such tabu acts herself, she was curious about them. I confessed that I'd always had middle-class ideas about such things myself. She said that there were more middle-class people than I thought who secretly did such things. So I said that I'd try to overcome any inhibitions I might have.

This conversation took place after we'd been discussing Nietzsche. I'm not sure how Zarathustra could have had such a liberating influence, but I'm sure that the woman-hating German philosopher who created Zarathustra would not have approved the events following. In any event, I found out that Felicia was polymorphous perverse (a marvelous phrase!) and that I shed my supposed inhibitions as easily as a snake sheds its skin.

Felicia claimed that she'd had no experience in such acts She'd only read about them. If this were true she was a hell of a good student. I didn't care, though I did wonder sometimes if she was just using me. Not that I was bothered about this. She seemed to be as fond of me as I was of her. Neither was in love with the other but I did have a bad time when she told me, ten months later, that we couldn't see each other any more. She would be getting married very soon; her fiancé would be in Peoria for the marriage within a week, her parents wouldn't like it if she kept dating me.

I've often wondered if she ever converted her husband to her ways or if she was lying to me about him or if she now and then took a lover. Whatever the situation, she was a wonderful woman, and I've always been grateful to her. (She died a few years ago of cancer.)

I suppose many of my youthful readers will wonder why I even bring up this story. What they don't realize, can't "feel," is that 1938 was a far different world from 1978. It was only five years before I met Felicia that Prohibition had been repealed and James Joyce's *Ulysses* could be legally printed in the United States. We could have been sent to jail for many years if caught, and we would have been regarded as rotten perverts. The main point of the Felicia story, though, is that, despite an intense conditioning against such sexual activity, I resisted it. My inborn temperament did not allow the conditioning to get a hold on me.

In the summer of 1939 I was able to return to school. But since I still didn't have much money, I decided to go to Bradley. This was a small college which had only a few years before been a polytechnic institute and still had an associated horological school, one of the best in the nation. Many I had known in high school were seniors there. I enrolled as an English literature major with a minor in philosophy. One of my teachers was a Harvard graduate the other, a Wellesley graduate. When I became a candidate for a creative writing scholarship, these two decided that I should win it. A third member of the committee, a Dr. Bell, didn't think I deserved it. But while the decision was pending, Bell went on a trip to Arkansas and was killed in an automobile accident. That effectively removed his objection, and I got the much-needed scholarship.

However, it turned out that my being on the football and track team also had something to do with being awarded the scholarship. This so disgusted me that I quit football as soon as I had the scholarship in my hands. Besides, practice was taking too much time, and I'd lost all my enthusiasm for the sport. The coach never forgave me.

Dr. Kinsey came to Bradley to interview male students about their sexual habits, and I was one of those who got to be questioned by this great man. His pioneering work didn't come out until years later, however.

In 1940, I helped establish a Lambda Chi Alpha chapter on the campus. A local fraternity had decided to become a chapter of the national organization. Since I was the only one with any Lambda Chi Alpha experience, I did much of the groundwork. My best friend there, whom I'll call Autolycus, became the president and I was the vice-president. The second semester we had a crisis which matched closely one I'd witnessed when I was a pledge at Missouri. A youth whom I'll call Applebury wanted to pledge the frat. But when he was voted on, all but two blackballed him because he was too Jewish-looking. Autolycus and I said that we'd resign and make the reasons for it public if Applebury wasn't pledged. After some acrimonious dispute, the others gave in. Nobody, of course, ever told Applebury about this, and he became quite popular in the house.

When I was a pledge at Mizzou, two of the actives were of Syrian descent. One of them was my best friend; his brother was an asshole. Their cousin wanted to become a pledge, and this caused a secret meeting of the actives, excluding the two brothers, of course. Some actives said that Lambda Chi Alpha already had two Jewish-looking members. That was enough. A third would break the camel's back. I had no vote in this meeting since I was only a pledge, but an active told me about it later on. The dilemma was solved, however, when the cousin decided to go to another school in Missouri.

The brothers never had to face the problem of a Negro wanting to pledge. At that time American blacks weren't admitted to Missouri. Blacks were admitted to Bradley, but there were very few because of the tuition. Most Peoria blacks went to state universities. At that time, however, there were very few who went to institutions of higher learning unless they were outstanding athletes.

My friend Autolycus was a native Peorian whose uncle had been a governor of Arkansas and whose father was a policeman. We ran around a lot, stuffed the ballot box in the campus elections, and vomited cheap whiskey behind the trees on the campus. Though we double-dated a lot, he would never go out with me on Saturday or Sunday. I finally found out why. He was earning the money to put himself through college by running the Peoria syndicate's gambling money to the St. Louis syndicate on weekends. He'd leave at midnight with the illicit cargo under the back seat and hope that no cop stopped him and searched the car. He'd gotten the job through his father, the cop.

Despite his criminal career, Autolycus became a very respectable member of the community. He was a civilian air instructor for the Army during the war, then became a pilot for American Airlines. At the same time, he studied law and eventually had two law practices going, one at Los Angeles and one at Chicago. The last I heard of him he'd retired from American and was in full-time practice as a well-known lawyer in Los Angeles. I never asked him whom he represented there.

I met Bette Virginia Andre soon after she entered Bradley College in 1940. She had a musical scholarship and played the lead in a college musical stage play. We got rather serious, but in the winter semester of 1941 I decided to transfer back to Missouri. Bradley had no courses in classical Greek, but Missouri did. If I was ever going to be able to read Homer in the original, I'd have to go where Greek was taught. Also, I was afraid of being too near to proposing marriage to Bette. I wasn't ready for that. Marriage was a tremendous responsibility, and my prospects for being able to support a wife and children were dismal.

Arriving at M.U., I found I'd have to wait until the fall semester to take Greek. Never mind. I'd take other courses. I moved into the Lambda Chi Alpha house, a larger one than that I'd tenanted in 1936-37. Looking back now, I can see that there was a subtle difference in the students of 1941 and those I'd known when I was a freshman. The Zeitgeist was slightly different. The frat brothers seemed to be a little more grim and serious, as if the clouds of the coming war were casting dark shadows. These students were anything but unaware of Hitler and the warlords of Japan.

I took another creative writing course and entered a long story in a contest. If I'd won, I'd have had some money to apply toward my room and board. I lost, though my teacher thought I should have won. Perhaps, it was the theme of the story which kept it from winning in that state. It was about a Peoria Negro, a superb athlete with a high intelligence and high ambitions, who was constantly frustrated and denigrated by whites. Finally, he explodes into verbal and then into physical violence. This story would be the germ of *Fire and the Night*, though I used very little of it in the novel.

Though my writing teacher, a fine old gentleman from the Deep South, thought that the story should have won because of its vivid characterization and descriptive details, he also said that he had never met a black like my protagonist. He didn't think that blacks were harboring the deep resentment and sullen rage of the hero. Of course, he didn't *know* any like Elkanah Lee. No black with any regard for his life would have expressed such feelings to any southern white. I didn't know any one like my hero, either. But all I had to do was put myself into the shoes of Elkanah and imagine how he felt.

There was an election for the student governing body in the spring, and Lambda Chi Alpha was voting as a body for one of the three parties campaigning for these posts. The chief opposing party always hung up a big standard before a tavern and guarded it with big athletes armed with the heavy wooden paddles used to thwack the rear ends of pledges. The tradition was that the party to which my frat belonged would try to steal the standard or take it by force.

I watched one such effort, a sudden raid which failed when the raiders were beaten back with the paddles. They were actually hitting each other with them! I thereupon determined to try to steal the standard all by myself, though I wasn't sure I'd have the guts to do it. I hung around with the guards, who didn't know me because I was a transfer and thought I was one of them. About half an hour before dusk, the guards took the standard down, rolled it up around the pole, and started to carry it toward the Sigma Chi house for safekeeping overnight. I grabbed the middle of the pole and helped them carry it.

When we were a block away from the tavern and at a corner street, I suddenly gave an Indian yell and tore the standard from the hands of the men holding each end. They yelled and cursed at me, and as I sped down the street, I saw whirling paddles fly by me, some very close. Knowing that I'd probably be beaten or at least roughly manhandled by the angry pursuers, I really put on the steam. I was in good shape and fear pumped adrenalin into me. By the time I got to the Lambda Chi Alpha house, I was half a block ahead of the closest pursuer. I was also breathing very hard, and my sides hurt. I couldn't have gone much farther, and a block ahead were other furious men who'd cut up the other block to head me off.

I staggered into the house where I could expect safety in numbers. But the only ones there were the very old housemother and a big football player. I told him what had happened. He told me to help him lock the doors and windows. Then I went up to the attic and put the standard there. Meanwhile, a mob had collected in front of the house. It yelled and screamed and hollered and demanded that the standard be returned—or else. The football player made a lot of phone calls to summon help. It did arrive, but by then the mob had left.

Not, however, before some went to a local warehouse and purchased dozens of eggs. When they returned, they pelted the front of the house with the eggs and a few rocks. Some windows were broken, causing the eighty-year-old housemother to go into hysterics. More eggs were brought up and hurled. The porch and front of the house and the windows became a gooey mess. Finally, seeing that they weren't going to get the standard back unless they broke into the house, and afraid to do that because the police might be called in, the mob dispersed. Just in time, since here came the rescuers, a big angry mob armed with paddles.

There was a lull for a while during which I explained what had happened. Then a convertible crammed with the opposition raced by, and eggs flew from it. The mob, our guys, wiped the shells and yolks off and went down to the warehouse to buy hundreds of the ovarian ammunition themselves. For an hour or more there was a great egg-fight, and raiders pelted the Sigma Chi and several other frat houses. A lot of innocent bystanders got smeared, too, independent party students caught crossing the campus or emerging from the tavern. Even a couple of professors were bombarded.

Then the chief candidate for the opposition phoned our leader and challenged him to a fistfight. They hated each other's guts, and one had stolen the other's girlfriend the semester before. So we piled into cars and drove to the Sigma Chi house. Here there were many actives and pledges of both parties, all spoiling for a fight though I think most of them hoped it would just be between the two big shots. These were in the center of the crowd when I got there each cursing and accusing the other. But after a while it became evident that neither was going to throw the first punch, and people began drifting away. Finally, our leader, still hurling threats, got into a car and drove away.

This was one of the big highlights of my life, and I was a hero for a day. In 1953 I wrote a twelve-thousand-word novelette based on this incident. But the hero was a freshman who nerved himself to steal the standard because he wanted to impress a beautiful senior girl. The title was "The Face That Launched a Thousand Eggs." It was too long for *Playboy* and the two mainstream magazines I sent it to. So I put it in the trunk. However, I plan to use it in a projected novel, *Pearl Diving in Old Peoria.* The locale will be shifted from the Missouri campus to Peoria University. Old P.U., based on Bradley College.

The Shakespeare professor I'd had at Bradley was very good, but the one at Missouri was a fireball, a genius scholar and lecturer with his own original interpretation of *King Lear.* He convinced me then, and I still believe, that this is the Bard's greatest play. Another professor who could set his students on fire was the Milton teacher, a witty Oscar Wilde-like character.

Meanwhile, I missed Bette so much that I began hitchhiking weekends, leaving Friday after class and usually getting to Peoria late that night. I'd spend Saturday with her and start thumbing rides on Sunday morning to travel the three hundred miles to Columbia. In June we decided to get secretly married, and when she came down on the bus for the big fraternity dance, we did get hitched.

Summer came, and since my parents had moved out to a farmhouse, I lived in the Lambda Chi Alpha house while working for the streetcar company. Then the draft threatened, and I became an aviation cadet in the Army Air Force. I'd had a semester of pilot instruction in the student CAA course at

Bradley. On my final checkout flight I'd put the Piper Cub into a spin and came out as required, but the motor conked out. Unable to get it going again, I had to glide in and make a deadstick landing. I didn't hit the telephone wires bordering the field, but I did miss the runway. The instructor got mad at me because we had difficulty getting the plane out of the mud. He said that he was doubtful about giving me my pilot's license, but, if I meant to take the next advanced course, he'd do so. I didn't think I'd be around so I said I wouldn't be taking the intermediate course.

After this experience I had no business becoming a cadet, but I wanted to fly. While at the preflight school at Kelly Field, Texas, I heard the news over the radio of the attack on Pearl Harbor. I was by no means the only one there who had a sinking feeling. After preflight, I was transferred to a primary field near a small town north of Abilene. It was fun flying Stearman biplanes with their open cockpits. Twice, a friend of mine and I flew out of sight of the officers at the field and had simulated dogfights. We also buzzed the cattle and horses until complaints from the ranchers stopped that.

Then I was sent from primary to basic at Randolph Field, the "West Point of the Air." I went down with five others in a car and spent two days in San Antonio. When we left in the morning to report to the field, we passed a tavern. Knowing that we'd be restricted to the base for a month, we decided we'd have one last drink. Three days later, we showed up at Randolph, hung over, red-eyed, our uniforms stained with beer, whiskey, and gravy. We were properly chewed out and in a few days were court-martialed. Our punishment was to walk fifty hours (not all at once) in full dress under the watchful eye of Major Taber. In addition, some of us accumulated some demerits which caused more hours to be tacked on.

Since the barracks were very crowded and I deserved to be punished even more, I didn't get to share a room with anybody. I had to sleep on a cot out in the hall. That didn't bother me. I was spared the many sudden inspections of the room for cleanliness and neatness. All I had to do was to arrange my bed and footlocker while the other cadets were working their asses off cleaning their quarters. At the same time that the officers were on our necks, the upperclassmen were hazing us. There was no justice in this, and there wasn't supposed to be. The good thing about this was that when you became an upperclassman, you could haze the lower class. I never did.

Though I'd had no trouble flying at primary, I did in basic. I could understand only half of what my instructor said through the earphones, and that drove him crazy. He was a maniac, anyway, a very nervous man with the biggest feet I've ever seen and a too close physical resemblance to the detestable

Dr. Bell of Bradley. I went to the Army doctor for a hearing examination. He told me my auditory apparatus was fine, and he intimated that perhaps I didn't want to hear my instructor. I didn't tell the doctor that the instructor had accused me of laughing at him behind his back. This was untrue, though I may have grinned at him.

Finally, I decided to apply for another instructor. Too late. I was washed out, and since I didn't want to stay in the Air Force if I couldn't be a pilot, the controller of the plane, I asked to be discharged. At that time those who'd entered the air force before the war began were allowed to leave it. I was given an honorable discharge, but it noted that I had an anxiety neurosis. I already knew that. I went home and waited for the draft to take me. I was thinking about joining the cavalry, and then I found out that this branch of the army had replaced horses with tanks.

I moved in with Bette's folks, and I got a job at the Keystone Steel & Wire Company, depicted under the name of Helsgets' in *Fire and the Night*. It was to be just a temporary job. So, eleven and a half years later, I quit the steel mill. I was never drafted. My son, the future Buddhist of the Nichiren sect, was born, followed three years later by my daughter, the future Roman Catholic. Their father, the village atheist and working stiff, slaved at the very hot, heavy, and sometimes dangerous labor in the blooming mill of Keystone. But he was reading voraciously in many fields and spasmodically writing stories or fragments thereof. The Bellman's map had very few lines on it, and the Bellman himself was still getting the rudder mixed up with the bowsprit.

I wrote several stories which I sent off to the *Saturday Evening Post* and a few other slicks. These were, of course, bounced. Why did I ever think that the Post would take a story about a young man who sneaked down at nights to bed his mother-in-law? Or a story about a woman in a small town, a very respectable and prudish wife and mother, who liked to expose herself in a window when the nearby trains went by?

I was reading the Gold Medal softcovers then, too, most of which were private eye stories or violent adventures. I especially admired John D. MacDonald. I started a novel with Gold Medal in mind but never finished it. I also wrote about one hundred pages of what was to be a long novel about a freshman at the University of Missouri (called Shomi). I was under the influence of Thomas Wolfe then, and the novel shows it. It was titled *The Green Knight*, which I later changed to *The Unruly Lance*. I was reading Whit Burnett's quarterly, *Story*, then. This paid nothing but prestige, as I remember it, but editors and critics read it and noted the works of its contributors. Its literary quality was usually high, and the fiction often consisted of stories which wouldn't be acceptable in the national magazines because of their too-specific erotic or violent content or their social views.

I wrote a short story titled "The Doll Game" and sent it to Burnett. It took place in Suburbia and was about two very young neighboring children who had witnessed the adulterous encounter of their parents and simulated this in a game with their dolls. Whit liked it very much but his wife said it was "too rough." I never did find out if she meant that the prose or the theme was too rough. I put it in the old trunk, and years later I sent it to Judy Merril when she was editing a mainstream anthology. She accepted it, but her publisher withdrew his support, and she lost the manuscript. I also wrote a fifty-word story for *Esquire*, which now and then published such midgets. The editor was all for it, but his publisher turned it down on the grounds that he wasn't printing puzzles for his readers. The punch line was obvious to me and the editor, but that didn't mean a thing to the man in power.

Meanwhile, conditions in Bette's parents' house were miserable. Her father was a salesman for local grocers, though at one time he'd been a big-shot lawyer in Burlington, Iowa, a member of the legislature, and had been groomed to be the Republican candidate for governor. Then he became involved in some scandal and was a fugitive from justice for a while, though it turned out that he needn't have run. Bette's mother came from a wealthy Dutch family in the very small village of Hartsburg, Illinois, but was now reduced to being a saleslady for Montgomery Ward. She was always the chief provider of the two. He was given to long periods of abysmal melancholy which usually ended when Bette, always defending her mother, forced him to reveal what he was so sad about. There would be an explosion of verbal violence, and then her father would be okay for a while. The big traumatic event in Bette's life had occurred when she was eight, when her father took off without a word and was hiding for four years. This made her "protect" her mother though in recent years she's seen that the fault wasn't entirely her father's.

Bette was suffering from grand mal seizures; our son got rheumatic fever. And then I came down with both typhoid fever and malaria. What? Malaria in mid-Illinois? Yes, I was one of three cases in Illinois that year. Later I'd find out that malaria was still a danger in the state, though not, statistically, a great one. I'd also discover that malaria killed far more pioneers in the Midwest than the Indians ever did.

In 1945 I wrote a twelve-thousand-word story, "O'Brien and Obrenov," about the meeting in central Germany of the Russian and American forces and their simultaneous capture of a Nazi war criminal, Scheissmiller. I sent it to *Saturday Evening Post*, which returned it with a note that the editors liked it very much but couldn't print it unless I deleted a big drunken banquet scene. I refused to do this since it would water the effect of the story too much. I sent it to *Argosy*, and the editor liked it but said it was too long for his magazine. However, he'd sent it on to the editor of *Adventure*, and Kenneth White bought it. Its appearance in a 1946 *Adventure* was euphoric for me. Just maybe I could sell many more and quit the sweating drudgery and deadening swing shifts of Keystone. And get out of the house I'd been a prisoner in for a long time. But my next two stories, one about the historical little Jack Horner, were rejected. They were said to be too "frenetic."

Most of the money I was making seemed to go for doctor bills. Then Bette's sister and her husband, with their two children, moved into the house. The situation was already bad enough, especially with my claustrophobic tendencies. It got worse, and one day I exploded under intense provocation and started to choke my sister-in-law. I never lost enough self-control, however, that I really meant to kill her. The result of this was that Bette's parents decided to loan us the money to put a down payment on our own house. (Her father had come into some money with the death of his mother.) We moved into a house on Barker Street, four blocks away. But it seemed light-years distant.

Bette, always the prime mover in our physical or metaphysical moves, thought that it would be a good idea if we joined a church. I went along with it, and then after a while I became charmed and overwhelmed by the brilliant intellect of the chief preacher. (Who later became a big shot in the World Council of Churches.) I joined and was baptized into the Disciples of Christ. (Which I found out last year was also the church of my eighteenth and nineteenth-century Dooley ancestors. Is there a psychic heredity?) However (there always is a however or but in my life), I eventually became aware of the rationalizations in this liberal church just as I'd become aware of the rationalizations in Fundamentalism. So I backslid. Fell from grace, whoever she is. But whereas I'd been an atheist before this conversion, I became an agnostic after it.

In the meantime, Bette said that I was wasting my talent and brains by working at Keystone. There was no future in it. So why didn't we go back to Bradley and finish our education? If I got an M.A., I could be a teacher. Then I'd have the time to write and be in an academic atmosphere, one conducive to writing. This premise was false, but we didn't know it then. To do this, I had to arrange with the bosses and fellow workers at Keystone a schedule which would permit me to work nights from 11:00 PM. to 7:00 A.M. The only way it would work out for me was to put in forty-eight hours a week. This meant that I'd have to put in an extra night. On the other hand, I'd be making more money.

I enrolled for seventeen hours of classes per week at Bradley, which by then had become a university. The campus was crowded, the formerly large open areas of lawn now being covered with Quonset huts to house the extra faculty and some of the students there on the GI Bill. The Zeitgeist at Bradley had changed enormously in nine years. Where B.C. had been almost a semirural college, B.U. was now truly a university, though its cosmopolitanism was perhaps rawer than that at the University of Illinois or of Chicago. Also, because master's and doctor's degrees were now available there, there were many older students, mostly ex-GI's.

Mornings, Bette and I would leave the house, walking the six long blocks to Bradley while our two children set off in the opposite direction for their grade school. Bette was taking courses which would, after hospital training, give her a license as a medical laboratory technician. I had a year and a half to complete toward a B.A. and then would get an M.A. and a job teaching English. After I was through with my morning and some early afternoon classes, I'd come home and sleep until suppertime. Then I'd study until it was time to go to work at the steel mill.

Despite this rigorous and hard schedule, we had an extensive and sometimes rigorous social schedule. We fell in with a group of the older students whose Bohemian pre-Beatnik ways earned us the title of "The Bearded Ones," though only two had beards. Since we were the only ones who had a house, the group made it the headquarters for parties. These lasted through Saturday evening and Sunday morning. One of the distinguishing features about this group was the eagerness of its members to learn. It may have been the last such at Bradley, since a professor there tells me that most of its students are distinguished now by their apathy.

In any case, we took courses in such subjects as semeiotics and advanced anthropology and spent much time between or after classes sitting in the student union and discussing philosophy, psychology, and, of course, sex. Copies of Henry Miller and Frank Harris, smuggled into the United States, were passed through the group. When L. Ron Hubbard's book on dianetics came out, some of us took turns being auditors and auditees. During one session I smashed lamps and tore up the furniture. I also experienced the sensation of sliding beyond my moment of conception in my mother's womb to an earlier life. It was the commonness of this phenomenon which led Hubbard to formulate the stage beyond dianetics, Scientology.

A few nonstudents came into the group. For instance, our new next-door neighbor was a minister who'd been kicked out of his church because he preached that flying saucers were vehicles for angels. He later became a Scientologist auditor. Another member was a Bradley professor, a brilliant but drunken and adulterous radical left-winger whose wife was an oral nymphomaniac. After one year he was asked to leave, not because of his alcoholism or his lechery but because of his politics. One man later got his Ph.D. in psychology at Florida U. and then returned to Bradley to teach a fanatical brand of behaviorism. Another taught school in San Francisco, but the last I heard of him he was in prison for selling drugs.

My best friend, depicted as Rohrig in *The Dark Design*, did blow his first oral examination for his M.A. as described in this novel. After graduation he got a job teaching English at a rural high school in Iowa but lost it, partly because he insisted on teaching his students Greek drama instead of English. Then he was a construction worker and architect of graveyards and then became the first mate on a Mexican ship carrying shrimp from Vera Cruz to Brownsville. As of now he's a sculptor in Florida and doing quite well. He also had great ability as a poet and painter.

Two of the group were the first persons I'd ever met who admitted to being homosexuals. (The Zeitgeist was really changing.) One was an excellent painter, but he ended up in Chicago's skidrow area, a hopeless wino. The other was a massively built lesbian, a barber who eventually became a lifelong tenant of psychiatrists' couches. Part of the group, after graduation, purchased an old yacht, repaired it, and voyaged down the Illinois, the Mississippi, and through the Gulf of Mexico to Florida. They never came back. Bette and I and the children were invited to come along, but we didn't want to be on a boat where every member of the crew was a Captain Ahab.

I graduated in 1950 after so many start-stop-starts, but my father wasn't able to attend the ceremony and see his ambition for me fulfilled. He died of pneumonia after being paralyzed for several weeks from a stroke. A series of smaller strokes previously had mentally befuddled him and changed his personality. Instead of being happy and proud of me, as I'd expected, he became sarcastic and bitter and obviously jealous. I was bewildered and hurt by this because I didn't know about the small strokes. Not until he had the major one did my mother tell me about them. She was a Christian Scientist and hence loath to admit that my father was sick.

After graduation I came down with a case of nervous exhaustion (that's what the doctor called it) for a few weeks. When I returned to work, I was forced to give up nights and to return to the regular swing shift. It was impossible for me to attend the day classes at Bradley on a regular basis. After taking two courses, I gave up my ambitions of getting an M.A. By then I'd decided that I didn't want to be an English teacher, anyway.

In the meantime I'd added the new *Magazine of Fantasy & Science Fiction* and *Galaxy* to my reading list. I sent two short stories to John Campbell of *Astounding*, but he rejected them. Then, in mid-1950, while I was read-ing a book on entomology, I had the basic inspiration for the story that would be called "The Lovers." I wrote this evenings and weekends, and when it was done sent it in to my hero, Campbell. It came back with a note to the effect that it nauseated him. Though he didn't say so, he must have also thought that his readers would be equally repulsed by this story about inter-phylum sexual intercourse and the use of the word "orgasm," among a number of other things.

I was crushed, though not for long. I sent the story to Horace Gold, and he had a similar reaction. "The Lovers" seemed to me to be too long for the *Magazine of Fantasy & Science Fiction*, though I may have been wrong about that. In any event, instead of putting the manuscript away after several rejec-tions, as I'd done with my manuscripts in the past, I meant to send it until all possible markets were exhausted. I believed that I had something that was real-ly revolutionary or at least really novel.

I purchased copies of *Startling Stories* and *Thrilling Wonder*, neither of which I'd ever read before, and perused the contents. The letter and fan columns were illuminating. For the first time, I became aware that there was a well-organized and vigorous fan world. It even had conventions. But though the stories didn't encourage me to think that "The Lovers" would be any bet-ter received by Sam Mines than by Campbell or Gold, I sent it in anyway.

I've been told that it was Jerome Bixby, the assistant editor, who picked it out of the slush pile. He gave it to Sam Mines, the senior editor, to read with his enthusiastic recommendation. Then, knowing that I must have sent the story to better-paying and more prestigious markets first, he phoned Gold, edi-tor of Galaxy. He said something like, "Hey, Horace, you silly son of a bitch, did you really reject 'The Lovers' by Philip José Farmer?" Horace stammered for a while, then began the first of a number of revisionist explanations for his rejection, none of which matched the one he'd given me. Bixby didn't phone Campbell because, I suppose, nobody talked to the colossus of science fiction as he'd talked to Horace.

Finally, after what seemed a long time but wasn't, I got a letter of acceptance from Mines. And then in the issue of *Startling* preceding the September issue, in which "The Lovers" was to appear, was a glowing comment by Mines about the forthcoming work by a new author. Sam really hyped it. He sounded almost like John the Baptist announcing the coming of the Messiah.

I was near delirious with joy, though I tried to appear very cool. At last, at long last, I might be able to quit working at Keystone, which had slowly been driving me nuts, and if I sold a few more stories, I could justify going into full-time writing. I thought I had the world by the tail. But, as it turned out, there was a tiger at the other end.

Part 2, dealing with the years 1952-80, will appear in a later book in this series. Or, if not there, somewhere.

Religion and Myths

First published in *The Visual Encyclopedia of Science Fiction,* 1977.

Phil: "Then there's the theory we were once gods but have devolved into Homo sapiens."

⁂

My basic religious education was in the Church of Christ, Scientist. It's a little difficult to imagine Mary introducing Jesus as "my son, the scientist," yet it's appropriate that a science-fiction writer should have had this peculiar background. So many SF writers write stories which combine science (or pseudo-science) with saviourism. That is, an SF writer often tells you how humanity can be saved if it follows the right path or how it will go to hell if it doesn't.

As I grew older, I became an agnostic, then an atheist. But I was only fooling myself when I thought that I was truly indifferent to religion. I wrote *Flesh* (1960), which projected a revival in the far future of the ancient vegetation religions. Later, my mainstream novel, *Fire and the Night* (1962), dramatised the more sophisticated idea that sex and religion were only two sides of the same coin.

At the same time, I was writing stories (*Night of Light* et al) about an interstellar priest, Father John Carmody. Even when I was an atheist, I was powerfully attracted by the Roman Catholic faith. But I still believed that religion was only Homo sapiens' conscious expression of the instinctive drive for survival in the unconscious cells in humankind's bodies.

The brain, knowing that a person can't live forever in this world, rationalises a future, or other-dimensional, world in which immortality is possible. In other words, religion is the earliest form of science fiction.

Nevertheless, I had, and I have, a contradictory belief that the possibility of immortality is not a fiction.

I've extrapolated on many religious themes in my writings. The ultimate is the premise, now being developed in my Riverworld series, that immortality won't be given us by supernatural means. We'll have to make it ourselves and

720 PHILIP JOSÉ FARMER

do so by physical means, by science. ("We" includes all sentient beings in the universe.) This is part of the Creator's plan, a sort of do-it-yourself book which we are in the process of writing for ourselves. It (the sexless Creator) has given us intelligence and self-consciousness so that we may bring about our own resurrection. We will then provide immortality, which will give us time for developing our psychic evolution towards the ideal.

It may seem idiotic or naïve to express belief in the attainment of immortality of everybody who's existed or will exist. But, without immortality, there is no meaning in life.

For me, only those stories concerned with this one vital issue are serious stories. All others, no matter how moving or profound, are mere entertainments. They do not deal with that which is our gravest concern. Without a belief in eternal life for us, the terrestrial existence is something to be gotten through with as little pain and as much pleasure as possible.

If this conclusion is the triumph of irrationality over logic, so be it. After all, irrationality is the monopoly of sentients.

Creating Artificial Worlds

First published in *Pulsar,* Summer 1979.

This article is a speech given by Farmer at *Facts about SF: The Writers Speak* a ten week series of SF lectures, April 5 - June 7 1978. Farmer takes his novel *Two Hawks from Earth* as an example and explains what research and extrapolating he did about the world where the story takes place, an Earth where North and South America never rose from the oceans.

✥✥✥✥✥

Our subject is Creating Artificial Worlds. In the first place, that is a misnomer. Nobody creates anything; Artists, in which I include writers, poets, sculptors, painters, and so forth, do not create; all they do is take the materials at hand and put it together. In other words, we are all "makers." There is only one original Creator and some people doubt whether He exists or not. He was the only one who ever took nothing and made something out of it. But all of us so-called artists only make things, we never create things.

Science fiction writers are known for constructing artificial worlds. When you say artificial worlds you immediately think of a science fiction writer. But the truth is that all writers in any genre, mainstream, historical, gothic or western, construct artificial worlds. A lot of mainstream writers like to think of themselves as being very realistic. But the truth is that even the most intensely realistic writer never matches reality one by one. Mainstream writers construct worlds that are entirely artificial.

All of us think that we see reality. Each of us—through this thing behind our eyes, these windows of perception—look out and we see certain items that we have agreed exist. But the truth is that none of us ever ever agree one hundred percent on just what this thing is, just how it exists, and how it operates. The only thing in which the science fiction writer differs from the other genres, is that he differs in degree, not in kind. But he does have a much harder job than the writer of mainstream or any of the other non-science fiction genres.

The mainstream writer, for instance, has all his materials at hand. He doesn't have to invent the world. He has a hard enough job as it is writing a story of a world that everybody knows about. Of course, the historical novelist has a harder job than a person who writes a contemporary novel because he has to do a tremendous amount of research. On the other hand, he is writing about the worlds that did exist. Whereas the science fiction writer writes about worlds that do not exist, that never existed, and that probably won't exist.

Now, I know some of you are thinking that there are a lot of writers who mostly deal with contemporary society. Like Harlan Ellison, for instance. But if you were to study Harlan carefully you would find that though he tends to operate mainly in the contemporary, the worlds that he constructs are not reality, one by one. There is a tremendous amount of fantasy in there and by the time he has gotten through the major part of the story, you are in a world that is as remote as Mars was supposed to be at one time...or as alien, I should say. I'm specifically thinking of Edgar Rice Burroughs' Barsoom or Heinlein's Mars. Harlan has taken the contemporary world, given you a background that many of you recognize, but by the time he is through—by the time he has looked at our world through his own particular doors of perception and then written a story—he has taken the material at hand and shaped them not into a mainstream novel—this might make him mad because he doesn't want to be known as a science fiction writer—he has taken his materials at hand and shaped them into a very alien world. Actually, his worlds are as strange and fascinating as any of Heinlein's. But whether you prefer Harlan or Heinlein is a matter of taste.

What I am trying to say is that all writers and all artists create artificial worlds, it doesn't matter what the genre. But then, as I said, it is a matter of degree, not of kind.

As my subject is constructing artificial worlds, I will take as an example one of my lesser novels, titled *The Gate of Time*. This was put out by Belmont quite a few years ago, reprinted once, but I have a contract now to rewrite it with its original title. I called it *Two Hawks from Earth*, and Belmont for some reason re-titled it *The Gate of Time*. I do not know why because it is not a time story, it is a parallel universe story. Belmont did a lot to the book. They cut out scenes here and there so that by the time I got it I didn't even recognize it. I imagine some other writers could tell you the same thing about some of their works.

A lot of people come up and ask me: "Where do you get your ideas from?" And I tell them, "I really don't know." I've gotten ideas from just hearing a phrase in an eavesdropped conversation; I've gotten them from reading poetry and prose; I've gotten them from dreams—a lot of ideas from dreams—

I've gotten them from booze…By the way, while you can get ideas sometimes when you drink, don't ever try to write while you're drinking. It doesn't work. There used to be a lot of legends about Hemingway and some of the other boozers of his period. It was claimed that he would sit down at his typewriter with a full quart of whiskey and drink it all one day while he was writing. I don't believe that. Or, if he did, then he had to re-write the next day while he sobered up. Which probably didn't work either. Don't try to write while you're sobering up.

What happened was that I was reading a book on the evolution of horses some years ago and I came across several statements which said that the horse family originated in North America, as did the camel family. They originated here and eventually spread over to the Old World, and then they died out in 8000 B.C., or perhaps a little later. I had known this for years but it had just never occurred to me that it might be an idea for a story. So while I was reading this book I said, "Ahh!"—you know, just like that, I didn't have to hit my head or anything—what if the North American and South American continents never rose from the sea?

There's your basic premise. We have already created an artificial world.

What this would mean, just to begin with, is that there are no horses or camels in the Old World. I suppose some of you are thinking, "So what?" Well, what this means is that transportation, communication, and warfare would have been considerably reduced. You see, without horses or camels trade goods, for instance, would have to be carried either on boats or on the backs of human beings.

Some of you are saying, "Well, what about oxen and elephants?" And I say that is a good point. Except that oxen are a very slow method of transportation. They are no good for anything like the horse for warfare. You can't get on the back of an ox and ride into battle…Elephants could be used a great deal more than they were in olden times, and that is something I overlooked when I wrote the first version of the book. But I'll change that. I would also like to point out that there is an old myth that African elephants can't be tamed, that only Indian elephants can. But that is not true at all. Hannibal of Carthage used African elephants to great effect taking him up through Spain. I'm just throwing that in.

What are other important things that wouldn't exist if there are no Americas? There would be no potatoes, tomatoes, turkeys, syphilis, pumpkins, squash, rubber, quinine to treat malaria—malaria has taken a tremendous toll of human lives in history—tobacco, maize or Indian corn.

Another big thing is that the American Indian supposedly originated in Central Asia or up in Siberia. They were supposed to have been—according to the theory, not provable, just a theory—a blend of archaic Caucasian and Mongolian peoples. After all of these tribes were mixed up in Central Asia or Siberia, or both, the American Indian was formed.

About 40,000 years ago, or maybe 100,000, the first Indian came across the Bering Bridge. But in an Americaless world there is no Bering Bridge. So what happens, according to my book, anyway, is that the Amerinds are frustrated. They go up to the Bering Strait, which is not a strait but part of the Atlantic Ocean look around and decide to come back. Instead of all being pushed out of Asia to America, where they developed their own culture, they turned inland. So my thesis is that they absorbed the Turkish-speaking peoples, became a very potent force, and so went back to the Old Stone Age.

Coming up to modern times in my parallel universe, they have drifted westward and they have also drifted southward. In the south they form an empire in what we now call in our world, Earth I, northern China. Their push kept the people—I'm going to speak particularly of the Finnish-speakers—from drifting westward and going across the Aegean and then into Russia and eventually forming the dual nations of Finland and Estonia. Instead, they were shunted eastward and they got to the Japanese Island before the Japanese did. The Japanese, according to the theory, were originally a Southeast Asian people who wandered on up and then went over to the Japanese Islands where they found the Ainu, who were an archaic Caucasian people. They just pushed them to the less-desirable areas and in time subjugated them. In Earth II, the Finnish speakers got to Japan first; the Japanese were thwarted, so they settled in Southeast Asia and what we call the Japanese Islands was called Saariset, which is Finnish for Islands.

What happened in Europe is that the Amerinds, by the time my story opens, occupy what we call Russia. These people speak a language that is related to Nahua, which is the same language the Aztecs and Toltecs spoke. They occupied most of Russia except for the extreme southern part.

The Iroquois, my favorite Indians, moved into what is now Bulgaria and Rumania, and formed a nation there. An Algonquin-speaking people which we call the Kinnikinuk, which is an actual Indian word, now quite distorted, the original meant "mixture," moved into what is Czechoslovakia. Now, all this is possible, given my premise.

By the time the story opens, which would be analogous to our 1944, because it starts out in World War II, there are no Slavs. They did not come out of their swamplands but were overrun by a group of Amerinds on one side and Lithuanians on the other side and absorbed. According to the theory, if I remember correctly, the Slavs lived in a huge swampland in Poland. What happened was that a group of Mongolians came in and conquered and enslaved them all, brought them out, and sent them to various colonies. That it why they are called Slavs, coming from the Latin word for slaves. Then, in a couple hundred years, the slaves overthrew their conquerors and they started to expand into different parts of Europe. But in my world, Earth II, this didn't happen.

I hope you bear with me because I'm not working up to an entirely different world, but a world based on the premise that the two Americas did not exist. I'm trying to show you how to extrapolate.

The people who in our world are the Lithuanians, and the old Prussians (who were Baltic not German), and the Latvians found a vacuum for a while and they expanded. As a matter of fact, back in the medieval period the Lithuanians at one time covered a tremendous stretch of country in Russia and Poland and so forth. The end result was that when the story starts, the Baltic-speaking nation Perkunisha occupies the territory called Denmark, Germany, Poland, Holland and Austria in our world, Earth I. The reason I call this Perkunisha is that Perkunis was the original chief god of the old Prussians. Again, I stress that they were not German. Prussia is called Prussia today because when the Germans came in they conquered the Prussians and absorbed them and eventually their language died.

The Perkunishans of the Americaless world live in this huge heartland in Central Europe. They had actually absorbed all the people that gave rise to what we call modern Germany in Earth I. In lower Norway and Sweden, in Earth II, there were people who spoke a form of Scandinavian. In England and Ireland are people who spoke a form of English. I'm going to get to that in a moment because I want to show you that when you create a whole new world you have to deal with every aspect of it. I want to show you what it takes to do this.

So, we have Europe and Asia. The Indians go up to the Bering Strait, find out there is nothing but water out there, and they turn around and go down to Central Asia and China, and their presence there causes a bumping effect, a fall of dominoes. Now remember, this process took thousands of years, not all at once.

You have to remember that the Incans of our world would not be like the Incans of Earth II, for the simple reason that they are subject to entirely different influences. The Chinese of that period outnumbered them; even though they were conquered for a while, they absorbed the American Indians eventually. But Quechua was spoken in the upper part of China and Chinese in the lower.

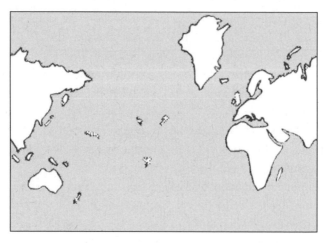

This is a map of Earth II, showing the lack of the North and South American Continents. In the center are (clockwise from 1:00) the Rockies, the Andes, and the Serra Nevada mountain ranges.

The Amerindians come into here (pointing to a map drawn with chalk on the blackboard (reproduced above—Editor)) where our Aztecs and Toltecs settled. And as a result of all this westward bumping, the Greeks, who in our world originated in the Danube area, were bumped from this area into Italy. The Hittites, due to the vacuum created by the Greeks not being there, came over to the Hellenic peninsula and conquered the aborigines, and so Greece is called Hatti. The Greeks eventually conquered the whole Italic peninsula and absorbed the aborigines—either killed them off or intermarried—their language conquers and as a result there is no Latin, which means that there won't be any Roman Empire, and the languages relating to the Latin such as the French, Italian, Spanish, and so forth are all absorbed.

Originally, on Earth I, the Phoenicians, who lived north of Palestine, came and founded a colony in west North Africa called Carthage which, if I remember correctly, in Phoenician, means New City.

This time there is no Roman Empire for the Greeks to battle with. The Greeks are still highly individualistic; they can't get together like the Romans did; they didn't have this empire-building complex that the Romans did. Therefore, the Grecians beat them out and they settle in Iberia or Spain and Portugal. Eventually, at the time our story opens, Greece holds Morocco, Algeria, Tunisia, Libya, and Egypt, which was in later times conquered by Greece, so it was Greek-speaking.

On our Earth in Classical times the Etruscans had a great civilization up in northern Italy, which was eventually absorbed by the Romans. The Etruscans, who, on Earth I, theoretically came from Asia Minor and settled in Italy, on Earth II never did. They were chased out by the Greeks and settled in what we (Earth I people) call France. So, in this story, there is of course no French language because there is no Latin language. They speak a language descended from the Etruscan. And In England and Ireland we have a form of English, and in what is now Normandy and Brittany there is a Germanic-speaking country, and in France south of the Seine and also in Belgium. These are all called the Six Kingdoms.

The reason northern Europe is warm, even though it's so far north, is because of the Gulf Current. But since there is no Gulf of Mexico, there is no Gulf Current. Therefore, Europe is still in an Ice Age, or the end of an Ice Age, or something comparable to an Ice Age. Now this makes Scotland and Northern Ireland and the upper parts of the Scandinavian peninsula very cold. In fact, all of Western Europe has long winters and short summers. The winters are very cold, very harsh, and the summers are very short and not as warm as on Earth I.

That means that when Perkunisha, the Lithuanian (Old Prussian) speak-ing nation, had spread over a good part of Europe, it looked south for new conquests, especially North Africa. You see, back in 8,000 B.C. when the Ice Age was ending, the Sahara was a vast area, still green, very fertile, and with lots of rivers, elephants, hippos, antelopes—a happy hunting ground for the natives. It began to dry out slowly, but even in Classical times North Africa was still green enough to be the granary of the Roman Empire.

What I overlooked when I first wrote this book, and that was because I wrote too fast, was the North African countries with their vast agricultural regions. They would have been very important in the world of Earth II. In fact they would have been so powerful that Northern European nations would be comparably weak. Industry and technology hasn't kept up with these people.

The story takes place in 1944 and later but, due to the lack of camels and horses, which caused a delay in fast communications and trade, and due to some of the other factors I mentioned, the 1944 of Earth II is technologically behind the 1944 of Earth I. When our hero enters the story, Europe is going through the transition from steam to internal combustion engines and has dis-covered oil. You might say that their technology in some respects is about what ours was in 1912. But in others, comparable to that of 1880. What you don't want to do in a case like this is just say that these people are 100 to 150 years behind and then take the Earth of 50 or 80 years ago and transplant it. You have to sit down and think about what form of technology they would have;

what forms of technology of 1880 and 1912 Earth I had that they lacked. You have to work out the whole thing.

Okay. We've got the geographical set-up, we've got the climatological set-up, we have the racial and the national set-up. Now, there are a lot of things that will be in the novel that I haven't told you about. There are a lot of things that I thought of that I wouldn't put in because I don't want to slow down the book too much.

I was talking about applying extrapolation not only to geography and geology and the vast migrations and so forth but I'm also talking about language. My premise is that English developed much more slowly in Earth II than it did here, so it's an archaic and sort of creole language. You can do it easy, if you want to. You can go to an Old English text and read it and pick up a few phrases here and there and perhaps put a few phrases down and you'll look very wise and very learned. The only thing is, is that it wouldn't work that way. I mean, not in reality. You see, I'm assuming that there was an English language but in its later stages was subject to different influences than those of Earth I. Let's take as a base Wessex, which is one of the forms of Old English. Actually, standard English is much more influenced by Mercian, for instance, for which we don't have too many manuscripts. If you study Old English, you study Wessex because most of the manuscripts are preserved in Wessex. Well, that isn't going to stop me any because I'm assuming that Wessex was the basis of modern English of Earth II.

I'd like to give you one example of a conversation between Roger Two Hawks and Lady Ilmika Thorrsstein. Two Hawks kisses her hand—remember, she's a member of the nobility—and he says, "Ur Huskarleship," which means "Your Ladyship."

And she says, "Hu far't vi thi, lautni Tva Havoken?" which means, "How goes it with you, Freeman (or Mister) Two Hawks?"

Now, if you are an Old English expert, I bet you don't recognize that (lautni). That's because it is not English, it is Etruscan. It comes from an Etruscan word meaning "freeman."

And he replies, "Ik ar farn be'er," or "I am doing better." Then, "Ur Huskarleship ar mest hunlich aeksen min haelth of," which means, "Your Ladyship is most gracious in asking about my health."

What I did was to take Old English and figure the influences it had been subjected to on Earth II and try and work out the way it might have gone. What I'm trying to say is that if you want to make your world sound authentic and make it ring true, try and cover every aspect that you have in the story. Do some research.

If you want to make up your own language, you don't have to make up the whole grammar and syntax and so forth, but you should at least, in order to be authentic, figure out what sounds are in the language. That is, what sounds are rejected and what sounds are used; what sound clusters are there so that when you make up names for your characters you can given them a true ring. Be sure that the language has certain rules and that you do not use any sounds that just happen to come into your mind because all languages accept certain sounds and reject others, and also combinations of certain sounds. Be consistent.

So, in 1944 there was a big oilfield in Ploesti, Rumania, and the Ninth Air Force decides they are going to knock it out, little knowing that the Germans referred to it as Festung Ploesti, that is, Fortress Ploesti, and so they are in for a big shock.

Roger Two Hawks comes from around Syracuse and is part Onondaga Indian—I'm very fond of American Indians; I think they make great heroes, anyway—and he is in a B-24 bomber. The Germans are really rigged up—boy, are they ready for him. They've got haystacks all over the place with anti-air-craft machine guns behind them, behind every haystack and bush, every place, and a heavy concentration of fighter planes.

The bombers come up from Cyrenaica, North Africa, and Roger Two Hawks is the pilot. They come zooming in, and Roger notes that his leader has gone off in the wrong direction. He tries to call him, then he follows him a little bit, and then here comes a fighter plane. They collide, cutting each other's wings off. Roger Two Hawks and Pat O'Brien, his gunner, are the only two who survive. They don't know it, but the guy flying the German plane also survives.

They land—pretty hard, too—and the place pretty much looks like Rumania. It doesn't look like Ploesti, but they figure they have parachuted on the outskirts, and they are out in the country someplace. They skulk around and find some peasants. They are a lot darker than they should be, and they don't speak Rumanian or German and have never heard of English. At least not the type that Roger speaks. Well, eventually, it dawns on Roger, who reads a lot—I like heroes who have read a lot because that enables them to explain things. I don't want him to be too dumb. Roger tells Pat that just before that German fighter hit them he had a strange, weird feeling of dissociation, but it only lasted two seconds. And he says what he thinks happened is that they went through a momentary gate or opening between Earth I and Earth II; they must be in a parallel universe. Pat O'Brien doesn't understand this, and he has a very hard time adapting to this world.

If people were transported to a parallel universe, some people would be able to adapt and others wouldn't. Eventually, Pat just dies; he just can't take it any more. He is a good gunner, but when he finds himself on Earth II surrounded by all these Indians...and no cigarettes or potatoes...he can't take it.

Remember that in this Earth II, except for a Celtic speaking nation in Switzerland and our Iroquois nation of Hotinohsinoh, which means housebuilder, there are no democracies, they are all monarchies. Some good, some bad, as Monarchies go. England is not called England, it is called Blodland, or Bloodland, because for a thousand years it was fought over by various invaders. English is not called English, it is called Inioinetalu. The word "Angle," or English, is originally supposed to come from one of the early Germanic gods, Ing, and probably originated in Denmark, or near there when the Anglos and Saxons lived there.

Well, we have our noble lady, Ilmika Thorrsstein, and though she is English, her first name is Greek and her second name is actually Old Norse. But her father was ambassador to what we call Hungary, but which is another Indian nation, and when the bad Perkunishans, who are an analog of the Nazis, invaded this land, and he got killed, our heroine fled and, naturally, she runs into Roger Two Hawks.

Here is another method of extrapolation. The Iroquolans, I'll call them that, can not believe Roger Two Hawks' story; they think he is either a spy or he is crazy. They decide that they will give him a break after they rough him up more than somewhat. They put him under the care of the Iroquolan equivalent of a psychiatrist. The ancient Iroquois of Earth I, our world, did have shamans who had a form of psychiatry in which they interpreted dreams. When the sick Iroquolan came in, the shaman would ask him to repeat his dreams. And he, quite often, would interpret the dreams just as they do nowadays. So they sent Roger Two Hawks and Pat O'Brien to this Iroquolan equivalent of a psychiatrist.

Again, you can not just pick up Freudian terms or Jungian and so forth and use them in Iroquolan psychiatry. You have to figure out how some other form of psychiatry used by the shamans developed in a modern nation. Because they do not live in teepees, and they no longer live in long houses, and they have had contact with the European nations and have been tremendously influenced by western culture. Therefore, you can not take the Iroquois tribes of 1780 of Earth I and transport them to Earth II without changes. You have to consider all the factors, everything that would influence the Hotinohsinoh: language, architecture, costumes, ways of raising children, everything.

Roger Two Hawks and Ilmika Thorrsstein flee Iroquola when the Perkunishans invade. They work their way up to what we call Russia but Earth II calls Itskapintik, a Nahuath speaking people. The two get to Tyrsland (Sweden) and, from thence, they take a boat and go to Blodland.

One good reason for having them escape and have all these adventures is it gives us a chance to go up here (indicates the map) and find out how the Nahuas developed. Then they get captured by the Perkunishans and find out how rotten they are. And when he is captured by the Perkunishans he runs into a guy named Horst Raske, who, it turns out, speaks German. He is the only German speaker in Earth II. And what happened was that he was piloting the German fighter plane that crashed; he went through the momentary opening between the two universes at the same time.

Anyway, Horst Raske is an engineer and he's given the Perkunishans a lot of advice on how to build faster airplanes that will enable them to shoot down the dirigibles and the primitive airplanes. Which will enable them to conquer Central Europe, sweep into Rasna, which is the Etruscan state, and eventually get down through Greece or as it is called Akhaivia.

Eventually—boy, I wish I could tell you that surprise ending. It has to do with Raske and Roger Two Hawks...So, after many adventures, they have to flee to a string of islands way off past what we call the Atlantic—these are the tops of the Rockies. What has happened is that a group of Polynesians came from Hawaii or someplace else a long time ago and the tops of the Rockies are populated by Polynesians. And that is where the surprise ending comes.

Phonemics

First published in *Gegenschein,* Number 27, 1976.
Here are a few comments sent to the editor of *Gegenschein* regarding their efforts to push phonemic spelling (not phonetic).

Phonemics is the study of the sound system of a given language and the analysis and classification of its phonemes.

Phonemes are the smallest phonetic unit in a language that is capable of conveying a distinction in meaning.

The font used for the phonemic character set is Lucida Sans Unicode.

"Eny" for "any" is fine for Australia. But what about standard American, which generally pronounces "any" as "iny"?

I got interested in phonemic spelling when I was taking a graduate course in linguistics at Arizona State University. I like the idea of such, because an eight-year old child could be taught to spell properly in two weeks, maybe less.

However, dialectical differences cause some trouble. Englishmen would spell their words (many of them, anyway) somewhat differently than an Australian or a Scot or an American. I don't see that this presents any great difficulty, however. For instance, the adjustment of a Midwesterner to the spelling of a Texan would be slight.

But the big objection would be economic. All books worth reprinting would have to be issued with the new phonemic spelling. Also, after a new generation has grown up, it would be cut off from the old literature. Only scholars among the new generation could read the old stuff.

Also, the conservatives, who would in this case include most of the population of the US (and I imagine that of any English-speaking country) would oppose, perhaps violently, any such change. (Even if anyone could learn to read the phonemic alphabet in two weeks or less.)

Theodore Roosevelt tried to introduce some simplified spellings in government documents during his presidency. Such stuff as "thru" for "through". The reaction was so energetic and vociferous that he had to abandon the idea.

However, I'm all for it. Why don't you spell "any" as "eniy"? The "iy" stands for the diphthong.

hwat duw Өiŋk əv ðis aydiyə? ay ləv it. meybiy səmdey itəl kætc on. bət ay daut it.

in phonemic spelling, capital letters can be discarded. you know when a new sentence begins because the previous one ends with a period or a question or exclamation mark or semicolon. izənt ðæt rayt, erik?

(erik: tuw bludiy rayt, fil. Or is "right" "rat" in Aussie dialect?)

but do you base the phonemic spelling on English as it is supposed to be spoken? or on rapid speech, which is slurred, contracting? what do you say = hwat duw yuw sey? = hwədyə sey?

Or, ay gat youw = ay gače?

· Diacritical marks make writing slower, so č and š could be spelled ch and sh, though that isn't completely phonemic.

I'd like to see the very useful and natural *ain't* restored as standard English and to hell with the absurd pedantical prejudice against it. eynt ðæt rayt?

ay intend tuw rayt n artik'l n is s bjikt s m dey.

best, filip howzéy farm r

Lovers and Otherwise

First published in *Fantastic Worlds,* Volume 1, Number 3, Spring 1953.

᠅

The history of "The Lovers" is, I think, worth reading. It is divided into two segments: (1) the actual conception and writing, and (2) what happened to it after it was written. The latter is especially intriguing because it illustrates so well the relationship between authors and editors. And the reverberations that may take a long time a-bouncing before there is complete understanding and agreement between the two species.

I was reminded of that when Mrs. H. L. Gold, known professionally as Evelyn Paige, was introduced to me during the World Science Fiction Convention in Chicago. Mrs. Gold is a striking brunette. She has very dark hair and very white teeth, a quite noticeable and very pleasing contrast. She smiles often, is energetic, intense, articulate, and devoted to her husband, whom she mentions frequently during her conversation. She has, both as wife and as assistant editor for *Galaxy,* been very much wrapped up in its spectacular leap to a place on the top roost of science fiction. (That's a mixed metaphor, but so is the story of "The Lovers'" fate.)

Mrs. Gold was emphatic in asking if I would please broadcast the truth about "The Lovers" and its reception at *Galaxy.* Many people had asked Mr. Gold why he had rejected "The Lovers;" she wished that I would inform those interested that he had not.

I said I'd be glad to. In fact, I was thinking of telling the story in an article for *Fantastic Worlds.* So, before the genesis and development of the story itself is told, I'd like to go sidewise in time. Science fiction fans or anybody interested in the-behind-the-story dealings of editors and writers should be intrigued.

When I finished the MS of "The Lovers," I was sure I had a pretty good story. Of course, during the writing and even after I'd completed it, I had qualms, moments of doubt, and impulses to rise and throw the pages in the furnace. But these, I'm told, are universal emotions during composition, especially to those who've sold little or nothing. Despite these little plunges into gloom, my general impression was that the story was, in some respects, fresh and original. This in spite of the fact that the story was framed in a setting as old as science fiction itself.

On finishing, I did what every author does. Look around for the highest-paying magazine. Money mattered. Respect for the editors and prestige of their magazines didn't enter the picture. All three of the editors that I thought of submitting to had my highest respect. And as far as prestige goes—there is no such thing.

Rather, I should say that prestige is a very subjective thing. What you consider the highest ranking, the next fellow thinks is rank. Read the fan columns in the various publications; check my statement. I'm continually amazed that so many people can't see what I do. And vice versa.

Anyway, not having an agent, and getting my information about rates for words, reprint rights, etc., from *Writer's Digest,* I decided that *Galaxy* would be a wonderful place to send it. Mr. Gold had announced, I believe, that a great deal of freedom would be allowed to writers in his magazine. A close and eager reading of *Galaxy* from its inception had convinced me of that.

Moreover, Mr. Gold was one of that triumvirate of science fiction editors who had been kind enough to criticize previous efforts. Believe me, that is one of the best things an editor can do to encourage up-and-coming talent. It's heartening to receive a note, even a small one, in which the defects and virtues of the rejected MS are pointed out.

After having written and having had turned down about twelve science fiction stories, mostly short-shorts, I began forming a liking for these three men. Perhaps the note was a brief statement to the affect that the story was trite, or that it had an original idea but was treated too heavily. But I preferred that by far to the cold and stony printed slip.

And I noticed as time passed that my stories were receiving lengthier and more favorable comments. I was getting some place and I *knew* it. That was the thing. I could have been closer to my goal, and if I'd not been informed so in so many words—if nothing but formal forms kept popping out of the manila envelopes—how would I know? I might have given up when I was just on the verge of acceptance.

Believe me, I was—and am—grateful for the efforts taken by these very busy men. The result was that I soon began grading editors—from a writer's, not a fan's, viewpoint—into two echelons, upper and lower. Not so strangely, those ranked in the upper echelon also edited, in my opinion, the best and most mature and most entertaining magazines.

So, taking into consideration various factors, I mailed it to Mr. Gold. And became convinced from what it cost me for stamps that "The Lovers" had better sell the first or second time, or I'd go broke kicking it around the weary reject circuit. Actually, though, with the undying optimism of the congenital idiot—I mean, author—I didn't think it would come back.

My only doubt, aside from its sexual-biological content, was its length. The peculiarity of the story was that it had to be wrapped in one package to get its full impact. It wouldn't do for it to be serialized. And that, to my naive mind, offered a problem. *Galaxy* and *ASF*, I knew, had a limit of 25,000 words for their one-shot novels. *Thrilling Wonder* printed novels of about 30,000; *Startling*, 40-45,000.

Here was the difficulty. I wanted the story to be about 45,000, just dandy for *Startling*. Full development of all I wanted to put in demanded it. Moreover, at that time there were only two editors whom I thought were taboo-free enough to consider "The Lovers." Or three, rather, but Mr. Boucher's magazine did not publish stories that long.

The pot of gold at the end of the rainbow twinkled. Three cents a word versus one point seven. So I compromised. I made it a little too long for *Galaxy* and a little too short for *Startling*. I cut hell out of it, threw out scenes, characters, and action that would have explained the fascinating—to me—social and political set up of the Ozagens. Also, there was much about the Haijac development of Dunne's theories of time that I sliced. The result was that, unless you'd read Dunne or read of him, you wouldn't understand fully the peculiar synthesis of religion and chronoscience.

However, I tried to show through action just how it worked. The reader who knew little or nothing of Dunne but who was intelligent should be able to deduce the needed facts.

After much heartburning blue-penciling, though I was, in a way, relieved because it meant less typing of the final MS (typing drives me to frantic, frantic drives me to beer, beer gives me an eye-ache so I can't type), I ended up with a 30,000-word story. This was too long for *Galaxy*, but I thought that if it were good enough it might be published in that length. I didn't think it could be reduced any more without its being weakened.

———⁂———

So I waited the normal period and formed nerves on my nerves, got a bad case of mailboxitis. And so, in normal process, the suitcase-sized package returned.

Gods! Blasphemy! Tearing of garments, gnashing of teeth, pouring of ashes on my heads! *Quelle horreur! Ia! Ia! Cthulhu fhtagn! Ph'nglui mglw'nafh!*

Home again baby?

My tear-filled eyes read the letter enclosed. And found that *The Lovers* was not rejected—in toto. Mr. Gold admitted that my story had a good idea, but that he couldn't accept it in its present form and live with himself. Whatever my attitude toward minorities might be, the story was dangerous. It, in effect, justified discrimination because minorities *might*, if they ever achieved domination, become dictatorial. As far as he, Mr. Gold, was concerned, it didn't matter *now* if they would or they wouldn't. The present fact was that the minorities were under direct or latent attack. And he wouldn't care to add fuel to that blaze.

However, my notion of imitation females could be excellent *sans* racial overtones, if I developed it in a Fortean manner to explain various mysterious phenomena. It would be kept on this planet, and it wouldn't have the elaborate stage I gave it. Should I be interested, and if I thought I could do something with the perceptions and integration of research that E. F. Russell did in his "Sinister Barrier," he would want to see it. He was even kind enough and interested enough to offer to help in the plotting, though it wouldn't be easy by mail.

In any case, I was to let him know.

That gave me to pause.

As to the first objection, about the dangerous implications, I hadn't even thought about them. At first, I didn't understand what he meant. It was something I wouldn't have dreamed of. It shook me.

The second idea—having the story take place on Earth—had already occurred to me. Indeed, I was halfway through "The Lovers" when such a thought collided head on with me. I stopped and turned it over to examine every facet. And then continued with my original plan. To carry that out would have meant wiping out Ozagen, Fobo, the tavern beetles, etc. I wasn't a world-wrecker; I couldn't do it.

I would have if I'd thought the story and the characters weren't jelling. But they were.

Besides, I was too lazy.

So I sent a long letter to Mr. Gold in which I very carefully—and probably too passionately—defended my position in regard to minorities, persecutions, and prejudices.

Mr. Gold took the trouble and time—and for a very busy science fiction editor this involves a sacrifice—to write a two-page single-spaced reply. In his very forceful and articulate style, he made it clear that, concerning "The Lovers," he didn't consider me bigoted. If he had, he'd have merely returned the story and kept me tagged for future rough handling.

This impressed me as a very mild and conservative attitude. If I were editor, and I received a story from a bigot, I would have voiced in no uncertain terms my opinions and told said author I wanted no more of his stories, even if they were world masterpieces and had nothing to do with racial derogation.

However, I'm not an editor.

Mr. Gold went on to the fact that two friends of mine had read the story before I'd sent it in. Both were involved with discrimination, ethically and personally. One was a preacher; the other, a freethinker of Jewish parentage. Neither had objected to anything in the story or even noticed anything that might be misconstrued. But Mr. Gold said that that should not convince me that my view was correct. The real test would be to give it to someone who *was* bigoted.

I couldn't do that. None of the bigoted people I know read science fiction, nor would they be persuaded to read what they call "that crap." Which speaks volumes for the kind of people they are and illustrates the high type of person, generally speaking, that inhabits the world of science fiction.

Mr. Gold maintained that a bigot would, on reading the story, have the same reaction as any other bigot. The only difference you might get would depend on his literate level. The uneducated would comment that the behavior of the Israeli Republics in the colonization of depopulated France would be just what you'd expect from a Jew or a Negro. Give them a chance and they'd be worse than the worst white men. The educated would have stated the same thing in well-turned phrases and a semblance of logic.

This was not based on guesswork. Part of his opinion was founded on his own dealings with bigots. But most of it came from the reaction stirred up both among biased and militantly unbiased people whenever he'd published a tale with a racial theme. He was, I suppose, referring especially to that wonderful story "Dark Interlude" by Mack Reynolds and Fredric Brown.

The latter people have always been against discrimination. Several of the stories Mr. Gold then had in inventory would, he believed, evoke the same angry reaction. One division of readers, the biased, acutely conscious of the message, would furiously deny its validity. And the unbiased would raise Cain because he'd had a character use the word "nigger"—even when his and its significance should be obvious to them.

If you took "The Lovers" apart, you'd find the neo-Judaic society a vicious one. The reader, who must identify himself with a character, is pleased by the revolt against society. A bigot, he'll have his own prejudices fortified by this idea of a culture that hasn't developed and probably never will. A tolerant person will find his emotions fighting each other. Aware there is no Haijac Union, he can be depended upon to recall the Bible and how it tells with remarkable candor the treatment by Hebrews of some of their neighbors. Thus, he might wonder if the same events might not occur again, only on a larger scale.

As Mr. Gold explains it, the tale had mental fishhooks of which I wasn't aware. His response on reading the story and my explanation was the same as the prayer of Voltaire: "Save me from my friends; I can handle my enemies."

Though he knew that I had the best of intentions, he considered my story potentially more dangerous than the most outrageous rantings of a minority-hater. Why? Because it was well intentioned and obviously sympathetic and very logical.

By the time I'd received Mr. Gold's second letter, I'd sold the story to Sam Mines.

——➤●◄——

For some time I'd watched the standards of *Thrilling Wonder* and *Startling Stories* rise under Sam Merwin, Jr. When he quit for freelancing and Sam Mines took over, I noticed that he had used Merwin's work as a sort of base and took off at right angles, like a rocket with the devil on its tail. Changes were frequent and evident and all for the better. Those who've followed the two magazines know what I'm talking about. Very pleasing to the science fiction heart.

Sam Mines, aided and abetted by Jerry Bixby, announced a policy whose only restrictions would be those of good taste. This, I thought, is my meat, for "The Lovers" will certainly test that policy. I'd made up my mind that I didn't want to rewrite the tale. To do so would have been composing a brand new story. And I didn't, I want to make clear here, think that there would be much, if any, reaction to the use of the Israeli or Haijac societies. The fact that the Haijac was vicious meant nothing. There have been and are sub-societies founded on similar principles. But this is not because the principles are vicious. Far from it. It is because these groups have taken the great and true teachings originated and promulgated by the Hebrew prophets and have hypocritically perverted them.

They have taken what was pure and magnificent and dirtied and twisted it. Sometimes this has been done honestly; sometimes not. In either case, there has been malformation.

So the Haijac Union.

Anyway, I read Sam's letter of acceptance with even more interest than you would expect. Sam stated that he liked "The Lovers" very much, with certain minor reservations. It was off-trail for *Startling* being basically a sex story. But he was serious in his policy of no taboos and anxious to impose no throttling hands upon authors who showed originality and freshness. Some small revisions seemed necessary; he and Jerry could work them out, but he thought I might prefer to do them myself.

Three points needed clarifying:

(1) The ship's purpose and mission ought to be made clear at once instead of late in the story. The reader wonders too long what the humans are after and what their relationship with the wogs is.

(2) Sam thought the love story would be benefited by an elevation from a simple and slightly sordid sex affair to something a little more noble. The hero could have *some* unselfish motive in offering shelter to the girl besides a desire to get in bed with her. His training in celibacy was strong. His breakdown should be gradual and logically motivated.

(3) And tying the theology of the future to the ancient Hebrews seemed strained, unlikely, and capable of offending the more tolerant who would resent being linked with suppressive totalitarianism. The story wouldn't suffer in the slightest if the theology were a mythical one, with a mythical god instead of Jahveh. My effect would be the same—might even be better—since it would sound more like the future and less like the past. I could even base it upon the new gods—Einstein, Freud, Edison, Jung, etc.

These changes were slight and would I let him know if I wanted to do them?

Point 1. O.K. I wrote the prolog.

Point 2. I replied that the hero did have some unselfish motive in offering shelter to the girl. She was human (so he thought), she was hiding from the wogs (so he thought), and she would be impounded and treated like a lab animal if he turned her over to his fellows (he knew).

The above was stated or at least implicit in the story. Besides, it was in the nature of the *lalitha* to go to bed with a desirable man and no bones about it. Their whole evolution pointed towards that.

His training in celibacy was very strong, true. On the other hand, a year or two in a space ship, plus that old devil Sex Urge, plus a congenital rebel, would lead to a quick breakdown. Moreover, Hal Yarrow had a corner on the market. She was the only available human female on the whole wide planet. Such a number of factors would go to a man's head.

Besides, had he ever met Jeannette? Did he know what she could do to a man?

I knew how she was. Take my word for it. St. Anthony himself would have fallen.

As to point three, as you've read, I'd encountered that before. Seeing it again, from another much-admired editor, gave me to pause. Maybe I was wrong.

So I wrote another long letter defending my viewpoint. The gist of it: The Hebrews have, among other things, been noted for the invention of the world's first *really* great religion. It is one so virile, so fecund, so strong in concept and truth, as far as basics go, that it has survived no matter what its enemies do and has given birth to two worldwide religions: the Mohammedan and the Christian.

The latter has split into many sects and sub-sects, and where it'll go nobody knows. Such a religion as the Hebrews', having already borne two great ones, might yet deliver another. Especially if it were coupled with a historical figure, Isaac Sigmen, the Forerunner, who lived long enough, due to longevity serums, not only to found but to cement the structure of his ideas. One who used scientific gobbledegook to justify his religion and a totalitarian setup—all for the good of his people, of course!—to keep his society static.

Moreover, the reader will see that whereas the neo-Judaic Haijacs were vicious, their enemies, the Israelis, were not. This last point will be made more clearly in the sequel to "The Lovers"—the story called "Moth and Rust."

I couldn't buy Sam's idea about a new religion based on the new gods - Einstein, Freud, Jung, etc.

Why?

Because they're scientists, not religious prophets. People don't follow scientists in matters of faith, not religious faith, anyway. And there's nothing in the scientists' works to whip up enthusiasm among disciples. You might take some of their ideas and tie them in with certain aspects or potentialities (for good or bad) of an already established religion. But that's what Sigmen did. I didn't think that the above-named scientists taught anything that could by the longest stretch of imagination be called religious.

Old lightning-wielding Jahweh still lives—in many forms—and it is from Him that you will get your true tablets of stone. Not from pen-wielders.

———

However, in order to avoid any such thing as Mssrs. Gold and Mines had objected to, I thought it'd be all right if a certain passage were struck out. That is the one referring to the division of France between the Israeli Republic (of Midi) and the Haijacs. A checking upon the story when it appeared in the magazine showed that Sam had come to the same conclusion as mine. Be realistic and logical and trust to the good sense of science fiction fandom, in general, to see what is meant.

After all, a bigot will seize upon anything you say and twist it. As to the militantly unbiased, I'm one, and I wrote the story. I would await the reaction. And while, at the time of writing this article, I haven't seen the letter response in the TEV[1] section of *Startling*, I've been told by Sam and Jerry that it's been terrific, unbelievably enthusiastic. The gripes are extremely few.

Another reason I wanted to keep the Israeli Republics. The Hebrews have suffered so much because of their religion, been so persecuted, so much, in short, a minority, that it tickled me to portray a future in which they've become a majority. After millennia of hanging on, they win out. Sheer guts and genius enable them to survive and become, finally, top dog. And, as I'll show in "Moth and Rust" they are the best among the four great unions left in my highly hypothetical but by no means impossible future. But I don't portray them as superhuman or subhuman. Just human, with the strength and weaknesses of men. Individuals, not types.

I took a chance on being misunderstood, but I think I was, in the main, justified.

As to whether "The Lovers" would have been a better story if set in a modern Terran background, no one will ever know. I'll concede that Mr. Gold might have been right. But I was just too fond of Fobo and my tavern beetles and Jeannette (whose death I regret but could not logically avoid) and the triumphant Israelis to kill them off. Besides being too lazy to do all that rewriting.

But I'm very well satisfied with the way things turned out. So are a number of other people.

Mr. Gold and I did not agree on certain points, but we parted amiably enough. I left still convinced that he was a great science fiction editor, and he probably left convinced that I was a peculiarly hard-headed author, but one who was, apart from that, not so bad.

During my conversation with Evelyn Paige, she told me that her husband was a man who could do the hardest thing in the world, that is, admit he might be wrong. Such honesty and flexibility are things to admire; they are the criteria of a real man. Mr. Gold has done just that; he has evidently changed his mind about one of the objections he had to "The Lovers." For he has published a story in the August issue of *Galaxy* "Education of a Martian," by Joseph Shallit, whose point is that a despised and persecuted person may himself hold towards another group the same attitude from which he suffers.

A bigot could deduce from this that if you don't keep a minority down, they might some day rise and keep you down.

---

[1] "The Ether Vibrates"—The magazine's letter pages.

But Mr. Gold has decided that bigots are the rara avis in science fiction fandom and that you may show that minorities possess weaknesses without having someone cry "Shame!" Or that if they do, enough people will understand what you're driving at.

I hope I've summed up fairly this tempest in a teapot.

I'd like to point out that up to three years ago or even later, such a story as "The Lovers" would have been unprintable as it was. Even today, with the policy adopted by Sam Mines in his search for new things in science fiction, such a sexual-biological story has to be offered with a certain amount of trepidation as to its reception. It took courage to print it.

That it has been given such an enthusiastic welcome is a true indication of the so-called "maturity" of science fiction. Basically biological, unavoidably sexual, the story is not sexy or sensational. It is, simply, a realistic treatment of an imaginative theme, one I tried to do honestly.

I'd like to thank Sam Mines and Jerry Bixby for their faith in allowing the story to remain virtually unchanged and the editors of *Fantastic Worlds* for having asked me to do an article on how I wrote "The Lovers." It's true I never got around to doing that, that I talked mainly of its course after being written.

Sometimes, the sideshow is more entertaining than the main attraction.

A Fimbulwinter
Introduction

First published in *Apart*, Number 3, August 1976.

Phil realized his ambition to write *Escape from Loki* some fifteen years later.

⁂

I was born in the Fimbulwinter of January, 1918. At that time I little realized that, in addition to Baron von Richthofen and Mick Mannock and other great aces, G-8 and The Shadow were also aerial crusaders. Come to think of it, nobody else did either. I moved from my native town, North Terre Haute, Indiana before I was one, though with my parents' consent. At the age of six I came to live in Peoria, Illinois, where I've spent most of my life but by no means all.

Before I even knew pulp magazines, I was reading in the local library such authors as Frank L. Baum and Crump, and then, later, Doyle, London, Verrill, Hope et al. At a very early age, however, I encountered Swift, Stevenson, Twain, and Homer. I believed then, and still believe, that Homer's *The Odyssey* is the greatest adventure story ever written. I fell under E.R. Burroughs' spell at the age of nine, and in 1929 additional fabulous worlds were opened for me when I purchased the first glorious copies of Gernsback's *Air Wonder Stories* and *Science Wonder Stories*. I determined at this time that I, too, would become a writer of stories of the far-off and the exotic.

This ambition wasn't realized until many many years later when I sold "The Lovers" to *Startling Stories* Magazine in 1952. I had sold one to *Adventure Magazine* (published in 1946), but this took place in Germany during World War II. Though a rather imaginative tale, it still was not science fiction.

My favorite pulp-magazine characters during my childhood and youth were Doc Savage, The Shadow, and heroes from the old *Argosy*; Singapore Sammy, Thibaut Corday, Bellow Bill Williams, Gillian Hazeltine, Peter the Brazen, Jimmie Cordie and his gang. *The Blue Book Magazine* provided some others, most notable of whom in my memory is Kioga.

This was during the Depression, however, and the dimes I had to spend on magazines were not many. So, when I had a choice to make between Doc Savage and The Shadow, I spent the dime on Doc. *The Shadow* and *Argosy* were begging, though I usually managed to borrow copies to read from my more affluent schoolmates.

College, in 1936, introduced me to classical literature. I had to quit in 1937 (because of the Depression) but I read the classics on my own. In 1939 I returned to college and in 1941 got married. My interest in Tarzan and the pulps waned for a long time; I was too busy working in a steel mill, being involved in the raising of two children, and in reading modern mainstream and the classics. I even lost interest in science fiction, though I still read *Astounding* and, occasionally, some of the other SF magazines.

In the meantime, I had returned to college, graduating in 1950. I regained my enthusiasm for SF, and by the time I'd sold "The Lovers," it was in full bloom again. The reprinting of the Doc Savage tales by Bantam Books rekindled an interest that I had thought died. Nostalgia never really perishes, however. The child in us may be deep, but it is ready to rise up if the lid is even momentarily lifted.

This time, on rereading the Savage tales and the long-ago-loved sagas from my collection, I had the advantage of knowing mainstream and classical literature. I began seeing certain valuable and significant elements in pulp fiction of which I had been entirely ignorant when I first read them. These elements will be described and amplified in my speech at the Classical Con.

From 1956 through part of 1969, I was an electromechanical technical writer for the space-defense industry. A month before the first moon landing, I decided to go into full-time writing. Two years later I moved from Los Angeles to Peoria, and I've been here ever since. As of now, I've had published about thirty-three novels, two "biographies," and fifty-three short stories. My plans include doing biographies on Allan Quatermain, Arsene Lupin (the French equivalent of Raffles and Jimmy Dale), and the Wizard of Oz. I'll continue the Ancient Opar and the Lord Grandrith-Doc Caliban series, among others. And some day I hope to get permission to write *Escape from Loki*, the novel in which young Doc Savage meets the Fearsome Five in a German prison camp during World War I.

On A Mountain Upside Down

First published in *JD Argossy*, Number 55, June 25th 1960.

This piece is set at the time when Phil was living in Arizona and working as a technical writer for Motorola's military electronics division.

Phil: "This is true or as true as I can remember it. I look back on my life and wonder if I was always nuts."

To stand on your head on top of a narrow mountain is not always easy. I did it once several months ago. Two paths led me there: yoga and the lure of the West.

Although not a conventional Beatnik, I became interested in the physical aspects of yoga to slough off the fat and tighten the slack muscles that working in an office have given me these last three years. One of the first exercises suggested is standing on the head for five minutes. Nehru, I found out, stands on his head half an hour every day, but look at the mess India is in. However, I tried it for three minutes at first, then over a lengthy period of three days built up my endurance to five and a half minutes. To time myself, I placed a clock in front of my face and had no trouble reading the time upside down. At first, the blood drained into my head, and I felt as if my eyes would pop out from pressure. My legs felt empty of all fluid, and my neck muscles quivered.

I also had trouble with my male Siamese sealpoint cat. He is a creature who does not like his routine disturbed, and his slave standing on his head was something he did not care for at all. After pacing back and forth crying (Siamese cats never meow), his tail stiff with extended hairs, he attacked me. He did this by leaping upon my crotch and hanging there—so over he and I went to the floor. I tried again, but this time he bit my face, not enough to bring blood but enough to warn me to quit this crazy posture.

Into the bathroom he went. The door locked on him, his piteous wails ringing through the house, his slave went back to his head-standing. The next day he paced back and forth while I was propped up against the wall, but he did not attack. And now he ignores me, having accepted it as part of routine that I stand on my head for five minutes every night before going to bed.

If you want to get a fresh slant on your living room, stand on your head. The world looks upside down; you get the strange sensation that you are wearing an anti-gravity belt and doing spin-turns through the house. Sometimes, if you stay in this position long enough, you begin to think that it is quite normal for the tables and chairs and sofa and lamps and rugs to be suspended from the ceiling. You get fond of this position; you are sure that people who are content to keep their feet on the ground are a bunch of damn bourgeois. And you are right.

This exercise is supposed to result in improved circulation of blood and will cure anything from colds to cancer. However, though I did begin to feel more stimulated, less tired, I think it was due to changing my routine and a fresher outlook on life. For, about three weeks after I began standing on my head, I came down with one of the worst colds of my life. Had to take almost a week off from work.

And this was in dry sunny Arizona.

Which leads me, unnaturally, to speak of other perils besides sinus and sore throats, in which Arizona is rich. The morning I was to return to work I awoke an hour early. I felt a tingling in my lower lip, which made me think that the damned cat was at his usual practice of getting me up at dawn so I could let him out. But no, he was sleeping on the foot of the bed. Then I felt the tingling increase, and I arose and went into the bathroom to look into the mirror. Suspicion verified. My lower lip was swelling at an alarming rate, ballooning up before my eyes.

By the time the rest of the family was up, the lip was stretched out so huge and taut I looked like a male white Ubangi, or half-Ubangi. I did not go to work but went instead to see a doctor. He did not think I had been bitten by a spider or nonpoisonous scorpion. He was insistent that the swelling was caused by psychosomatic reasons. Even though I showed him the slight break in labial skin which could have been caused by an insect bite, he wanted to know if I was under unusual pressure, was worried about anything in particular, etc. I told him I wasn't any more nervous or strained that usual. He was dissatisfied with my secure neurological state but gave me a shot of anti-histamine in the hip, which hurt worse than the insect bite (?) and some pills whose chemical composition I don't remember. Probably a placebo, anyway. The swelling went down in two days and I returned to work with my story, which was greeted with guffaws and stares of incredulity.

No matter. The following week-end I went with the Old Prospector on a safari into the desert near the Kofa Mts. The desert in Arizona is guaranteed to cure you of anything unless you get bitten by a rattlesnake or run out of water. And even these have their end.

The Old Prospector is a technical writer who slaves away at the desk beside mine. He is an ex-electrical power engineer who has at least thirty claims staked out all over Arizona and parts of California and Utah. On this trip we were headed for Bronco Ledge, which he is testing for gold or whatever he finds through the equipotential method. This consists of driving a number of iron rods into the grounds and sending a current into the earth to measure the resistance. He says it is a sure-fire method of locating ore deposits; other engineers I've talked to say it is highly unreliable in the type of ground he deals with. I do not care, though I would like to see George strike it rich. While he and his partners slave away, I roam the desert, looking for animals, Indian artifacts, and breath-taking views. On this trip four of us went, two electrical engineers and two technical writers. I rode with George in his pick-up truck; the engineers followed behind in their jeep. After reaching Hassayampa, we cut off the state highway onto a country dirt road, then left that to make our own trail. Our destination for that evening was Clanton Well.

Out here you have to cross washes by the scores. And often, if your vehicle can't make it down or up a steep bank, you have to build your own road, pile rocks to make a causeway, then fill the gaps in between with sand. And push the truck when it gets stuck in the sand of the wash-beds. Hard work, but a lot of fun. While you're jolting over the rough rocks, going this way and that around the saguaro, mesquite, cholla, and palo verde vegetation and the mala-pi rocks, jumping out now and then to push or make a road, the moon comes up over the mountains, the biggest orange you ever saw, and the desert is painted with a thin spray of shining tequila-juice. At least, that's how it feels, because you get drunk with its harsh beauty.

Sometimes, you have to go down a wash to see if there's a good crossing for the truck, and you wonder if any big pussycats are around. You know there's a good chance, for your flashlight has picked up many tracks of deer, bobcats, coyotes and mountain lions. How the hell they live out here where the nearest water is forty miles away, you don't know. Maybe they drink each other's blood.

Our first big stopping-place was the abandoned mine which the Clanton boys, and their poppa dug. Very few people have seen this; I felt thrilled. We roamed around a while but didn't go down into the mine because we didn't have a rope ladder. We said that the next time we came out this way we'd bring one. One of the men staked a claim to the mine, just for the hell of it, and we pushed on.

We drove down a wash with very narrow sides and very sandy bottom. The cat-claws reached out and scraped the truck-side; you had to keep your elbows in. George said that this wash was once a road the military had built. After they abandoned it, nature took it back and turned it into a course for the spring floods which come down from the snow melting in the mountains.

Our next stop was the Stardust mine. This was once worked by the parents of George's partner (who wasn't with us that night). After the gold vein seemed to peter out, the mine was deserted. But George thinks it might turn up again later on; he's been doing some work on it from time to time. We went down several levels, climbing down a rickety wooden ladder with only our flashlights for illumination. When we reached the bottom, we were a hundred and fifty under. But this wasn't the lowest level. After walking down a high corridor about fifty feet long, we took a tunnel that descended at a fortyfive degree angle into the rock. Went down another wooden ladder, and reached the bottom. Here we found a strange thing; two dried-up corpses of animals intertwined. One looked like a large rat; the other, like a jackrabbit. Apparently these two rodents had locked in mortal combat on the ground above and had fallen down the shaft and been killed when they struck the rock floor. Some of their bones were broken.

Before we left the mine, George gave us sticks of dynamite to carry out for him; these had been stored for some time. But George looked them over to make sure the dynamite wasn't crystallized; when the nitro starts to form crystals, the dynamite is likely to go off with a slight jar.

Our next stop, the final for that night, was Clanton Well. This is where the Clanton clan had a ranch before they went off to Tombstone and became famous. The military had dug a well here, used it as a watering place. Then they abandoned it, and the Clantons moved in with their cows. The Clantons didn't pay much attention to the cattle. They spent most of their time prospecting, knowing that the cows wouldn't stray far because this was the only place they could get water for forty miles roundabout. Now there's nothing left of the old Clanton ranch but a few timbers piled under a tree; somebody had built a cattle-chute and fences here, and a rusty iron windmill stands above the well. There's still water in it, but we had no way of operating the pump.

The next day we pushed on, and by noon got to Bronco Ledge. This heap of malapi rock is only a few miles east of the Kofa Game Refuge; the only sign of civilization is a narrow trail made by the state and the inevitable beer and bean cans. Even these are so few they don't distract.

Part of the afternoon we shot with our pistols and rifles at a beer can in which was a stick of dynamite. Once George, as a joke, threw a stick of dynamite at me, hollering, "Catch!" I didn't jump, because I knew—or hoped—he wouldn't throw crystallized dynamite. Even if it was inclined to explode, there wasn't anything I could do.

One of the engineers, who shall be nameless, had already shown his fear of the explosive in the Stardust. When George asked us to help him carry the stuff out, he had taken up the ladder without a word. I won't say he was pale, but he did look shaken. However we all have our idiosyncrasies; one man's foolishness is another man's fear.

George is quite the practical joker. That first morning at Clanton Well, he rose early and fired his .38 close to the ear of one of the men sleeping under the truck. Naturally, he raised his head, and also, a bump. George laughed and said he'd seen a fox and shot at it.

After target practice was over, and George had gotten a big laugh out of me jumping into the air when a stick went off when I was cooking lunch, having completely forgotten about their practice, I hooked my canteen onto my G.I. belt, filled my knapsack with goodies, and stuck my .32 Husquevarna six-shooter into my holster. Then I took off for Puka Peak, a mountain about five miles away, though it looked only two. On its topmost peak was a lone saguaro cactus; I decided to climb the peak and keep it company.

I hadn't gotten more than fifty yards away when I heard a rattle, and there, sure enough, was a diamond-back. He was no danger to me, being too far away, but I didn't want to take a chance of running into him later, so I broke his back and smashed in his head with a malapi. I was genuinely sorry to have to do that, for I think a rattler is a beautiful creature, but I don't like to think about getting bitten. I walked another mile up, and down the hills and across a very steep wash—where there were mountain lion tracks—and then came across the biggest tarantula I've ever seen outside of a zoo. He wanted nothing to do with me, and I wasn't scared because they're not poisonous, contrary to what folk-lore says. But I was leery; they look as if they belong on the surface of Mars, that is, in Arizona, which from where I was, looks as strange and desolate as the surface of the red planet. He scuttled off into a hole.

I entered a valley which was absolutely soundless. No sign that man had ever been there. But I did flush up a jackrabbit, who bounded off toward the west. And the sun shone through the transparent upper parts of his ears, making them look like pale blood. This was, to me, a weird and unforgettable sight, the sun shining pinkly through his ears.

When I reached the bottom of Puka Peak and looked up, the saguaro on top presented the appearance of a sorrowful saint or some hooded figure. It bulged at the top to form a chin and the outline of a face. I named it Saint Puka.

The climb was steep and breath-taking. Being out of condition, I had to stop often and get my wind back and wait until my heart quit pounding. And there were places which were precipitous enough to impress me, though a real mountain-climber wouldn't have given them a second thought. However, being alone, I had to be extra careful.

Close to the top, I passed caves. These looked as if they could harbor big pussycats, but I doubt it, for the climb up and back wouldn't be worth the effort for them.

Finally, I reached the top by the lone saguaro and here sat down to look over the scene. Too bad you couldn't have been there; you could see for over fifty miles away, and all around were the heads of mountains mightier than the one I was on, mountains with strange shapes indeed. One looked like a Chinese pagoda; another, like an eagle's tail. I strained my eyes, but I couldn't see the Shithouse Mountains, which are designated on the topographical maps as the SH mountain range. These got their name from a series of peaks which look from a distance like a row of outhouses.

From the ridiculous to the sublime. I stood on my head on top of this peak. There was just enough room so that if I lost my balance I wouldn't fall off; my feet would hang over the edge. And I had folded my shirt under my head to keep its top from being hurt by the rock floor.

It was a strange thing, seeing all those mountains hanging down from the upside down earth. Strange, but nothing beyond the imagination to conceive. I rotated slowly, pivoting from east to west, until I was facing the sinking sun. The sun, as anybody knows, looks the same downside up as the other way. Being round has its disadvantages.

Finally, having exhausted the possibilities of this position, and sure that nobody else had stood on their head on this particular peak, or probably on any in Arizona, sure also that nobody but myself gave a damn, I sat down. All was quiet; even the hawk that had been circling this peak and crying as I climbed up was gone; no sound but my breathing. Far away I could see the sun glitter from the white top of the truck at the base of Bronco Ledge; at least, it should have been the truck, for I was too distant from it to make out its outline.

Here, I thought, if a man wanted to practice some aspects of Zen, or just be simpatico with Nature, here is the place. For a while, at least. Eventually, a man would miss his kind; he'd have to climb down and find someone to talk to; after all, Man is part of Nature, too.

I did decide to climb down. By the time I reached the bottom of the mountain, twilight had fallen. And in a short time, darkness. The sky had become clouded over, a rare thing in this part of the country, and the moon and stars were hidden. Fortunately, though the camp was five miles away, I had lined up the intersection of two hills to aim for, knowing the camp would not be too far away. Even in the darkness, the twins loomed up.

Nevertheless, I was nervous. There were mountain lions, bobcats, and the stickly cholla cactus to run into me. And I had not taken along my flashlight. I could have lit up my path for fifty yards ahead by touching off the inflammable needles of cholla; these blaze up like tar torches and give an excellent light. But I did not want to do this; Somehow, it seemed more romantic to be sneaking through the desert night without a light. Though you could hardly call my noisy progress sneaking. Once, I heard a loud snort, then a crash as some large animal bounded away. Undoubtedly a deer. If it had been a cougar I'd have heard nothing.

I put my .32 in my hand and walked along, whirling every now and then to see if some glowing-eyed big cat was trailing me. Naturally, there were none; if they'd wanted me they'd have made sure I didn't see them until it was too late.

Eventually, I passed through the little valley between the two hills and suddenly saw the campfires. It took me half an hour to reach them, for I had to take a roundabout way to avoid climbing other hills. When I did get there, I asked them if they had seen me through their binoculars. They said they had. They didn't say a thing about my having stood on my head, so I didn't. I did tell them about filing a claim on top, which I left in an empty Prince Albert tobacco can. Why claim that useless knob of rock? they asked. Just so anybody else who climbed up there would know he wasn't the first, I replied. But somebody else may have been there before you and didn't leave any record of it, they said. Without evidence to the contrary, I am the first, I said, and we left it at that.

On PJF

Afterword—
The Mother of Pearl

**From Michael Croteau—fan, collector and webmaster
of the Official Philip José Farmer website**

The book you hold in your hands contains stories, articles and poems that
it took me seven years to find. Even today with the internet making book collecting much easier than ever before, some of these items are still extremely
hard to obtain. Or at least they were. We could have named this book, *The
Short Cut to Collecting Philip José Farmer*.

The genesis of this book goes back several years. I began collecting the
works of Philip José Farmer in earnest when I began my original "unofficial"
web page in 1996. After discovering and reading all his books I then began to
collect all the short stories he wrote for anthologies, magazines and fanzines.
Then the non-fiction articles he wrote for magazines and fanzines. Each piece
I added to my collection, and then the web page, being more obscure and hard
to find than the last.

It wasn't long however, before most of my favourite pieces by Phil were not
the works he was famous for: "The Lovers," "Riders of the Purple Wage," the
Riverworld and World of Tiers series. Instead my favourites became the more
obscure pieces like: "A Scarletin Study," "Heel," and "Seventy Years of Decpop"
- among others, and I especially relish the autobiographical articles: "The Tin
Woodman Slams the Door," "On a Mountain Upside Down," "Lovers and
Otherwise" and "Maps and Spasms."

After self-publishing an illustrated collector's guide to Philip José Farmer
in 1998 and enjoying the sensation of being a publisher more than being published, I started thinking about how few of Phil's books were currently in print.
I wrote up a very grandiose business plan on how I would print many of his
paperback originals in hardcover for the first time, print previously unpublished material, print collections of his "fictional author" stories, his uncollect-
ed stories, his obscure articles... the possibilities were endless. The reason you
have not seen any of *these* books in print was the one weakness of my proposal. I had just enough money to print maybe 100 copies each of two or three of
the books. As the money came in I would pay Phil his royalties each month

and put the rest of the money into printing more books. In a perfect world it would have been great.

But, here in the real world, Phil had absolutely no reason to give up the rights to his works to someone who had nearly no experience as a publisher. And even though my royalty payments would have been much more generous than is standard, any author who agrees to be paid by a publisher as the books sell, needs to have his head examined. So Phil politely declined my proposal and that dream died away.

However, there is something so maddening about so much of Phil's work being out of print that people kept coming to my webpage and asking me why I, or someone, didn't reprint this book or that book. At one time or another Craig Kimber, Rick Beaulieu and Zacharias Nuninga all asked me this question in one manner or another. It wasn't until Paul Spiteri asked me this question, and then talked about it with Bette Farmer during a visit that things started to happen. Not exactly in the manner we expected though.

Besides the four fans mentioned above and myself, two writers, Tracy Knight and Roger Crombie got involved in a plan to print a previously unpublished novel, a collection of rare Farmer items and anything else we could get Phil to agree to. We were going to pool our money and pay Phil his royalties in advance, we would get our money back when the book sold. Phil agreed in principle to give it a go, so all we had to do was find a binder.

Embracing what we felt was the future of publishing we found a print-on-demand publisher who would print as many copies of the book up front as we wanted and sell them to us at the author's discounted rate. Then the book would be available at their website as well as online outlets like amazon.com. We thought we were all set and sent a proposal to Phil. It turns out that while the thought of us printing a limited edition small print run of an unpublished novel was ok with Phil, the whole print-on-demand scenario was just too big. His agent had already told him about print-on-demand publishers and that the industry was too new and too risky. It's hard to get paid from a dot com that has gone bankrupt.

Back to the drawing board. The seven of us started looking around for a publisher when a publisher found us. Phillip Rose, of The Rose Press, contacted me at the, now "official," PJF website and asked specifically about printing a limited edition hardcover of *As You Desire*. (A previously unpublished adult novel written by Phil in 1965). Phil said that he no longer had that manuscript. Not to be deterred, Phillip Rose decided that he was very equally interested in publishing a collection of Phil's hard to find articles and stories.

So the seven of us started typing up all the items in this book. Frankly we were not moving fast enough so we recruited two more fans, Lee J Barrie and

Christopher Carey to help with the typing. Craig Kimber graciously offered to let us include "A Rough Knight for the Queen," a long unpublished manuscript that he owns the only known copy of. Paul Spiteri once again became the motivating force behind the project and took on the task of sorting this collection into some sort of order. He then took on the task of trying to add even more contextual value to this book by writing the introductions to the stories and articles. Christopher Carey was once again asked to help by contributing his writing skills. I too wrote some of the introductions.

While putting this collection together, Paul continued to take on more and more responsibility until he fell into the role of full-blown editor. Some of the pieces have been renamed, with Phil's permission, and these all came from Paul, who now continues the story…

From Paul Spiteri—Fan, collector and Editor of *Pearls from Peoria*

I read of Phil long before I read anything by Phil.

I was always a voracious reader and whilst mostly of fiction, I loved information, especially of the weird variety (if only I'd known about *The Fortean Times* then; I would have been an avid fan and reader!) and loved *The People's Almanac* by David Wallechinsky and Irving Wallace. For those that have not come across these books, they're full of fascinating, but mostly unnecessary, facts or lists. The 10 greatest crime capers, 6 positions for sexual intercourse—in order of preference, Orson Welles's 10 favourite films and so on. One list (in *The People's Almanac* #3) was "11 planets discovered by Science Fiction writers." Coming in at number 9 was Riverworld. The description was extraordinary: the whole of humanity, 36 billion people, who had lived and died, all reborn along the banks of an enormous river! The concept blew my mind.

A few months later I was in my local bookstore browsing the SF shelves and saw a title that sent neural connections in my brain racing to bridge the gap. The book was *Riverworld and Other Stories*. I remembered the description I'd read, though not the actual title (which would have been *To Your Scattered Bodies Go*). So I bought the book. It was only a few hours from purchase of book to having read the title story. I marvelled at the imagination that gave us an early Hollywood actor travelling along a mighty river with Jesus Christ. I read the rest of the collection but I was fascinated by Riverworld.

I now faced the daunting, but absolutely necessary, task of tracking down more Farmer books. The best source was Forbidden Planet, then on Denmark Street in London. An oasis for SF lovers, I found many Farmer titles there. (Unknown to me at the time, Phil did a book signing session there in the early 1980s.)

I reread the small biographical introductions countless times. Phil Farmer lived in Peoria. I got an atlas and found it. At that time I truly believed I would never get to meet my literary hero.

In 1999 I won an auction for a signed copy of the *World Fantasy Convention Program, 1983*—where "The Monster on Hold" premiered. The seller was Phil's fellow Illinoisan, and author, Tracy Knight. We struck up an email conversation and he bowled me over when he said he knew Phil and had actually been at a signing with him just a week or two previously.

Tracy and I kept up an email friendship and when, with my family, I visited the States in 2000, Tracy and I arranged to meet up. The hope being that Tracy could arrange an introduction with Phil. As it turned out Phil was out of town but we were still very keen to meet up with Tracy and his wife Sharon. We each took on a 3 or 4 hour journey to meet up in Peoria (which seemed apposite).

It was a miserable, stormy drive across the prairie and when we did finally meet up and expressed our concern over tornadoes (only half joking), Tracy 'reassured' us with the fact that tornado season was still a week or two away!

We kept in touch with the Knights and the following year went back to the States. This time we were luckier and whilst staying in Carthage (where Tracy and Sharon lived at the time) we took a trip up to Peoria. We'd been invited to the Farmers' along with Tracy and family. It turned out to be Phil and Bette's 60th wedding anniversary. It was a real honour to be invited to help celebrate such an auspicious milestone. Pulling up outside Phil's house I started to feel nervous and disconnected. Was I really going to meet Phil? Would he want to talk to me?

We walked in to a hum of happy conversation. Greetings were warm and friendly and soon Phil was asking me about my genealogy. (It really is a passion with him!) The evening was perfect and when things quietened down a bit later we descended to Phil's basement library. I have a photo, treasured beyond worth, of Phil, Tracy and me sitting on a sofa. It has always sat on my sideboard, at the front.

I came away that evening feeling very mellow. I had met a hero of mine and it was an experience I knew I would always treasure. I've heard it said that you should not meet your heroes; you'll only be disappointed. Nothing could have been further from the truth, meeting Phil and Bette that day was the start of a strong friendship that exists to this day.

The next year we were back and were present as friends and fans celebrated with Phil the 50th anniversary of the publication of *The Lovers*. It was amazing to see him lionised by so many people who care for him and love his work.

Shortly after this visit Mike Croteau and I started to discuss a Phil Farmer publishing project. We had hoped to publish a novel entitled *Up from the Bottomless Pit*. This is a previously unpublished ecological disaster story. Unfortunately the project floundered but in the midst of our disappointment along came Phillip Rose and wanted his new publishing venture to put out a Phil Farmer collection.

The scope of the anthology was enormous; a collection of all the rare pieces that had taken avid collectors literally years to pull together, coupled with a full retrospective of Phil's work. His fiction, researches, reviews, poems and autobiographical pieces. We even got agreement to include some previously unpublished pieces—a real coup!

But how to order the book? With over 60 pieces it was important that the presentation allowed the reader to fully appreciate the breadth of the work they were about to read. I considered a strictly chronological order but that made the collection seem haphazard; jumping about too much from subject to subject. Grouping the work into themes seemed more sensible and I gave up on the chronological idea. Once in groups it was much easier to see a progression that had less to do with the date of writing and more to do with the development of ideas. As I review the contents list now it's hard for me to appreciate the hours of soul searching and head scratching that went into the final manifest.

This book has hundreds of pages, thousands of words and over a million letters. Phil has always been an extremely imaginative writer and, for me, a particularly appealing aspect is the way Phil plants such clear images in your mind. Having the right artwork was very important; identifying the right artists was paramount. Mike and I agreed that we should approach artists who were also Farmer fans. Mike was able to give me the names of four artists who had contributed to his website: Jason Robert Bell, Charles Berlin, Keith Howell and Mario Zecca. I contacted them all and, to a man, they were all thrilled at the idea of having their interpretation of some part of Phil's work published in a Philip José Farmer book. I hope you are as thrilled with the results as I am.

Unfortunately, due to printing issues totally outside of Philip Rose's control, he was not able to realise his plan to physically publish the book. It is characteristic of the man that he was happy to stand aside and it was at this point, a real nadir on the project, that Bill Schafer from Subterranean Press came to the fore. Subterranean Press were just putting the finishing touches to *The Best of Philip José Farmer* and agreed to take on *Pearls from Peoria*. All of us involved are just so grateful for this timely intervention.

It's taken well over two years to get to this point. A long time, I know, but everyone involved in this project has given his or her time gratis. This volume only exists because of the effect Phil's writing has had on the lives of a special group of people and how they felt they wanted to give something back. As much as anything this book is our tribute to Phil. I can't stress just how much this book is a labour of love, from copy typing, to proofreading, to artwork, to researching copyright and penning introductions. Everybody involved has worked hard and long and I truly believe we have created something special. Even the dimensions of this book proclaim loudly, Phil Farmer is a major talent.

The works included here start in the 1940s with Phil's first published piece and go right through to Phil's latest short stories from the 1990s. There are also a number of pieces printed here for the first time and, for one story ("Some Fabulous Yonder"), an early unpublished draft from Phil.

As well as an expanse of time, this compilation spans a multitude of subject matters; from pulp heroes to genealogy, from poems to witches, from autobiography to biography. Phil is a polymath, for those who already know that this book will be a joy, for those that don't this book will be a revelation.

May 2006

The Artwork and the Artists

Keith Howell

With this portrait of Ralph Von Wau Wau, I took liberties with the character, but I think Phil would be ok with that. In Phil's stories, Ralph is not anthropomorphized, but continues to look and act like a dog (albeit a large dog) who just happens to be extremely intelligent and have a mechanical voice box allowing him to talk. I have not anthropomorphized Ralph, but I have portrayed him posing up on his back legs. If someone were to see the undersketching, they would find that I sketched Ralph's dog body under the trenchcoat so that I could rightly envision how it would drape and fall if it were on a real dog.

My inspiration for the portrait was an old Sam Spade publicity shot of Humphrey Bogart. If you look carefully at Ralph's eyes, those are Bogie's eyes. I think that odd conflation of features makes Ralph very intriguing as a portrait and illustration.

Accompanying "A Scarletin Study"

Keith Howell

I love Tarzan of the Burroughs (and Farmer) books and the chance to publish a portrait of the true-life inspiration for the famous ape-man was a "can't miss" opportunity. The single best and most effective portrait of Tarzan I've ever seen was a Jeffrey Jones painting of Lord Greystoke. It was a face portrait and it was Lord Greystoke back in his ancestral home, clean shaven, cut and styled hair, in his proper aristocratic clothes. Yet, in his eyes, you see the repressed beast within this apparently proper English Lord. I wanted to accomplish something similar in my portrait, that is, in Grandrith's face, body, and eyes, you know the character - you see into his soul. In this portrait, I used the bright full moon as the light source for the image. Since Lord Grandrith is "Lord of the Trees," I felt it imperative to place him in a tree. I sketched around with ideas such as letting loose his guttural yell or swinging from tree to tree. I settled on this image of the noble savage reclining in the tops of the trees late in the evening.

While the portrait is realistic, it is also stylized. The musculature of Lord Grandrith has its inspiration in the Tarzan comic strip art of Burne Hogarth. One of Hogarth's drawings was used for one of the paperback covers of Phil's *Tarzan Alive*. Hogarth has his artistic critics because he frequently and freely ignored even the illusion of realistic anatomy when it served his dramatic purpose. Even so, I appreciate his work and the dynamic movement he evoked in flat drawings. In this drawing, I am attempting to give the viewer the feeling of movement even as Grandrith is still. For the tree, I have taken the stylistic musculature I used on Grandrith's body and reproduced it in the tree to drive home the spiritual and physical connection between Grandrith and the trees of his jungle home.

Accompanying "The Princess of Terra"

Keith Howell

A standard pose of Doc, Pauncho, Barney, and Trish. To further drive home the Doc Caliban/Doc Savage connection, I took the classic Doc Savage logo and converted it to "Doc Caliban" and placed it in a carved-from-stone style in the background. For Pauncho and Barney, I wanted to evoke Monk and Ham, but make them seem more "real" physically. I also aged them a bit, which gave them both more character. Trish was simply based on a tall model that I saw once who had a unique cheek structure and eyes that I feel exemplfied Phil's description of Trish.

Doc Caliban, himself, was a fun project on his own. I know that Phil has expressed disdain for the James Bama design for Doc Savage that includes the extreme widow's peak hair style. However, I remember an old Doc adventure (perhaps *The Black Spot?*) where Doc's hair was described as looking like a skull-cap "helmet" and having qualities that caused water to just bead up and drip off. This stuck with me for all these years and I've always assumed this was what inspired Bama's design. Personally, I prefer the Baumhoffer design with that thick bronze curl of hair. So, what you see in my portrait is an attempt to combine the two. I have included the extreme widow's peak and skull-cap style, but I have made sure that the hair coloring is darker—evoking the dark bronze of Phil's description and Baumhoffer's illustrations.

Just because I love the Bama-style design choice of always portraying Doc with that torn shirt, I have done so as well. It creates an automatic backstory as if Doc has just finished battling some great evil.

Accompanying "Writing Doc's Biography"

Charles Berlin

It seems as though I always wanted to illustrate Philip José Farmer. This desire began with reading *Tarzan Alive*, completing it in one sunny Saturday afternoon. On those sacred weekends as a youngster, I was invariably at the drawing table laboring over a new sketch or out in the neighboring forest exploring unconquered territory, but when I got his incredible book, I knew this would be part of the perfect Saturday. In Farmer, I found a kindred creative spirit, heavily influenced by the great archetypes of Pulp. As a Muse for this artist, Farmer is "The Hero of a Thousand Works of Art": I always come away from his work ready to create.

As I grew, I remained fascinated with the many worlds of this author. I began to discover not only was he a master of epic adventure, but of intricate, layered symbolism as well. To this day, I can reread Farmer and always find a new key to a different gate of understanding.

Illustrating stories in this collection was an experience which I will put beside the golden memory of opening that very first Farmer book on that amazing Saturday afternoon.

Accompanying "Nobody's Perfect"

*Accompanying
"Wolf, Iron and Moth"*

Charles Berlin

Accompanying "Evil, be my good"

Accompanying "Hunter's Moon"

Accompanying "Savage Shadow"

Jason Robert Bell

I first became aware of Philip José Farmer when I picked up a copy of *Flesh*; it was the Signet 1969 edition. The reason why I bought the book was that instead of some cheesy airbrushed laser-gun packing muscleman with raised extruded type floating above him, the book's cover had the quirky flatfooted cartoon of the horned hero hiding his "manhood" behind a motionless white stag. After reading the book I was hooked. Farmer had taken all the standard pulp fodder turned it on its ear and shot it full of holes with a double barrel shot gun loaded with Robert Graves, Sigmund Freud, and Joseph Campbell.

A Feast Unknown changed my life. Here Farmer took all the negative critiques of action adventure; that it is basically homo-erotic power fantasy escapism, and embraced it, creating a masterful parody that is so devoid of internal irony that it is almost unreadable, pure genius!

I first did my version of Caliban (PJF's Doc Savage pastiche) confronting the "monster" from "The Monster on Hold." I saw Caliban as the most extreme testosterone pump Overman, and the monster as the female polar opposite: she is a Ray Harryhausen-esque gorgon.

The second illustration came out of Paul Spiteri and me e-mailing ideas back and forth. He mentioned doing a portrait of Farmer similar to the hydra at the end of, the now late, Tony Randall's masterpiece, *The Seven Faces of Dr. Lao*, with each of the head being one of Farmer's characters. That is exactly what I did.

Accompanying
"The Monster on Hold"

Accompanying "Maps and Spasms"

Accompanying
"The Source
of the River"

Mario Zecca

No single author has entertained and enlightened me more than Philip José Farmer. He spoke to a secret part of me, the part where the sleeping heroes of adventure wait to arise, where mythology and the imagination reside, where escape more than transcends reality; enhancements to the waking life dream.

By adding a bizarre background story of near immortals and homicidal-sexuality to the Tarzan saga in *A Feast Unknown*, he made that childhood hero of mine a complex and more real invention. That novel and the two shorter pastiches that follow, seem to me, the greatest, if uncompleted, adventure story ever written. I was introduced to Doc Savage, another noble champion, equal and in some ways, superior to the Lord of the Trees, through those stories and the biography Mr. Farmer wrote. He wrote many great SF and fantasy adventures that I have loved getting lost in. The World of Tiers and Riverworld series, very popular and revelatory, but the single story efforts shine just as brightly in my memory; *The Stone God Awakens, Lord Tyger, A Barnstormer in Oz, The Wind Whales of Ishmael, Time's Last Gift* and the two Opar books come to mind.

In the Tarzan and Doc Savage biographies, *Tarzan Alive* and *Doc Savage His Apocalyptic Life*, Philip José Farmer links the family trees of the heroes of literature, whose common ancestors are radiated—and their offspring's genes beneficially mutated by the Wold Newton Meteor. Aside from finding the notion immensely amusing, the concepts have influenced my own output of drawing and writing. Philip José Farmer has inspired my speculative thinking.

Thank you Mr. Farmer for giving me valuable lessons in imaginative freedom, for sometimes being a light in the darkness, and especially for being so much fun to read.

Accompanying "Oft Have I Travelled"

Photo Montages

*Harry Harrison, Ray Bradbury and Phil in
Pasedena California on 15 January 1986*

*From Philcon 89 where Phil
was Prinicple Speaker*

Late 1990s

*Phil, Robert Bloch, Forrest Ackerman
and Arnold Schinlder at Bloch's
house in the early 1990s*

*Early 1980s at the grave of
Sir Richard Francis Burton, UK*

10 August 2002 Lovers 50th celebration

1993; Phil and Bette

*Phil and Bette in 1993 at Bradley University where
Phil has been named a 'Distinguished Scholar'*

Phil the student athlete

Phil holding his first Hugo award, won in 1953 as the Most Promising New Talent of 1952

Phil's awards, on display at his home

Phil (rose in mouth!) in front of Tarzan's Coat of Arms; as commissioned by Phil

Phil giving a Tarzan' yell, Fort Lauderdale 1990

Phil and Bette on their 60th wedding anniversary

Phil, Tracy Knight and Paul Spiteri in 2001

Bette Farmer in Phil's writing room, 2003

Phil and Bette, 2003

Phil. Photo taken after meeting to discuss Pearls from Peoria, 2003